D0653075

Dorset Libraries
Withdrawn Stock

THE
SKULL
THRONE

THE
SKULL
THRONE

PETER V. BRETT

HARPER
Voyager

HarperCollins*Publishers*
1 London Bridge Street
London SE1 9GF

www.harpercollins.co.uk

Published by Harper*Voyager*
An imprint of HarperCollins*Publishers* 2015
1

A catalogue record for this book
is available from the British Library

ISBN: 9780007425686

Set in Sabon LT Std by Palimpsest Book Production Limited,
Falkirk, Stirlingshire

Printed and bound in Great Britain by
Clays Ltd, St Ives plc

Map by Andrew Ashton

For Lauren

Acknowledgements

I may have written this book, but there are many people whose patience and hard work on the completed work of art that's made its way to you – in whatever form you're enjoying it – deserve credit.

Cassie, my perfect daughter, whose care forced me to unplug regularly and live in the now, and who has helped me see the world in completely different ways. My mom, who does much of the copy editor's and proofreader's jobs without them ever knowing. My agent Joshua, the single most in-depth editor I have, and his amazing team at JABberwocky Literary, and their international affiliates.

Myke Cole, who reads all the versions and understands all the trials. Jay and Amelia, who always make time to read.

My assistant Meg, who does more than she realizes to keep me sane.

Larry Rostant, whose ability to capture my characters makes me feel they've stepped right from my mind. Lauren K. Cannon, who designed the wards, and Karsten Moran who made me look respectable in my new author photo.

My audio narrators, Pete Bradbury and Colin Mace, who make me feel like a kid listening to Grandpa reading me a story, and the cast and crew at GraphicAudio, whose productions bring it all to life.

My publishers all around the world – editors who have always believed in me and a small army of design, editorial, production, and marketing people who work behind the scenes to make me look more awesome than I deserve, and especially my translators, whose work is Herculean.

Coffee. You are my true friend.

But above all, thank you to Lauren Greene, who has been there for every moment, giving comfort and invaluable advice – both personal and professional. More important, thank you for showing by example how to be awesome and successful at life.

Contents

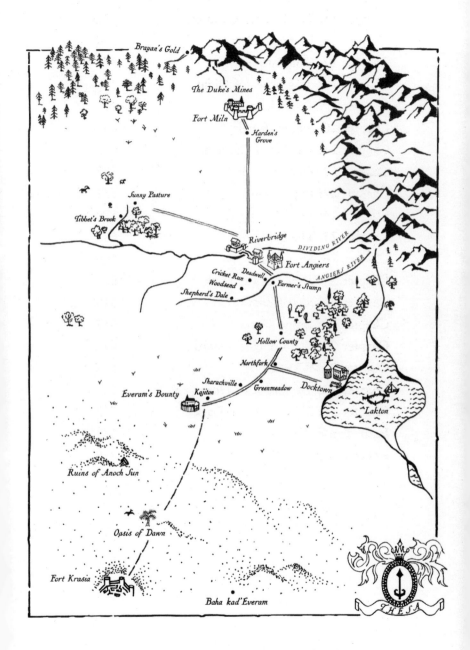

Prologue

No Victor

333 AR Autumn

'No!' Inevera reached out, clutching empty air as the Par'chin pitched himself and her husband over the cliff.

Taking with them all the hope of the human race.

On the opposite side of the circle of combat, Leesha Paper let out a similar cry. The strict ritual laws of *Domin Sharum* were forgotten as witnesses from both sides rushed to the precipice, crowding together to peer into the darkness that had swallowed the combatants.

In Everam's light, Inevera could see as clearly in darkness as brightest day, the world defined by magic's glow. But magic was drawn to life, and there was little below save barren rock and dirt. The two men, glowing as fiercely as the sun a moment ago, had vanished into the dull gloom of ambient magic as it vented to the surface.

Inevera twisted her earring, the *hora* stone within attuned to its mate on her husband's ear, but she heard nothing. It could be out of range, or broken in the fall.

Or there might be nothing to hear. She suppressed a shiver as a chill mountain wind blew over her.

She glanced at the others clustered at the edge, reading their expressions, searching for a hint of betrayal, a sign one of them had known this was coming. She read the magic that emanated

I

from them, as well. The circlet of warded electrum coins she wore did not let her read spirits as fluidly as her husband did with the Crown of Kaji, but she was getting more and more skilled at reading emotions. Shock was clear throughout the group. There were variations from one to another, but this was not the outcome any of them had expected.

Even Abban, the smug liar, always hiding something, stood horrified. He and Inevera had been bitter rivals, each attempting to undo the other, but he loved Ahmann as much as an honourless *khaffit* could, and stood to lose more than any, should he prove dead.

I should have poisoned the Par'chin's tea, Inevera thought, remembering the guileless face of the Par'chin the night he appeared from the desert with the Spear of Kaji. *Pricked him with a venom-dipped needle. Put an asp in his pillows as he dozed before* alagai'sharak. *Even claimed offence and killed him with my bare hands. Anything but leave it to Ahmann. His heart was too true for murder and betrayal, even with the fate of Ala in the balance.*

Was. Already she used the past tense, though he had been gone only seconds.

'We must find them.' Jayan's voice sounded miles away, though her eldest son stood right beside her.

'Yes,' Inevera agreed, thoughts still spinning, 'though it will be difficult in the darkness.' Already, the cries of wind demons echoed off the cliffs, along with the deep rumble of the mountain stone demons. 'I will cast the *hora* to guide us.'

'Core with waitin' on that,' the Par'chin's *Jiwah Ka* said, shouldering Rojer and Gared aside as she dropped to her belly and swung her legs over the edge of the cliff.

'Renna!' Leesha grabbed for her wrist, but Renna was too fast, dropping quickly out of reach. The young woman glowed brightly with magic. Not so brightly as the Par'chin, but brighter than any other she had ever seen. Her fingers and toes drove into the cliff face like a demon's talons, cracking stone to create her holds.

Inevera turned to Shanjat. 'Follow her. Mark your trail.'

To his credit, Shanjat showed none of the fear that ran through his aura as he looked at the cliff. 'Yes, Damajah.' He punched a fist to his chest and slung his spear and shield over his back, dropping to his belly and swinging over the edge, picking his way carefully down.

Inevera wondered if the task might be beyond him. Shanjat was as strong as any man, but he had killed no demons this night, and did not possess the inhuman strength that allowed Renna am'Bales to claw her own path.

But the *kai'Sharum* surprised her, and perhaps himself, using many of the fissures the Par'chin's wife made for his own holds. Soon he, too, vanished into the gloom.

'If you're going to throw your bones, do it now, so we can begin the search,' Leesha Paper said.

Inevera looked at the greenland whore, suppressing the snarl that threatened her serene expression. Of course she wanted to see Inevera cast the dice. No doubt she was desperate to learn the wards of prophecy. As if she had not stolen enough from Inevera.

None of the others knew, but the dice had told her Leesha carried Ahmann's child in her belly, threatening everything Inevera had built. She fought the urge to draw her knife and cut the babe free now, ending the trouble before it began. They would not be able to stop her. The greenlanders were formidable, but no match for her sons and two *Damaji sharusahk* masters.

She breathed, finding her centre. Inevera wanted to heap all her anger and fear upon the woman, but it was not Leesha Paper's fault that men were proud fools. No doubt she'd attempted to dissuade the Par'chin from his issuing his challenge, much as Inevera had tried to dissuade Ahmann from accepting it.

Perhaps their battle had been inevitable. Perhaps Ala could not suffer two Deliverers. But now there was none, and that was worse by far.

Without Ahmann, the Krasian alliance would crumble, the *Damaji* devolving into bickering warlords. They would kill Ahmann's *dama* sons, then turn on one another, and to the abyss with Sharak Ka.

Inevera looked to Damaji Aleverak of the Majah, who had proven the greatest obstacle to Ahmann's ascension, and one of his most valuable advisors. His loyalty to Shar'Dama Ka was without question, but that would not stop him from killing Maji, Ahmann's Majah son, that he never supplant the Aleverak's son Aleveran.

An heir could still unite the tribes, perhaps, but who? Neither of her sons was ready for the task, her dice said, but they would not see it that way, nor give up interim power once granted. Jayan and Asome had always been rivals, and powerful allies would flock to them both. If the *Damaji* did not tear her people apart, her sons might do it for them.

Inevera moved wordlessly into the ring where the two would-be Deliverers had fought mere moments before. Both men had left blood on the ground, and she knelt, pressing her hands where it had fallen, wetting them as she took the dice in hand and shook. The Krasians formed a ring about her, keeping the greenlanders at bay.

Carved from the bones of a demon prince and coated in electrum, Inevera's dice were the most powerful set any *dama'ting* had carried since the time of the first Damajah. They throbbed with power, glowing fiercely in the darkness. She threw and the wards of foretelling flared, pulling the dice to a stop in that unnatural way they had, forming a pattern of symbols for her to read. It would have been meaningless to most. Even *dama'ting* argued over the interpretations of a throw, but Inevera could read them as easily as words on parchment. They had guided her through decades of tumult and upheaval, but as was often the case, the answer they gave was vague, and brought little relief.

—There is no victor—

What did it mean? Had the fall killed them both? Did the

battle still rage below? A thousand questions roiled within her and she threw again, but the resulting pattern was unchanged, as she had known it would be.

'Well?' the Northern whore asked. 'What do they say?'

Inevera bit back a sharp retort, knowing her next words were crucial. In the end, she decided the truth – or most of it – was as good an answer as any to hold the plotting of the ambitious minds around her at bay.

'There is no victor,' she said. 'The battle continues below, and only Everam knows how it will end. We must find them, and quickly.'

It took hours to descend the mountain. The darkness did not slow them – all of this elite group could see by magic's glow – but rock and stone demons haunted the trail now, blending in perfectly with the mountainside. Wind demons shrieked in the sky, circling.

Rojer took up his instrument, coaxing the mournful sounds of the *Song of Waning* from its strings, keeping the *alagai* at bay. Amanvah lifted her voice to accompany him, their music enhanced by *hora* magic to fill the night. Even amidst the despairing wind that threatened to bend the palm of her centre to breaking, Inevera found pride in her daughter's skills.

Wrapped in the protections of the son of Jessum's strange magic, they were safe from the *alagai*, but it was slow going. Inevera's fingers itched to take the electrum wand from her belt, blasting demons from her path as she raced to her husband's side, but she did not wish to reveal its power to the Northerners, and it would only attract more *alagai* in any event. Instead, she was forced to keep the steady pace Rojer set, even as Ahmann and the Par'chin likely bled to death in some forgotten valley.

She shook the thought away. Ahmann was the chosen of Everam. She must trust that He granted His Shar'Dama Ka some miracle in his time of greatest need.

He was alive. He had to be.

Leesha rode in silence, and even Thamos was not fool enough to disturb her. The count might share her bed more oft than not, but she did not love him as she had Arlen . . . or Ahmann. Her heart had torn watching them fight.

It seemed Arlen held every advantage going in, and if she'd had to choose, she would not have had it another way. But Arlen's tormented soul had found a kind of peace in recent days, and she'd hoped he could force a submission from Ahmann and end the battle without death.

She'd cried out when Ahmann stabbed Arlen with the Spear of Kaji – perhaps the only weapon in the world that could harm him. The battle had turned in that moment, and for the first time her anger at Ahmann had threatened to become hate.

But when Arlen pitched them both over the cliff rather than lose, her stomach had wrenched as Ahmann dropped from sight. The child in her belly was less than eight weeks formed, but she could have sworn it kicked as its father fell into darkness.

Arlen's powers had been growing ever stronger in the year since she met him. Sometimes it seemed there was nothing he could not do, and even Leesha wondered if he might be the Deliverer. He could dissolve and protect himself from the impact. Ahmann could not.

But even Arlen had his limits, and Ahmann had tested them in ways no one had expected. Leesha remembered vividly the fall, mere weeks past, that had left Arlen a broken spatter on the cobblestones of the Hollow, his skull cracked like a boiled egg struck against the table.

If only Renna had not rushed after them. The woman knew something of Arlen's plans. More than she was telling.

They doubled back long before reaching the mountain's base, avoiding the pass watched by scouts from both their armies. Perhaps war was inevitable, but neither side wished for it to begin tonight.

The mountain paths wound and split. More than once, Inevera had to consult the dice to choose their path, kneeling on the ground to cast while the rest of them waited impatiently. Leesha longed to know what the woman saw in that jumble of symbols, but she knew enough not to doubt there was real power in the foretellings.

It was nearing dawn when they found the first of Shanjat's markers. Inevera picked up her pace and the others followed, racing along the trail as the horizon began to take on a purplish tinge.

They had not been noticed by the Watchers stationed at the base of the mountain, but Inevera's bodyguards Ashia and Shanvah had crept unseen up the slope and silently fell in with them. The greenland prince glanced at them but shook his head dismissively when he noticed they were women.

At last they came upon Renna and Shanjat, the two watching each other warily as they waited. Shanjat moved quickly to stand before Inevera, punching his chest with a bow. 'The trail ends here, Damajah.'

They dismounted and followed the warrior to a spot not far off where a man-sized depression lay, dirt and shattered stone telling of a great impact. Blood spattered the ground, but there were footprints, as well – signs of continued struggle.

'You've followed the trail?' Inevera asked.

Shanjat nodded. 'It vanishes not far from here. I thought it best to await further instruction before ranging too far.'

'Renna?' Leesha asked.

The Par'chin's *Jiwah Ka* was staring at the bloody crater with a glazed look in her eyes, her powerful aura unreadable. She nodded numbly. 'We've been circling the area for hours. It's like they grew wings.'

'Carried off by a wind demon?' Wonda ventured.

Renna shrugged. 'Reckon it's possible, but hard to believe.'

Inevera nodded. 'No demon could ever touch my sacred husband, but that he willed it.'

'What of the spear?' Jayan asked. Inevera looked at him sadly. It came as no great surprise that her eldest son cared more for the sacred weapon than his own father, but it saddened her nonetheless. Asome, at least, had the courtesy to keep such thoughts to himself.

Shanjat shook his head. 'There has been no sign of the holy weapon, Sharum Ka.'

'There is fresh blood,' Inevera said, looking at the horizon. Dawn was minutes away, but she might manage one last foretelling. She reached into her *hora* pouch, gripping her dice so tightly the edges dug painfully into her hand as she went to kneel by the crater.

Normally she would not have dared to expose the sensitive dice to even predawn light. Direct sunlight would destroy demon bone, and even indirect light could cause permanent damage. But the electrum she had coated them in protected them even in brightest sun. Like the Spear of Kaji, their power would deplete rapidly in the light, but they could be charged again when night fell.

Her hand shook as she reached out. She needed to breathe for several seconds to find her centre before she could continue, touching the blood of her husband for the second time this night and using it to seek his fate.

'Blessed Everam, Creator of all things, give me knowledge of the combatants, Ahmann asu Hoshkamin am'Jardir am'Kaji, and Arlen asu Jeph am'Bales am'Brook. I beseech you, tell me of the fate that has befallen them, and the fates yet to come.'

The power throbbed in her fingers and she threw, staring hard at the pattern.

When questioned on things that were, or had been, the dice spoke with cold – if often cryptic – assurance. But the future was always shifting, its sands blowing with every choice made. The dice gave hints, like signposts in the desert, but the farther one looked, the more the paths diverged, until one became lost in the dunes.

Ahmann's future had always been filled with divergences. Futures where he carried the fate of humanity, and ones where he died in shame. Death on *alagai* talon was the most common, but there were knives at his back always, and spears pointed at his heart. Those that would give their lives for his, and those waiting to betray.

Many of those paths were closed now. Whatever happened, Ahmann would not return soon, and likely not at all. The thought set a cold fear writhing through Inevera's gut.

The others held their collective breath, waiting on her words, and Inevera knew the fate of her people lay upon them. She remembered the words of the dice so many years ago:

—*The Deliverer is not born. He is made.*—

If Ahmann did not return to her, she would make another.

She looked at the myriad dooms that awaited her love, and plucked one from the rest. The only fate that would let her hold power until a suitable heir could be found.

'The Deliverer has passed beyond our reach,' Inevera said at last. 'He follows a demon to the abyss itself.'

'So the Par'chin is a demon after all,' Ashan said.

The dice said no such thing, but Inevera nodded. 'It would appear so.'

Gared spat on the ground. 'Said "Deliverer". Din't say "Shar'Dama Ka".'

The *Damaji* turned to him, regarding him the way a man might look at an insect, wondering if it was worth the effort to crush. 'They are one and the same.'

This time it was Wonda who spat. 'Core they are.'

Jayan stepped in, balling a fist as if to strike her, but Renna Tanner moved to interpose herself. The wards on her skin flared, and even Inevera's impulsive eldest son thought better of challenging her. It would not do to be beaten down by a woman before the very men he must convince to let him take the throne.

Jayan turned back to his mother. 'And the spear?' he demanded.

'Lost,' Inevera said. 'It will be found again when Everam wills it, and not before.'

'So we are to simply give up?' Asome asked. 'Leave Father to his fate?'

'Of course not.' Inevera turned to Shanjat. 'Find the trail again and hunt. Follow every bent blade of grass and loose pebble. Do not return without the Deliverer or reliable news of his fate, even if it takes a thousand years.'

'Yes, Damajah.' Shanjat punched his chest.

Inevera turned to Shanvah. 'Go with your father. Obey and protect him on his journey. His goal is your goal.'

The young woman bowed silently. Ashia squeezed her shoulder and their eyes met, then father and daughter were off.

Leesha turned to Wonda. 'You have a look as well, but be back in an hour.'

Wonda grinned, showing a confidence that filled Inevera with envy. 'Wan't planning to hunt till my hair turns grey. Deliverer comes and goes, but he'll be back, you'll see.' A moment later she, too, was gone.

'Goin' too,' Renna said, but Leesha caught her arm.

The woman glared at her. Leesha quickly let go but did not back down. 'Stay a moment, please.'

Even the Northerners are afraid of the Par'chin and his woman, Inevera noted, filing the information away as the two women moved off to speak in private.

'Ashan, walk with me,' she said, looking to the *Damaji*. The two of them stepped away as the others remained dumb-struck.

'I cannot believe he is gone,' Ashan said, his voice hollow. He and Ahmann had been as brothers for over twenty years. He had been the first *dama* to support Ahmann's rise to Shar'Dama Ka, and believed in his divinity without question. 'It seems like a dream.'

Inevera did not preamble. 'You must take the Skull Throne

as Andrah. You are the only one who can do it without inciting a war and hold it against my husband's return.'

Ashan shook his head. 'You are mistaken if you think that, Damajah.'

'It was the Shar'Dama Ka's wish,' Inevera reminded him. 'You swore an oath before him, and me.'

'That was if he were to fall in battle at Waning, with all to see,' Ashan said, 'not killed by a greenlander on some forgotten mountainside. The throne should go to Jayan or Asome.'

'He told you his sons were not ready for that burden,' Inevera said. 'Do you think that has changed in the last fortnight? My sons are cunning, but they are not yet wise. The dice foretell they will tear Everam's Bounty asunder vying for the throne, and should one climb to the top of the bloodied steps and sit, he will not rise on his father's return.'

'If he returns,' Ashan noted.

'He will,' Inevera said. 'Likely with all the Core behind him. When he does, he will need all the armies of Ala to answer his call, and have neither time nor desire to kill his son to regain control.'

'I don't like it,' Ashan said. 'I have never coveted power.'

'It is *inevera*,' she told him. 'Your likes are irrelevant, and your humility before Everam is why it must be you.'

'Be quick,' Renna said, as Leesha led her aside. 'Wasted enough time already waitin' on you lot. Arlen's out there somewhere and I need to find him.'

'Demonshit,' Leesha snapped. 'I don't know you that well, Renna Bales, but well enough to know you wouldn't have waited ten seconds on me if your husband was still unaccounted for. You and Arlen planned this. Where has he gone? What's he done with Ahmann?'

'Callin' me a liar?' Renna growled. Her brows tightened, fingers curling into fists.

For some reason, the bluster only made Leesha all the more sure of her guess. She doubted the woman would really strike her, but she held a pinch of blinding powder and would use it if need be.

'Please,' she said, keeping her voice calm. 'If you know something, tell me. I swear to the Creator you can trust me.'

Renna seemed to calm a bit at that, relaxing her hands, but she held them palms up. 'Search my pockets, you'll find no answers.'

'Renna,' Leesha struggled to maintain her composure, 'I know we had an ill start. You've little reason to like me, but this isn't a game. You're putting everyone at risk by keeping secrets.'

Renna barked a laugh. 'If that ent the night callin' it dark.' She poked Leesha in the chest, hard enough to knock her back a step. 'You're the one got the demon of the desert's baby in your belly. You think that ent puttin' folk at risk?'

Leesha felt her face go cold, but she bulled forward, lest her silence confirm the guess. She lowered her voice to a harsh whisper. 'Who told you that nonsense?'

'You did,' Renna said. 'I can hear a butterfly flap its wings across a cornfield. Arlen, too. We both heard what you said to Jardir. You're carrying his child, and setting the count up to take the blame.'

It was true enough. A ridiculous plot of her mother's that Leesha had foolishly brought to fruition. It was doubtful the deception would last past the child's birth, but that was seven months to prepare – or run and hide – before the Krasians came for her child.

'All the more reason I find out what happened to Ahmann,' Leesha said, hating the pleading tone that had slipped into her voice.

'Ent got a notion,' Renna said. 'Wastin' time should be spent lookin'.'

Leesha nodded, knowing when she was beaten. 'Please don't tell Thamos,' she said. 'I'll tell him in time, honest word. But not now, with half the Krasian army just a few miles off.'

Renna snorted. 'Ent stupid. How'd a Gatherer like you get pregnant, anyway? Even a dumb Tanner knows to pull out.'

Leesha dropped her eyes, unable to keep contact with Renna's intense gaze. 'Asked myself that same question.' She shrugged. 'History's full of folk whose parents knew better.'

'Din't ask about history,' Renna said. 'Asked why the smartest woman in the Hollow's got wood for brains. No one ever tell you how babes are made?'

Leesha bared her teeth at that. The woman had a point, but she'd no right to judge. 'If you won't tell me your secrets, I've no reason to trust you with mine.' She swept a hand out at the valley. 'Go. Pretend to look for Arlen till we're out of sight, then go and meet him. I won't stop you.'

Renna smiled. 'As if you could.' She blurred and was gone.

Why did I let her get to me? Leesha wondered, but her fingers slipped to her belly, and she knew full well.

Because she was right.

Leesha had been drunk on couzi the first time she'd kissed Ahmann. She hadn't planned to stick him that first afternoon, but neither had she resisted when he moved to take her. She'd foolishly assumed he wouldn't spend in her before marriage, but Krasians considered it a sin for a man to waste his seed. She'd felt him increase his pace, beginning to grunt, and could have pulled away. But a part of her had wanted it, too. To feel a man pulse and jerk within her, and corespawn the risk. It was a thrill she'd ridden to her own crescendo.

She'd meant to brew pomm tea that night, but instead found herself kidnapped by Inevera's Watchers, ending the night battling a mind demon by the Damajah's side. Leesha took a double dose the next day, and every time they had lain together since, but as her mentor Bruna said, 'Sometimes a strong child finds a way, no matter what you do.'

Inevera eyed Thamos, the greenland princeling, as he stood before Ashan. He was a big man, tall and muscular but not without a share of grace. He moved like a warrior.

'I expect you'll want your men to search the valley,' he said.

Ashan nodded. 'And you, yours.'

Thamos gave a nod in return. 'A hundred men each?'

'Five hundred,' Ashan said, 'with the truce of *Domin Sharum* upon them.' Inevera saw the princeling's jaw tighten. Five hundred men was nothing to the Krasians, the tiniest fraction of the Deliverer's army. But it was more men than Thamos wished to spare.

Still, the princeling had little choice but to agree, and he gave his assent. 'How do I know your warriors will keep the peace? The last thing we need is for this valley to turn into a war zone.'

'My warriors will keep their veils up, even in the day,' Ashan said. 'They would not dare disobey. It's your men I worry over. I would hate to see them hurt in a misunderstanding.'

The princeling showed his teeth at that. 'I think there'd be hurt enough to go around. How is hiding their faces supposed to guarantee peace? A man with his face hidden fears no reprisal.'

Ashan shook his head. 'It's a wonder you savages have survived the night so long. Men remember the faces of those who have wronged them, and those enmities are hard to put aside. We wear veils in the night, so that all may fight as brothers, their blood feuds forgotten. If your men cover their faces, there will be no further blood spilled in this Everam-cursed valley.'

'Fine,' the princeling said. 'Done.' He gave a short, shallow bow, the barest respect to a man who was a dozen times his better, and turned, striding away. The other greenlanders followed.

'The Northerners will pay for their disrespect,' Jayan said.

'Perhaps,' Inevera said, 'but not today. We must return to Everam's Bounty, and quickly.'

1

The Hunt

333 AR Autumn

Jardir woke at sunset, his mind thick with fog. He was lying in a Northern bed – one giant pillow instead of many. The bedcloth was rough, nothing like the silk to which he had become accustomed. The room was circular, with warded glass windows all around. A tower of some sort. Untamed land spread into the twilight, but he recognized none of it.

Where in Ala am I?

Pain lanced through him as he stirred, but pain was an old companion, embraced and forgotten. He pulled himself into a sitting position, rigid legs scraping against each other. He pulled the blanket aside. Plaster casts running thigh-to-foot. His toes, swollen in red, purple, and yellow, peeked from the far ends, close, yet utterly out of reach. He flexed them experimentally, ignoring the pain, and was satisfied with the slight twitch that rewarded him.

It harkened back to the broken arm he'd suffered as a child, and the helplessness of his weeks of healing.

He reached immediately to the nightstand for the crown. Even in day, there was magic enough stored within to heal a few broken bones, especially ones already set.

His hands met empty air. Jardir turned and stared a long moment before the situation registered. It had been years since he had let himself be out of arm's reach of his crown and spear, but both were missing.

Memories came back to him in a rush. The fight atop the mountain with the Par'chin. How the son of Jeph had collapsed into smoke as Jardir struck, only to solidify an instant later, grabbing the spear shaft with inhuman strength and twisting it from his grasp.

And then the Par'chin turned and threw it from the cliff as if it were nothing more than a gnawed melon rind.

Jardir licked cracked lips. His mouth was dry and his bladder full, but both needs had been provided for. The water at his bedside was sweet, and with some effort he managed use of the chamber pot his searching fingers found on the floor just underneath the bed.

His chest was bound tightly, ribs grinding as he shifted. Over the bandages he was clad in a thin robe – tan, he noted. The Par'chin's idea of a joke, perhaps.

There was no door, simply a stair leading up into the room – as good as prison bars in his current state. There were no other exits, nor did the steps continue on. He was at the top of the tower. The room was sparsely furnished. A small table by the bedside. A single chair.

There was a sound in the stairwell. Jardir froze, listening. He might be bereft of his crown and spear, but years of absorbing magic through them had remade his body as close to Everam's image as a mortal form could be. He had the eyes of a hawk, the nose of a wolf, and the ears of a bat.

'Sure you can handle him?' the Par'chin's First Wife said. 'Thought he was going to kill you out on that cliff.'

'No worries, Ren,' the Par'chin said. 'He can't hurt me without the spear.'

'Can in daylight,' Renna said.

'Not with two broken legs,' the Par'chin said. 'Got this, Ren. Honest word.'

We shall see, Par'chin.

There was a smacking of lips as the son of Jeph kissed his

jiwah's remaining protests away. 'Need you back in the Hollow keepin' an eye on things. Now, 'fore they get suspicious.'

'Leesha Paper's already suspicious,' Renna said. 'Her guesses ent far from the mark.'

'Don't matter, long as they stay guesses,' the Par'chin said. 'You just keep playin' dim, no matter what she says or does.'

Renna gave a stunted laugh. 'Ay, that won't be a problem. Like makin' her want to spit.'

'Don't waste too much time on it,' the Par'chin said. 'Need you to protect the Hollow, but keep a low profile. Strengthen the folk, but let them carry the weight. I'll skate in when I can, but only to see you. No one else can know I'm alive.'

'Don't like it,' Renna said. 'Man and wife shouldn't be apart like this.'

The Par'chin sighed. 'Ent nothin' for it, Ren. Bettin' the farm on this throw. Can't afford to lose. I'll see you soon enough.'

'Ay,' Renna said. 'Love you, Arlen Bales.'

'Love you, Renna Bales,' the Par'chin said. They kissed again, and Jardir heard rapid footsteps as she descended the tower. The Par'chin, however, began to climb.

For a moment Jardir thought to feign sleep. Perhaps he might learn something; gain the element of surprise.

He shook his head. *I am Shar'Dama Ka. It is beneath me to hide. I will meet the Par'chin's eyes and see what remains of the man I knew.*

He propped himself up, embracing the roar of pain in his legs. His face was serene as the Par'chin entered. He wore plain clothes, much as he had when they first met, a cotton shirt of faded white and worn denim trousers with a leather Messenger satchel slung over one shoulder. His feet were bare, pant and shirt cuffs rolled to show the wards he had inked into his skin. His sand-coloured hair was shaved away, and the face Jardir remembered was barely recognizable under all the markings.

Even without his crown, Jardir could sense the power of those symbols, but the strength came with a heavy price. The

Par'chin looked more like a page from one of the holy scrolls of warding than a man.

'What have you done to yourself, old friend?' He had not meant to speak the words aloud, but something pushed him.

'Got a lot of nerve callin' me that, after what you did,' the Par'chin said. 'Din't do this to myself. *You* did this to me.'

'*I?*' Jardir asked. 'I took ink and profaned your body with it?'

The Par'chin shook his head. 'You left me to die in the desert, without weapon or succour, and knew I'd be corespawned before I let the *alagai* have me. My body was the only thing you left me to ward.'

With those words, all Jardir's questions about how the Par'chin had survived were answered. In his mind's eye he saw his friend alone in the desert, parched and bloodied as he beat *alagai* to death with his bare hands.

It was glorious.

The Evejah forbade the tattooing of flesh, but it forbade many things Jardir had since permitted for the sake of Sharak Ka. He wanted to condemn the Par'chin, but his throat tightened at the truth of the man's words.

Jardir shivered as a chill of doubt touched his centre. No thing happened, but that Everam willed it. It was *inevera* that the Par'chin should live to meet him again. The dice said each of them *might* be the Deliverer. Jardir had dedicated his life to being worthy of that title. He was proud of his accomplishments, but could not deny that his *ajin'pal*, the brave outsider, might have greater honour in Everam's eyes.

'You play at rituals you do not understand, Par'chin,' he said. '*Domin Sharum* is to the death, and victory was yours. Why did you not take it and claim your place at the lead of the First War?'

The Par'chin sighed. 'There's no victory in your death, Ahmann.'

'Then you admit I am the Deliverer?' Jardir asked. 'If that is so, then return my spear and crown to me, put your head to the floor, and have done. All will be forgiven, and we can face Nie side by side once more.'

The Par'chin snorted. He set his satchel on the table, reaching inside. The Crown of Kaji gleamed even in the growing darkness, its nine gems glittering. Jardir could not deny the desire the item stirred in him. If he'd had legs to stand, he would have leapt for it.

'Crown's right here.' The Par'chin spun the pointed circlet on a finger like a child's hoop toy. 'But the spear ent yours. Least, not 'less I decide to give it to you. Hidden where you can never get it, even if your legs wern't casted.'

'The holy items belong together,' Jardir said.

The Par'chin sighed again. 'Nothing's holy, Ahmann. Told you once before Heaven was a lie. You threatened to kill me over the words, but that doesn't make 'em any less true.'

Jardir opened his mouth to reply, angry words forming on his lips, but the Par'chin cut him off, catching the spinning crown in a firm grip and holding it up. As he did, the wards on his skin throbbed briefly with light, and those on the crown began to glow.

'This,' the Par'chin said of the crown, 'is a thin band of mind demon skull and nine horns, coated in a warded alloy of silver and gold, focused by gemstones. It is a masterwork of wardcraft, but nothing more.'

He smiled. 'Much as your earring was.'

Jardir started, raising his hand to touch the bare lobe his wedding ring had once pierced. 'Do you mean to steal my First Wife, as well as my throne?'

The Par'chin laughed, a genuine sound Jardir had not heard in years. A sound he could not deny he had missed.

'Not sure which would be the greater burden,' the Par'chin said. 'I want neither. I have a wife, and among my people one is more'n enough.'

Jardir felt a smile tug at his lips, and he let it show. 'A worthy *Jiwah Ka* is both support and burden, Par'chin. They challenge us to be better men, and that is ever a struggle.'

The Par'chin nodded. 'Honest word.'

'Then why have you stolen my ring?' Jardir demanded.

'Just holding on to it while you're under my roof,' the Par'chin said. 'Can't have you calling for help.'

'Eh?' Jardir said.

The Par'chin tilted his head at him, and Jardir could feel the son of Jeph's gaze reaching into his soul, much as Jardir did when he had the gift of crownsight. How did the Par'chin do it without the crown at his brow?

'You don't know,' the Par'chin said after a moment. He barked a laugh. 'Giving me marriage advice while your own wife spies on you!'

The derision in his tone angered Jardir, and his brows drew tight despite his desire to keep his face calm. 'What is that supposed to mean?'

The Par'chin reached into his pocket, producing the earring. It was a simple hoop of gold with a delicate warded ball hanging from it. 'There's a broken piece of demon bone in here, with its opposite half in your wife's ear. Lets her hear everything you do.'

Suddenly so many mysteries became clear to Jardir. How his wife seemed to know his every plan and secret. Much of her information came from the dice, but the *alagai hora* spoke in riddles as oft as not. He should have known cunning Inevera would not rely on her castings alone.

'So she knows you've kidnapped me?' Jardir asked.

The Par'chin shook his head. 'Blocked its power. She won't be able to find you before we're finished here.'

Jardir crossed his arms. 'Finished with what? You will not follow me, and I will not follow you. We stand at the same impasse we found five years ago in the Maze.'

The Par'chin nodded. 'You couldn't bring yourself to kill me then, and it forced me to change how I see the world. Offering you the same.' With that, he tossed the crown across the room.

Instinctively, Jardir caught it. 'Why return it to me? Won't this heal my wounds? You may have difficulty holding me without them.'

The Par'chin shrugged. 'Don't think you'll leave without the spear, but I've drained the crown in any event. Not a lot of magic venting from the Core makes it this high,' he waved his hand at the windows circling the room on all sides, 'and the sun cleans out this room each morning. It'll give you crownsight, but not much else until it's recharged.'

'So why return it to me?' Jardir asked again.

'Thought we might have a talk,' the Par'chin said. 'And I want you to see my aura while we do. Want you see the truth of my words, the strength of my convictions, written on my very soul. Perhaps then, you'll come to see.'

'Come to see what?' Jardir asked. 'That Heaven is a lie? Nothing written on your soul can do that, Par'chin.' Nevertheless, he slipped the crown onto his head. Immediately the darkened room came alive with crownsight, and Jardir breathed deep in relief, like the blind man in the Evejah, given his sight back by Kaji.

Through the windows, land that had been nothing but shadows and vague shapes a moment ago became sharply defined, lit with the magic that vented from Ala. All living things held a spark of power at their core, and Jardir could see strength glowing in the trunks of trees, the moss that clung to them, and every animal that lived within their branches and bark. It ran through the grasses of the plains and, most of all, in the demons that stalked the land and rode the winds. The *alagai* shone like beacons, waking a primal desire in him to hunt and kill.

As the Par'chin had warned, his cell was dimmer. Small tendrils of power drifted up the tower walls, Drawn to the wards etched into the glass windows. They flickered to life, a shield against the *alagai*.

But though the room was dim, the Par'chin shone brighter than a demon. So bright it should be difficult to look at him. But it was not. Quite the contrary, the magic was glorious to behold, rich and tempting. Jardir reached out through the crown, attempting to Draw a touch of it to himself. Not so much the Par'chin might sense the drain, but perhaps enough to speed his healing. A wisp of power snaked through the air towards him like incense smoke.

The Par'chin had shaved his brows, but the wards above his left eye lifted in an unmistakable expression. His aura shifted, showing more bemusement than offence. 'Ah-ah. Get your own.' Abruptly, the magic reversed its flow and was Drawn back into him.

Jardir kept his face calm, though he doubted it made a difference. The Par'chin was right. He could read the man's aura, seeing his every feeling, and had no doubt his old friend could do the same. The Par'chin was calm, centred, and meant Jardir no harm. There was no deception in him. Only weariness, and fear Jardir would be too rigid to give his words fair consideration.

'Tell me again why I am here, Par'chin,' Jardir said. 'If your goal is truly as you have always said, to rid the world of *alagai*, then why do you oppose me? I am close to fulfilling your dream.'

'Not as close as you think,' the Par'chin said. 'And the way you're doing it disgusts me. You choke and threaten humanity to its own salvation, not caring the cost. Know you Krasians like to dress in black and white, but the world ent so simple. There's colour, and more than a fair share of grey.'

'I am not a fool, Par'chin,' Jardir said.

'Sometimes I wonder,' the Par'chin said, and his aura agreed. It was a bitter tea that his old friend, whom he had taught so much and always respected, should think so little of him.

'Then why did you not kill me and take the spear and crown for your own?' Jardir demanded. 'The witnesses were honour-bound. My people would have accepted you as Deliverer and followed you to Sharak Ka.'

Irritation ran like wildfire across the Par'chin's calm aura. 'You still don't get it,' he snapped. 'I'm not the ripping Deliverer! Neither are you! The Deliverer is all humanity as one, not one as humanity. Everam is just a name we gave to the idea, not some giant in the sky, fighting back the blackness of space.'

Jardir pressed his lips together, knowing the Par'chin was seeing a flare across his aura at the blasphemy. Years ago he had promised to kill the Par'chin should he ever speak such words again. The Par'chin's aura dared him to try it now.

Jardir was sorely tempted. He had not truly tested the crown's power against the Par'chin, and with it at his brow, he was no longer as helpless as he seemed.

But there was something else in his *ajin'pal's* aura that checked him. He was ready for an attack, and would meet it head-on, but an image loomed over him, *alagai* dancing as the world burned.

What he feared would come to pass, if they did not find accord.

Jardir drew a deep breath, embracing his anger and letting it go with his exhalation. Across the room, the Par'chin had not moved, but his aura eased back like a *Sharum* lowering his spear.

'What does it matter,' Jardir said at last, 'if Everam be a giant in the sky, or a name we have given to the honour and courage that let us stand fast in the night? If humanity is to act as one, there must be a leader.'

'Like a mind demon leads drones?' the Par'chin asked, hoping to snare Jardir in a logic trap.

'Just so,' Jardir said. 'The world of the *alagai* has ever been a shadow of our own.'

The Par'chin nodded. 'Ay, a war needs its generals, but they should serve the people, and not the other way 'round.'

Now it was Jardir who raised an eyebrow. 'You think I do not serve my people, Par'chin? I am not the Andrah, sitting fat on my throne while my subjects bleed and starve. There is no hunger in my lands. No crime. And I personally go into the night to keep them safe.'

The Par'chin laughed, a harsh mocking sound. Jardir would have taken offence, but the incredulity in the Par'chin's aura checked him.

'This is why it matters,' the Par'chin said. 'Because you actually *believe* that load of demonshit! You came to lands that were not yours, murdered thousands of men, raped their women, enslaved their children, and think your soul is clean because their holy book's a little different from yours! You keep the demons from them, ay, but chickens on the chopping block don't call the butcher Deliverer for keeping the fox at bay.'

'Sharak Ka is coming, Par'chin,' Jardir said. 'I have made those chickens into falcons. The men of Everam's Bounty protect their own women and children now.'

'As do the Hollowers,' the Par'chin said. 'But they did it without killing one another. Not a woman raped. Not a child torn from its mother's arms. We did not become demons in order to fight them.'

'And that is what you think me?' Jardir asked. 'A demon?'

The Par'chin smiled. 'Do you know what my people call you?'

The demon of the desert. Jardir had heard the name many times, though only in the Hollow did any dare speak it openly. He nodded.

'Your people are fools, Par'chin, as are you if you think me the same as the *alagai*. You may not murder and you may not rape, but neither have you forged unity. Your Northern dukes bicker and vie for power even as the abyss opens up before them, ready to spew forth Nie's legions. Nie does not care about your morals. She does not care who is innocent and who is corrupt. She does not even care for Her *alagai*. Her goal is to wipe the slate clean.

'Your people live on borrowed time, Par'chin. Loaned to you against the day of Sharak Ka, when your weakness will leave them meat for the Core. Then you will have wished for a thousand murders, a thousand thousand, if that's what it took to prepare you for the fight.'

The Par'chin shook his head sadly. 'You're like a horse with blinkers on, Ahmann. You see what supports your beliefs, and ignore the rest. Nie doesn't care because She doesn't ripping *exist.*'

'Words do not make a thing so, Par'chin,' Jardir said. 'Words cannot kill *alagai* or make Everam cease to be. Words alone cannot unite us all for Sharak Ka before it is too late.'

'You talk of unity, but you don't understand the meaning of the word,' the Par'chin said. 'What you call unity I call domination. Slavery.'

'Unity of purpose, Par'chin,' Jardir said. 'All working toward one goal. Ridding the Ala of demonkind.'

'There is no unity, if it depends on one man alone to hold it,' the Par'chin said. 'We are all mortal.'

'The unity I have brought will not be so easily cast aside,' Jardir said.

'No?' Arlen asked. 'I learned much during my visit to Everam's Bounty, Ahmann. The Northern dukes have nothing on your people. Your *dama* will not follow Jayan. Your *Sharum* will not follow Asome. None of the men will follow Inevera, and your *Damaji* would as soon kill one another as eat at the same table. There is no one who can sit the throne without civil war. Your precious unity is about to crumble away like a palace made of sand.'

Jardir felt his jaw tighten. His teeth whined as he ground them. The Par'chin was correct, of course. Inevera was clever and could hold things together for a time, but he could not afford to be gone for long, or his hard-forged army would turn on itself with Sharak Ka only just begun.

'I am not dead yet,' Jardir said.

'No, but you won't be returning any time soon,' the Par'chin said.

'We shall see, Par'chin.' Without warning, Jardir reached out through the crown, Drawing hard on the Par'chin's magic. Caught off guard, the Par'chin's aura exploded in shock, then distorted as Jardir hauled in the prize.

Power rushed through Jardir's body, knitting muscle and bone, making him strong. With a flex, the bandages around his chest ripped and the plaster about his legs shattered. He sprang from the bed, crossing the room in an instant.

The Par'chin managed to get his guard up in time, but it was a *Sharum*'s guard, for he had not been trained in Sharik Hora. Jardir easily slipped around it and caught him in a submission hold. The Par'chin's face reddened as he struggled for air.

But then he collapsed into mist, as he had in their battle on the cliff. Jardir overbalanced when the resistance ended, but the Par'chin reformed before he hit the floor, grabbing Jardir's right arm and leg, throwing him across the room. He struck the window so hard even his magic-strengthened bones snapped, but the warded glass did not so much as crack.

There was a thin flow of magic on the surface of the wards, and Jardir instinctively Drew on it, using the power to mend his bones even before the pain set in.

The Par'chin vanished from across the room, appearing in close, but Jardir was wise to the trick. Even as the mist began to reform he was moving, dodging the Par'chin's attempted hold and striking two hard blows before he could melt away again.

They struggled thus for several seconds, the Par'chin disappearing and reforming before Jardir could do any real damage, but unable to strike in turn.

'Corespawn it, Ahmann,' he cried. 'Ent got time for this!'

'In this, we agree,' Jardir said, having positioned himself correctly. He threw the room's single chair at the Par'chin, and predictably, the man misted when he could as easily have dodged.

Your powers are making you lax, Par'chin, he thought as he sprang the open distance to the stairwell.

'You ent goin' anywhere!' the Par'chin growled as he reformed, drawing a ward in the air. Jardir saw the magic gather, hurtling at him, a blast that would knock him away from the stairs like a giant hammer. With no time to dodge, he embraced the blow, going limp to absorb as much of the shock as possible.

But the blow never came. The Crown of Kaji warmed and flared with light, absorbing the power. Without thinking, Jardir drew a ward in the air himself, turning the power into a bolt of raw heat. Enough to turn a dozen wood demons to cinders.

The Par'chin held up a hand, Drawing the magic back into himself. Jardir, dizzied by the sudden drain, stared at him.

'We can do this all night, Ahmann,' the Par'chin said, melting away and reappearing between Jardir and the stairwell. 'It won't get you out of this tower.'

Jardir crossed his arms. 'Even you cannot hold me forever. The sun will come, and your demon tricks and *hora* magic will fail you.'

The Par'chin spread his hands. 'I don't have to. By dawn, you'll stay willingly.'

Jardir almost laughed, but again the Par'chin's aura checked him. He believed it. He believed his next words would sway Jardir, or nothing would.

'Why have you brought me here, Par'chin?' he asked a final time.

'To remind you of the real enemy,' the Par'chin said. 'And to ask your help.'

'Why should I help you?' Jardir asked.

'Because,' the Par'chin said, 'we're going to capture a mind demon and make it take us to the Core.

'It's time we brought the fight to the *alagai*.'

2

Vacuum

333 AR Autumn

Inevera wasted no time when they returned to the Krasian camp. Even as Ashan quietly selected warriors to begin the search and ordered others to break camp, she summoned Abban to her private audience chamber in the pavilion of the Shar'Dama Ka.

Already the *Sharum* were questioning why the Deliverer had not returned to them. There had been no formal announcement, either of the battle itself or of its sudden end. Yet soon word would spread, and the ambitious would seek to exploit her husband's absence. The cunning had plotted for this day, and would be quick to act once it was clear the search was in vain. The rash might be quicker still.

It was clear Abban knew this, approaching the pavilion surrounded by his *kha'Sharum* warriors. The *dal'Sharum* still sneered at warriors in tan, but the eunuch spies Inevera had sent to Abban's compound had been found dead, and that spoke volumes for the *khaffit* warriors' skill. She had seen, too, the glow of power in their weapons and equipment, carefully disguised with worn leather and paint to hide their fine quality. Not even the elite Spears of the Deliverer, with their shields and spearheads of warded glass, were equipped better.

You have grown formidable, khaffit. The thought did not please her, but neither did it worry her as it once had. She had not understood weeks ago when the dice told her Abban's fate was intertwined with her own, but it was clear now. They were Ahmann's closest, most trusted advisors and, up until a few hours ago, had been untouchable with vast discretionary powers. But with her husband gone, much of that power would evaporate. Inevera would have to work quickly and carefully to install Ashan, but once the reins were passed it would still be his voice, not hers, that led their people. Ashan was not as wise – or as pliable – as Ahmann.

Abban was in an even worse position. Formidable though his *kha'Sharum* were, the crippled merchant would be lucky to live another day once his enemies ceased to fear Ahmann's wrath should he be harmed. Not long ago the thought of his death would have pleased her greatly. Now she needed him. The *khaffit* knew every last draki in the Deliverer's treasury, every debt of the throne, every grain in his silos. More, Ahmann trusted him with schemes and secrets he did not even share with the *Damaji*. Troop movements. Battle plans. Targets.

The fat *khaffit*'s smile as he limped into her audience chamber showed he knew her need, Everam damn him.

At Abban's back was the giant *kha'Sharum* bodyguard that had become his shadow in recent weeks. The deaf man who had been one of the first to answer the Deliverer's call. He had given up his weapons to enter, but seemed no less formidable as he loomed over the *khaffit*'s shoulder. Abban was not a short man, even stooping to lean on his crutch, but his bodyguard stood head and shoulders above him.

'I commanded we meet in private, *khaffit*,' Inevera said.

Abban bowed as deeply as his camel-topped crutch allowed. 'Apologies, Damajah, but the *dal'Sharum* no longer have Ahmann to hold their leash. Surely you will not deny me a modicum of security? Earless is deaf as a stone, and will hear nothing of our words.'

'Even a deaf man may hear,' Inevera said, 'if he has eyes to watch a speaker's mouth.'

Abban bowed again. 'This is so, though of course the Damajah's veil prevents this, even if my humble servant had learned the art, which I swear by Everam he has not.'

Inevera believed him – a rare occurrence. Her own eunuch guards had given up their tongues to protect her secrets, and she knew Abban would value a man who could not overhear and be made to betray his many intrigues. Still, it was best not to yield too much.

'He may guard the door,' Inevera said, turning to saunter to the pillows on the far side of the chamber with a swing to her hips. Abban had never dared ogle her before, but she wondered if he might now, with Ahmann gone. That would be something she could use. She glanced over her shoulder, but Abban was not looking. He made a few quick gestures to the giant, who moved with a silent grace that belied his great size to stand by the door.

Abban limped over, easing himself carefully down onto the pillows across from her. He kept his inviting smile in place, but a flick of his eyes at his bodyguard betrayed his fears. He knew Inevera could kill him long before the giant could cross the room, and even Earless would fear to strike the Damajah. She could kill the *kha'Sharum* as well, in any of a hundred ways – not the least of which was a whisk of her fingers to her own bodyguards, Ashia, Micha, and Jarvah, hidden just out of sight.

There was a silver tea service between them, the pot still steaming. At a nod from her, the *khaffit* poured and served.

'You honour me with your summons, Damajah.' Abban sat back with his cup. 'May I ask the reason why?'

'To offer you protection, of course,' Inevera said.

Abban looked sincerely surprised, though of course it was an act. 'Since when does the Damajah place such value upon poor, honourless Abban?'

'My husband values you,' Inevera said, 'and will be wroth

if you are dead upon his return. You would be wise to accept my help. The dice tell me your life will be short indeed without it. My sons hate you even more than the *Damaji*, and that is a very great deal. And do not think Hasik has forgotten who cut his manhood away.'

Inevera had expected the words to rattle the *khaffit*. She had seen his cowardice reveal itself in the face of danger before. But this was the bargaining table, and Abban knew it.

He has a coward's heart, Ahmann once told her, *but there is steel in Abban to put* Sharum *to shame, when the haggling has begun*.

Abban smiled and nodded. 'It is so, Damajah. But things are no less dire for you. How long will the *Damaji* let you sit atop the seven steps without your husband? A woman sitting above them is an insult they have never borne well.'

Inevera felt her jaw begin to tighten. How long since any save her husband had dared speak to her thus? And from a *khaffit*. She wanted to break his other leg.

But for all the audacity, his words were true enough, so Inevera let them pass over her like wind.

'All the more reason we must ally,' she said. 'We must find a way to trust, as Ahmann commanded, or both of us may walk the lonely path before long.'

'What are you asking?' Abban said.

'You will report to me as you did to my husband,' Inevera said. 'Bring your tallies and schemes to me before they are presented to the council of *Damaji*.'

Abban raised an eyebrow. 'And in return?'

Inevera smiled, visible through the gossamer lavender veil she wore. 'As I said, protection.'

Abban chuckled. 'You'll forgive me, Damajah, but you have fewer warriors at your command than I, and still not enough to protect me should one of the *Damaji* or your sons decide to be rid of me at last.'

'I have fear,' Inevera said. 'My sons fear me. The *Damaji* fear me.'

'They *feared* you, yes,' Abban agreed, 'but how much of that fear will last when a new backside sits the Skull Throne? Absolute power has a way of emboldening a man.'

'No power is absolute save that of Everam.' Inevera held up her dice. 'With Ahmann gone, I am His voice on Ala.'

'That, and three draki, will buy you a basket,' Abban said.

The phrase was a common one in Krasia, but it put Inevera on edge nevertheless. Her mother was a basket weaver with a successful business in the bazaar. No doubt Abban – who controlled half the commerce in Everam's Bounty – had dealings with her, but Inevera had worked tirelessly to ensure her family remained safely anonymous, out of the politics and intrigues that ruled her world.

Were they just words, or a subtle threat? Useful or not, Inevera would not hesitate to kill Abban to protect her family.

Again, Inevera wished she could see into the hearts of men and women as her husband did. The thick canvas walls of the pavilion let her see the *khaffit*'s aura, albeit dimly, but the subtle variations and patterns of shifting colour that Ahmann read as easily as words on a page were a mystery to her.

'I think you'll find my words carry more weight than you think,' Inevera said.

'*If* you secure your position,' Abban agreed. 'We are discussing why I should help you do that. Not every man in the Deliverer's court is a complete fool, Damajah. I may never enjoy the power I did with Ahmann, but I could still find protection and profit if I side with another.'

'I will grant you a permanent position at court,' Inevera said. 'To witness firsthand every dealing you can twist into a way to fill your greedy pockets.'

'Better,' Abban said, 'but I have spies throughout the Deliverer's court. More than even you can root out.'

'Do not be so sure,' Inevera said. 'But very well. I will offer something even you cannot refuse.'

'Oh?' Abban seemed amused at the thought. 'In the bazaar,

those words are a threat, but I think you will find I am not so easily bullied as I may appear.'

'No threats,' Inevera said. 'No bullying.' She smiled. 'At least not for coercion. They will be a promise, should you break our pact.'

Abban grinned. 'You have my fullest attention. What does the Damajah think my heart desires above all?'

'Your leg,' Inevera said.

'Eh?' Abban started.

'I can heal your leg,' Inevera said. 'Right now, if you wish. A simple matter. You could throw your crutch on the fire and walk out on two firm feet.' She winked at him. 'Though if I know sly Abban, you would limp out the way you came, and never let any know until there was profit in doing so.'

A doubtful look crossed the *khaffit*'s face. 'If it's such a simple matter, why didn't the *dama'ting* heal me when it was first shattered? Why cost the Kaji a warrior by leaving me lame?'

'Because healing is the costliest of *hora* magics,' Inevera said. 'At the time we did not have warded weapons to bring us an endless supply of *alagai* bones to power our spells. Even now, they must be rendered and treated, a difficult process.' She circled a finger around her teacup. 'We cast the dice for you, all those years ago, to see if it was worth the price. Do you know what they said?'

Abban sighed. 'That I was no warrior, and would provide little return on the investment.'

Inevera nodded.

Abban shook his head, disappointed but unsurprised. 'It is true you have found something I want. I do not deny this is something my heart has longed for.'

'Then you accept?' Inevera asked.

Abban drew a deep breath as if to speak, but held it instead. After a moment, he blew it out, seeming to deflate as he did. 'My father used to say, *Love nothing so much you cannot leave it at the bargaining table.* I know enough of the ancient tales to know that magic always has its price, and that price is ever higher than it appears. I have leaned on my crutch for twenty-five years. It is a part of me. Thank you for your offer, but I fear I must refuse.'

Inevera was becoming vexed and saw no reason to hide it. 'You try my patience, *khaffit*. If there is something you want, be out with it.'

The triumphant smile that came over Abban's face made it clear this was the moment he had been waiting for. 'A few simple things only, Damajah.'

Inevera chuckled. 'I have learned nothing is simple where you are concerned.'

Abban inclined his head. 'From you, that means everything. First, the protection you offer must extend to my agents, as well.'

Inevera nodded. 'Of course. So long as they are not working counter to my interests, or caught in an unforgivable crime against Everam.'

'And it must include protection from you,' Abban went on.

'I am to protect you from myself?' Inevera asked.

'If we are to work together,' Inevera noticed he did not say that he would work *for* her, 'then I must be free to speak my mind without fearing for my life. Even when it is not things you wish to hear. Especially then.'

She will tell you truths you do not wish to hear, the dice had once told Inevera of her mother. There was value in an advisor like that. In truth, there was little value in any other kind.

'Done,' she said, 'but if I choose not to act on your advice, you will support my decisions in any event.'

'The Damajah is wise,' Abban said. 'I trust she would not act wastefully once I have given her the costs.'

'Is that all?' Inevera asked, knowing it was not.

Abban chuckled again, refilling their teacups. He took a flask from the inner pocket of his vest and added a splash of couzi to the drink. It was a test, Inevera knew, for the drink was forbidden by the Evejah. She ignored the move. She hated couzi, thought it made men weak and foolhardy, but thousands of her people smuggled the tiny bottles under their robes.

Abban sipped at his drink. 'At times I may have questions.' His eyes flicked to the *hora* pouch at her waist. 'Questions only your dice can answer.'

Inevera clutched the pouch protectively. 'The *alagai hora* are not for the questions of men, *khaffit*.'

'Did not Ahmann pose questions to them daily?' Abban asked.

'Ahmann was the Deliverer . . .' Inevera caught herself, '. . . *is* the Deliverer. The dice are not toys to fill your pockets with gold.'

Abban bowed. 'I am aware of that, Damajah, and assure you I will not call upon you to throw them frivolously. But if you want my loyalty, that is my price.'

Inevera sat back, considering. 'You said yourself magic always comes with a price. The dice, too, can speak truths we do not wish to hear.'

'What other truth has value?' Abban asked.

'One question,' Inevera said.

'Ten, at least,' Abban said.

Inevera shook her head. 'Ten is more than a *Damaji* has in a year, *khaffit*. Two.'

'Two isn't enough for what you ask of me, Damajah,' Abban said. 'I could perhaps manage with half a dozen . . .'

'Four,' Inevera said. 'But I will hold you to your word not to use this gift frivolously. Waste the wisdom of Everam with petty greed and rivalries, and every answer will cost you a finger.'

'Oh, Damajah,' Abban said, 'my greed is never petty.'

'Is that all?' Inevera asked.

Abban shook his head. 'No, Damajah, there is one more thing.'

Inevera brought the scowl back to her face. It was art, but

easy enough. The *khaffit* could try even her temper. 'This bargain is beginning to outgrow your worth, Abban. Spit it out and have done.'

Abban bowed. 'My sons. I want them stripped of the black.'

There was commotion in the Krasian camp when Abban limped away from the audience. Inevera caught sight of Ashan striding towards her rapidly.

'What has happened?' Inevera asked.

Ashan bowed. 'Your son, Damajah. Jayan has told the warriors his father has disappeared. The Sharum Ka acts as if it is a foregone conclusion that he will sit the Skull Throne on our return.'

Inevera breathed, finding her centre. This was expected, though she had hoped for more time.

'Bid the Sharum Ka to lead the search for his lost father personally, and leave a handful of warriors to maintain a camp. The rest of us must ride for Everam's Bounty with all haste. Leave behind anything that may slow us.'

They pressed for home as fast as the animals would allow. Inevera sent *Sharum* to kill *alagai* as soon as the sun set and used their power-rich ichor to paint wards of stamina on the horses and camels to strengthen them enough to continue on in the night.

It was a risk, using *hora* magic so openly. The quick-minded might glean some of the mysteries the *dama'ting* had guarded for centuries, but it could not be helped. The dice advised she return as quickly as possible – and warned it might not be fast enough.

There were countless divergences over the coming days, a struggle that threatened to rend the fragile peace Ahmann had forged among the tribes and cast them back into chaos. How many feuds had been set aside on the Deliverer's order, but still nursed in the hearts of families that had stolen wells and blooded one another for generations?

Despite her precautions, Jayan and the Spears of the Deliverer reached Everam's Bounty before them. The fool boy must have given up the search early and ridden cross-country with his warriors, pushing their powerful mustang to their limits and beyond. Her trick with the ichor to strengthen the animals could be replicated by warriors who killed demons in the night, the wards on their spears and the steel-shod hooves of their mounts absorbing power even as they turned the *alagai*'s strength back on them.

'Mother!' Jayan cried in shock, turning to see Inevera, Ashan, Aleverak, and Asome storm into the throne room where he had gathered the remaining *Damaji* and his most trusted lieutenants.

Inevera's group was followed by the twelve *Damaji'ting*, Qeva of the Kaji and Ahmann's eleven wives from the other tribes. All were loyal to Inevera and her alone. Ashan was shadowed by his powerful lieutenants, Damas Halvan and Shevali, all three of whom had studied with the Deliverer in Sharik Hora. Ashan's son Asukaji, speaking for the Kaji in his absence, waited with the other *Damaji*.

Abban limped into the throne room as fast as his crutch would allow, practically unnoticed in the commotion. He slipped quietly into a dark alcove with his bodyguard to observe.

It was good that she had pushed her entourage. Jayan had clearly expected more time to rally the *Damaji* to his favour. He had barely been in the Bounty a few hours, and had not yet had the audacity to climb the seven steps to sit the Skull Throne.

It would not have been claim enough if he had, with the Deliverer's inner council and the most powerful *Damaji* absent, but he would have been far more difficult to unseat without open violence. Inevera loved her son for all his faults, but she would not have hesitated to kill him if he'd dared such a blatant grab at power. Ahmann had curtained off the great windows of the throne room that he might use his crownsight and give Inevera access to her *hora* magic in the day. The electrum-coated forearm of a mind demon hung from her belt, warm with pent energy.

'Thank you for gathering the *Damaji* for me, my son,' Inevera said, striding right past his gaping face to ascend the steps and take her customary place on the bed of pillows beside the Skull Throne. Even from a few feet away, the great chair throbbed – perhaps the most powerful magic item in existence. Below, the holy men and women assembled as they had for centuries, the *Damaji* to the right of the throne, and the *Damaji'ting* to the left. She breathed a bit of relief that they had arrived in time, though she knew the coming struggle was far from over.

'Honoured *Damaji*,' she said, drawing a touch of power from a piece of warded jewellery to carry her voice through the room like the word of Everam. 'No doubt my son has informed you that my divine husband, Shar'Dama Ka and Everam's Deliverer, has disappeared.'

There was a buzz of conversation at the confirmation of Jayan's tale. Ashan and Aleverak were nodding, though they were not foolish enough to give any detail until they learned what exactly Jayan had said.

'I have cast the *alagai hora*,' Inevera said after a moment, her enhanced voice cutting through the chatter without being raised. She held up the dice and called upon them to glow brightly with power. 'The dice have informed me the Deliverer pursues a demon to the very edge of Nie's abyss. He will return, and his coming shall herald the beginning of Sharak Ka.'

Another rash of conversation broke out at this, and Inevera gave it just a moment to build before pressing on. 'Per Ahmann's own instructions, his brother-in-law Ashan will sit the Skull Throne in his absence, as Andrah. Asukaji will become *Damaji* of the Kaji. Upon the Shar'Dama Ka's return, Ashan will greet him from the base of the dais, but retain his title. A new throne will be built for him.'

There was a collective gasp, but only one voice cried out in shock.

'What?!' Jayan shouted. Even without Ahmann's talent for reading auras, the anger radiating from him was unmistakable.

Inevera glanced to Asome, standing quietly beside Ashan, and saw simmering rage at the injustice in his aura as well, though her second son was wise enough not to show it. Asome had ever been groomed for the role of Andrah, and had chafed since his brother took the Spear Throne, seeking the white turban more than once.

'This is ridiculous,' Jayan shouted. 'I am the eldest son. The throne should fall to me!' Several of *Damaji* murmured their agreement, though the strongest wisely kept silent. Aleverak's dislike of the boy was well known, and Damaji Enkaji of the Mehnding, the third most powerful tribe, was known to never publicly take sides.

'The Skull Throne is not some bauble, my son, to be passed without a thought,' Inevera said. 'It is the hope and salvation of our people, and you are but nineteen, and have yet to prove worthy of it. If you do not hold your tongue, I despair you never will.'

'How are we to know it was the Deliverer's wish that his own son be passed over?' Damaji Ichach of the Khanjin tribe demanded. Ichach was ever a thorn in the council's ass, but there were nods from many of the other *Damaji*, including Aleverak.

'A fair question,' the aged cleric said, turning to address those gathered, though his words were no doubt meant for Inevera. With Ashan's claim for the throne announced, he had relinquished control of the council of *Damaji*, and none dared challenge venerable Aleverak as he assumed the role. 'The Shar'Dama Ka did not speak them openly, nor even in private that we know of.'

'He spoke them to me,' Ashan said, stepping forward. 'On

the first night of Waning, as the *Damaji* filed from the throne room, my brother bade me take the throne, if he should fall against Alagai Ka. I swore by Everam's name, lest the Deliverer punish me in the afterlife.'

'Lies!' Jayan said. 'My father would never say such a thing, and you have no proof. You betray his memory for your own ambition.'

Ashan's eyes darkened at that. He had known the boy since birth, but never before had Jayan dared speak to him so disrespectfully. 'Say that again, boy, and I will kill you, blood of the Deliverer or no. I argued in your favour when Ahmann made his request, but I see now he was right. The dais of the Spear Throne has but four steps, and you have yet to adjust to the view. The dais of the Skull Throne has seven, and will dizzy you.'

Jayan gave a growl and lowered his spear, charging for Ashan with murder in his heart. The *Damaji* watched with cool detachment, ready to react when Jayan closed in.

Inevera cursed under her breath. Regardless of who won the fight, they would both lose, and her people with them.

'Enough!' she boomed. She raised her *hora* wand and manipulated its wards with nimble fingers, calling upon a blast of magic that leapt forth, shattering the marble floor between the men.

Both Jayan and Ashan were knocked from their feet by the shock wave, along with several of the *Damaji*. As the dust settled, there was an awed silence, save for the sound of debris falling back to the floor.

Inevera rose to her feet, straightening her robes with a deliberate snap. All eyes were upon her now. The *Damaji'ting*, schooled in the secrets of *hora* magic, retained their serenity, though the display was one none of them could match. A scorched crater now stood in the centre of the thick marble floor, big enough to swallow a man.

The men stared wide-eyed and openmouthed. Only Ahmann himself had ever displayed such might, and no doubt they had thought they could quickly erode Inevera's power with him gone.

They would be rethinking that assessment now. Only Asome kept his composure, having witnessed his mother's power on the wall at Waning. He, too, watched her, eyes cold, aura unreadable.

'I am Inevera,' she said, her enhanced voice echoing throughout the room. The name was pregnant with meaning, literally translating as 'Everam's will'. 'Bride of Everam and *Jiwah Ka* to Ahmann asu Hoshkamin am'Jardir am'Kaji. I am the Damajah, something you seem to have forgotten in my husband's absence. I, too, witnessed Ahmann's command to Damaji Ashan.'

She raised her *hora* wand high, again manipulating the wards etched in the electrum, this time to produce a harmless flare of light. 'If there are any here who would challenge my command that Ashan take the throne, let them step forward. The rest will be forgiven your insolence if you touch your foreheads to the floor.'

All around the room, men dropped to their knees, wisely pressing their foreheads to the floor. No doubt they were still scheming, grating at the indignity of kneeling before a woman, but none, even Jayan, were fool enough to challenge her after such a display.

None save ancient Aleverak. As the others fell to the floor, the ancient *Damaji* strode to the centre of the room, his back straight. Inevera sighed inwardly, though she gave no outward sign. She had no wish to kill the *Damaji*, but Ahmann should have killed him years ago. Perhaps it was time to correct that mistake and end the threat to Belina's eldest son, Maji.

The submission of the other tribes had been total. Only Aleverak had fought Ahmann and lived to tell the tale. The old man had earned so much honour in the battle that Ahmann had foolishly granted him a concession denied the others.

Upon the hour of his death, Aleverak's heir had the right to challenge Ahmann's Majah son to single combat for control of the Majah tribe.

Ahmann no doubt thought Maji would grow into a great warrior and win out, but the boy was only fifteen. Any of Aleverak's sons could kill him with ease.

Aleverak bowed so deeply his beard came within an inch of the floor. Such grace for a man in his eighties was impressive. It was said he had been Ahmann's greatest challenge as he battled to the steps of the Skull Throne. Ahmann had torn the *Damaji*'s arm off, but it had done nothing to strike fear into his heart. It was not surprising her blast of magic similarly failed to deter him.

'Holy Damajah,' Aleverak began, 'please accept my apologies for doubting your words, and those of Damaji Ashan, who has led the Kaji people, and the council of *Damaji*, with honour and distinction.' He glanced to Ashan, still standing at the base of the dais, who nodded.

'But no Andrah has been appointed since the position was first created,' Aleverak went on. 'It runs counter to all our sacred texts and traditions. Those who wish to wear the jewelled turban must face the challenges of the other *Damaji*, all of whom have a claim to the throne. I knew well the son of Hoshkamin, and I do not believe he would have forgotten this.'

Ashan bowed in return. 'The honoured *Damaji* is correct. The Shar'Dama Ka instructed me to announce my claim without hesitation, and kill any who stand in my path to the throne before any of the *Damaji* dare murder his *dama* sons.'

Aleverak nodded, turning to look Inevera in the eye. Even he had lost a moment's composure at her show of power, but his control was back, his aura flat and even. 'I do not challenge your words, Damajah, or the Deliverer's command, but our traditions must be respected if the tribes are to accept a new Andrah.'

Inevera opened her mouth to speak, but Ashan spoke first. 'Of course, Damaji.' He bowed, turning to the other *Damaji*.

Tradition dictated that they could each challenge him in turn, starting with the leader of the smallest tribe.

Inevera wanted to stop it. Wanted to force her will on the men and make them see she could not be denied. But the pride of men could only be pushed so far. Ashan was the youngest *Damaji* by a score of years, and a *sharusahk* master in his own right. She would have to trust in him to make good his claim, as Ahmann had.

She cared nothing for the *Damaji* – not a one of them worth the trouble they caused. She would as soon be rid of the lot of them and let her sister-wives take direct control of the tribes through Ahmann's *dama* sons.

Aleverak was the only one that worried her, but *hora* magic could ensure that Maji win out against the ancient *Damaji*'s heirs.

'Damaji Kevera of the Sharach,' Ashan called. 'Do you wish to challenge me for the jewelled turban?'

Kevera, still on his knees with his hands on the floor, sat back on his ankles to look Ashan in the eyes. The *Damaji* was in his sixties, but still robust. A true warrior-cleric.

'No, Damaji,' Kevera said. 'The Sharach are loyal to the Deliverer, and if it was his wish that you take the jewelled turban, we do not stand in your way.'

Ashan nodded and called upon the next *Damaji*, but the answer was the same. Many of them had grown lax since taking the black turbans, no match for Ashan, and others were still loyal to Ahmann, or at least afraid of his return. Each man had his own reasons, but as Ashan went up through the tribes, none chose to face him.

Until Aleverak. The one-armed old cleric stepped forward immediately, barring Ashan's path to the steps of the dais and assuming a *sharusahk* stance. His knees were bent, one foot pointed towards Ashan, and the other perpendicular, a step behind. His single arm was extended forward, palm up and stiffened fingers aimed at Ashan's heart.

'Apologies, Damaji,' he said to Ashan, 'but only the strongest may sit the Skull Throne.'

Ashan bowed deeply, assuming a stance of his own. 'Of course, Damaji. You honour me with your challenge.' Then, without hesitation, he charged.

Ashan stopped short when he came in range, giving Aleverak a minimum of momentum to turn against him. His punches and kicks were incredibly fast, but Aleverak's one hand moved so quickly it seemed to be two, batting them aside. He tried to latch on, turning the energy of the blows into a throw, but Ashan was wise to the move and could not be caught.

Inevera had never thought much of *dama sharusahk*, having learned a higher form among the *dama'ting*, but she grudgingly admitted to herself that the men were impressive. They might as well have been relaxing in a hot bath for all their auras told.

Aleverak moved like a viper, ducking and dodging Ashan's kicks. He spun around a leg sweep and came out of it with a kick straight into the air that was impressive even for a *dama'ting*. Ashan tried to pull back out of range, but the blow was so unexpected he was clipped on the chin and knocked back a step, out of balance.

Inevera breathed out the tension as the ancient *Damaji* moved to take advantage of Ashan's momentary imbalance. His fingers were like a speartip as he thrust his hand at Ashan's throat.

Ashan caught the blow just in time, twisting Aleverak into a throw that would break the old man's arm if he resisted.

But Aleverak did not resist. Indeed, it became clear he was counting on the move, using Ashan's own strength to aid his leap as he scissored his legs into the air, hooking them around Ashan's neck. He twisted in midair, throwing his weight into the move, and Ashan had no choice but to go limp and let himself be thrown to the floor, lest Aleverak break his neck.

But Ashan was not finished. As he rebounded off the floor with Aleverak above him, he used the energy to punch straight up. Even wooden Aleverak could not instantly embrace such a blow, and Ashan tucked his legs in, kicking himself upright and whirling to face the *Damaji* on even footing once more.

Aleverak was angry now. Inevera could see it, a thin red film crackling on the surface of his aura. But the emotion did not claim him. His energy was centred, channelled into his movements, giving him terrifying strength and speed. He wielded his one hand like a knife, showing surprising knowledge of the pressure points *dama'ting* used in their own *sharusahk*. Ashan took a blow to the shoulder that would leave his right arm numb for a minute, at the least. Not long in Everam's great scheme, but a lifetime in battle.

Inevera began to wonder how much control she could keep if Aleverak ascended to the throne.

But again Ashan surprised her, taking a similar stance to Aleverak and focusing his efforts on defence. His feet beat rapidly on the marble floor, back and forth, keeping Aleverak dancing but always stopping short of full attacks that might give the aged *Damaji* free energy to turn against him. Again and again Aleverak struck at him, but Ashan batted his hand aside every time, keeping up the dance. Aleverak's kicks were dodged, or blocked smoothly with thighs, shins, and forearms.

He kept it up, his aura calm, until, at last, Aleverak began to tire. Whatever reserves of energy the ancient *Damaji* had called upon depleted, and his moves began to slow.

When he next stepped forward, he was not quick enough to stop Ashan from stomping on his foot, pinning it. Aleverak stabbed his right hand in, but Ashan caught the wrist, holding it as he snapped his hips around to add torque to a devastating punch to the chest with his now recovered right arm.

Aleverak gasped and stumbled, but Ashan locked his arm and added several more punches before his opponent could recover, driving sharp knuckles into the shoulder joint of the *Damaji*'s one arm. He swept Aleverak's feet from him and put him down hard on his back. The retort as he struck the marble echoed throughout the chamber.

Aleverak looked up at Ashan, his eyes hard. 'Well done, Andrah. Finish me with honour and take your place atop the steps.'

Ashan looked at the ancient *Damaji* sadly. 'It was an honour to face you, Damaji. Your fame among the masters of *sharusahk* is well earned. But tradition does not demand I kill you. Only that I clear you from my path.'

He began to turn away, but Aleverak's aura flared, as close to a loss of control as Inevera had ever seen. He clutched the hem of Ashan's robe with quivering fingers.

'Maji is still in his bido!' Aleverak coughed. 'Kill me and let Aleveran have the black turban. No harm will come to the Deliverer's son.'

Ashan glanced up to Inevera at this. It was a tempting offer. Maji would be safe from the foolish vow Ahmann had made, but in exchange the Majah would have a younger *Damaji* who might rule for decades to come. She gave a slight shake of her head.

'Apologies, Damaji,' Ashan said, pulling his robe free of the old man's grasp, 'but the Deliverer still has need of you in this world. It is not yet your time to walk the lonely path. And should any harm come to the Deliverer's Majah son apart from an open challenge in court on the hour of your natural death, my respect for you will not stop me from having your entire male line killed.' He turned again, striding for the seven steps leading to the Skull Throne.

Asome met him there, blocking the path.

Inevera hissed. What was the fool boy doing?

'Apologies, Uncle.' Asome gave a formal *sharusahk* bow. 'I trust you understand this is not personal. You have been as a father to me, but I am the eldest *dama* son of the Deliverer, and have as much right as any assembled to challenge you.'

Ashan seemed genuinely taken aback, but he did not dispute

the claim. He bowed in return. 'Of course, nephew. Your honour is boundless. But I would not leave my daughter a widow, nor my grandson without his father. I ask this once that you step aside.'

Asome shook his head sadly. 'Nor would I leave my cousin and wife without a father. My aunt without a husband. Renounce your claim and allow me to ascend.'

Jayan leapt to his feet. 'What is this?! I demand . . .!'

'Silence!' Inevera shouted. There was no need to enhance her voice this time, the sound echoing around the room. 'Asome, attend me!'

Asome turned, climbing the steps swiftly to stand before Inevera's bed of pillows. There was a flare in his aura as he passed by the throne. Was it covetousness? Inevera filed the information away in her mind as she manipulated polished stones on a small pedestal beside her, covering some wards and uncovering others. She could use the stones to control a number of effects, powered by *hora* placed around the room, and now placed a wall of silence around her pillows, that none save her son should hear her words.

'You must give up this foolish claim, my son,' Inevera said. 'Ashan will kill you.' Having seen Asome's *sharusahk*, she wasn't certain this was true, but now was not the time to flatter the young man.

'Have faith, Mother,' Asome said. 'I have waited my entire life for this day, and I will prevail.'

'You will not,' Inevera said. 'Because you will not continue your challenge. This is not what Everam wants. Or your father. Or I.'

'If Everam does not wish me to take the throne, I will not,' Asome said. 'And if He does, then it should be Father's and your wish as well.'

'Wait, my son,' Inevera said. 'I beg you. We have always meant the jewelled turban for you, but it is too soon. Jayan will drive the *Sharum* into revolt if you take it now.'

'Then I will kill him, too,' Asome said.

'And rule over a civil war with Sharak Ka on our heels,' Inevera said. 'No. I will not allow you to kill your brother. If you persist, I will cast you down myself. Recant, and you will have the succession on Ashan's death. I swear it.'

'Announce it now,' Asome said. 'Before all assembled, or cast me down as you say. My honour will be appeased with nothing else.'

Inevera drew a deep breath, letting it fill her, and flow back out, taking her emotions with it. She nodded, sliding the stones on her pedestal to remove the veil of silence.

'Upon Ashan's death, Asome will have the right to challenge the *Damaji* for the jewelled turban.'

Jayan's aura swirled with emotion. The anger was still present, but he seemed mollified for the moment. There was no telling what he would have done if his younger brother had been given the chance to fight for a throne that sat higher than his. But seeing Asome thwarted had always brought Jayan pleasure. Ashan was not yet forty, and would stand between Asome and ascension long enough for Jayan to claim his father's crown.

He stamped his spear loudly on the marble, and turned without leave to exit the throne room. His *kai'Sharum* followed obediently behind, and Inevera could see in them, and many of the *Damaji*, a belief that the Deliverer's eldest son had been robbed of his birthright. The *Sharum* worshipped Jayan, and they outnumbered the *dama* greatly. He would be a growing danger.

But for the moment he was dealt with, and Inevera felt the wind ease as Ashan at last climbed the dais to sit the Skull Throne. He looked out at the assembled advisors and said the words Inevera had instructed, though she could tell they were sour on his lips.

'It is an honour to hold the throne for the Shar'Dama Ka, blessings be upon his name. I will keep the Deliverer's court much as he left it, with Damaji Aleverak speaking for the council, and Abban the *khaffit* retaining his position as court scribe and master of logistics. As before, any that dare hinder or harm him or his interests will find no mercy from the Skull Throne.'

Inevera twitched a finger to Belina, and the Majah *Damaji'ting* stepped forward with *hora* to heal Aleverak. Soon the *Damaji* was rising shakily back to his feet. The disorientation would soon pass, leaving him even stronger than before. His first act was a bow of submission to the Skull Throne.

Satisfying as that submission was, it was nothing compared to the flick of Ashan's eyes to her, obviously asking if this scene was at its end. She gave a subtle nod and Ashan dismissed the *Damaji* and moved to meet with Asukaji and Asome, as well as his advisors, Halvan and Shevali.

'Little sisters,' Inevera said, and the *Damaji'ting* remained as the men filtered out, clustering at the base of the dais to take private audience with her.

'You did not tell all, Damajah. My dice foretell that Ahmann may never return.' Belina kept her voice steady, but her aura was like a raw nerve. Most of the *Damaji'ting* appeared the same. They had lost not only a leader, but a husband as well.

'What has happened? Truly?' Qasha asked. Less disciplined than Belina, the Sharach *Damaji'ting* could not keep her voice steady. The last word cracked with a whine like a flaw forming in glass.

'Ahmann spared the Par'chin in secret after claiming the spear,' Inevera said, disapproval in her tone. 'The man survived and challenged him to *Domin Sharum*.'

The women began to chatter at this. *Domin Sharum* literally meant 'two warriors', the name given to the ritual duel first fought by Kaji himself against his murderous half brother Majah three thousand years ago. It was said they battled for seven days and nights atop Nie's Breast, the tallest of the southern mountains.

'Surely there is more to the tale than that,' Damaji'ting Qeva said. 'I have trouble believing any man could defeat the Shar'Dama Ka in fair combat.'

The other women voiced their assent. No man nor demon they could imagine could stand against Ahmann, especially with the Spear of Kaji in his hands.

'The Par'chin has covered his skin in inked wards,' Inevera said. 'I do not understand it fully, but the symbols have given him terrifying powers, not unlike a demon himself. Ahmann held sway in battle and would have won, but as the sun set the Par'chin began misting like an *alagai* rising from the abyss, and the Shar'Dama Ka's blows could not touch him. The Par'chin cast them both from the cliff, and their bodies were never found.'

Qasha gave out a wail at that. Damaji'ting Justya of the Shunjin moved to comfort her, but she, too, had begun to sob. All around the semicircle of women, there was weeping.

'Silence!' Inevera hissed, her enhanced voice cutting through the sobs like a lash. 'You are *Damaji'ting*, not some pathetic *dal'ting jiwah*, weeping tear bottles over dead *Sharum*. Krasia depends on us. We must trust that Ahmann will return, and keep his empire intact until he can reclaim it.'

'And if he does not?' Damaji'ting Qeva asked, her words a calm breeze. She alone of the *Damaji'ting* had not lost a husband.

'Then we hold our people together until a suitable heir can be found,' Inevera said. 'It makes no difference in what we must do here and now.'

She looked out over the women. 'With Ahmann missing, the clerics will try to leach our power. You saw the magic I displayed to the *Damaji*. Each of you has combat *hora* you have been husbanding against need. You and your most powerful *dama'ting* must find excuse for displays of your own. The time to hide our strength is over.'

She looked around the semicircle of women, seeing determined faces where a moment ago there had been tears. 'Every *nie'dama'ting* must be put to preparing new *hora* for spells, and all should be embroidering their robes with the Northlander's wards of unsight. Abban will have spools of gold thread sent to every *dama'ting* palace for the task. Any attempts to prevent us walking in the night should be ignored. If men dare hinder you, break them. Publicly. Kill *alagai*. Heal warriors near death. We must show the men of Krasia we are a force to be feared by man and demon alike, and not afraid to dirty our nails.'

3

Ashia

333 AR Autumn

Ashia stiffened as her husband challenged her father for the Skull Throne. It was unthinkable that she should interfere, but she could not deny the outcome would greatly affect her, whomever the victor.

She breathed, finding her centre once more. It was *inevera*.

Shifting slightly, she relaxed some muscles as she tensed others to maintain the pose that held her suspended over the alcove to the left of the Skull dais, braced against the arched ceiling with toes and fingers. In this way she could hold the position indefinitely, even sleeping without losing her perch.

Across the room, her spear sister Micha mirrored her in the opposite alcove, silently watching through a tiny pinhole in the ornate carving above the archway. Jarvah was positioned behind the pillar just past the Skull Throne, where none save the Deliverer and Damajah could tread without invitation.

Cloaked in shadow, the *kai'Sharum'ting* were imperceptible even to those stepping into the alcoves. But should the Damajah be threatened they could appear in an instant, launching a spray of sharpened, warded glass. Two breaths later, they could interpose themselves between her and any danger, spears and shields at the ready.

The *kai'Sharum'ting* and their growing number of spear

sisters guarded the Damajah openly when she was on the move, but Inevera preferred them to keep to the shadows whenever possible.

At last the court was adjourned and the Damajah was left alone with her two most trusted advisors, Damaji'ting Qeva and her daughter, nie'Damaji'ting Melan.

The Damajah gave a slight flick of her fingers, and Ashia and Micha dropped silently from their perches. Jarvah appeared from behind the pillars, all three moving as escort to the Damajah's personal chambers.

The Deliverer's *dal'ting* wives, Thalaja and Everalia, were waiting with refreshment. Their eyes drifted to their daughters, Micha and Jarvah, but they knew better than to speak to the *kai'Sharum'ting* while they guarded the Damajah. There was little to say, in any event.

'A bath has been prepared for you, Damajah,' Thalaja said.

'And fresh silks laid,' Everalia added.

Ashia still could not believe these meek, obsequious women were wives of the Deliverer, though her holy uncle had taken them many years before coming to power. She had once thought the women hid their skills and power, much as she herself had been taught.

Over the years, Ashia had come to see the truth. Thalaja and Everalia were wives in name only now that the usefulness of their wombs had faded. Mere servants to the Deliverer's wives in white.

But for inevera, Ashia thought, *that could have been me.*

'I will need new silks,' Inevera said. 'The Deliverer is . . . travelling. Until his return, I will wear only opaque colours.' The women nodded, moving hurriedly to comply.

'There is more news.' Inevera turned back, first meeting the eyes of Qeva and Melan, then letting her gaze drift to rest on Ashia and her spear sisters.

'Enkido is dead.'

Ashia pictured the palm, and bent before the wind that rushed over her. She bowed to the Damajah. A step behind, Micha and Jarvah mirrored her. 'Thank you for telling us, Damajah.' Her voice was steady and even, eyes carefully on the floor, seeing all in periphery. 'I will not ask if he died with his honour intact, for it could be no other way.'

Inevera nodded. 'Enkido's honour was boundless even before he severed his tongue and tree to serve my predecessor and learn the secrets of *dama'ting sharusahk*.'

Melan stiffened slightly at the mention of Inevera's predecessor, Qeva's mother and Melan's grandmother, Damaji'ting Kenevah. It was said the Damajah choked the old woman to death to wrest control of the tribe's women from her. Qeva gave no reaction.

'Enkido was killed by an *alagai* changeling, bodyguard to one of Nie's princelings,' Inevera went on. 'These mimic demons can take on any form, real or imagined. I watched the Deliverer himself in pitched battle with one. Enkido died doing his duty, protecting Amanvah, Sikvah, and their honoured husband, the son of Jessum. Your cousins live because of his sacrifice.'

Ashia nodded, bending her centre to accept the news. 'Does this . . . changeling still live?' If so, she would find a way to track and kill it, even if she had to follow it all the way to Nie's abyss.

Inevera shook her head. 'Amanvah and the son of Jessum weakened the creature, but it was the Par'chin's *Jiwah Ka* who at last took its unholy life.'

'She must be formidable indeed to succeed where our honoured master failed,' Ashia said.

'Beware that one, should your paths ever cross,' the Damajah agreed. 'She is nearly as powerful as her husband, but both, I fear, have drunk too deeply of *alagai* magic, and made the madness that comes with it a part of them.'

Ashia put her hands together, eyes still on the floor. 'My spear sisters and I beg the Damajah's leave to go into the night and kill seven *alagai* each in his honour, one for each pillar of Heaven, to guide our lost master on the lonely road.'

The Damajah whisked her fingers. 'Of course. Assist the *Sharum*.'

Ashia's hand worked with precision, painting wards on her nails. They were not long in the fashionable way of pampered wives and some *dama'ting*. Enkido's students kept a warrior's cut, barely past the nub, the better to handle weapons.

But Ashia had no need to claw at the *alagai*. A knife or speartip served best for that. She had other intentions.

Out of the corner of her eyes, she watched her spear sisters, silent save for the sounds of oil and leather, stitching and polishing as they readied weapons for the coming night.

The Damajah had given her *kai'Sharum'ting* spears and shields of warded glass, much like the Spears of the Deliverer. The blades needed no sharpening, but the grips and harnesses were just as important, and Enkido had inspected all their equipment regularly, never satisfied. A single crooked stitch on a shield strap, barely visible and irrelevant to performance, and he would rip out the thick leather with his bare hands, forcing the owner to replace it entirely.

Other infractions were treated less gently.

There were three *kai'Sharum'ting* remaining in Everam's Bounty. Ashia, Micha, and Jarvah. Micha and Jarvah were full daughters of the Deliverer, but born to his *dal'ting* wives, Thalaja and Everalia. They, too, had been refused the white.

Their blood might have ranked them above the Deliverer's nieces, but Ashia was four years older than Micha, and six older than Jarvah. The girls walked in women's bodies thanks to the magic they absorbed each night, but they still looked to Ashia to guide them.

More women were becoming *Sharum'ting* every day, but

only they were blood of the Deliverer. Only they wore the white veils.

Only they had been trained by Enkido.

That dusk, the gates of the city opened to release the *Sharum* into the vast territory they dubbed the New Maze. Two hours later, when full night had fallen, the three *kai'Sharum'ting* and half a dozen of their new spear sisters slipped quietly over the wall.

The Damajah's command to 'assist' the *Sharum* was very clear. They would hunt the outer edges of the New Maze, where demons were thickest, and patrol for foolhardy *Sharum,* so drunk on magic and eager for carnage they let themselves be surrounded.

Ashia and her spear sisters would then step in to rescue the men. It was meant to create blood ties with as many *Sharum* as possible, but being saved by women stung the warriors' pride. This, too, was part of the Damajah's plan, for they were to invite challenges from the men, killing or crippling enough to send clear examples to the others.

Miles melted away under their fleet steps. Their black robes were embroidered with wards of unsight to render them invisible to the *alagai,* their veils with wards of sight to let them see as clearly in night as in day.

It wasn't long before they found four overeager Majah *dal'Sharum* who had ranged too far from their unit and been caught by a reap of field demons. Three of the demons were down, but so was one of the *Sharum,* clutching a bloodied leg. His fellows ignored him – and their training – fighting as individuals when a formation might yet save them.

Drunk on alagai *magic,* Ashia signed to her sisters. The madness of magic's grip was known to them, but it was easily ignored by a warrior who kept her centre. *We must save them from themselves.*

Ashia herself speared the field demon that would have killed the abandoned *Sharum* as Micha, Jarvah, and the others waded into the dozen remaining demons in the reap.

The jolt of magic as she speared the demon thrummed through her. In Everam's light, she could see the magic running like fire along the lines of power in her aura. The same lines drawn in the Evejah'ting, and tattooed on her master's body. The Riddle of Enkido.

Ashia felt the surge of strength and speed, understanding how easily one could get drunk upon it. She felt invincible. Aggression tugged at her centre. She bent her spirit as the palm in the wind and let it pass over her.

Ashia examined the deep wound in the *Sharum*'s leg. Already it was closing as the *alagai* magic he had absorbed turned its workings inward to repair. 'Next time, angle your shield properly.'

'What would a woman know of such things?' the warrior demanded.

Ashia stood. 'This woman saved your life, *Sharum*.'

A demon leapt at her, but she bashed it aside with her shield, sending it sprawling near one of the other *dal'Sharum*, who speared it viciously. It was a killing stroke, but the man tore free his spear and stabbed again and again, roaring in incoherent fury.

Another demon leapt for his back, and Ashia had to shove the warrior aside to stab at it. She struck a glancing blow, but the angle was poor, and the force of the *alagai*'s leap knocked the weapon from her grasp.

Ashia gave ground for two steps, batting aside flashing paws with her shield. The demon tried to snap at her, and she shoved the edge of the shield into its jaws, lifting to bare its vulnerable underbelly. A kick put it onto its back, and before it could recover its feet she fell on it, pinning its limbs as she stuck her knife into its throat.

She was getting to her feet when something struck her across the back of the head. She rolled with the blow, coming up to face the *Sharum* she had just rescued. His eyes were wild, and there was no mistaking the aggression in his stance.

'You dare lay hands on me, woman?' he demanded.

Ashia cast her eyes about the battlefield. The last of the demons was down, her *Sharum'ting* unscathed and standing in a tight unit. They watched the *Sharum* with cold eyes. The injured one was still on the ground, but the others were moving to surround her.

Do nothing, Ashia's fingers told them. *I will handle this.*

'Find your centre!' she shouted to the man as he advanced on her again. 'You owe me your life!'

The *Sharum* spat. 'I would have killed that *alagai* as easily as I did the other.'

'The other I knocked senseless at your feet?' Ashia asked. 'As my sisters slew the reap that would have killed you all?'

The man's answer was a swing of his spear, meant to knock her across the face. Ashia caught the spear shaft and twisted until she felt the warrior's wrist break.

The others were coming in hard now, the magic thrumming in them multiplying their natural aggression and misogyny. To fail in battle and need to be saved was shame enough. To be saved by women . . .

Ashia spun behind the warrior, rolling across his back to kick the next man in the face. He fell away as she charged the third, slapping his spearpoint aside and striking her open palm against his forehead. Stunned, he stumbled until Ashia caught him in a throw that sent him tumbling into the other two, struggling back to their feet.

When the men recovered, they found themselves surrounded by *Sharum'ting*, spearpoints levelled at them.

'Pathetic.' Ashia lifted her veil to spit at the men's feet. 'Your *sharusahk* is as weak as your control, allowing yourself to become drunk on *alagai* magic. Pick up your fellow and return to your unit before I lose all patience with you.'

She did not wait for a reply, whisking off into the night with her spear sisters in tow.

Our spear brothers would as soon strike us as accept our aid, Jarvah signed as they ran.

For now, Ashia signed. *They will learn to respect the Sharum'ting. We are blood of the Deliverer, who will remake this rabble before Sharak Ka.*

And if my holy father does not return? Jarvah signed. *What state will the Armies of Everam be in without him?*

He will, Ashia signed. *He is the Deliverer. In his absence, we must set an example to all. Come. We have killed not half the* alagai *needed to ease our master's passage into Heaven.*

They ranged farther, but most *Sharum* respected the night – and their own limitations – and they found nothing else needing attention. Deeper they went, leaving the *dal'Sharum* patrols behind as they passed from the Maze into what Northerners called the naked night.

Ashia found the tracks of a large passing reap, and the others followed silently as she tracked them. They fell upon nearly thirty *alagai* unawares, cutting into the centre of the reap and forming a ring of shields. Ashia trusted her sisters to either side to keep her safe, and they she. Free from fear of counterattack, they began to stab at the demons with calm efficiency, like snuffing candles, one by one. Each kill sent a jolt of magic through the group, making them stronger. The power pushed against their control, but it was only a gentle breeze to the centred women.

Half the reap was dead before the demons got it in their heads to flee. By then Ashia and her sisters had coaxed them into a narrow ravine with steep sides not suited for their loping strides. At a signal from Ashia, her sisters broke into smaller formations, each cornering several demons.

Ashia let a group of *alagai* cut her off from her sisters, baiting them to surround her and draw close. She could see the lines of power that ran through their limbs, and closed her eyes, breathing deeply.

In your honour, master. Her spear and shield fell from limp fingers as she opened her eyes, dropping into a *sharusahk* stance.

The demons shrieked and launched themselves at her, but Ashia could see the strikes before they came, written clearly in the lines of their auras. Stolen magic gave her speed as she bent and turned a half circle, slapping the jaw of the quickest to redirect the full force of its attack into the path of two others. She sidestepped the jumble, stabbing stiffened fingers into one demon's belly to knock it aside.

The wards on her fingernails flared with power, and the magical feedback that came from direct contact was a hundred times stronger than that which filtered through the wood of her spear. The field demon was thrown back, rib cage scorched and flattened, and struggled to rise. Ashia kicked the strength from another demon's leg just as it was about to spring, sending it sprawling. The next she chopped to the temple, blinding it.

How dare that man strike her from behind? She should have killed him as an example to the others.

The *alagai* slashed wildly at her, but two simple blocks diverted sharp talons, walking her to her next strike. Inside the creature's guard, she stabbed her fingers into its throat. The skin stretched and tore, as much from the strength of the blow as the searing magic that accompanied it.

Ashia shoved her entire forearm into the demon's chest. Inside, the creatures were as vulnerable as any surface animal. She caught a grip where she could and yanked free a fistful of gore. The magic was thunder in her soul now.

The Deliverer gone. The Damajah living on a knife's edge. Enkido dead. And her own spear brothers would as soon kill her for emasculating them as accept her aid. It was too much to bear.

She grew more aggressive, leaving her neutral stance to pursue retreating demons instead of lulling them in. She had scolded the *dal'Sharum* for this very thing, but she was blood of the Deliverer. She was in control.

She caught the next demon to leap at her by the head, turning a circle to use its own strength to break its neck.

Ashia took another pass, kicking, punching, and positioning

herself for deadly strikes of her fingernails to the *alagai* lines of power.

Her vision grew red around the edges, and all she could see was the next demon. She did not even look at their bodies, only their true forms, the lines of power in their auras. It was these alone she saw, these alone she struck.

Suddenly her vision went dark, and she stumbled in her next strike. Another target appeared and she struck hard, but it rebounded off a shield of warded glass.

'Sister!' Micha cried. 'Find your centre!'

Ashia came to her senses. She was covered in ichor, and all around her lay dead *alagai*. Seven of them. The ravine was cleared, and Micha, Jarvah, and the others were staring at her.

Micha caught her elbow. 'What was that?'

'What?' Ashia said. 'I was honouring our master with *sharu-sahk*.'

Micha's brows tightened as she lowered her voice to a harsh whisper the others could not hear. 'You know what, sister. You lost control. You seek to honour our master, but Enkido would be ashamed of you for such a display, especially in front of our little sisters. You are lucky the *Sharum* did not see as well.'

Ashia had been struck many times over the years, but no blow had ever hit as hard as those words. Ashia wanted to deny them, but as her full senses returned she saw the truth.

'Everam forgive me,' she whispered.

Micha gave her elbow a comforting squeeze. 'I understand, sister. I feel it too, when the magic is high. But it has always been you we look to for example. With our master dead, there is only you.'

Ashia took Micha's hands in hers, squeezing tightly. 'No, beloved sister. There is only *us*. With Shanvah gone, the *Sharum'ting* will look to you and Jarvah as well. You must be strong for them as you have been for me, this night.'

Ashia's robes were still wet with demon gore as she made her way back to the palace chambers she shared with Asome and their infant son, Kaji.

Normally she would change from her *Sharum* robes to proper women's blacks before returning, that she might not further the rift with her husband. Asome had never approved of her taking the spear, but it was not his decision to make. Both had petitioned the Deliverer to divorce them when he named her *Sharum'ting*, but her uncle had refused the request, his wisdom a mystery.

Ashia was tired of hiding, though, tired of pretending to be a helpless *jiwah* in her chambers even as she broke men and bled *alagai* in the night. All to protect the honour of a man who cared nothing for her.

Enkido would be ashamed of you. Micha's words echoed in her mind. What was her husband's displeasure compared to that?

She was silent as a spirit, but there was no sign of Asome – her husband likely sleeping in Asukaji's embrace in the new *Damaji*'s palace. The only one present was Ashia's grandmother Kajivah, asleep on a divan outside the nursery. Her first great-grandchild, the Holy Mother doted on the boy, refusing a proper nurse.

'Who could love the boy better than his own grandmother?' she would always say. Implicit in that statement, of course, was her belief that Ashia herself was unsuitable, now that she had taken up the spear.

Ashia slipped by without disturbing her, closing the nursery door behind her as she looked down upon her sleeping son.

She had not wanted the child. She had feared what bearing would do to her warrior's body, and there was no love lost between her and Asome. Her brother's need to have his own sister bear his lover's child had seemed an abomination.

But Kaji, that perfect, beautiful child, was no abomination. Having spent months with him suckling at her breast, sleeping in her arms, reaching his tiny hands up to touch her face, Ashia could not bring herself to wish any change upon her life that might undo him. His existence was *inevera*.

Enkido would be ashamed of you.

There was a creak, and the edge of the crib broke off in her hands with a loud crack. Kaji opened his eyes and let out a shriek.

Ashia tossed the broken wood aside, reaching for the boy. Always his mother's touch could calm him, but this time Kaji thrashed in her arms, struggling wildly. She tried to still him, but he screamed louder at her clutch, and she saw his skin bruising at her touch.

The night strength was still upon her.

Quickly, Ashia laid her son back in his pillows, seeing in horror his soft, smooth skin bruised and stained with the demon ichor that still clung to her. The stink of it was thick in the air.

The door slammed open, and Kajivah stormed into the room. 'What are you doing, disturbing the child at this hour?!'

Then she saw the child, bruised and covered in ichor, and let out a wail. She turned to Ashia, enraged. 'Get out! Get out! You should be ashamed of yourself!'

She shoved hard, and Ashia, fearing her own strength, allowed herself to be driven from the room. Kajivah took the child in her arms, kicking the door shut behind her.

For the second time that night, Ashia lost her centre. Her legs turned to water as she stumbled to her room, slamming the door and slumping to the floor in darkness.

Perhaps the abomination is me.

For the first time in years, Ashia put her hand to her face and wept. She wanted nothing more than the comforting presence of her master.

But Enkido was on the lonely path, and like her grandmother, he would be ashamed of her.

4

Sharum Blood

327—332 AR

'Sit up straight,' Kajivah snapped. 'You're a princess of the Kaji, not some *kha'ting* wretch! I despair of ever finding you a husband worthy of your blood who will take you.'

'Yes, Tikka.' Ashia shivered, though the palace baths were warm and steamy. She was but thirteen, and in no rush to marry, but Kajivah had seen the reddened wadding and seized upon it. Nevertheless, she straightened as her mother, Imisandre, scrubbed her back.

'Nonsense, Mother,' Imisandre said. 'Thirteen and beautiful, eldest daughter of the *Damaji* of Krasia's greatest tribe, and niece to the Deliverer himself? Ashia is the most desirable bride in all the world.'

Ashia shivered again. Her mother had meant the words to calm her, but they did the opposite.

Kajivah was apt to be vexed when her daughters disagreed with her, but she only smiled patiently, signalling her daughter-in-law Thalaja to add more hot stones to the water. She always held court thus, from the nursery to the kitchen to the baths.

Her subjects were her five *dal'ting* daughters – Imisandre, Hoshvah, Hanya, Thalaja, and Everalia – and granddaughters Ashia, Shanvah, Sikvah, Micha, and Jarvah.

'It appears Dama Baden agrees,' Kajivah said.

Every head turned sharply to look at her. 'His grandson Raji?' Imisandre asked.

A wide grin broke across Kajivah's face now that the secret was out. 'They say no man has ever offered such wealth for a single bride.'

Ashia couldn't breathe. A moment ago she would have put this moment off for years, but . . . Prince Raji? The boy was handsome and strong, heir to the white and a fortune that dwarfed even the Andrah's. What more could she want?

'He is not worthy of you, sister.'

All eyes turned to Ashia's brother Asukaji, standing in the doorway with his back to the women. It was not an uncommon sight. No man would have been allowed entry to the women's bath, but Asukaji was but twelve and still in his bido. More, he was *push'ting*, and all the women knew it, more interested in the gossip in a woman's head than what was under her robes.

All the women of the family adored Asukaji. Even Kajivah did not mind that he preferred men, so long as he did his duty and took wives to provide her with grandchildren.

'Beloved nephew,' Kajivah said. 'What brings you here?'

'My last visit to the women's bath, I am afraid,' the boy said, to a chorus of disappointment. 'I was called to *Hannu Pash* this morning. I will be taking the white.'

Kajivah led the cheers. 'That's wonderful! Of course we all knew it would be so. You are the Deliverer's nephew.'

Asukaji gave a shrug. 'Are you not the Deliverer's mother? His wives and sisters, his nieces? Why is it none of you is in white, yet I should be?'

'You are a man,' Kajivah said, as if it were obvious.

'What does that matter?' Asukaji said. 'You ask whom Ashia should be worthy of, but the true question is what man is worthy of *her*?'

'Who in the Kaji is higher than Dama Baden's heir?' Ashia asked. 'Father wouldn't marry me into another tribe . . . would he?'

'Don't be an idiot,' Kajivah snapped. 'The very notion is absurd.'

But there was doubt on her face as she looked to her grandson. 'Who is worthy, then?'

'Asome, of course,' Asukaji said. The two boys were nearly inseparable.

'He is our cousin!' Ashia said, shocked.

Asukaji shrugged. 'What of it? The Evejah speaks of many such unions in the time of Kaji. Asome is the son of the Shar'Dama Ka, beautiful, rich, and powerful. More, he can cement the ties between my father and the house of Jardir.'

'*I* am of house Jardir,' Kajivah said, her voice strengthening. 'Your father is his brother-in-law, and I, his mother. What further tie is required?'

'A direct one,' Asukaji said. 'From the Deliverer and father to a single son.' He dared to look into the room for a moment, meeting Ashia's eyes. 'Your son.'

'You *have* a direct one,' Kajivah said. 'I am the Holy Mother. You are all blood of the Deliverer.'

Asukaji turned back away and bowed. 'I mean no disrespect, Tikka. Holy Mother is a fine title, but it has not turned your black robes white. Nor my blessed sister's.'

Kajivah fell silent at that, and Ashia began to consider. Marrying a first cousin was not unheard of in powerful families, and Asome *was* beautiful, as Asukaji said. He had taken after his mother in appearance, and the Damajah's beauty was without equal. Asome had her face and slender build, and he wore them well.

'Why not Jayan?' she asked.

'What?' Asukaji said.

'If I should marry a cousin as you say, why not the Deliverer's firstborn?' Ashia asked. 'Unless he weds his sister, who is more worthy than I, Shar'Dama Ka's eldest niece?'

Unlike slender Asome, Jayan took after the Deliverer in form – broader and thick with muscle. He was not kind, but Jayan radiated power enough to make even Ashia flush.

Asukaji spat. '*Sharum* dog. They are animals bred for the Maze, sister. I would as soon let you marry a jackal.'

'That is enough!' Kajivah snapped. 'You forget yourself, boy. The Deliverer himself is *Sharum*.'

'Was *Sharum*,' Asukaji said. 'Now he wears the white.'

That very day, Kajivah set a fire under Ashan and dragged Ashia, Shanvah, and Sikvah before the Shar'Dama Ka, demanding they be made *dama'ting*.

But one did not make demands of the Deliverer and Damajah. Kajivah and her daughters were given white veils. Ashia and her cousins were sent to the Dama'ting Palace.

'It is good, sister,' Asukaji said, as the girls were pushed towards the waiting Damajah. 'There is no reason why our father or the Deliverer should refuse your match to Asome now.'

Kajivah did not seem satisfied, but Ashia could not see why. The Deliverer had named them his blood and heaped honour upon them. Ashia had no wish to be *dama'ting*, but who knew what mysteries she might learn in their palace?

Kai'ting. She liked the sound. It was powerful. Regal. Shanvah and Sikvah were afraid, but Ashia went gladly.

The Damajah escorted the girls out of the great chamber through her own personal entrance. An honour in itself. There waited Qeva, *Damaji'ting* of the Kaji, and her daughter and heir, Melan, along with one of the Damajah's mute eunuch guards.

'The girls will be taught letters, singing, and pillow dancing for four hours each day,' the Damajah told Damaji'ting Qeva. 'The other twenty, they belong to Enkido.'

She nodded to the eunuch, and Ashia gasped. Shanvah clutched at her. Sikvah began to cry.

The Damajah ignored them, turning to the eunuch. 'Make something worthy out of them.'

Nie'Damaji'ting Melan led them through the Dama'ting Underpalace. It was said the *dama'ting* could heal any wound with their *hora* magic, but the woman's hand and forearm were horrifically scarred, twisted into a frightening claw not unlike those in the paintings Ashia had seen of *alagai*.

Sikvah was still weeping. Shanvah had her arms around her, her own eyes wet with tears.

You are an example to every other young woman in the tribe, her father told her once. *And so I shall be harsher with you than any other, lest you ever shame our family.*

And so Ashia had learned to hide fear and keep tears at bay. She was as terrified as her cousins, but she was eldest, and they had always looked to her. She kept her back arched proudly as they were brought to a small door. Enkido put his back to the wall beside the portal as Melan led through to a large tiled chamber. The walls were lined with pegs holding white robes and long strips of white silk.

'Remove your robes,' Melan said as the door closed.

Her cousins gasped and hesitated, but Ashia knew it was foolish – and useless – to argue with a Bride of Everam. Keeping her dignity intact, she removed her hood and pulled her fine black silk robe over her head. Beneath, a wide strip of silk around her chest flattened the beginnings of her woman's shape. Her bido, too, was fine black silk, wrapped in a loose, simple weave for ease and comfort.

'Everything,' Melan said. Her eyes flicked to Shanvah and Sikvah, still hesitating, and her voice became a lash. 'Now!'

A moment later, all three girls stood naked, and they were taken out the far side of the room into the baths, a great natural cavern lit by wardlights in the stone far above. The floor was tiled marble, deep with water. Ornate fountains kept the water moving, and the air was hot and thick with steam. It put even Kajivah's baths to shame.

There were dozens of girls in the water, ages ranging from children to just shy of a woman grown. All stood washing in the stone bath, or lounged on the slick stone steps at its edges, shaving and paring nails. As one, they looked up to regard the new girls.

Ashia and the others were no strangers to bathing alongside other girls, but there was a frightening difference between these baths and those in the women's wing of her father's palace – here every girl's head was shaved bald.

Ashia reached up, touching the lush, oiled hair she had cultivated for a lifetime, in hope of pleasing her future husband.

Melan caught the look. 'Enjoy the touch, girl. It will be your last for some time.'

Her cousins gasped, and Shanvah put her hands to her head protectively.

Ashia forced herself to let go, dropping her hands to her sides, drawing a calming breath. 'It is only hair. It will grow back.' Out of the corner of her eyes, she watched her cousins calm as well.

'Amanvah!' Melan called, and a girl Sikvah's age came forward. She was too young for a woman's curves, but her eyes and face were much as the Damajah's.

Ashia felt a wave of relief. Holy Amanvah was their cousin, firstborn daughter of the Deliverer and Damajah. Once, they had been as close as Asome and Asukaji.

'Cousin!' Ashia greeted her warmly, holding her arms out. It had been years since she had last played with Amanvah, but it did not matter. She was their blood, and would help them in this strange and unfamiliar place.

Amanvah ignored her, refusing to meet Ashia's eyes. She was years younger and inches shorter than Ashia, but her bearing made it clear she considered her cousins beneath her now. She moved with liquid grace, stepping around the girls to face Melan, meeting the *nie'Damaji'ting*'s eyes boldly for a Betrothed.

'Here to study pillow dancing?' she smirked. It was common for young women, mostly from poor families, to be taken into the palace for pillow dancing lessons before they were sold to the great harem. Some were returned to their fathers, brides that could bring a fortune in dowry.

Melan nodded. 'An hour each day. And an hour of singing. Another at writing, and a fourth to bathe.'

'And the other twenty?' Amanvah asked. 'You cannot mean they will be granted the Chamber of Shadows.' Ashia's skin goosebumped at the name, and she struggled not to shiver despite the hot air.

But Melan shook her head. 'The other twenty, they will study *sharusahk*. They belong to Enkido.'

There were gasps from some of the other girls, and even Amanvah's face lost its smug look.

Ashia suppressed a snarl. She was blood of the Deliverer. Enkido was but half a man. She might have to obey his instruction, but Nie take her before she think herself his property.

'Shave them, and teach them the bido weave,' Melan said.

Amanvah bowed. 'Yes, Nie'Damaji'ting.'

'Thank you, cous . . .' Ashia began, but as soon as Melan left, Amanvah turned away. She snapped her fingers, pointing to three of the older girls, who immediately went over to Ashia and the others, leading them to the water.

Amanvah went back to a group of other girls, resuming an idle conversation and totally ignoring Ashia, Shanvah, and Sikvah as the *nie'dama'ting* cut away their beautiful hair and shaved their heads. Ashia stared forward, willing herself not to feel the loss as her heavy locks fell away.

The *nie'dama'ting* came at her with a cake of soap and a razor next. Ashia froze as the girl lathered her scalp, wielding the blade with expert strokes.

Amanvah returned when they were finished. Kept her gaze above their heads, letting none meet her eyes. 'Dry off.' She pointed to a pile of pristinely white, freshly folded drying cloths. 'Then follow.'

Again she turned away, as Ashia and the others dried off and followed their haughty cousin back to the dressing area. Behind trailed the same three girls who had cut their hair.

Amanvah walked past the many rolls of white bido silk to a lacquered box at the far end of the chamber. 'You are not *dama'ting.*' She threw them each a roll of the black silk from the box. 'Unworthy to wear the white.'

'Unworthy,' the older girls echoed at their backs. Ashia swallowed at that. Betrothed or not, they were blood of the Deliverer, not some common *dal'ting*.

Enkido was waiting for them when they emerged from the baths with thin, black silk scarves and robes over their bidos. Shanvah and Sikvah had stopped weeping, but still they clutched at each other, eyes on the floor.

Ashia boldly raised her gaze to meet the eunuch's eyes. She was blood of the Deliverer. Her father would cut off more than this man's cock if he dared lay a hand on her. She would not be afraid.

She would *not.*

The eunuch paid her no mind, staring instead at Sikvah, who shook like a hare before the wolf. He made a sharp, dismissive gesture. Sikvah only stared, uncomprehending, beginning to weep once more.

Enkido raised a finger sharply in Sikvah's face, causing the girl to gasp and stand up straight. Her eyes, wide with fear, crossed as they watched the finger.

Again, Enkido made the dismissive gesture. As if his finger in the air alone had been supporting her, Sikvah bent again, sobbing harder. This put Shanvah over the edge as well, the two of them clutching each other as they shook.

'She doesn't understand what you want!' Ashia cried. She couldn't tell if the eunuch was deaf as well as mute, for he did not look at her.

Instead, Enkido's hand whipped out, slapping Sikvah's cheek so hard her head struck Shanvah's and they were both driven hard into the wall.

Ashia was moving before she knew it, interposing herself between the eunuch and the other girls. 'How dare you?!' she cried. 'We are princesses of the Kaji, blood of the Deliverer, not camels in the bazaar! The Shar'Dama Ka will see you lose that hand.'

Enkido regarded her a moment. Then his hand seemed to flicker, and she was launched backward, an odd tingling in her jaw. She heard more than felt the rebound of the rock wall as she struck it. The sound echoed in her head as she struck the floor, and she knew pain would soon follow.

But Shanvah and Sikvah needed her. She put her hands under her, struggling to rise. She was the eldest. It was her duty to . . .

Her vision blurred at the edges, then darkened into black.

Enkido, Shanvah, and Sikvah were in the same positions when she woke. It seemed a mere eyeblink, but the dried blood caking her cheek to the marble floor told another story. The girls had stopped crying, standing with their backs straight. They watched her with terrified eyes.

Ashia managed to push herself up to her knees, then rose shakily to her feet. Her face throbbed with more pain than she had ever known. Rather than terrify her, the feeling made her angry. Perhaps he might strike them, but the half-man would not dare kill them. He was just trying to make them afraid.

She set her feet, daring once more to raise her gaze to Enkido. She would not be so easily cowed.

But the eunuch did not acknowledge her at all, simply turning away and walking down the hall, beckoning them with a wave.

Wordlessly, the girls followed.

Enkido stood before the three frightened girls in a large circular chamber lit only by dim wardlight. Like the rest of the under-palace, the floor and walls were stone, cut with wards and worn to a smooth polish by generations of use. The wards on the floor were arranged in concentric circles, like a marksman's target.

There were no furnishings save myriad weapons hanging from the walls. Spears and shields, bows and arrows, *alagai*-catchers and short melee knives, throwing blades and batons, weighted chains and other weapons Ashia could not even put a name to.

They had been forced to remove their robes again, placing them on hooks by the door, standing in only their bido weaves.

Enkido, too, wore only his bido. It was barely a strip of silk, for of course he had no manhood to cover. His muscular body was shaved smooth, covered in hundreds of tattooed lines and dots. It was a chaotic design, but Ashia sensed a pattern that was just beyond her ability to discern.

There was a riddle in them. The Riddle of Enkido. Ashia had always been skilled at riddling games. Riddles were taught to girls at a young age, that they might keep their husbands entertained.

The mute *Sharum* took a *sharusahk* pose. The girls looked at him blankly for a moment, but as his eyes darkened, Ashia took his meaning and assumed the same pose. *Sharusahk* was forbidden to *dal'ting*, but Ashia and her cousins had been taught dance as well as riddling. This was not so different.

'Follow him,' she told the others.

Shanvah and Sikvah complied, and Enkido circled them, inspecting. He grabbed Ashia's wrist hard, pulling her arm straight as he roughly kicked her legs farther apart. She could feel his grip long after he let go and turned to Shanvah.

Shanvah cried out and hopped from the loud smack to the meat of her thigh, and then Enkido took the stance again. No fool, Shanvah was quick to resume her imitation. She was closer this time, but Enkido kicked her legs out from under her, dropping her to the floor. Sikvah jumped back at that, and even Ashia let her pose slip, turning to face them.

Enkido pointed at her, and that simple gesture made her heart stop. Ashia resumed her pose as Sikvah continued to back away. Eventually she fetched up against the wall and did her very best to sink into it like a spirit.

Once again Enkido took the pose, and Shanvah was quick to scramble to her feet and mimic him. Her feet were set correctly this time, but her back was not straight. Enkido grabbed the strands of bido silk that connected the weave around her shaved head to that covering her nethers. He pulled hard, pressing a thumb into Shanvah's spine. She cried out in pain, but was helpless to resist as he pulled her back straight.

Enkido let go and turned towards Sikvah. The girl was backed against the wall in terror, hands covering her nose and mouth, eyes wide and tearing. The eunuch flowed smoothly into the pose again.

'Pose, you little fool!' Ashia snapped when the girl did not respond. But Sikvah only shook her head, mewling as she tried to shrink away farther into an unyielding wall.

Enkido moved faster than Ashia could have thought possible. Sikvah tried to run as he came for her, but he was on her in an instant, yanking her arm to turn the momentum of her attempt to flee into a throw. She cried out as she tumbled across the floor to the centre of the room.

Enkido was there in an eyeblink, kicking her in the stomach. Sikvah was thrown over onto her back and hit the ground hard. There was blood on her face and she groaned, limbs limp as fronds of palm.

'For Everam's sake, get up!' Ashia cried, but Sikvah didn't – or couldn't – comply. Enkido kicked her again. And again. She wailed, but she might have been crying to a statue of stone for all the eunuch took heed. Perhaps he truly was deaf.

He didn't appear to be trying to maim or kill her, but neither was there any hint of mercy, or sign that the onslaught would end if she did not rise and take the pose. He paused after each strike, giving her the chance to rise, but Sikvah was beyond comprehension, crippled with fear.

The blows began to accumulate. There was blood running from Sikvah's nose and mouth, and another cut at her temple. One of her eyes was already beginning to swell. Ashia began to think Enkido truly might kill her. She glanced to Shanvah, but the other girl stood frozen, staring helplessly at the scene.

So fixed was the eunuch on Sikvah, he did not notice as Ashia dropped her pose, sliding silently to the wall. Sacred law forbade her or any woman to touch a spear, so she selected a short, heavy baton, banded with steel. It felt good in her hand. Right.

Years of dance told in the grace of her swift and silent approach, as she carefully kept unseen at Enkido's back. When she was close enough she didn't hesitate, swinging the baton hard enough to shatter the eunuch's skull.

Enkido seemed not to have noticed her, but at the last moment he twisted, putting his littlest finger against her wrist. Ashia barely felt the feather-touch, but her swing missed Enkido's head by a wide margin. His calm eyes met hers, and Ashia knew then he had been waiting, baiting her to see if she would defend her cousin.

Sikvah lay forgotten, a quivering mass of blood and bruise. *He would have killed her*, Ashia thought, *just to test me*. She bared her teeth, pulling back and swinging again at his head, arcing her blow in from another angle.

It was a feint, and she spun before Enkido could react, moving to smash his kneecap.

But the mute eunuch was unsurprised, again sending her blow out wide with only the barest touch. Again and again Ashia swung the baton at him, but Enkido blocked her effortlessly. She felt a mounting fear at what he might do when he decided the lesson was over and struck back.

A moment later she learned, as he caught her wrist with the thumb and forefinger of his left hand, twisting. The hold was delicate, but Ashia's arm might have been set in stone for all she could move it. Enkido's other hand wove around her arm, a single hard finger poking her shoulder joint.

Immediately Ashia's arm went numb, falling loosely to her side as Enkido released it. What had he done? She did not feel her fingers lose their grip on the baton, but heard it clatter to the floor. She looked down, willing her fingers to clench, her arm to rise, but it was futile. She cursed the limb for its betrayal.

Enkido lunged at her, and she instinctively raised her other arm to shield herself. He jabbed a finger, and that arm, too, fell to her side. She tried to back away, but he struck again. Just a tap, and her legs would no longer bear her weight. She collapsed in a heap on the floor, head rebounding off the stone like the clapper of a bell.

With an effort she rolled onto her back, her vision spinning as she watched Enkido stalk over to her. She held her breath, determined not to cry out as the final blow came.

But Enkido squatted at her side, reaching gently to take her face in his hands, as comforting as a mother's touch.

His fingers found her temples and pressed hard. The pain was beyond anything Ashia could have imagined, but she bit her lip till she tasted blood, refusing to give him the satisfaction of seeing her scream.

The fingers tightened. Ashia's vision narrowed, then began to blacken at the edges. A moment later, sight vanished entirely. For a few moments, there was a swirl of colour, then that, too, fell away, leaving her in darkness.

Enkido let go the hold and rose, moving away towards her cousins.

She knew not how long she lay there, limp, listening to their cries. But then the shrieks and whimpers fell away. Ashia wondered if she had passed out, or the others had. She strained her ears, hearing gentle sighs, steady breathing, and a soft rustling.

A golden pall came over her vision like a sandstorm, and she began to make out vague shapes. However the eunuch had blinded her, it seemed not to be permanent.

Experimentally, she tried to clutch her numbed fingers. The jolt through her arm had little effect, but already it was a far cry from the seeming death of the limb minutes ago.

She could see the vague shape of the eunuch carrying one

of her cousins off. Another was still lying nearby. *Shanvah*, she realized when her sight began to sharpen. The eunuch returned and carried her off as well. Ashia was left alone in the centre of the room, twitching and struggling to control her slowly wakening limbs. Every thrash was agony, but so was her feeling of helplessness. And that, she would fight to the death.

The eunuch returned to her, a large blur of dark against the field of gold. She felt him lay his hand flat upon her bare chest, and held her breath.

Enkido pressed hard, compressing her lungs to force that breath free. When Ashia tried to take another breath, she found herself unable. He held her that way for a long time. She jerked and thrashed, trying to get her limbs to obey, to strike at him.

Still he held, and at last Ashia had not the strength or control even to thrash. Her slowly returning vision began to darken again.

Back to sleep, she thought, almost with relief.

But then the eunuch eased his hand slightly. Ashia tried to take a breath, and choked. Her lungs still could not expand fully. But she could take a short breath, and did. It was sweeter than any breath she had ever taken, but it was not enough, and so she took another. And another.

She found a steady rhythm in the short breaths, and again her vision began to return, her limbs to reawaken. But she did not thrash, focused solely on those fluttering, life-giving breaths.

And then Enkido eased his hand once more. She was allowed a half breath, and accepted it greedily, again finding a steady rhythm to compensate for the missing half.

He raised his hand again, laying it gently on her breast. Ashia took a full breath, and knew it was his gift to her. No pleasure of her life could match the perfection of that single breath.

Then he pushed slowly down again. Ashia went limp, letting him force the air from her lungs. He raised his hand a moment later, and Ashia breathed again. For several minutes, she let him guide her breaths. After struggling so mightily for air, this was complete rest, letting Enkido breathe for her.

She thought that she might fall asleep to that soothing feeling, But he took his hand away, and began massaging her temples, tending the very spot he had brought such agony upon.

Ashia's return to sight increased rapidly now, the haze before her focusing into the eunuch's muscular form. Ashia had never before seen a man without his robes and knew she should lower her eyes, but the tattoos on his body called to her once more. The Riddle of Enkido.

The eunuch's skilful fingers moved from her temples to her still-numb arm. There was a tugging feeling as he worked, but she could not feel his touch on her skin. But then there was a stab of pain that made Ashia jerk. She whipped her head around, seeing Enkido massaging a tiny bruise on her shoulder. An almost perfect circle of purple flesh where his fingertip had struck.

The pain faded quickly, spreading out into a gentle feeling of pins and needles as Ashia's limb came fully alive once more.

He turned slightly, and Ashia caught sight of a tattoo almost identical to her bruise on the eunuch's shoulder.

There were others on his temples, right where he had squeezed Ashia. Her eyes flickered over his body, following the lines that connected the points. There were many convergences, some great and some small. Enkido next moved to a bruise on her lower back. She twisted to better see, but she had already seen its tattooed mate on Enkido's back.

She knew even before the eunuch began to work that her legs would soon be full of pins and needles as well.

He's teaching, she realized. *The very lines on his body are the sacred text.*

She looked up at Enkido, and his face as he massaged her injury seemed almost one of kindness. She reached out, tentatively touching the convergence point on Enkido's back. 'I see it now. I understand, and will tell the others . . . master.'

Enkido bent towards her. For a moment she thought she was imagining it. But no. He held it too long.

Enkido bowed to her, as a teacher to a pupil, before scooping her up in his arms and carrying her, gentle as a babe, to the warm mass where her cousins slept. He laid her there, and brushed gentle fingertips over her eyelids, closing them for her.

Ashia did not resist, putting her arms protectively about her cousins and falling into a deep sleep.

They woke with a start. Enkido might be mute, but he could still bring thunder from the polished ram's horn at his lips. It felt like the very walls were shaking. The girls shrieked and covered their ears, but the noise did not cease until they were on their feet. Ashia had no idea what time it was, but they must have slept for hours. She felt refreshed, if still sore.

The eunuch replaced the horn on the wall and handed them each a towel, silently leading the way from his training room to the bath. They walked in a line, but Ashia stole glances back at her cousins. Shanvah's face was frozen, thoughts far away. Sikvah walked with a limp, drawing sharp breaths as they went down a series of steps.

As before, Enkido waited outside as they entered the dressing chamber. They could hear the trickle of the fountains while they unwove their bidos, but it was otherwise quiet. Indeed, they found the bath empty.

Shanvah and Sikvah looked about nervously, dwarfed by the great chamber. Ashia clapped her hands, drawing their attention. 'Nie'Damaji'ting Melan said we were to have an hour a day in the bath. Let us not waste it.' She waded out into the water, leading them to the largest, most central fountain. There were benches of smooth stone at the base where bathers could lie, immersing themselves in the hot flow.

Sikvah groaned as she lay in the steaming water. 'There, sister,' Ashia said, coming to her side to inspect the bruise on her thigh, gently massaging as Enkido had done. 'The bruise is not great. Let the hot water soak the pain, and it will heal quickly.'

'There will be others,' Shanvah said, her voice flat and lifeless. 'He will never stop.' Sikvah shuddered, her skin pimpling even in the warm air.

'He will,' Ashia said, 'when we solve the riddle.'

'Riddle?' Shanvah asked.

Ashia pointed to the bruise on her shoulder. Shanvah had a matching one, as did Sikvah. 'There is a mark just like this on the master's flesh. When struck, the arm dies for a time.'

Sikvah began to cry again.

'But what does it mean?' Shanvah asked.

'A *dama'ting* mystery,' Ashia said. 'Melan said we were to learn *sharusahk*. The Riddle of Enkido is a part of it, I'm sure.'

'Then why give us a teacher who cannot speak?' Sikvah demanded. 'One who . . . who . . .' She sobbed again.

Ashia squeezed her thigh reassuringly. 'Fear not, cousin. Perhaps this is simply the way. Our brothers all came back from *sharaj* with *sharusahk* bruises. Why should we be different?'

'Because we're not boys!' Shanvah shouted.

Just then, the doors opened and the three girls froze. A group of Betrothed entered, led by Amanvah.

'Perhaps not,' Ashia said, drawing the other girls' eyes back to her. 'But we are blood of the Deliverer, and there is nothing common boys can endure that we cannot.'

'You're using our fountain,' Amanvah called as she and the others strode over. She pointed to a small fountain at the far end of the pool. 'Black bidos wash over there.'

The other *nie'dama'ting* laughed at that, squawking like trained birds. Amanvah was only eleven, but girls years her senior, some close to taking the white veil themselves, deferred to her, eager to curry favour.

Sikvah's leg had gone tense, and Ashia could sense Shanvah, too, was ready to bolt like a hare.

'Pay the chatter no mind, little cousins,' Ashia said. 'But come.' She took each of them by an arm, pulling them gently to their feet and ushering them away while she glared at Amanvah. 'A smaller fountain and the laughter of girls is a cheap price for our hour of peace.'

'Not girls,' Amanvah said, grabbing Ashia's arm. '*Nie'dama'ting*. Your betters. Something you'd best learn.'

'Why are you doing this?' Ashia demanded. 'We are cousins. Our blood is your blood. Blood of the Deliverer.'

Amanvah pulled at Ashia's shoulder, at the same time sliding a leg behind hers. Ashia was thrown into her cousins, the three of them falling to the water with a splash.

'You are nothing,' Amanvah said when they came sputtering out of the water. 'The Deliverer has spoken, sending you here in black. You are the products of his useless, *dal'ting* sisters, fit for breeding wolves to run the Maze and nothing else. Your blood is not holy, and you are no cousin of mine.'

Ashia felt her sense of calm slip away. She was two years older than Amanvah, bigger and stronger, and she would not be bullied by her younger cousin.

She struck the water, sending a splash that Amanvah instinctively threw a hand up to shield from her face. Quick as an asp, Ashia darted in and struck, fingers bunched and stiffened, for the point on her shoulder where Enkido's tattoo had been. The place she and all her cousins carried bruises.

Amanvah gave a shrill, satisfying cry as she fell onto her backside in the water. The other girls froze, no one sure how to react.

Amanvah's eyes were wide as she stared at her numb, lifeless arm. Then she scowled, rubbing at the spot until the numbness faded. She flexed her arm experimentally, and it responded, if slowly.

'So Enkido has managed to teach you something of *sharusahk* already,' Amanvah said, getting to her feet and taking the same stance Enkido had demonstrated the day before. She smiled. 'Come, then. Show me what you have learned.'

Ashia already knew what was coming, and steeled herself. *If the* Sharum *can endure this, then I can as well.*

The thought calmed her a bit, but did nothing to shield her from the pain as Amanvah administered the beating. She flowed around Ashia's punches as if she were standing still, and her own strikes were quick and precise, twisting and jabbing points meant to deliver maximum pain. When she tired of the game, she easily grappled Ashia to the pool floor, twisting her arm so far Ashia feared she might break it off. She struggled to keep her head above water, and knew, to her shame, that if the younger girl wished to drown her, there was nothing she could do to stop her.

But Amanvah was content with pain, pulling at Ashia's arm until she had screamed herself hoarse.

At last Amanvah let her go, dropping her with a splash. She pointed to the small fountain. Her eyes taking in all three of her cousins.

'To your kennel, *nie'Sharum'ting* dogs.'

The horn sounded, and Ashia was on her feet before her mind was fully awake. She crouched in a defensive stance, presenting as low a profile as possible as she scanned for the threat.

No attack came. Enkido casually replaced the horn on the wall while the girls stood at the ready. There were five of them now, her cousins Micha and Jarvah joining them not long after the Damajah gave them to Enkido. The new girls were years younger, but seemed to adapt to Enkido's world the faster for it, and for the example Ashia set.

For months, Enkido's training room had been the centre of their world. They slept and ate there, meals and rest earned only with pain. Lessons always ended with one of the girls nursing numbed limbs or worse maladies. Sometimes they could not smell. Other times deaf for hours. None of the effects was permanent.

If he was pleased with them, Enkido would massage and stretch away their pain, restoring lost limbs and senses, speeding healing.

They learned quickly that hard work pleased him. And stubborn resolve. A willingness to continue even when hurt or in pain. Complaints, begging, and disobedience did not.

They had not been allowed a full sleep since that first night. Twenty minutes here, three hours there. The eunuch would wake them at odd hours and expect them to perform complex *sharukin*, or even spar. There seemed no pattern to it, so they learned to sleep when they could. The perpetual state of exhaustion made the first weeks seem a blurred dream.

Lessons with the *dama'ting* came and went like mirages in the desert. They obeyed the Brides of Everam without question. Enkido always knew if they had displeased one of the women in white, and made it known without words why the mistakes should never be repeated.

I would kill for a full sleep, Shanvah's fingers said.

Most of the lessons the *dama'ting* gave were of little interest to the girls, but the secret code of the eunuchs, a mixture of hand signs and body language, had been embraced fully. Complex conversations could be had in code as easily as speech.

Enkido gave occasional commands or bits of wisdom in code, but the eunuch still preferred to silently teach by example, forcing them to guess the full meaning for themselves. Sometimes days went by without a word in code.

But while it did little to foster communication with their master, it had become their primary means of communication with one another. Enkido, it turned out, was not deaf. Quite the contrary, the slightest whisper could bring pain and humiliation that kept the girls silent in his presence. Ashia was sure he had caught them speaking in code more than once, but thus far he had chosen to ignore it.

As would I, Ashia's fingers replied, shocked to find she truly meant it.

I haven't the strength to kill, Sikvah said. *Without sleep, I may die.* As usual, Micha and Jarvah said nothing, but they watched the conversation closely.

You won't die, Ashia replied. *As the master taught me to survive on shallow breaths, so too is he teaching us shallow sleep.*

Shanvah turned to meet her eyes. *How can you know that?* her fingers asked.

Trust your elder, little cousins, Ashia replied, and even Shanvah relaxed at that. Ashia could not explain, but she had no doubt of the master's intent. Sadly, understanding did not give her endurance. That had to be earned.

There was an unexpected reprieve as Enkido made his most beloved gesture, pointing towards the towels. They must have slept longer than they thought. All five girls had a spring in their step as they collected their towels and lined by the door. The eunuch dismissed them with a wave.

Twenty hours a day with Enkido, as the Damajah commanded. Three more studying with the *dama'ting*. And that one, blessed hour between, when they were in the baths. The one place Enkido could not follow. The one hour they could speak freely, or close their eyes without permission. Showing submission to the *nie'dama'ting* was a small price for the peace.

The Betrothed sneered at them in the baths, the halls, at lessons, laughing at the *nie'Sharum'ting*, as Amanvah had dubbed them. The black bidos forever marked Ashia and her cousins from the other girls in the palace. Even the *dal'ting* girls sent to learn pillow dancing seemed above them. They were allowed to keep their hair, and not beaten for their errors.

Ashia and her little cousins had learned to keep quiet and to themselves, passing unnoticed whenever possible, showing submission when not.

As usual, they were the first to the baths. The *nie'dama'ting* would not arrive for a quarter hour, but Ashia led them directly to the small fountain at the edge of the pool, even though the water was not as hot, so far from the wards that heated it. There they washed the sweat from their skin, and helped one another massage sore muscles, sand calluses, and treat blistered skin. Enkido's lessons on massage and healing were invaluable in the baths.

There was a shout as the doors opened. The *nie'dama'ting* entered in a knot, and clearly a confrontation was going on at their centre.

Ashia was not fool enough to stare, but she casually sat atop the fountain, right by the flow of water, to grant a better view from the side of her eyes. Wordlessly, her cousins did the same, pretending to groom one another as they watched.

This was not the first time they had witnessed the Betrothed fighting. They called one another sister, but there was little love among them, each vying for influence over the others and the favour of Amanvah. Outside, they used debate and logic, but in the privacy of the baths, where the Brides of Everam would not see, they were as apt to use cutting words, or even *sharu-sahk*.

The argument was between two older girls, Jaia and Selthe. They seemed ready to come to blows, but both glanced first to Amanvah, seeking favour.

Amanvah turned her back on them, giving them permission to fight. 'I see nothing.'

The other Betrothed did the same, repeating the words and turning their backs until the older girls faced each other alone.

Who will take the match? Ashia's fingers asked.

Selthe, Sikvah answered without hesitation. *It is said she will soon finish her dice and take the white.*

She will lose, and badly, Ashia disagreed.

Her form is strong, Shanvah noted. Micha and Jarvah did not comment, but they followed the conversation with their eyes.

There is fear in her eyes, Ashia said. Indeed, Selthe took a step back as Jaia moved in. A moment later, Selthe's head was being held under the water. Jaia kept her there until Selthe ceased struggling and slapped her submission on the surface of the pool. Jaia pushed her farther under, then let go and took a step back. Selthe rose with a splash, gasping for air.

Weak lungs, too, Ashia said. *She was barely under the water a full minute.*

'I see your fingers chattering, *Sharum* dogs!' Amanvah's cry snapped their heads up. The girl strode angrily their way, several other Betrothed at her back.

'Behind me, little cousins,' Ashia said softly as Amanvah approached. 'Eyes down. This is not your fight.' The girls complied as Ashia raised her gaze to meet Amanvah's. The act seemed to double the younger girl's ire as she pulled up, close enough to reach out and touch.

The kill zone, Enkido's fingers had called the space between them.

'You saw nothing,' Amanvah said. 'Say it, *nie'Sharum'ting.*'

Ashia shook her head. 'The large fountain is not worth fighting over, cousin, but nothing you can do will make me lie to my master, much less the *dama'ting.* I will not volunteer the information, but if asked, I will tell the truth.'

Amanvah's nostrils flared. 'And what is that?'

'That the *nie'dama'ting* lack discipline,' Ashia said. 'That you call one another sister but do not know the meaning of the word, bickering and fighting like *khaffit.*' She spat in the bath, and the other girls gasped. 'And your *sharusahk* is pathetic.'

Amanvah's eyes flicked to her target an instant before she struck, but it was more than enough for Ashia to block and plot her next three blows. The Betrothed spent two hours each day studying *sharusahk.* Ashia and her cousins spent twenty, and the difference had come to tell.

Ashia could have put Amanvah under the water as easily as Jaia did Selthe, but she wanted the beating to last, as had the one Amanvah delivered on their second day in the palace.

Two knuckles into the armpit, and Amanvah howled with pain. A chop to the throat cut off the sound, and Amanvah's eyes bulged as her lungs seized. The heel of Ashia's hand to her forehead left Amanvah stunned as the force of the blow knocked her backward into the water.

Ashia could have continued the beating, but she stayed her hand as Amanvah rose choking to her knees, coughing out bathwater. 'If you walk away now, I will not have to tell the *dama'ting* you are fools, as well.'

It was a goad, of course, forcing Amanvah to willingly prolong the beating, lest she appear weak in front of the other *nie'dama'ting*.

The other girls held their collective breath as Amanvah slowly got to her feet, water dripping from her skin. Her eyes promised murder, but they also told Ashia where she would strike next.

The eyes tell all, Enkido's fingers had said. Ashia stood calmly, breathing in steady rhythm, her guard low, inviting the attack.

Amanvah was more cautious now, keeping her guard in place and using feints to set up her true attacks.

It was all to no avail. Ashia could see the moves before Amanvah even made them, blocking a series of blows without retaliating, simply to show the ease of it.

Up to their thighs in water, Ashia kept her feet planted, blocking and dodging with her upper body alone, but Amanvah needed her feet. It made her slow, and she soon began to breathe hard.

Ashia shook her head. 'You Betrothed are soft, cousin. This lesson was overdue.'

Amanvah glared at her with open hatred. Wrapped in the soft cocoon of her breath, Ashia was calm, but she put a smile on her lips, if only to goad her cousin further. She already knew what Amanvah was planning, though she wanted to believe the girl was not so stupid as to actually attempt it.

But in her desperation, Amanvah took the bait, delivering a series of feints before trying a kick.

Her legs already tired and underwater, the kick was pathetically slow. Amanvah was counting on surprise, but even that would not have been enough. Ashia caught her ankle, yanking the leg upward.

'One stupid enough to kick in water does not deserve the use of their leg.' She struck hard, driving her stiffened fingers hard into a precise point on Amanvah's thigh. Amanvah screamed from the pain, and then the leg went limp in Ashia's hand.

Ashia spun her as she fell, easily slipping into a submission hold as she held Amanvah under.

Jaia tried to intercede, but Shanvah moved in without a word, striking two quick blows that collapsed the older girl's legs. She fell to the water, thrashing to keep her head above the surface. Selthe could have stepped in to help her, but she and the other *nie'dama'ting* stood frozen in place. Sikvah, Micha, and Jarvah lined up next to Shanvah, blocking their path to the combatants.

Amanvah thrashed at first, and then went still. Ashia waited for her to slap the surface of the water in submission, but to her credit, the girl never did. She knew she was the Deliverer's daughter, and even Ashia would not dare kill her in front of everyone.

She pulled Amanvah's head free of the water, letting her gasp a breath.

'*Sharum* blood of the Deliverer. Say it.'

The girl looked at her in fury, spitting in Ashia's face.

Ashia did not let her draw another breath before putting her back under, twisting her arm painfully for long moments.

'*Sharum* blood,' Ashia said, pulling her into the air. 'Everam's spear sisters. Say it.' Amanvah shook her head wildly as she gasped and thrashed, so Ashia put her under again.

This time she waited long minutes, her hands in tune with Amanvah's body. The muscles tensed one last time before consciousness was lost. When she felt it, she pulled Amanvah out into the air a third time, leaning in close.

'There is no *hora* magic in the bath, cousin. No *dama'ting*, no Enkido. There is only *sharusahk*. We can do this every day if you wish.'

Amanvah eyed her with cold rage, but there was fear there as well, and resignation. '*Sharum* blood of the Deliverer, Everam's spear sisters,' she agreed. 'Cousin.'

Ashia nodded. 'An admission that would have cost you nothing, when I came to you in friendship.' She let go her hold and stepped back, pointing. 'I think it is the Betrothed who will use the small fountains where the water is cool from now on. Everam's spear sisters claim the large one.'

She looked out over the assembled *nie'dama'ting* and was satisfied to see them all rock backward under her gaze. 'Unless any wish to challenge me?'

Shanvah and the others broke their line as if the move had been rehearsed, giving room for a challenger to approach, but none was so foolish. They made way as Ashia led her sisters to the large fountain, where they continued their bath as if nothing had happened. The Betrothed helped Amanvah and Jaia onto benches, massaging life back into their limbs. They watched Ashia and the others dazedly, their own bathing forgotten.

That was incredible, Shanvah's fingers said.

You should not have interfered, Ashia replied. *I ordered you to stand back.*

Shanvah looked hurt, and the others genuinely surprised.

But we won, Micha signed.

Today we won, Ashia agreed. *But tomorrow, when they come at us together, you will all need to fight.*

The *nie'dama'ting* did indeed attack the next day. They entered the bath en masse, moving to surround the large fountain where Ashia and her spear sisters bathed, outnumbering them three to one.

Six *nie'dama'ting* were carried from the bath by their sisters that day, limbs too numb to support them. Others limped or nursed black bruises. Some were dizzy from loss of air, and one had still not recovered her sight.

They went through lessons fearing reprisal, but if the *dama'ting* asked questions about the state of them, the *nie'dama'ting* saw nothing.

When they returned to Enkido, they found him kneeling at the head of a small table with six steaming bowls. Always, the girls had knelt by the wall as they ate their small bowls of plain couscous. The room had never before held any piece of furniture beyond training equipment.

But even more shocking was the scent that came from the bowls. Ashia turned and saw dark meat atop the couscous, moist with juice and dark with spices. Her mouth watered, and her stomach lurched. Food such as she had not tasted in half a year.

As if in a daze, the girls followed their noses to the table. It felt like floating.

The head of the table for the master, Enkido signed.

The foot, for Nie Ka. He indicated that Ashia kneel at the opposite end. He beckoned Shanvah and Sikvah to kneel on one side, Micha and Jarvah the other.

Enkido swept his hands over the steaming bowls. *Meat this one night, in honour of* Sharum *blood.*

He thumped his fist on the table, making the bowls jump. *The table, always, for Everam's spear sisters.*

From that day forward, they always ate together, like true family.

He punished their failures, yes, but Enkido gave rewards, too.

No meat had ever tasted sweeter.

Years passed. At sixteen, Ashia and the other girls had been commanded to begin growing back their hair. It seemed heavy now, clumsy. She kept it carefully pinned back.

At seventeen, her father sent for her. It was the first time she had left the Dama'ting Palace in over four years, and the world outside looked strange to her now. The halls of her father's palace were bright and garish, but there were places to hide, if one was limber and quick. She could disappear in an instant if she wished, trained to be invisible.

But no, she was here to be seen. It was an alien concept, half remembered from another life.

'Beloved daughter!' Imisandre rose and went to embrace her when she entered the throne room.

'It is a pleasure to see you, honoured mother.' Ashia kissed her mother's cheeks.

Her brother stood to the right of the throne, draped in the white robes of a full *dama*. He nodded to her, but did not presume to speak before their father.

Ashan did not rise, watching her coolly, searching still for some imperfection to judge. But after Enkido, her father's expectations were met effortlessly. Back straight, eyes down, every fibre of her black robes in place, she silently approached. At the precise distance from the throne, she stopped and bowed, waiting.

'Daughter,' Ashan said at last. 'You are looking well. Does the Dama'ting Palace agree with you?'

Ashia straightened, but kept her eyes at her father's sandals. He had two *Sharum* guards by the door, too far to assist him in time. A Krevakh Watcher lurked in the columns behind the throne. She might not have noticed him when she was younger, but now he might as well have been wearing bells. Pitiful protection for the *Damaji* of the Kaji and his heir.

Of course, Ashan himself was a *sharusahk* master, and could see to his own defence against most any foe. She wondered how he and her brother would fare against her now.

'Thank you, honoured Father,' she said. 'I have learned much in the Dama'ting Palace. You were wise to send me and my cousins there.'

Ashan nodded. 'That is well, but your time there has come

to an end. You are seventeen now, and it is time you were married.'

Ashia felt as if she had been punched in the gut, but she embraced the feeling, bowing again. 'Has my honoured father selected a match at last?' She could see the smile on her brother's face, and knew who it was before her father spoke again.

'It has been agreed between fathers,' Ashan said. 'You are released from the Dama'ting Palace to marry the Deliverer's son Asome. Your palace chambers are as you left them. Return there now with your mother to begin preparation.'

'Please.' Having dismissed her, Ashan was already looking to his advisor Shevali when Ashia spoke.

'Eh?' he asked.

Ashia could see storm clouds gathering on her father's brow. If she were to attempt to refuse the match . . .

She knelt, putting her hands on the floor with her head between them. 'Excuse me, honoured Father, for disturbing you. It was my hope, only, to see my cousins one last time before I go with my honoured mother to follow the path Everam has laid before me.'

Her father's face softened at that, the closest he had ever come to a show of affection. 'Of course, of course.'

She held her tears until she reached the training chamber. Her spear sisters were practising *sharukin*, but they stood straight, bowing. Enkido was not to be found.

Nie Ka, you have returned, Shanvah signed. *Is all well?*

Ashia shook her head. *Nie Ka no longer, sister. That title will be yours now, and the care of our little sisters. I am to marry.*

Congratulations, sister, Sikvah signed. *Who is the groom?*

Asome, Ashia signed.

An honour, Micha signed.

What will we do without you? Jarvah's hands asked.

You will have one another, Ashia signed, *and Enkido, until such time as we are reunited.* She embraced each in turn, and still refused to cry.

But then the door opened, and Enkido appeared. With a wave, the other girls filed out of the room, dismissed.

Ashia looked at her master, and then, for the first time since she was sent to the Dama'ting Palace, she wept.

Enkido opened his arms, and she fell into them. From his robes he took a tear bottle. He held her, steady as stone, stroking her hair with one hand as he collected her tears with the other.

'I'm sorry, master,' she whispered when it was done. It was the first time in years anyone had spoken aloud in the training chamber. The sound echoed to her sensitive ears, seeming wrong, but what did it matter now?

Even the palm weeps, when the storm washes over it, Enkido signed, moving to hand her the bottle. *The tears of Everam's spear sisters are all the more precious for how seldom they fall.*

Ashia held up her hands, pushing the bottle away. 'Then keep them always.'

She looked down, even now unable to meet his eyes. 'I should be overjoyed. What greater husband could a woman dream of than the Deliverer's son? I thought that fate was taken from me when I was sent to you, but now that it has come again, I do not wish it. Why was I sent here, if only to be given to a man who would have had me regardless? What point in the skills you have taught, if I am never to use them? *You* are my master, and I want no other.'

Enkido looked at her with sad eyes. *I had many wives before giving myself to the* dama'ting, his fingers said. *Many sons. Many daughters. But not one has made me as proud as you have. Your loyalty makes my heart sing.*

She clutched at him. 'Asome may be my husband, but you will always be my master.'

The eunuch shook his head. *No, child. The command of the*

Deliverer cannot be denied. It is not for me or you to speak against his blessing, and I will not shame the Deliverer's son by coveting what is rightfully his. You will go to Asome a free woman, unbound to me.

Ashia pulled away, walking to the door. Enkido did not follow.

'If you are no longer my master,' she said, 'then you cannot command my heart.'

The wedding was everything she might have dreamed as a girl, fit for a prince and princess of Krasia. Her spear sisters stood beside her as she waited for her father to escort her to where Asome waited with Jayan at the foot of the Skull Throne in Sharik Hora.

Enkido was in attendance as well, guarding the Damajah and watching over the proceedings, though none of the guests knew it. She and her sisters knew the signs, saw the slight ripples he left to mark himself to them.

The oaths and ceremony were a blur. Two thrones had been provided for the bride and groom at the feast, but Ashia sat alone, waiting on her husband as he accepted gifts and spoke to the guests, Asukaji at his side.

No expense had been spared, but the rich, honeyed cakes were bland to Ashia's tongue. She longed to be back safe underground, eating plain couscous at the foot of Enkido's table.

But for all she walked through the day in a daze, it was the wedding night that brought home her true fate.

She waited in the pillow chamber for Asome to come and take her as a husband, but hours passed in silence. Ashia looked more than once at the window, dreaming of escape.

At last, there was a sound in the hall, but it never reached the door.

There was a vent above the archway. Ashia was up the wall

in an instant, her fingers easily finding holds in the minute cracks between the stones. She put her eye and ear to the vent, seeing the back of Asome's head, with Asukaji facing him. They looked to be arguing.

'I cannot do this,' Asome was saying.

'You can, and you will,' Asukaji said, taking her husband's face in his hands. 'Ashia must give you the son I cannot. Melan has thrown her dice. If you take my sister now, it will be done. One time, and the ordeal be over.'

Realization was a slap in the face.

It was no sin for men to love their own gender. It was common enough in the *sharaj*, boys forming pillow friendships to pass the years before they were old and experienced enough for their first wife. But Everam demanded new generations, and so all but the most stubborn *push'ting* were eventually bound to marry and share the pillows, if only long enough to produce a son. Everam knew, Kajivah had said as much to Asukaji many times.

But she had never thought *she* would be a *push'ting* bride.

They entered a moment later. Ashia had plenty of time to get back in the pillows, but her mind was reeling. Asome and Asukaji were *push'ting* lovers. She had never meant anything to them save as a womb to carry the abomination they wanted to bring into the world.

They ignored Ashia, Asukaji undressing her husband and stiffening him with his mouth until he could do the deed. He joined them in the pillows, coaxing them together.

His touch made Ashia's skin crawl, but she took shallow breaths, and endured.

Despite his words, there was jealousy in her brother's eyes, his face darkening as Asome gasped and saw Everam, seeding her. As soon as the deed was done, Asukaji pulled them apart and the two men fell into an embrace, seeming to forget she was even there.

Ashia thought then about killing them both. It would be simple. They were so lost in each other she doubted they would notice until it was too late. She could even make it seem an accident, as if the act had been too much for poor Asome's heart. Her brother, distraught at his lover's death, would have taken a knife to himself rather than live without.

Enkido had taught her to do those things, so cleanly that the Deliverer himself would never know.

She closed her eyes, living the fantasy fully, not daring to move lest she make it reality. She breathed, and eventually her centre returned. She rose from the pillows, pulling her wedding robes back on, and left.

Her husband and brother did not notice.

5

Kajivah

333 AR Autumn

Ashia looked up in shock as wardlight flooded the room where she wept. How long since someone had been able to sneak past her guard? Had she forgotten everything her master taught?

Enkido would be ashamed of you, Micha said, and it was true. How could she lead the *Sharum'ting* when she could not even lead herself?

She turned to the doorway expecting to see Kajivah, but her heart sank farther at the sight of her husband. Perhaps it was *inevera* that Asome should find her so, eyes puffed and wet, as much a failure at motherhood as she was in *alagai'sharak*. He would tell her now, as so many times before, that she should give up her spear. And perhaps he was right.

'Tikka was having one of her fits.' Asome produced a spotless white cloth from his sleeve, handing it to her to dry her eyes. 'But I wore her down with patience, though Everam knows, a mountain does not have enough.'

Ashia laughed, sniffing into the cloth.

'Word of your exploits in the night has already reached the palace, *jiwah*,' Asome said.

Ashia looked at him weakly. He knew. Everam damn him, he already knew of her loss of control out beyond the Maze.

Would he have her stripped of her spear, now that the Deliverer was not there to stop him? Asome and her father had both argued long and hard to keep her from *alagai'sharak*. With Ashan on the Skull Throne, this was all they needed. Even the Damajah could not stop them.

'Those men were foolish to leave their unit behind,' Asome went on. 'It was only by Everam's infinite mercy that you should have been there to save them from themselves. You have done well, *jiwah*.'

Relief flooded Ashia, though it was mixed in a sickening swirl of guilt. Was she less a fool?

Even more confusing was the source of the praise. Had Asome ever spared a compliment for her? Words failed as she watched him, waiting for the twist.

Asome crossed the room to the greenland bed in her pillow chamber. He sat, sinking into the feathered mattress, then immediately stood back up.

'Everam's beard,' he said. 'Do you actually sleep on that?'

Ashia realized her husband had never even seen her sleeping chambers before. She shook her head. 'I fear it will swallow me. I sleep on the floor.'

Asome nodded. 'The greenland ways threaten to make us as soft as they.'

'Some, perhaps,' Ashia said. 'The weak of will. But it is to us, the blood of the Deliverer, to show them a better way.'

Asome looked at her a long time, then began to pace the room, arms crossed behind his back, hands thrust into his sleeves.

'I have failed you as a husband,' he said. 'I knew I would never be good at it, but I did not realize what it would drive you to.'

'My path was laid down by Everam before you took me to wife,' Ashia said. 'I am what the Damajah made me, a spear sister of Everam. She knew this, and advised against the match, but our fathers would not listen.'

Asome nodded. 'Nor Asukaji, who pressed for the match at

every turn. But perhaps it is *inevera*. My mother told me on Waning that a great man does not fear his wife will steal his glory. He uses her support to reach even higher.'

He moved over to her, offering a hand to pull her to her feet, mindless of the greasy black ichor that stained her fingers. 'It seems I am not a great man, but perhaps, with your help, it is not too late.'

Ashia's eyes narrowed. She ignored the hand, curling her legs and kicking herself to standing. 'What are you saying, husband? You must forgive me if I require plain words, but we have had many misunderstandings. What support do you wish from me?'

Asome bowed. Not so long and deep as to show deference, but still a sign of respect that surprised her. Her husband had not bowed to her since their wedding day. 'This night? Nothing save a peace between us, and a renewed hope to preserve our marriage, as the Deliverer has commanded. Tomorrow . . .' He shrugged. 'We shall see what the dawn brings.'

Ashia shook her head. 'If by "preserving our marriage" you mean I submit to your touch again and bear you further sons . . .'

Asome held up a hand. 'I have eleven *nie'dama* brothers, and dozens more among the *nie'Sharum*. Soon I shall have nephews in the hundreds. The house of Jardir, nearly extinct a generation ago, is thriving once again. I have done my duty and produced a son and heir. I need no further children. What child could be greater than our Kaji?'

Asome cast his gaze to the floor. 'We both know I am *push'ting*, *jiwah*. I do not crave a woman's touch. That night was . . .' He shook his head vigorously, as if to throw the image from his mind. Then he looked up, meeting her eyes. 'But I am proud of you, my *Jiwah Ka*. And I can still love you in my way, if you will allow it.'

Ashia looked at him a long time, considering. Asome and her brother had been dead in her heart since the wedding night. Was there any return from the lonely path?

'Why are you proud of me?' she asked.

'Eh?' Asome said.

'You said you were proud of me.' Ashia crossed her arms. 'Why? A fortnight ago you stood before the Shar'Dama Ka crying shame and demanding divorce.'

Now it was Asome's turn to stare while he sifted his feelings and chose his words. 'And you stood there beside me, fierce and certain of your place in Everam's plan. I envy that, cousin. Heir to Nothing, they call me. When have I understood my place in it?'

He swept a hand her way. 'But you. First of the *Sharum'ting*, giving glory to Everam in sacred *alagai'sharak*.'

He paused, and his eyes flicked to the floor. He let out a sigh and raised them again, meeting her eyes and holding them. 'I was wrong to try to deny your wishes, *jiwah*. It was jealousy, and a sin against Everam. I have repented before the Creator, but the sin was against you. I beg that you accept my apology.'

Ashia was stunned. An apology? From Asome, son of Ahmann? She wondered if she were sleeping, and this some bizarre dream.

'Jealousy?' she asked.

'I, too, crave the right to fight in the night,' Asome said. 'An honour denied me not by sex, but the colour of my robe. I was . . . bitter, that a woman should be given the right to do what I may not.'

'Traditions change every day, as we approach Sharak Ka,' Ashia said. 'The Deliverer was vexed when he forbade you to fight. Perhaps when he returns . . .'

'And if he does not return?' Asome said. 'Your father sits the throne now, but he does not have a warrior's heart. He will never allow the *dama* to fight.'

'The same was said of my spear sisters,' Ashia said. 'If this is what you want, you should be making peace with the Damajah, not me.'

Asome nodded. 'Perhaps. But I do not know how to begin. I always knew Jayan was not worthy to succeed my father, but I did not know until today that I, too, had failed my parents.'

'The Damajah has promised you the succession of the Skull Throne,' Ashia said. 'That is no small thing.'

Asome waved his hand. 'A meaningless gesture. Ashan is young. Sharak Ka will likely have come and gone before Everam calls him to Heaven, with me left watching from the minarets.'

Ashia laid a hand on his shoulder. He stiffened at the touch but did not pull away. 'The Damajah is under more strain than you know, husband. Go to her. She will show you the path to honour.'

Asome reached out, entwining their arms as he, too, reached for her shoulder. Ashia stiffened in return. It was a sign of trust among those who studied *sharusahk*, both of them giving the other opportunity for leverage and attack.

'I will do what I can,' Asome said. 'But her first command was that I make peace with you.'

Ashia squeezed his shoulder. 'I have not broken your arm, husband. Nor you, mine. That is peace enough to build upon.'

Inevera lounged in her new robes on her bed of pillows beside the Skull Throne. Still scandalous by Krasian standards, the bright colourful silks were a shock to the eyes in a culture where every decent woman was in black, white, or tan.

But now the thin silk was opaque. No more would men have a glimpse of the flesh beneath, always ready for the Deliverer's pleasure. She kept her hair uncovered, but now the locks were tightly woven and banded with gold and jewels instead of falling free for the Deliverer to stroke.

She let her gaze slip across the auras of the men in the room. All of them, even Ashan, were afraid of her. He shifted on the throne, uncomfortable.

That, too, was good.

'The Sharum Ka!' the door guard called as Jayan strode into

the room and past the *Damaji*, climbing to stand opposite Asome on the fourth step.

It was an agreement that had only come after hours of negotiation between their camps. The fourth step was high enough to advise quietly, but low enough that their eyes were below sitting Ashan, and level with each other. The dice had predicted blood in the streets should either stand a step higher or lower.

Jayan's entourage remained on the floor. Hasik, Ahmann's disgraced eunuch brother-in-law, now heeled Jayan like an attack dog. With him stood *kai'Sharum* Jurim, who commanded the Spears of the Deliverer in Shanjat's absence, and Jayan's half brothers, *kai'Sharum* Icha and Sharu, eldest sons of Ahmann by Thalaja and Everalia. Both were seventeen, raised to the black mere months earlier, but already they commanded large contingents of *Sharum*.

'Sharum Ka.' Ashan accorded Jayan a nod of respect. The Andrah had never cared for Inevera's firstborn, but he was not fool enough to let the rift between them deepen. 'How fare the defences of Everam's Bounty?'

Jayan bowed, but it was a shallow courtesy, showing none of the obeisance due an Andrah from his Sharum Ka. 'They are strong . . . Andrah.' Inevera could almost hear his jaw grinding at the title as he looked up at his uncle. 'Not a single demon has been spotted within miles of the throne since Waning. The *Sharum* must venture far to even wet their spears. We have built new defences and established additional fire brigades in the *chin* villages worthy of salvage after the demons burned the fields, and turned others into new Mazes to trap and harry *alagai* in the night, further culling their forces after their defeat at Waning.'

Defeat. A political choice of word. Even Jayan knew better. The only thing that truly defeated the *alagai* on Waning was the sun. They would return, as strong as ever.

Ashan nodded. 'You have done well, Sharum Ka. Your father will be proud on his return.'

Jayan ignored the compliment. 'There is another matter I must bring before the court.' Inevera frowned, though the dice had already told her this was coming.

Jayan clapped his hands, and fourteen muscular young men in black bidos entered the throne room, dropping to one knee in a precise line behind him. All carried shields on their backs and spears in hand. Inevera looked at them, seeing her husband's handsome features on each of their sixteen-year-old faces. One of them was her third son, Hoshkamin, the others second sons of Everalia and Thalaja, and the firstborn of all the *Damaji'ting* save Qeva.

'The Andrah no doubt recognizes my brothers, sons of Shar'Dama Ka,' Jayan said. 'Their elder brothers,' he indicated Icha and Sharu, 'even I, myself, took the black at seventeen. But while young, my brothers have our father's *Sharum* heart. When they learned of his absence, all demanded the right to stand in the night. Their training in both *sharaj* and Sharak Hora has been without flaw, and I saw no reason to refuse. I myself stood as *ajin'pal*, blooding them in the New Maze. Each has personally sent more than one demon back to the abyss. I ask they be made *kai'Sharum*, in accordance with Evejan law.'

Ashan glanced to Inevera. Raising new warriors to the black could only be done with the approval of the *dama'ting* who cast the bones for them, and only Inevera and her *Jiwah Sen* could cast for the Deliverer's sons.

Jayan was wilier than Inevera had given him credit for. The dice told her he had been the one to demand the boys fight, but none had been unwilling. The moment they donned black robes with white veils, each of Ahmann's sons would command great power among their tribe's warriors, and all would owe their allegiance to Jayan. Raising them would increase her son's power greatly at a time when he might still try to usurp the throne.

But neither could she easily refuse. Inevera's power over her sister-wives was great, but even she would be a fool to insult them all in one move. She had cast the bones for all the boys in their birthing blood, and by law, if they had stood in the night and taken *alagai*, they could claim their birthrights.

She nodded her permission, keeping her face serene.

'It is done,' Ashan said, relieved. 'Rise, *kai'Sharum*. Everam looks upon the Deliverer's sons with pride.'

The boys rose smoothly, but did not whoop or cheer, bowing to the throne and standing with tight discipline. Jayan, however, could not keep the smug smile from his face.

'These are difficult times for Krasia, with the Deliverer abroad,' Asome said. 'Perhaps it is time his *dama* sons took the white robes, as well.'

It was like a bucket of camel water thrown on the *Damaji*. They stood shocked a moment, their indignation building, and Inevera savoured it. She was well in favour of raising Ahmann's *dama* sons. The sooner the boys were given the white, the sooner they could take control of the tribes and spare her the endless grumblings of these old men.

'Ridiculous!' Aleverak snapped. 'No boy of fifteen has ever been raised to the white.' If he had been cowed by his defeat the day before, it did not show. Healed by Belina's magic, the *Damaji* looked haler than he had in years. But if he felt any debt to Ahmann's Majah wife, it did not stop him from opposing her son's advancement. Aleverak stood to lose more than the others if Maji was raised to *dama*.

A chorus of agreement rose from the other *Damaji*, and Inevera breathed, holding her centre. Everam grant she soon be free of these vile men, more interested in holding their own power than helping their people.

'Many things will happen for the first time before Sharak Ka is upon us,' Asome said. 'We should not deny our people leaders when the *dama* are already stretched thin keeping peace in the *chin* villages.'

Ashan considered, eyes flicking around the room. As *Damaji*, he had been a strong leader for the Kaji, but he seemed more diplomat than Andrah, eager to please all and secure his position.

Still, Ahmann had ordered him to take the throne to keep his sons alive, and it didn't take a great mind to see that would be easier with them in white.

'Take them,' she breathed. Wards carried the words to his ears alone.

'Age is irrelevant,' Ashan said at last. 'There are tests for the white, and they will be administered. It will be upon the sons of the Deliverer to pass them. Asome will observe the testing personally and report back to me.'

Inevera could see the flush of pleasure in the auras of the *Damaji'ting* at the unexpected pronouncement, a mirror image of the sour cloud around the *Damaji*. Reading auras was subtler even than the dice, but with every passing day she grew more adept.

The next order of business was the matter of the night's new *Sharum'ting*. Since Ahmann's creation of the *Sharum'ting* – to give rights to a *chin* woman, no less – there had been a growing movement among women to kill *alagai*, thus gaining the rights of men to own property, bear witness, and have liberty to refuse a man's touch. Women came to the Dama'ting Palace every day, many in secret, begging to be trained. Inevera had given them to Ashia, and not regretted the decision.

Chin women, unused to the yoke of Evejan law, came in numbers, often with the encouragement of their husbands. Krasian women came at a trickle. Three thousand years of subservience had been beaten into them, and while the movement was growing, it was still overpowered by the fierce and near-unanimous opposition of Krasian men, husbands, fathers, brothers – even sons still in tan. Many women were prohibited from leaving their homes without escort, and brutally beaten when they tried to slip away to the palace.

Even those raised to the black were not safe. With the aid of warded weapons, all had taken *alagai*, but the best of them had weeks of training compared to the lifetime of most *Sharum*. More than one of the women had been found beaten, raped, or killed.

But there was always blood for the *alagai hora*, and when Inevera found the assailants, Ashia and her spear sisters soon paid a visit. The crime was returned tenfold, and their remains left where others would find them and remember the lesson.

As if summoned by the thought, Ashia entered the throne room, escorting two groups of women to the dais. The larger group, twenty women trained in the Dama'ting Palace, knelt in tight lines as they awaited judgement. Some wore *dal'ting* black, others the more varied dress of *chin*.

Ashia kept a hard eye on the women, but Inevera could see the pride in her aura. Her growing knowledge of *alagai* lines of power and points of convergence had allowed her to design *sharukin* more dependent on leverage and accuracy than strength of arm. She called the fighting style Everam's Precise Strike, and taught the women well.

The other group was more curious. Seven common *dal'ting*, huddled together on their knees, fear and determination in their collective aura. Several women had bloodied bandages showing under their blacks, signs of *alagai* wounds. One had her entire arm and part of her face wrapped in white cloth that was already stained brown. Firespit. She could see the deep burns in the woman's aura. Without magic, she would never recover fully.

Another woman had blackened eyes and what looked like a broken nose under her veil. Inevera didn't need to probe further to know those injuries had not come from a demon.

'Daughter.' Ashan acknowledged Ashia with a nod. He remained displeased with her new station, but was wise enough not to publicly undermine her. 'Who have you brought before the Skull Throne?'

'Candidates for the spear, honoured Andrah,' Ashia said. She gestured to the women she had trained. 'These women were all trained in the Dama'ting Palace, and have taken demons in *alagai'sharak*. I ask that they be made *Sharum'ting*.'

Ashan nodded. He wasn't pleased at the idea of presiding over women taking the spear, but had seen Ahmann do it often enough that he did not resist. He looked to Damaji'ting Qeva. 'Have the bones been cast?'

Qeva nodded. 'They are worthy.'

Ashan whisked a hand at the women. 'Rise, *Sharum'ting.*'

The women rose and bowed deeply before Ashia dismissed them.

Ashan regarded the group of fearful *dal'ting* huddling before the dais. 'And the others?'

'Untrained *dal'ting* from a Khanjin village,' Ashia said. Damaji Ichach stiffened. 'Their honour is boundless. They took it upon themselves to come to the Deliverer's call, going out into the night and killing a demon. They ask for the rights the Deliverer promised them.'

'That's one way of putting it,' Jayan said.

Ashia nodded to him. 'My cousin does not agree.'

Ashan's aura darkened. 'You will address the Sharum Ka with the respect he is due, daughter.' His voice was a deep boom, far from the quiet tones he had used a moment ago. 'You may serve the Damajah, but Jayan is still your superior.'

Ashan turned to Jayan. 'I apologize for my daughter's rudeness, Sharum Ka. I assure you she will be disciplined.'

Jayan nodded, waving a hand. 'Unnecessary, Uncle. A warrior my cousin may be, but she is a woman, and cannot be expected to control her emotions.'

'Indeed,' Ashan agreed. 'What does the Sharum Ka have to say on this matter?'

'These women are outlaws,' Jayan said. 'They have brought shame to their families with their reckless actions, endangering their fellow villagers and causing the death of an innocent woman.'

'Serious accusations,' Ashan said.

Jayan nodded. 'With deliberate planning and forethought, they violated the curfew of the local *dama* and disobeyed the commands of their *Sharum* husbands, sneaking out of their homes at night and crossing the village wards. They lured a lone flame demon into a crude trap and surrounded it. Using improvised weapons and shields, poorly painted with stolen wards copied from their honoured husbands' equipment, they attacked. Without training, one woman was killed, and several others injured. The fires started in their battle threatened to burn the entire village down.'

'That isn't . . .!' one of the women blurted, but the others grabbed her, covering her mouth. Women were not to speak in the Andrah's presence save when spoken to, and under Evejan law, they could not bear legal witness in any event. Their husbands would speak for them.

Jayan's eyes flicked to the commotion, but he said nothing. They were only women, after all.

Ashia bowed deeply, an artfully executed show of deference, just enough to mock without giving true offence. 'The words of the honoured Sharum Ka of Krasia, firstborn son of the Deliverer, my cousin the esteemed Jayan asu Ahmann am'Jardir am'Kaji, may he live forever, are true, Father, if exaggerated in detail.'

Jayan crossed his arms, the hint of a smirk at the corner of his mouth.

'They are also irrelevant,' Ashia said.

'Eh?' Ashan said.

'I, too, violated curfew and disobeyed my husband to go into the night,' Ashia said. 'The curfews are designed to make it illegal for any woman to go into the night.' She met her father's eyes. 'You debated these very points with the Deliverer on the day he named me *Sharum*, and they did not deter him then. They should not deter you now. By the Shar'Dama Ka's own words, any woman who kills a demon is to be made *Sharum'ting*.'

Ashan frowned, but Jayan was not finished.

'Indeed,' he said. 'But I count seven women, and only one demon killed. Who is to say who struck the killing blow? Or if all of them struck at all?'

'Also irrelevant,' Ashia said, drawing a glare from Jayan. 'All warriors share kills, especially when blooding *nie'Sharum*. By your measure, there is not a warrior in Krasia who does not claim more than are his due. The Deliverer himself was one of more than a dozen spears in the push guard on his first night in the Maze.'

'The Deliverer was twelve years old that night, daughter,' Ashan said, 'and was sent to Sharik Hora for five more years before he was given his blacks.'

Ashia shrugged. 'Nevertheless, if you discount shared kills, you will need to strip the blacks from every warrior raised before the Deliverer returned fighting wards to us, and half the rest. The purpose of the blooding is not to kill a demon unassisted. It is to test a warrior's courage in standing fast against the *alagai*. These women have done so. In truth, their test was the greater for the lack of proper training and equipment. Are these not the very hearts we need with Sharak Ka nigh?'

'Perhaps,' Ashan agreed.

'And perhaps not,' Damaji Ichach cut in. 'Andrah, surely you cannot mean to raise these women? They are Khanjin. Let me see to the matter personally.'

'I do not see that I have a choice, Damaji,' Ashan said. 'I am of no tribe at all, and must follow the Deliverer's commands.'

'You are Andrah,' Aleverak snapped. 'Of course you have a choice. Your daughter twists the Deliverer's words to trap you, but she does not speak the whole truth. "Any woman who takes a demon in *alagai'sharak* shall be *Sharum'ting*," the Deliverer said. I do not believe this qualifies. *Sharum* blooding does not come without the approval of a drillmaster. *Alagai'sharak* is a sacred ritual, not some fools stealing out into the night on a whim.'

The other *Damaji* grunted along, and Inevera felt her jaw tighten. Again the rasping chorus as the old men quoted scripture, related irrelevant anecdotes, and warned sagely against being too free with the rights of *Sharum*. She stroked the *hora* wand at her belt, imagining for a moment what it would feel like to blast the lot of them into the abyss.

'Did any men witness the event?' Ashan asked when the

hubbub had faded. He still had not consulted the women themselves, and likely would not.

Jayan bowed again. 'Andrah, the women's husbands are waiting outside, and beg to speak before you make your decision.'

Ashan nodded, and the men were brought in. All wore blacks, though by their look and equipment none was a warrior of note. Their auras were coloured with rage, shame, and awe at the grandeur of the throne. One of the men was particularly distraught, barely contained violence radiating from him like a stink.

The widower. Inevera shifted slightly on her bed of pillows. *Watch that one*, her fingers said.

I see him, Damajah. Ashia's hand hung loose at her side, her reply a whisper of nimble fingers.

'These women killed my wife, Holy Andrah,' the distraught warrior said, pointing. 'My Chabbavah would not have disobeyed me and acted so foolishly without their foul influence. I demand their lives in recompense.'

'Lies!' another of the men shouted. He pointed to his own wife, the *dal'ting* who had been beaten. 'My wife fled to me after the disaster, and made clear Chabbavah had been one of the ringleaders pressuring the others. I regret my spear brother's loss, but he has no right to claim vengeance for his own failings as a husband.'

The widower turned and struck at him, and for a moment the two warriors traded blows. Ahmann had tolerated no violence in his court, but none of the men, even Ashan, seemed inclined to stop them until the second man had put the widower onto the floor in a painful hold.

Ashan clapped his hands loudly. 'The argument stands. Everam would not give victory to a liar.'

Inevera breathed. Not a liar. Only a warrior who had beaten his wife.

The second man bowed. 'I ask the holy Andrah to remand these women to us, their rightful husbands, for punishment.

I swear by Everam they will not bring shame to their families, our tribe, or your throne again.'

Ashan sat back on the throne, steepling his fingers and staring at the women. Ashia had made a compelling case, but Inevera could see in his eyes that the new Andrah would still refuse them. Given the opportunity, Ashan would take the spears from every *Sharum'ting*, Ashia included.

She should have brought the women to me first, Inevera thought. But perhaps this, too, was Everam's will.

Living in the Northland where women had as many rights as men had shown Krasian women that there was an alternative to living their lives under a husband's sandal. The greenlanders had not been able to stand against the Krasian spears, but they had struck at the very heart of their enemy in the Daylight War. More and more women would seek their due, and sooner or later the clerics must be confronted on the matter.

Inevera did not want to overrule Ashan publicly on his first day on the Skull Throne, but if he would not see reason, so be it.

She opened her mouth to speak, but was checked as Asome loudly cleared his throat and spoke with a voice that carried through the room. 'My honoured wife is correct.'

Ashan's face went slack with surprise, and even Inevera was struck dumb as Asome stepped down from the dais to take the floor. The boy had argued vehemently against the formation of *Sharum'ting* and his wife and cousin's raising.

'It is true my honoured father said that the demons must be taken in *alagai'sharak*,' Asome said, 'but what is *alagai'sharak*, truly? It literally means "demon war", and war is no ritual. The *alagai* have made all humanity, male and female, their enemy. Any battle against them is *alagai'sharak*.'

Jayan snorted. 'Leave it to my *dama* brother to fail to understand war.'

It was the wrong thing to say in a court dominated by clerics, further proof of Jayan's tendency to speak without thought. Ashan and the *Damaji* all turned angry glares upon him.

At last, Ashan found his spine, using the same deep boom he had used on his daughter a moment before. 'You forget your place, Sharum Ka. You serve at the will of the white.'

Jayan blanched, and anger blossomed in his aura. His hand tightened on his spear, and if he had been a single grain more the fool he might have used it, even if it plunged all Krasia into civil war.

Asome was wise enough to keep his expression neutral, but it did not save him from the dark gaze Ashan turned his way. 'And you, *nie'Andrah*. Did you not argue long and hard against women taking the spear before this very throne not long ago?'

Asome bowed. 'Indeed I did, Uncle. I spoke with passion and belief. But I was wrong, and my honoured father was right to ignore my pleas.'

He turned, sweeping his eyes over the room. 'Sharak Ka is coming!' he boomed. 'Both the Deliverer and the Damajah have said it is so. Yet still we stand divided, coming up with petty excuses why some should be allowed to fight while others stand by and do nothing. But I say when the Deliverer returns with all the armies of Nie biting at his heels, there will be glory and honour enough for all in the great battle. We must be ready, one and all, to fight.'

He pointed to Ashia. 'It is true I argued against my wife taking the spear. But she has brought us nothing save honour and glory. Hundreds owe their lives to her and her spear sisters. They carry the Damajah's honour on the field, trusted with her protection. They elevate us all. Women give us strength. The Deliverer was clear on this. *All* who have the will for Sharak Ka must be allowed to stand.'

He paused, and Asukaji stepped into the gap as smoothly as if it had been rehearsed. The two were ever the first to support each other.

Ashan shook his head. 'Everam, not you, too.'

Asukaji pointed to the *Sharum* husbands. 'What have these men to hide, that they fear the witness their wives might bear against them if raised? Perhaps the threat of it will make some husbands wiser. These women have fought *alagai*. Should our walls fail, they will be the last defence of our children. With so much resting upon them, why should they not have rights?'

'Why not indeed?' Inevera asked, before any of the older men had time to formulate a retort. She smiled. 'You men argue as if the choice were yours, but the Deliverer gave the *Sharum'ting* to *me*, and *I* will decide who shall be raised and who shall not.'

Ashan's scowl was belied by the relief in his aura, spared responsibility for a decree that would make him enemies regardless of how he ruled.

'Umshala.' She beckoned her sister-wife, *Damaji'ting* of the Khanjin. 'Foretell them.'

Eyes widened. Foretellings were private things. The *dama'ting* were secretive with their magic, and with good reason. But the men needed reminders that there was more than politics at work here. It was Everam's will that should guide them, not their own petty needs.

The women knelt in a crescent about Umshala's casting cloth. All of them wore reddened bandages, and the *Damaji'ting* touched her dice to the wounds, wetting them with blood for the prophecy.

Inevera dimmed the wardlight in the chamber. Not to aid the casting, for wardlight did not affect the dice. Rather, she did it so all would see the unmistakable glow of the *hora*, pulsing redly with Umshala's prayers. Hypnotized, men twitched at the flash of light each time she threw.

At last, Umshala sat back on her heels. She turned, ignoring Ashan to address Inevera. 'It is done, Damajah.'

'And what have you seen?' Inevera asked. 'Did these women stand fast in the night? Are they worthy?'

'They are, Damajah.' Umshala turned, pointing to the woman who had been beaten. 'Save for this one. Illijah vah Fahstu faltered in her strike and fled the demon, causing the death of Chabbavah and the injury of several others. The kill is not hers.'

Illijah's aura went white with terror, but the other women stood by her, reaching out in support – even the woman who had been badly burned. Inevera gave them a moment for pity's sake, but there was nothing she could do. The dice cut both ways.

'Six are raised,' she said. 'Rise, *Sharum'ting*. Illijah vah Fahstu is returned to her husband.' It was a cruelty, but better than if Inevera had left her fate to Damaji Ichach, who would likely have had her publicly executed for bearing false witness before the throne.

Illijah screamed as Fahstu walked up behind her, grabbing the top of her hair in one thick fist, dragging her backward off her knees. She stumbled, unable to rise fully, as Fahstu dragged her from the room, her wails echoing off the walls as the *Damaji* watched with cold satisfaction.

Bring me the hand he uses to drag her before the sun sets, her fingers told Ashia.

Ashia's fingers replied in their customary hidden whisper. *I hear and obey, Damajah.*

'Wait!' one of the women cried, drawing everyone's attention. 'As *Sharum'ting*, I wish to testify on Illijah's behalf to bring witness against the crimes of Fahstu asu Fahstu am'Ichan am'Khanjin.'

Inevera waved, and the guards lowered their spears, preventing Fahstu from leaving the throne room. Illijah was released, and both were escorted back to the throne.

Damaji Ichach threw up his hands. 'Is this what the Andrah's court has become? A place for ungrateful women to complain about their husbands like gossiping washerwomen?'

Several of the *Damaji* nodded with agreement, but Damaji Qezan of the Jama, Ichach's greatest rival, smiled widely.

'Surely not,' Qezan said, 'but your tribe has brought such drama to the court, we of course must see it through.' Ichach glared at him, but other *Damaji*, even some of those who had supported him a moment ago, nodded. They might not be washerwomen, but the *Damaji* loved gossip as much as any.

'Speak,' Ashan commanded.

'I am Uvona vah Hadda am'Ichan am'Khanjin,' the woman said, using a man's full name for the first time in her life. 'Illijah is my cousin. It is true she ran from the *alagai*, and is not worthy to stand in the night. But her husband, Fahstu asu Fahstu am'Ichan am'Khanjin, has been forcing her to prostitute herself for years to earn money for his couzi and dice. Illijah is an honourable daughter of Everam and refused his initial demands, so Fahstu beat her so badly she was forced to keep to her bed for days. I witnessed her shame personally.'

'Lies!' Fahstu cried, though Inevera could see the truth in his aura. 'Do not listen to this vile woman's falsehoods! What proof does she have? Nothing! It is the word of a woman against mine.'

The woman whose arm and face were wrapped to cover her firespit burns moved to stand beside Uvona. Pain lanced across her aura, but she stood straight, and her voice was firm. 'Two women.'

The other four moved in, the women standing together as one.

'Six women bear witness to your crime, Fahstu,' Uvona said. 'Six *Sharum'ting*. We went into the night not to claim rights for ourselves, but for the sake of Illijah, that she might be free of you.'

Fahstu turned to Ashan. 'Andrah, surely you will not take the word of women over a loyal *Sharum*?'

Umshala looked up as well. 'I can consult the dice if you wish, Holy Andrah.'

Ashan scowled, knowing as well as any what answer the dice would bring. 'Do you wish to confess, son of Fahstu, or shall we clear your name with *hora*?'

Fahstu blanched, then glanced around, seeking support where there was none. At last he shrugged. 'What difference does it make what I do with my own wife? She is my property, and no *Sharum'ting*. I have committed no crime.'

Ashan looked to Ichach. 'He is your tribesman, Damaji. What say you to this?'

'I rule in favour of the husband,' Ichach said without hesitation. 'It is a wife's duty to work and support her husband. If he cannot pay his debts, the failing is hers and she should pay the price, even if he decide it be on her back.'

'Or her knees,' Damaji Qezan said, and the other men laughed.

'The *Damaji* of the Khanjin has spoken,' Inevera said, drawing looks of surprise. 'For prostituting his wife, Fahstu shall not be punished.' A wide smile broke out on Fahstu's face at the words, even as the eyes of the new *Sharum'ting* fell. Illijah began to weep once more, and Uvona put an arm around her.

'However, for the crime of lying to the Skull Throne,' Inevera went on, 'he is found guilty. The sentence is death.' ,

Fahstu's eyes widened. 'What?'

'Umshala,' Inevera said.

The *Damaji'ting* reached into her *hora* pouch, pulling out a small black lump – a piece of breastbone from a lightning demon. The *Damaji'ting* knew to avert their eyes, but the rest of the room looked on and was blinded by the flash of light, deafened by the thunder.

When their eyes cleared, Fahstu son of Fahstu lay halfway to the great doors, his chest a charred, smoking ruin. The smell of cooked meat permeated the room.

'You push fast and too hard, Damajah,' Qeva said. 'The *Damaji* will revolt.'

'Let them, if they are such fools,' Belina said. 'Ahmann will not weep if he returns to find the entire council reduced to a scorch on his throne room floor and his sons in control of the tribes.'

'And if he does not return?' Melan asked.

'All the more reason to cow the *Damaji* and recruit as many *Sharum'ting* as possible now,' Inevera said. 'Even Abban the *khaffit* has more soldiers than I.'

'*Kha'Sharum*,' Qeva said derisively. 'Not true warriors.'

'Tell that to Hasik,' Inevera said. 'The Deliverer's own bodyguard, brought down and gelded by the *khaffit*. They say the same about the *Sharum'ting*, but I would take any of Enkido's spear daughters over a dozen Spears of the Deliverer.'

They reached Inevera's private gardens, a botanical maze filled with carefully manicured plants, many cultivated from seeds brought all the way from Krasia. There were medicinal herbs and deadly poisons, fresh fruit, nuts and vegetables, as well as grasses, shrubs, flowers, and trees cultivated for purely aesthetic value.

It was easy for Inevera to find her centre in the gardens, standing in the sun amidst so much flourishing vegetation. Even in the Palace of the Deliverer in Krasia, such a garden would have been impossible to maintain. The land was too harsh. In Everam's Bounty, it seemed one had but to throw seeds in any direction and they would thrive unaided.

Inevera breathed deeply, only to be thrown from her centre as she caught a hint of the perfume that always signalled an end to tranquillity.

'Flee while you can, little sisters,' she said quietly. 'The Holy Mother waits within the bowers.'

The words were enough to send her sister-wives hurrying from the garden as fast as their dignity would allow. As his *Jiwah Ka*, Ahmann's mother was Inevera's responsibility, a position the women were all too happy to yield.

Inevera envied them. She, too, would have fled had she been able. *Everam must be displeased, not to have warned me in the dice.*

Only Qeva, Melan, and Asavi dared to remain. Ashia had vanished into the leaves, though Inevera knew she was watching, never more than a breath away.

Inevera breathed, bending to the wind. 'Best get it over with,' she muttered, and strode ahead to where the Holy Mother waited.

Inevera heard Kajivah before she saw her.

'By Everam, keep your back straight, Thalaja,' the Holy Mother snapped. 'You're a bride of the Deliverer, not some *dal'ting* merchant in the bazaar.'

The scene came into sight as Kajivah reached and snatched a pastry from her other daughter-in-law. 'You're putting on weight again, Everalia.'

She looked to one of the servants. 'Where is that nectar I asked for? And see they chill it this time.' She rounded on another servant, holding a ridiculous fan. 'I didn't tell you to stop fanning, girl.' She fanned herself, hand buzzing like a hummingbird. 'You know how I get. Everam my witness, the entire green land is as humid as the baths. How do they stand it? Why, I have half a mind—'

The woman mercifully broke off as Inevera entered the bower. The other women looked as if they were about to be rescued from a coreling. Kajivah might treat every other woman like a servant, but she was wise enough to respect the *dama'ting*, and Inevera most of all.

Usually.

'Where is my son?!' Kajivah demanded, storming over to Inevera. She wore the black robes and white veil of *kai'ting*, but had added a white shawl as well, similar to Ahmann's mode of dress. 'The palace buzzes with gossip, my son-in-law sits the Skull Throne, and I am left the fool.'

Truer witness was never given, Inevera thought.

Kajivah grew increasingly shrill. 'I demand to know what's happened!'

Demand. Inevera felt a coil of anger in her centre. Had the woman forgotten who she was talking to? Even Ahmann made no demands of her. She imagined herself blasting Kajivah across the gardens like Fahstu at court.

Oh, if it could be so easily done. But while Ahmann would be forgiving if she vaporized the entire council of *Damaji*, he would hunt his mother's killer to the ends of Ala, and with his crownsight, there would be no hiding the crime.

'Ahmann is hunting a demon on the edge of the abyss,' Inevera said. 'The dice favour his return, but it is a dangerous path. We must pray for him.'

'My son has gone to the abyss?!' Kajivah shrieked. 'Alone?! Why are not the Spears of the Deliverer with him?'

Inevera reached out, grabbing Kajivah's chin. Ostensibly it was to force her to make and hold eye contact, but Inevera put pressure on a convergence spot, breaking some of the woman's energy.

'Your son is the Deliverer,' she said coldly. 'He walks in places none may follow, and owes no explanations to you, or even me.'

She released Kajivah, and the woman fell back, weakened. Thalaja caught her and tried to usher her to one of the stone benches, but Kajivah straightened, pulling from her grasp and meeting Inevera's eyes again.

Stubborn, Inevera thought.

'Why was Jayan passed over?' Kajivah demanded. 'He is Ahmann's eldest heir, and a worthy successor. The people worship him.'

'Jayan is too young and headstrong to lead in Ahmann's stead,' Inevera said.

'He is your son!' Kajivah shouted. 'How can you . . .'

'ENOUGH!' Inevera barked, causing everyone to jump, most of all Kajivah. It was rare for Inevera to raise her voice, especially in front of others. But more than anyone else alive, Inevera's mother-in-law could test her patience. 'You have forgotten yourself, woman, if you think you can speak to me so of my own children. I forgive you this once, for I know you are worried for your son, but do not cross me. All of Krasia needs me, and I do not have time to soothe your every anxiety. Ashan sits the Skull Throne by Ahmann's own command. That is all you need know of the matter.'

Kajivah blinked. How many years had it been since someone

dared speak to her like that? She was the Holy Mother, not some common *dal'ting*.

But for all the liberties she took and influence she had, Kajivah had no true powers. She was not even *dama'ting*, much less Damajah. Her wealth and servants were a stipend from the throne Inevera could easily rescind in Ahmann's absence, though there would be others quick to try to gain her favour with gifts of gold.

'Mother.' Inevera and the other women turned to see Asome enter the bower. He had been silent as Enkido in his approach. Asome bowed. 'Grandmother. It is good to see you both.'

Kajivah brightened immediately, opening her arms for her grandson. He moved into her embrace and accepted the kisses she gave through her veil with grace and dignity, though the treatment was below his station.

'Tikka,' Asome said, using the informal Krasian word for 'grandmother' Kajivah had instilled in all her grandchildren even before they began to speak. Just the sound of it from Asome's lips made the woman melt into agreeability as if drugged. 'Please be gentle with my honoured mother. I know you fear for Father, but she is his *Jiwah Ka*, and no doubt her worry is as great as yours.'

Kajivah nodded as if dazed and looked to Inevera, her eyes respectfully down as she nodded. 'Apologies, Damajah.'

Inevera wanted to kiss her son.

'But why were you and your brother passed over?' Kajivah asked, regaining something of her resolve.

'Passed over?' Asome asked. 'Tikka, Jayan sits the Spear Throne, and I am next in line for the Skull. Asukaji has been made *Damaji* of the Kaji. Your firstborn grandsons are all *kai'Sharum* now, and soon the second sons will take their places as *nie'Damaji*. Thanks to you, the line of Jardir, so close to ending twenty years ago, is set to control all of Krasia for generations.'

Kajivah seemed mollified at that, but pressed still. 'But your uncle . . .'

Asome cupped her chin in his hand much as Inevera had, but instead of touching a pressure point, he laid his thumb on her veil. He touched her lips as gently as a feather, but it silenced Kajivah as effectively as Inevera's more forceful move.

'The Evejah teaches us all *dama'ting* possess the Sight,' Asome said, 'the Damajah most of all. If she has allowed my honoured uncle to sit the throne, it is likely because she sees Father returning soon, though of course she cannot speak of such things directly.'

Kajivah glanced at Inevera, a touch of fear in her eyes. The Sight was revered in Krasia, the source of *dama'ting* power. Inevera played along, giving Kajivah a measured stare and the slightest hint of a nod.

Kajivah looked back at Asome. 'It is bad fortune to speak of fortune.'

Asome bowed with convincing deference as Kajivah mangled the ancient proverb. 'Wisely said, Tikka.' He looked at Inevera. 'Perhaps there is something my honoured grandmother could do to praise Everam and help pray for Father's safe return?'

Inevera started, Asome's words reminding her of the advice her own mother Manvah had given her with regard to the Holy Mother. She nodded. 'Waning will be upon us in less than two weeks, and with the Deliverer abroad, morale will be low even as the forces of Nie gather once more. A great feast to give heart to our warriors and join the voices of many as one in beseeching Everam for Ahmann's victory in his latest trial . . .'

'A wonderful idea, Damajah,' Melan said, stepping forward. Inevera looked at her old rival, thankful for the support.

'Indeed,' Asome said. 'Perhaps the Holy Mother could even give the blessings over the food and drink?'

'I was going to see to it personally . . .' Inevera lied.

As Manvah had predicted, Kajivah leapt at the bait. 'Think on it no more, Honoured Damajah. Many are the burdens upon you. Let me lift this one, I beg.'

Indeed, Inevera felt a great burden lifting. 'One feast may not be enough, I fear. We may have need of another at Waxing, and on until Sharak Ka is won.'

Kajivah bowed, deeper than Inevera had seen in years. 'It would be my great honour to see to it, Damajah.'

'I will ask the Andrah to assign a generous stipend from the treasury for the feasts,' Inevera said, knowing Ashan would be as pleased as her to have the woman out of their hair. He would agree to anything and call it a bargain. 'You will need help, of course. Florists and chefs, scribes to prepare invitations . . .' *People who can read and do sums,* she thought derisively, for of course Kajivah could do neither, even after twenty years of palace life.

'I would be honoured to assist the Holy Mother,' Melan said.

'I, too, will assist, as my responsibilities will allow,' Asome said, looking pointedly at Inevera. She had no doubt it was a debt he would one day collect upon, but she would pay it gladly. This was a favour beyond price.

'It is settled, then,' she said, giving Kajivah a nod. 'All of Krasia will owe you a debt for this, Holy Mother.'

6

A Man Is Nothing
333 AR Autumn

Abban leaned heavily on his crutch as he descended the palace steps, gritting his teeth at each stab of pain in his twisted calf. Knives were being sharpened throughout the court of the Deliverer, but sometimes it felt the palace steps were his greatest challenge each day. He could bear most anything for a profit, but embracing pain for its own sake had never been a skill he'd mastered.

Not for the first time, he regretted his stubborn refusal to let the Damajah heal him. It was wise to remind her she could not bribe him with comforts – especially ones she could as easily take away – but the thought of stairs without pain was an image worth killing for. Still, there was something he had wanted far more, and soon he would have it.

Drillmaster Qeran walked beside him, faring far better on the steps. The drillmaster's left leg was missing at the knee, replaced with a curved sheet of spring steel. The metal bowed slightly with each step, but easily supported the large man's weight. Already, Qeran was close to the fighting skill he had once claimed before the injury, and he continued to improve.

Abban's *kha'Sharum* were not allowed at court, but the drillmaster had trained the Deliverer himself, and his honour was boundless. Even in Abban's employ, he was welcome most anywhere, including the palace. A useful thing for a bodyguard. Now none was fool enough to harass Abban as he passed.

Earless was waiting for them at the foot of the stairs, holding open the door to Abban's carriage. Two *kha'Sharum* sat the driver's seat, spears in easy reach, and two more at a high bench at the carriage rear, these armed with Northern crank bows. Qeran sprang easily into the carriage, taking Abban's crutches as the deaf giant lifted Abban into the carriage as easily as a man might pick up his child, sparing him the dreaded steps.

Too big to comfortably fit inside, Earless closed the door and climbed the first step, holding a handle to ride outside. He knocked on the carriage wall, and the drivers cracked the reins.

'Have the *Damaji* accepted Ashan as Andrah?' Qeran asked.

Abban shrugged. 'It is not as if the Damajah gives them a choice, with her displays of power. Ashan is her puppet, and none fool enough to challenge her.'

Qeran nodded. He knew the Damajah well. 'The *Sharum* do not like it. They believe the Sharum Ka should have taken his father's place. They fear a *dama* on the throne will take focus away from *alagai'sharak*.'

'What a tragedy that would be,' Abban said.

Qeran looked at him coldly, not amused. 'If Jayan calls, the spears will flock to him. It would be easy for him to put Ashan's and the *Damaji*'s heads up on spears and take the throne.'

Abban nodded. 'And easier still for the Damajah to reduce him to ash. We waste our time, Drillmaster, pondering shifts above our station. We have our duty.'

They arrived at Abban's compound, a high, thick wall heavily manned with armed *kha'Sharum*. The gates opened before them as the drivers gave the proper signal, revealing the squat, blocky buildings within.

The compound was strong and secure, but Abban was careful – on the surface at least – to give it no quality others might covet. There was no aesthetic to the architecture, no gardens or fountains. The air was thick with the smoke of forges and the sound of ringing hammers. Men laboured everywhere, not an idle hand to be seen.

Abban breathed deep of the reeking air and smiled. It was the smell of industry. Of power. Sweeter to him than any flower's perfume.

A boy scurried up as Earless deposited Abban back on the ground. He bowed deeply. 'Master Akas bids me inform you the samples are ready.'

Abban nodded, flipping the boy a small coin. It was a pittance, but the boy's eyes lit up at the sight. 'For swift feet. Inform Master Akas we will join him shortly.'

Akas managed Abban's forges, one of the most important jobs in the entire compound. He was Abban's cousin by marriage, and was paid more than most *dama*. One of Abban's best *kha'Sharum* Watchers lurked in his shadow, ostensibly for his protection, but as much to deter or report anything hinting of treachery.

'Ah, Master, Drillmaster, welcome!' Akas was in his fifties, his bare arms thick with muscle in the way of those who worked the forge. Despite his age and size, he moved with the nervous excitement of a younger man. A *khaffit* like Abban, he was without a beard, though a rough stubble clung to his chin. He stank of sweat and sulphur.

'How is production?' Abban asked.

'The weapons and armour for the Spears of the Deliverer are on schedule,' Akas said, gesturing to pallets piled with spearheads, shields, and armour plates. 'Warded glass, indestructible so far as we can determine.'

Abban nodded. 'And for my Hundred?' He used the term for the hundred *kha'Sharum* Ahmann had given him, but in truth they were one hundred and twenty, with close to a thousand *chi'Sharum* to supplement them. Abban wanted all of them armed and with the best equipment money could buy.

Akas scratched at his stubble. 'There have been . . . delays.'

Qeran crossed his arms with a glower, not even needing a cue from Abban. Akas was a big man, but not fool enough to mistake the gesture. He put up his palms placatingly. 'But progress has been made! Come and see!'

He darted over to a group of pallets, these shields and spearheads shining like mirrors. He selected a spearhead and brought it over to a squat, heavy anvil.

'Warded glass,' Akas said, holding up the spearhead, 'silvered as you requested to hide its true nature from the casual observer.'

Abban nodded impatiently. This was not news. 'Then why the delay?'

'The silvering process weakens the glass,' Akas said. 'Watch.'

He put the spearhead on the anvil, holding it in place with banded clamps. Then he took up a long, heavy sledge, the handle three feet long and the head thirty pounds at least. The master smith swung the hammer with practised smoothness, letting its weight and momentum do more work than his considerable muscles. It came down with a sound that resonated through the forges, but Akas did not stop, putting all his strength behind two more swings.

'A waste to make that man *khaffit*,' Qeran said. 'I could have made a great warrior of him.'

Abban nodded. 'And had no weapons or armour for him to wield. The sagas may tell tales of cripples working the forge, but it is a strong man's labour, and not without honour.'

After the third blow, Akas unclamped the spearhead and brought it over for inspection. Abban and Qeran held it to the light, turning it this way and that.

'There,' Qeran said, pointing.

'I see it,' Abban said, staring at the tiny flaw in the glass, near the point of impact.

'Ten more blows like that, and a crack will form,' Akas said. 'A dozen, and it will break.'

'Still stronger by far than common steel,' Qeran said. 'Any warrior would be lucky to have such a weapon.'

'Perhaps,' Abban said, 'but my Hundred are not just any warriors. They have the greatest living drillmaster, the richest patron, and should have equipment to match.'

Qeran grunted. 'I'll not argue, though mirrored shields bring some advantage over clear glass. We used mirrors to herd *alagai* in the Maze. They are easily fooled by their own reflections.'

'That's something, at least,' Abban said, looking back to Akas. 'But you spoke of progress?'

Akas broke into a wide, conspiratorial smile. 'I took the liberty of making a set with the new alloy.'

The alloy was electrum, a rare natural mix of silver and gold that was in short supply and valuable beyond imagining. The Deliverer had already confiscated all the known metal for the Damajah's exclusive use. Abban had secured his own source, and had agents seeking more, but the consequences would be dire if the Damajah caught him hoarding the sacred metal.

'And?' Abban asked.

Akas produced a spearhead and shield from beneath a cloth. Both shone bright as polished mirrors. 'As strong as the warded glass, at least. We cannot melt or break either one. But the new alloy lends . . . other properties.'

Abban kept the twitching smile from his lips. 'Do go on.'

'When we charged the equipment, the warriors made some startling discoveries,' Akas said. 'The shield did more than block *alagai* blows. It absorbed them. The warrior took a full lash of a rock demon's tail without shifting his feet an inch.' Qeran looked up sharply at that.

'Once charged, the *alagai* could not even approach the shield for the length of a spear. The warrior had to turn the shield aside just to strike.'

'That is as much a weakness as strength,' Qeran said, 'if one must give up protection to strike a blow.'

'Perhaps,' Akas said, 'but what a blow! The speartip split the rock demon's scales as easily as plunging into water. Observe.'

He took the spearhead back to the anvil, using a different clamp to secure it vertically, point down. Again he lifted the sledge and struck hard. There was a great clang, and Abban and Qeran both gaped to see the speartip embedded over an inch into the iron. Again Akas struck, and again, each blow hammering the spearhead in like a nail into wood. On the fourth blow, the anvil split in half.

Qeran moved to the anvil, touching the cracked metal reverently. 'The Andrah must hear of this. Every warrior must have one. Sharak Ka will be ours!'

'The Andrah already knows,' Abban lied, 'as do the Deliverer and Damajah. On your life and hope of Heaven, Qeran, you will speak of it to no other. Just the thin sliver used in the glass is worth more than a *Damaji*'s palace, and there is not enough to equip even a fraction of our forces.'

Abban's lips curled in a smile as Qeran's own fell away. 'But that doesn't mean my drillmaster and his most trusted lieutenants should not have these.'

The drillmaster's mouth opened, but no sound came out.

'Come, Drillmaster,' Abban said. 'If you stand there gaping, we shall be late for our appointment.'

Drillmaster Qeran kept pace with Abban as they strode through the new bazaar, a huge district of Everam's Bounty determined to recapture – and exceed – the vast glory of the Great Bazaar of Krasia.

Already, there had been great strides. The Northerners had not taken well to Evejan law, but they understood commerce, and there were as many *chin* as there were *dal'ting* and *khaffit* working and shopping in the hundreds of kiosks and stalls lining the streets. To Abban, it felt almost like home, save without the ever-present heat and dust.

Evejan law meant little in the bazaar. For every merchant loudly hawking wares, another was quietly whispering of items and services forbidden by the Evejah, or otherwise prohibited by the *dama*. Gambling. The flesh of pigs. Couzi. Weapons. Books. Relics from before the Return. All could be found in the bazaar if one had money to pay and knew whom and how to ask.

For the most part, this was permitted. Indeed, some of the biggest consumers of illegal goods were the *dama* and *Sharum* themselves, and no one would dare arrest *them*. Women and *khaffit* were less fortunate, and were occasionally condemned and made public examples of by the *dama*.

Standing well over six feet tall, armed with spear and shield and Everam only knew how many hidden weapons, Qeran still looked uncomfortable. His eyes flicked everywhere, as if expecting ambush at any moment.

'You seem nervous, Drillmaster,' Abban said. 'How is it a man who stands fast before the *alagai* in darkness should fear to walk a street in the brightness of day?'

Qeran spat on the ground. 'This place is as much a Maze as any used to trap *alagai*.'

Abban chuckled. 'That is so, Drillmaster. The bazaar is made to trap purses instead of demons, but the idea is much the same. Customers are drawn in easily, but find egress more difficult. Streets twist and dead-end, and armies of merchants are ready to pounce on the unwary.'

'It's easy to know who the enemy is in the Maze,' Qeran said. 'Men are brothers in the night, and *alagai* don't come offering gifts and lies.' He looked around warily, dropping a hand to his purse as if to reassure himself it was there. 'Here, everyone is an enemy.'

'Not when you're with me,' Abban said. 'Here, I am Andrah and Sharum Ka both. Even now, people mark us together. Return tomorrow, and they will fall over themselves to find your favour, in hopes that you might bring good word of them to me.'

Qeran spat again. 'I have wives to shop the bazaar for me. Let us be about our business and be gone from this place.'

'Soon enough,' Abban said. 'You know your part?'

Qeran grunted. 'I have been breaking boys and building men from the pieces since before you were born, *khaffit*. Leave it to me.'

'No lectures about the sacred black?' Abban asked.

Qeran shrugged. 'I have seen the boys. They are lax. Weak. Jurim and Shanjat spoiled them to turn them against you, and it will take a firm hand to turn them back. They will need to feel as *nie'Sharum* again.'

Abban nodded. 'Do this for me, Drillmaster, and you will be compensated beyond dreams of avarice.'

Qeran dismissed the offer with a wave of disgust. 'Pfagh. You have given me back *sharak*, son of Chabin. This is the least I can give in return. A man is nothing without the respect of his sons.'

'This is the place,' Abban said, pointing to an eating establishment. The front porch was filled with patrons at low tables, taking midday meal, smoking, and drinking bitter Krasian coffee. Women scurried to and fro, bringing a steady stream of full cups and bowls from inside, returning with empties and jingling purses full of draki.

Abban led them into the alleyway, rapping his crutch on a side entrance. A boy in tan opened the door, deftly catching the coin Abban flipped him as he escorted them down a rear stair.

The clatter of dice and shouted bets filled the air, a sweet haze of pipe smoke. They stopped behind a curtain, watching as a group of *Sharum* drank couzi over a dicing table piled high with coin.

'The *dama'ting* should . . . ah,' Abban said, spotting Asavi coming down the main stair. Her white robes stood out in the dark basement, but the men, intent on the wards carved into the dice faces, did not notice her approach until she was upon them.

'What is this?!' Asavi shouted, and the *Sharum* all jumped. One of the men – Abban's son Shusten – whirled towards her, spilling his cup. The *dama'ting* pretended to step back, but gave the sleeve of her robe a masterful flick, catching the spill.

There was a tense silence as Asavi regarded her sleeve, none of the warriors even daring to breathe.

Asavi touched the wetness, bringing her fingers to her nose. 'Is this . . . *couzi*?' She shrieked the last word, and the men nearly pissed their bidos. Even Abban felt terrified, though he himself had arranged the meeting. It was a scene not unlike the one thirty years past, when his father, Chabin, accidentally spilled ink on a *dama*'s robe, and was put to death on the spot. He swallowed a lump at the memory. Perhaps it was fitting his sons should take a similar lesson.

'Forgive me, *dama'ting*!' Shusten cried, snatching a cloth of dubious cleanliness and reaching out to grab her sleeve, blotting ineffectually at the stain. 'I will clean . . .'

'How dare you?!' Asavi cried, pulling her sleeve free of his grasp. She caught his wrist, pulling the arm straight and whirling to slam her open palm into the back of Shusten's elbow. His arm broke with an audible snap, much as Chabin's neck had.

Shusten screamed, but it was choked off as the *dama'ting* struck again, this time at his throat. 'You will clean it with your blood, fool!' She bent forward, kicking her right leg back and curling it up and over her head, kicking him in the face.

'Beautiful,' Qeran whispered, watching her art. Abban glanced at him. He would never understand warriors.

Shusten fell back, nose shattered, and crashed into the dicing table, sending coin and couzi scattering in all directions. The *Sharum* broke away, far less worried about their money than the *dama'ting*'s wrath.

Asavi strode in, continuing the beating. Shusten attempted to crawl away, but a kick to his thigh collapsed his leg. The next kick was to his balls and even Qeran winced at the whimper Shusten gave at the blow, blood bubbling from his broken nose.

A bit of the spray of blood and snot spotted Asavi's robe, and she gave a growl, pulling the curved knife from her belt.

133

'No, *dama'ting*!' Fahki, Shusten's elder brother, cried, rushing to interpose himself. 'Mercy, for Everam's sake!'

Fahki was unarmed, hands open in supplication. He was careful to avoid touching the *dama'ting*, but Asavi moved like a dancer, slipping a leg in his path. Her cry was quite convincing as Fahki stumbled into her, bearing them both to the dirty wooden floor.

'Your cue, Drillmaster,' Abban said, but Qeran was already moving. He threw open the curtain, careful not to reveal Abban's presence, and strode into the room.

'What is the meaning of this?!' Qeran roared, his voice like thunder in the low-ceilinged room. He snatched Fahki by the collar of his robe, hauling him off the *dama'ting*.

Asavi glared at him. 'Are these drunkards your men, Drillmaster?' she demanded.

Qeran bowed deeply, slamming Fahki's head into the floorboards in the process. 'No, Dama'ting. I was taking my meal in the establishment above and heard the commotion.' Still holding Fahki, who choked and gagged at the grip on his collar, he reached a hand out to Asavi.

The *dama'ting* took the offered hand and he pulled her to her feet, turning to cast a glare over the men cowering against the walls. 'Shall I kill them for you?'

It seemed a ludicrous statement, a single warrior threatening to kill close to a dozen men, but it was a threat all took very seriously. One did not take on the red veil of a drillmaster easily, and Qeran was well known to all the warriors of the Kaji, a living legend in both *alagai'sharak* and the training grounds.

Asavi, too, cast her eyes over the men for long, tense seconds. At last, she shook her head.

'You men,' she called to the cowering warriors. 'Tear the black from these two.'

'No!' Fahki screamed, but the men, his spear brothers a moment before, were deaf to his cries as they moved in. Qeran threw him to the men and one of them caught him with a spear shaft under the chin, choking out any resistance as half a dozen men eagerly tore his *Sharum* robes from him. Shusten was unable to put up even a token resistance, moaning as the remaining warriors stripped him.

How quickly the fabled loyalty of Sharum *fades when put to the test*, Abban mused. They would do anything to get back in the *dama'ting*'s good grace.

'You are *khaffit* now,' Asavi told the naked men. She looked at Fahki's shrivelled manhood and gave a snort. 'Perhaps you always should have been. Return to your fathers in shame.'

One of the warriors knelt before her, placing his hands and forehead on the floor in absolute supplication. 'They are brothers, *dama'ting*,' he said, 'their father is *khaffit*.'

'Fitting,' Asavi said. 'The fig lands close to the tree.' She turned to regard the other warriors. 'As for the rest of you, you will go to Sharik Hora and repent. You will not take food or drink for three days in penance, and if I learn you have so much as *touched* a cup of couzi – or dice – again, you will share their fate.'

The warriors gaped a moment, until Asavi clapped her hands in a sharp retort that made them all jump. 'Now!'

Practically pissing their bidos, the warriors hurriedly backed out of the room, bowing repeatedly and saying 'Thank you, Dama'ting,' over and over. They stumbled into one another as they bottlenecked at the stairwell, turning and running up the steps as fast as their sandalled feet could carry them.

Asavi cast one last disgusted glance at the naked men. 'Drillmaster, dispose of these pitiful excuses for men.'

Qeran bowed. 'Yes, Dama'ting.'

Fahki and Shusten blinked in the dim lamplight as the hoods were pulled from their heads. They were tied to chairs in an underground chamber. Both had been 'softened', as Qeran put it, bruises still swollen and red, not yet gone to purple. Shusten's arm had been set in plaster and his nose splinted. Both had been dressed in ragged shirts and pants of *khaffit* tan.

'My prodigal sons return,' Abban said. 'Though perhaps not as proud as when I saw you last.'

The boys looked at him, squinting until their eyes adjusted to the light. Qeran stood a step behind Abban, arms crossed, and Fahki's eyes widened at the sight of him. Abban could see understanding dawn.

Perhaps they are not total fools, he thought, pleased. Warrior sons were bad enough. If they proved fools as well, he would just as soon kill them and have done. He had other sons, though none more by Shamavah, the only wife who truly mattered to him. For her sake, he must try to pull these back into his fold.

'Why are they bound?' Abban asked. 'Surely my own sons pose no threat to me. There is no need for such shameful treatment.'

Qeran grunted, pulling a knife as he went over, cutting their bonds. The boys groaned, massaging ankles and wrists to restore blood flow. Shusten looked weak and chastened, but Fahki still had defiance in his eyes.

'Abban.' He spat on the floor, a pinkish froth of blood and saliva. He looked to his brother. 'Our father is bitter we proved his betters and rose above his station. He has found a way to bribe a *dama'ting* to drag us back to his world of commerce and *khaffit*.'

'You are *khaffit* now, too,' Abban reminded him.

'You took our blacks in deception,' Fahki growled. 'We are still *Sharum* in the eyes of Everam, better than all the *khaffit* scum in Everam's Bounty.'

Abban put a hand to his chest. '*I* took your blacks? Was it me who put cups of couzi and dice in your hands? Was it me who tore the robes from your backs? Your own brothers were happy to do it, to save themselves. Your loss of status is a product of your own foolishness. I warned you what would happen if you kept to dice and drink. The black does not put you above Everam's law.'

Fahki rolled his eyes. 'Since when do you care for Everam's law, Father? Half your fortune comes from couzi.'

Abban chuckled. 'I do not deny it, but I am smart enough not to dice away my profits, or to drink in public.'

He limped over to the third chair in the room, easing himself down and peering at them between the humps of his camel-headed crutch. 'As for your being better than *khaffit*, we shall soon put that to the test. You will be fed and given a night's sleep. In the morning, you'll be given a spear and shield and set against one of my *kha'Sharum* guards. Any one. You may choose.'

Fahki snorted. 'I will kill him in less time than it took you to limp your fat carcass across the room, old man.'

Qeran barked a laugh at that. 'If you last five minutes, I will give you the robes off my back and my own good name.'

The smug look fell from Fahki's face at that. 'Why do you serve this *khaffit*, Drillmaster? You trained the Deliverer himself. You sully your good name with every order you take from beneath you. What price did you demand, to sell your honour to a pig-eater?'

Qeran walked over to Fahki, bending low as if to whisper an answer. Fahki, the fool boy, leaned in to hear.

Qeran's punch knocked him out of his chair and onto the floor. Fahki coughed, spitting a wad of blood and the shards of a broken tooth onto the stone floor.

'Your father may allow you to speak to him with such disrespect . . .' Qeran said.

'For now,' Abban cut in.

'For now,' Qeran agreed. 'But as you say, I am a drillmaster of the *Sharum*. I have trained countless warriors, and claim their kills as my own. A million *alagai* have I shown the sun, boy, and I owe you no explanations. For every insolent word you cast my way, I will break a part of you.'

Qeran smiled as Fahki glared at him. 'Yes. Come at me. I see it in your eyes. Come and test your mettle. Abban has two sons. Perhaps he won't miss one.'

'I daresay I don't need either, if they are fool enough to attack you, Drillmaster,' Abban said.

Fahki breathed deeply, muscles knotted, but he stayed on the ground.

Abban nodded. 'The beginning of wisdom. Perhaps there is hope for you yet.'

Fahki chose the smallest and weakest looking of the *kha'Sharum* to challenge in the yard the next day. Skinny and bespectacled, the man seemed no match for Fahki, who was tall and thick like his father.

All of clan Haman was summoned to witness the event. Abban had the inner ring around the combatants filled with women, Fahki's sisters, cousins, aunts, and stepmothers. The *kha'Sharum* and *chi'Sharum* watched eagerly, as did all of the workers in Abban's employ, given time off simply to add to the boy's humiliation.

Fahki circled warily, spinning his spear in an impressive – if pointless – display. The spectacled *kha'Sharum* watched him coolly, not bothering to circle. He was Sharach, and carried an *alagai*-catcher instead of a spear. The long hollow pole ended in a loop of woven cable that the warrior could tighten with a lever on the shaft.

A vendor made his way through the crowd, selling candied nuts.

At last Fahki's tension reached a breaking point, and he charged, spear leading. The warrior batted the point aside and had the loop around Fahki's neck in an instant, whipping the pole and turning the momentum of his attack against him. Fahki had to leap head over heels and flip himself onto his back simply to keep from having his neck broken.

A twist of the pole, and Fahki was on his stomach. Abban nodded to his daughter Cielvah, and the girl stepped forward, carrying a short leather lash.

'Apologies, brother,' she said, pulling Fahki's pantaloons and bido down. The boy thrashed, but the *kha'Sharum* tightened the noose and kept him prone.

Abban looked to Shusten, standing by his side. His son had his eyes on the ground, unable to watch, but he flinched with every sound of the lash, and wept at his brother's humiliation.

'I trust, my son, this lesson is not lost on you,' Abban said.

'No, Father,' Shusten said.

Abban nodded. 'Good. I hope your brother is as wise. If you prove worthy, Qeran will train you and Fahki properly, and you will rise to *kha'Sharum*.'

The Sharach warrior escorted Fahki over to Abban at the end of his pole. The boy's face was red with shame under the tear-streaked grime of the yard. Abban nodded to the warrior, who released Fahki and stood at attention.

'This is Lifan,' Abban said, gesturing to the Sharach. 'He will be your tutor.'

Shusten looked at him. 'You said Drillmaster Qeran . . .'

'Would teach you to fight, yes,' Abban said. '*If* you prove worthy. Lifan will tutor you in reading, writing, and mathematics. Lessons your mother began, abandoned when you were called to *Hannu Pash*. You will hop to his every command. When you can read without moving your lips and do sums without your fingers, we shall discuss whether you will be allowed to hold a spear again.'

7

More Sack Than Sense
333 AR Autumn

Jardir gaped at the Par'chin, seeking signs of deceit – or madness – in his aura. But the Par'chin was calm, focused, and very serious.

Jardir opened his mouth, then closed it again. The Par'chin laughed.

'If this is some jest, Par'chin, it will be the end of my patience . . .'

The son of Jeph remained relaxed, waving him down. In a show of trust, he backed away till his back struck the window, then slid down to sit on the floor amidst the broken bits of his chair. 'No jest. Know it's a lot to wrap your thoughts around. Plenty of questions, ay? Take your time, and start throwing them when you're ready.'

Jardir stiffened, unsure. The heat of battle was fading, but his muscles were bunched for action, knowing the Par'chin could be upon him the moment he let down his guard.

But in his heart, he did not believe it. The Par'chin was many things, but he was not a liar. His casual posture reminded Jardir of the countless hours they had spent interrogating each other, talking about everything under the sun as they fought to understand each other's language and culture. The Par'chin's relaxed demeanour had always put Jardir at ease in a way he never was with his own people.

He looked to the bed, but like the chair it was a wreckage, broken by the force of his leap. Instead he backed to the window opposite the Par'chin, sliding to the floor to mirror him. He remained alert to attack, but the Par'chin was right. There was nothing to be gained in fighting each other before dawn came to even the odds.

Rivalries must be put aside when night falls, the Evejah said.

'How can we get to the abyss?' Jardir asked, picking a question at random out of the many swirling in his thoughts. 'You can mist as the *alagai* do, but I cannot.'

'Don't need to,' the Par'chin said. 'There are land routes. The minds take human captives and keep them alive in the Core.' He spat on the floor. 'Keeps their brains fresh.'

'We must journey to the underworld to save those lost souls,' Jardir guessed. 'Then Everam will . . .'

The Par'chin sighed loudly, rolling his eyes. 'If you're going to make a fresh guess at "Everam's plan" every time I tell you something new, we're going to be here a long time, Ahmann.'

Jardir scowled, but the Par'chin had a point. He nodded. 'Continue, please.'

'Dunno if there's much worth saving in any event.' The Par'chin's eyes were sad and distant. 'The minds consider empty brains a delicacy. Imagine dozens of generations, living and dying in darkness, eating moss and lichen, cattle for the slaughter. Denied clothes or even language. Ent human any more. Become something else. Dark, twisted, and savage.'

Jardir suppressed a shudder.

'Point is,' Arlen said, 'there are a number of routes we can follow to the Core, but it's a long, winding trail. Lots of forks, dead ends, pitfalls, and dangerous crossings. Not something we could ever do on our own. Need a guide.'

'And you want that guide to be one of Alagai Ka's princelings,' Jardir said. The Par'chin nodded. 'How will we make it betray its own kind and guide us?'

'Torture,' the Par'chin said. 'Pain. Demons have no sense of loyalty, and rail against captivity. We can use that.'

'You sound unsure,' Jardir said. 'How can we trust a prince of lies in any event?'

'It's a weak point in the plan,' the Par'chin admitted. He shrugged. 'Need to catch one, first.'

'And how do you intend to do that?' Jardir asked. 'I've killed two. One I took by surprise, and had help from Leesha Paper and my *Jiwah Ka* with the other. They are formidable, Par'chin. Given a moment to act, they can—'

The Par'chin smiled. 'What? Turn into mist? Draw wards in the air? Heal their wounds? We can do these things, too, Ahmann. We can set a trap even Alagai Ka could not escape.'

'How can we even find one?' Jardir asked. 'After I killed one the first night of Waning, its brothers fled the field. They kept their distance the following nights, moving quickly.'

'They fear you,' the Par'chin said. 'They remember Kaji, the mind hunter, and the many he killed with the crown and spear and cloak. They will never come within miles of you willingly.'

'So you admit Kaji was the Deliverer, and I am his heir,' Jardir said.

'I admit Kaji was a general the mind demons feared,' the Par'chin said, 'and when you faced them with his spear and crown, they came to fear you, too. Doesn't make you heir to anything. If Abban wore the crown and held the spear, they'd piss themselves and run from him, too.'

Jardir scowled, but it was pointless to argue. Despite his doubtful words and the Par'chin's disrespect, he felt hope kindling in his breast. The Par'chin was building to something. His plan was madness, but it was *glorious* madness. Madness worthy of Kaji himself. He embraced the barb and pressed on. 'How can we know where to set wards to trap one?'

The Par'chin winked at him. 'That's the thing. I know where they're going on new moon. All of them.

'They're going to Anoch Sun.'

Jardir felt his blood go cold. The lost city of Kaji, where the Par'chin's theft of the spear had set everything in motion. 'How can you know this?'

'You're not the only one who's fought minds, Ahmann,' the Par'chin said. 'While you struggled with one in your bedroom, I fought its brother north of the Hollow. Would've had me, if not for Renna.'

Jardir nodded. 'Your *jiwah* is formidable.'

The Par'chin accepted the compliment with a nod, but sighed deeply. 'Maybe if I'd listened to her, I wouldn't have been caught with my bido down by three of them last month.' His eyes dropped to the floor, and his aura coloured with shame. 'Got inside my head, Ahmann. Couldn't stop them. Rooted around my memories like a rummage trunk. Most of all, they wanted to know where I found the wards . . .'

'Raise your eyes, son of Jeph,' Jardir said. 'I have never met a man who fought the *alagai* harder than you. If you could not stop them, they could not be stopped.'

Gratitude flushed in the Par'chin's aura as he lifted his chin. 'Wasn't all bad. Even as they looked into my thoughts, I got a glimpse into theirs. They mean to return to the lost city and do what three thousand years of sandstorms could not. Dunno if it's fear the city has secrets yet to divulge, or a wish to shit upon their ancient foes, but they will exhume the sarcophagi and raze the city.'

'We must stop them at any cost,' Jardir said. 'I will not have my ancestors profaned.'

'Don't be a fool,' Arlen snapped. 'Throw away all strategic advantage over a handful of dusty corpses?'

'Those are heroes of the First War, you faithless *chin*,' Jardir snapped. 'They carry the honour of mankind. I will not suffer them to be sullied by the *alagai*.'

The Par'chin spat on the floor. 'Kaji himself would command you leave them.'

Jardir laughed. 'Oh, you claim to speak for Kaji now, Par'chin?'

'I've read his treatise on war, too, Ahmann,' the Par'chin said. '*No thing is more precious than victory.* Kaji's words, not mine.'

Jardir balled his fists. 'You're free with the holy scripture when it suits you, son of Jeph, and quick to dismiss it as fantasy when it does not.' His crown began to glow fiercely. 'Kaji also commanded we honour the bones of those who have given their lives in *alagai'sharak* above all others, and let none profane them.'

The Par'chin crossed his arms, the wards on his flesh flaring to match the crown. 'Tell me I'm wrong. Tell me you will give up our one chance to take the fight to the demons just to preserve the honour of empty shells whose spirits have long since gone down the lonely path.'

Our cultures are a natural insult to each other, Par'chin, Jardir had once said. *We must resist the urge to take offence, if we are to continue to learn from each other.*

The son of Jeph's aura was plain. He believed he was in the right, but had no wish to fight over the matter.

'You are not wrong,' Jardir admitted, 'but you are a fool if you think I will stand idle and watch a demon shit upon the bones of Kaji.'

The Par'chin nodded. 'And I do not ask you to. I ask that if it comes to it, you watch them shit upon Isak. Maji. Mehnding. Even Jardir, should they find him.'

'They will not,' Jardir said, relieved. 'My holy ancestor is interred in the Desert Spear. We can move the body of Kaji there.' Still, the thought of letting the *alagai* desecrate the bodies of the great leaders of the Evejah horrified him. Even with all Ala at stake, he did not know if he could witness such a thing and not act to stop it.

'And what advantage do we gain by this . . . sacrifice?' Jardir asked through bitter tones.

'We do not steal Kaji away,' the son of Jeph said. 'The first Shar'Dama Ka will serve his people once more, baiting the trap we will set upon his tomb. Anoch Sun is enormous. We cannot predict precisely where the mind demons will strike, save that one crypt, seen so clearly in my memory. They are coming there, Ahmann. They are coming in force. And we will be there to meet them, hidden in Cloaks of Unsight. When they enter the chamber, we will capture one, kill as many as we can while surprise holds, and flee.'

Jardir crossed his arms, looking sceptical. 'And how are we supposed to accomplish this?'

'We use the crown,' the Par'chin said.

Jardir raised a brow.

'The Crown of Kaji's warding field can repel any demon, even an army of them, up to half a mile,' the Par'chin said.

'I am aware of this,' Jardir said. 'It is my crown.'

The Par'chin smiled. 'Are you also aware that you can raise the field at a distance? Like a bubble, keeping demons out, or as in the Maze . . .'

'. . . keeping them in,' Jardir realized. 'If we get in close . . .'

'. . . you can trap them in with us,' the Par'chin said.

Jardir clenched a fist. 'We can destroy Nie's generals before the first sallies of Sharak Ka even begin.'

The Par'chin nodded. 'But it won't do much good if their queen can lay more.'

Jardir looked at him. 'Alagai'ting Ka. The Mother of Demons.'

'Just so,' the Par'chin said. 'Kill her, and we've a shot at winning the war. If not, they'll come back again, even if it takes another three thousand years. Eventually, they'll wear us down.'

'What if I do not agree to this plan, Par'chin?' Jardir asked. 'Will you steal the crown and try alone?'

'Half right,' Arlen said. 'Minds are coming to Anoch Sun on new moon and I'll be there with or without you. If you can't see the value in that, then you're not the man I thought you were. Take your crown, slink back to your ripping throne, and leave Sharak Ka to me.'

Jardir gritted his teeth. 'And the spear?'

'The spear is mine,' Arlen said. 'But you swear by the sun to do this with me, I'll give it to you free and clear and call it a bargain. If not, I'll take it to the Core and put it through the demon queen's heart myself.'

Jardir stared at him a long time. 'That will not be necessary,

Par'chin. It grates me to be given what is already mine, but what kind of *ajin'pal* would I be if I let you walk such a road alone? You may think Everam a lie, Par'chin, but truly He must love you, to grant you such courage.'

The Par'chin smiled. 'My da always said I had more sack than sense.'

Arlen bustled about the kitchen, his hands a blur as he worked. He had never been a great cook, but years spent alone on the road had made him efficient enough at boiling potatoes and pan-frying meat and vegetables. He used no fire; heat wards etched into the pots and pans did the work, powered by his touch.

'May I assist?' Jardir asked.

'You?' Arlen asked. 'Has the self-proclaimed king of the world ever even touched unprepared food?'

'You know me well, Par'chin,' Jardir said, 'but not as well as you think. Was I not *nie'Sharum* once? There is no menial task I have not bent my back to.'

'Then bend your back to setting the table.' The banter was familiar, something Arlen hadn't realized he had missed all these years. It was easy to fall into their old patterns, brothers in all but name. Jardir had stood with Arlen on his first night in the Maze, and in Krasia, that was as great a bond as blood. Greater.

But Jardir had been willing to kill him for power. He had not done it with malice, but he had done it all the same, and even now, Arlen had to wonder if he would do it all over again if he had the chance . . . or if the chance came again in the future. He searched Jardir's aura for a clue, but he could discern little without Drawing magic through him and Knowing him fully – an intrusion Jardir would no doubt sense, and have every right to take offence to.

'Ask, Par'chin,' Jardir said.

'Ay?' Arlen asked, surprised.

'I can see the question that gnaws at your spirit,' Jardir said. 'Ask, and let us have it done.'

Arlen nodded. 'Soon enough. Some things are best done on a full stomach.'

He finished preparing the meal, waiting patiently as Jardir said a prayer over the food before they set to eating. A single serving was enough for Arlen, but Jardir had suffered serious wounds in their battle on the cliff, and while magic could heal them in an instant, it couldn't make flesh and blood from nothing. He emptied three bowls and still reached for the fruit plate while Arlen cleared the table.

When he returned he sat quietly, watching Jardir gnaw the bowl down to stem, seed, and core.

'Ask, Par'chin,' Jardir said again.

'Did you decide to kill me in the heat of the moment that night in the Maze,' Arlen asked, 'or was our friendship a lie from the start?'

He watched Jardir's aura carefully, taking some small pleasure as hurt and shame coloured it for an instant. Jardir mastered himself quickly and looked up, meeting Arlen's eyes as he let out a long exhale, nostrils flaring.

'Both,' he said. 'And neither. After she threw the bones for you that first night, Inevera told me to embrace you like a brother and keep you close, for I would one day need to kill you if I was to take power.'

Something tightened in Arlen, and unbidden, the ambient magic in the room rushed to him, making the wards on his flesh glow.

'That don't sound like both,' he said through gritted teeth. 'Or neither.'

Jardir could not have missed the glow of his wards, but he gave no indication, keeping his eyes fixed on Arlen's. 'I knew nothing of you then, Par'chin, save that the *Sharum* and *dama* nearly came to blows over your request to fight in the Maze. You seemed a man of honour, but when your rock demon broke the wall, I did not know what to think.'

'You talk like One Arm was a piece of livestock I tried to sneak past the gate,' Arlen said.

Jardir ignored the comment. 'But then, as the *alagai* poured through the breach and despair took hold in the hearts of the bravest men, you stood fast and bled at my side, willing to give your life to capture the rock demon and put things right.

'I did not lie when I called you brother, Par'chin. I would have given my life for you.'

Arlen nodded. 'Nearly did more'n once that night, and Creator only knows how many times since. But it was all a show, ay? You knew you'd live to betray me one day.'

Jardir shrugged. 'Who can say, Par'chin? The very act of foretelling gives us a chance to change what is seen. They are glimpses of what *might* be, not what *will*. What would be the point, otherwise? If I thought myself immortal and began to take foolish risks I would otherwise have avoided . . .'

Arlen wanted to argue, but there was little he could say. It was a fair point.

'Inevera's prophecies are vague, and often not what they seem,' Jardir went on. 'I spent years pondering her words. *Kill*, she had said, but the symbol on her die had other meanings. Death, rebirth, conversion. I tried to convert you to the Evejah, or find you a bride and tie you to Krasia, in hope that if you ceased to be a *chin* and were reborn as an Evejan, it would fulfill the prophecy and allow me to spare you.'

Almost every man Arlen knew in Krasia tried to find him a bride at some point, but none so hard as Jardir. He never would have guessed it was to save his life, but there was no lie in Jardir's aura.

'Reckon it came true after a fashion,' Arlen said. 'Part of me died that night, and was reborn out on the dunes. Sure as the sun rises.'

'When you first presented the spear, I knew it for what it was,' Jardir said. 'I sensed its power and had to force down my desire to take it from you then and there.'

Arlen's lip curled, showing a hint of teeth. 'But you were too much a coward. Instead you conspired and lured me into a trap, letting your men and a demon pit do the dirty work for you.'

Jardir's aura flared, a mix of guilt and anger. 'Inevera too told me to kill you and take the spear. She offered to poison your tea if I did not wish to sully my hands. She would have denied you a warrior's death.'

Arlen spat. 'As if I give a demon's piss. Betrayal's betrayal, Ahmann.'

'You do,' Jardir said. 'You may think Heaven a lie, but if you were given to choose your death, you would face it with a spear in your hand.'

'Didn't have a spear when death came for me, Ahmann. You took it. All I had were needles and ink.'

'I fought for you,' Jardir said, not rising to the bait. 'Inevera's dice have ruled my life since I was twelve years old. Never before or since have I so defied them, or her. Not even over Leesha Paper. Had Inevera not proven so . . . formidable, I would have hurt her when my arguments failed. I left for the Maze determined. I would not kill my brother. I would not rob him.'

Arlen tried to read the emotions in Jardir's aura, but they were too complex, even for him. This was something Jardir had wrestled with for years, and still not come to terms with. It did little to ease his sense of betrayal, but there was more, and Arlen wanted to hear it.

'What changed?' he said.

'I remembered your words,' Jardir said. 'I watched from the wall as you led the *Sharum* to clear the Maze, the Spear of Kaji shining bright as the sun in your hands. They shouted your name, and I knew then they would follow you. The warriors would make you Shar'Dama Ka, and charge Nie's abyss if you asked it.'

'Afraid I'd take your job?' Arlen asked. 'Never wanted it.'

Jardir shook his head. 'I did not care about my *job*, Par'chin. I cared about my people. And yours. Every man, woman, and child on Ala. For they would all follow you once they saw the *alagai* bleed. I saw it in my mind's eye, and it was glorious.'

'Then what, Ahmann?' Arlen asked, losing patience. 'What in the Core happened?'

'I told you, Par'chin,' Jardir said. 'I remembered your words. *There is no Heaven*, you said. And I thought to myself, Without hope of Heaven, what reason would you have to remain righteous when all the world bowed to you? Without being humble before the Creator, what man could be trusted with such power? Nie corrupts what She cannot destroy, and it is only in our submission to Everam that we can resist Her whispers and lies.'

Arlen gaped at him. The truth of the words was written on Jardir's aura, but his mind boggled at the thought. 'I embody everything you hold dear, willing to fight and die in the First War, but you'd betray me because I do it for humanity, and not some figment in the sky?'

Jardir clenched a fist. 'I warn you, Par'chin . . .'

'Corespawn your warnings!' Arlen brought his fist down, the limb still thrumming with power. The table exploded with the blow, collapsing in a spray of splinters. Jardir leapt back from the broken boards and shrapnel, coming down in a *sharusahk* stance.

Arlen knew better than to attempt to grapple. Jardir was more than his match at hand-fighting. He'd fought *dama* before, and been lucky to escape with his life. Jardir had studied for years with the clerics, learning their secrets. Even now, when Arlen was faster and stronger than anyone alive, Jardir could take him like a boy to the woodshed. Much as Arlen wanted to meet Jardir on even terms, there was nothing to be gained, and everything to lose.

Jardir's superior *sharusahk* skill was irrelevant in any event. His understanding and control over his magic was rudimentary at best, self-taught and unpractised. It would be some time before he was in full control of his abilities, and even then he could not match with *hora* relics what Arlen, who had made magic a part of him, could do. If he wanted to kill Jardir, he could.

And doom them all. Arlen might be able to make the crown work without Jardir, but there wasn't much chance he could escape Anoch Sun alive without help, and he'd never make it to the mind court alone. The Core would call to him, its song more insistent the closer he drew.

Nie corrupts what she cannot destroy. Words of faith, but there was wisdom in them all the same. Every child had heard the proverb in the Canon that power corrupts, and absolute power corrupts absolutely. The Core offered absolute power, but Arlen dare not touch it. He would lose himself, absorbed and burnt away like a match thrown into a Solstice bonfire.

He breathed deeply to calm himself before he did something rash. Jardir kept his guard up, but his aura showed he had no desire to fight. They both knew what was at stake.

'I made a promise to you that night as I left you on the dunes, Par'chin,' Jardir said. 'I threw you a waterskin and promised I would find you in the afterlife, and if I had not kept true and made the Ala a better place, we would have a reckoning.'

'Well it's come early,' Arlen said. 'Hope you're ready for it.'

Jardir looked at the sky as they exited the tower, trying to deduce where they were from the position of the stars. South and west of Everam's Bounty, but that told him little. Millions of untamed acres lay between the great city and the desert flats. He might manage to find his way back on his own, but Everam only knew how long it would take.

He didn't need to ask the Par'chin his purpose in leading them from the tower. It was written clearly on his aura, mirrored in Jardir's own. The hope that fighting side by side against the *alagai*, as they had done so many times before, could begin to eat away at the anger and mistrust that lay between them still.

Unity is worth any price, the Evejah said. Kaji had called it the key to Sharak Ka. If he and the Par'chin could find unity of purpose, then they stood a chance.

If not . . .

Jardir breathed deep of the night air. It was fitting. *All men are brothers in the night*, Kaji had said. If they could not find unity before the *alagai*, they were unlikely to find it elsewhere.

'They'll catch our scent soon enough,' the Par'chin said, reading his thoughts. 'First thing to do is recharge your crown.'

Jardir shook his head. 'The first thing is for you to return my spear to me, Par'chin. I have agreed to your terms.'

The Par'chin shook his head. 'Let's start slow, Ahmann. Spear's not going anywhere just yet.'

Jardir gave him a hard look, but there was nothing for it. He could see the Par'chin would not budge on the point, and it was useless to argue further. He raised his fist, knuckles scarred with wards Inevera had cut into his skin. 'The crown will begin to recharge when my fist strikes an *alagai*.'

The Par'chin nodded. 'No need to wait, though.'

Jardir looked at him. 'You suggest I take more from you?'

The Par'chin gave him a withering look. 'Caught me off guard the once, Ahmann. Try that trick again and you'll regret it.'

'Then how?' Jardir asked. 'Without an *alagai* to Draw from . . .'

The Par'chin cut him off with a wave of his hand, gesturing at their surroundings. 'Magic's all around us, Ahmann.'

It was true. In crownsight, Jardir could see as clearly at night as in day, the world awash in magic's glow. It pooled at their feet like a luminescent fog, stirred by their passage, but there was little power in it, any more than smoke had the power of flame.

'I don't understand,' Jardir said.

'Breathe,' the Par'chin said. 'Close your eyes.'

Jardir glanced at him, but complied, his breathing rhythmic

and even. He fell into the warrior's trance he had learned in Sharik Hora, soul at peace, but ready to act in an instant.

'Reach out with the crown,' the Par'chin said. 'Feel the magic around you, whispering like a soft breeze.'

Jardir did as he asked, and could indeed sense the magic, expanding and contracting in response to his breath. It flowed over the Ala, but was drawn to life.

'Gently Draw it,' the Par'chin said, 'like you're breathing it in.' Jardir inhaled, and felt the power flow into him. It was not the fire of striking an *alagai*, more like sunlight on his skin.

'Keep going,' the Par'chin said. 'Easy. Don't stop with your exhales. Just keep a steady pull.'

Jardir nodded, feeling the flow continue. He opened his eyes, seeing magic drifting to him from all directions in a steady current, like a river heading to a fall. It was a slow process, but eventually the chasm began to fill. He felt stronger.

Then his elation cost him his centre, and the flow stopped.

He looked to the Par'chin. 'Amazing.'

The Par'chin smiled. 'Just gettin' started, Ahmann. We've got a lot more to cover before we're ready to face a court of mind demons.'

'You do not trust me with the Spear of the Kaji, but you give me the secrets of your magic?'

'Sharak Ka comes before all else,' Arlen said. 'You taught me war. Only fair I teach you magic. The rudiments, anyway. Spear's a crutch you've leaned on too long.' He winked. 'Just don't think I'm teaching you all my tricks.'

They spent several more minutes thus, the Par'chin gently coaching him in how to Draw the power.

'Now hold the power tight,' the Par'chin said, producing a small folding knife from his pocket. He opened it and flipped the blade into his grip, passing the handle to Jardir.

Jardir took the small blade curiously. It wasn't even warded. 'What am I to do with this?'

'Cut yourself,' the Par'chin said.

Jardir looked at him curiously, then shrugged and complied.

The blade was sharp, and parted his flesh easily. He could see blood in the cut, but the magic he'd absorbed was already at work. The skin knitted together before it could begin to well.

The Par'chin shook his head. 'Again. But keep a tighter grip on the power. So tight the wound stays open.'

Jardir grunted, slicing his flesh again. The wound began to close as before, but Jardir Drew the magic from his flesh into the crown, and the healing stopped.

'Healing's great when your bones are in the right place and you've got power to spare,' the Par'chin said, 'but if you're not careful, you can heal twisted, or waste power you need. Now let out just a touch, sending it straight where it's needed.'

Jardir let out a measured trickle of magic, and watched the cut seal away as if it had never been.

'Good,' the Par'chin said, 'but you might've done with less. Two cuts, now. Heal one, but not the other.'

Holding tight to the power, Jardir cut one forearm, and then the other. He closed his eyes and breathed deeply, releasing a fraction as much magic as before and willing it to his left arm alone. He could feel the tingle run along the limb, and opened his eyes to see the cut slowly sealing, the other still oozing blood.

There was a howl not far off, the sound of field demons. Jardir looked in that direction, but the *alagai* were still too far off.

'Draw power from that direction,' the Par'chin said. 'Take it in through your eyes.'

Jardir did so, and found that even though there was no direct line of sight, he could see the creatures in the distance, running hard for their position.

'How?' he asked.

'All living things make an imprint on the ambient magic,' the Par'chin said, 'spreading out like a drop of dye in water. You can read the current, and see beyond the limits of your eyes.'

Jardir squinted, studying the approaching creatures. A full

reap, more than a score of demons. Their long, corded limbs and low torsos glowed fiercely with power.

'They are many, Par'chin,' he said. 'Are you certain you do not wish to return the spear to me?' He scanned the sky. There were wind demons beginning to circle as well, drawn to the glow of their power. Jardir reached for his Cloak of Unsight, ready to pull it close, but of course the Par'chin had taken that, too.

The son of Jeph shook his head. 'We can't take them with *gaisahk* alone, then we got no business in Anoch Sun.'

Jardir looked at him curiously. The meaning of the word was clear enough, a conjunction of the Krasian *gai*, meaning 'demon', and *sahk*, meaning 'unarmed', but he had never heard it before.

'*Sharusahk* was designed for men to kill one another.' The Par'chin held up a warded fist. 'Needed to change it up a bit to bring the wards to bear properly.'

Jardir crossed his fists before his heart and gave a shallow bow, the traditional bow of *sharusahk* pupil to master. The move was perfectly executed, but doubtless the Par'chin could see the sarcasm in his aura.

He swept a hand at the rapidly approaching field demons. 'I eagerly await my first lesson, Par'chin.'

The Par'chin's eyes narrowed, but there was a hint of smile on his lips. His face blurred momentarily, and his clothes fell away, leaving him in only his brown bido. It was the first time Jardir had truly seen what his friend had become. The Painted Man, as the Northerners called him.

It was easy to see why the greenlanders thought him the Deliverer. Every inch of his visible flesh was covered with wards. Some were large and powerful. Impact wards. Forbiddings. Pressure wards. Like Jardir, a demon could not touch the Par'chin, but that he willed it, and his punches, elbows, and kicks would strike the *alagai* like scorpion bolts.

Other wards, like those than ran around his eyes, ears, and mouth, were almost too small to read, conveying more subtle powers. Midsized ones ran up and down his limbs. Thousands in all.

That in itself was enough to amaze, but the Par'chin had always been an artist with warding. His patterns, simple and efficient, were rendered with such beauty they put Evejan illuminators to shame. *Dama* who had spent a lifetime copying and illustrating sacred text in ink made from the blood of heroes.

The wards Inevera had cut into Jardir's flesh were crude by comparison. She would have needed to flay him alive to approach what the Par'chin had done.

Magic ran along the surface of those wards, crackling like static on a thick carpet. They pulsed and throbbed, brightening and dimming in a hypnotizing rhythm. Even one without wardsight could see it. He didn't look like a man any more. He looked like one of Everam's seraphs.

The field demons were close now, racing hard at the sight of prey. They stretched out in a long line, a few loping strides apart. Too long spent fighting the first would have the second upon him, and on and on, till he was fighting all of them. Jardir tensed, ready to race to his friend's aid the moment he began to be overwhelmed.

The Par'chin walked boldly to meet them, but it was warrior's bravado. No man could fight so many alone.

But again his friend surprised him, slipping in smoothly to grab the lead demon and turn its own momentum against it in a perfect *sharusahk* circle throw. Cracked like a whip, the field demon's neck snapped a split second before the Par'chin let go. His aim was precise, crashing the dead *alagai* into the next in line, sending both tumbling to the ground.

The Par'chin glowed brightly now. In the seconds of contact, he had drained considerable magic from the first demon. He charged in, stomping down on the living demon's head with an impact-warded heel. There was a flare of magic, and when the Par'chin turned to meet the next in line, Jardir could see its skull had been crushed like a melon.

A crash and shriek stole Jardir's attention. While he had been focused on the Par'chin, a wind demon had dived at him, hitting hard against the warding field that surrounded Jardir's crown for several paces in every direction. Including up.

Everam take me for a fool, Jardir scolded himself. In his younger days, he would never have been so reckless as to lose track of his surroundings. The Par'chin feared that the spear had made him lax – and perhaps it had – but the crown was more insidious. He'd begun to drop his guard. Something that would cost him in Anoch Sun. The demon princelings had shown at Waning there were still ways they could strike at him.

Jardir collapsed the field, dropping the wind demon heavily to the ground. It struggled to rise, more dazed than harmed, but as Drillmaster Qeran had taught so many years before, wind demons were slow and clumsy on the ground. The thin bone that stretched the membrane of its wings bowed, not meant to support the demon's full weight, and at rest the creature's hind legs were bent fully at the knee, unable to straighten fully.

Before it could manage to right itself, Jardir was on the demon, kicking its limbs out and using his own weight to knock the breath from it once more. The wards scarred onto Jardir's hands were not as intricate as the Par'chin's, but they were strong. He sat on the demon's chest, too high for it to bring its hind talons to bear, and pinned its wings with his knees. He held its throat with his left hand and the pressure ward cut into his palm glowed, building in power as he punched it repeatedly in the vulnerable bone of its eye socket, just above the toothed beak. Impact wards on his knuckles flashed, and he felt the bone crack and finally shatter.

Then, as the Par'chin had shown him, he Drew, feeling the *alagai*'s magic, absorbed deep in the centre of Ala, flood into him, filling him with power.

Another wind demon dove for him while he was engaged,

but this time Jardir was ready. He had learned in lessons long ago that wind demons led their dive with the long, hooked talons at the bend in their wings. They could sever a head with those talons, then spread their wings wide, arresting their downward momentum as they snatched their prey in their hind talons and launched back skyward with a great wingstroke.

Flush with magic, Jardir moved impossibly fast, catching the demon's wing bone just under the lead talon. He pivoted and threw himself forward, preventing the demon from spreading its wings and throwing it to the ground with the full force of its dive. Bones shattered, and the demon shrieked, twitching in agony. He finished it quickly.

Looking up, he saw the Par'chin fully engaged now. He had killed five of the field demons, but the rest, more than three times that number, surrounded him.

But for all that, he did not appear to be in danger. A demon leapt at him and he collapsed into mist. The *alagai* passed through him and crashed into one of its fellows, the two going down in a tangle of tooth and claw.

An instant later he reformed behind another of the beasts, catching it under the forelegs and locking his fingers behind its neck in a *sharusahk* hold. There was an audible snap, and then another demon came at him. He misted away once more, reforming a few feet away, in place to kick a demon in the belly. Impact wards on his instep flashed, launching the *alagai* several feet through the air.

Jardir was the greatest living *sharusahk* master, and even he could barely hold his own against the Par'chin's mist-fighting. Against the *alagai*, with their powerful bodies and tiny brains, it was devastating.

'You cheat, Par'chin!' Jardir called. 'Your new powers have made you lax!'

The son of Jeph had caught an *alagai*'s jaws in his hands, and was in the process of forcing them open well past their limit. The demon let out a high-pitched squeal, thrashing madly, but it could not break his hold. He looked over to Jardir, amusement on his aura. 'Says the man hiding behind his crown's warding field. Come and show me how it's done, if you've had your rest.'

Jardir laughed, pulling open his robe. The Par'chin's body was wiry and corded like cable, a sharp contrast to the heavy bulk of Jardir's muscles, a broad canvas Inevera had painted with her knife. He pulled the crown's warding field in close and strode into the press. A field demon leapt at him, but he caught its foreleg and snapped it with an effortless twist, dropping it in time for a spin-kick that took the next demon at the base of its skull. The impact ward on his instep was enough to break its spine, killing it instantly.

The other demons, their ravenous fury turned to a more cautious aggression after their battle with the Par'chin, circled, issuing low, threatening growls as they looked for an opening. Jardir glanced at the Par'chin, who had stepped back to observe. His wards of forbiddance glowed fiercely, and Jardir could see the edge of the warding field they formed. It bordered several feet in every direction around the Par'chin, like an invisible bubble of impenetrable glass.

His own warriors had been ready to name the Par'chin Deliverer that night in the Maze. Jardir had thought it due only to the Spear of Kaji at the time, but it seemed the Par'chin was destined to power. It was *inevera*.

But destined to power did not mean he was Shar'Dama Ka. The Par'chin baulked at the final price of power, refusing to take the reins his people thrust at him. There was still much he had to learn.

'Observe, Par'chin,' Jardir said, making a show of setting his feet as he took one of the most basic *dama sharusahk* stances. He breathed in, taking in all his surroundings, all his thoughts and emotions, embracing them and letting them fall away. He looked at the demons with calm, relaxed focus, ready to react in an instant.

He lowered his guard, pretending distraction, and the *alagai* took the bait. The ring around him burst into motion as all the field demons moved at him together with all the precision of a push guard.

Jardir never moved his feet, but his waist, supple as a palm frond, twisted and bent as he dodged the attacks and turned them away. He seldom needed more than the flat of his hand to redirect tooth or talon, slapping at paws or the side of a field demon's head just enough to keep them from touching him. The creatures landed in confused tumbles, dazed, but unharmed.

'You fighting, or just playing with them?' the Par'chin asked.

'I am teaching, Par'chin,' he replied, 'and you would be wise to attend the lesson. You may have skill with magic, but the *dama* would laugh at your *sharusahk*. There is more than dogma taught in the catacombs beneath Sharik Hora. *Gaisahk* has merit, but you have much to learn.'

Jardir sent a pulse of power through the crown, knocking the *alagai* back in a tumble as if from the press of a shield wall. They shook themselves off, growling and beginning to circle once more.

'Come,' Jardir beckoned, making a show of setting his feet. 'Plant your feet and let us begin the lesson.'

The Par'chin melted into mist, reappearing right at his side, feet set in a perfect imitation of Jardir's stance. Jardir grunted his approval. 'You will fight without misting. *Sharusahk* is the eternal struggle for life, Par'chin. You cannot master it if you do not fear for yours.'

The Par'chin met his gaze, and nodded. 'Fair's fair.'

As the demons came back at them, Jardir gave the Par'chin a mocking wink. 'But do not think I am teaching you *all* my tricks.'

Jardir watched the sun strike the bodies of the *alagai* they had used as *sharusahk* practice dummies. Demons more powerful than field and wind had arrived as the night wore on, drawn to the sound of battle. In the end he and the Par'chin had been forced to drop their easy pretence and fight hard to take them with *gaisahk* alone.

But now their foes lay broken at their feet, and he and the Par'chin stood to show them the sun.

If Jardir lived to be a thousand, he would never tire of the sight. The demons' skin began to char instantly, glowing like hot coals before bursting into bright fire, casting a flush of heat over his face. It was a daily reminder that, no matter how dark the night, Everam would always return in strength. It was the one moment of every day when hope overpowered the burden of his task to free his people of the *alagai*. It was the moment when he felt as one with Everam and Kaji.

He looked to the Par'chin, wondering what his faithless *ajin'pal* saw in the flames. His crownsight was fading as shadows fled, but there was still a hint of his *ajin'pal*'s aura, and the hope and strength of purpose that filled it in that moment.

'Ah, Par'chin,' he said, drawing the man's gaze. 'It is so easy to remember our differences, I sometimes forget the similarities.'

The Par'chin nodded sadly. 'Honest word.'

'How did you find the lost city, Par'chin?' Jardir asked.

Arlen could not read Jardir's aura in the daylight, but the sharp, probing look in his eyes told him this was no random question. Jardir had been holding it, biding his time, waiting until Arlen was relaxed and unsuspecting.

And it had worked. Arlen knew his face in that instant told Jardir much he would have preferred to keep secret. His thoughts offered up a dozen lies, but he shook them away. If they were to walk this road together, it must be as brothers, honest and with trust, or their task was doomed to failure before it even began.

'Had a map,' he said, knowing it would not end there.

'And where did you get this map?' Jardir pressed. 'You could not have found it out in the sands. Such a fragile thing would have long since crumbled away.'

Arlen took a deep breath, straightening his back, and met Jardir's eyes. 'Stole it from Sharik Hora.' Jardir's nod was calm, the act of a disappointed parent who already knows what his child has done.

But despite his posture, Arlen could smell his mounting anger. Anger no wise person would ignore. He readied himself, wondering if he could defeat Jardir in the light of day if it came to blows.

Just need to get the crown off him, he thought, knowing it sounded far simpler than it was. He'd rather climb a mountain without a rope.

'How did you accomplish this?' Jardir asked with that same tired tone. 'You could not have penetrated Sharik Hora alone.'

Arlen nodded. 'Had help.'

'Who?' Jardir pressed, but Arlen simply inclined his head.

'Ah,' Jardir said. 'Abban. He's been caught bribing *dama* many times, but I did not think even he could be so bold, or that he could have lied to me for so long without being discovered.'

'He ent stupid, Ahmann,' Arlen said. 'You'd have killed him, or worse, done some barbaric shit like cutting out his tongue. Don't you deny it. Wasn't his fault, anyway. He owed me a blood debt, and I wanted the map in payment.'

'That makes him no less accountable,' Jardir said.

Arlen shrugged. 'What's done is done, and he did the world a favour.'

'Did he?' Jardir asked. His calm façade dropped as he glared at Arlen, striding in till they were nose-to-nose. 'What if the spear was not meant to be found yet, Par'chin? Perhaps we were not ready for it, and you denied *inevera* by bringing it back before its time? What if we lose Sharak Ka over your and Abban's arrogance, Par'chin? What then?'

His voice grew in power as he went on, and for a moment

Arlen felt himself wilt under it. Stealing the scroll had never seemed right, but even now, he would do it again.

'Ay, maybe,' he agreed. 'And it's on me and Abban if it's so.'

He straightened, leaning back in and meeting Jardir's glare with one of his own. 'But maybe our best chance to win Sharak Ka was three hundred years ago, when humanity numbered millions, and your ripping *dama* kept the fighting wards from us by locking those maps up in a tower of superstition. Who bears the weight of arrogance then? What if *that* was what denied Everam's ripping plan?'

Jardir paused, losing a touch of his aggressive posture as he considered the question. Arlen knew the sign and stepped back quickly. He stood arms akimbo, offering neither aggression nor submission. 'If Everam's got a plan, he ent shared it with us.'

'The dice—' Jardir began.

'—are magic, and no denying,' Arlen cut him off. 'That don't make them divine. And they never told Inevera to have you stop me going to Anoch Sun. They just told you to use me when I got back.'

The anger further left Jardir's scent as he considered this new possibility. His old friend could be a fool over his faith, but he was an honest fool. He truly believed, leaving him forever hamstrung as he tried to reconcile the hypocrisies of the Evejah.

Arlen spread his hands. 'Got two choices here, Ahmann. Either we stand around arguing abstractions, or we fight Sharak Ka the best we can with what we've got and sort out who's right after we win.'

Jardir nodded. 'Then there is only one choice, son of Jeph.'

The days passed, and their tentative accord held. Jardir felt more in control of his magic than ever before, stunned at the breadth of power at his fingertips, and his previous narrow vision of it.

But for all their progress, Waning drew closer by the hour.

He and the Par'chin could run at great speed when the magic filled them, but even so, Anoch Sun was not close, and they still had to lay their traps.

'When will we leave for the lost city?' he asked one morning, as they waited to show the night's kill the sun.

'Tonight,' the Par'chin said. 'Lesson time's done.'

With those words, he melted away into mist. Jardir watched closely with his crownsight as he slipped down into one of the many paths that vented magic onto the surface of Ala. Everam's power of life, corrupted by Nie.

He was gone for but an instant, but when he rose back out of the path, the current of magic that came with him told Jardir he had travelled a long way, indeed.

In his hands, he carried two items: a cloak and a spear.

Jardir was reaching for the spear before the Par'chin had fully solidified. His hand passed through it at first grasp, but he snatched again, and took hold at last, pulling it from the Par'chin's hands.

He held the spear before him, feeling the thrum of its power, and knew it was the genuine Spear of Kaji. Without it, he had felt empty. A shell of himself. Now it was returned, and at last his heart eased.

We shall not be parted again, he promised.

'You'll be needing this, too.' Jardir looked up just as the Par'chin tossed Leesha Paper's Cloak of Unsight to him. His arm darted out to catch it before the edge touched the ground.

He eyed the Par'chin in annoyance. 'You insult Mistress Leesha by treating her wondrous cloak so disrespectfully.'

Leesha's gift did not have the hold over his fate the spear did, but he could not deny that the feel of the fine cloth, and the invisibility it gave him against even the most powerful *alagai*, made him feel their mad plan might have a chance.

'How will you hide, when the *alagai* come to Kaji's tomb?' he asked when the Par'chin gave no reply. 'Have you a cloak as well?'

'Don't need one,' the Par'chin said. 'I could trace the wards of unsight in the air, but even that's too much trouble.'

He held out his arms, wrists turned outward. There, on his forearms, were tattooed the wards of unsight.

The wards began to glow, even as the others on the Par'chin's skin remained dark. They became so bright Jardir lost sight of the individual symbols as the son of Jeph faded, much as when he became insubstantial – translucent and blurry. Jardir felt dizzied at the sight of him. Something urged him to look away, but he knew in his heart that if he did, he would not be able to find the Par'chin when he looked back, even if the man did not move.

A moment later, he returned to focus. The glow faded from the wards, and they became readable once more. Jardir's eyes danced over them, and his heart caught in his throat. Warding was like handwriting, and these were traced in the distinct looping script of Leesha Paper, embroidered in detail all over his cloak.

Normally it made his heart sing to see the art of his beloved's warding, but not here.

'Did Mistress Leesha ward your flesh?' He did not mean the question to come out as a growl, but it did. The idea of his intended touching the Par'chin's bare skin was unbearable.

To Jardir's relief, the Par'chin shook his head. 'Warded them myself, but they're her design, so I copied her style.' He stroked the symbols almost lovingly. 'Keeps a part of her with me.'

He wasn't telling all. His aura practically sang with it. Jardir probed deeper with his crownsight, and caught an image that burned his mind's eye. Leesha and the Par'chin naked in the mud, thrusting at each other like animals.

Jardir felt his heart thudding in his chest, pounding in his ears. Leesha and the Par'chin? Was it possible, or just some unfulfilled fantasy?

'You took her to the pillows,' he accused, watching the Par'chin's aura closely to read the response.

But the Par'chin's aura dimmed, the power Drawn beneath the surface. Jardir tried to probe, but his crownsight struck an invisible wall before it got to his *ajin'pal*.

'Just 'cause I let you read my surface aura now and then don't give you the right to break into my head,' the Par'chin said. 'Let's see how you like it.'

Jardir could feel the pull as the Par'chin Drew magic through him and absorbed it, Knowing him as intimately as a lover. He tried to stop the pull, the Par'chin caught him unaware, and by the time he could raise his defences, it was done.

Jardir pointed the spear at him. 'I have killed men for less insult, Par'chin.'

'Then you're lucky I'm more civilized,' the Par'chin said, ''cause the first insult was yours.'

Jardir tightened his lips, but he let it go. 'If you have been with my intended, I have a right to know.'

'She ent your intended, Ahmann,' the Par'chin said. 'Heard her tell it to your face on the cliff. She'll be corespawned before she becomes your fifteenth wife, or even your First.'

The Par'chin was mocking him. 'If you heard those private words, Par'chin, then you know she carries my child. If you think for a moment you have a claim to her . . .'

The Par'chin shrugged. 'Ay, she's a fine woman and I shined on her a bit. Kissed her a couple times, and once, something more.'

Jardir's grip tightened on the spear.

'But she ent mine,' the Par'chin said. 'Never was. And she ent yours, either, Ahmann. Baby or no. If you can't get that, you'll never have a chance.'

'So you no longer desire her?' Jardir asked incredulously. 'Impossible. She shines like the sun.'

There was a sound of galloping hooves, and the Par'chin smiled, turning to watch his *Jiwah Ka* riding hard in the predawn light. She rode bareback on an enormous mare, leading four similarly huge horses. Their hooves, bright with magic, ate the distance at more than twice the speed of a Krasian racer.

'Got my own sun, Ahmann,' the Par'chin said. 'Two is asking to be burned.'

He pointed to Jardir as he strode out to meet his wife. 'You already got enough sun to turn the green lands into another desert. Think on that.'

Renna flew from the saddle, and Arlen caught her in his arms, returning her kiss. He concentrated, activating the wards of silence on his shoulders. Jardir would see the magic and know they were masking their words, but Arlen didn't think he would say anything. A man was entitled to private words with his wife.

'All well in the Hollow?' he asked.

Renna saw the magic, too, and kept her face buried in his chest as she spoke to hide the movement of her lips. 'Well as can be expected. Hope you're right about this being a light moon. They ent ready for much more, especially without us.'

'Trust me, Ren,' Arlen said.

Renna thrust her chin at Arlen, but he could tell she was gesturing past him, at Jardir. 'You tell him yet?'

Arlen shook his head. 'Was waiting for you to come back. Tell him soon as the sun comes up.'

'Might regret giving him the spear back first,' Renna said.

Arlen shrugged and gave her a smile. 'This ent *Domin Sharum* with a bunch of rules on fighting fair. Got Renna Bales at my back if things go sour, don't I?'

Renna kissed him. 'Always.'

Jardir averted his eyes, giving the Par'chin and his *jiwah* privacy in their greeting. Her arrival with the horses meant their trip to face the *alagai* princes was nigh, and Jardir was eager for the test, but there was disappointment, as well. Alone, he and the Par'chin had begun to find accord at last. The addition of his unpredictable *Jiwah Ka* could upset that precarious balance.

The sun crested the horizon at last, and Jardir breathed

deeply, falling into his morning meditation as the bodies of the *alagai* began to smoke and burn. Everam always returned things to balance. He must keep faith in *inevera*.

When the flames had died down, they took the horses to the stable beside the hidden tower. Up close, the animals were enormous, the size of camels. The wild mustang that roamed the green lands had grown powerful in their nightly struggle with the *alagai*. His *Sharum* had captured and managed to train hundreds of them, but these were magnificent specimens, even so.

The black stallion that nuzzled the Par'chin's hand, its body covered in warded armour and its head adorned with a pair of metal horns that could punch through a rock demon, could only be his famed horse Twilight Dancer. His *jiwah*'s piebald mare was almost of a size with it, wards painted on its spots and cut into its hooves. A simple leather girth wrapped its belly to help her keep her seat.

There were two other stallions and a mare, all of them with warded saddles and hooves. Powerful beasts – it was surprising even Twilight Dancer could keep them all in line. They stamped and pranced, but followed the lead into the stalls.

'Why are there five horses, if there are only three of us?' he demanded. 'Who else have you taken upon yourself to invite to undertake this sacred journey, Par'chin? You claim to need my help, but you keep me blind to your plans.'

'Plan was for it to be the three of us, Ahmann, but it hit a snag. Hoping you'll help me get it unstuck.'

Jardir looked at him curiously. The Par'chin sighed and nodded to the back of the stable. 'Come with me.'

He lifted an old rug out of the way, shaking off a camouflage of dust and hay. Underneath was a pull-ring to a trapdoor. He lifted the trap and descended into the darkness below. Jardir followed warily, aware that the Par'chin's *jiwah* followed behind. Jardir did not fear her, but the strength of her aura told him she was powerful. Enough to give the Par'chin a telling advantage should they come to blows.

His crownsight returned as they slipped back into darkness, but the Par'chin's wards began to glow anyway, sending the shadows fleeing as he led them to a heavy door, banded with steel and etched with powerful wards.

The Par'chin opened the door, casting light on the man and woman, clad only in their bidos, imprisoned within.

Shanjat and Shanvah looked up from their embrace, squinting in the sudden light.

8

The True Warrior
333 AR Autumn

'Deliverer!' Shanjat and Shanvah leapt to their feet, moving to stand apart. Without veil or robe, there was nothing to hide the blush of their skin or the guilty looks on their faces.

Indeed, their auras matched the look, shame and embarrassment palpable. Jardir assessed the situation, and his eyes darkened. Even if Shanvah had lain with him willingly, she was Shanjat's daughter, and Jardir's niece. Whether his spirit was penitent or not, Jardir would have no choice but to sentence his old friend to death.

He considered the thought grimly. Shanjat had served him loyally since the two of them were children in *sharaj*, and proven a good husband for his sister Hoshvah. More, Jardir needed Shanjat and the *Sharum* he commanded at his side when the First War began in full. Perhaps he could commute the sentence until after Sharak Ka. Give his loyal servant a chance to die on *alagai* talons and bring that his honour with him on the lonely path before he stood before Everam to be judged.

'Forgive us, Deliverer, we have failed you!' Shanjat cried before Jardir could utter a word. He and Shanvah fell to their knees, pressing hands and foreheads to the dirt floor. 'I swear by Everam we tried every method in our power to escape and continue our search for you, but the Par'chin—'

'—is using *hora* magic to strengthen our cell,' Shanvah cut in. Her fingernails were raw and dirty. In wardsight, Jardir could see the scratches where she and her father had tested every inch of their prison.

He looked around the room, seeing no robes or veils. Of course the Par'chin would have stripped and searched them before imprisoning them. Even he was not such a fool as to leave them tools to escape. The only other thing in the room was a covered chamber pot, too small and fragile to make an effective weapon.

Suddenly Jardir was the one to feel ashamed. Was the caress of parent and child, trapped in a lightless cell, a crime? He had been ready to assume the worst, to sentence one of his oldest friends to death, when his only guilt stemmed from the fear they had failed in their duty to him.

'Always quick to turn on a friend,' the Par'chin murmured, and Jardir gritted his teeth.

'Rise in honour, brother, niece,' he said. 'The Par'chin is beyond your power. There is no shame in defeat at his hands.'

Both stayed on their knees. When Shanjat hesitated, Shanvah spoke in his place. 'It was not the Par'chin who captured us, Deliverer.'

Most fathers would have been enraged at the face lost having their daughter speak for them before the Deliverer, but Shanjat only looked at her with gratitude, and a pride Jardir had not seen him show either of his sons.

'Was me,' the Par'chin's *jiwah* said. Jardir turned a sceptical eye on her. He knew the woman was formidable, but Shanjat and his daughter were *kai'Sharum*, Krasian warrior elite.

Shanvah raised her eyes to give the Par'chin's *jiwah* an appraising look. 'Her *sharusahk* is pathetic, Deliverer. A child could defeat her. But her magic is strong. Even with our night strength, she was beyond us. Our shields and spears lay broken.'

The words sent anguish through Shanvah's aura. Jardir Drew through her as the Par'chin had taught him, seeing a vision around her. Inevera commanding Shanvah to seek the missing

Deliverer. Her first assignment, one of such immense honour she could barely contain her pride. A chance to show the Deliverer and Damajah her worth.

And she had failed. Utterly.

Another vision arose, her defeat at the hands of the Par'chin's *jiwah*.

'The Par'chin brought me down in the same way, niece,' he said. 'You have been trained well, but you would be unwise to challenge his *Jiwah Ka* . . .'—he met Renna's eyes—'. . . in the night. In day, she will be more vulnerable to *sharusahk*, and no match for you.'

The Par'chin's *jiwah* glared at him. Jardir felt the weight of auras shift as face in the room was restored to balance. Shanvah looked at Renna in a new way. A predator's appraisal.

Jardir waved for his warriors to rise and turned angrily to face the Par'chin. 'If my brother-in-law and niece have been mistreated . . .'

'They haven't.' The Par'chin whisked a hand. 'Ask 'em yourself.'

'We have not, Deliverer,' Shanjat said as Jardir looked back to him. 'We have been given food, water, and rest after days spent tracking you. The Par'chin treated the wounds we suffered when his *Jiwah Ka* subdued us.'

He looked at his daughter, and his aura shone with love. 'And I do not regret having time to know my daughter.'

Jardir could well understand. He knew little about his own daughters, taken into the Dama'ting Palace when they were very young. They had been locked in the room as strangers, but trapped alone in the dark, father and daughter had found each other again.

'Thought a few days to reflect might do 'em some good,' the Par'chin said.

'And now?' Jardir said. 'I will not allow you to shame them with further imprisonment, Par'chin.'

'Wouldn't have shown 'em to you, I'd meant to keep 'em locked up,' the Par'chin said. 'We're leaving at dusk, and won't be around to feed 'em and empty the chamber pot. Taking 'em with us.'

Jardir shook his head. 'They are not prepared for the path we must walk, Par'chin. Set them free. One way or another, our task will be done before they find their way back to Everam's Bounty.'

The Par'chin shook his head.

Jardir eyed him dangerously. 'And if I free them anyway? What will you do then?'

'I'll be done trusting that you put Sharak Ka first,' the Par'chin replied. 'Mind demons can eat a person's memories like a snack. Leave 'em not even knowing anything happened. They can plant commands that hold force in daylight. There could be spies anywhere, Ahmann, and we only get one throw at this. The less people know we're still alive, the better.'

'Shar'Dama Ka!' The shout shocked Jardir. When was the last time Shanjat had spoken out of turn? He turned to his old friend, who bowed deeply. 'If you walk a dangerous path, Deliverer, it is our duty to guard you with our lives.'

Shanvah nodded. 'The Damajah bade us not return without you. She will not forgive us if we abandon you in your time of need.'

'They can help us in Anoch Sun, if they have the courage,' the Par'chin said. 'Shouldn't underestimate the princes. Your power will be limited while you maintain the field. Even with Renna, we'll be overmatched.'

'If two warriors might shift the balance, why not bring an army?' Jardir asked.

'And hide them where?' the Par'chin asked. 'I can draw wards of unsight in the air around two, but more will alert the minds to our presence, and all will be for naught.'

Jardir sighed. He could not deny the comfort the two gave him, balancing the shift in power when the Par'chin's *jiwah* arrived. 'Very well.'

173

'We'll make the lost city in five days if we trample demons to charge the horses to speed,' the Par'chin said as they packed supplies, laying in food and water for the desert crossing. There would be little if anything to replenish their stores once they reached the clay flats. 'Four if we really push.'

'That does not give us much time to prepare before Waning, Par'chin,' Jardir said.

The Par'chin shrugged. 'Don't want any sign we been there, so the less the better. Ent much to do once we get there save wait in any event. Better off readying ourselves than the tomb.'

'Shanjat and Shanvah will need new spears and shields,' Jardir said.

'Got a cache of weapons we can raid out in the desert,' the Par'chin said. 'Meantime, I can stain their skin with blackstem wards, and we can all work on our *gaisahk* together.'

'Wise,' Jardir said. 'I know my warriors' skill, but I have not seen your *jiwah* fight.'

'Started teaching her a few months ago,' the Par'chin said. 'She learns fast.'

Jardir nodded patiently, and called the five of them to practise while the sun was still high. The Par'chin and his *jiwah* produced brushes and painted impact wards on Shanjat's and Shanvah's fists, elbows, and feet. They cut the sleeves from their returned robes to bare the symbols to the air.

As expected, his warriors took quickly to *gaisahk*, but the Par'chin's *jiwah* had forms even a novice could best. Shanvah had not been unfair in her assessment. If anything, she had been kind.

'You continue to place your feet wrong,' Jardir told her as she finished a *sharukin*. He had already corrected her stance a dozen times, but still she failed to give it her full attention.

'What's the difference?' she asked. 'Would've punched right through a demon's face with that move.'

'The difference, fool, is that if there had been another at its back, you would have been off balance,' Jardir snapped. '*Alagai'sharak* is no game, where the loser can play another day.'

'Know that,' Renna said. The words were sullen, but he believed them. She was trying to place her feet right, but the move was beyond her. It was not fair of him to expect her to master in days what his warriors practised their whole lives, but they did not have time to coddle her.

'Shanvah will tutor you each day when we stop under the sun to rest and water the horses,' he ordered.

'What?!' both women exclaimed at once.

Jardir looked to his niece. 'She is not to be harmed. You must put aside any emotion over your imprisonment.'

Shanvah embraced her emotion and crossed her fists, bowing. 'Your will, Deliverer.'

'Goes double for you, Ren,' the Par'chin said. 'You need these lessons, but don't forget you're a lot stronger'n her, and we need you both in one piece come new moon. You're learnin', not fightin'.'

Renna spat in the dust. 'Won't break anything can't heal.'

The two moved off to begin the lesson, and the Par'chin shook his head. 'Gonna regret sayin' that, isn't she?'

'More than you know, Par'chin,' Jardir said. 'But I have seen the pride in her aura. All warriors must understand their own weakness if they are to overcome it.' He looked at the departing women. 'Shanvah will show her, delivering the same lesson your *jiwah* did to her.'

The Par'chin laughed. 'Maybe that makes *her* the Deliverer, then.'

Hours later, Arlen paced the stable, watching the sun falling in the sky. In a few hours, they would be off, and he was anxious to begin. They were gambling the fate of everyone in the world on his plan.

What if I'm wrong? he wondered. *Just some dumb Bales from Tibbet's Brook going to poke the hive with a stick, thinking I'm so much smarter than the hornets.*

But in his heart, he knew this was the only way. The people they were leaving behind were strong now. They would hold. They had to. Waiting behind the wards for each successive new moon was a losing strategy. The demons had the advantage in numbers, and people couldn't ward the entire world. Cities built on greatwards might one day reach critical mass, but only with a head start.

There was a creak of floorboards, and Renna appeared, stealing him from his reverie. He was relieved until he took a look at her. She was bruised and bloody, with a swollen eye. Tears streaked the blood on her face, and she cradled her broken right arm with her left.

'You okay, Ren?' he asked.

Renna paused, surprised to see him. No doubt she had come to the stable to be alone. She gave a tired shrug, brushing past him as she went into Promise's stall. She put her back to the divider and slid down to the floor. Promise nickered and nuzzled her cheek as she pulled the arm straight with a hiss, holding it in place while she waited for the magic in her blood to knit it back together.

Arlen nodded, leaving her in privacy. Inside the tower, he saw Shanvah laughing with her father as they prepared supper. The girl was seven years Renna's junior and didn't have Ren's ability to heal, but there wasn't a mark on her. She looked fresh as sunrise.

Oh, Ren. He shook his head. Jardir was right. This was a lesson Renna sorely needed. One Arlen had tried – and failed – to teach her himself. She liked being strong enough to bully folk a little too much for anyone's good. Considering what she'd been through it wasn't surprising, but . . .

Nie does not care about a warrior's problems, he heard Jardir say.

But there was a difference between understanding the need for Renna to learn a little humility, and looking at his love, his wife, bloody and beaten. The only thing stopping him from setting Shanvah straight about the difference between lessons and fighting was the fact he knew Renna wouldn't want him to.

Night, she'd never forgive him.

You weren't any different, your first time in Krasia, he thought to himself. Ragen had taught him to fight – he'd thought as well as any man could. Then he met the Krasian drillmasters.

Arlen hadn't wanted help, either. The Krasians would never have respected him if he'd asked for it, and it wasn't any different with Renna. She would win Shanvah's respect, given time.

That night, when they rode down a reap of field demons on the road to Anoch Sun, Renna's *sharusahk* was noticeably better. She had healed good as new after a few hours' rest, but strode into the fray more cautiously now. She lost none of her savagery when the time came to strike, but she waited for that time, now, and thought more than one move in advance.

He feared there would be another confrontation with Shanvah once Ren's blood was up and she had her full night strength, but the two women kept their distance as they fought.

Only once did their paths cross. Shanvah braced herself for three field demons charging her when Renna lifted a hand and drew quick wards in the air. The demons burst into flame, burning away to ashes before they could reach the *Sharum'ting*.

Satisfaction was palpable on Renna's aura as she turned away without waiting for a response. Shanvah could likely have taken the demons herself, but it was a strong reminder that her advantage was temporal. In the night, Renna Bales had powers she could not hope to match.

The next afternoon Renna still returned bruised and bloodied after their lesson, but she had a smirk on her face.

It was a start.

The Par'chin led them down cool stone steps, away from the desert heat. The beating sun was a familiar trial, but not one

Jardir had missed. He better understood now why Everam had sent his people there to be tested and made hard. Already, the temperate clime and abundant resources of the green lands were having a softening effect on his people.

Sharak Ka had best come soon, he thought, but it was a fool's wish. They needed time most of all. The Northern dukes would not kneel before him without a fight. It would be a decade at least to unite the green lands into any semblance of unity. And without unity, they had no hope of winning the First War.

'Take what you like,' the Par'chin said to Shanjat and Shanvah when they reached the bottom of the steps, 'but don't weigh yourselves too much. Ent gonna stand and fight once we've got what we're after. Gonna run like all the Core's after us.'

The words were casual, but as they slipped into darkness he drew light wards in the air, and the warriors stood transfixed, staring at the arsenal before them. Portable warding circles, bows of various sorts, dozens of spears and shields, hundreds of arrows and bolts. Piles of other weapons – hammers, axes, picks, and knives. Anything the Par'chin could find, it seemed. All intricately warded in his unmistakable hand.

Jardir expected the warriors to rush in, but they hesitated, like *khaffit* taken into a *Damaji's* treasure room and told they could take any prize they wished. What to choose from the vast riches before them? And, they both glanced at the Par'chin, would there be a hidden price?

'Go,' Jardir bade them. 'Explore. Find the weapons that best fit your hands. We will not leave until after sunset. You have several hours. Use them well. The fate of all mankind may ride on your choices.'

The warriors nodded, moving reverently into the room. Hesitantly at first, then with more confidence, they began to lift weapons, testing their weight and balance. Shanjat spun a spear through an intricate set of *sharukin* while Shanvah did the same with every shield until she found one to her liking.

'Where are the other rooms?' Jardir asked the Par'chin. 'I would rest and refresh myself before our journey continues.'

The Par'chin shrugged. 'Just got the one. Wasn't sleeping much back when I used to frequent this place. 'Fraid there's no fancy pillow chambers for Your Grace.' He pointed to a workbench, beside which lay a bundle of rags. It had been many years since Jardir had been in *sharaj*, but he knew a bedroll when he saw one.

A memory flashed in his mind – curled with Abban on a hard, dirty floor, sharing a thin blanket that didn't even cover them. Jardir remembered the bitter choice between cold shoulders and cold feet. He'd been fortunate to have Abban, that they might pool their warmth. Other boys were forced to sleep alone, or to accept the price older boys often demanded in exchange for a partner. Jardir had fallen asleep shivering, listening to their muffled grunts.

How long since he last slept in such squalor? The Par'chin had done it for years, living in isolation from all other men, focused only on his sacred tasks, making weapons to face the *alagai* in the day, and killing them in the night.

Not all greenlanders are soft, he reminded himself.

'I can try to hunt up a goose, if you need a feather pillow,' Renna offered when he had been silent a while, staring at the bedroll. The Par'chin laughed.

Insolent. Jardir embraced the insult, swallowing a barbed retort. He ignored the woman, turning to meet the Par'chin's eye. 'I live in palaces because they are my due, Par'chin, but as Kaji tells us in the Evejah, *The true warrior—*'

'*—need only bread, water, and his spear,*' the Par'chin finished. He shrugged. 'Guess I ent a true warrior, then. Always liked a blanket.'

Jardir laughed, breaking much of the tension in the room. The others relaxed visibly. 'I too, Par'chin. If I live to complete the Ahmanjah, I will add a blanket to the proverb.'

He went to the cool stairwell, putting his back to the side of the stairs and sliding to the ground. They had been riding for three days, resting only when the animals reached the very limits of their endurance. Magic kept them running hard through the night, but in the day, they were as mortal as any. Even Jardir needed to close his eyes for an hour or two.

But sleep was elusive. His mind spun, trying to comprehend what they were about to attempt. The Par'chin's plan was bold and larger than life, but it lacked detail. As with any battle, the opening blows might be planned, and an exit readied, but beyond that . . . *inevera*.

Inevera. He could use her advice now. He would even have welcomed her accursed dice. Was she all right? Had she installed Ashan as Andrah as they had agreed if he should fall? Or had the *Damaji* already killed her and all his sons? Or had Jayan killed Asome and seized power? Were his people in the midst of civil war even now?

He watched his warriors while he wondered after the fate of everyone he loved. Perhaps Shanjat and Shanvah were safer with him after all.

They had already chosen spears, shields, and knives, familiar weapons they could use like extensions of their arms. Now they were inspecting the bows curiously.

Ranged weapons were not considered dishonourable in Krasia, exactly, but shooting an *alagai* from a distance was a lesser glory by far than facing one at spear's length, and before the fighting wards were returned bows could not harm the demons in any event. They had fallen from use, only the bare rudiments part of a warrior's training. A single tribe, the Mehnding, had kept the practice, manning the slings and scorpions on the walls of the Desert Spear, and now specializing in killing from afar with their short bows, often from horseback.

But Shanjat and Shanvah were Kaji, not Mehnding, and the long Northern bows had little in common with their southern cousins. They held the weapons uncomfortably. So much that even the Par'chin noticed. He took a quiver of arrows, tossing it to Shanjat.

'Shoot me,' he commanded, moving to stand at the far side of the room.

Shanjat nocked an arrow, but glanced at Jardir.

'Do as he says,' Jardir said, whisking a hand. It was doubtful an arrow could do the Par'chin any lasting damage even if it struck, and looking at Shanjat's tense grip on the weapon, a hit seemed unlikely.

Shanjat loosed, and the arrow missed the Par'chin by more than a foot.

'I'm standing still, warrior,' the Par'chin called. 'The *alagai* will not be so thoughtful.'

Shanjat held his hand out, and his daughter slapped another arrow into it.

'Stop standing there and ripping shoot me!' The Par'chin slapped the large ward at the centre of his chest. Again Shanjat loosed, this time missing by inches.

'Come on!' the Par'chin cried. 'A pig-eating son of a *khaffit* can shoot better than that!'

Shanjat growled, pulling another arrow to his cheek. He had the weapon's measure now, and his next shot would have taken the Par'chin in the shoulder, had he not caught the arrow in midair the way a quick man might snatch a horsefly.

'Pathetic,' the Par'chin growled, holding up the arrow. He turned to look at Shanvah. 'Your turn.'

No sooner had he spoken than Shanvah had her bow raised, firing. Jardir had not even known she was holding it.

The shot was true, and the Par'chin gasped, dematerializing just in time to evade the missile. It struck behind him, embedding in the wall.

Jardir was impressed. Even he was a novice with the bow, but Shanvah and her spear sisters were trained by Enkido, whose name was legend in the Maze before he was even born.

'Better,' the Par'chin admitted as he solidified. 'But you shoot straight, like you've got a short bow. Fine in close, but you'll have more power and range if you arc your shots.'

'I'll teach her,' the Par'chin's *jiwah* said. Jardir expected Shanvah to protest, but she only nodded.

'As for you . . .' the Par'chin said, turning back to Shanjat.

Shanjat threw the bow to the ground. 'I do not need this coward's weapon. My spear will suffice.'

'Reckon it'll come down to spears and fists before the end,' the Par'chin agreed, 'but there's more at stake here than your personal glory, Shanjat. You need to be able to shoot if you're to protect your master.'

'Am I to master this weapon in a day?' Shanjat asked. 'I have my pride, Par'chin, but not so much as that.'

'Don't need to.' The Par'chin lifted one of the cross-shaped crank bows the Northern women favoured. It had a wooden stock, shod with steel like the bow and firing mechanism. The 'string' was a weave of thin wire.

Shanjat, too, recognized the device. 'A woman's weapon? Shall I dance in veils for the *alagai* next?'

The Par'chin ignored him, taking a heavy shield, warded steel riveted onto a thick wood frame, and set it against the wall. He moved across the room to stand by Shanjat. With two fingers he tugged the thick bowstring back until it clicked in place, fitting a bolt.

'Like this,' he said, bracing the weapon against his shoulder and bringing it level with the floor, sighting down its length. He handed the bow to Shanjat, who held it as he had been shown.

'Finger off the trigger until you're ready to shoot,' the Par'chin said. 'Put your target between the lines at the end, keep steady, and squeeze.'

KA-CHUNG! The bow recoiled, surprising Shanjat enough that he took a step back.

'Missed,' he said. There was shame in his aura, but his face was grim as he moved to hand the weapon back.

'Did you?' the Par'chin asked.

Shanvah was across the room in an instant, lifting the shield to inspect it. All could see the finger she poked clear through from back to front. 'A clean hole.' She looked behind her, then stepped away so the others could see the bolt, embedded in the rock wall.

'Everam's beard,' Shanjat said, looking at the weapon with new respect. He tried to draw the string back as the Par'chin had, but strong as he was, it was beyond him.

'Crank it.' The Par'chin pointed to the mechanism.

Shanjat turned the crank, growing frustration on his face. At last it clicked into place and he looked up. 'I could have thrown three spears in that time, Par'chin.'

The Par'chin nodded. 'And then you would be out of spears. Don't worry over the draw. With night strength you won't need the crank.'

Shanjat nodded, but he selected three light throwing spears in addition to the bow and quarrels.

'Sleep while you can,' Jardir bade. 'We'll be in Anoch Sun before dawn, with only two days to prepare.' Immediately, Shanjat and Shanvah found a space by the wall to curl up. Jardir closed his eyes.

9

Anoch Sun

333 AR Autumn

As the sun rose, Arlen looked out over the lost city of Anoch Sun with a heavy heart. The Krasians had been reckless in their looting. When Arlen was living in the ruins seeking the secrets of demon fighting, he had been careful to preserve the place, digging carefully, leaving everything intact. The only relics he removed were weapons and armour, that he might study their wards. He had returned most of the items once he learned their secrets.

The Krasians had given no such consideration to preserving their antiquity. The city now looked like a crop field after a swarm of locusts and an army of voles. Massive piles of dirt and sand everywhere, shattered stone that had stood strong for thousands of years. The land was dotted with holes where roofs had been broken into for easier access to underground chambers, exposing them to the elements for the first time in millennia.

Only the great burial chambers were still intact. The Krasians had taken everything else of value, but even they baulked at moving the sarcophagi and disturbing the rest of their sacred ancestors.

'And you were ready to kill me for taking one spear,' he muttered.

'It wasn't yours to take, Par'chin,' Jardir replied. 'It is a place of *my* people. Krasians, not greenlanders.'

Arlen spat over the side of his horse. 'Wern't so worried about cultural rights when you sacked Fort Rizon.'

'That was conquest, not grave looting,' Jardir said.

'So robbing living folk you have to beat and kill is more honourable than ones been dead thousands of years?' Arlen asked.

'The dead cannot defend themselves, Par'chin,' Jardir said.

'And yet you destroyed the resting place of your ancestors,' Arlen said. 'Night, your logic just whirls around like a dust devil, doesn't it?'

'I had a hundred thousand people to feed, and nothing here to sustain them,' Jardir said. He was keeping his outward calm, but his words were beginning to tighten. 'We had to work fast. There was no time to peel the layers of the city back with brushes and hand tools.'

He looked curiously at Arlen. 'How did you manage it, Par'chin? There is nothing to eat here, and without baggage, you cannot have carried much from the Oasis of Dawn.'

Arlen was thankful his aura was hidden in the morning sun. The question cut close to one of the few secrets he was not yet willing to share with Jardir. Likely he never would. He had eaten demon meat to sustain himself in the weeks he spent in Anoch Sun, something he knew the Krasians would never understand, despite the power it brought.

'Went out and brought back supplies,' Arlen said. It wasn't a lie, precisely.

He shook his head to clear it. There was nothing to be gained, continuing to bicker. They needed to work together, now more than ever. He glanced at Shanjat and Shanvah to find their predatory eyes locked on him and Renna, as if awaiting Jardir's command to kill them while the sun kept their full powers at bay.

But Jardir gave no such command. For better or worse, they were allies.

'Just as well you took anything of value,' Arlen said, 'now that the demons know of it. That's my fault, I'll admit. Let them get in my head.'

'*Inevera*,' Jardir said. 'It may be your failing is what saves us. Just this once, we know where our enemy will strike. Just this once, we have advantage. We *must* seize it.'

'First thing we need to do is find a spot near the tomb to stake the horses,' Arlen said. 'We'll paint wards of unsight around the place. Might need to ride out of here in a hurry.'

'And then what?' Jardir asked.

'We go to Kaji's tomb and dig a secret exit,' he said. 'Then we find places to hide, and we wait.'

'And then?' Jardir asked.

Arlen blew out a breath. *Core if I know.*

'Bit to the left,' Renna said, looking down the shaft of the arrow Shanvah pointed to the sky. 'Wind's stronger that high. Got to account for it.'

She stood behind the younger woman, raised on the balls of her feet to put her sight in line with Shanvah's. Renna had never thought herself short, but even the average Krasian was tall by Tibbet's Brook standards. Her heel was only a little off the ground, but she resented that inch.

Shanvah accepted the correction with a nod, and loosed. Her arrow arced high over the dunes, then came down hard on the sand-filled bag they were using as a target. It wasn't a perfect shot, but from such distance it was impressive nonetheless.

'How did you learn this?' Shanvah asked, lowering her bow. There was more respect in her tone now, though Renna was not fool enough to think them friends. 'By your own words, you were no warrior until recently, but you handle that weapon too comfortably for the Par'chin to have been your only teacher.'

Renna shook her head. 'My da taught me. Wern't always

enough food to go around back home. Everyone who liked eatin' needed to go out and hunt sometimes.'

Shanvah nodded. 'Among my people, women were not allowed to even touch weapons until recently. You are fortunate to have had such a father. What was his name?'

'Harl.' Renna spat. 'But wern't no fortune in him as a da.'

'In Krasia, we carry the honour of our fathers, daughter of Harl,' Shanvah said. 'The pride of their victories, and the shame of their failures.'

'Got a lot to make up for, then,' Renna said.

'If we succeed tonight,' Shanvah said, 'you will have cleaned the slate and dipped it in gold, even if your father is Alagai Ka himself.'

'Far as me and my sisters went, might as well have been.' Renna felt a throb in her temple. Thoughts of her father, of that corespawned farm, always made her angry. Less the memories themselves than the reminder they brought. The reminder of the old Renna. Weak. Scared. Useless. Sometimes she wished that part of her was a limb she could cut away and cast off forever.

Shanvah was staring at her. Why were she and Shanvah sharing stories like square girls, anyway? They might need to fight the same side, but neither trusted the other, and Renna saw no reason for that to change.

'You said you faced one of them,' Shanvah said. 'An *alagai* prince.'

As if talk of Harl's farm hadn't been personal enough. Renna remembered the horror, the violation, as the demon had taken over her mind, burrowing deep and nestling in like a tomato bug. It was the last thing she wanted to talk about, but this, Shanvah had a right to know. Soon she would be face-to-face with them.

'Ay,' Renna said. 'Keep your mind wards sharp that night. Paint 'em right on your brow. Don't trust a headband. They get inside your mind, swallowing everything that makes you . . . you. Swallow it, and then spit out just the parts that cut the ones you love.'

Shanvah nodded. 'But you killed it.'

Renna bared her teeth, magic boiling in her blood at the memory. 'Arlen killed it. I put my knife right through its ripping back, and it kept fighting.'

'How is my bow supposed to make a difference against such a creature?' Shanvah asked.

Renna shrugged. 'Honest word? Probably won't. Against a mind demon, you strike a killing blow, or you might as well not have struck at all. Wouldn't trust that to a bow.'

She looked at Shanvah. 'But the minds are for Arlen and Jardir to worry about.' Shanvah stiffened at the informal reference to her uncle, but she kept her mouth closed. 'Up to us to keep their guards away while it's done,' Renna went on. 'Minds can call other demons from miles around, and make 'em fight smart.'

Shanvah nodded. 'So I have been told.'

'You heard about their bodyguards?' Renna asked. 'The mimics?'

'Only whispers,' Shanvah said.

'Smarter'n other corelings,' Renna said. 'Able to lead and summon lesser demons, but that ent the worst of it.'

'Shapeshifters,' Shanvah whispered, as much a question as a statement.

Renna nodded. 'Turn into anything they can think of. One second you're fighting the biggest damn rock demon you ever saw, and a second later it's got tentacles, or wings. Think you got a grip and suddenly it's a snake. Think you've got help coming, but in the blink of an eye it looks just like you, and your friends don't know who to shoot.'

Shanvah gave no sign, but a trickle of fear came into her scent, and that was good. She needed to know what was coming and respect it, if she was going to live.

'Last one I fought killed over two dozen men before we brought it down,' Renna said. 'Cut through a unit of *dal'Sharum* like a nightwolf in a henhouse. Killed half a dozen, along with Drillmaster Kaval and Enkido. And more Cutters than I can remember. Hadn't been for Rojer and . . .'

She broke off, looking at Shanvah's wide eyes. The young woman had stopped listening, staring at her openmouthed. Her scent changed dramatically, filling with mounting horror and grief as tears began to well in her eyes. It was more emotion than Renna had ever seen her show.

'What'd I say?' Renna asked.

Shanvah looked at her silently for a long time, her mouth moving slowly, as if needing to limber before forming words.

'Master Enkido is dead?' she asked.

Renna nodded, and Shanvah wailed. It went on till her breath caught, and she coughed out a sob.

She fumbled desperately at a pouch on her belt even as she wept, producing a tiny glass vial that slipped from her shaking fingers.

Renna caught the vial before it hit the ground, holding it out to her, but Shanvah made no move to take it. 'Please,' she begged. 'Catch them before they are lost.'

Renna looked at her curiously. 'Catch what?'

'My tears!' she wailed.

It seemed a bizarre request, but Renna had seen the Krasian women doing this when they came for their dead after new moon. She unstoppered the vial, looking at its wide rim, the edge almost sharp, ideal for scraping a streaking tear from a cheek. She stepped close, catching one drop just before it fell, and then tracing its path back up with the vial's edge.

Shanvah's sobbing only increased, as if she were throwing herself intentionally into the emotion for this sole purpose. Fast as she was, Renna was hard-pressed to keep up. Shanvah filled two bottles before she was done.

'What happened to the demon?' Shanvah asked, when it was over.

'We killed it,' Renna said.

'You're sure?' Shanvah pressed, leaning forward to grip her arm.

'Cut its head off myself,' Renna said.

Shanvah slumped back, looking as defeated as Renna had

ever seen her, and she had beaten the woman unconscious just weeks earlier.

'Thank you,' Shanvah said.

Renna nodded, deciding it was best not to mention that she, too, had fought Enkido when they first met.

They reached Anoch Sun by the first morning of Waning. Arlen led them down to Kaji's tomb, and they set to work preparing the chamber.

In the darkness beneath the sands, Anoch Sun was a place of strong magic, ancient and deep. It was embedded in every speck of dust, leached from the Core with powerful wards over thousands of years. Arlen reached tendrils of his own magic to join with it, and immediately felt the city come to life, like an extension of his own body. It hummed with power, lending him strength for the trials to come.

Jardir led a prayer to Everam, and Arlen swallowed his cynicism long enough to bow his head and be polite. He could see the honest belief in the auras of the Krasians, and the strength it gave them.

Even Renna shone with belief, in spite of all that had been done to her in the name of the Canon.

Night, wish I could share it. The others in the room were convinced they were marching in the Creator's great plan. Arlen alone understood they were making things up as they went along.

'That's enough,' he said at last, when it seemed the chanting would go on forever and he could stand it no more. 'Night's falling. Take your places, and no more noise.'

Jardir looked at him with irritation. The sun had not yet set. Still, he nodded. This was no time for discord. 'The Par'chin speaks wisely.'

Shanjat and Shanvah had made an ambush pocket off to one side, cut from the wall, which Arlen had etched with wards of camouflage. The wall would appear unbroken to demon eyes.

Renna drew her Cloak of Unsight about herself and went to stand ready to one side of the small doorway into the tomb. Arlen moved to stand opposite her, cutting himself off from the magic of Anoch Sun, lest the coreling princes sense his presence.

The next hour was the longest of his life. As the minutes ticked by, he almost wished they could go back to prayers.

Night fell, but attack did not come right away. Arlen knew it was a risk, but after an hour he could not stand it, and opened himself up to the magic of Anoch Sun, reaching out his senses for sign of the enemy.

They were out there. Night, there were thousands of them.

The mind demons had been in his head. They knew the layout of the city, and exactly where the tomb of Kaji lay.

But they were in no hurry. They had three days to desecrate and destroy the city, and obviously meant to savour the task. The ground shook as the demons began to tear down the city.

All night Arlen and the others waited, silent and still, the deep, booming vibrations of the corelings' assault their only company. But in the end, the demons never came anywhere near them.

They were saving Kaji for last.

Dawn came to find everyone tense and exhausted, massaging sore muscles as they looked questioningly at Arlen.

'You promised they would come, Par'chin,' Jardir growled. 'Here! To this very spot! You swore on your honour. Instead I insult Kaji by hiding in—'

'They will!' Arlen insisted. 'Didn't you feel it? Tonight was just the opening act.'

'How can you possibly know that?' Jardir growled.

'City told me,' Arlen said.

Jardir's glower became uncertain. 'The . . . city? Are you mad, Par'chin?'

Arlen shrugged. 'Reckon more'n a little, but not about this. There's old magic here, Ahmann. Magic that's been at the heart of this city since it was alive with your ancestors. Open yourself to it, and it will speak to you.'

Jardir spread his feet and closed his eyes. Arlen could see the magic flowing to him, but a few moments later he shook his head, opening his eyes to look at Arlen. 'There is power as you say, Par'chin, but Anoch Sun is silent to me.'

Arlen looked to Renna, who had already closed her eyes and Drawn as Jardir had. After a minute she opened her eyes and shrugged.

'It's there,' he asserted, shoving aside the very real possibility he might indeed be mad. 'Just need to practise listening.'

'So what happened?' Renna asked.

'They've made a ring around the city,' Arlen said, 'with the tomb at the centre. Burning their way inward. Reach us soon enough. Won't leave a stone intact by the end of Waning.'

'Think I might lose my mind spending another night on edge like that, much less two,' Renna said, moving for the doorway. 'Goin' up for some air.'

Arlen moved to block her way. 'Don't think that's a good idea. Can't have the demons pickin' up our scent.'

'So what, we're supposed to spend three days buried in a tomb?' Renna demanded.

'If that is what's required,' Jardir said. 'We will die in here, if need be.'

Arlen began to nod, but Jardir went on. 'But I am not convinced that is what is required. I would see the devastation with my own eyes, to ensure the voice speaking to you is not your own madness. If the *alagai* are attacking with such abandon as to raze the entire city in a single Waning, then they are not snuffing about for scents.'

He strode to the exit, slow enough to give Arlen a chance to try and stop him, but his aura made clear it would be foolish to do so. Arlen nodded.

Carefully they removed the heavy warded stone fitted in the entryway and went up to the surface, where a grim sight awaited them.

Jardir looked over the devastation of Anoch Sun with a heavy heart. The Par'chin had accused his people of destroying the place – not without cause – but the Krasians had barely scratched the surface compared to the wrath of the *alagai* princes.

The minds had let their drones play, digging up buried sandstone only to grind and burn it back down to sand and glass. As the Par'chin had said, a ring of destruction miles wide circled the area like a moat. A deep crater was filled with the pulverized remains of what had once been a sprawling and vibrant city. There was no piece of rubble larger than Shanvah's small fist.

Save for the bodies.

At the edge of the ring, the demons had laid the sarcophagi of Anoch Sun's great leaders as each was stripped from its tomb. Jardir lifted the lid from one, then turned away in horror, dropping the lid to gag.

Inside, the sarcophagus was filled to the rim with an oily black filth, the stench of which was overpowering. Jardir had to forcibly swallow back the remains of his last meal, putting his silk night veil up over his mouth and nose.

It did little to help. His eyes stung and teared from the noxious fumes, but he forced himself to step close again, seeing bits of the cloth used to wrap his ancestor's body floating in the muck. Khanjin, Kaji's second cousin and one of the sacred twelve, lay within, desecrated.

Renna stepped closer, then she, too, recoiled. 'Night, what is that?'

'Mind demon shit.' Even the Par'chin looked green. 'They eat only brains, to make it extra disgusting. Gives it that slick, oily quality. Sticks to everything it touches.'

'Will it burn?' Jardir asked.

'Ay,' the Par'chin began, 'but . . .'

'I will not leave my ancestors like this, Par'chin,' Jardir said.

'You will,' the Par'chin snapped. 'Maybe you're right and the corelings won't scent us, but sure as the sun rises they'll notice if we burn their little display. We go back. Now. Wait for them to come right to us, and then pay them back in person.'

Jardir wanted to argue. Every fibre of his being screamed to alleviate the dishonour to his holy ancestors. But the Par'chin was right. The only way he could hope to balance the scales was to make the *alagai* pay dearly for the insult.

Arlen kept feeling his chest constrict, and had to remind himself to breathe. He dared not touch the power of Anoch Sun to learn anything of the foe. It was the third night of Waning, and the sounds of destruction had grown ever closer, until it felt as if the whole chamber would collapse in on itself. Then abruptly the cacophony stopped, the only sound the dust still falling all about them.

Even without reaching out his magic, Arlen could sense the minds' approach. Not just one, but many. Too many, if they did not claim every surprise and every advantage. Even then, perhaps.

Creator, he thought, feeling the fool even as he did, *if you're up there, now's the time to throw in.*

There was no response, of course. Arlen had not expected one, but this was one time he would have been glad to have been wrong.

Renna wiped the sweat from her palms on her tight-laced vest, flexing her fingers. Her hand kept drifting down to stroke the handle of her knife.

Across the room, Shanjat shifted his feet, adjusting his grip on his spear. Only Shanvah showed no sign of unease. She had not moved in hours, her aura so flat and even that Arlen might have thought her sleeping, if not for her open eyes.

There was a hissing outside, and the sound of scraping as the demons marred the wards barring their entry. Arlen looked at the wards of unsight he had set around the ambush pocket, wondering if they would be enough. He activated his own, and watched as Renna pulled her cloak in tight.

There was a boom as the great stone exploded inward, spraying the room with shrapnel. Renna cried out in surprise, but off to the side of the entrance, she was safe from the worst of it. Others were not so lucky. Shanvah got her shield up in time, but was knocked from her feet. A large chunk of stone struck Shanjat on the head, and he collapsed. Shanvah caught him as he fell, keeping him within the safety of the concealing wards, but it was clear he was out of the fight.

Dust was still falling when the mimic rolled into the room, shapeless, flowing over the floor like liquid. In normal light it would have looked like boiled tar, but in wardsight it was bright with core magic. Everyone tensed, watching, waiting to see if they were noticed.

It always felt thus when shielded by the magic, wondering if this would be the time the corelings pierced the veil. Arlen's chest grew tight, and he forced himself to breathe.

But if the mimic sensed them, it gave no sign. It completed a circuit of the room, flowing around the great warded sarcophagus and returning to pool in the doorway. A lump grew in the centre of that pool, and like a man climbing from a vat of molasses, the demon formed, rising until its shoulders nearly touched the low ceiling. It grew wide and squat, with short, powerful legs and long muscular arms ending in huge obsidian claws.

A mind demon entered the chamber and Arlen smiled, holding up a hand to stay the others until the time was right. The coreling was small, like the minds he had encountered, with spindly limbs and delicate claws. The horns on its huge, bulbous head were vestigial, and its gigantic eyes were inky, reflective pools.

His smile faded slightly as another mind entered the chamber. And another after that. They kept coming until the room was crowded with them, six in all. They moved towards the sarcophagus, and its wards began to glow fiercely, holding them at bay. Arlen could see the forbidding, an impenetrable barrier surrounding the stone like a bubble. The demons could get close, but not enough to touch. Kaji's wards were too powerful.

The minds stood silently for a time, studying the wards, their knobbed craniums throbbing as they silently communicated with one another. Arlen could feel the vibrations in the air, but with his mind wards in place, it was a buzzing and nothing more.

Then, as one, they turned their backs and bent their knees. The stubs of what might once have been tails lifted, and there was a horrid squelch as they released a spray of black, oily faeces.

The stench that filled the tiny room was overwhelming. Arlen's eyes stung and teared, and his lungs burned with it. He envied the veils of the Krasians, though he doubted they helped much. There was a slight ripple in her camouflage as Renna put a hand to her mouth to keep from retching, but the corelings, intent on the sarcophagus, did not notice.

The mind demons glowed bright with magic, far more than the mimic, which held more power than any other demon breed. But coreling princes controlled their power completely, and relinquished none of it as they eliminated. The spray was magic-dead, covering the wards and blocking their power. Their glow dimmed and faded to nothing as they were covered. Open to the air, the vile stool quickly dried, hardening to a layer like crete.

Arlen readied himself. It was almost time. He forced his hand to keep from shaking as he prepared to give the sign. They would not have a second chance at this.

But a crunch of talon on dirt in the hall outside stayed him. Suddenly the other minds straightened and stepped away from the sarcophagus, moving close to the walls and kneeling, talons on the floor and necks bared as another mind entered. One stood so close Renna could reach out and touch him if she wished. Another was in spear's reach of where Shanvah crouched protectively over her father's unconscious form.

In physical appearance, this demon was little different from the others, small and frail with fine needle teeth and talons that seemed almost fragile, like an Angierian noblewoman's painted nail.

But the power this one demon held was staggering. More than Arlen had ever sensed in a single creature, as much as a Hollow greatward. It might not have been a match for all six of the other minds, but it was close. Arlen knew the coreling princes had a hierarchy of sorts based on age and power, but in his only other experience it had been more one of grudging respect and slight deference than outright submission. This one must be ancient and strong indeed to make the others hug the walls and bare their necks.

Powerful enough to spot them despite the concealing wards? His muscles knotted, readying to attack at the slightest hint they were discovered. He felt the burning in his chest again, but did not dare to breathe as the demon passed him by, moving to stand before the sarcophagus.

Its cranium throbbed and the mimic was moving instantly, reaching out to grasp the heavy stone lid in its talons, tossing it aside. The powerful mind sprang with surprising grace and strength, leaping lightly to stand spread-legged, balanced atop the narrow rim as it looked down at the mummified form of its kind's greatest foe. It squatted, its vestigial tail lifting to bare its anus.

And that was when Jardir, hidden in the coffin wrapped in his Cloak of Unsight, struck.

Before the demon even knew he was there, Jardir had snapped the shaft of the Spear of Kaji up between its legs, lifting it clear off its clawed feet. At the same instant, his crown activated, trapping it in an impenetrable bubble of energy as he leapt up and struck again.

'Now!' Arlen cried, leaping at the closest mind demon even as Renna and Shanvah struck. Renna cut the head clean off her target, her father's great hunting knife passing through its scrawny neck like Hog's cleaver through a chicken.

Shanvah, too, went right for the kill, her speartip piercing a demon prince's heart and twisting to tear the organ to shreds. The minds could heal most any injury with terrifying speed, but even they were not proof against a killing blow.

The mind was just turning his way as Arlen grabbed its horns, adding the force of his leap to the twist that snapped its neck. Unwilling to leave it there, lest the creature heal even that terrible wound, he put a foot on its chest and kept twisting, turning the head until scaled skin and sinewy muscle began to tear. With a roar, he ripped it free of the body.

The psychic death cries of the three minds exploded outward in a wave. Experience had shown the death of a mind would kill or drive mad every drone for a mile in every direction. Even Arlen, his mind warded, could hear it, like the air itself screamed. The remaining minds and mimic took it worse, putting claws to their heads and howling.

Arlen gave them no time to recover, pulling hard at the old magic of Anoch Sun. The power responded instantly, as if eager to avenge the city's destruction. He drew heat and impact wards, scattering the minds and keeping them confused. The stone shook from the explosion, cracks forming in the pillars that held the roof in place. He dare not call such power again. If their goal had been to simply kill the demons, Arlen would not have hesitated to give all their lives, but they were playing a different game.

He charged one of the demons, spinning into a warded kick that would take it right in the throat. Shanvah and Renna were already moving to support him.

But the mind demon met Arlen's eyes just before the blow landed, and the creature collapsed into mist, quickly fleeing the room and finding a path to the Core. Arlen's kick shattered one of the stones of the wall, and more dust fell from the weakened ceiling.

The other minds did the same, fleeing without a thought. Arlen expected no less. The mind demons might show submission to one more powerful, but loyalty was an alien concept to them. They were more than happy to let others of their kind die and lose their chance to mate. Only the mind demon Jardir had trapped and its mimic bodyguard remained.

Jardir had the coreling prince on the ground, wrestling, but the demon was stronger than it appeared, and while the crown kept it from summoning help or fleeing, Jardir could not access its other powers while he maintained the trap.

The demon prince shrieked, and its mimic responded, moving to come to its aid. Arlen drew a cold ward in the air, freezing it solid, and Renna delivered a kick that snapped one of its legs right off. The limb struck the ground and shattered as she spun to deliver a killing blow.

But before the blow could land, the mimic melted into a puddle, and she overbalanced as the kick struck only air. Instantly, tentacles formed, whipping out from the pool of goo. The wards on Renna's flesh and Shanvah's shield prevented the blows from making contact, but the rebound against the forbidding still knocked both women from their feet.

But these were no novice fighters. Shanvah never lost control of her tumble, landing in a crouch and coming right back in. Renna was less graceful, but with her night strength she caught herself quickly and was ready before the demon could reform.

The mimic demon was not to be underestimated. Brute bodyguards of the minds, they were also captains of the coreling forces, with intelligence beyond that of simple drones. Already, Arlen could sense it calling for reinforcements. All the drones close by were dead or insane, but soon the mimic's call would carry to those beyond the reach of the minds' psychic screams. They could not rise inside the warded tomb, but the tunnel outside would soon be thick with scale and claw.

Arlen looked back to Jardir, locked in his struggle with the mind, and knew where his priority must lie.

'Kill the mimic!' he shouted to Renna and Shanvah. 'Ware reinforcements!'

And with that, he turned from the women and launched himself into battle with the mind.

Renna and Shanvah struck as one, Renna's knife stabbing into the reformed mimic's chest even as Shanvah struck it in the back.

Neither blow hit home. The demon's flesh melted away from the warded weapons as wax from a flame. Shanvah's speartip passed within inches of Renna's face as her thrust overbalanced.

'Guard the door!' Renna shouted. 'I'll deal with this!' The demon struck at her, but her mimic wards flared, and its huge talons only knocked her back instead of cutting her in half.

Shanvah looked at her doubtfully, but nodded, running to the doorway and readying her bow.

Renna drew a mimic ward in the air as Arlen had taught her, Drawing hard on the magic of Anoch Sun to power the symbol. The demon was thrown into the far wall, and again the ceiling shook. She tried to draw others, trapping it, but the mimic's claws sank into the wall, pulling free a great sandstone block and hurling it at her. Renna flung herself to the side, but she wasn't fast enough and felt the stone clip her shoulder, spinning her to the ground. Her head struck the stone floor and she saw a flash of light.

It took only seconds for her to recover, Drawing magic to heal the damage and clear her senses, but the demon had already pulled another stone free, heedless of the impending collapse of the tomb, and would have crushed her if not for Shanvah. Her first arrow took it in the arm, causing it to drop the stone. The second took it in the face, the wards sending streaks of killing magic through its body. The demon shrieked before melting away. The arrow hung in the air a moment before dropping to the ground even as the coreling reformed.

It grabbed a third stone to hurl at Shanvah, but Renna threw her knife, skewing its aim. The stone exploded off the door frame, and Shanvah was able to throw up her shield in time. Before the mimic could recover, Renna was in close, punching and kicking with warded fists and feet. Some of the blows landed hard, and she felt a touch of the demon's power leach into her, but others met only mist, and while the demon could not touch her skin, the impact of its return blows against her wards was not easily shrugged off.

A glance at Shanvah saw the woman pressed as well. She was firing rapidly down the corridor leading to the tomb entrance, and Renna could hear the shrieks of the sand demons struggling to answer the mimic's call.

Arlen watched as Jardir and the mind demon writhed in the demon shit covering the tomb floor. Jardir had managed to get behind it, the Spear of Kaji held crosswise under its chin, pulling back its bulbous head as it hissed and gasped. Its flesh sizzled and smoked where the shaft of the spear touched it.

Seeing that Jardir held it prone, Arlen paused a moment to Know his foe before attacking. While it remained distracted, he pulled a touch of magic through the coreling prince and tried to absorb it into himself, reading for weaknesses.

But the mind was wise to the trick, and even amidst its

struggle with Jardir, it caught the magic Arlen Drew and held it fast, revealing nothing.

And then the mind began to swell, soft skin toughening and growing sharp, spiny ridges. The minds were not changelings like their bodyguards, but while they might consider physical conflict beneath them, they were not helpless.

Nearly seven feet tall now, the mind demon struggled to its feet, lifting Jardir clear off the floor. It was unable to flee or call for help so long as Jardir maintained the field, but the other powers of the crown were denied him while he did, and he could not bring the point of the spear to bear lest he kill the foe and all this be for naught.

Arlen came in fast before Jardir lost the advantage, punching the demon repeatedly in the ribs and face. It was like striking a wall. He felt the coreling's bones crack under his warded fists, but even with his inhuman speed, he knew they were already knitting together before he could pull back for another blow.

The demon leapt back, smashing Jardir against the wall and driving its sharp spines deeply into him. Jardir grunted but held on as it took a step forward, that it might smash backward again.

Arlen gave it no chance, kicking hard at its knee and collapsing the limb. It dropped to one knee, trying to pull at the choking spear, but the wards kept its talons from gaining purchase. Again and again Arlen hammered at the bulbous head, giving the demon no chance to counterattack.

But then suddenly the demon shrank, smaller even than it had been in the beginning. It slipped from the loosened hold and drew a quick ward that burst the stones at their feet, knocking Arlen and Jardir onto their backs.

The Crown of Kaji slipped askew in the tumble, and in that instant, the demon dematerialized and attempted to flee.

But Arlen had worked too long and hard for this moment, and had no intention of letting it go. Instantly he dissolved and gave chase. He had faced demons in the immaterial between-state before, and knew battle there was more a matter of will than power. Three minds had proven his undoing, but he was confident in his strength against one. With all humanity at stake, there was no way the demon's will could match his.

The tomb was warded, and the cut-stone blocks of the floor offered no paths to the Core. The demon raced for the entryway where Shanvah worked her bow, desperately trying to hold back an assault from demons fighting to answer the call of the mimic, vibrating in the air.

Arlen caught it before it could cross the room, mingling his essence with its, locking on as he forced his will upon the creature.

But this mind was like nothing he had ever faced. Even the three he fought at once had not breached his defences as effortlessly as this one did, slipping into his mind as easily as a man might pull on an old pair of boots. As he had done instinctively in his first confrontation with a mind, Arlen let go his own defences as lost, striking hard against the mind's own thoughts, hoping to find a weakness, but he might as well have tried to run through the great wall of Fort Krasia. The mind's thoughts were impenetrable even as it raked through his own memories – his very being – with ease.

Had he a voice, Arlen would have screamed.

It was Jardir who saved him. In the moment Arlen delayed the demon's escape he had reestablished the barrier, and now he raised the Spear of Kaji, firing a lightning strike into the cloud of mist that was the struggling combatants. Whether he had sensed Arlen's lost advantage and had chosen to risk killing them both – or he simply did not care – was unclear, but the surge of agony through them both broke the demon's hold for an instant, and Arlen quickly solidified, dropping heavily to the floor, his mind wards back in place.

He breathed a sigh of relief. Not for the first time, his overconfidence had almost proven his undoing. He would be a fool to match wills with this one again. They would have to find another way.

Jardir moved to his side, but did not offer a hand as Arlen struggled to his feet, never taking his eyes off the glowing mist of the mind demon, floating just out of reach at the edge of the barrier. In its immaterial state, the demon could not draw wards, or do anything to harm them. It drifted along the edge of the forbidding, seeking a gap it could exploit to escape. Across the room, Renna and Shanvah fought for their lives, but they dare not take their attention from the mind, even for a moment.

'What do we do, Par'chin?' Jardir asked. 'We cannot wait like this forever.'

'No,' Arlen said, 'but we can wait a lot longer than it can.' He moved to the wall, pulling aside the heavy stone that led to their secret tunnel to the surface. 'Drag it up with us. Sunrise'll be soon enough.'

But with those words, the demon solidified and attacked.

Renna was hurled into the wall again, the breath blasted from her body. She pushed off hard, dropping back onto her hand even as the lid of Kaji's sarcophagus, hundreds of pounds of stone, smashed against the wall where she had just been.

In an instant she was back up, punching and kicking, striking with elbows and knees, hammering at the demon. She could see its magic drain slightly each time it healed, but it was no different for her. One of them would exhaust its supply first, but it was anyone's guess who it would be.

The mimic remained solid, gripping a large piece of the shattered lid in its talons, slashing with it like a blade. Renna dodged one blow, but it caught her on the recoil, breaking her jaw and shattering teeth.

She rolled with the blow, ignoring the pain, knowing that to lose focus was to die. She was drawing heat and impact wards even as she hit the ground, and the remaining stone exploded in the demon's face before it could strike her again.

The drain dizzied her, but she Drew hard on the magic beneath her, flooding herself with more power. So much it burned her from the inside, drying her throat and sinuses. She put all of it into a mimic ward that threw the demon into the wall so hard it shattered a pillar and part of the ceiling collapsed atop it. Crushed, black ichor squirted from the debris, but it flowed with purpose, and Renna knew it would soon reform. She choked on dust, her dried eyes stinging. Night, was there no killing this creature?

She glanced at Arlen and Jardir, still locked in battle with the mind, and Shanvah, battling with spear and shield to hold the door, and knew it was up to her to hold the line. The mimic could tip the balance if she let it, destroying all their hopes.

She drew a magnetic ward, and her knife, lying amidst the rubble, flew to her hand. A tentacle formed from the mass of black slime pooling on the floor, and she caught it, cutting the limb free. It was melting even as she threw it aside, turning back into a lifeless black stain. It could heal, but it could not regrow flesh she cut away.

If need be, she would take the demon apart a piece at a time.

The demon knew it, too, and the puddle fled her, running up the wall to gather on the ceiling. Renna leapt high to stab at it, but there was nothing vital to target, nothing to cut off. The gelatinous lump flowed away from the blade, growing another tentacle that slapped her down from behind.

It only took her a second to reorientate, but the demon, fully formed once more, dropped down from above. Her blackstem wards were weak, her flesh coated in ancient dust, stuck to the oily blood and sweat that covered her in a sheen. It grabbed at her with two great claws and she caught its wrists, but even as she strained to hold the creature back, its wrists stretched, talons closing about her throat, crushing.

Renna kicked hard, but the demon had her now, and accepted the blows, its grip only tightening. Her face swelled, head throbbing as she desperately tried to draw breath that would not come. She watched as the demon's great maw opened wider and wider, growing row after row of teeth. She twisted and put her heel into them, shattering a handful even as she tore open her foot. Unlike hers, the demon's teeth grew back even as her vision began to go black.

She had to get away. Had to escape. She pulled uselessly at the demon's arms, but they were harder than steel. She tried to draw wards, but it grew tentacles to slap at her hands, preventing her from forming the precise symbols. She tried to shift its weight, but it had driven talons into the floor, holding fast.

Her vision was gone when she felt its teeth sink into her, but she had no voice to scream.

Jardir had not dropped his guard and had his spear at the ready when the demon solidified, but instead of dropping down into their midst, the *alagai* prince hovered in midair as if standing on solid ground. It extended a single talon, drawing complex wards in the air as easily as Jardir, who approved hundreds of documents a day, might sign his name.

The effect was immediate. Jardir had the spear ready to absorb a blast of killing magic, but he was unprepared as the sandstone floor beneath him turned to mud and he slipped under with a wet sucking sound.

Jardir stifled his gasp before he swallowed a lungful of muck, flailing to find purchase. The tip of his spear scraped stone, telling him it was only a local effect, but his attempts to reach the edge failed. Like most Krasians, Jardir had never learned to swim.

There was no knowing what was happening above, but Jardir knew the Par'chin's life, and that of all the Ala, depended on him maintaining the trap. He embraced his fear, concentrating on the crown's forbidding, keeping the demon trapped.

His lungs burned as his frantic movements only seemed to

pull him farther down. At last he gave in, sweeping his arms to push himself under, stretching his toe downward until at last he touched bottom.

He relaxed, folding his legs under him and using the spear to Draw magic into himself, strengthening his legs for a desperate leap to freedom.

But then things went deathly cold, enough to make winter nights in Krasia seem a summer day. The mud around him froze hard, and he, too, was trapped.

Arlen started to reach for Jardir as he slipped below the surface of the mud, but knew that was just what the demon wanted. Its spell did not have the range to take them both.

He coiled his legs instead, leaping high to strike at the demon, but he passed through an illusion. The real demon had to be close – and solid, if it was drawing wards – but apparently it could cloak itself from sight as easily as Arlen.

He bounced off the ceiling, coming down in a shower of stones and half landing in the muck that trapped Jardir. Before he could extricate himself, the mind drew more wards, freezing the muck solid, trapping his leg.

Arlen grabbed the largest stone he could reach, throwing it into the air and drawing an impact ward. The sandstone exploded, and in the spray he saw the outline of the demon, raising its arms to shield itself. Arlen threw his warded knife at it as hard as he could, then planted his hands and tore his leg free of the frozen mud. Cracks spiderwebbed out from the spot, and they were deepened and multiplied a moment later as the rock bowed upward.

Jardir was still fighting.

The demon hit the ground hard, losing its cloak of distortion. It reached to pull the knife from its ribs, but its talons smoked as it tried to grip the handle, and Arlen smiled. He drew the same series of wards the mind had used a moment earlier, but the demon was wise to the trick, floating atop the mud as easily as solid ground. It dissipated and Arlen's favourite knife fell free, sinking into the mud, lost.

With the trap still in place, the mind could not go far, and in its ethereal state, it was unable to draw wards or absorb magic. Arlen sketched a quick series of wards to send a shock of magic through the cloud, forcing it to solidify.

The floor shook again, and the Spear of Kaji broke the surface of the stone. Arlen used the moment of distraction, closing the distance in an instant. He caught the demon's horns in his sizzling grasp, pulling hard as he slammed the impact ward tattooed on the top of his head right between its eyes.

Arlen felt the ground shake again as Jardir worked to tear himself free of the trap, but he refused to be distracted, hammering the demon's conical head over and over. The coreling prince had swollen again, as big as a wood demon and stronger by far. Arlen had to draw his own defensive wards in close in order to strike, giving the demon the ability to strike back. It shoved hard, and they hit the ground, grappling.

'Even the creatures of Nie draw breath, Par'chin!' Jardir called. Arlen gritted his teeth, accepting the claws and spiny ridges that cut at him as he worked his way into a choke hold.

There was a sound, and he realized it was his own screams, but still he held on.

Renna wanted to lose consciousness, but even as the demon began to eat her, she could not give in. She pulled at the magic of Anoch Sun, hoping, praying for some help, but she could not focus the power with wards, or use it to create air in her burning bloodstream.

But then, as if from a great distance, she heard it.

The call of the Core.

Through the cracks of the shattered stone, deep in the Ala, a song resonated, just as Arlen had described it so long ago. Calling to her like a Jongleur to a reel, or her mother's arms to a warm embrace. There would be no pain there. No more struggle. Nothing but the warm glow of the Creator's power.

She reached for it, and the pain fell away. The demon's claws closed on empty air as she sank beneath the surface, racing to touch that infinite power, leaving behind all the pain of the surface. No more demons. No more people, as apt to hurt as help.

No more sunrises, burning her as they took away the magic she absorbed in the night.

No more Arlen, holding her and whispering his love.

She pulled up short. How far had she gone? The Core was closer, its song a roaring now, the surface a distant thing. She strained her senses along the path behind her, and could still make out, just barely, the sounds of battle.

Arlen, fighting alongside his greatest enemy for the sake of the human race. Shanvah, ignoring her father as he bled to death, holding back a demon horde. And her, fleeing for a warm embrace.

She reversed course, flowing back out of the cracks in the floor. She saw the mimic hammering at the forbidding surrounding Arlen, Jardir, and the mind demon, but even as it kept the mind in, the barrier kept the demon out. At last it turned its attention to Shanvah, moving for her unprotected back.

Renna reached out to stop it, but she had no limbs, her body still insubstantial. She willed herself back to solidity, but as Arlen had warned, it was not so easily done. She felt the cloud her body had become drawing back together, but it was slow to respond. She concentrated, remembering her limbs and willing them back into existence, but knew it would not happen in time. Claws leading, the mimic struck.

KA-CHUNG!

A crank bow bolt tore through the demon's throat, exploding

out the other side in a spray of ichor. The demon turned to Shanjat, even this grievous wound healing, as the warrior dropped the bow to hang from its strap as he charged in with his spear.

'Nie take me, demon, before I let you touch my daughter!' Shanjat's attack was uneven, the blow to his head and loss of blood taking much of his strength and balance, but his aim was true. The spear sank deep into the demon, and it howled as its magic was drained and turned against it as waves of killing power. Just a fraction of that energy flowed up the shaft as feedback, but Renna could see how it restored balance to Shanjat's aura, bringing him fully into the fight once more.

The demon melted away from the spear, reforming, but Renna, too, was solid again, fully healed and feeling stronger than ever before. Her punch crumpled the demon's face, knocking it across the chamber once more.

'Hold the door!' she cried, and then crossed the tomb in an eyeblink, hammering at the demon, keeping it off balance and unable to focus. It burst into mist, but this time Renna joined it, remembering Arlen's description of his battle with the mind on the path to the Core. She intermingled with its essence, latching onto it with her own, and touched its will.

The demon was not intelligent by human standards. Perhaps as wise as a child, though that was far more than the mindless drones that dominated demonkind.

Not intelligent, but its will was strong. It wanted only to protect its mind, would do anything to achieve that end. Renna stood in its way, and it struggled against her desperately.

But while the demon's will was focused on protecting its mind, for Renna, all humanity was at stake. All humanity, and Arlen most of all. If she did not stop it, everything would be lost, and she might as well have fled to the Core. Might as well have given in and let her father have his way, as Lainie had. What good was her entire worthless life, if she could not do this?

She caught the mimic's will in the vice of her own and crushed it, scattering its essence. It burst apart in a shower of magic, and was gone.

Jardir drove the butt end of the Spear of Kaji into the frozen stone one last time, shattering the final piece that held him. The Par'chin was howling in agony as he wrestled the *alagai* prince, but his *Sharum* spirit remained undiminished. He held.

A single throw of the spear, and he could end them both. His greatest rival and the most powerful *alagai* he had ever faced. He could end them, and return triumphant to Everam's Bounty, setting right whatever chaos had arisen from his absence. Without the Par'chin to flock to, the greenlanders' resistance would collapse, and in the abyss, Nie's servants would shake with terror at the power of Everam's warriors.

All he had to do was throw, and live with betrayal a second time. A heavy price, perhaps, but was any price too great, if it meant advantage in Sharak Ka?

We must not become demons in order to fight them. The Par'chin's words echoed in his mind.

Nie take me, he thought, *before I betray my true friend again.*

He slipped the spear into its harness on his back, pulled the hood of his Cloak of Unsight over his head, and reached into the pouch at his waist.

The demon was weakening. Arlen could feel it. While he could Draw upon the power of Anoch Sun, the mind was cut off by the forbidding, and its reserves were fast emptying. Still, it was proving his match. He had needed to cut power to the wards that kept it from touching his skin in order to maintain the choke hold, and the bones and skin of its scrawny neck had hardened into what felt like diamond. He was hurting his hands as much as the demon.

But I can breathe, he thought. *It can't.*

The demon's mouth opened in a silent scream, baring black gums and dozens of needle teeth. The jaws stretched impossibly, bringing the teeth closer and closer to his face. He could taste the foul reek of its rancid breath. Its spittle struck his cheek, and he retched.

But then a fist struck the jaws, shattering teeth and knocking them away from him. He looked over, expecting to see Jardir, but it was Renna who stood there, as bright with magic as he had ever seen her. Her face was set with hard determination, and her aura shone with strength.

He felt tears welling in his eyes and wanted to speak, but it was all he could do to keep his hold as she hammered the demon again and again.

Then, suddenly, Jardir appeared behind the demon, whipping the silver chain Arlen had spent countless hours warding over its head. Before it could catch a breath, Arlen let go his hold, and Jardir pulled the chain tight, its wards flaring.

The demon shook violently, attempting to dissipate, but that power was robbed from it now. It shrank back to its former slender size, hoping to find some slack, but Jardir kept the chain tight, and when the demon seemed unable to shrink farther, Arlen slipped a warded padlock into the links, snapping it shut.

All three of them hammered at it now, Jardir twisting with the smooth efficiency of *sharukin* as he caught each of the demon's limbs in twists of the silver chain like he was tying a hog at the Solstice festival. It fell to one knee, then face-first on the ground. After a moment it ceased to struggle, and its aura went flat. Arlen snapped another lock two links looser about its throat and undid the first, letting the unconscious creature draw a shallow breath.

They had fought too hard to let it die now.

Only then did he turn his attention to the rest of the room, stone shattered and parts of the ceiling collapsed in the struggle. There was no sign of the mimic apart from a few blackened stains on the rock.

In the doorway, battle still raged. Shanvah, quiver empty and spear broken, held her shield on one arm and her father's on the other, using both to hold back the tide of demons pressing at the door. Her feet had put cracks in the sandstone floor as she held against the press.

Shanjat stood a pace back, holding his crank bow. Shanvah shifted, opening a gap in her shields, and Shanjat quickly fired through. She closed the gap immediately as he pulled the heavy bowstring back with two fingers and snapped a new bolt in place, then opened another in a different place for him to fire again.

Before Arlen or Jardir could react, Renna burst into mist and shot across the room. He gaped as she passed the two warriors blocking the door as easily as a strong wind, and he could hear the sounds of battle on the far side. The press eased, giving Shanvah and Shanjat a moment to catch their breath.

Then the whole chamber shook as Renna collapsed the tunnel. Heavy stones began to shake loose from the ceiling, sand pouring down at an alarming rate as the whole chamber groaned.

'Time to go,' Arlen said.

'Kaji—' Jardir began.

'—will be buried forever on the spot where his heirs defeated the most powerful *alagai* the surface has seen in millennia,' Arlen finished for him.

Jardir nodded. 'Shanjat! Shanvah! Clear the path for our escape!'

The two warriors stepped back from the door. Shanvah tossed her father back his shield and the two of them ran for the hidden escape tunnel.

Renna materialized at Arlen's side. It took her a bit longer than it did him, but she was already faster than he had been in the first months he had experimented with dissipation.

He wanted to ask her about the new power, to tell her how proud he was, how great his love, but there was no time, and he trusted it was written on his aura for her to see.

'Skate ahead and ready the horses,' he told her. 'Need to be miles from here before sunrise.'

Renna smiled and gave a wink, then collapsed into mist once more.

10

The *Chin* Rebellion

333 AR Autumn

Inevera woke to a buzzing in her ear. Never a deep sleeper, and even in less troubling times, she drifted on its bare edge in recent days and came awake swiftly.

The vibration came from one of her earrings, gifts given to her most trusted servants and advisors, a way to contact her, and a way to spy. Ahmann's had been silent since he fell, the mountain where he had fought the Par'chin far out of range. She wore it still, praying to Everam each dawn that this would be the day it sounded again, signalling his return.

But it was not her husband's ring that sounded now. Inevera slid a finger along the cartilage of her ear, counting down until she felt the hum. The eighth. No sacred number for the *khaffit*.

She twisted the ball dangling from the ring until it clicked, changing the alignment of the wards in circumference around the two hemispheres that housed the bit of demon bone. With the link open, she spoke, knowing her words resonated in its twin.

'It is not yet dawn, *khaffit*,' she said quietly. 'This had better be important or I'll have your—'

'While I do love the artistry of your threats, Damajah, I'm afraid we have no time for them, if you wish to have my news before it reaches the ears of the *Damaji*.'

Abban's words were as flip as ever, but his clipped tone left no doubt that his news would put her fragile rule to the test at a time when Krasia could ill afford further instability.

'What is it?' she said.

'I am surrounded by your lovely bodyguards outside, and cannot speak freely,' the *khaffit* said, 'and this news is best discussed in person. Invite me in, please.'

Invite him in. To her private pillow chamber. The one she shared with the Deliverer himself. The *khaffit* invited death with the very suggestion. Simply entering this wing of the palace carried a hundred sentences far worse, if he should be seen. Was he mad?

No. Abban was many things, but mad was not one of them. If he was here, it was only because he was certain the news could not wait, and was more valuable than his life should he delay. Her fingers gave a quick dance, and a shadow flitted across the room. A moment later, Ashia returned with the *khaffit*.

'Speak,' Inevera said.

Abban glanced at Ashia, hovering disapprovingly at his side. He looked back at Inevera and inclined his head slightly towards the door.

'You forfeited your life the moment you walked through that door, *khaffit*,' Inevera said. 'If you do not pay me its worth in the next few seconds, Ashia will collect it.'

Abban paled, the usual smug demeanour fallen from his face. Inevera could see the sudden fear that washed over his aura. It was not a mask.

'Speak,' she said again. 'Ashia guards my sleep. There is nothing I do not trust her with.'

'The *chin* are in rebellion,' Abban said.

It took a moment for the words to register. Rebellion? From the greenlanders?

'Impossible,' she said. 'Unthinkable. The *chin* of Fort Rizon broke like slate to the hammer when our armies came, and the villages gave up without a fight. They would not dare oppose us.'

'Slate may break easily,' Abban said, 'but it leaves behind a thousand shards that may cut those who do not take care.'

Inevera felt her stomach twist. She breathed, finding her centre. 'What has happened?'

'The *sharaji* in seven of the *chin* villages are ablaze,' Abban said. 'All at once, at the sounding of the horns ending *alagai'sharak*, while all the warriors and eldest *nie'Sharum* were afield.'

'The children?' Inevera asked. The eldest *nie'Sharum*, boys of twelve or more, acted as spotters and signal runners for the Watchers in *alagai'sharak*, but the younger boys, ranging from seven to eleven, should have been asleep in their barracks.

'Taken before the fires were set,' Abban said. 'Krasian children as well as *chin*. The *dama* watching over them were brutally killed.'

Inevera's jaw tightened. It all came to the children. Taking them for *Hannu Pash* had been the hardest demand the Krasians placed upon the *chin* after they surrendered and placed their foreheads on the ground before the *dama*.

For their children, the *chin* would fight. She wondered how long they had been meeting in secret, planning this. More insidious was the matter of the Krasian children, young enough to have their wills broken. Raised as *chin*, they would make valuable spies for the greenlanders.

Seven fires. Seven villages. Not a fraction of the hundreds of villages throughout Everam's Bounty, but a significant number. A sacred number. It could not be coincidence.

'Which tribes were struck?' she asked, already guessing the answer.

'Shunjin, Halvas, Khanjin, Jama, Anjha, Bajin, and Sharach,' Abban said. 'The seven smallest. Those that would be stung most deeply by the loss of a *sharaj* and class of *nie'Sharum*.'

Inevera was not surprised. Their enemies had studied them well.

'Have you caught the men responsible?' Inevera asked.

Abban shook his head. 'They are not mine to catch, Damajah.

And the *Sharum* are still fighting the fires, lest they spread. The culprits are vanished into the darkness.'

A darkness they feared before our armies came, Inevera thought. *We taught them to stand tall in the night, and they use it against us.*

'You say the fires still burn,' Inevera said. 'How is it you have this information so quickly? Before the *Damaji* who rule those villages, or the Andrah himself?'

Abban smiled and gave a shrug. 'I have contacts in every village in Everam's Bounty, Damajah, and pay well for news that can bring me profit.'

'Profit?' Inevera asked.

'There is always profit to be found in chaos, Damajah.' Abban glanced at Ashia. 'Even if one must buy back one's life first.'

Inevera gave a wave, and Ashia withdrew, vanishing again into the shadows. She did not leave the room, but after a moment even Inevera lost track of her.

'How long until the *Damaji* hear of this?' Inevera asked.

Abban shrugged. 'An hour, at most. Likely less. There will be blood, Damajah. Rivers of it, when they fail to find the guilty parties.'

'What makes you so certain they will fail?' Inevera asked, though she did not disagree.

'Six months and more since we conquered them, Damajah, and the local *dama* do not so much as speak the *chin* language, much less understand their ways,' Abban said. 'Instead we force our language on them, our ways.'

'The ways of the Evejah,' Inevera said. 'Everam's ways.'

'Kaji's ways,' Abban said. 'Interpreted by corrupt *Damaji* to their own ends over the centuries.'

Inevera pressed her lips together. She had listened in many times as Abban whispered blasphemy into her husband's ear, and in truth she often agreed with his words, but it was a different thing to ignore words she was never supposed to have heard than to ignore them spoken to her face.

'Have a care with your blasphemy, *khaffit*,' she said. 'I know your value, but I will not be so tolerant as my husband.'

Abban smiled, giving a shallow bow. 'My apologies, Damajah.' There was no hint of the fear that had taken his aura a few moments earlier. Inevera would indeed tolerate much from Abban. More and more she understood the insidious nature of the *khaffit*. So long as he was loyal, she would overlook most anything.

And Abban knew it.

'Your husband and I went to a village called Baha kad'Everam when we were *nie'Sharum*, Damajah.'

Inevera had heard of the *khaffit* village. The pottery master Dravazi had lived there, and many of his works adorned her palace. 'The Bowl of Everam lost contact with the Desert Spear many years ago. Taken by demons, I believe.'

Abban nodded. 'Clay demons, to be precise. They infest the place. Would have killed me, if not for Ahmann. They nearly killed the Par'chin years later, when I sent him there on an errand.'

'Why are you telling me this, *khaffit*?' Inevera kept her serene exterior, but she was paying close attention. Abban couldn't know that her dice had told her the Par'chin was as likely the Deliverer as her husband. Her own mother was the only person she had trusted with the information, though Ahmann had later guessed it with the aid of his crownsight.

The fact that both would-be Deliverers had visited some obscure, distant village in connection with Abban was too great a coincidence to ignore. Everam's hand was in it. She would have to learn everything there was to know about the place.

Not for the first time, she wondered at Everam's plan for Abban. The dice had been vexingly vague on the subject.

'Fascinating creatures, the clay demons,' Abban said. A touch of fear rippled across his aura. 'They blend, you see. Their armour is the exact texture and colour of Baha's adobe. You can stare right at one – on the steps, clinging to the walls, peeking from the rooftops – and not see it until it moves.'

'The *hora* see things the eyes cannot,' Inevera said.

Abban nodded. '*Inevera*, I pray it so. For the greenlanders in Everam's Bounty outnumber us six to one. They are the adobe, and the *chin* who seek to strike terror in our hearts with these attacks are clay demons. The *dama* will not see them until they move again, and shame will force them to look for others to punish, that they might save face.'

'A move that will only deepen the wedge and strengthen the *chin* resolve,' Inevera mused.

'If we do not step carefully, these attacks will worsen,' Abban said. 'Seek and kill the true culprits, but every greenlander we harm beyond those who held the torches will be a martyr to their cause.'

—They are aided from the north.—

Inevera sat vexed on her bed of pillows beside the Andrah as the *Damaji* angrily strode into the throne room. Her sons and nephew already waited below them as the other men were granted entry.

She spent close to an hour casting after Abban was dismissed and the runners sent, but that was the only useful bit of information to be gleaned about the rebels.

—They are aided from the north.—

It was easy to assume that meant the Hollow tribe. They stood to gain the most from something like this, especially if the Par'chin had survived. But it was seldom wise to assume more than the dice told. The rebels could as easily be supplied and funded by any of the Northland dukes. Euchor of Miln, perhaps, or Rhinebeck of Angiers. Even Lakton, mostly to the east, was north of Everam's Bounty, and they had already been warned by Leesha Paper that they would be the next Krasia would conquer. Would Duke Reecherd and his dockmasters be fool enough to provoke the attack?

No. It was the Hollow. It had to be, hadn't it? Or was she

letting her hatred of Leesha Paper colour her judgement? It would be just like the Northern whore to smile to their faces and light fires behind their backs, and Inevera would welcome the excuse to kill the witch and Ahmann's child growing in her belly.

There were times she hated the dice. They had ever been vague hints and riddles, even to Inevera, who was more gifted in their reading than any *dama'ting* in three thousand years. The more important the question, the more the answer would shift the course of the future, the more the dice grew opaque. She had cast thrice daily, seeking her husband's fate, but the bones told her nothing more than they had in the mountain valley where Ahmann fell, and even that was more than they would tell of the rebels.

Perhaps Everam's plan required the *chin* rebellion, or a civil war in Krasia, and knowledge of how to stem them before the time was right would run counter to *inevera*. Or perhaps she had displeased Him, and Everam had chosen another to speak through.

Perhaps the Northern whore's child is inevera, *as well.* The thought nauseated her. She was almost thankful when the *Damaji* began to shout, drawing her thoughts back·into the present.

'I have said from the beginning that we were too gentle pacifying the *chin*,' Damaji Qezan groused. 'We let them bend when they should have been broken.'

'I agree,' Damaji Ichach said, as if to remind Inevera how bad things had gotten. If Qezan and Ichach were agreeing, the sun might as well rise in the west.

Of the Andrah's court, the dice had been more forthcoming. Ashan she could control, for now. Her sons would look at the rebellion not as a crisis, but as a chance to find glory in its defeat. The *Damaji*, however, were old men grown to comfort in Everam's Bounty's largesse. The danger to their new holdings terrified them more than the children of Nie.

'We should burn the villages where the attacks took place to the ground,' Damaji Enkaji said. 'Hang the butchered bodies of every man, woman, and child from the trees and let the *alagai* feast on them.'

'Simple words, Damaji, when it was not your lands attacked,' Damaji Chusen said. The attack against the Shunjin had taken place in his tribe's new capital.

'The *chin* would not dare attack Mehnding lands,' Enkaji boasted, and Inevera wondered at that. The rebels had avoided the lands of the five most powerful tribes – Kaji, Majah, Mehnding, Krevakh, and Nanji – but if they were being aided by the north this was only the beginning.

'Food is scarce enough after the *alagai* burned the fields on Waning,' Ashan said. 'We cannot burn more fields – or butcher those who tend them – if we wish to see the spring.'

'What is to stop the *chin* from burning fields next?' Semmel of the Anjha asked. 'Even the great tribes do not have men to protect the land from its very inhabitants.'

'You cannot let this go unpunished, Andrah,' Aleverak said. 'The *chin* attacked us in the night, when all men are brothers, killing *dama* and burning sacred ground. We must respond, and quickly, lest we embolden the enemy.'

'And we shall,' Ashan said. 'You are correct this cannot be tolerated. We must find those responsible and execute them publicly, but we will only feed the rebel ranks if we hold all the *chin* responsible for the actions of a few.'

Inevera hid her smile. Ashan had said the words exactly as she had instructed him, though his first reaction to the attacks had not been far from that of Enkaji.

'Your pardon, Andrah, but all the *chin are* responsible,' said Damaji Rejji of the Bajin. 'They are hiding the rebels and the children. What difference if they set a fire or offer their cellar as a hiding place?'

'We must show them their defiance comes at a price,' Jayan said, thumping his spear. 'A high price, paid by all, so that the next rebels are turned over by their own people in fear of our wrath.' Many of the *Damaji* nodded eagerly at the words, turning back to Ashan with sceptical eyes.

'My brother is correct,' Asome said loudly on cue, drawing their gazes. 'But the trail is still warm, and we would be fools to muddy it. We can decide how to punish the collaborators once we have executed the rebels and recovered the missing children.'

Jayan looked at him with open mistrust, but he took the bait. 'That is why I will take the Spears of the Deliverer and kick in every door, dig out every cellar, and put every relative of the boys taken under question. We will find them.'

The *Damaji* were nodding again, but Asome tsked loudly and shook his head. 'My brother would cut a tree down to harvest its fruit.'

Jayan glared at him. 'And what does my wise *dama* brother propose instead?'

'We send the Watchers,' Asome said, nodding to the veiled *Damaji* of the Krevakh and Nanji tribes. They never spoke in council, each beholden to a greater tribe. The Krevakh served the Kaji, and the Nanji the Majah.

The Watcher tribes trained in special weapons and combat, and controlled the Krasian spy network. Many of their interrogators spoke the *chin* tongue, and had contacts throughout Everam's Bounty. Even their lesser *Sharum* could move without being seen, and pass barriers as easily as *alagai* drift up from the abyss.

'Find the children, and we will find the rebels and their sympathizers,' Asome said.

'And then?' Jayan asked.

'Then we execute all three,' Ashan said. 'Rebels, sympathizers, and even the *chin* children, to remind the greenlanders of the futility of resistance, and its consequence. We will make the other *chin nie'Sharum* watch, and the next time, the boys themselves will fight their rescuers.'

Inevera kept her centre, even as Ashan deviated from her script. Killing a handful of children was still a mercy compared to the wholesale slaughter Jayan favoured, but she did not know if she could allow it when the time came.

'Very well,' Jayan said. 'As you command, I will send the Watchers.'

I. It was a dangerous word. Jayan was assuming control of the search regardless. As Sharum Ka, it was his duty and right, but Inevera had intended the Watchers to report to the throne – her – to avoid unintended brutality.

She breathed, keeping her centre. Sacrifices must be made. She had spies enough in the Sharum Ka's court, and her Krevakh and Nanji sister-wives could put their *dama'ting* on alert to pass on anything they heard.

Ashan gave her seven breaths to speak, and then struck his staff of office. 'It is settled. Send your Watchers, Sharum Ka. We expect regular reports on your progress.'

Jayan threw a smug glance at Asome and turned on his heel, striding for the door where Hasik, his new bodyguard, waited.

Three days passed, with no sign of the rebels or the stolen *nie'Sharum*, and Abban could sense a black mood on the streets. In the bazaar, it was worse.

Dal'ting, *khaffit*, and *chin* had begun to find a level of comfort with one another in the marketplace, but all that changed with the attacks on the *sharaji* and kidnappings. Krasians gave the *chin* a wide berth now, eyeing them with mistrust. They kept their purses closed as well, starving the *chin* of trade.

Dama patrols in the marketplace had increased markedly, with the *dama* not even bothering to hang the *alagai* tails from their belts or lean on their whip staves. The weapons were always in motion, if only to clear the path around them of *chin*, or to get the attention of one they sought to question.

And those questionings, the thing everyone in the bazaar from the lowest *chin* to Abban himself dreaded, were coming more and more frequently. The *Sharum* had been forbidden to kick in doors and search everywhere, but the *dama* were taking any excuse to conduct searches, and their jurisdiction was wide.

Abban watched from the flaps of his pavilion as a pair of Kaji *dama* tore the back of a *chin* woman's dress open in the middle of a market street, whipping her with their staves for not being properly veiled.

It had been around her neck, simply slipped during the bustle of the day and not hurriedly replaced.

Abban closed the flap to muffle her screams.

'I pray to Everam we find the rebels soon,' he said. 'This is bad for business.'

'If it can be done, the Krevakh will do it,' Qeran said. 'It was my honour to serve with many of them in *alagai'sharak*. No better trackers exist on Ala.'

The drillmaster still looked uncomfortable in the market-place, but Abban could no longer afford the luxury of leaving him in his compound to train recruits. He depended on Qeran's status and experience to keep him alive.

They retired to Abban's private office. The *khaffit* opened a hidden panel on his writing desk, removing a sheaf or parchment and handing it to Qeran. 'I have some plans I need you to review before I present them to the throne.'

Qeran raised an eyebrow. Unlike most *Sharum*, drillmasters were literate, needing to keep lists and tallies in the running of *sharaji*, and to understand the equations to calculate tensile strength and load in the building of fortifications. But compared to even the least of Abban's wives and daughters, this put him slightly above a trained dog. Abban would not have trusted him with even the simplest clerical task, and they both knew it.

The unexpected request aroused Qeran's curiosity, and the man laid the papers on the desk and began to rummage through them. He spread out the map, squinted at the tallies, and his eyes widened.

'Is this what I think it is?' he asked.

'It is, and you will speak of it to no one,' Abban said.

'Why do you have this, and not the Sharum Ka?' Qeran asked.

'Because the Sharum Ka was a figurehead until a fortnight ago,' Abban said. 'But fear not. Soon he will think all this was his own idea.'

The next morning, Abban rode in his palanquin to the palace. His finest *kha'Sharum* surrounded the muscular *chin* slaves who carried the poles, guarding him from all sides. The curtains, heavy things with a layer of metal mesh that could stop a spear, were pulled tight, leaving him alone with his thoughts.

The Damajah always made him nervous, even if he was wise enough not to show it. She had a way of putting him off guard, a sense she was looking right through him, seeing his dissembling as easily as she might a streak of dirt on his face.

How would she see his plans without Ahmann to bless and implement them?

BOOM!

Even through the thick curtains the sound was horrific. Abban was thrown into the lacquered ceiling as the palanquin fell. He could hear the shouts of his men, and as the palanquin came to an abrupt and jarring stop, he found himself face-to-face with one of his bearers, thrust through the curtain as the whole vehicle fell on him. He groaned, eyes glazed.

Ignoring the man, Abban reached for his cane, struggling against his lame leg to put his feet under him.

'Master!' one of his guards called. 'Are you all right?'

'Fine, fine!' Abban snapped, sticking his head out the curtain atop the carriage. 'Help me out of . . .'

He stopped short, gaping.

Sharik Hora was burning.

Everyone had been thrown from their feet, even this far from the blast. Closer to where the fires raged, passersby lay bloodied in the street, struck by debris that had once been the great walls and stained-glass windows of the largest temple to Everam in the green lands.

Qeran was the first back to combat readiness, berating the others to their feet as he moved to Abban's side. Tempered in the heat of battle, the drillmaster was able to put his feelings aside and maintain the chain of command, but even he had a look of horror as his eyes touched the burning temple.

'What could have done such a thing?' he asked. 'A dozen flame demons could not spew such a blaze.'

'*Chin* flamework,' Abban said. Another mystery he had yet to unravel. 'Get the men up. We must make double pace to the palace now. Send Watchers to find out what happened and report en route.'

Inevera regarded the *khaffit* as he drank cool water and lay on the pillows in her receiving chamber. He was pale, covered in ash, and smelling of smoke. One of his eyes had filled with blood, and his clothes were torn and bloodied. Runners had already confirmed Sharik Hora was burning.

'What happened?' she demanded, when the silence began to grate on her.

'It appears the *chin* are bolder than we credit them for,' Abban said. 'The *sharaj* burnings were a distraction, drawing our attention to distant villages while they struck at our heart.'

'An odd coincidence that you should be there to witness the event,' Inevera said. 'Especially after being the first to come to me with news of the rebellion.'

Abban looked at her flatly. 'I am flattered the Damajah thinks me capable of such a complex weave of deceit, but I am not such a martyr as to get in range of a blast just to add credence to some mysterious plot. Every inch of me aches, my ears still ring, and my thoughts are cloudy.'

That last concerned Inevera. She needed Abban, now more than ever. His body was of little use to her, but his mind . . .

She might have been a tunnel asp, the way the *khaffit* fell back as she moved to examine him. He squeaked like a woman.

'Be still and comply,' she snapped. 'I am Damajah, but am still *dama'ting*.'

Though Inevera seldom treated any other than Ahmann, she had lost none of her skill at healing after decades in the *dama'ting* healing pavilion. The *khaffit*'s dilation, the slow way he tracked her fingers, the long pauses in his speaking, all were indicative of head trauma.

She reached into her *hora* pouch for her healing bones, a collection of warded mind demon fingers, coated in a thin sheen of electrum to focus their power and shield them from the sun. She deftly manipulated the wards with her fingertips until the configuration was right, and then activated them.

The blood drained from his eye, and minor scrapes on his face crusted and dried in an instant. Still Inevera kept the power flowing, making sure there was no swelling or damage to the brain.

At last Abban gasped and pulled back. His eyes had regained their familiar twinkle.

He laughed aloud. 'It is no wonder the *Sharum* say the magic is stronger than couzi. I haven't felt so sharp and strong in twenty years.'

He looked at his leg curiously, then moved to stand, leaving his crutch on the pillows. For a moment he seemed steady, but when he bent his knees to give a delighted hop, the leg buckled. It was only thanks to a lifetime of practice that he managed to fall back onto the pillows and not the floor.

Inevera smiled. 'You refused my offer to heal your leg, *khaffit*. I may offer again some day, but never for free.'

Abban nodded, grinning in return. 'The Damajah would do well in the bazaar.'

Indeed, Inevera had grown up in the bazaar, but it was more than she wanted Abban – or anyone – to know. Her family depended on their anonymity for their safety, and already there were too many who might know the secret.

'Am I to take that as some kind of compliment, that you think me as worthy as some *khaffit* merchant's daughter?' she snapped.

Abban bowed. 'It is the greatest compliment I am worthy to give, Damajah.'

She grunted, pretending to be mollified. 'Enough time wasted. Tell me everything you recall about the attack.'

'Seventeen dead in the blast, a *dama* among them,' Abban said. 'Another forty-three wounded, along with severe structural damage to the temple. Many of the heroes' bones adorning its walls were destroyed.'

'How is that even possible?' Inevera asked. 'The blast was in broad daylight – it could not have been *hora* magic.'

'I believe the *chin* used thundersticks to effect the blast,' Abban said.

'Thundersticks?' Inevera asked.

'*Chin* flamework,' Abban said. 'Ours is mostly liquids and oil, but the chin have powders. Mostly just light and noise for celebration, but rolled with paper into sticks, they are useful in mining and construction. I have seen Leesha Paper use them to great effect against the *alagai*.'

Inevera scowled, forgetting herself for a moment. She quickly put her mask back in place, but no doubt the *khaffit* had said the name intentionally, and watched for her reaction.

'You risk more using that name than you did approaching my pillow chamber unannounced,' she said. 'Do not think me such a fool as to miss your hand in my husband's indiscretions with the Northern whore.'

Abban shrugged, not bothering to deny it. 'Leesha Paper is the least of the Damajah's worries now.'

If only, Inevera thought. 'I want detailed notes on the making of these flamework weapons.'

Abban blew out a breath. 'That will be a problem, Damajah. I have a few of the sticks themselves, confiscated from the mining operations we took over when the Deliverer claimed Everam's Bounty, but their making remains a mystery. The *chin* custom is for their Herb Gatherers to pass the information orally to their apprentices rather than write it down.'

'And none of your bribes and spies have been able to turn one of them into giving up the formula?' Inevera asked. 'I'm disappointed.'

Abban shrugged. 'It is a rare skill, even amongst the Gatherers, and all deny the knowledge. They are not such fools as to think we won't turn it against them.'

'I will give you writs of arrest,' Inevera said. 'If the women will not respond to bribes, then question them harder. And bring me samples of these thundersticks. This is too powerful a weapon for the *chin* to hold over us.'

Abban nodded. 'Treat them with utmost care, Damajah. Two of my men were killed in a blast when they tried to move a batch that had lain too long in storage.'

'Do we have any suspects in the crime?' Inevera asked.

Abban shook his head. 'The flamework has a short fuse, but none were seen running from the building prior to the blast. There were *chin* amongst the dead. One of them must have lit the fuse and martyred himself.'

'The *chin* have steel in them, after all,' Inevera said. 'A pity they waste it in Daylight War and not *alagai'sharak*.'

'The *Damaji* will not stand for this,' Abban said. 'Everam's Bounty will run with blood.'

Inevera nodded. 'More will flock to Jayan. There will be no stopping his *Sharum* from taking control of the city.'

'For its own protection,' Abban said, sarcasm more in his aura than his words.

'Just so,' Inevera agreed.

'All the more reason to send him away,' Abban said.

Inevera looked at him curiously. She would like nothing more, but what could . . .? There. She saw it in his aura. Clever Abban had a plan. Or at least, he thought he did.

'Out with it, *khaffit*,' she snapped.

Abban smiled. 'Lakton.'

This was his plan? Perhaps Inevera gave the *khaffit* too much credit. 'You cannot possibly think Lakton is still a priority, with Ahmann gone and a rebellion just outside the palace walls.'

'All the more reason,' Abban said. 'The Laktonians make their harvest tithe to the duke in barely more than a fortnight. We need that harvest, Damajah. I cannot stress that enough. If the *alagai* continue to strike our food supply, it may be the only thing that keeps our armies intact through the winter. The preparations have all been made.'

'And how am I supposed to convince the Sharum Ka and *Damaji* to send their warriors on a week's hard march with Sharik Hora still aflame?' Inevera asked.

'Pfagh.' Abban pointed to Inevera's *hora* pouch. 'Wave the dice around and tell them the dockmasters are behind the attacks. Demand that your eldest son go forth as Everam's hammer to crush them and take the city.'

Inevera raised an eyebrow. 'You suggest I mislead the council of *Damaji* about what I see in the sacred dice?'

Abban smiled. 'Damajah, please. Do not insult us both.'

Inevera had to laugh at that. She hated to admit it, but she was beginning to like the *khaffit*. The idea had merit.

She reached into her pouch for the dice with her left hand, drawing her curved dagger with her right. 'Hold out your arm.'

The *khaffit* paled visibly, but he did not dare refuse. When the *hora* were wet with his blood, he watched in horrified fascination as she shook them and they began to glow.

'Everam, Creator of Heaven and Ala, Giver of Light and Life, your children need guidance. Should we follow the *khaffit*'s plan and attack the city on the lake?'

The dice flared as she threw, spinning out of their natural

trajectory as the magic took them. It was a familiar sight to Inevera, but Abban gaped as she scanned the symbols for an answer.

—Unless given something to fight, the *Sharum* will tear themselves apart.—

A surprisingly clear answer, for the dice had been opaque of late, but vexing all the same. They stopped short of endorsing the move.

She shook again. 'Everam, Creator of Heaven and Ala, Giver of Light and Life, your children need guidance. Will an attack on Lakton be successful?'

—The city on the lake will not fall easily, or without wisdom.—

Inevera stared at the symbols. Wisdom was not easily found in the armies of the Deliverer.

'What do they tell you?' Abban asked.

Inevera ignored him, gathering the dice. 'This still leaves us with a rebellion on our hands, and a risk that Jayan will return with increased glory and an even stronger claim to the throne.'

Relief flooded Abban's aura. He believed her convinced. 'You will have an easier time rooting out the rebels with Jayan far away. A chance to secure your own power.' He grinned. 'Perhaps we will be lucky, and he will catch a stray arrow.'

Inevera slapped him, her nails drawing blood as the fat *khaffit* was knocked from the pillows. He held his face in pain, eyes wide with fear.

Inevera pointed at him, calling a harmless but dramatic flare of wardlight from one of her rings. 'However he may vex me, have a care when you speak of my oldest son, *khaffit*.'

Abban nodded, rolling to his knees with a wince and putting his forehead on the floor. 'I apologize, Damajah. I meant no offence.'

'If I regret this decision even a little, *khaffit*, you will regret it ten thousandfold. Now be gone from here. The council will meet soon, and I will not have you seen skulking from my chambers.'

The *khaffit* gathered his crutch and limped from the room as quickly as his lame leg would allow.

When the door closed behind him, she bent to the dice again. She had not cast for her husband's fate in over a day, but it would have to wait longer still. With this latest attack and Abban's mad plan, it was easy to forget it was the first day of Waning. If it was anything like the last, her people would be lucky to survive without Ahmann.

'Everam, Creator of Heaven and Ala, Giver of Light and Life, your children need guidance. What will Waning bring to Everam's Bounty this night, and how can we prepare?'

She shook and threw, reading the meanings behind the symbols as easily as words on a page.

—Alagai Ka and his princelings will not come to Everam's Bounty this Waning.—

Curious. Her eyes scanned the rest of the symbols and she started. For the first time in weeks, the one day she had not cast for Ahmann's fate, the dice gave her a glimpse.

And her world collapsed.

—They go to defile the corpse of Shar'Dama Ka.—

Abban watched the Andrah's closed circle of advisors – Asome, Asukaji, Aleverak, and Jayan – from the safety of his small writing desk in the shadow of the Skull Throne. The open circle, including all twelve *Damaji*, would not be called until Inevera took her place and the internal debate finished. Already Abban could hear them bickering in the hall.

Both circles tended to ignore Abban unless he spoke, and some of them even then. Abban was wise enough to encourage this, speaking only when spoken to, a rare thing now that Ahmann was gone.

Inevera had been in her chamber a long time. What in Nie's abyss could be keeping her? There were riots in the streets, and the *Damaji* were close to losing control.

'First they strike us at night,' Aleverak shouted, 'and now on the first day of Waning, profaning the bones of our heroes and the very temple of Everam! It is outrageous!'

'No thing happens, but Everam wills it.' Damaji Asukaji's forearms had disappeared up the wide opposite sleeves of his robes, clutching his elbows as he had taken to doing now that he and Asome were forced to stand apart. Leader of the largest tribe in Krasia, his smooth face betrayed a boy of but eighteen. 'It is a sign we must not ignore. The Creator is angry.'

'This is what comes of being gentle with the *chin* after their cowardly attacks on the *sharaji*!' Jayan said. 'Our show of weakness has only emboldened them to further aggression.'

'For once, I must agree with my brother,' Asome said. 'The attack on Sharik Hora cannot go unanswered. Everam demands blood in response.'

Everam, Abban prayed as he penned their words, *set a cup of couzi before me now, and I will give one of my wives to the* dama'ting.

But as ever, the Creator did not listen to Abban. All of them, Jayan, Asome, Asukaji, were children forced into roles beyond their experience. They should have had Ahmann's guiding hand for decades to come. Instead, the fate of the world might rest upon their shoulders.

He suppressed a shudder at the thought. 'He shall have a lake full of it.' None had noticed the Damajah exit her private chamber. Even Abban had been unaware, though she stood mere feet from him. He only glanced at her a moment, but it was long enough to note she had applied fresh makeup, though it did not mask entirely the puff around her eyes.

The Damajah had been weeping.

Everam's beard, he thought. *What in Heaven, Ala, and Nie's abyss could make that woman weep?* Had she been a lesser woman, he might have attempted to offer comfort, but he respected the Damajah too much for that, and turned back to his parchment, pretending not to notice.

The others, oblivious, had no need to pretend. 'Have you found the rebels at last, Mother?' Jayan asked.

Abban did not have Ahmann's ability to see into hearts, but such skills were hardly necessary to read the eager gleam in the young Sharum Ka's eyes. Jayan stood to win threefold this day. Once for appearing right when all his rivals were wrong, once for the glory he stood to gain when he quelled the rebellion, and once for his brutal nature, which already relished the prospect of inflicting pain and suffering on the *chin*.

'The rebels are puppets.' Inevera rolled her dice thoughtfully in her hand. 'Vermin placed in our silos by our true enemies.'

'Who, Mother?' Jayan could not hide the eagerness in his voice. 'Who is to blame for these cowardly attacks?'

Inevera called a touch of power from the dice, causing them to glow. They cast her face in an ominous light that lent the will of Everam to her answer. 'Lakton.'

'The fish men?' Ashan gaped. 'They dare strike at us?'

'They were warned by Leesha Paper,' Inevera could not keep the venom from her voice at the name, 'that we might attack as soon as spring. No doubt the dockmasters seek to sow discord to keep our armies at home.'

It was perfectly plausible, if patently false – at least so far as Abban knew. He suppressed a smile as the others accepted the accusation without question.

'I will crush them!' Jayan clenched a fist in the air. 'I will kill every man, woman, and child! I will burn—'

Inevera rolled the dice in her fingers, manipulating the symbols, and their soft glow became a flare of light that cut Jayan's words short as he and the others turned away, blinking spots from their eyes.

'Sharak Ka is coming, my son,' Inevera said. 'We will need every able man that can lift a spear before it is done, and food for their bellies. We cannot afford to punish all in their lands for the actions of Lakton's foolish princelings. You will keep to the Deliverer's plan.'

Jayan crossed his arms. 'And what plan is that? Father told us he meant to march just over a month from now, but no plan was ever discussed.'

Inevera nodded to Abban. 'Tell them, *khaffit*.'

Jayan and the others turned incredulous looks his way.

'The *khaffit*?!' Jayan demanded. 'I am Sharum Ka! Why does this *khaffit* know of battle plans when I do not? I should have been advising Father, not some pig-eater.'

'Because Father spoke to Everam,' Asome guessed, 'and did not need your "advice".' He glanced to Abban. 'He only needed the tallies.'

Something about the cold assessment of Asome's stare frightened Abban in ways Jayan's aggression did not. He used his crutch to stand, then left it leaning on his desk. The men would give more weight to his words if he stood on his own two feet to deliver them. He cleared his throat, moulding the clay of his face into a look of nervous deference to put his 'betters' at ease.

'Honoured Sharum Ka,' Abban said. 'The losses to our food stores during the last Waning are greater than the Deliverer wished known. Without a fresh supply, Everam's Bounty will starve before spring begins to bud.'

That got everyone's attention. Even Ashan leaned towards Abban now, rapt. 'Sixteen days from now is the date the Laktonians observe the *chin* holy day first snow. The beginning of winter.'

'What of it?' Jayan snapped.

'It is also the day the *chin* deliver their harvest tithe to the dockmasters of Lakton,' Abban said. 'A tithe that would keep our army fed until summer. The Deliverer made a bold plan to capture the tithe and the *chin* lands in one move.'

Abban paused, expecting an interruption at this point, but the closed circle remained silent. Even Jayan hung on his next words.

Abban signalled Qeran, who pulled out the carpet Abban's wives had carefully woven to match the maps of the *chin* lands to the east, setting the rug on the floor and unrolling it with a kick. Abban limped over as the others moved to stand around it.

'It was Shar'Dama Ka's intention to send the Sharum Ka and the Spears of the Deliverer, along with two thousand *dal'Sharum*, overland in secret,' he traced a path over the open territory with the tip of his crutch, avoiding the Messenger road and *chin* villages, 'to take the village of Docktown, here, the morning of first snow.' He tapped the large town at the lake's edge with his crutch.

Jayan's brow furrowed. 'How will capturing a single village give us the city on the lake?'

'This is no simple village,' Abban said. 'Closest to the city proper, seventy percent of Lakton's docks are in Docktown, and all will be brimming with ships waiting to be loaded with the tithe once the talliers have counted it. Take the city on first snow, and you can take the tithe, the fleet, and the closest landfall to the city. Without the stores, or ships to go in search of more, the fish men will be ready to offer you the head of their duke, and his dockmasters besides, in exchange for a loaf of bread.'

Jayan clenched a fist at the thought, but he was not satisfied. 'Two thousand *dal'Sharum* is enough to take any *chin* village, but not enough to hold and guard any length of shoreline through the cold months. We will be surrounded by enemies that outnumber us greatly.'

Abban nodded. 'This is why the Deliverer, in his wisdom, planned to send a second force of five thousand *dal'Sharum* up the main road a week after to conquer the Laktonian villages one by one, levying them for Sharak Ka. They will act as spearhead, clearing the path for forty *dama* and their apprentices, ten thousand *kha'Sharum*, and twenty thousand *chi'Sharum* who will settle the land in their wake, sending for their families and assisting the local *dama* in instituting Evejan law. Before any true snow falls, you will have seven thousand of your finest *dal'Sharum* at hand.'

'Enough to smash anyone fool enough to stand against us,' Jayan growled.

Asukaji slipped his hands from his sleeves and he and Asome began speaking rapidly in their personal sign language. Normally the code was so subtle it could easily be missed by someone staring right at them, but now there was too much to say, and too little time. Fortunately, the others in the room were distracted.

Abban could not begin to follow the conversation, but he could easily guess its content. They were debating the relative advantages and disadvantages of having Jayan out of Everam's Bounty fighting Sharak Sun for an extended time, and whether they could stop it in any event.

They must have decided not, for the two men, the most likely to oppose the plan, remained silent.

Aleverak turned to Ashan. 'What says the Andrah to this plan? Is it wise to send the bulk of our forces on the attack when we have a growing rebellion at home?'

Ashan's eyes flicked to Inevera's. They, too, had a silent language, but he caught the slightest hint of her lips moving, and knew that she had given him a *hora* ring as well.

'The dice have spoken, Damaji,' Ashan said. 'The dockmasters have been financing the attacks to keep us from taking the offensive against them. We must show them the futility of this strategy.'

'In the meantime, Waning is upon us,' Inevera said. 'Alagai Ka and his princelings will walk the Ala tonight. Even the *chin* know what that means. Put them under curfew and muster every able warrior, including the *Sharum'ting*. The dice tell me the First Demon will turn his eyes elsewhere this cycle, but we must not relax our guard. Even the least of his princes can turn the mindless *alagai* into a cohesive force.'

There was none of the usual arrogance in Jayan's bow, even at the command to include women in the fighting. He was wise enough to keep quiet when all was going better than he could possibly have imagined. 'Of course, Mother. It will be done.'

'If every able body is needed, I propose the *dama* be allowed to fight, as well,' Asukaji said.

'I agree,' Asome said immediately, a rehearsed scene if ever Abban had seen one.

'Preposterous!' Aleverak sputtered.

'Out of the question,' Ashan said.

'So we are in such dire need of warriors that you will take women over those trained in Sharik Hora?' Asome demanded.

'The Deliverer forbade it,' Ashan said. 'The *dama* are too important to risk.'

'My father forbade it last Waning,' Asome corrected, 'and only for that cycle. He forbade the *Sharum'ting* then as well, but tonight they will muster to the Horn of Sharak. Why not the *dama*?'

'Not all the *dama* are young, strong men as you and my son, nephew,' Ashan said.

'None should be forced to fight,' Asukaji amended, 'but those who wish it should not be denied Everam's glory in the night. Sharak Ka is coming.'

'Perhaps,' Ashan said. This time, he did not so much as glance at Inevera. 'But it is not here yet. The *dama* will remain behind the wards.'

Asome pressed his lips together, and again, Abban was reminded how young he was. Jayan cast a hint of smirk his way, but Asome arched his back, holding hard to his pride and pretending not to see.

'It is decided,' Inevera said. 'On the first dawn following Waning, Jayan and his warriors will depart to strike a crushing blow in Everam's name.'

Jayan bowed again. 'Docktown will be ours and Lakton in a submission hold before they even know we are close.'

Inevera nodded. 'Of that I have no doubt. We will need a strict accounting of all your expenses, however, and of the captured harvest.'

'Eh?' Jayan asked. 'Am I a *khaffit*, to be spending my time with ledgers and lattices when my men are shedding blood?'

'Of course not,' Inevera said. 'That is why Abban will accompany you.'

'Eh?' Abban asked, feeling his stomach drop into his balls.

11

Docktown

333 AR Winter

'Damajah, there must be some mistake,' Abban said. 'My duties here—'

'Can wait,' Inevera's voice in his ear cut him off. That she had refused to see him, deigning only to speak via *hora* ring, said more than any words about the finality of the decision.

'You have made your case too well, *khaffit*,' the Damajah continued. 'We must have the Laktonian tithe to keep our forces strong, and we both know Jayan is more likely to shit in the Laktonian grain for spite than he is to tally and ship it back to Everam's Bounty. You must see to that.'

'Damajah, your son hates me,' Abban said. 'Out beyond your reach . . .'

'It may be you who catches a stray arrow and does not return?' Inevera asked. 'Yes, that is true. You will need to take care, but so long as you handle the aspects of war he does not wish to, Jayan will see the value in letting you live.'

'And his bodyguard Hasik, who my own men castrated?' Abban asked.

'It was you let out that djinn, *khaffit*,' Inevera replied. 'It is up to you to find a way to close it. Hasik's passing would fill no tear bottles.'

Abban sighed. With Qeran and Earless at his side at all times,

Hasik was unlikely to strike at him, and he could make himself useful enough to Jayan to ingratiate for a short time. Undoubtedly, there was a fortune to be made in Lakton. Many fortunes, for one with a sharp eye.

'So I may return with the tithe?' he asked. He could last a few weeks, surely.

'You may return when Lakton flies a Krasian flag, and not before,' Inevera said. 'The dice say wisdom will be needed in the taking, and of that, my son's court has little. You must guide them.'

'Me?' Abban gaped. 'Conduct war and give orders to the Deliverer's son? These things are above my caste, Damajah.'

Inevera laughed at that. '*Khaffit*, please. Do not insult us both.'

As Inevera had predicted, Waning had brought no unusual levels of attack from the *alagai*, but even the rebels amongst the *chin* were not fool enough to weaken the defences in the dark of new moon. Dawn after the third night came all too soon.

'As soon as the road is secure, I want daily updates on every operation,' Abban told Jamere.

Jamere rolled his eyes. 'You've told me that seven times now, Uncle.'

'A *dama* should know that seven is a holy number,' Abban said. 'Holier still is seven times seventy, and that is how many times I will tell you, if that is what it takes to penetrate your thick head.'

There were few *dama* in the world a *khaffit* could take such a tone with – lacking a wish to journey the lonely path – but Jamere was Abban's nephew. He had become arrogant and insufferable since being raised to the white, but Abban would never have taken the boy in if he had not been clever. Clever enough to understand his life of ease was entirely dependent on keeping his uncle happy. He would leave the running of the business to the women of the family, Abban's sisters and wives, and act as a figurehead to sign papers and threaten any who dare encroach on Abban's territory in his absence.

'By Everam and all that is holy, I swear I shall send you missives daily,' Jamere said with a cocksure bow.

'Everam's balls, boy,' Abban chuckled. 'I trust that promise least of all!'

He hugged the boy, as close to a son as any of his own spawn, and kissed his cheeks.

'Enough filling tear bottles like wives at dusk,' Qeran snapped. 'Your new walls are strong, Abban, but they will be put to the test if the Sharum Ka must come and collect you.'

The drillmaster sat atop one of the giant greenland horses. There was no sign of the drunken cripple Abban had found in a pool of his own piss mere months ago. Qeran's right stirrup was specially designed to fit his metal leg, and he handled the animal expertly, unhindered.

'Every. Day,' he whispered in Jamere's ear one last time.

Jamere laughed. 'Go, Uncle.' He gave Abban a gentle shove towards his camel, steadying the ropes of the cursed stepladder with his own weight as Abban struggled to climb.

'Shall I have them fetch a winch?' Jamere asked.

Abban put the foot of his crutch down on the young cleric's fingers, putting weight on them as he ascended another step. Jamere gasped and pulled his hand away as the weight lifted, but he was still smirking as he shook the pain from it.

Abban reached the top of the beast's back at last, strapping himself in. Unlike Qeran, Abban could not ride a horse for any length of time without pain beyond his ability to endure. Easier to lounge in the canopied seat atop his favourite camel. The animal was stubborn, as apt to bite or spit as obey, but it was as fast as a Krasian charger when whipped, and speed would be of the essence in an overland march.

He kept his eyes ahead until the procession was through the gates, then paused, turning back to give one last longing look at the thick walls of his compound. It was the first place he'd felt secure since Ahmann led his people from the Desert Spear. The crete was hardly dry on the walls, his guards only just accustomed to their routines, and already he had to leave the place behind.

'Not as pretty as a *Damaji*'s palace,' Qeran said at his side, 'but as strong a fortress as the Desert Spear.'

'Return me to it alive, Drillmaster,' Abban said, 'and I shall make you richer than a *Damaji*.'

'What need have I for wealth?' Qeran asked. 'I have my honour, my spear, and Sharak. A warrior needs no more.'

The drillmaster laughed at Abban's worried look. 'Fear not, *khaffit*! I have sworn to you now, for better or worse. Honour demands I return you safely, or die in the attempt.'

Abban smiled. 'The former, if you please, Drillmaster. Or both, if need be.'

Qeran nodded, kicking his horse and starting the procession. Behind them followed Abban's Hundred, *kha'Sharum* hand-picked and trained by Qeran. The Deliverer's decree granted him one hundred warriors and one hundred only, but Abban had taken one hundred twenty in case some failed or were crippled in training.

Thus far all had excelled, but the training had only just begun. Abban would return them when the Skull Throne demanded it and not a moment before. He wished he could take them all to Lakton, and his five hundred *chi'Sharum* as well, but Jamere and Abban's women needed men to guard his holdings, and it would not do to show his full strength to Jayan's court. At least a few of them could count past a hundred.

The Sharum Ka was giving last-minute instructions to his younger brother Hoshkamin when they found him in the training grounds. Jayan had dropped jaws in the Andrah's court when he announced that Hoshkamin, just raised to the black, would sit the Spear Throne in his absence.

It was a bold move, and one that showed Jayan was not

blind to the danger of leaving his seat of power. Hoshkamin was too inexperienced to truly lead, but like Jamere, the Deliverer's third son and his eleven half brothers were intimidating stewards.

Jayan may yet take the Skull Throne, Abban thought. *I had best ingratiate myself while I still can.*

'Horses, I said, *khaffit*,' Jayan snapped, looking down his nose at Abban's camel. 'The *chin* will hear that beast braying a mile off!'

The other warriors laughed, all save Hasik, who glared at Abban with open hatred. Rumour had it the man had become even more sadistic since Abban had cut his balls off. Denied the brutal but simple release of rape, he had become . . . creative. A trait Jayan was said to encourage.

'A *khaffit* in our company is an ill omen, Sharum Ka,' Khevat said. 'And this one, in particular.' Dama Khevat sat straight-backed and stone-faced on his white charger. The man hated Abban nearly as much as Hasik, but the cleric was too experienced to reveal his feelings. Not yet sixty and still vital, Khevat had trained both Ahmann and Abban in *sharaj*. He was now the ranking *dama* in all Krasia, father to the Andrah and grandfather to the *Damaji* of the Kaji. Perhaps the only man powerful enough to keep Jayan in line.

Perhaps.

Next to Khevat, on a smaller, if equally pristine white charger, was Dama'ting Asavi. Other *dama'ting* would ride in a carriage with the supply train, but it seemed Inevera was taking no chances on this mission. No doubt the sight of a woman, even a *dama'ting*, riding a horse like a man set the rest of the Sharum Ka's court on edge, but she was a Bride of Everam, and none would hinder her.

Asavi's gaze was even harder to read than Khevat's. Her eyes gave no indication they had ever met. Abban was pleased Inevera had another agent close at hand, but he was not fool enough to think he could depend on her to protect him should he anger his host.

'I cannot sit a horse, Sharum Ka,' Abban said. 'And I will, of course, remain behind while you conquer the city. My noisy camel and I will only approach Docktown when you have claimed victory and need to begin tallying the spoils.'

'He will slow our progress through the *chin* lands, Sharum Ka,' Hasik said. He smiled, revealing a gold tooth that replaced the one Qeran had knocked out in *sharaj* a quarter century ago, earning him the nickname Whistler. 'This is not the first time Abban has been dead weight to a march. Let me kill him now and have done.'

Qeran nudged his horse forward. The drillmaster had trained the Deliverer himself – even Jayan was respectful to him. 'You will need to get through me first, Hasik.' He smiled. 'And none know your failings as a warrior better than I who instructed you.'

Hasik's eyes widened, but his look of surprise was quick to turn into a snarl. 'I am not your student any more, old man, and I still have all my limbs.'

Qeran snorted. 'Not all, I hear! Come at me, Whistler, and this time I will take more than your tooth.'

'Whistler!' Jayan laughed, breaking the tension. 'I'll need to remember that! Stand down, Hasik.'

The eunuch closed his eyes, and for a moment Abban thought it was a ruse precluding attack. Qeran was relaxed as he watched, but Abban knew he could react in an instant if Hasik made a move.

But Hasik was not fool enough to disobey the Sharum Ka. He had fallen far since Abban had castrated him for raping his daughter, and only Jayan had offered him a chance to restore his honour.

'Our reckoning will come, pig-eater,' he growled, easing his heavy mustang back.

Jayan turned to Abban. 'He is right, though. You will slow us, *khaffit*.'

Abban bowed as low as he could from his saddle. 'There is no need for me to slow the swift march of your warriors,

Sharum Ka. I will travel a day behind with my Hundred and the supply trains. We will meet you at the camp a day before the attack, and join you in Docktown by noontime on first snow.'

Jayan shook his head. 'Too soon. There may still be fighting throughout the day. Best you come the following dawn.'

You and your men need a day to properly loot the town, you mean, Abban thought.

He bowed again. 'Apologies, Sharum Ka, but for the mission to be successful, there cannot be delay. There must not. As you told the council, you must seize the town and secure the tithe before they know you are upon them. Strike hard and fast, lest they escape on their ships, or fire the harvest simply to deny it to us.'

He lowered his voice for Jayan alone to hear as the young Sharum Ka's face darkened at the tone. 'Of course my first duty in the tallies will be to see to it the Sharum Ka has his share of the spoils before they are shipped to Everam's Bounty. The Skull Throne has empowered me to give you ten percent, but there is some, ah, flexibility in these matters. I could arrange fifteen . . .'

Jayan's eyes flashed with greed. 'Twenty, or I will gut you like the pig you are.'

Ah, Sharum, Abban thought, suppressing his smile. *All the same. Not a haggler among you.*

He blew out a breath, moulding his face into a look of worry – though of course the number was meaningless. He could weave such a web of lists and tallies Jayan would never penetrate it, or realize whole warehouses and thousands of acres had disappeared from the ledgers. Abban would make the Sharum Ka think he had taken fifty percent, and give him less than five.

At last he bowed. 'As the Sharum Ka commands.'

Perhaps this would not be so bad after all.

Abban lounged with his distance lens in the comfortable chair he'd had placed atop the small rise as the attack fell upon Docktown. Qeran, Earless, and Asavi preferred to stand, but he didn't begrudge them that. The warrior and holy castes had ever been masochists.

He had chosen the knoll for its fine view of the town and docks from a direction refugees were unlikely to flee when the fighting broke out. The day was clear enough that Abban could just make out the city on the lake with his naked eye, a blur colouring the edge of the horizon. It was clearer with his distance lens, though all he could make out were docks and ships. Accounting for the distance, it was much larger than he had anticipated.

Shifting back to Docktown and adjusting his lens, Abban could clearly see individual workers on the docks. They moved easily, unaware what was about to befall them.

Even from this distance, Abban could hear the thunder of the Krasian charge. The first Dockfolk they encountered looked up at the sound just in time to die, impaled on light spears thrown from moving horses. The *dal'Sharum* were brutal, uneducated animals, but at killing they were second to none.

They spread out as they made the town, some riding into the streets to create havoc and subdue the Dockfolk as others flanked the town to either side and put on speed, racing to come at the docks from both directions, before the sailors even realized what was happening.

Now the screams began, cries of victims cut quickly short, and the prolonged wails of those left in the wake. Abban took no pleasure in the sounds, but neither did he feel remorse. This was not senseless killing. There was more profit to be made in a quick submission than an extended siege. Let the *Sharum* have their fun, so long as they captured the docks, the ships, and the tithe.

Fires began to crop up as the warriors sought to sow confusion and chaos while they made their way to their objective. As a rule, Abban hated fire as a tool of war. Indiscriminate and expensive, it inevitably destroyed things of value. *Sharum* lives were cheaper by far.

Horns began to sound, followed by the great bell on the docks. Abban watched as the sailors dropped the cargo they were loading and raced for the ships.

The air around the docks turned sharp as Mehnding archers loosed their arrows and *Sharum* hurled throwing spears, killing first the men on deck – frantically trying to cast lines and raise sail – and then the fleeing workers.

Abban smiled, turning his lens out onto the water. A few approaching ships turned away, but one found a clear stretch of dock and swept in, throwing down planks for women and children fleeing the attack.

The planks bowed under the weight of the rush, and more than one refugee fell into the water. Able men joined the press, pushing and shoving until it seemed more than not were falling into the water. No one bothered to help the fallen – all were focused on getting aboard.

At last the ship reached capacity, dipping noticeably deeper in the water. The captain shouted something into his horn, but the fleeing townsfolk kept trying to get aboard. The sailors kicked out the planks before they sank the ship, and turned the sails to the wind, moving swiftly away from water churning with desperate, screaming refugees.

Abban sighed. He might feel no remorse, but neither did he wish to watch people drown. He moved his lens back over the town, where the *Sharum* appeared to have taken firm control. He hoped they would douse the fires quickly, already there was too much smoke . . .

Abban started, moving the lens quickly back to the docks.

'Everam's balls, not again,' he said. He turned to Qeran. 'Ready the men. We're going in.'

'It is hours before noon,' Qeran said. 'The Sharum Ka—'

'Is going to lose this war if he doesn't get his camel-fucking idiot warriors under control,' Abban snapped.

'They are burning the ships.'

'What difference does it make?' Jayan demanded. 'Capture the tithe, you said. Do not let the ships escape, you said. We have done both, and still you dare come shouting before me?'

Abban took a deep breath. His blood was up as high as Jayan's, and that was a dangerous thing. He might speak to Ahmann as if he were a fool, but his son would not tolerate such words from a *khaffit*.

He bowed. 'With respect, Sharum Ka, how are we to get your warriors to the city on the lake to conquer it without boats?'

'We will build our own. How hard can it . . .' Jayan trailed off, looking at the huge cargo vessels with their intricate rigging.

'Put them out!' he cried. 'Icha! Sharu! Get those fires under control. Move the remaining ships away from the flames!'

But of course the *Sharum* had no idea how to move the ships, and the Everam-cursed things seemed to catch sparks as if oiled. Abban watched in horror as a fleet of almost forty large ships and hundreds of smaller ones – along with much of the docks – was reduced to ten scorched ships and a scattering of smaller vessels.

Jayan glared, as if daring Abban to speak of the lost fleet, but Abban kept wisely silent. The ships were a concern for springtime, and winter had only just begun. They had the tithe, and if they had lost the ships, so, too, had Lakton lost its link to the mainland.

'My congratulations on a fine victory, Sharum Ka,' Abban said, reading the stream of reports from his men as they catalogued the spoils of the attack. The grain would mostly be sent back to Everam's Bounty, but there were countless barrels of strong drink Abban could make vanish, and turn to profit, as well as other precious items and real estate. 'The Damajah will be most pleased with you.'

'You will learn soon enough, *khaffit*,' Jayan said, 'my mother is never pleased. Never proud.'

Abban shrugged. 'The treasure is vast. You can hire a thousand mothers to follow you and shower you with praise.'

Jayan looked at him sidelong. 'How vast?'

'Enough to give lands, holdings, and ten thousand draki apiece to all your most trusted lieutenants,' Abban said. A year's pay to most *Sharum*, the number seemed grand, but it was a pittance spread amongst a few dozen men.

'Don't be so quick to give away my fortune, *khaffit*,' Jayan growled.

'Your fortune?' Abban asked, seeming hurt. 'I would not be so presumptuous. These are anticipated costs of war covered in the budget I gave the Andrah before leaving. Your purse will be free to begin settling your outstanding debt to the Builders' Guild. I can arrange payment directly, if you wish.'

Like all men, Jayan had little tells as his blood began to rise. He cracked his knuckles, and Abban knew he had struck a nerve.

Jayan's weakness was his palace. He was determined it be greater than any other, as befit the Skull Throne's true heir. Coupled with his complete inability to count past his fingers, the quest had left the firstborn prince with stale air in his coffers and more interest accumulating each day than he could hope to pay. More than once he had come before the Skull Throne begging money for the 'war effort' simply to keep his creditors at bay. Construction on the palace of the Sharum Ka had stopped midway, an embarrassment that followed Jayan everywhere.

It had to be dealt with, if the boy were to ever become pliable.

'Why should I pay those dogs?' Jayan demanded. 'They have suckled at my teat too long! And for what? My palace dome looks like a cracked egg! No, now that I have this victory, they will resume work or I will have them killed.'

Abban nodded. 'That is your right, of course, Sharum Ka. But then you would be short of skilled artisans, and those remaining would have no materials to work with. Or will you kill the quarrymen as well? The drainage pipe makers? Will threats keep the pack animals alive without money for feed?'

Jayan was silent a long time, and Abban allowed him a moment to simmer.

'Frankly, Sharum Ka,' Abban said, 'if you were to kill anyone, it should be the moneylenders for the ridiculous interest rate they are charging you.'

Jayan clenched his fists. It was well known that he had exhausted a line of credit with every moneylender in Krasia. He opened his mouth to begin a tirade that would likely end in him commanding something quite bloody and stupid.

Abban cleared his throat just in time. 'If you will allow me to negotiate on your behalf, Sharum Ka, I believe I can eliminate much of your debt, and begin payments that will see work on your palace resume without emptying your purse.'

He dropped his voice lower, his words for Jayan alone. 'Your power and influence will only increase with a reputation as a man who pays his debts, Sharum Ka. As your father was.'

'Do not trust the *khaffit*, Sharum Ka,' Hasik warned. 'He will whisper poison in your ear.'

'Do,' Abban said, pointing his chin at Hasik, 'and you'll be able to give your dog a golden cock to match his tooth.'

Jayan barked a laugh, and the rest of his entourage was quick to follow. Hasik's face reddened and he reached for his spear.

Jayan put two fingers to his lips and gave a shrill whistle. 'Whistler! Heel me!'

Hasik turned to him incredulously, but the cold look the young Sharum Ka gave him made clear how he would deal with insolence. Hasik's head drooped as he moved to stand behind Jayan.

'You have done well, *khaffit*,' Jayan said. 'Perhaps I won't need to kill you after all.'

Abban worked hard to keep his face and stance relaxed as he watched the warriors surround the warehouse, but his jaw was tight. He had begged Jayan to let him send his Hundred for the delicate mission instead of the *dal'Sharum*, but was dismissed out of hand. There was too much glory to be had.

The massive dockfront warehouse had great windows facing the three great piers jutting into the water like a trident. The local merchant prince, Dockmaster Isa, had reportedly barricaded himself and his guards inside.

According to Abban's spies, the dockmasters were the real power in Lakton. Duke Reecherd was the strongest of them, but unless there was a tie, his vote had little more weight than any other.

'You shame him with that task,' Qeran said.

Abban turned to the approaching drillmaster, who was nodding at Earless. The rest of Abban's Hundred ranged all over the town, surveying and preparing reports.

'Earless is one of the finest close fighters I have ever seen,' Qeran went on, free with his praise, knowing the warrior could not hear him. 'He should be out killing *alagai*, not shading a fat *khaffit* afraid of a little sun.'

Admittedly, the *kha'Sharum*, seven feet of roped muscle and bristling with weapons, did look a bit foolish holding the delicate paper parasol over Abban. Mute, he could not protest, not that Abban would have cared. He thought he knew sun after a lifetime in the Krasian desert, but the refection off the lake water was something else entirely.

'I pay my *kha'Sharum* very well, Drillmaster,' Abban said. 'If I wish them to put on a woman's coloured robes and do the pillow dance, they would be wise to do it with a smile.'

Abban turned back to watch the *Sharum* kick in the doors and storm the warehouse. Bows were fired from the second and third floor windows. Most deflected off round warded shields, but here and there a warrior screamed and fell.

Still the warriors pressed, bottlenecking at the door. Above, a cask of oil was dumped on their heads, followed by a torch, immolating a dozen men. Half of them were wise enough to run off the pier and leap into the water, but the rest stumbled about screaming, setting others alight. Their warrior brethren were forced to turn spears on them.

'If he has half a brain,' Abban said, 'Earless prefers the parasol.'

It was the first real organized resistance Jayan's men had encountered, killing and wounding more warriors than the rest of the town combined. But there were hundreds of *Sharum* and only a handful of Isa's guards. They were quickly overwhelmed and the fires extinguished before they could destroy the grand building Jayan had already claimed as his Docktown palace.

'Everam,' Abban said, 'if ever you have heard my pleas, let them bring the dockmaster out alive.'

'I spoke to the men just before the assault,' Qeran said. 'These are Spears of the Deliverer. They will not fail in their duty just because a few men were sent down the lonely path. Those men died with honour and will soon stand before Everam to be judged.'

'The best trained dog will bite unbidden if pressed,' Abban said.

Qeran grunted, the usual sign he was swallowing offence. Abban shook his head. *Sharum* were full of bold speeches about honour, but they lived by their passions, and seldom thought past the moment. Would they know the dockmaster from one of his guards?

The clear signal was given, and Abban, Qeran, and Earless moved in to join the Sharum Ka as the prisoners were brought out.

A cluster of women came first. Most of them were in long dresses of fine cloth in the greenland fashion. Whorish by Krasian standards, but demure by their own. Abban could tell by their hair and jewels that these were women of good breeding or marriage, used to luxury. They were largely unspoiled, but through no mercy of the warriors. Jayan would be given his pick of the youngest, and the rest would be divided by his officers.

A few of the women were dressed in breeches like men. These bore bruises, but their clothing was intact.

The same could not be said of the *chin* guards marched through the doors next. The men had been stripped in shame, arms bound behind them around spear shafts. The *dal'Sharum* drove them outside with kicks, shoves, and leather straps.

But they were alive. It gave Abban hope that this once, the *Sharum* might exceed his low expectations.

Some women watched the scene in horror, but most turned away, sobbing. One, a strong woman in her middle years, watched with hard eyes. She was dressed in men's clothing, but of fine cut and quality. Other women clutched at her for support.

The warriors kicked *chin*'s knees out and put boots to their naked backs, holding their heads to the ground in submission as Jayan approached.

'Where is the dockmaster?' Jayan demanded in accented but understandable Thesan.

Hasik knelt before him. 'We have searched the entire building, Sharum Ka. There is no sign of him. He must have disguised himself among the fighting men.'

'Or escaped,' Abban said. Hasik glared at him, but he could not deny the possibility.

Jayan approached a man at random, kicking him so hard the man was flipped onto his back. He squirmed, naked and helpless, but his face was defiant as Jayan put the point of his spear to the man's heart.

'Where is the dockmaster?' he demanded.

The guard spat at him, but his angle was wrong, and the spittle landed on his own naked belly. 'Suck my cock you desert rat!'

Jayan nodded to Hasik, who gleefully kicked the man between the legs until his sandals were bloody and there was nothing left to suck.

'Where is the dockmaster?' Jayan asked again, when his screams had turned to whimpers.

'Go to the Core!' the man squeaked.

Jayan sighed, putting his spear through the man's chest. He turned to the next in line, and Hasik kicked this one onto his back as well. The man was weeping openly as Jayan stood over him. 'Where is the dockmaster?'

The man groaned through his teeth, tears streaking his face. The boardwalk grew wet around him. Jayan leapt back in horrified disgust. 'Pathetic dog!' he growled, drawing back his spear to thrust.

'ENOUGH!'

All eyes turned to the speaker. The woman in fine men's clothing had broken away from the others to come forward a step. 'I am Dockmaster Isadore.'

'Mistress, no!' one of the bound men cried. He tried to get to his feet, but a heavy kick put him back down.

Isadore? Abban thought.

Jayan laughed. 'You?! A *woman?*' He strode over and grabbed the woman by the throat. 'Tell me where the dockmaster is, or I will crush the life from you.'

The woman seemed unfazed, meeting his savage stare. 'I told you, I am the dockmaster, you ripping savage.'

Jayan snarled and began to squeeze. The woman kept her defiant stare a few moments longer, but then her face began to redden, and she pulled helplessly at Jayan's arm.

'Sharum Ka!' Abban called.

All eyes turned to him, Jayan never losing his grip on the woman, supporting her by her throat as the strength left her legs. Khevat and Hasik especially watched him, ready to strike at the first sign of Jayan's disfavour.

Abban was not beyond kneeling when it was called for, and quickly lowered himself, hands and eyes on the wooden boardwalk. 'The ways of the greenlanders are strange, Most Honoured Sharum Ka. I heard the dockmaster's name as Isa. This woman, Isadore, may be telling the truth.'

He left unsaid the words he had hammered into the boy privately. The dockmaster was worth far more alive than dead.

Jayan gave the woman an appraising look, then released her. She fell purple-faced to the boardwalk, coughing and gasping for air. He pointed his spear at her.

'Are you Dockmaster Isa?' he demanded. 'Know that if I find you have lied to me, I will put every man, woman, and child in this *chin* village to the spear.'

'Isa was my father,' the woman said, 'dead six winters today. I am Isadore, and took his seat after the funeral barge was burned.'

Jayan stared at her, considering, but Abban, who had been watching the other prisoners as well, was already convinced.

'Sharum Ka,' he said. 'You have taken Docktown for the Skull Throne. Is it not time to raise the flag?'

Jayan looked at him. This was a plan they had discussed in detail. 'Yes,' he said at last.

Horns were blown, and the *Sharum* drove the captured *chin* villagers towards the docks at spearpoint to watch as Dockmaster Isadore was marched to the flagpole and made to lower the Laktonian flag – a great three-masted sailing vessel on a field of blue – and raise the Krasian standard, spears crossed before the setting sun.

It was a purely symbolic gesture, but an important one. Jayan could now spare the remainder of her entourage, and accede her status as a princess of the *chin* without appearing weak.

'A woman,' Jayan said again. 'This changes everything.'

'Everything, and nothing, Sharum Ka,' Abban said. 'Man or woman, the dockmaster has information and connections, and her treatment will influence those in power in the city on the lake. Let the powerful think they will keep their titles and holdings, and they will deliver their own people to us on a platter.'

'What is the point of taking the city, if I let the *chin* keep it?' Jayan asked.

'Taxes,' Khevat said.

Abban bowed in agreement. 'Let the *chin* keep their boats and bend their backs to the fishing nets. But when they come to your dock, three of every ten fish will belong to you.'

Jayan shook his head. 'This dockmistress can keep her title, but the fish will be mine. I will take her as *Jiwah Sen.*'

'Sharum Ka, these are savages!' Khevat cried. 'Surely you cannot truly mean to taint your divine blood with the camel's piss that runs in the veins of *chin.*'

Jayan shrugged. 'I have a Kaji son and *Jiwah Ka* to carry on my blood. My father knew how to tame the *chin*, as he did with the tribes of Krasia. Become one with them. His mistake was in letting Mistress Leesha keep her title before she accepted, giving her liberty to refuse. I will not be so foolish.'

Abban coughed nervously. 'Sharum Ka, I must agree with the great Dama Khevat, whose wisdom is known throughout all Krasia. Your father acknowledged Mistress Leesha's title and gave her liberty, for a child's claim to her power depended upon that legitimacy. If she only has the title you give her, then she has no title for you to claim.'

Jayan rolled his eyes. 'Talk and worry, worry and talk. It's all you old men do. Sharak Ka will be won with action.'

Abban turned his own eye roll away as Khevat took a turn.

'She is too old, in any event.' Khevat spoke as if the very words were foul upon his tongue. 'Twice your age, or I'm a Majah.'

Jayan shrugged. 'I have seen women older than her with child.' His eyes flicked to Asavi. 'It can be done. Yes, Dama'ting?'

Abban's eyes flicked to Asavi, waiting for the *dama'ting* put an end to this foolishness.

Instead, Asavi nodded. 'Of course. The Sharum Ka is wise. There is no greater power than the blood. A child of your blood put upon the dockmistress will make the town yours.'

Abban hid his gape. It was terrible advice, and would add months at least to their siege of Lakton. What was the *dama'ting* playing at? Was she purposely undermining Jayan? Abban would not fault her for it. Everam, he would willingly help, but not without knowing the plan. He was used to being a player and not a pawn.

'At least let me negotiate the terms,' Abban said. 'A short delay, for appearances' sake. A month at most, and I can deliver . . .'

'There is nothing to negotiate and no need for delay,' Jayan said. 'She and all her holdings will be my property. The contract will be signed tonight, or neither she nor her court will see the dawn.'

'This will inflame the *chin*,' Abban said.

Jayan laughed aloud. 'What of it? These are *chin*, Abban. They do not fight.'

'I do.' Dockmaster Isadore wept as she said the words.

Abban's spies had worked frantically, learning everything he could about the woman before the ceremony. Her husband had been among the men who fell protecting her. Abban had told this to Jayan in hope the fool boy would at least give her the seven days to grieve as prescribed in the Evejah.

But the Sharum Ka would hear no reason. He eyed the woman like a nightwolf eyeing the oldest sheep in the herd. He had warmed to the idea of taking her this very night, and would not be swayed. When he thought no one was watching him, he squeezed himself through his robes.

Ah, to be nineteen and stiff at the very idea *of a woman,* Abban lamented. *I don't even remember the feeling.*

Isadore had children, as well. Two sons, both ship captains already bound for Lakton when Jayan's forces struck. They would keep the line hard against the Krasians, knowing Jayan must kill them to assure title for his son – should he manage to get one on the aging woman with the aid of Asavi's spells.

The two moved to the pitiful excuse for a contract. Krasian marriage contracts typically filled a long scroll. Those signed by Abban's daughters were often several scrolls long, each page signed and witnessed.

Jayan and Isadore's contract was barely a paragraph. As he promised, Jayan had negotiated nothing, taking all and offering Isadore only her title – and the lives of her people.

Isadore bent to dip the quill, and Jayan tilted his head to admire the curve of her back. He squeezed his robes again, and everyone, including Khevat himself, dropped their eyes, pretending to ignore it.

And in that moment, Isadore struck. Ink splashed across the parchment like *alagai* ichor as she spun and leapt at Jayan, burying the sharp quill in his eye.

'Stop moving, if you ever hope to see again,' Asavi snapped. It was a tone few would ever dare take with the young Sharum Ka, but his mother had instilled a deep fear of the *dama'ting* in Jayan, and Asavi was his aunt in all but blood.

Jayan nodded, gritting his teeth as Asavi used a delicate pair of silver tweezers to pull the last slivers of feather from his eye.

The Sharum Ka was soaked in blood, little of it his own. When Jayan at last turned from the altar, panting and growling like an animal, the feather that jutted from his eye bled remarkably little.

The same could not be said for Dockmaster Isadore. Abban never ceased to marvel at how much blood a human body could contain. It would be days before Khevat's *nie'dama* servants could clean it sufficiently for Khevat to formally reconsecrate the temple as Everam's and begin indoctrination of the *chin*.

'I will take a thousand *chin* eyes, if I lose this one,' Jayan swore. He hissed as Asavi dug deep. 'Even if not. There will not be a two-eyed fish man left before I am through.'

He glared at Abban, Qeran, and Khevat with his one good

eye, daring them to argue. Daring them to even *hint* that this *might* be his own fault for not listening to their advice. He was like a dog looking for someone to bite, and everyone in the room knew it. They all kept their eyes down and mouths shut as Asavi worked.

This test is for you alone, Sharum Ka, Abban thought. *It will temper you, or it will unleash you.*

It was not difficult to lay odds on which it would be. If any were fool enough to take the bet, Abban would stake his fortune on the lake turning red in the spring.

'This would be easier if you would let me give you a sleeping potion,' Asavi said.

'NO!' Jayan shouted, but he shrank back from the glare Asavi gave in return. 'No,' he said more calmly, regaining control. 'I will embrace the pain, that I may remember it always.'

Asavi looked at him sceptically. Most *dama'ting* patients were not given a choice when *hora* magic was to be used, sedated heavily so they would remember nothing and not interfere with the delicate work.

But Jayan grew up in a palace where *hora* magic was used constantly, his father famous for his refusal of sedation while his injuries were tended.

'As you wish,' Asavi said, 'but the sun is approaching. If we do not power the spell before then, you will lose the eye.'

The slivers removed, Asavi carefully cleansed the wound. Jayan's hands and feet clenched, but his breathing was steady and he did not move. Asavi took a razor to his eyebrow, clearing a path for her wardings.

'Hang what remains of the *chin* whore's body beneath the new flag at dawn,' Jayan said when the *dama'ting* turned to ready her brush and paint.

Qeran bowed. Jayan had made his father's teacher one of his advisors, knowing it gave him further legitimacy in the eyes of the warriors. 'It will be done, Sharum Ka.' He hesitated a moment as Asavi began her work. 'I will prepare the men in case the *chin* find their spines and attack.' It was an old drill-master's trick, giving instructions to an inexperienced *kai* in the form of following assumed commands.

'What is to prepare?' Jayan snapped. 'We will see their sails long before they get close enough to threaten us. The docks and shallows will run red.'

Asavi pinched Jayan's face. 'Every time you speak, you weaken a ward, and I do not have time to draw them again.'

Qeran remained in his bow. 'It will be as the Sharum Ka says. I will send messengers to your brothers on the road, asking them to send reinforcements.'

'My brothers will be here in less than a month,' Jayan said. 'I have taken the *chin*'s measure. I will go to the abyss if we cannot hold this tiny village that long against them.'

'May I at least install scorpions on the docks?' Qeran asked.

'Have them ready to poke those ships full of holes.' Jayan nodded.

'Nie's black heart!' Asavi shouted, as his nod smeared her warding. 'Everyone not missing an eye get out!'

Qeran dipped lower in his bow, using the steel of his leg to spring upright. Abban and Khevat were already moving for the door, but Qeran reached it in time to hold it for them.

Jayan refused sleep, pacing out the sunrise in front of the great window as his advisors watched nervously. Even Jurim and Hasik kept their distance.

The Sharum Ka's eye was clouded white. He could see blurred shapes, as through a filthy window, but little more.

Twenty great Laktonian ships stood at anchor on the horizon, watching the town as the sun's bright fingers reached for it.

No doubt their captains were looking through their distance lenses even now, seeing the dockmaster's remains, wrapped in her merchant house colours, hanging beneath the crossed spears of Krasia's flag. Horns were blown, and they set sail for the town. Out on the docks, the Mehnding Qeran had sent worked frantically to get scorpions in place.

'At last!' Jayan clenched a fist and ran for his spear.

'You should not be fighting,' Asavi said. 'Your sight will try to trick you with only one eye. You will need to grow accustomed to it.'

'I would not have to, if you had healed it properly,' Jayan said acidly.

Asavi's veil sucked in as she drew a sharp breath, but she accepted the rebuke serenely. 'You would be seeing from two perfect eyes had you allowed me to sedate you. As it is, I have saved the eye. Perhaps the Damajah can heal it further.'

Again, Abban wondered at her motives. Had he truly been beyond her skills, or was this one more bit of leverage for Inevera to rein in her passionate son?

Jayan waved a disgusted hand her way and headed out the door, spear in hand. His bodyguard, the Spears of the Deliverer, appeared in growing numbers at his back as he marched through the rooms.

As the Sharum Ka predicted, there was plenty of time to assemble the disciplined *Sharum* on the docks and beach around the city before the boats could attempt to make landing. They gathered in tight formations on the docks and beach, ready to lock shields and protect the scorpions against the inevitable waves of arrow fire before the larger ships drew close enough to unload men on the docks. Smaller boats would make right for the shore.

Abban ran his distance lens across the water, counting boats and calculating their relative sizes against the cargo holds he had seen in the captured vessels. The maths did not reassure him.

'If those ships are fully loaded,' he said, 'the Laktonians can field as many as ten thousand men. Five times the number of *Sharum* we have.'

Qeran spat. '*Chin* men, *khaffit*. Not *Sharum*. Not warriors. Ten thousand soft men funnelled down narrow docks, or slogging through shallow water. We will crush them. A dozen will fall for every board of dock they take.'

'Then let us hope their will breaks before they push through,' Abban said. 'Perhaps it is time to send for reinforcements.'

'The Sharum Ka has forbidden it,' Qeran said. 'You worry too much, master. These are Krasia's finest warriors. I would count on *dal'Sharum* to cut down ten fish men apiece even on an open field.'

'Of course you would,' Abban said. '*Sharum* are only taught to count by adding zeros to fingers and toes.'

Qeran glared at him, and Abban glared right back. 'Do not forget who is master here simply because the Sharum Ka favours you, Qeran. I found you in a puddle of couzi piss, and you'd still be there if I hadn't spent precious water cleaning you off.'

Qeran drew a deep breath, and bowed. 'I have not forgotten my oath to you, *khaffit*.'

'We attacked Docktown for the *tithe*,' Abban said, as if speaking to an infant. 'Everything else is secondary. Without it our people starve this winter. We have barely begun tallying it, much less shipped it to our own protected silos. That idiot boy is jeopardizing our investment, so you'll forgive me if I'm not in the mood to listen to *Sharum* boasting. Jayan has needlessly provoked an attack against a foe with superior numbers, even with time on our side to wait the fish men out all winter.'

Qeran sighed. 'He wishes a great victory, to give credence to his claim on his father's throne.'

'All of Krasia wishes that as well,' Abban said. 'Jayan has never impressed anyone in his life, or he would already be on the Skull Throne.'

'It does not excuse his reckless leadership.' Qeran winked. 'I did not send for reinforcements, but I did send messages to Jayan's half brothers that we were about to engage the enemy. The sons of the Deliverer crave glory above all. They will come, even without orders.'

Abban remembered the way Qeran used to casually beat

him as a child, trying to force him into a *Sharum* mould. Abban had hated Qeran then, and been terrified of him. He had never dreamed that one day he might command the man, much less actually *like* him.

He turned back to the window as the boats drew close enough for scorpion fire. Jayan gave the signal, and the Mehnding teams manning the weapons called numbers and adjusted tensions, aiming at the sky as twenty bolts, bigger and heavier than *Sharum* spears, were thrown like arrows. They climbed into the sky, dark and ominous as they reached the apex and arced down. Abban adjusted his distance lens to observe the results.

They were less than inspiring.

Mehnding scorpions could turn a charging sand demon into a pincushion at four hundred yards, more than twice the distance a bowman could manage. The teams were so fast, fresh bolts were loaded before the first struck their targets.

Or missed them.

Six bolts fell harmlessly into the water. One glanced off a ship's railing. One passed through an enemy sail, causing a small tear that did not seem to impede the vessel. Two struck harmlessly from thick enemy hulls.

The teams adjusted and fired again, with similar results.

'What in the abyss is the matter with those fools?' Abban demanded. 'Their entire tribe only has one skill! A Mehnding who can't aim is worth less than the shit on my sandal.'

Qeran squinted, reading the hand signals of the men on the docks. 'It's this cursed weather. It was never a problem in the Desert Spear, but since coming to the green lands we learned the scorpion tension springs don't like the damp and cold.'

Abban looked at him. 'Please tell me you're joking.' Qeran shook his head grimly.

While the Mehnding fell into disarray, the Laktonian ships grew ever closer. Watchers blew horns when they came in bow range, and the *Sharum* returned instantly to their formations, shields raised, locked together like the scales of a snake.

Arrows fell like rain upon the shields, most splintering or skittering away, but some stuck quivering. Here and there were cries of pain from men with arrowheads in their forearms.

In their other hands they readied spears. The boats would be drawing in to the docks in just a few moments. They would wait out the bowfire, then come out of the shield formation and crush the invaders as they disembarked.

But volley after volley came down on the warriors, with more and more penetrating shields or slipping through cracks that formed in the scales as men were hit.

Abban looked up to see that the ships had pulled up, staying just in range to strike at the docks.

'Cowards!' Qeran spat. 'They are afraid to fight us as men.'

'That just shows they're smarter than we are,' Abban said. 'We will need to adapt, if we're to survive till the Sharum Ka's brothers arrive with reinforcements.'

Long-armed rock slingers were loaded on the Laktonian decks. There was a horn and all loosed at once, arching small casks at the *Sharum*, blind in their formation.

The projectiles shattered, spattering a viscous fluid across the shield scales. Abban's stomach clenched in dread as another enemy slinger fired, launching a ball of burning pitch.

The ball hit only one group of *Sharum*, but as the liquid demonfire – another secret of the greenland Herb Gatherers – flared white hot, it seemed to leap along the dock, the slightest ember or spark lighting shields soaked in the infernal brew. Men screamed as the fire slid through the cracks and rained on them like acid. They broke formation, those on fire shoving – and igniting – their fellows as they raced for the water.

Just in time for another withering volley of arrows from the enemy ships. Without their formations, hundreds were struck.

'This is fast becoming an embarrassment for Jayan, rather than a victory,' Abban said. Qeran nodded, even as Abban began calculating how much of the tithe they could get away with if the town was overrun.

Many fell to the planking as more casks of demonfire were

hurled in, spreading the fire so fast it seemed the entire board-walk was ablaze, with the fire running fast towards their vantage.

An arrow pierced the glass, missing Abban by inches. He collapsed his distance lens with a snap. 'Time to go. Signal the Hundred to gather as many grain carts as possible. We will head down the Messenger road and rendezvous with the re-inforcements.'

Qeran had his shield up to protect Abban. 'The Sharum Ka will not be pleased.'

'The Sharum Ka already thinks *khaffit* cowards,' Abban said as he moved for the door as quickly as his crutch would allow. 'This will do nothing to change his opinion.'

There was a pained look on Qeran's face. The drillmaster had worked hard to make the Hundred into warriors that would be a match for any *Sharum*, and indeed they were well on their way. This would not bode well for their reputation, but it was more important they escape alive. Abban would happily watch a thousand *Sharum* fall before risking one of his Hundred in a pointless battle.

By the time they made the street, there was smoke and fire abounding, but Jayan was not defeated. Hundreds of Dockfolk had been rounded up at spearpoint and marched to the docks, clutching one another in fear.

'The boy isn't a complete idiot, at least,' Abban said. 'If the enemy can see . . .'

They could, it seemed, for the rain of arrows ceased, even as the Mehnding began to return fire. The scorpion teams still struggled, but they were improving. Rock slingers began hurling burning pitch at enemy sails as the *Sharum* archers took their toll.

'Already fleeing, *khaffit*?' Jayan said, coming up to them with his lieutenants and bodyguard.

'I am surprised to see you here, Sharum Ka,' Abban said. 'I expected you to be standing at the front of the docks, ready to repel the invaders.'

'I will kill a hundred of them when the cowards finally step off their ships,' Jayan said. 'Until then, the Mehnding will do.'

Abban looked to the Laktonian vessels, but they seemed content to sit safely out on the water at the edge of bow range. Catapults continued to rain fire at any open areas of dock.

'The ships!' Abban cried, fumbling with his distance lens and turning towards the stretch of docks holding the captured vessels. It seemed there might still be time. The Laktonians had not yet attacked their precious ships, and there was movement on the decks.

'Quickly!' he told Qeran. 'We must wet them, before . . .'

But then his lens focused, and he saw that the movement on the decks was not a bucket line, but Laktonian sailors, many of them shirtless and dripping, frantically working lines and unfurling sails.

There were bowmen as well, and the moment the *Sharum* noticed them, they began to fire, buying precious time as the moorings were cut.

The first ship away was the largest and finest of the lot. Its pennant showed a woman's silhouette looking into the distance as a man holding a flower at her back hung his head.

A cheer came from the Dockfolk. 'Cap'n Dehlia came back for the *Gentleman's Lament*!' one man cried. 'Knew she wouldn't leave it in the hands of the desert rats!' He put fingers to his lips, letting out a shrill whistle. 'Ay, Cap'n! Sail on!'

Jayan personally speared the man, his bodyguard beating down anyone who dared cheer with the butt of a spear, but the damage was done. Two more of the larger captured vessels sailed away, the sailors hooting and baring their buttocks to the *Sharum* as they went.

Warriors leapt onto the remaining vessels, ensuring that no more were lost. The sailors did not even bother to fight, shattering casks of oil and putting fire to them before leaping over the sides and swimming to small boats waiting nearby. The *Sharum*, none of whom could swim, threw spears at them, but it was an ineffectual gesture. In the distance, the other Laktonian vessels ceased fire, taking up the cheer as they turned away. Six stopped at the halfway point and dropped anchor as the rest sailed back to the city on the lake.

Jayan looked around, taking in the lost ships, wounded *Sharum*, and destruction of the docks. Abban did not wait to see who the Sharum Ka would vent his anger upon, quickly getting out of sight.

'This is a disaster,' Qeran said.

'We still have the tithe,' Abban said. 'That will have to do, until we can beat some wisdom into the Sharum Ka.

'Have the men claim a warehouse we can fortify and use as a base,' he added. 'We're going to be here a long time.'

12

Filling the Hollow
333 AR Autumn

'Should be out huntin',' Wonda growled, 'not answerin' the same rippin' questions every night and pushin' scales like one of yur patients tryin' to get their strength back.'

'It's the only way to get accurate results, dear,' Leesha said, making a notation in her ledger. 'Add another weight to the scale, please.'

Leesha watched through warded spectacles, her young bodyguard ablaze with magic as she pressed five hundred pounds the way another woman might open a heavy door. Leesha had been painting blackstem wards on Wonda's skin for almost a week now, carefully recording the results.

Arlen made her swear not to paint wards on skin, then turned around and did it to Renna Tanner. If the practice was as dangerous as he claimed, would he have risked it on his own bride?

She'd meant to confront him about it before breaking her oath, but Arlen was gone a month, and had hidden his true plans from her. Even Renna lied to her face. When neither of them appeared at Waning, it was time to take matters into her own hands.

You are all Deliverers, Arlen had told the Hollowers, but had he meant it? Truly? He spoke of all humanity standing as one, but had been stingy with the secrets of his power.

And so Leesha spent a week testing Wonda to establish baselines for her metabolism, strength, speed, precision, and stamina. How much sleep she averaged per day. How much food she consumed. Every bit of data she could gather.

And then the warding began. Just a little, at first. Pressure wards on the palms. Impact wards on the knuckles. The weather had turned chill, and the blackstem stains were easily hidden under Wonda's gloves during the daylight hours.

At night, they hunted alone, stalking and isolating lone corelings to gradually test the effects. Wonda began by fighting with her long knife in her dominant right hand, delivering warded slaps and punches with her off hand as she experimented with the utility.

Soon, she was fighting unarmed with confidence, growing stronger and faster each night. Tonight had been her most intense kill thus far, slowly crushing the skull of a wood demon with her bare hands.

Wonda eased the bar down until the basket touched the ground, then moved over to the carefully stacked pile of steel weights. Each was exactly fifty pounds, but Wonda picked up two in each hand as easily as Leesha might carry teacup saucers.

'One at a time, dear,' Leesha said.

'I can lift lots more than that,' Wonda snapped, irritation clear in her voice. 'Why waste the whole night lifting one at a time? I could be out killin' demons right now.'

Leesha made another note. That was the eleventh time in the last hour Wonda had mentioned killing. She'd absorbed more magic in a few moments than an entire Cutter patrol did in a full night, but rather than feeling sated – or overwhelmed, as Leesha predicted – it only made her desperate to absorb more.

Arlen had warned her about this. The rush of magic was addictive – something she'd witnessed firsthand with the Cutters. Those warriors Drew magic by feedback from their warded weapons. It remade them as perfect versions of themselves, healed wounds, even granted temporary levels of inhuman strength and speed.

But warded skin was something else altogether. Wonda's body was Drawing directly with none of the loss experienced through feedback. It made her a lion amongst house cats, but the signs of addiction were frightening.

'You've killed enough for tonight, Wonda,' she said.

'Ent even midnight!' Wonda said. 'I could be savin' lives. Ent that more important than marks on a page? S'like ya don't even care . . .'

'Wonda!' Leesha clapped her hands so hard the young woman jumped.

Wonda dropped her eyes and took a step back. Her hands were shaking. 'Mistress, I'm so so—!' Her words choked off with a sob.

Leesha went to her, reaching her arms out for an embrace.

Wonda tensed and took a quick step back. 'Please, mistress. I ent in control. Y'heard how I spoke to ya. I'm magic-drunk. Coulda killed ya.'

'You would never harm me, Wonda Cutter,' Leesha said, squeezing Wonda's arm. Night, the girl was shaking like a frightened rabbit. 'It's why you're the only one in creation I trust to test this power with.'

Wonda remained stiff, looking at Leesha's hand sceptically. 'Got upset. Really upset. Don't even know why.' She looked at Leesha with frightened eyes. For all her size, strength, and courage, Wonda was only sixteen.

'Never hit ya in a million years, Mistress Leesha,' she said, 'but I might've . . . dunno, shaken ya or something. Don't know my own strength right now. Might've torn yur arm off.'

'I'd have drained the magic from you before that happened, Wonda,' Leesha said.

Wonda looked at her in surprise. 'You can do that?'

'Of course I can,' Leesha said. She *thought* she could, in any event. She had drugged needles and blinding powder ready, if not. 'But it's on you to see I never need to. The magic will try to sweep you up, but you need to account for it, like you're aiming your bow in the wind. Can you do that?'

Wonda seemed to brighten at the comparison. 'Ay, mistress. Like I'm aiming my bow.'

'I never doubted it,' Leesha said, going back to her ledger. 'Please add the next weight to the scale.'

Wonda looked down and seemed surprised to find she still held two fifty-pound weights in each hand. She put one on the scale, restacked the others, and went back to the bar.

Leesha tried to take up her pen, but her fingers were stiff with tension. She squeezed her hand into a fist so tight her knuckle cracked, then flexed the fingers back to dexterity before dipping for fresh ink. The vein in her temple throbbed, and she knew a headache was coming.

Oh, Arlen, she wondered. *What was it like for you, going through this alone?*

He had told her some of it, on the many nights they spent in her cottage, teaching each other in wardcraft and demonology. In between the lessons they shared hopes and stories like lovers, but never so much as held hands. Arlen had his couch and she hers, a table carefully between them.

But she always walked him to the door, and offered a farewell embrace. Sometimes – just sometimes – he put his nose in her hair, inhaling. Those times she knew he would accept a fleeting kiss, savouring it a moment before pulling away, lest it lead to more.

She lay awake in bed after he left, feeling his lips on hers and imagining what it would be like if he were beside her. But that was out of the question. Arlen had many of the same fears and mood swings as Wonda, terrified of hurting her, or getting her with a magic-tainted child. Her offers to take pomm tea were not enough to persuade him.

But like warding skin, all that had changed when Renna Tanner came along. She was nearly as strong as he was, and could take the punishment he'd feared to unleash in passion with Leesha. The whole town knew about the noise those two made.

Creator, Arlen, where have you gone? she wondered. There were questions she needed to ask, things only he or Renna could understand.

I don't care if we never kiss again, just come home.

'Have a look at this,' Thamos said. He had his shirt off, and it was a moment before Leesha realized he was holding a coin in his hand. He flipped it to the bed, where she caught it.

It was a lacquered wooden klat, the common coin of Angiers. But instead of the seal of the ivy throne, the coin was stamped with a standard warding circle of protection, the lines sharp and clear.

'This is fantastic!' Leesha said. 'No one will ever be left without wards for the night again when every coin in their pocket is a guide.'

Thamos nodded. 'Your father made the original mould. I have half a million ready to disperse, and the presses are running day and night.'

Leesha flipped the coin over, and laughed out loud. Stamped there was Thamos' likeness, looking stern and paternal. 'It looks like you when one of the Hollowers forgets to bow.'

Thamos put his face in his hand. 'My mother's idea.'

'I would have thought she'd want the duke's face,' Leesha said.

Thamos shook his head. 'We're making them too fast. The Merchants' Guild feared the value of the duke's klats would plummet if it were tied to entitlements in the Hollow.'

'So the coins will be worthless in Angiers,' Leesha said.

Thamos shrugged. 'For a time, but I mean to make them worth as much as Krasian gold.'

'Speaking of which,' Leesha said. 'Smitt is going to complain about Shamavah stealing his business again today.'

Thamos sat back down on the bed, putting his arm around Leesha and pulling her close. 'He insisted Arther add it to the agenda. I can't say he doesn't have a point. Trading with the Krasians has risks.'

'As does refusing it,' Leesha said. 'We don't need to be abed with the Krasians to want civil relations and contacts in Everam's Bounty, and those are made through trade.'

Thamos looked at her, eyes probing, and she regretted her choice of words. *Abed. Idiot. Why not just slap him in the face with it, as Mother would have?*

'Besides,' she added quickly, 'Smitt's motives are far from pure. He's less interested in politics and security than he is in keeping down a rival.'

There was a knock on the bedchamber door. Early in her relationship with the count the servants made Leesha jump, especially when she was in a state of undress. But she had grown accustomed to the constant, discreet presence of Thamos' staff. Most of his intimate servants had been with his family for generations, their loyalty beyond question.

'Let me handle them.' Leesha put on stockings and stepped back into her dress, then rang the bell. Thamos' manservant Lord Arther entered silently with an older maid. Tarisa had been Thamos' nurse since he was in swaddling. The count was one of the most powerful men in the world, but he still jumped when Tarisa snapped for him to sit up straight.

'Your Highness, my lady.' Arther glided across the room, eyes down, not daring to so much as glance at Leesha's bared back as Tarisa came to tighten the laces.

'How is my lady this morning?' the woman asked. Her voice was kind, and whatever she might think of finding an unmarried woman in the count's bedchamber, she had never once given an inkling. Of course, with Thamos' reputation, she had likely seen far worse.

'Very well, Tarisa, and you?' Leesha said.

'I'd be better if you'd let me do something with this hair,' the old woman said, taking a brush to Leesha's dark tresses. 'Things have gotten so dull for me since His Highness learned to count past his fingers and wipe his own bottom.'

'Nanny, please,' Thamos groaned, burying his face in his palm. Arther pretended not to notice, and Leesha laughed.

'Yes, nanny, please go on,' she said. 'Do whatever you wish, so long as you relate every last detail of His Highness' privy training.'

She watched the old woman's face in the mirror. Her smile lines became great fissures as she began to efficiently section and pin Leesha's hair. There was nothing Tarisa loved more than telling stories of her lord as a boy.

'I called him the little firefighter,' Tarisa said, 'for he sprayed like a hose all over the . . .'

Tarisa had many stories, but the nanny's nimble fingers never stopped working as she spoke. Leesha's hair was pinned up exquisitely, her face powdered and lips darkened. Somehow the woman had even talked her into a new gown, one of the many Thamos had presented her with.

All the preening and posturing for appearances at court would once have been anathema to her, but slowly, her association with the ever style-conscious Thamos had begun to wear her defences. She was a leader that her people looked up to. There was no shame in presenting herself at her best.

Wonda was waiting as Leesha left Thamos' chambers, falling in behind her wordlessly. The girl looked calmer now – Leesha had sent her for a walk in the sun to burn off the excess power while she met with the count. Wonda had no illusions about how she and Thamos spent their time, but like Arther and Tarisa, she never spoke, never judged.

Thamos was still inside, fussing over clothes and the trimming of every last hair on his beard, though Leesha knew it was as much that he might make an entrance after his councillors had been kept waiting a bit, and to give her time to leave in secret and enter properly.

Leesha exited by a side door to her private herb garden

within the count's walls. As the Royal Gatherer, His Highness' health was her responsibility, so it was perfectly normal to be seen leaving the garden on her way to the main doors.

The deception seemed unnecessary for an open secret, but surprisingly it was Thamos who insisted they keep appearances, if only to keep his mother at bay. Araine seemed to approve the match, and – from what Leesha knew of the old woman – likely didn't care what they did abed, but appearances were everything at court.

Leesha's hand drifted to her belly. Soon enough, it would swell and force the issue. All would assume it belonged to the count, and there would be pressure from every direction for them to marry. When that happened, she would have to make a choice between evils.

Thamos was a good man. Not brilliant, but strong and honourable. He was prideful and vain, demanding obeisance from his subjects, but he would give his life for the least of them in the night. Leesha found she wanted nothing more than to spend the rest of her life sharing his bed and his throne, leading the Hollow together. But when Ahmann's child was born with olive skin, it would all tear apart. Leesha was no stranger to being the centre of scandal in the Hollow, but this . . . This they would not forgive.

But the alternative, revealing the child's parentage when it was still vulnerable in her womb, would be all the more dangerous. Inevera and Araine would wish the child dead, and be happy to send Leesha off with it.

Leesha felt the muscles in her temple twitch. Morning sickness had faded, but the headaches were worse than ever as the pregnancy progressed, and it only took a little stress to trigger one.

'Mistress Leesha!' Darsy was waiting at the pillars by the main entrance to the count's manse. The big woman fumbled with her papers as she dipped an awkward curtsy. Leesha had nearly cured her and the other Gatherers of such needless formality when the count came to the Hollow, but Thamos, accustomed to palace life, expected such treatment, and it was a hard habit to break. Now Leesha left a trail of bows and curtsies wherever she went.

'Looked in the garden,' Darsy said. 'Guess I missed you.'

Leesha breathed deeply, her smile warm and serene. 'Good morning, Darsy. Are you taking good care of my hospit?'

'Doin' my best, mistress,' Darsy said, 'but need your word on a dozen things.'

She began handing Leesha papers as they walked, and one dozen turned into two before they made their way to the council chamber. Leesha made notations on patient cases, approved shift rotations and allocations of resource, signed correspondences, and anything else Darsy could shove in front of her.

'Can't wait till Vika gets back from Angiers,' Darsy grumbled. 'Been gone for months! Ent cut for this. I'm better at setting bones and settling fights between the apprentices than planning shift rotations and recruiting volunteers to give blood and help with the wounded.'

'Nonsense,' Leesha said. 'There's no one better for setting bones, it's true, but you do yourself a disservice if you think your worth ends there. I wouldn't have made it this last year without you, Darsy. You're the only one I trust to tell me things everyone else is afraid to.'

Darsy coughed, her face reddening. Leesha pretended not to notice, giving her time to collect herself. The reaction told Leesha she didn't compliment the woman nearly enough. Darsy vexed her at times, but every word she'd said was true, and Darsy deserved to hear it.

As they reached the council chamber, she turned to Darsy one last time. 'The Gathering is set?'

Darsy nodded. 'Every hospit will have apprentices covering the day. Almost every Gatherer is planning to attend.'

Leesha smiled. 'Not a word of it inside.'

Darsy nodded. 'Gatherers' business.'

The other council members were already in attendance when they opened the door. Lord Arther led the way as the men rose to their feet and bowed, waiting for Leesha to sit before doing the same. Such formalities seemed out of place in the Hollow, but Thamos expected no less in his council chambers, and Arther had browbeaten even the most stubborn until they adapted.

It was said in Angiers one always knew where they stood with a host by the chair they were given. There were twelve seats around the great table. Rojer, Lord Arther, Captain Gamon, Hary Roller, Smitt, Darsy, and Erny all sat in armless chairs, their legs and hard backs carved of fine goldwood in the ivy scrollwork of the Angierian royal family. The feathered cushions were green silk embroidered in brown and gold.

Inquisitor Hayes and Baron Gared faced each other at the middle of the table, both with narrow, high-back armchairs to denote their status. The Tender sat with quiet dignity on his velvet cushion. Child Franq was at his side, sitting on a simple backless stool, his posture perfect. Gared looked squeezed into his, like an adult in a throne built for a child. His legs stretched far under the table, and his huge hands seemed in constant danger of snapping the arms off if he moved too quickly.

Leesha's chair at the foot of the table wasn't quite a throne, but it was far more than would normally ever be accorded to a Royal Gatherer. It was wider than the baron and Inquisitor's together, soft-cushioned and richly upholstered with wide arms and room for her to curl her legs under her if she wished.

But if Leesha felt her chair ostentatious, she had only to look at the gold-and-velvet monstrosity of Thamos' throne at the head of the table, looming over the other chairs like Gared loomed over other men. Even empty as it was now, it was a reminder to all of his power.

A few minutes later, a boy came in to signal Lord Arther, who again was the first to stand at attention. The others followed, and all bowed as the count entered. Leesha gave him a wry smile as she dipped into her curtsy.

'Apologies for keeping you waiting,' Thamos said, meaning

no such thing. No doubt he had paced his room, counting to a thousand after the pages informed him the last of his council was seated. 'Arther, what is first on the agenda?'

Arther made a show of consulting his writing board, though of course he knew it all by heart. They had rehearsed while dressing.

'The same as ever, Highness. Elections, land, and entitlements.' Arther had learned to mask much of his distaste at that last word, but his lips still puckered as if it soured his tongue. 'Mistress Leesha's invitation to the Laktonians continues to grow the population of Hollow County at an alarming rate.'

Entitlements. Leesha hated the word, too, but not for the same reason as Arther. It was a cold word, used by those with full bellies to bemoan feeding those without.

Leesha smiled. 'The Hollow is strong, my lord. Not just because of our leaders, or our magic. It is people that give us that strength, and we must welcome with open arms as many as will come. Already Cutter's Hollow and three other baronies are off the programme, and providing substantial tax revenue to Hollow County.'

'Four out of nearly twenty, mistress,' Arther noted. 'Three more still being rebuilt, and another dozen in their infancy. The cost exceeds the revenue by a firm margin.'

'Enough,' Thamos said. 'I was sent here to grow Hollow County, and that work cannot be done on empty stomachs.'

'Nor shall it,' Leesha said. 'The fertilizers and farming techniques Darsy and I prepared this summer more than tripled our yield. They will be implemented in every barony before spring.' Silently, she thanked her mentor Bruna for the books of old world science that made much of it possible.

She looked to Smitt. 'How are the rabbits breeding?'

Smitt laughed. 'Like you'd expect. Bees and chicks, too. Shipments go out like clockwork. We've got hives, burrows, and hatcheries in every barony. Even the ones that are just a bunch of tents.'

Thamos looked to Gared. 'Baron, how are the Cutters progressing on the new greatwards?'

'Should finish another this week,' Gared said. 'Land's mostly clear, just digging foundations and clipping the hedges.' *Clipping the hedges* was the Cutter term for shaping the outer perimeter of the tree line to meet the exact specifications of the Warders. He cocked his head towards Erny, who had been made master of the Hollow Warders' Guild.

The difference between the two men was multiplied tenfold by the difference in their seats. Leesha's father looked like a mouse next to a wolf.

Again Leesha's mind flashed back to the night she had caught Gared and her mother coupling. She shook her head sharply to throw off the image. No one else noticed, but Thamos raised an eyebrow at her. She forced a smile and winked in return.

'The ward should activate in the next day or two,' Erny said, 'but the area is well patrolled. Now that new moon is past, folk can begin moving in and building. We won't have full potency until buildings, walls, and fences reinforce the shape.'

Arther passed Thamos a list. 'These are the proposed names for the new baronies, and the barons and baronesses elected to lead them for your approval. All are willing to kneel and swear oath to you and to the ivy throne.'

Thamos grunted, glancing at the paper. He was still not pleased about letting the refugees elect their own leaders, but the count and the Wooden Soldiers he brought to the Hollow were fighting men, not politicians. Better to let the groups govern themselves as much as possible, so long as they kept the peace and did their part for Hollow County.

'And recruitment?' Thamos asked.

'Got men making the rounds at every barony, letting folk know there's training to help protect their own if they join the Cutters. Raw wood comes in every day, and more men are ready to stand each night.'

Thamos looked to Smitt. 'And how are we equipping the raw wood? Have the weapons shortages continued?'

'The fletchers are struggling to keep up with demand, Highness, but we have more than enough spears.' Smitt glanced at Erny. 'The delay is in warding them.'

Erny set his mouth as all eyes turned on him. He might not stand up for himself with his wife, but at the council table, he was not to be trifled with. 'I'll leave it to Your Highness to decide which takes longer, making a stick, or warding it. My Warders are working as fast as they can, but we don't have nearly enough to meet demand.'

Thamos was not cowed. 'Then train more.'

'We are,' Erny said. 'Hundreds, but one doesn't learn wardcraft overnight. Would you want to wager your life on a first-year student's warding?'

Smitt coughed, breaking the tension and drawing attention back to himself. 'These things take time, of course. There will be more horses, in the meantime.'

Thamos sat up at that. He had lost his favourite horse, and much of his cavalry, at new moon six weeks past. He had bought a giant Angierian mustang much like Gared's own stallion Rockslide since, and he talked of it so often Leesha had once suggested he might prefer sticking the mare to her.

Gared nodded. 'Jon Stallion hired a bunch of Hollowers out at his ranch. Big as a town now, with hundreds out catching and taming mustang. Says you'll have all the Wooden Soldiers lost and to spare by spring. Cost is a bit more than we'd like . . .'

Arther rolled his eyes. 'Of course.'

'Pay it,' Thamos said. 'I need my cavalry back, Arther, and don't have time to dicker over klats.'

Arther's mouth was a flat line as he gave a shallow bow from his seat. 'Of course, Your Highness.'

'Perhaps Darsy might give us an update on the convalescent initiative?' Leesha asked. In addition to the loss of cavalry, thousands of Hollowers had been injured in the attacks. Leesha used *hora* magic to heal those with the most critical cases or important positions, but the vast majority were required to heal naturally after the Herb Gatherers stitched them back together. Many were just beginning to use broken bones again, and needed proper exercise and attention to return to self-sufficiency.

Darsy gave an awkward move that Leesha took as a seated curtsy. 'Got local gatherers making rounds throughout the county. Volunteers gather in town squares to help the injured build their strength walking, stretching, and lifting weights.' She thrust her chin at Rojer and Hary. 'Jongleurs been touring, keeping spirits high as folk struggle to rebuild.'

Rojer nodded. 'More than touring. Teaching. Town squares are more than just rehabilitation for the injured. Starting kids playing as soon as they can hold a bow or pluck a string.

'We've sent for instrument makers from Angiers,' Rojer continued tentatively, taking a sheet of parchment from his leather case. 'The cost . . .'

'I'll take that, Master Halfgrip,' Arther said, reaching for the paper. Rojer had been promoted to master by the Jongleurs' Guild with the last Messenger, but the title still sounded fresh to Leesha's ears. The lord scanned the contents, passing it to the count with a frown.

Even Thamos gave a profound sigh as he read the numbers. 'You're quick to claim the Jongleurs as your own and not subject to me, Master Halfgrip, until you need coin. If you would reconsider your position as royal herald of the Hollow, it would be easier to secure funds for you.'

Rojer pursed his lips. He had refused the count when he first made the offer, months ago, but Leesha felt his resolve weakening as it became more and more likely that she would soon be countess. Rojer had a stubborn streak, though, and didn't care to answer to anyone. Thamos pushing like this was only going to strengthen his resolve.

'With all due respect, Your Highness, we're not asking for luxuries,' Rojer said. 'Those instruments will save as many lives as your horses and spears.'

Thamos' nostrils flared, as did the pain in Leesha's temple. She wondered if Rojer would be a good herald in any event. He had a knack for saying the wrong things.

'How many of your Jongleurs died on Waning, Master Halfgrip?' Thamos asked quietly. They both knew the answer. None. It wasn't a fair comparison, but Thamos wasn't always fair.

Hary cleared his throat. 'We're working with what we've got in the meantime, Your Highness. Everyone's got a voice, and most can be taught to carry a tune. Not every barony has a Holy House yet, but they've all got choirs. Master Rojer and his, ah, wives have seen to that. On Seventhday you can hear the *Song of Waning* for miles around. Enough to hold an entire copse of wood demons at bay.

'Master Rojer even wrote a lullaby version,' Hary went on. 'One that can protect a parent and child even as it soothes the babe's cries.' Thamos looked unconvinced, but he let the matter drop.

'Amanvah and Sikvah have been giving *sharusahk* lessons, as well,' Rojer added. 'Simple *sharukin* to help the healing stretch muscles and scars back to full flexibility.' The Hollowers might still look askance at the Krasians in their midst, but they had all taken to *sharusahk*. Arlen had begun to teach the Cutters, but now it was a craze that spread throughout Hollow County.

'Krasian songs in the Holy Houses,' Inquisitor Hayes griped. 'Krasian exercises in the town square. Bad enough we have a heathen priestess teaching choirs of the Creator, but now we must corrupt our people further by teaching them to murder in the fashion of the desert rats?'

'Ay!' Gared said. 'Lot of Cutters alive who wouldn't be without Rojer's music and Krasian fighting moves. Don't like the desert rats any more'n you, but we're forgettin' the real enemy if we turn noses up at what's keeping folk strong in the night.'

Leesha blinked. Wisdom from the baron. Wonders never ceased.

'It's not just that,' Hayes amended. 'What of the silks this Shamavah is selling? Women are parading about like harlots, forgetting all decency and putting sin in the minds of men.'

'I beg your pardon,' Leesha snapped, lifting a silk kerchief she had purchased just last week. Abban's First Wife Shamavah had come to the Hollow with her, and set up a Krasian restaurant in town that never had an empty seat. She had set up a pavilion out back, selling southern goods at shockingly low prices, and a steady stream of supply carts had come from Everam's Bounty since with much-needed trade.

'If all it takes to put sin in the minds of men is women flashing a bit of silk,' Leesha said, 'perhaps the problem is with your sermons, Inquisitor, and not the Krasians.'

'Still got a point,' Smitt cut in. 'Shamavah's selling on the cheap to cut into my business, but she's making up for it in the back waving gold in workers' faces then paying them klats. Getting folk dependent on our enemies for things we can do without or make here in the Hollow.'

'I think you've gotten too used to being the only store in town, Smitt Inn,' Leesha said. Indeed, the Speaker of the Hollow had many connections with the Merchants' Guild in Angiers, and had grown steadily wealthier even as those around him suffered the depredations of the last year. 'I've seen what you charge hungry folk for a loaf of bread. A little competition will do you good.'

'Enough,' Thamos cut in. 'We're in no position to refuse the trade right now, but as of today there will be an import tax on all goods from the Krasian lands.'

Smitt and Hayes broke into wide grins at that, but the count checked them with a finger. 'But you're both going to have to get used to a little silk and competition in exchange. Don't make a habit of wasting my time with these petty complaints.'

Leesha held back her own smile as the curve fell from the other men's lips.

'I trust the new cathedral is not a petty matter?' Hayes said testily.

'Not at all, Inquisitor,' Thamos said. 'In fact, it vexes Arther daily when he prepares the tallies. You've barely broken ground, and by all accounts already exceeded your yearly budget and every line of credit available.'

'There are no braver men or women in all Thesa than the Hollowers, Your Highness, but they are woodsmen,' Hayes said, the derision in his tone almost undetectable. 'Canon – and wisdom – demand a Holy House be built in stone. In Angiers, where stoneworkers are more common, the cost would be a third as much.'

Smitt coughed. He was one of the many creditors waiting on the Inquisitor for payment.

'You have something to add, Speaker?' Thamos asked.

'Begging Your Highness' pardon, and no disrespect to the Inquisitor,' Smitt said, 'but that just ent true. Demons did most of our quarrying for us at new moon. Stone is cheap in the Hollow, and so is muscle. Wasn't our idea to make this the first building in history in the shape of a ripping greatward.'

'Ent the whole barony a greatward?' Gared asked.

'Even the baron agrees it's a redundant waste,' Smitt said.

Gared's face took on the strained look it did when someone said something he didn't understand. 'A what?'

Child Franq ignored him, glaring at Smitt. 'How dare you question the Inquisitor? Hollow Cathedral will be the last refuge if the corelings take the county, as they nearly did at new moon.'

'A project that will take decades to finish properly,' Erny said, 'and leave you with irregularly shaped rooms with vastly wasted footage. A basic wardwall would be cheaper and far more efficient.'

'Demons make it all the way into the centre of the Hollow,' Gared said, 'ent no wall or ward gonna stop 'em. Better to use the place to pray for the Deliverer to return.'

'Mr Bales himself denies he is the Deliverer,' Hayes reminded him. 'By his own words. We must continue to look to the Creator for true succour.'

Gared's hands curled into fists at the words. He had become

more pious of late, but it was due to his belief – shared by tens of thousands across Thesa – that Arlen Bales was the Deliverer, sent by the Creator to lead humanity against the corelings.

The Inquisitor had been sent to the Hollow by the Tenders of the Creator in Angiers to study these claims, preferably disproving them and outing Arlen as an imposter. But the Inquisitor was no fool. A public stance against Arlen would turn the entire Hollow against him.

'With all due respect, Inquisitor,' Leesha said, 'Arlen Bales never said any such thing. He denies he is the Deliverer, true, but it was one another he told us to look to.'

Gared's fists thumped the table, rattling goblets and making papers jump. All eyes in the room turned to his dark glare. 'He *is* the Deliverer. Don't understand why we're still talking like he ent.'

Inquisitor Hayes shook his head. 'There is no proof . . .'

'*Proof?!*' Gared boomed. 'He saved us when we'd all have been et. Gave us back the power to save ourselves. Ent none can deny that. You all saw him floating in the sky, throwing lightning from his *rippin'* hands, and you still want *rippin'* proof? How about how there wan't a mind demon attack last Waning?'

He looked to the count. 'You heard him during the fight. "You're my last piece of business before I take the fight to the Core", he told Jardir.'

'Demons still come every night, Baron,' Thamos said. 'Homes burn. Warriors bleed. Innocent people die. I'll not deny what Mr Bales has done, but neither do I feel "delivered".'

Gared shrugged. 'Maybe he did the hard part, and we've the rest to do ourselves. Maybe it's gonna get hard again, an' he just bought us time to grow strong. Ent no Tender. Don't pretend to know the Creator's whole plan. But I know one part, sure as the sun rises. Creator sent Arlen Bales to deliver the fighting wards back to us and show us how to fight.'

He looked back at the Inquisitor. 'Rest we'll see when we

get down the road. Maybe we'll be worthy an' win back the night, and maybe our sins'll weigh us an' we'll fail.'

Hayes blinked, caught for a reply. Leesha could see the man warring within himself, trying to reconcile Arlen's 'miracles' with the desire of his order to hold on to power.

'So we are supposed to bow down to Arlen Bales?' Thamos demanded, giving the thought voice. 'All the Tenders and Shepherds – I and my brother and Euchor of Miln? All of us voluntarily abdicate power to him?'

'Abdi-what?' Gared asked. 'Course not. You've met him. Mr Bales dun't care about thrones and papers. Dun't think the Deliverer cares about anythin' 'cept keepin' us safe in the night. So where's the harm in givin' him credit for what he's done, 'specially now when he's gone on to the Core itself for us?'

'We have only his word on that, Baron,' Child Franq noted.

Gared turned a cold glare at him. 'You callin' him a liar?'

The Child shrank back, clearing his throat. 'Of course not, I, ah . . .'

Hayes laid a hand on his arm. 'The Child will be silent.' Immediately, a look of relief crossed Franq's face, and he dropped his eyes, withdrawing from the debate.

'I don't see what difference it makes,' Leesha cut in. Gared glared at her, but she met his gaze coolly. 'If Arlen had wanted to be called the Deliverer, he wouldn't have spent his every other breath denying it. Whether he is or isn't, he thinks folk won't put their backs into the fight if they're waiting to be saved.'

The Inquisitor nodded, perhaps too eagerly. Leesha turned to him next. 'As for your plans, Inquisitor, I'm afraid I must agree with my father, Speaker Smitt, and the baron. They are impractical and wasteful.'

'That is not for you to decide, Gatherer,' Hayes snapped.

'No, but it is for me to decide how it will be paid for.' Thamos' voice had taken on the quiet tone that showed his patience was at an end and folk should listen well.

All eyes returned to the count. 'If you insist on continuing the cathedral in this fashion, Inquisitor, the Tenders are welcome to shoulder the cost. There will be no more talk of royal funds until you change plans to something more sensible.'

Hayes gave Thamos a cold look, but he dipped a shallow bow. 'As you wish, Highness.'

'As for the matter of Arlen Bales,' the count said, 'I can assure you, Baron, this will be a topic addressed during your visit to court. You'll have the opportunity to make your case to Shepherd Pether and the duke in person.'

The zealous look on Gared's face melted away. 'Ent no Speaker, Highness. Plenty others got better words'n me on the topic. Tender Jona—'

'Has been questioned at length on the matter,' Thamos said. 'But my brothers remain unconvinced. You have witnessed his rise firsthand. If you truly believe Arlen Bales is the Deliverer, you will speak for him. If you haven't the courage, it will say even more than your words.'

Gared's jaw tightened, but he nodded. 'Deliverer told me life ent always fair. If the weight's on me, I'll carry it and more besides.'

The meeting went on for some time, each councillor in turn asking the count for funds to pay for one project or another. Leesha rubbed her temple as she tried to follow each councillor's accounting, and calculate the true numbers they sought to hide. Even when she disagreed with his choices, she didn't envy Thamos in having to make them. She wished she were at the other end of the table by his side, so she could touch him and whisper advice only he would hear.

She was surprised at how strongly the image resonated with her. The more she thought of it, the more she wanted to be countess.

She took her time gathering her papers when the session ended and the other councillors began to file out. She hoped to steal another moment with Thamos before heading to the hospit, but the Inquisitor moved over to him, stealing the opportunity.

Leesha left the room slowly, passing as close to them as possible, ears open.

'Your mother and brother will hear of this,' the Inquisitor warned.

'I'll tell them myself,' Thamos snapped back. 'And that you're being a ripping fool.'

'How dare you, boy,' the Inquisitor growled.

Thamos raised a finger. 'I'm not beneath your cane any more, Tender. Try to swing it at me again and I'll break it over my knee and send you on the next coach back to Angiers.'

Leesha clutched her papers, smiling as she left the room.

Smitt was lingering outside, speaking to his wife, Stefny, and their youngest son, Keet. The Speaker looked at her, bowing. 'My apologies if I offended you earlier, mistress.'

'The council chamber is meant for debate,' Leesha said. 'I hope you know that the Hollow owes you a great debt for your service as Speaker in these difficult times.'

Smitt nodded, slapping Keet on the shoulder. 'Just telling the boy here to see if we can't lower the price of bread, like you asked. If there's a way, he'll find it. Good head for numbers, just like his da.'

Out of his line of sight, Stefny rolled her eyes at Leesha. They both knew the boy was not really Smitt's son, but the illegitimate son of the Hollow's late Tender, Michel.

Both Leesha and Bruna had used the knowledge like a lash against Stefny when the woman was out of line, but now, with an illegitimate child of her own growing in her belly, Leesha knew she had been wrong to do so.

'A word,' she said to Stefny, as the two men walked off.

'Ay?' the woman asked. They had never been anything approaching close, but both had faced down corelings for the sake of wounded Hollowers, and there was respect between them now.

'I owe you an apology,' Leesha said. 'I've threatened you

with Keet before, but I want you to know I would never have done it, to Smitt or to the boy.'

'Nor Bruna, whatever the witch might have said,' Stefny agreed. 'I may not agree with everything you do, girl, but you keep your Gatherer's oath. You can keep your apology with it.'

She tilted her head at Smitt and the boy. 'Even if you hadn't, Smitt never would have believed you.' She shook her head. 'Funny thing about children. People see in them what they wish to see.'

Rojer smiled to see Amanvah's coach waiting in the courtyard of Thamos' keep. Heavily warded and powered with *hora*, the princess' coach was as safe as any building in the Hollow.

Pulled by four brilliant white mares with golden traces, the coach was painted to match. The white and gold was typical of austere Krasian artisans, but in the North, where a typical Jongleur's Wagon looked like the vomit of a rainbow and every two-klat Messenger had his own colours, the stark white was louder than even Thamos' royal coach.

Inside, it was a Jongleur's paradise, with multicoloured silks and velvet on almost every surface. Rojer called it the motley coach, and he loved it so.

The driver was Coliv, the Krevakh Watcher Jardir had sent to escort Leesha's entourage back to the Hollow. The man was a cold and efficient killer, and like the other *Sharum*, had looked at Rojer like a bug they were waiting for the order to squash.

But they had shed blood together at new moon, and that seemed to change everything. There were not friends – the Watcher gave new depths to the word *taciturn* – but Rojer now received a nod of respect when he saw the warrior, and it made all the difference.

'They inside?' he asked.

The Watcher shook his head. '*Sharusahk* in the Alagai

Graveyard.' His words were even, but Rojer could sense the tension in them. Since the death of Amanvah's bodyguard Enkido, Coliv had appointed himself to the role, and never let Amanvah out of shouting distance, save at her direct command. Rojer was not convinced the man ever slept or even took a piss.

Maybe he wears a sheep's bladder under those loose pants. Rojer kept his Jongleur's mask in place, giving no sign of his amusement. 'Let's go see them.'

He could sense Coliv's relief. He was cracking the reins before Rojer had even closed the door behind him. He was thrown into the pillows as the coach started with a jerk. He inhaled his wives' perfume and sighed, missing them already.

Had he been anywhere else, Sikvah at least would have been waiting inside to greet him in her coloured silks. But some fine point of Krasian honour kept them from coming within a mile of the count's keep without a formal invitation – which happened all too infrequently for Amanvah's satisfaction. They were blood of the Shar'Dama Ka, after all.

He saw them in the bandshell as the coach pulled into the Corelings' Graveyard, stretching in the gentle – yet strenuous – movements of *sharusahk*. In the square, nearly a thousand women, men, and children practised with them.

They slipped into scorpion, a pose even Rojer, a professional acrobat, had trouble with. Rojer saw shaking limbs as many struggled to hold the pose – or their closest approximation of the impossible thing – but their faces were all serene, their breathing even. They would hold as long as they could, and every day, they would get stronger.

More and more dropped out. First the men, and then the children. Soon the women began to drop off, as well. And then there were but a few, including Kendall, Rojer's favourite apprentice. And then none. Still Amanvah and Sikvah held the pose effortlessly, like marble statues.

Rojer called them *Jiwah Ka* and *Jiwah Sen*, and he loved them so. Arrick had taught Rojer to fear marriage like a plague, but what the three of them had was unlike anything Rojer ever dreamed.

Sikvah seemed to sense when he wanted to be alone and would vanish, reappearing as if by magic the moment he needed something. It was uncanny, and amazing. She was warm and inviting, caressing him and giving his every word and wish – not to mention every twitch in his motley pants – her utmost attention and effort. He confided in her as they lay in the pillows, knowing full well it would get back to Amanvah.

Sikvah was the heart of their little family, and Amanvah, of course, was the head. Always serious, always in control, even in lovemaking. And usually, Rojer had learned, right. Amanvah demanded surrender in all things, and Rojer had learned it was best to give it to her.

Unless the fiddle demanded it. Since the night they first used their music to kill corelings, his wives had known that in this, he led. Amanvah was the head and Sikvah the heart, but Rojer was the art, and art must be free.

They finished the session at rest position on their backs, then kicked themselves upright. Their students remained on their backs, treating Rojer to a chorus of panting and groans while he approached the bandshell, kissing his wives as they came down the steps from the stage, their breathing calm.

Kendall was the first of the Hollowers on her feet, coming over to them. Amanvah and Sikvah treated his other apprentices like servants, but Kendall they had taken to. She was the most skilled of the lot, turning their musical trio into a quartet, and limber enough to have a real chance at even the most difficult *sharusahk* moves one day. Her breathing was deep and even, but it was quick with exertion.

'You did well today, Kendall am'Hollow,' Amanvah said in Krasian, giving that rare, dignified nod that meant more from his *Jiwah Ka* than the loudest praise. Kendall had been included in the Krasian lessons they gave Rojer, which was a great help to him, allowing him a practice partner who struggled as much as he.

Kendall beamed, pulling her loose motley pants into an impressive curtsy. 'Thank you, Your Highness.'

Her practice robe fell open a bit as she rose, and Rojer's eyes dipped, catching sight of the line of thick scars on her chest.

Kendall caught him looking, smiling at first until she glanced down and realized he was staring at the scars and not her exposed cleavage. Suddenly the girl blushed, pulling the robe to cover herself. Rojer quickly looked away. The shame in her eyes made him wish he was cored.

Amanvah picked up on the discomfort in the air immediately. She tilted her head slightly at Kendall, and immediately Sikvah took the girl's arm.

'You are ready for more advanced *sharukin*,' Sikvah said, 'if you can perfect your scorpion pose.'

'Thought I had that one,' Kendall said.

'Better than any of the *chin*, perhaps,' Sikvah said, 'but you must reach a greater standard if you are to be instructed in higher forms. Come.'

Kendall glanced at Rojer, but allowed herself to be led a short distance away to practise. Amanvah watched the women go, then turned back to Rojer the moment they were out of earshot. 'Husband, explain. You often lament at how your people behave at the sight of your *alagai* scars, yet you do the same to your apprentice.'

Rojer swallowed. Amanvah had a way of cutting right to the heart of a matter. He was more than a little afraid of her sometimes.

'It's my fault she got them,' he said. 'I wanted to show off how good she was at charming demons with her fiddle. Pushed her to solo before she was ready, then wandered too far from her side. She made a mistake, and I wasn't there to keep her from being cored.'

His vision blurred with tears. 'It was Gared who saved her. Waded right into a pack of demons and carried her out. She nearly died as Leesha operated. I gave blood till I felt I might pass out, but it was barely enough.'

Amanvah looked at him sharply. 'You gave her your blood?'

The tone pulled Rojer up short like a bucket of cold water. Krasians had a thousand laws and customs when it came to blood, but Rojer had never grasped more than the rudiments. Giving Kendall his blood might make her his sister, or it might mean she and Sikvah needed to have a knife fight. Creator only knew.

Amanvah lifted a finger towards Sikvah. She and Kendall had barely done anything at all, but immediately Sikvah began complimenting Kendall's improvement. In moments, they rejoined Rojer and Amanvah. Kendall looked confused, but she, like Rojer, had learned it best to simply ride along when his wives began acting strangely.

'You must join us for lunch.' Amanvah's words were as much command as invitation, an honour that could not easily be refused.

Kendall dipped another curtsy. 'Be honoured, Your Highness.'

They all climbed into the motley coach, riding to Shamavah's restaurant. The count had forbidden the Krasians from owning property, but that had done little to slow Shamavah when she saw the building, a large ranch house not far from the centre of town. Abban's First Wife had deep pockets filled with gold, and it had taken her only one session of haggling with the owner to walk away with a century lease that would stand in any magistrate's court in Thesa. Craftsmen had been at work night and day, adding extensions and additional floors. Already it was unrecognizable as the more modest building it had been before.

First to be finished were luxury quarters for visiting Krasian dignitaries. His wives, finding their room at Smitt's Inn unacceptable, had transferred their things immediately. Rojer had not been consulted, but could hardly complain. Shamavah showered them in splendour while they waited on construction of Rojer's manse.

Manse. He shook his head at the thought. He'd never truly had a home at all, and since Arrick died, he'd never had more than a single room to lay his head. Soon he'd be able to house an entire acting troupe with room to spare.

A crowd was forming outside Shamavah's, waiting for tables at the bustling establishment. Many of the Hollowers had developed a taste for spicy Krasian cooking, and no sooner did one backside lift from the pillowed floor than another took its place.

But Amanvah was Krasian royalty, and Shamavah never failed to greet her – or even Rojer – personally. 'Your usual table, Highness?'

'*Inevera*,' Amanvah said. It meant 'If Everam wills', but as with Kendall, all knew it was a command. 'But first, a bath to wash away the sweat of *sharusahk*.'

Rojer had neither seen nor smelled a hint of sweat on his wives, but he shrugged. Those two bathed more than every noble in Angiers. He had plenty of papers to review in the meantime.

He escorted the women to the large bathing chamber, where Shamavah's people were already carrying in steaming buckets to heat the water. 'I'll be in the—'

'—bath with us,' Amanvah said, her tone pleasant and relaxed, as if his refusal was unimaginable.

Rojer and Kendall exchanged an uncomfortable glance. 'I bathed just this morning . . .'

'A clean body is Everam's temple,' Amanvah said, her grip on his arm like a steel vice as she led him into the steamy, wood-floored room. Sikvah had a similar hold on Kendall. Both of them resisted as the women began to pull at their clothes.

Amanvah clicked her tongue. 'I will never understand you greenlanders. You bare flesh enough on the streets to bring a flush to the cheeks of a pillow wife, yet you baulk at the thought of seeing one another in the bath.'

'Thought men ent supposed to see women naked unless they're married,' Kendall said.

Amanvah waved a hand dismissively. 'You are unbetrothed,

Kendall am'Hollow. How would you ever find a husband if men were not allowed to inspect you?'

Sikvah began unbuttoning Kendall's vest. 'The *dama'ting* will ensure your honour remains intact, sister.'

Kendall relaxed, letting herself be undressed, but Rojer felt something akin to panic rising as Amanvah did the same for him. Her quiet tone was gently scolding. 'You will wrap your apprentice in the intimacy of your music, but not share hot water with her?'

'She can have all the water she wants,' Rojer replied quietly. 'Don't need to see her bare bottom for that.'

'It's not her bottom you fear,' Amanvah said. 'And that cannot stand. You will face her scars and make your peace with them, son of Jessum, or by Everam, I will—'

'Ay, ay,' Rojer said, not even wanting to know the rest of the threat. 'I get it.' He let her finish stripping him and moved to the bath.

Rojer's wives never failed to tend him in the bath, and normally by this point he was fully aroused. *Don't want her thinking I'm trying to stick her.*

Never stick your apprentices, Master Arrick used to say. *No good can come of it.*

Thankfully, Rojer's nerves were taut and fraying, and he remained slack. But then Kendall gave him an appraising look, and he was suddenly nervous about that, as well.

A woman will forgive a small cock sooner than a limp one, Arrick taught. Rojer turned to angle his crotch from her as he hurriedly slipped into the water. His wives followed, and Kendall was the last to join them.

Rojer had spent so much time looking away from his apprentice, he had never truly seen her. She was young, yes, but not the child he thought of her as.

And her scars . . .

'They're beautiful.' Rojer had not meant to say the words aloud.

Kendall looked down. Rojer realized she was once again

unsure what he was staring at. He made a show of dropping his eyes lower for a moment, then looked up, meeting her with a grin. 'Those are beautiful, too, but I meant your scars.'

'Then how come you ent looked at me for more than a second since I got them?' Kendall demanded. 'All of a sudden you put a river between us.'

Rojer dropped his eyes. 'My fault you got them.'

Kendall gave him an incredulous look. 'I'm the one that screwed up. I'm the one so busy trying to impress you I didn't keep my mind on the strings.'

'I never should have pushed you to solo,' Rojer said.

'I never should have pretended to be ready when I knew I wasn't,' Kendall countered.

Amanvah tsked. 'The water will grow cold before you finish this argument. What does it matter? It was *inevera*.'

Sikvah nodded. 'Nie sent the *alagai*, husband, not you. And Kendall lives, while they were shown the sun.'

Rojer held up his three-fingered hand, the crippled thing that had earned him the name Halfgrip. 'My wives' people understand the beauty of scars, Kendall. The missing part of my hand is where my mother gave her life for me. I treasure it every bit as much as my thumb.'

He nodded to the raised scars that ran across Kendall's chest from the demon's claws and the puckered half-moon on her shoulder from its bite. 'Seen a lot of people get cored, Kendall. Hundreds. Thousands. Seen the ones who live to tell the tale, and the ones who don't. But I ent seen many that get it like that and make it through. They're a portrait of your strength and will to live, and I have never seen anything so beautiful.'

Kendall's lip quivered. Water ran down her face, not all of it from the steam in the air. Sikvah moved to hold her. 'He's right, sister. You should be proud.'

'Sister?' Kendall asked.

'Our husband gave you his blood the night you received these.' Amanvah traced a finger along Kendall's scars. 'We are family, now. If you wish it, I will accept you as Sikvah's *Jiwah Sen*.'

'Ay, what?!' Rojer had relaxed into the hot water, but now he sat up with a splash.

Sikvah bowed to Kendall, her breasts dipping into the water. 'I would be honoured to accept you, Kendall am'Hollow, as my sister-wife.'

'Hold on, now,' Rojer said.

Kendall snorted uncomfortably. 'Doubt we'll find a Tender willing to perform *that* ceremony.'

'Inquisitor Hayes won't even acknowledge Sikvah,' Rojer noted.

Amanvah shrugged, not taking her eyes from Kendall. 'The heathen Holy Men are irrelevant. I am a Bride of Everam and the daughter of the Deliverer. If you swear the marriage oath before me, you will be wed.'

Like I'm not even here, Rojer thought, as the bathing women negotiated his *third* marriage. He knew he should protest further, but words failed him. He never set foot in a Holy House any time he didn't absolutely have to, and a Tender's words had never meant a corespawned thing to him. Creator knew he, and his master before him, had led many a wife to forget her marriage vows. For a few hours, at least.

But that kind of thing always led to trouble. The Creator might not care, but maybe the Tenders had a bit of wisdom in their dogma.

'Ay,' Kendall said, looking down at the water, and Rojer felt a thrill run through him. She raised her eyes and met Amanvah's. 'Ay, all right. I do. I will.'

Amanvah nodded, smiling, but Kendall held up a hand. 'But I ent swearing any oaths in the bath. Want to know more about this *Jiwah Sen* business, and I'll need to tell my mum.'

'Of course,' Amanvah said. 'No doubt your mother will wish to negotiate your dower, and seek the blessing of your patriarch.'

Rojer relaxed a bit at that, and Kendall seemed to settle as well.

'Ent got a patriarch,' Kendall said. 'Corelings took everyone but my mum.'

'Now that you are intended, she, too, will have a man to care for her,' Amanvah promised. 'Rooms for you both will be added to our husband's new manse.'

'Ay, wait,' Rojer said. 'Don't I get a say in this? All a sudden I'm intended, *and* have to live with my new mother-in-law?'

'What's wrong with my mum?' Kendall demanded.

'Nothing,' Rojer said.

'Corespawned right,' Kendall said.

'A grandparent will be a great assistance when the children begin to come, husband,' Amanvah said.

'What happened to my needing to be free?' Rojer asked. The words sounded like a mouse squeak, and all the women, even Kendall, laughed.

'May I make a confession, sister?' Sikvah asked.

'Of course,' Kendall said.

Sikvah's demure smile curled just a touch. 'I lay with my husband in the bath before we were wed.'

Rojer expected Kendall to be scandalized, but instead she, too, gave a sly smile, turning to meet his eyes. 'Ay? Honest word?'

Leesha glanced at the water clock, shocked to find it was nearly dusk. She had been working for hours, but it seemed only moments had passed since she went down into her cellar laboratory. Working *hora* magic had a similar effect to what happened to warriors who fought the corelings with warded weapons. She felt energized, strong despite all the time spent hunched over her workbench.

For the past year she'd used the cellar almost exclusively for brewing flamework and dissecting demons, but since her return from Everam's Bounty it had become a warding chamber. She had learned many things in her travels, but none more compelling than the secret of *hora* magic. In the past, she had been able to do her warding in sunlight, needing dark and demons only to power its effects. Now, thanks to Arlen and Inevera, she understood far more.

A dark, ventilated shed had been built on her land, far enough from her cottage to keep the stench away, where the bodies of slain demons, rich with magic, slowly desiccated. The ichor was collected in special opaque bottles for powering spells, and the polished bones and mummified remains were warded and coated in silver or gold to give permanent, rechargeable powers to weapons and other items. Some few even worked in daylight.

It was an incredible advancement, one that could change the course of the war with demons. Leesha could heal wounds once thought beyond repair, and blast corelings from a distance without ever having to risk a life. Already her apron needed more pockets for her growing assortment of wardings. Some of the Hollowers called her the ward witch, though never to her face.

But for all the power of the discovery, warding and *hora* magic was too much work for her to make a difference alone. She needed allies. More ward witches to help with the making, and to spread word and make sure these powers were never lost again.

She went up the stairs, careful to close the thick curtain before lifting the trap and coming into her cottage. There was still a bit of light left in the windows, but Wonda had already lit the lamps.

Leesha had just enough time to wash and put on a fresh dress before women began to arrive for the Gathering. Her tendons twisted like a tourniquet in those few minutes. She felt as if she might snap as the first coach came up the warded road.

But then Wonda opened the door, and Leesha saw Mistress Jizell, a heavyset woman now in her fifties, with great streaks of grey in her hair and deep smile lines on her face.

'Jizell!' Leesha cried. 'When you never wrote back, I assumed . . .'

'That I was too coward to brave a few nights on the road with the demons to come when family calls?' Jizell demanded. She swept Leesha into one of her crushing hugs, stealing her breath and making her feel safe and protected. 'Love you like my own daughter, Leesha Paper. I know you wouldn't have asked us to come if you didn't truly need us.'

Leesha nodded, but she did not loosen her hold, keeping her head on Jizell's comforting bosom just a moment longer. She shivered, and suddenly she was weeping.

'I'm so frightened, Jizell,' she whispered.

'There, poppet.' Jizell stroked her back. 'I know. Got the world on your shoulders these days, but I ent seen a stronger pair in all my days. If you can't hold it, no one can.'

She squeezed tighter. 'And me and the girls will always be there to lend our backs to it.'

Leesha looked up. 'The girls?'

Jizell let go and took a step back, reaching into her cleavage and producing a kerchief with a wink. 'Dry your eyes and say hi to your new old apprentices.'

Leesha took a deep, calming breath, drying her eyes. Jizell kept close, the big woman giving her the privacy to compose herself before opening the coach doors again. Roni and Kadie, apprentices that had been Leesha's students up until she returned to the Hollow last year, veritably leapt from the coach into her arms. Their excitement was palpable, and Leesha laughed with the joy of it.

'We saw the greatward light up, mistress!' Kadie squeaked. 'It was amazing!'

'Not as amazing as the men we saw,' Roni said. 'Are all the Hollowers so tall, mistress?'

'Night, Roni,' Kadie rolled her eyes, 'we're standing out in the open in the dark and all you can think of is boys.'

'Men,' Roni corrected her, and even Leesha snickered.

'Enough, giggleboxes,' Leesha said, falling easily back to her stern instructor's voice. 'We can talk warding and boys later. Tonight, there's work to be done.' She pointed to the freshly built operating theater at the far end of the yard. 'Go and help Gatherers to their seats as they arrive.' The girls nodded, running off.

'My new old apprentices?' Leesha asked.

'Long as you can stand their prattle,' Jizell said. 'They'll learn far more in the Hollow than they will in Angiers.'

Leesha nodded. 'And have more asked of them. We often don't have the luxury of a clean hospit to work in, Jizell. Before long, they'll be cutting and stitching folk right where they fell, just to get them back to the hospit alive.'

'World's marching off to war, one way or the other. Gatherers can't afford to hide behind the walls any more.' Jizell put a hand on Leesha's shoulder. 'But if someone's got to teach them the lesson, I'd rather it be you. Proud of you, girl.'

'Thank you,' Leesha said.

'How many weeks since you last bled?' Jizell asked.

Leesha's heart stopped. Her voice caught in her throat and she froze, wide-eyed.

Jizell gave her a wry look. 'Don't look so surprised. You're not the only one of us trained by Mistress Bruna.'

From all over Hollow County, Herb Gatherers came up the warded road. Some on foot from the hospit just over a mile away by the Corelings' Graveyard. Others in coaches sent to collect them from the outermost baronies, and everywhere in between. There were even a few from the migrant refugee villages that had not yet been absorbed.

'Bandits,' Wonda said, after they greeted a few of the lean, hard-eyed women.

'That's enough of that talk, Wonda Cutter,' Leesha said. 'This is a Gathering. Every woman here has taken oaths to save lives, and you will treat them all with respect. Is that clear?'

Wonda's eye quivered, glistening just a little, and Leesha wondered for a moment if she had been too harsh. But then the girl swallowed hard and nodded. 'Ay, mistress. Din't mean no disrespect.'

'I know you didn't, dear Wonda,' Leesha said. 'But you must never forget the real enemy comes from the Core. Their attack at new moon was little more than a feint, and they almost destroyed us, even with Arlen and Renna in the Hollow.'

Wonda clenched a fist. 'He'll come back, mistress.'

'We don't know that,' Leesha said. 'And if he did, he'd tell you himself that we'd best make every ally we can.'

'Ay, mistress,' Wonda said. 'Still say you should've let me hide the silver.'

Leesha shook her head, counting the women already in the theatre and those still on the road. The parked carriages stretched out of sight now, and every Gatherer arrived on foot.

Amanvah and Sikvah were the last to arrive, leaving Rojer waiting in the yard with the other men as they followed Leesha and Jizell into the theatre. The chatter of the women grew markedly louder at the sight of the Krasian women standing behind Leesha at the entrance to the floor.

Leesha took a deep breath. Jizell gave her shoulder a comforting squeeze, and she stepped out into the centre of the theatre floor. The din died instantly.

Leesha turned a full circle, trying to meet every eye in the theatre, if only for a moment. Nearly two hundred women leaned forward, waiting expectantly for the ward witch to speak.

It wasn't nearly enough. As near as the talliers could tell, Hollow County and its environs had swollen to almost fifty thousand inhabitants. Few in number even before these troubled times, many Gatherers had been captured or killed on the road as they fled the Krasian invasion, or fallen prey to the destruction at new moon.

Less than half the women were true Gatherers. Leesha knew many of them from correspondence and interviews when they first came to the Hollow. Some few had real skill and knowledge of old world techniques, but others were glorified midwives, grandmothers who could pull a babe from its mother and brew a few simple cures. Few if any of them could read, and almost none of them, even Jizell, could ward.

The rest were apprentices. Some young girls in training, others older, women drafted into the hospits when the wounded began to mount, likely with no more skill than boiling water and bringing fresh linen.

You're all Gatherers now, Leesha thought.

'Thank you all for coming,' Leesha called, her voice strong and clear. 'Many of you have travelled great distance, and I welcome you most of all. There hasn't been such a Gathering in the Hollow since my teacher, Mistress Bruna, was young.'

Many of the women nodded to themselves. Bruna was known to all of them, the legendary Herb Gatherer who had lived to be one hundred and twenty before the flux had taken her.

'Gatherings used to be commonplace,' Leesha said. 'After the Return, it was the only way left to us to pool the secrets of the old world and try to gain back something of what we lost when the demons burned the great libraries.

'It must be so again. There are too few of us, and too much to share, if we are to survive the coming moons. We must recruit as heavily as the Cutters, and train together as they do. My apprentices have been copying my books of chemics and healing – all of you will be sent home with your own copies to study. And from this day forward, there will be regular lessons in this theatre, covering everything from healing and warding to demon anatomy. Even some of the secrets of fire. For some I will be the teacher. For others,' she looked back to Jizell and Amanvah, 'I too will be a student.'

'Ay, you can't expect us to take lessons from some Krasian witch!' one old woman had the guts to cry. Many others echoed their approval. Too many.

Leesha looked back at Amanvah, but for all the pride she knew the young princess carried, she remained serene, refusing to be baited. Leesha gave a clap, and her apprentices carried in an injured Cutter on a stretcher. He had been given a sleeping draught, and the girls grunted as they lifted the burly man's dead weight onto the operating table.

'This is Makon Orchard, from the barony of New Rizon,' Leesha said, drawing the white cloth that covered him down to his waist, revealing black and purple bruising around a neat line of stitches that stretched across his abdomen. 'He was injured clearing land for a new greatward three nights ago. I spent eight hours cutting and stitching him back together. Are there any here who witnessed this?'

Six Gatherers and a score of apprentices raised their hands. Still, Leesha pointed to the old woman who had called out. 'Gatherer Alsa, isn't it?'

'Ay,' the old woman said with a suspicious look. She was one of the migrant refugee Gatherers, come from one of the many hamlets that had fled the Krasian invasion. It was true that many of the migrants had turned to banditry, but their desperation had not happened without cause.

'Will you come and inspect the wound, please?' Leesha asked.

The Gatherer grunted, thumping her walking stick and pushing to her feet. Roni moved to escort her, but Alsa swatted at her and the girl wisely kept her distance as the old woman shuffled down to the theatre floor.

Despite her gruff exterior, Gatherer Alsa seemed to know her business, inspecting Makon's injury with firm but gentle hands. She squeezed the stitches and rubbed her thumb and forefinger under her nose, sniffing.

'You do good work, girl,' Alsa said at last. 'Boy's lucky to be alive. But I don't see what this has to do with us sharing secrets with desert rats.' She pointed her stick rudely at Amanvah. The young *dama'ting* eyed the stick, but maintained her calm.

'Lucky to be alive,' Leesha echoed. 'Even so, it will be months before Makon can walk, or pass a stool without blood and pain. He will be on a liquid diet for weeks, and may never be able to fight or do hard labour again.'

She gestured to Amanvah, who stepped forward, careful to

keep her distance from Alsa. She produced a curved silver knife.

'Ay, what are you doing?' Alsa demanded coming forward, her stick held ready to strike. Leesha checked her with an outstretched hand.

'Patience I beg, mistress,' she said.

Alsa looked at her incredulously, but stayed her hand as Amanvah skilfully cut away Leesha's neat stitches, pulling them free and tossing them aside. She held out a hand and Sikvah placed a fine horsehair brush in it, producing a porcelain ink bowl for dipping.

Makon's chest and belly had been freshly shaved, leaving a clean, smooth surface for Amanvah to work. She dipped the brush and wiped the excess ink on the edge of the bowl, painting precise wards around the wound. She worked quickly and with confidence, but it was still several minutes before she finished. When she was done, there were two concentric ovals of wards surrounding the line of stitches.

She then reached into her *hora* pouch, producing a demon bone that looked like a chunk of charcoal. She passed this slowly over the wound, and immediately the wards began to glow. Softly at first, then brighter. The two ovals seemed to rotate in opposite directions, wards flaring brighter and brighter until those closest had to shield their eyes.

The light faded a few moments later, and Amanvah brushed her hands as the bone crumbled to dust. Sikvah came forward again, this time with a bowl of hot water and a cloth. Amanvah took it and wiped away the crusted blood and ink wards, then stepped back.

There were gasps throughout the theatre. All could see that Makon's skin had gone from black and purple to pale pink, and the wound was gone.

Alsa shoved past Leesha, moving to inspect the warrior, running her hand over the scarless flesh, pressing, squeezing, and pinching. At last she looked up at Amanvah. 'That ent possible.'

'All things are possible with Everam's grace, mistress,' Amanvah said. She turned to address the Gathering.

'I am Amanvah, First Wife of Rojer asu Jessum am'Inn am'Hollow. We are Krasian, yes, but my sister-wife and I are Hollow tribe now. Your warriors are our warriors, and regardless, all who stand against the *alagai* are the charges of the *dama'ting*. With *hora* magic, many of those who might have died can be saved, and many left crippled will be able to fight again. Tomorrow night, Makon am'Orchard will once again lift the spear with his brothers in defence of Hollow County.'

She turned, looking Gatherer Alsa in the eye. 'If you let me, I will teach you to do the same.'

Out in the yard, Rojer couldn't make out many of the words in the Gathering theatre, but his trained ear could still pick out voice and tone, Leesha's most of all. He'd spent hours training her to dominate the theatre by projecting like a Jongleur. Leesha took well to the lessons, especially with the masterful performances of the count to study. Thamos could speak a normal tone to those closest to him without eavesdroppers catching a word, and project whispers across his entire courtroom clear as day. Trained from birth to command, the Royals of Fort Angiers could put an entire acting troupe to shame. Obedience was assumed so they were free to be genial unless pressed, and dignified even then.

Rojer had seen personally how quickly that affable tone could turn into a lash. Just a subtle shift, not losing a touch of politeness, could express displeasure without ever giving offence, and let everyone else in the room know how their leader expected them to behave.

Now Leesha's voice rang through the theatre in the same manner. Polite. Respectful. And utterly in control.

She would make a brilliant countess, once she and Thamos stopped sticking in the dark and announced the inevitable match. He hoped it was soon. If there was anyone in the world due for a bit of happiness, it was Leesha Paper. Night, even Arlen found a wife, and he was crazier than a mustang stampede.

The theatre went silent and he saw the pulsing lights of Amanvah's performance. When it was over, his *Jiwah Ka*'s voice took over the Gathering, thrumming throughout the theatre in a powerful spell.

Amanvah needed no training from Rojer. Even common Krasians rivalled the Angierian royal court for dramatic performances, and where Thamos had been raised prince of a duchy, his First Wife had been raised princess of the world. She closed her speech with such a tone of finality Rojer expected the women to come filing out soon after, but the Gathering went on for hours as they lectured, debated, and argued about what form Leesha's new Gatherers' Guild would take. That Leesha would be guildmistress was never in question, but the women had plenty to say on the rest.

Rojer didn't mind the wait, idly testing new tunes on his fiddle as his head spun with thoughts of Kendall. The scent of her, the talent, the beauty. The way she kissed.

It was only a few hours ago, but already it seemed a dream. *But it ent*, he thought. *It really happened. Tomorrow Amanvah's going to visit Kendall's mother and all the Core's gonna break loose.*

He felt his nerves clench and played the lullaby his mother used to sing until he calmed again.

Not like they can run you out of town, he told himself. *You're the Painted Man's fiddle wizard. Hollow needs you.*

But he'd already given them the *Song of Waning*. Did they *really* need him any more?

Got to have a private talk with Leesha, he realized. *She'll know what to do. Not like she's got a leg to stand on when it comes to scandal.*

He took a deep breath as the Gathering finally broke and women started filing out. His wives wasted no time in coming to him, ignoring the stares of the other women and moving with dignified haste until they were safely in the motley coach.

'Let us go quickly,' Amanvah said. 'I may have agreed to teach *hora* healing to these women, but I have no desire to weather their stares any longer than I have to. As if I were to blame for their foolish and cowardly flight from my father's glorious coming.'

'One way to look at it,' Rojer said. 'Doubt they see things the same way, what with all the fire and murder chasing them out.'

'All training leaves scrapes and bruises, husband,' Amanvah said. 'They will understand when my father leads them to victory in Sharak Ka.'

Rojer knew better than to argue. 'You'll make no friends here with that sort of talk.'

Amanvah gave him a withering look. 'I am not a fool, husband.'

Rojer sketched a bow. 'Forgive me, *Jiwah Ka*. I never meant to suggest such.'

He thought the sarcasm in his tone might get him in trouble, but like many Royals, Amanvah took obsequious words as her due. 'You are forgiven, husband.' She inclined her head at the carriage steps. Rojer had still not climbed in. 'May we go?'

'You go on ahead,' Rojer said. 'Need to talk to Leesha.'

Amanvah nodded. 'To discuss Kendall, of course.'

Rojer blinked. '. . . and you've no protest?'

Amanvah shrugged. 'Mistress Paper acted as your sister in arranging our own marriage, husband, and spoke honestly and true. If you wish her advice on the contract, that is your right.'

Advice on the contract, Rojer thought. *Meaning she can dicker the dower, but the marriage is happening.*

'And if she tells me it's a bad match?' Rojer said.

'It is a sister's right to raise such concerns.' Amanvah gave Rojer a cold look. 'But she had best have good reason, not some greenland prudishness.'

Rojer swallowed, but he nodded. He closed the door and stepped away as Amanvah rang her bell and the driver took off for Shamavah's restaurant.

Gatherers were filing away to their own coaches or heading down the road in groups, chatting animatedly and clutching the books Leesha was handing out as they left.

'I'm too old to be an apprentice again,' one hag was saying as he approached. She smelled like incense and tea, dry and stale.

'Nonsense,' Leesha said.

'Not as fit as I used to be,' the woman continued as if Leesha had not spoken. 'Can't be coming all the way out here all the time.'

'I'll arrange lessons in your own barony,' Leesha said. 'I have apprentices who can teach you the basics of warding, and help train your own.'

'Corespawned if I'm going to take lessons from some girl that ent reddened her wadding yet,' the woman snapped. 'Ent had an apprentice in a dozen years. I was retired before the Krasians came.'

Leesha's eyes grew hard. 'Times are dark for everyone, Gatherer, but you'll take your lessons, and apprentices, too. Hollow County won't lose a single life because you're too stubborn to change your ways.'

The woman's eyes widened, but she wisely did not argue further. Leesha saw Rojer waiting and turned to him, dismissing her as expertly as the Duchess Mum.

'Not going back with your wives?' Leesha asked.

'Need to talk to you,' Rojer said. He, too, had a trained voice, and his tone made clear the seriousness of the matter.

Leesha drew a deep breath, ending in a faint shudder. 'Need to talk to you, too, Rojer. Mum's got my head in a spin.'

Rojer smiled. 'Creator, what are the odds? That only happens on days when the sun comes up.'

Leesha barked a nervous laugh at that, and Rojer wondered what could rattle her so. She signalled Darsy and Wonda to hand out books and make farewells. She and Rojer made their way into her cottage.

Only to find Renna Bales waiting for them.

''Bout time,' Renna said. 'Startin' to think I'd be waitin' all night for you to finish up.'

Leesha put her hands on her hips. She tired easily now, and arguing with every stubborn woman in the Hollow at once had left her drained of energy and patience. The only thing not feeling drained was her bladder, which was fit to burst. She was in no mood for Renna and her superior attitude.

'Perhaps if you'd let me know you were coming instead of sneaking into my home, Renna Bales, I might have accommodated you.' She put just a touch of emphasis on *might*.

''Pologies for disrespectin' your wards,' Renna said. 'Din't want folk seein' me.'

'And why not?' Leesha demanded. 'You were the only thing giving them hope when Arlen disappeared, and then you up and vanished for weeks on end. Where in the Core have you been?'

Renna crossed her arms. 'Busy.'

Leesha gave her a moment to elaborate, but Renna just stared at her, daring her to press.

'All right,' Rojer said, stepping between them. 'Everyone's got big paps. Can we stop comparing them and sit down?' He reached into his multicoloured bag of marvels, pulling out a tiny clay flask. 'I've got couzi to take the edge off.'

'Night, that's all we need.' Leesha had made some of the worst decisions of her life when she drank. 'Please, have a seat. I'll put on tea.'

Renna had already taken the flask and tipped it back hard. Leesha thought she would have spat fire after a gulp like that, but Renna gave only a slight cough, handing the bottle back to Rojer. 'Creator, did I need that.'

Leesha's head throbbed as she put the kettle on and set a tray of cups and saucers on the counter, but it was nothing compared to the pressure down below. She glanced at the privy, but could not bear to miss a word. Renna, like Arlen, had a tendency to vanish if one took their eye off her for even a moment.

'Glad you're all right,' Rojer was saying as she joined them in the sitting room. 'When new moon came with no sign of you, we all feared the worst. It's a miracle we survived without you.'

'Minds weren't coming to the Hollow last Waning,' Renna said. 'They had other business.'

'What business?' Leesha demanded. 'Enough vagaries. Where were you? Where is Arlen?'

'Don't expect to see either of us again after tonight,' Renna said. 'Hollow needs to stand on its own. We were the reason the mind demons came. We *draw* them.'

Leesha looked at her a long time. That would certainly explain Arlen's disappearance. If he was drawing the minds' attention to the Hollow, he would put himself as far away as possible. 'Why?'

'Mind demons take this Deliverer business seriously as Tenders,' Renna said. 'Scared as piss about it. Unifiers, they call us. Ones who get so strong they draw followings. Wern't gonna rest till we were dealt with, and you ent ready for that kind of demon attention. Need time to fill the Hollow.'

'So Arlen killed Ahmann and went into hiding?' Leesha demanded. 'What's to stop them going after Thamos, next?'

Renna waved a hand so dismissively Leesha was offended on her lover's behalf. ''Less he learns to shoot lightning from his arse, count's beneath the minds' notice.'

She looked at them pointedly. 'You two, on the other hand, need to step careful. Minds know who you are. Strike at you, they get the chance.'

Leesha felt her face go cold. Rojer looked like he might slosh up. 'How can you know that?'

Renna opened her mouth, but Rojer answered for her. 'She's right. Saw it myself at new moon. Stepped beyond the wards, and every demon on the field turned to me at once. Felt like I had a flaming bullseye on my chest.'

Leesha saw it in her mind's eye, imagining hundreds of cold coreling eyes turned upon her and the vulnerable life she carried within. The child would barely be bigger than her curled little finger, but she could have sworn it kicked. Her bladder cried out to empty, but she clenched her thighs and ignored it.

'So you're going to leave the Hollow at the mercy of the demons while you go off and . . . what? Take your honeymoon without a care?'

'Corelings ent got any mercy, Gatherer,' Renna said. 'You of all people should know that. Don't tell me I don't care. Hollowers been good to me like no others. Just because I ent here don't mean I ent fighting for 'em every corespawned night.'

'Then why'd you come back?' Rojer said. 'Just to tell us you ent coming back?'

'Ay,' Renna said. 'Owed you that much. Need to know help ent coming.'

'You could've just left a note,' Leesha said.

'Can't write,' Renna said. 'Not everyone grows up with a rich da and time to spend learnin' letters. Expect you've got questions, so make 'em quick.'

Leesha closed her eyes, breathing deeply. Renna had a way of infuriating her past her ability to think. She might ask directly if Arlen was alive, but there was little point. She didn't believe for one moment the woman would be so calm if he wasn't.

'Just tell me one thing,' Leesha said.

Renna crossed her arms, but she waited on the question.

'Did Arlen kill Ahmann?' Leesha asked. Her hand went to her belly as if to shield the child from the answer.

'He ent comin' back, either,' was all Renna said. 'Hollowers ent the only ones need to stand on their own.'

'That's not an answer,' Leesha said.

'Told you to ask,' Renna said. 'Din't say I would answer.'

Insufferable woman. Leesha eyed her. 'Why do you and Arlen have powers in the day, when no others do?'

'Eh?' Renna asked.

'In the count's throne room, you defeated Enkido,' Leesha said. 'His blow should have paralysed you, but instead you forced him back and threw him across the room. No woman your size could do that without magic, but it was broad day. How? It's more than just the blackstem, isn't it?'

Renna paused, choosing her words with care. The delay answered Leesha's second question if not her first.

Just as the woman was about to answer, the front door slammed open. 'Mistress Leesha!' Wonda cried.

Leesha only took her eyes off Renna for an instant, but when she looked back, the woman was gone.

'Creator!' Rojer cried, leaping to his feet as he, too, noticed the disappearance.

Wonda burst into the room an instant later. 'Mistress Leesha!' Her eyes were wild and terrified. 'You need to come quick!'

'What is it?' Leesha asked.

'Krasians,' Wonda said. 'Krasians attacked Lakton. Cutters found refugees on the road. They're bringing them in as they can, but there's wounded, and lots still out in the naked night.'

'Night,' Rojer said.

'Corespawn it,' Leesha growled. 'Send runners to catch the Gatherers and have them meet us at the hospit. The Cutters will be mustering, and I want volunteers to go out with them. You and Darsy go with Gared.'

Wonda nodded and vanished out the door. Leesha felt a gentle breeze, and looked back. There was a fog along the floor, barely noticeable an instant ago, but now it was pooling together, growing bigger, solidifying.

And then Renna stood before them again. Leesha should have been startled to see her dissipate and reform like Arlen, but for some reason it was no surprise. There were bigger matters at hand.

'You said the Hollow needs to stand on its own,' she said. 'Does that include the Laktonians, too?'

'Ent a monster,' Renna said. 'Every second we waste talkin' is a second I'm not looking out for those on the road. Send the Cutters out quick as you can. I'll see those farthest away last until help arrives.'

Leesha nodded. 'Creator watch over you.'

'And you,' Renna said, vaporizing right before their eyes.

Rojer and Leesha stood silent a long time before breaking the silence as one.

'I need to use the privy.'

13

Foul Meat

333 AR Winter

There was a loud sound and Renna's sight distorted, shattering entirely as her eyes were broken down into billions of tiny particles.

Human senses had little meaning in the between-state. Here, magic, in its endless tides, was the only sense that mattered. She could feel the wards in Leesha's cottage, gently tugging at her essence. The demon bones in the pockets of her apron. They were not on the Hollow greatward net, but she felt its contours as surely as running her hand along a wall. Its power was a beacon, its Draw a twister that threatened to pull her in and suck her dry.

Instead she reached out, seeking a path to the Core. There were a number of them out in the yard, all harnessed by wardnets like Ferd Miller's waterwheel back in Tibbet's Brook.

Like the woman herself, Leesha's wardnets had a powerful pull, but were simple enough to resist once their strength was known. Renna slipped into one and down, deep beneath the surface.

Immediately, she heard the call of the Core. It was distant on the surface, like Beni banging on a pot to call them from the field for lunch. But the moment she touched the path it gripped her in its beautiful song, filled with the promise of infinite power and immortality.

Beautiful as the song was, though, Renna knew it told only

a half-truth. When the demons attacked the Hollow on new moon, she had conducted magic to repel them – and even that small amount had nearly consumed her. The Core was infinitely stronger, the source of all the magic in the world. Her own magic, enough to make her one of the most powerful people in the world, was a candle held up to its sun. She could indeed become a part of the Core, but not while hoping to retain anything of herself. A raindrop falling on the great lake.

She went as far down as she dared, knowing the call would only get stronger, then reached out her senses, feeling for paths back to the surface. They ran in all directions, some great and others small, some touching ground nearby, and others meandering for miles before finally poking out onto the surface.

She had not intentionally left anything of herself on the path she had taken here, but it was marked nevertheless, as familiar as the smell of her own sweat. She followed it and the miles bled by in an instant. She materialized south of the Hollow, and searched again, finding the next path in her return journey the same way.

She skated across hundreds of miles in four quick hops, materializing in moments inside the tower. 'Ay, anyone here?'

When there was no answer, she gritted her teeth, stomping to the door and kicking it open. Arlen and Jardir were in the yard, checking the wards that held the prisoner.

'Ren?' Arlen asked. He and Jardir both saw her aura and stopped what they were doing, turning their full attention on her.

'Sons of the Core did it again!' Renna shouted.

'What—' Arlen began.

'Krasians took Docktown,' Renna cut him off, snapping an angry hand Jardir's way. 'Marchin' on the hamlets as we speak. Killin', burnin', and drivin' folk from their homes.'

'Not as we speak,' Jardir said. 'My people do not fight Sharak Sun in the night.'

'Like it makes a difference to all the folk you've thrown to the demons!' Arlen shouted. 'Did you know about this?'

Jardir nodded calmly. 'It was planned months ago that we

would strike Docktown on first snow, though I did not expect the attack to go forward without me.'

Arlen flew across the distance between them. Jardir reached for his spear, but Arlen batted the weapon across the yard and bulled forward, smashing Jardir into a goldwood tree. The trunk was five feet thick, but Renna heard the wood crack as they struck.

Arlen raised a fist, flaring bright with power as he Drew magic into the impact wards on his knuckles. 'Do lives mean nothing to you?!'

Jardir looked at the fist, unafraid. 'Do it, Par'chin. Strike. Kill me. Doom your own plan to failure. For if you do not, it is as much as admitting I was right.'

Arlen looked at him incredulously. 'How's that?'

Jardir flexed, breaking the hold and driving an open palm into Arlen's chest so hard he was thrown back several feet before he caught himself. The glare he threw back was terrifying.

'Bout time Arlen stomped some humble into that son of the Core, Renna thought, smirking.

Jardir seemed unconcerned, brushing himself off and straightening his robes. 'You are right, Par'chin. Greenlanders, and no doubt more than a few *Sharum*, are dying at my command. But you are wrong if you believe their lives mean nothing to me. Every life lost is one less for Sharak Ka, and we are outnumbered already.'

'And yet you senselessly . . .' Arlen began.

'Not senselessly.' Jardir's voice was still infuriatingly calm. Even his aura shone with righteousness. 'The greenlanders are weak, Par'chin. You know it to be true. Weak and divided like stalks of wheat. Sharak Sun is the coming of the scythe, that a grander crop can follow. The coming generation will be spears, ready to stand fast in Sharak Ka. Those lives lost are the price we pay for unity, for in that unity is the strength to save Ala.'

Arlen spat on him. 'You arrogant bastard, you don't know that.'

'And you don't know that I will be what tips you to victory in the Core.' Jardir wiped the spittle away without comment, though it was clear his patience was thinning. 'Yet you brought me here and healed my wounds despite what I've done. What I'm *doing*. Because a part of you knows there is more at stake than a few lives. It is the future of the human race, and we must hold every advantage.'

'What advantage does raping and killing and burning bring?' Arlen demanded. 'Making folk bow to a different Creator? How does that make us stronger? Folk in the Hollow are every bit as strong as your *Sharum*, and I didn't have to destroy their homes and families to get 'em there.'

'Because Nie did it for you,' Jardir said. 'I know the tale of your coming, arriving just before the *alagai* took the tribe forever, like I once did for the Sharach.'

'Hollowers were just the beginning,' Arlen said. 'Thousands have joined the Cutters since.'

'Refugees of my coming,' Jardir said. 'How many of your *chin* would take up the spear had I not driven them from their illusion of safety? You told me when we first met that many of your men would not raise a hand against the *alagai* even when their families were threatened.'

He squinted, reading something on Arlen's aura. Renna looked at him, but could not understand it as they did.

Yet.

'Your own father,' Jardir said, nodding as understanding came to him. 'Shamed himself, watching as the *alagai* came for you and your mother.'

Renna might not understand the subtler aspects of auras, but even she could not miss the humiliation and anger that washed across Arlen's.

Yet there was something in Jardir's aura, too. Pride. Respect. Her senses sharp in the night, she saw the apple of his throat tighten with emotion as he continued to Know Arlen. 'It was you who saved her. Barely old enough for *sharaj*, and you took to the field like a trained *Sharum*.'

'Wan't enough,' Arlen said. 'Still lost her. Just not as quick.'

'Do you regret standing in Nie's path for her?' Jardir asked.

'Not for an instant,' Arlen said.

'This is what it means to be Shar'Dama Ka,' Jardir said. 'To make the harsh decisions others cannot. The weak like your father must be shoved aside, that the strong might emerge.'

'Jeph Bales ent weak,' Renna said, drawing both men's attention to her. 'Took his lesson that same night, even if it was fifteen years before the test. When it was me out in his yard, bloody and with demons on my heel, he grabbed a tool and faced them down. Saved my life. You din't do that, Krasian. Tibbet's Brook stands tall now, and din't need half the folk to die to make it happen.'

'*Inevera*,' Jardir said. 'It matters not how people come to join in Sharak Ka, only that they come.' He looked to Arlen. 'It was you, Par'chin, who said we were beyond such things now. The strike on Docktown was Abban's plan, and Everam will deem whether he and Jayan or Lakton's dockmasters will prove the stronger.'

'Never should have trusted that slimy camel-thief,' Arlen growled.

Jardir chuckled. 'So I have said to myself many times over the years. The only thing anyone should trust Abban to do is be Abban. He follows his conscience only until there is profit in ignoring it.'

'Got half a mind to skate over to Docktown and knock him and your son on their asses,' Arlen said.

Jardir face darkened. 'Do that, Par'chin, and our pact is broken. Do that, and I will return to the Skull Throne and leave you to your mad scheme.'

Arlen's lip curled, and both men tensed, ready in an instant to resume fighting. They held the pose a moment, then Arlen shook his head. 'We'll see. Meantime, Ren and I need to see to the folk you've put out in the naked night.'

'That is not—' Jardir began.

'Shut it!' Arlen roared, so vehement even Jardir twitched. 'It's night, and I won't see our brothers and sisters face it alone.'

Jardir nodded. 'Of course there is no honour in that. I will summon Shanvah and Shanjat, and we—'

'Will stay right ripping here and guard the prisoner,' Arlen snapped.

'We are not your servants, Par'chin,' Jardir said, 'to be ordered to gaol duty.'

'Ent no common gaol,' Arlen said. 'You know what we're holding.'

Jardir stiffened at that. 'Alagai Ka.'

Arlen gave a curt nod. 'I come back and find less than three of you here guarding, and our pact will indeed be broken.'

Jardir bowed. 'Do not allow yourselves to be seen. Save your people in the night, but the Daylight War is no longer ours.'

Arlen scowled, but he nodded, turning to hold a hand out to Renna. She took it, holding tight to him even as they dissipated, as intimate as any connection of flesh. Linked, they slipped down a path to skate together.

Renna skated back to the tower, clumsily solidifying a few inches off the ground. Night after night of Drawing and skating had left her dizzy and drained of magic, insides weak and burning from conducting so much power.

The sudden drop twisted her ankle and sent her stumbling, but something caught her before she hit the ground. She tensed, ready to fight.

'Peace, sister,' Shanvah said. 'It is only me.'

Renna shook her head, getting her feet under her and pushing away from the woman's support. 'Since when am I your sister?'

'Since we shed blood together in the tomb of Kaji,' Shanvah said. 'We are spear sisters now.'

Her ankle throbbed painfully. Renna tried to heal it, but found she did not have the strength. She tried to Draw more power, but it made her whole body seem aflame. Easier to let the ankle throb.

Renna looked to the horizon. The sky was lightening, but dawn was still an hour away. She needed to feed before then, or she would be useless in the coming day. 'That only till sunrise, when we go back to being enemies?'

Shanvah shrugged. 'If the Shar'Dama Ka commands me to fight you, I will, Renna vah Harl, but it will not be as I would wish it. I see honour in you and the Par'chin, and I think Everam must have a plan for us.'

'Wish it was that simple,' Renna said.

'It is, and it isn't,' Shanvah said. 'Nothing on Ala is simple, or it would be as Heaven. Everam does not show his plan, but we know it is there.'

'Ay,' Renna agreed, though she did not agree at all. The woman was wasting time she needed to hunt, especially on a sore ankle. She drew her knife. 'Gonna hunt a bit. Get my strength back.'

Shanvah nodded. 'I will accompany you.'

'Core you will,' Renna snapped.

'You're exhausted, sister,' Shanvah said. 'There is safety in numbers.'

Renna shook her head. 'Don't need a sitter. You'd only slow me down.'

'But we . . .'

Shanvah's aura blossomed with genuine hurt, and it made Renna angry. 'We're what? Spear sisters? You think that means a corespawned thing to me when I just spent a week trying to save lives you desert rats put out in the night?'

She grabbed at her vest, showing the deep crimson stains. 'I'm covered in innocent blood because of your Shar'Dama Ka, Shanvah. Here, in the ripping night. So forgive me if I ent interested in having you at my back.'

She turned away sharply, storming off into the night without another word.

It was nearing dawn when Renna at last caught sight of her prey. The five of them had hunted the area around the tower down to nothing, and even as she ranged farther, many had already slipped back down to the Core's embrace to shelter them from the sun.

She had been tracking this demon for several minutes, and saw she was just in time. The field demon had retreated into the shelter of deep grass for the moment of vulnerability when it began to dematerialize. Lesser drones could not do it as quickly as the elite demons – or she herself – and they might as well be asleep for all they could defend themselves when they were in the dissipation trance.

She saw its muscles relax as the trance began and pounced on its back, hooking an arm and her legs around the demon's midsection as she rolled onto her back. The demon flailed and kicked helplessly as she drove her knife into its chest and pulled down sharply, laying its insides open.

Light began to peek over the horizon, the coreflesh beginning to smoke and sizzle. Desperate, Renna thrust her hands into the open wound, clawing free whatever meat she could find and cramming it into her mouth before the sun could burn it away.

There were several intense moments of messy mastication, and then a spark, as the ichor running down her chin caught fire. She cried out in surprise.

There was a sudden slash, a shining spearpoint cleaving the grass like a scythe. Shanvah stood there, spear raised to attack. But then she started, seeing the demon corpse.

Immediately she leapt back, bowing deeply. 'Apologies for not heeding your request, sister, but I was concerned. When you cried out, I thought . . .'

She looked up. 'But of course not. You are Renna vah Harl, and no demon can stand against . . .'

Her aura was lost in the rising sun, but Shanvah's eyes told Renna enough. She knew.

'Shanvah, wait . . .' she began, but the woman turned and raced away.

Everyone was back in the yard by the time Renna made it back, standing in the shadow of the tower. Shanvah was on her knees, head on the ground. Shanjat was holding his spear.

Arlen and Jardir looked ready to fight again, this time once and for all.

All eyes turned to her as she approached. Shanvah leapt to her feet, spear pointed Renna's way. 'She is a servant of Nie!'

'Impossible,' Jardir said. 'She stood with us against Alagai Ka himself.'

'She has been corrupted,' Shanvah said. 'Before Everam, on my honour and hope of Heaven, I swear, Deliverer. With my own eyes I saw her feasting on the foul meat of the *alagai*.'

'Impossible,' Jardir said again, pointing to the rising sun. He and the others were still in semidarkness, but Renna stood fully in the light. 'How could any servant of Nie stand in Everam's radiance if . . .'

But then he turned sharply, looking at Arlen. He closed the distance between them in a second, grabbing Arlen's hands as he probed deeper into his aura.

'It's true,' Jardir whispered. 'Everam preserve us, I trusted you, and all along, you served Nie.'

'Corespawn it, stop acting the ripping fool!' Arlen shouted. 'Why else would you profane your body with . . .!'

Arlen growled, shoving Jardir away so hard Shanjat had to leap out of the way to avoid being hit. Everyone tensed for battle, but Arlen held his ground, making no effort to continue the fight. 'You have the stones to ask *why*?! Night, you think I *wanted* this?'

He pointed an angry finger at Jardir. 'This is *your* doing, same as the ripping ink.'

'Now it is you being the fool, Par'chin,' Jardir said. 'I did not force demon meat down your throat.'

'No, you and Shanjat and the others left me for dead in the corespawned desert,' Arlen snapped, 'after beating me, robbing me, and trying to throw me to the demons for having the audacity to *win* the first night's *alagai'sharak* in three thousand years.'

Shanvah looked to Shanjat, eyes wide. 'Father, this cannot be true.'

The tip of Shanjat's ready spear dipped as he turned to her. 'It is true, daughter. We dishonoured ourselves with what we had to do that night, but the Par'chin had stolen the Spear of Kaji, and could not be allowed to keep it.'

'You parse words worse than any *khaffit* in the bazaar,' Arlen spat. 'No one had seen the spear in over three thousand years. Its power belongs to all humanity, and I brought it to Jardir honourably, to share with you.'

'The *Sharum* will be silent!' Jardir snapped, his gaze never leaving Arlen. 'You parse words, too, Par'chin. None of this explains why you have eaten of this foul meat.'

'Don't it?' Arlen said. 'Said yourself there was no food in Anoch Sun. It was why your people violated that place worse than the mind demons when you came through. Didn't have time to be respectful. You just wanted to loot the place.'

'I warn you, Par'chin . . .' Jardir began.

'Don't deny it,' Arlen said. 'Being Shar'Dama Ka means making the big decisions, ay? Then take responsibility for them.'

'I do,' Jardir said evenly.

'Me, too,' Arlen said. 'I wanted the secrets of Anoch Sun as much as you did. When I stumbled back to the Oasis of Dawn and warded my flesh, I had enough food to escape the desert . . .'

'Or return to Anoch Sun,' Jardir finished.

Arlen nodded. 'Spent a long time there, studying. Demons were the only thing to eat. Had to survive, I was to pass on what I learned.'

He raised a finger. 'But I left the place just like I found it. Bet your people didn't even notice I'd been there. So which of us is honouring Everam and battling Nie better?'

Jardir sneered. 'Speak not of Everam and Nie, Par'chin. You believe in neither.'

'And still better at your religion than you!' Arlen said, crossing his arms.

'You ate *alagai* meat,' Jardir said. 'Do you honestly think you can keep from being corrupted by it?'

Arlen laughed. 'You're such a ripping hypocrite! Your entire life, your rise to power, your conquest, all of it was dictated by *alagai hora*, and you talk to me of corruption? How in your twisted logic does the voice of Everam come from demon bones?'

Jardir pursed his lips. 'I have often wondered that, myself, but their power cannot be denied.'

'Of course not,' Arlen said. 'You can see the ripping magic.' He pointed to the spear. 'The Spear of Kaji has a demon bone core. So does the crown.

'Magic ent evil, and corelings ent foot soldiers in some eternal space war,' Arlen continued. 'Just animals, like us. Animals that spent millions of years living deep in Ala, bathed in the power of the Core. Evolved to absorb and hold some of that power, and we've learned to turn it against them. That's all.'

He held up a warded fist. 'Tattoos give me power, but no more than your scars. Real power comes from eating the meat. That's why I can dissipate and draw wards in the air. Do things you need your spear and crown for, or can't do at all. Got my own demon bone core now.'

'If they are just animals as you say,' Jardir said, 'you risk becoming one of them yourself, if you continue on this course.'

'Know that,' Arlen said. 'Ent eaten demon in years, but the power seems here to stay.'

'But you allow your *jiwah* to risk it, too,' Jardir said.

Arlen laughed again, but it was not a condescending sound this time. His mirth was genuine. 'Allow? Have you met Renna Bales? There's no allowing her.'

'Corespawned right,' Renna said, taking his hand.

Arlen looked at her, love in his eyes, but kept talking to Jardir. 'Asked her not to, but she knows what's at stake, and has been trying to catch up. Thinks I'll mist down to the Core and try to take on the *alagai* without her, she doesn't.'

'Don't say it like it's some crazy notion,' Renna said. 'Told me yourself it calls to you. Hear it too, now that I'm skating. But that ent a fight we can win alone.'

She expected Jardir to be aghast at the thought of the Core calling them, but he only nodded. 'Nie's call is strong, but indeed, you must resist. All Ala depends upon us. Put your faith in Everam and He will keep you strong.'

Arlen shook his head. 'Never been much good at putting faith anywhere but in me and mine.'

Jardir reached out gently, touching Arlen's chest. 'Everam *is* inside you, my friend. Whether we created Him, or He created us, is irrelevant. He is the Light inside you when all else is dark. He is the Voice that whispers right from wrong. He is the Strength you drew upon in your desert trials. He is the Hope that you carry in this mad scheme.' He smiled. 'He is the Stubborn inside you that refuses to admit the truth I bring.'

Arlen smiled. 'Grant you that last, at least.'

'Now that the cat's out, might be we don't need the prisoner,' Renna said. 'There's a shortcut to down below for all of us.'

Arlen shook his head. 'Don't trust anyone, even myself, to dissipate too close to the Core. Be like dumping a bucket into a river and expecting it to stay upstream.'

Jardir crossed his arms. 'Hypocrisy or not, my warriors and I will not profane our bodies with *alagai* meat.'

There were enthusiastic nods from Shanvah and Shanjat, and Renna could see the relief in their eyes.

'So we do it the hard way,' Arlen agreed. 'But for that, we need a way to get that ripping demon to talk.'

14

The Prisoner

333 AR Winter

The Consort huddled at the centre of the warding, presenting as little flesh as possible to the cursed day star.

His captors had been thorough. The chain and locks were carefully crafted from a true metal, and their warding was strong. They burned against his skin, keeping him corporeal.

His cell was circular and bereft of furnishing. Coloured stones lined the floor, cemented into a mosaic of warding that would keep him trapped even if he escaped the chain. The warding pulled at his magic with such strength the Consort needed to keep his power buried deep, lest it be drained.

There would be no restoring lost energy, for the demon prince's cell was high above the surface, with no vents to Draw from. The Consort powered his own prison, and was determined to give it as little as possible. He sipped at the store carefully.

There were wards outside the walls, as well. Wards to keep his prison hidden from prying eyes, both human and the drones that no doubt combed the surface, seeking sign of him. The Consort had tried to reach out to them, but the forbiddance was too strong. For the first time, his mind was cut off from both the base impulses of his drones and the beautiful complexity of his brethren's thoughts. The silence was maddening.

But worse than even that indignity was the day star. Thick

curtains had been pulled over the windows of the cell, overlapping and lashed tight. The darkness was so complete the surface stock were blind, but to the demon prince, even the barest light filtering in through the weaves was agony, sapping his strength and burning his skin. It was all the demon could do to squeeze his lidless eyes tight and curl on the floor until darkness returned.

At last, the star set, and the demon made a few quick, efficient motions to sit himself upright despite the unevenly wrapped lengths of chain that bound him. Slowly, the Consort Drew a bit of power, healing the flesh beneath an ever-thickening armour of burned and dead flesh.

Again he Drew, a spark for sustenance. His captors wisely did not get close enough to feed him.

Last, he shifted, pulling a particular lock against his flesh as he focused a last bit of power into it, slowly eroding the metal. Too much, and the chain would pull the power away, but just a touch could wear it like water dripping on stone.

The demon had studied his chains for half a cycle now, and knew them intimately. Shatter three locks at the shackle, and much of his mobility would be restored. Break two more links, and he could slip the chain.

Once free of the chain, he would need to disable the mosaic to dissipate out of the prison. That would go more quickly, but the patterns suggested he would not progress far enough before one of his captors noticed the attempt. Even the weakest of them could pull the curtain with a flick of the wrist, and sunrise mark his end.

The Consort could afford to be patient. It would be many cycles before he was ready to shatter the chain, and much could change in that time. The human minds wanted him alive, and it was a good opportunity to study and probe their weaknesses.

It was a delightful irony that the very shackles they used to keep him corporeal prevented the Consort from reshaping his throat and mouth to allow him to replicate the crude grunting that passed for speech among the surface stock. He could understand their questions, but not answer them.

This frustrated the minds, deepening the rifts between them. Unifiers they might be, but like any human, they were stupid. Emotional. Barely more intelligent than mimics.

Most of all, they were mortal. The time would come when their vigilance failed, and he would be free.

15

The Painted Children
333 AR Winter

'Corespawned if I'm letting you put your oily desert hands on my little girl!'

Leesha looked up, her hands full of a man's intestine, to see a thick-armed Laktonian man and his teenage son looming with balled fists over tiny Amanvah. The apprentices assisting her were all frozen with fear. Jizell, too, had paused in her surgery, but she could no more stop and involve herself than Leesha.

Amanvah did not seem perturbed. 'If I do not, she will die.'

'Ay, whose ripping fault is that?' the boy cried. 'You desert rats killed Mum and ran us out into the night!'

'Do not blame me for your cowardice and inability to protect your sister,' Amanvah said. 'Stand aside.'

'Core I will,' the man said, grabbing her arm. Sikvah took a step forward, but the man's son sidestepped to block her path.

Amanvah looked down as if he had rubbed shit on her white robe, pristine despite the hours she had spent in the surgery with Leesha. Then her hand shot up, snaking around the man's giant biceps and into his armpit. She stepped back in a half turn, bringing the man's arm out straight until the elbow locked. She twisted slightly, and the man roared with pain.

Amanvah used the locked arm to guide the man like a puppet, swinging him away from the operating table and right into his son. A well-placed kick set the boy stumbling towards the doors, and Amanvah walked the screaming man straight back after him, sweeping both men out of the room as easily as dust into a pan.

She let the man's arm go as the doors swung open, delivering a mule-kick into his solar plexus that sent both flying through the air, one landing heavily atop the other. Dozens of women working triage looked up in shock.

Leesha turned to Roni. 'Get out there and find the biggest Cutters you can. Post them at the surgery door and tell them I will bite their ripping heads off if anyone other than patients and Gatherers is allowed in.'

'Someone's got to carry the wounded in,' Roni said. 'Most of the Cutters are out in the night.'

'I'll find a few hands when I finish here,' Leesha said. 'Go.'

Roni nodded and vanished. Amanvah was already at work on the girl, badly bitten by field demons. These were not the first Laktonians to lose control at the sight of Amanvah's robes and dark skin, but folk would need to swallow it – along with a few teeth, if necessary.

Even with almost every Gatherer in the Hollow at hand, their resources were taxed. The apprentices could set a bone and stitch a gash, but there were few with the knowledge to cut into a patient, much less fix what they found. Amanvah was the best combat surgeon Leesha had ever seen. She could not afford to send the woman away.

There was a lull as they waited for the next wave. Leesha finished her work, leaving Kadie to stitch. She stretched her back as she made her way out of the surgery. The extra weight she was carrying did not make hours bent over the operating table any easier.

The hospit's main room was chaotic. It was more than a week since the refugees began to arrive but still wounded poured in as Cutter and Wooden Soldier patrols gathered groups on the road and guided them into the Hollow. Fleeing for days on end, many suffered from exhaustion and exposure; others had been wounded in the invasion, or by demons on the road.

But after the waves of refugees from Rizon and the losses at new moon, the Hollowers had gotten used to bringing order from chaos.

Off to the side, the two Laktonian men slumped on a bench, arms on their knees as they stared at the floor. She was in desperate need of a rest, but it was a stark reminder that others had it far worse.

Leesha understood the rage the refugees directed towards Amanvah. She felt it herself. Their strike on Docktown was too precise to have been a sudden inspiration. Ahmann had been planning it all along, even as he seduced her.

Part of her, angry and wounded, hoped Arlen had indeed killed him.

She made her way over to them. The father didn't even look up until she put her feet right in their field of vision. The son continued to stare.

'Your daughter will be all right,' she said. 'All of you will.'

''Preciate the thought, Gatherer,' the father said, 'but I don't things will ever be all right again. We've lost . . . everything. If Cadie dies, I don't know what I'll . . .' He choked off with a sob.

Leesha laid a hand on his shoulder. 'I know it feels that way, but I've been right where you are. More than once. All the Hollowers have.'

'Gets better.' Stela Inn had appeared with the water cart. She ladled a pair of cups and produced a rough blanket. 'Weather's gettin' chill. There'll be heat wards in the campsite, but they only work at night. Did they give you a site number?'

'Ah . . .' the man said. 'Boy out front said something . . .'

'Seven,' the son said, his eyes still on the floor. 'We're in site seven.'

Stela nodded. 'Pollock's field. What are your names?'

'Marsin Peat.' The man nodded to his son. 'Jak.'

Stela made a note on her pad. 'When's the last time you ate?'

The man looked at her blankly for a moment, then shook his head. 'Search my pockets.'

Stela smiled. 'I'll ask Callen to come by with the bread cart while you wait for word.'

'Creator bless you, girl,' the man said.

'See?' Leesha said. 'Getting better already.'

'Ay,' the boy said. 'Mum's gone, house is ashes, and Cadie's gonna die of demon fever. But we've got a blanket, so everything's sunny!'

'Ay, be grateful!' Marsin snapped, swatting his son on the back of his head.

'There will be more than just blankets and bread,' Leesha said. 'A pair of strong backs like yours can be put right to work cutting trees and building homes on one of the new greatwards.'

'Paid work,' Stela noted. 'Food credits at first, but then you'll start at five klats a day each.'

Leesha had scoffed, but the new coin was just what folk needed, dispersing among the refugees faster than they could be printed.

Marsin shook his head. 'Thought it was over for us tonight, when the demons got through our camp wards. But I gotta believe . . . Deliverer wouldn't've saved us if there weren't no reason.'

Leesha and Stella looked up sharply at that. 'You saw the Deliverer?' Stela asked.

The man nodded. 'Ay. And I wasn't the only one.'

'It was just a flash of wardlight,' Jak said.

'Ay,' Marsin agreed. 'But brighter than anything my hasty wards could make. Hurt to look at. And I saw an arm.'

'Could've been anythin',' Jak said.

'Anythin' didn't freeze the flame demon that bit Cadie solid,' Marsin said. 'Or set that woodie on fire so we could reach the Cutters on the road.'

Leesha shook her head. This wasn't the first tale of Renna's exploits she'd heard, but as yet none had seen more than a flitting shadow or a glimpse of warded flesh.

How is she doing it? Leesha wondered. Drawing wards in the air and dissipating like smoke, travelling miles in the time it took to draw a deep breath. It was more than blackstem wards could explain. Wonda had grown powerful at night, but nothing like that, and her abilities always faded back to mortal levels when the sun rose.

'Swear by the sun,' Marsin was saying. 'Deliverer saved me and mine.'

'Course he did,' Stela said. 'Deliverer's out there, watching over all of us.'

Leesha led the girl out of earshot of the men. 'Don't go making promises like that. You know as well as any even Arlen Bales can't be everywhere at once. Folk need to concentrate on saving themselves.'

Stela gave a curtsy. 'Ay, mistress, that's sunny and good when you're a Cutter with arms like tree trunks, or a Krasian princess who can throw men across the room like dolls. What's a Hollow girl like me to do?'

What indeed? Leesha wondered. Stela was healthy enough, but small and thin-limbed. The girl was helping as best she could, but she was right. She wasn't built for fighting.

'Would you fight if you could?' Leesha asked.

'Ay, mistress,' Stela said. 'But even if Grandda would let me, I can't so much as wind a crank bow.'

'We'll see about that,' Leesha said.

'Mistress?' Stela asked.

'Focus on your work,' Leesha said. 'We'll speak of this again soon.'

There was a boom as the front door to the hospit was kicked open. Wonda Cutter strode in, with two grown men slung over her shoulder and another carried in the crook of one arm. Her sleeves were rolled up, the blackstem wards glowing softly.

All around the room, folk pointed and whispered. Wonda caught Leesha's eye and shrugged apologetically.

'Din't have no choice, mistress,' Wonda said when they were alone. 'I was all out of arrows and the demon was going right for 'em. What was I supposed to do? Let 'em die?'

'Of course not, dear,' Leesha said. 'You did the right thing.'

'Whole town's talkin' about it by now,' Wonda said. 'Calling me your Painted Child.'

'What's done is done,' Leesha said. 'Pay it no mind. We couldn't hide it forever, and I've learned enough to begin expanding our experiment.'

'Ay?' Wonda asked.

Leesha nodded to the wards on Wonda's arms, still glowing softly. 'The glow should die down when your adrenaline does. Do your breathing until it fades, then go ask around for volunteers. Remember what I told you to look for.'

'Ay, mistress.' Wonda was already breathing in slow rhythm.

'And Wonda?' Leesha nodded her head across the room. 'Start with Stela Inn.'

The sun came up, and Wonda waited for the light to reach the yard, then stepped from the porch to begin slowly stretching through her daily *sharukin*. It was a chill morning, but she wore only a slight shift, exposing as much of her warded skin as possible to the sunlight.

'How do you feel, today?' Leesha asked.

'Wards itch when the sun first hits them in the morning,' Wonda said.

'Itch?' Leesha asked.

'Sting,' Wonda said. 'Like being whipped with nettle branches.' Wonda let out a slow breath as she eased into her next position.

'But don't worry none, mistress. Feeling only lasts a minute or two. I can handle it.'

'Ay,' Leesha said. 'I never would have known to look at you.'

'Ent gonna waste your time with every ache and pain, mistress,' Wonda said. 'Don't see you complaining, and you've had it worse than any of us.'

'You have to tell me these things, Wonda,' Leesha said. 'Now more than ever, you need to tell me everything. The magic is affecting you, and we need to make sure it's safe, for all their sakes.'

And for mine, she thought. *And my baby.*

'You haven't slept in over a week,' Leesha said. Few of the Cutters had. Wherever demon fighting was thickest for refugees on the road, Wonda and Gared were there with the original Cutters, those who had stood with Arlen at the Battle of Cutter's Hollow. By night, the wards cut into their horses' hooves ate the miles as they tracked packs of demons hunting the refugees, destroying them before they could strike. By day they helped guide the fleeing Laktonians to the warded campsites being built along the road.

'Neither have you, mistress,' Wonda pointed out. 'Don't think because I wan't here I din't have eyes on you. Girls tell me you ent caught more'n a few minutes since all this began. Magic's affecting you, too.'

It was true enough.

'It is.' Leesha hardened her voice just a touch. 'I've used more *hora* magic in the last week than in the months before. I'm not getting half the feedback you are since the blackstem, but enough to get a sense of what you're going through. I feel . . .'

'Like you could march on the Core itself, and put your toe up the Mother of Demons' ass.'

Leesha laughed. 'More colourful than I would have put it, but ay. The magic flows through you and washes fatigue away.'

Wonda nodded. 'By sunrise, feels like you've had a full night's sleep and a pot of coffee. Better. Like a bowstring, ready to loose.'

'Do you keep your bow drawn all the time?' Leesha asked.

'Course not.' Wonda paused in her workout to look at Leesha. 'Ruin a good bow like that.'

'It's unnatural to go so long without sleep,' Leesha said. 'Maybe we're not tired, but I feel something draining away. Without dreams to escape to—'

'—whole world's starting to feel like one,' Wonda finished for her. 'Ay.'

'I'm going to brew you a dash of tampweed and skyflower,' Leesha said. 'Should put you out for eight hours.'

'What about you?' Wonda said.

'I'll sleep tonight, when you take them out,' Leesha promised. 'Honest word.'

Wonda grunted, going back to her stretching. Leesha wondered what it was like for Arlen, or even Renna. Had they had a decent sleep in months? When did they last dream?

She was afraid of the answer. *Probably why they're both crazy as cats.*

Wonda finished her exercises and they went inside. Wonda took her wooden armour off its rack, readying her polishing tools. The armour was a gift from Thamos' mother, Duchess Araine, and Wonda prized it nearly as much as the bow and arrows Arlen had given her. Each morning she polished the weapons and armour as lovingly as a mother bathing an infant.

Leesha stole a moment to boil a kettle and take it to the bathing chamber. She nibbled on a biscuit and stripped for a quick rag bath before changing into a fresh dress.

She took a deep breath. It would get easier soon. The flow of refugees continued, but the Hollow's reach lengthened daily, now scooping folk still fresh on the road, with live animals and food on their backs. Several towns that had not yet broken were conducting organized evacuations under Cutter protection.

The Hollow would still need to absorb them, but it was more easily done when people came as settlers, with supplies and possessions in hand, rather than the first waves of exhausted folk, carrying nothing but their wounded.

Tonight, Leesha could afford to sleep. Perhaps. But already, young volunteers were gathering in her courtyard, being tested for strength and reflexes to serve as baselines and split into groups by her apprentices. The chatter of the assembled young Hollowers fell into an excited hush as Leesha and Wonda appeared at the door.

The volunteers were all in their late teens or early twenties, Hollowers who had volunteered to join the Cutters only to be turned away for one reason or another. One had trouble breathing. Another needed lenses to see. Others simply because they weren't large or strong enough to keep up.

A growing class of khaffit, *if we're not careful*, Leesha thought.

'They're staring at me,' Wonda said.

'Ay,' Leesha said. 'See how it feels, for once. You might as well be the Painted Man to these children.'

'Don't jest about the Deliverer,' Wonda said.

'We're all Deliverers,' Leesha said. 'His words. It's your job to inspire these children, same as he did for you. World needs all the Deliverers it can get.'

'Why not ward the Cutters and *Sharum*, then?' Wonda asked. 'Why only the rejects?'

'We're still testing,' Leesha said. 'We need a small group. A group we can control, to test the process before we try it on men the size of goldwood trees.'

There were three groups. Stela had made it into one. Her uncle Keet, only a couple of years her senior, another. None was the finest fruit the Hollow could provide in terms of warriors.

The first dozen, including her friend Brianne's son Callen Cutter, would be given specially designed spears Leesha had warded personally. They had short shafts and long warded blades, designed to maximize the magic leached from the corelings and fed back into the wielder.

The second group would be given weapons that appeared identical to the first, but contained slivers of *hora*, coated in warded silver. The spears would hold some limited power in day as well as night, and recharge when spent.

Finally, Stela's group, the most coveted of the three, would have blackstem wards painted on their skin, and study *sharusahk* with Wonda.

The testing would take months, but if Leesha's hypotheses were right, they could have an army of Deliverers waiting in the Hollow the next time the demon princes came calling.

Her Painted Children.

'There, finished.' It was dark by the time Leesha painted the last ward on Stela's skin. The others all waited with Wonda in the yard, marvelling at warded weapons and skin. All knew that soon they would be going out into the night, a place many seasoned warriors had gone, never to return.

Excitement was building in the air. A chance to die, yes, but also a chance to avenge, to show the Hollow that they were to be counted. None of them could keep still, shifting from foot to foot or pacing the yard, waiting for Stela, that they might begin.

Leesha sent her off, watching the girl with her warded spectacles. The yard was awash with magic, only a fraction of it visible to the naked eye. Some wards were designed to glow, casting light in the yard, but others thrummed with power unseen by any without wardsight.

She saw the power draught to Stela's ankles as it already had begun to do with the others. It danced up the blackstem wards on her legs, pulled along by the interlinked wards, swirling around her torso and out to her limbs and head like a heart pumping magic instead of blood. Just standing in the yard, the Painted Children would be feeling a tingle. At first it would feel like a strong stimulant tea, then an adrenaline rush. Soon after, their senses would expand, confusing them with every faint scent, every whisper heard from a mile away. It would be overwhelming until their thoughts sped as well.

Then they would begin to feel invincible.

'This here,' Wonda held up a long metal tube with braided steel rope extended in a loop at the end, 'is a Krasian weapon called an *alagai*-catcher.' She whipped the loop over a hitching post in the yard, tightening it in an instant with a twist and pull. 'Each of you go and take one. I set coreling traps in the Gatherers' Wood. We're going to use these to haul demons out so we can use 'em for practice.'

'Ay, just like that?' Keet asked. 'We ent gonna, dunno, practise in the yard a bit before going into the naked night?' Others murmured their agreement.

Leesha kept the smile from her face. Naked night, indeed. Leesha had greatwards and warded paths throughout her land. The children might feel they were out with the demons, but in truth they would be in safe succour almost the entire time.

But it was important they get in contact with demons as soon as possible, and the feeling of constant danger would keep them respectful. This was no game.

It was like a dream, watching Wonda lead the children away. The world had become fuzzed at the edges. Her focus remained sharp, even after ten straight hours of warding. Pain in her temple throbbed and turned her stomach, but it was a near constant companion now, and she had learned to shut it out.

But as the last of the children vanished into the darkness at the edge of her wardsight, she began to fill the vacuum with images. Callen Cutter screaming for his mother as he slowly bled out from talon wounds. Brianne would never speak to her again. Nor Smitt, if anything should happen to Stela or Keet. An image flashed across her mind of a wood demon biting Stela's head clean off. Her heart would still beat a few times before her body realized it was dead. The blood would jet high into the air.

She shook herself out of the vision, rubbing her eyes. At last. At last she was free to sleep, lest she go insane. If Arlen, Ahmann, and Thamos all walked into her yard this instant and began fighting one another for her hand, she would still go to bed.

Her stride was strong as she headed for her cottage door, but her mind was already in its nightgown, blowing out the candles. Her bed would be warm and soft.

'Mistress Leesha!' the frantic call came from behind. Leesha didn't recognize the voice, but the tone was clear. Having seen her, this was not someone who would stop until they spoke.

She took a deep breath, counting to five as her mind threw on a robe. Her countess smile was back in place as she turned to face the woman, recognizing her immediately from the hours she had spent at her daughter's bedside in the hospit. Lusy Yarnballer. Kendall's mother.

Yarnballer was not a proper surname, rather a jibe that had stuck when the spinner's apprentice had never developed a skill with the spindle. Lusy was a sweet but altogether unremarkable woman who had somehow managed to produce an exceptional daughter.

'A bit late for a social call, Lusy,' she said.

Lusy dipped a curtsy. 'Apologies, mistress. Wouldn't have bothered you if it weren't important.' She choked on a sob. 'Just don't know who else to turn to.'

Leesha's mind shook off its robe and put a dress back on. Her sigh was invisible as she went over to the woman and took her in her arms. 'There, child,' she said, though Lusy was years her senior. 'It can't be as bad as all that. Come inside and I'll brew some tea.'

Lusy blubbered interminably in Leesha's sitting room. Leesha sat in Bruna's rocking chair, the old woman's shawl wrapped around her. More than once her eyes slipped closed, and it was only the fall of her head as she drifted off that startled her awake.

At last, the mild sedative Leesha had put in the woman's tea took effect, and she calmed.

'All right, Lusy,' she said. 'I've enjoyed our visit, but it's time we got to the point.'

Lusy nodded. 'Sorry, mistress, I just don't know—'

'—what to do. Yes, you've said.' Leesha's patience was at an end. 'About what?'

'About Kendall and those Krasian witches!' Lusy all but shrieked.

Leesha looked at her curiously. 'Who? Amanvah and Sikvah?'

'Ay, you know what they did?' Lusy demanded.

'I'm sure I don't,' Leesha said, though she had a sinking suspicion. 'Why don't you take another sip of tea, lower your voice, and start at the beginning.'

Lusy nodded, taking a noisy slurp from her cup and letting out a long shuddering breath. 'They came to me this afternoon. Said they wanted to buy Kendall from me. Buy her! Like a ripping sheep!'

'Buy her?' Leesha asked, though she knew full well by now what the woman meant.

'As a whore for that coreson Rojer,' Lusy said. 'Seems two wives ent enough of an abomination for him. Wants my sweet Kendall for his harem, too. Plans to breed her like a cow, to hear them put it.'

'The Krasians can be . . . indelicate in these matters,' Leesha said carefully. 'Marriage is a contract to them, but when the negotiations are through they take their vows no less seriously than we. I am sure they meant no insult.'

'Like I give a demon's shit what they meant,' Lusy said. 'Told them Rojer could have Kendall over my dead body.'

Poor choice of words. Leesha wouldn't put it past Amanvah make it so.

'Them two harlots went off in a huff, acting like *I* was the one being rude,' Lusy continued. 'Then not twenty minutes later, Kendall is in my face, cryin' and screamin', saying she's marryin' Rojer and that's that. Told her no Tender would let her put hand to the Canon and vow to be a man's third wife, and you know what she said?'

'Do tell,' Leesha sighed.

'Said she didn't care. Said the Core with Canon and Tenders both. Said she'd make her oath on an Evejack—'

'Evejah,' Leesha corrected.

'Book of sin,' Lusy countered. 'Kendall's always had her eye on Rojer, but not like this. Girl's got no sense! Bad enough them Krasian tramps witched poor Rojer off the Creator's path, but I ent gonna let them take my daughter as well.'

'You may not have a choice,' Leesha said.

Lusy looked up at her, startled. 'Night, mistress, you can't possibly approve.'

'Of course not.' Leesha was already planning the scolding she was going to give Rojer. 'But Kendall's a grown woman with the right to choose her own path.'

'Don't think you'd be so calm,' Lusy said, 'it was your daughter being bid on like a laying hen.'

Leesha raised an eyebrow and Lusy started, suddenly remembering she was talking to the future Countess of the Hollow, a woman who had herself been the subject of Krasian bride bidding. She could not match Leesha's stare and looked down, trying to bury her face in her teacup. She gulped too fast, and coughed. 'Meant no offence, mistress. Course you understand.'

'I daresay I do,' Leesha said. 'I will speak to Rojer and Amanvah as soon as possible, and summon you again when it's done.'

'Thank you, mistress.' Lusy got to her feet, bowing awkwardly as she backed out of the room, turned, and scurried away.

'Are you out of your corespawned mind?' Leesha was already wearing Bruna's shawl. Never a good sign.

Rojer exaggerated his sigh just a touch for effect, taking his time hanging his motley Cloak of Unsight by the door. Leesha's face was ablaze, and it was always best to stall when she got this way. Leesha didn't have the stamina to be unreasonable for long. Not with him, anyway.

He wondered how he had once been so intimidated by her.

After dealing with Amanvah, Leesha Paper was a sunny stroll through the town square.

He left his fiddle case by the door, shut tight to ward away Amanvah's prying ears. He felt naked without his cloak and fiddle, but that was all the more reason to put them down now and again, lest they claim him completely.

Never let an act own you, Arrick had said, *or it will be all you do for the rest of your life. Rather go to the Core than have to tell the same ripping jokes every night from now till I die.*

Pointedly ignoring Leesha's aggressive stance and tone, he made his way into the sitting room, taking his favourite chair. He put his feet up on the stool and waited. A moment later, Leesha huffed into the room and sat in Bruna's chair. She did not offer tea.

Night, she must be furious, Rojer thought.

'Lusy paid you a visit, ay?' He had assumed this was why Leesha sent word she wanted to see him in the middle of the night. Not that he slept much at night. Few Hollowers did, any more. Wardlight lit the streets and paths, proof that all were safe from the corelings. People had taken to the new freedom with a vengeance, and now the streets were busy at all hours. Shamavah's bazaar and Smitt's General Store both kept night hours now.

'Course she did,' Leesha snapped. 'Someone needed to talk some sense into you.'

'You're my mother, then?' Rojer asked. 'Your job to wipe my bottom when it's dirty and smack it when I'm bad?' He stood up, pretending to fumble with his belt. 'You want I should just lay over your knees and we can have done?'

Leesha put a hand up to shield her eyes, but her scowl had fallen away. 'Rojer, you keep your pants on or I will give you such a dose of pepper!'

'These are my best pants!' Rojer said, aghast. 'I hear you cut your switches fresh, mistress. Sap on silk is impossible to clean.'

'I've never switched anyone in my life!' Leesha was fighting a smile now.

'How is that my fault?' Rojer scratched his head. 'I could give you pointers, I suppose, but it seems odd to teach someone how to switch you.'

Leesha choked on a laugh. 'Corespawn it, Rojer, this isn't a joke!'

'Ay,' Rojer agreed. 'But neither is it a breach at new moon. No one's bleeding and nothing's on fire, so there's no reason not to be civil. I'm your friend, Leesha, not your subject. I've shed as much blood for the Hollow as you have.'

Leesha sighed. 'You're right of course. I'm sorry, Rojer.'

'Ay,' Rojer's eyes grew wide as saucers, 'did Leesha Paper just admit she was wrong?'

Leesha snorted as she got up. 'Something to tell your grand-children about. I'll make tea.'

Rojer followed her to the kitchen, fetching the cups as she put the kettle on the fire. He kept his in hand. Mistress Jessa – madam of Duke Rhinebeck's brothel, where Rojer had spent much of his formative years – taught him never to trust a Herb Gatherer not to put something in your tea.

Even me, Rojer, Jessa said with a wink. *Night*, especially *me*.

Leesha put her hand on her hip, leaning against the counter while they waited for the kettle to boil. 'You can't have expected everyone to think it sunny, taking Kendall as your *third* wife. Two isn't enough for you? Night, she's only sixteen!'

Rojer rolled his eyes. 'A whole two years younger than me. The demon of the desert has, what, a dozen years on you? At least Kendall isn't trying to enslave everyone south of the Hollow.'

Leesha crossed her arms, a sign Rojer was getting to her. 'Ahmann is gone, Rojer. He had nothing to do with this attack.'

'Open your eyes, Leesha,' Rojer said. 'Just because a man curls your toes doesn't make him the Deliverer.'

'Ay, you should talk!' Leesha snapped. 'Not a season ago,

your precious little wives tried to poison me, Rojer. But they emptied your seedpods, so you went and married them anyway, no matter what I thought.'

Rojer's instinct was to snap back, but Leesha Paper was stubborn as a rock demon if you tried to lock horns with her. He kept his voice calm and quiet. 'I did. I ignored your advice and did what felt right. And you know what? I've no regrets. Don't need your permission to marry Kendall, either.'

'You need a Tender's,' Leesha said. 'It'll be easier to find a snowball in the Core.'

'Tenders' words don't mean a corespawned thing to me, Leesha,' Rojer said. 'Never have. Hayes wouldn't recognize Sikvah, either. You think we lose any sleep on it?'

'And Lusy?' Leesha asked. 'You plan to ignore her, as well?'

Rojer shrugged. 'That's Kendall's worry. She's old enough to promise whether her mum likes it or not. Just as well she disapproves. Less chance she'll want to move in with us.'

'So you're going through with it?' Leesha asked. 'You used to say marriage was a fool's game. Now you go and do it every time I turn 'round.'

Rojer chuckled. 'Tried to talk to you about it. Night of the Gathering, remember? But then Renna showed up . . .'

'And we all had bigger worries,' Leesha agreed.

'Had my doubts at first,' Rojer said. 'Never thought of Kendall like that. Honest word.' He looked at his hands, trying to find a way to express what he was feeling. He could do it easily with his fiddle, but notes always came to him more easily than words.

'This thing I have.' A woeful beginning. 'This . . . affinity with the demons, this way of influencing them with music that you and Arlen expected me to be able to teach – Kendall's the only one who really gets it. The Jongleurs, even Amanvah and Sikvah, can follow a lead and mimic the notes, but they don't . . . feel it like Kendall does. When she and I play together, it's as transcendent and intimate as anything in marriage. When the four of us play, it's a ripping choir of seraphs.'

He smiled. 'Only natural to want to kiss, after.'

'So kiss!' Leesha said. 'Night, stick each other silly. No one's business but yours and your wives. But marriage . . .'

'Told you, we don't need a Tender's blessing,' Rojer said. 'Kendall's my apprentice. Only natural she live with us. She'll have her Jongleur's licence soon, and we'll invite Lusy to stay. It's certainly better than the hovel the women are sharing.'

'You think no one will notice?' Leesha asked.

'Course they will,' Rojer said. 'Be the talk of the town. Rojer with his harem. I'll seed the tale myself.'

'Why?' Leesha said. 'Why invite scandal?'

'Because it's coming whether I like or not,' Rojer said. 'Amanvah and Kendall struck a deal before I knew what was going on, and it was a deal only a fool would turn down. So let people gossip now, and get used to it. I'll make them love me in spite of it, so when Kendall gets pregnant, no one's surprised when I ledger it a legitimate child.'

'Is that you talking, or Amanvah?' Leesha asked.

Rojer threw up his hands. 'Corespawned if I know.'

It was nearly midnight when Rojer finally left. Leesha watched him leave the yard, scripting her next meeting with Lusy.

If Kendall is willing, there's nothing you can do to stop this, she would say, pausing for the shock of the words to set in. *All you can do is delay it and hope the girl comes to her senses. Agree to negotiate, but ask for ridiculous things . . .*

She shook herself. There would be time for it in the morning. *If I get in bed right now, I might get six hours before Wonda and the children come back and folk start stomping on the porch.*

Leesha closed the door and went straight to her bedroom, leaving a trail of hairpins and shoes. Her dress was falling as she entered the room, the silk shift she wore underneath night-gown enough. She climbed into bed, forgoing even her nightly cleansing rituals. Her face and teeth would have to survive a few hours.

It felt like she had just closed her eyes when there was a pounding at the door. Leesha sat bolt upright, wondering how the night could have passed so soon.

But then she opened her eyes, and saw the room was still dark, lit only by the soft glow of wards.

The thumping continued as Leesha fumbled on her robe, staggering out of the room. She had deliberately not used *hora* tonight that she might sleep naturally, and now felt worse than she had the morning after she got drunk at Arlen's wedding. Her head throbbed with agony at every rap on the wood.

Either there's someone bleeding to death on the other side of that door, or there's going to be. Leesha made no effort to disguise her displeasure as she opened the door, only to find her mother on her front porch.

The Creator is punishing me, she thought. *It's the only explanation.*

Elona looked her up and down as she stood frazzled and fuming in the doorway. 'Putting on a little weight, girl. Folk are already whispering that the count may have an heir on the way.'

Leesha crossed her arms. 'Rumours you're no doubt fuelling.'

Elona shrugged. 'A wink here, a nudge there. Nothing to hold before a magistrate. You put your klats on the table when you got drunk and stuck the count in front of his carriage driver, Leesha. Too late to pull the bet now.'

'We didn't do it in front of . . .' Leesha began, but cut herself off. Why was she even engaging? Her bed still beckoned. 'Why are you here in the middle of the night, Mother?'

'Pfaw, it's barely midnight,' Elona said. 'Since when are you in bed so early?'

Leesha breathed. It was a fair point. She was used to receiving visitors at all hours, but most of them sent word first.

Elona tired of waiting for an invitation and pushed past

Leesha. 'Put the kettle on, that's a girl. Nights are turning chill as a coreling's heart.'

Leesha closed her eyes, counting to ten before closing the door and refilling the kettle. Elona, of course, didn't lift a finger to help. She was in the sitting room when Leesha brought the tray. Bruna's rocking chair was by no means the most comfortable place to sit, but Elona took it anyway, if only because she knew Leesha preferred it.

Leesha kept her dignity as she settled on a divan, back straight. 'Why are you here, Mother?'

Elona sipped her tea, made a face, and added three more sugars. 'Got news.'

'Good or bad?' Leesha asked, already knowing the answer. She could not recall a time her mother had ever delivered good news.

'Bit of both, from where you stand,' Elona said. 'I don't think you're alone.'

'Alone?' Leesha asked.

Elona arched her back, rubbing her free hand on her stomach. 'Might have my own scandal brewing, just in time to distract from yours.'

Leesha tried to speak, but no words would come. She stared at her mother a long time. 'You're . . .'

'Sick as a cat, and my flow ent come,' Elona confirmed. 'How that's even possible is beyond me, but there it is.'

'It's certainly possible,' Leesha said. 'You're only forty-f—'

'Ay!' Elona cut her off. 'No need to throw barbs! Ent talking about age. Quarter century ago Hag Bruna – your sainted teacher – told me you were my womb's last chance. Ent had a lick of pomm tea or made a man pull out since, but not an egg in the warmer. You mean to tell me all of a sudden I'm a fresh flower again?'

'Anything's possible,' Leesha said, 'but if I had to guess, I'd say it was the greatward.'

'Ay?' Elona said.

'Everyone in Cutter's Hollow has been living for nearly a

year on a ward that charges the very land with magic,' Leesha said. 'Even folk who don't fight are getting a bit of the feedback, making them younger, stronger—'

'—and more fertile,' Elona guessed. She lifted a biscuit, then gagged and put it back on her saucer. 'Ent all bad, I suppose. Your sibling and your child can crap the same crib and chase each other in the garden.'

Leesha tried to imagine that, but it was just too much. 'Mother, I have to ask . . .'

'Who's the da?' Elona asked. 'Core if I know. Gared was sticking me regular the last few years . . .'

'Creator, Mother!' Leesha cried.

Elona ignored her and went on. 'But the boy's gotten all religious since he stood up for the Painted Man. Hasn't touched me since you caught us on the road.'

She sighed. 'Could be your father's, I suppose, but Erny's not the man he used to be. You'd be amazed what I have to do just to get him stiff enough to . . .'

'Augh!' Leesha covered her ears.

'What?' Elona said. 'Ent you the town Gatherer? Ent it your job to listen to this kind of talk and help folk figure things out?'

'Well, yes . . .' Leesha began.

'So everyone else is good enough, but not your own mum?' Elona demanded.

Leesha rolled her eyes. 'Mother, no one else comes to me with stories like this. And what about Da? He's a right to know the child might not be his.'

'Hah!' Elona laughed. 'If that ent the night callin' it dark, I don't know what is.'

Leesha pressed her lips together. It was true enough.

'He knows, in any event,' Elona said.

Leesha blinked. 'He knows?'

'Course he knows!' Elona snapped. 'Your da has many failings, Leesha, but he ent dumb. Knows he can't plough the field well as it needs, and looks the other way when I get it done proper.'

She winked. 'Though I caught him watching a couple times. Didn't need help getting stiff those nights.'

Leesha put her face in her hands. 'Creator, just take me.'

'Point is,' Elona said, 'Erny's fine so long as no one rubs his nose in it.'

'Like you do every chance you get?' Leesha asked.

'I do no such thing!' Elona snapped. 'I may talk that way around you, but you're family. Ent like I'm telling the prissy wives at the Holy House that your da likes to—'

'Fine!' Leesha would rather give her mother the win than endure this conversation a moment longer. 'So we don't know who the father of your baby is. We can be run out of town together.'

'Core with that,' Elona said. 'We're Paper women. Town's just gonna have to get used to us.'

16

Demon's Heir

333 AR Winter

'Apologies, mistress,' Tarisa said, trying for a third time to fasten the back of Leesha's gown. 'The material appears to have shrunk. Perhaps you should choose another while I have the seamstresses let it out.'

Shrunk. Tarisa, bless her, was far too discreet to ever tell Leesha she was putting on weight, but it was clear as day in the silvered mirror. The face that stared back at her was plumper, a change shared by her bosom, which seemed to have doubled in size over the last fortnight. Thamos was paying them more attention, but had not yet put the evidence together. Tarisa, however, had a knowing look in her eye, and a hint of smile at the corner of her mouth.

'Please.' Leesha stepped behind the changing screen, running a hand over her stomach as she slipped out of the gown. It remained flat enough, but that wouldn't last. Her mother had told her the gossip was already beginning weeks ago. None dared speak of it to her face, but the moment her belly began to swell, there would be no stopping the goodwives from swarming her, causing such a stir Thamos couldn't help but notice.

Her hands clenched as panic took her. Her heart pounded, and it felt like her chest was bound tight, unable to draw a full breath. She gasped for air, eyes beginning to water, but she bit back her sobs. It would not do for Tarisa to see her so.

She fumbled for a kerchief, but none was to be found. She was about to lift the hem of her shift to dry her eyes when Tarisa's hand appeared, passing a clean cloth behind the screen.

'Tears will come and go, my lady,' the woman said. 'Better by far than sloshing up.'

She knows. It was not a surprise, but the confirmation still terrified Leesha. Her time was fast running out. In some ways, it was already too late.

'Had enough of both to last a lifetime,' Leesha said. 'Please fetch the green gown.' That one had laces more easily adjusted.

There was no council session this day, and Thamos had already left for his office. Tarisa, having planted the seed, kept her talk about frivolous things. She had made herself available if Leesha wished to talk, but knew her place too well to press. She and the other servants would no doubt be elated. They all loved the count, and had welcomed Leesha openly. Everyone wanted an heir.

What will they think when they discover the child is heir to the demon of the desert and not their beloved count?

Leesha hurried from the palace as quickly as possible, needing distance from prying eyes of the servants. Tarisa might not speak of her suspicions to Leesha directly, but no doubt gossip was rampant in the servants' quarters.

The hospit was little safer. The women might not see her in a state of undress as Tarisa did, but they saw with trained eyes. A good Gatherer was taught to suspect that every woman might be pregnant, and looked for the signs reflexively. Leesha hurried through the main floor to her office, closing the door. She sat at her desk and put her head in her hands.

Creator, what am I going to do?

There was a knock at the door, and Leesha swore under her breath. Was a moment's peace too much to ask?

She arched her back, drawing a deep breath and blocking away her own concerns. 'Enter.'

Amanvah slipped into the room, followed by Lusy Yarnballer, shooting daggers into the young priestess' back.

It was all Leesha could do not to burst into tears. Why couldn't it have been a rock demon?

Fortunately, the women were too involved in their own drama to even notice as Leesha composed herself. Both strode to the chairs in front of Leesha's desk, taking seats without invitation. Lusy's mouth was a hard line, veins throbbing at her temples. Just the sight of it made Leesha's own head ache.

Amanvah was more composed, but Leesha could tell it was an act. The woman looked ready to pull her silk veil aside and spit. 'We must speak with you, mistress.'

Leesha's nostrils flared. Amanvah was respectful, but she could not mask the imperious tone that came with her requests, as if they were mere formalities and complicity assured.

'The negotiations are not going well?' she asked, knowing well the answer.

Amanvah's serenity broke. 'She wants a palace. A palace! For a *chin* third wife whose family are servants to shepherds.'

'Ay!' Lusy cried.

'Do not be so quick to judge those of low station,' Leesha said. She had been the one to suggest the palace to Lusy, after studying Krasian marriage laws. 'Was not Kaji born to a family of lowly fruit pickers? Dozens of his wives had palaces of their own.'

'Kaji was the Deliverer, touched by Everam,' Amanvah said.

'By your own words, Rojer is touched by Everam as well,' Leesha noted.

Amanvah paused at that. 'He is . . .'

'And also by your own words, Kendall shares something of his gift. Does that not mean she, too, is touched?'

Amanvah leaned back, crossing her arms defensively. 'Everam touches all in some way. Not everyone gets a palace. Do I have one? Does Sikvah? We are Blood of the Deliverer. Should this Kendall be put above us?'

'Ay, that's right,' Lusy said. 'Maybe *she* ought to be *Jiwah* First or whatever.'

Amanvah's eyebrow twitched, and Leesha knew she had taken it too far.

'That's enough, Lusy.' She put a touch of lash into the words, and the woman started. 'I know you love your daughter and want the best for her, but what in the Core do you need a palace for? Night, have you ever even seen one?'

Lusy looked ready to cry. Not the sharpest spear. 'B-but you said . . .'

Leesha had no time to coddle her, cutting the woman off before she gave away the ruse. 'I never said for you to be insulting. Apologize. Now.'

Lusy, a terrified look on her face, turned to Amanvah, pulling her skirts in a clumsy, seated imitation of a curtsy. 'Sorry, your, er . . .'

'Highness,' Leesha supplied.

'Highness,' Lusy echoed.

'I think it's best we give this a little time for everyone to think it through,' Leesha said. 'Amanvah to remind herself Kendall is not some pack mule to haggle over, and Lusy to remind herself of the Canon's passages on greed. Roni will schedule a time we can meet again. Perhaps at full moon?'

Full moon was a blessed day to the Evejans, a day for oaths and alliances. It also happened to put the problem off for nearly a month, when she and Lusy would look for another reason to delay.

Amanvah nodded. 'That is acceptable.'

Lusy wasted no time getting out of her seat. She curtsied and was gone. Amanvah remained seated, shaking her head as the door closed behind her.

'Everam's balls, I am not sure if that woman is a bazaar grand master or a complete idiot.'

Leesha was shocked. 'Why Amanvah, I don't think I've ever heard you curse.'

'I am a Bride of Everam,' Amanvah said. 'If I cannot speak of His balls, who can?'

Leesha laughed at that – her first real laugh in what felt like forever. Amanvah joined her, and for a moment there was peace between them.

'Is something else on your mind, Amanvah?' she asked.

'You are carrying a child,' Amanvah said. 'I want to know if it is my father's.'

And just like that, the peace was gone. So, too, was Leesha's weariness and frustration. Adrenaline flooded her, every sense on alert. If Amanvah dared make the slightest threat to her child . . .

'I don't know what you're talking . . .'

Amanvah held up her *hora* pouch. 'Do not lie, mistress. The dice have already confirmed it.'

'But not whose it is?' Leesha asked. 'Curious things, these dice. Fickle, it seems. Unreliable.'

'That you are with child, there is no doubt,' Amanvah said. 'To know more, I would require blood.'

She looked at Leesha pointedly. 'Just a drop or two, and I could tell the father, the sex, even the very future of the child.'

'Even if I was, what business of yours is any of that?' Leesha asked.

Amanvah gave a rare bow. 'If the child is my half sibling, blood of the Deliverer, it is my duty to protect it. Few know better than I how many assassins a child of Shar'Dama Ka will draw.'

It was a tempting offer. The sex of the child might mean a difference of years in the coming war with Krasia, and Leesha desperately wished to know the path to keep the child safe.

But she did not hesitate to shake her head. Giving Amanvah even a drop of blood would let her cast a foretelling that could lay out Leesha's every weakness. No *dama'ting* would ever have the nerve to so bluntly ask another *hora* user for her blood. It was an insult that could create enmity to last generations.

Leesha turned her voice to a lash. 'You forget yourself, daughter of Ahmann. That, or you think me a fool. Begone from my sight. Now, before I lose patience with you completely.'

Amanvah blinked, but Leesha's stare was hard, her words sincere. Leesha was in her place of power. Everyone in the Hollow would turn on Amanvah if she so much as raised a finger. Most of them were waiting eagerly for the day.

The young priestess kept her dignity as she rose. Her quick strides to the door were not quite a scurry.

As the latch clicked shut, Leesha put her head back in her hands.

Amanvah had a queer look about her as she climbed into the motley coach. Rojer had become accustomed to her moods, reading them in her eyes and bearing as easily as he did with the corelings.

But no empathy could tell him what Amanvah was thinking now. Her manner was unprecedented, showing nothing of her usual haughtiness. She seemed almost shaken.

Rojer reached for her hand. 'Are you all right, my love?'

Amanvah returned the squeeze. 'All is well, husband. I am simply frustrated.'

Rojer nodded, though he knew how frustration looked on Amanvah, and this wasn't it.

'Mum still won't see reason?' Kendall asked.

'Surely Mistress Leesha has convinced her,' Sikvah said.

'Wouldn't count on that,' Rojer said. 'She may not openly oppose it, but Leesha ent thrilled about the idea, either.'

'It remains to be seen,' Amanvah said. 'Mistress Leesha appears willing to mediate the contract, but I am not convinced she is impartial. She may drive the dower beyond our ability to pay.'

'Don't care about any dower,' Kendall said. 'Let me talk to her . . .'

Amanvah shook her head. 'Absolutely not. It is not proper for you to involve yourself in these proceedings, little sister.'

'Ay, so everyone gets a say in my marriage but me?' Kendall said.

Rojer had to laugh at that. 'Had more say than me. Wasn't even asked if I wanted it.' When Kendall stared at him, he quickly added, 'Though of course I do. Sooner, the better.'

'This is exactly why both of you must be kept above the debate,' Amanvah said. 'You will both see the contract before you are asked to sign, but hearing your flaws laid bare as the haggling continues can only do harm. As it is written in the Evejah, *The cold of negotiating a marriage can douse the fires in which it must burn.*'

Kendall sighed. 'Just tired of having to sleep at my mum's. Don't care about some piece of paper.'

Rojer walked in the naked night, his warded cloak thrown back despite the chill air. He breathed deep, filling his lungs with winter's bite. He had suffocated in that cloak for too long.

Rojer and Kendall played an easy melody on their fiddles, subtly nudging corelings in the area away, while Amanvah and Sikvah sang a harmony to make them invisible to demon senses.

There were five of them in all. Kendall and Sikvah at the rear, joined in their music like lovers. He and Amanvah were similarly linked. He could feel her voice resonating inside him, more intimate than the touch of their sexes. All four played the same piece, but Amanvah's voice was led by Rojer's fiddle, while Sikvah followed Kendall's. This allowed them to break in two as needed, the blend of strings and voice enhancing each other's power. Ahead strode Coliv, vigilant, shield and spear at the ready.

They carried no light – the world lit by magic. Rojer and Kendall wore motley warded masks Amanvah and Sikvah had made, allowing them to see its glow. The princesses wore delicate gold nets in their hair, dangling warded coins that offered the same power. Amanvah had sewn the sight wards into Coliv's turban and veil that he might accompany them.

They walked until they found their favourite practice spot, a wide knoll that let them see far in every direction. Coliv was atop it in an instant, surveying the land. He gave sign all was clear, and the others followed.

When they were in position, Rojer lifted bow from string, his fiddle and Amanvah's voice falling silent as one.

Kendall nodded, changing the easy melody that kept the demons at bay to a call that reached far into the night, drawing corelings to them with promise of easy prey. Sikvah kept singing, her voice still masking their presence.

Wind demons were the first to reach them, two of the creatures circling down from above. Kendall drew them close, and then her music suddenly shifted. Sikvah smoothly dropped her masking spell, joining her voice to Kendall's music, and the demons shifted in midflight, colliding with one another and falling from the sky in a jumble of snapping beaks and slashing talons. They struck the ground so heavily Rojer almost could hear their hollow bones shattering.

He and Amanvah applauded, and Kendall and Sikvah bowed as he had taught them.

'Field demons to the west,' Coliv called. The reap was small, only five of the beasts, but five field demons could rend them to pieces in seconds.

Both women were calm as they turned to regard the approaching threat. Already Sikvah had resumed her song of unsight, masking the five humans atop the hill from the demons' senses as surely as a warded cloak.

As the reap came in, pulled by Kendall's insistent call, she knitted her brow and layered another melody over the first, wracking them with pain. Sikvah layered a harmony to match, keeping them hidden even as she added power to Kendall's attack.

Rojer's hand clenched on the neck of his fiddle as the demons closed, remembering the night she had been cored because of his failing.

But Kendall had been out in the naked night without him many times since, and it was time to stop coddling her.

'Too easy,' he called, as Kendall set the corelings fighting. 'Any two-klat Jongleur with one of my music sheets can make demons fight each other.' It wasn't entirely true, but Kendall was still being timid in her harmony with Sikvah. She needed to push herself.

Kendall smiled at him. 'Ay? How about if they fight themselves?'

She twisted the music like a knife in a wound, and the field demons turned their teeth and talons upon themselves. First Kendall made them claw their own eyes, leaving them stumbling blind in agony and rage. Soon after she had them lying on their backs, biting and clawing at themselves in a frenzy until the sheer number of wounds overwhelmed them. Hot, stinking ichor, glowing bright with magic, pooled like syrup around them.

After a few moments, only one of the demons was still kicking. It was a thickly armoured creature, the leader of the reap. Kendall eased her melody away, and it leapt to its feet, wounds already beginning to close. In minutes it would be fully healed, and those milky blind eyes would see once more.

Kendall gave it no time. She reached out tendrils of music, catching the demon fast and leading it in a blind charge right into an exposed rock face on the hilltop. It stumbled back, shrieking, but Kendall might as well have had it on a string, using the demon's own legs to smash its head back into the stone. Again and again, until there was only a wet slapping sound and the creature collapsed, its skull smashed.

Rojer gave a shrill whistle to accompany their applause. Even Coliv banged his spear on his shield. But then he pointed. 'Flame demons coming from the south. Wood from the east.'

Rojer looked and saw the approaching corelings, still a few moments away. 'Fiddle down, Kendall. Amanvah and Sikvah's turn.'

Amanvah glided over to join Sikvah, her voice lifting and falling naturally into Sikvah's song of unsight, weaving in a song of summoning.

Kendall was smiling proudly as she came to Rojer, pressing right up against him. He felt his heart quicken and his face flush. It took little, these days, for his apprentice to excite him. She was a whole new person to him now.

'You'll soon be as good as me,' Rojer said, meaning it.

Kendall kissed his cheek. 'Better.'

'From your lips to the Creator's ears,' Rojer said. 'I'd have it no other way.'

The flame demons came racing up the hill, but before they could reach the top, his wives seduced them. Rojer tried other words to describe it, but none was so apt. The corelings circled Amanvah and Sikvah, giving off a soft, rhythmic noise that sounded disturbingly like purring.

The copse of wood demons drew near, spreading out to surround the hilltop. Coliv dropped into a crouch, and Rojer and Kendall gripped their instruments, ready to raise them at a moment's notice.

Amanvah led the way as the singers dropped a pitch. The flame demons arched their backs, hissing, and darted to take up guard around the hilltop. They kept hissing as the woodies approached, and when they were in range, spat fire at them.

The resulting battle was fierce, but ultimately one-sided. Wood demons were wary of flame demons, but nevertheless killed them on sight. Flame demons could hurt them, even kill occasionally, but seldom before a wood demon crushed several of them.

Then Sikvah began a counterpoint to Amanvah's seduction, extending the song of unsight to cover their new allies. Woodies swung wildly, but the nimble flame demons danced around the lumbering blows, hawking great gobs of firespit. The spit stuck where it landed, burning with an intense flame that left Rojer seeing spots. He flexed his right hand, crippled where a flame demon had bitten off his index and middle fingers.

Soon the last of the wood demons had collapsed, bright pyres that burned out into a charred and blackened remain.

'Might as well have stepped into a sunbeam,' Kendall said, applauding.

'Ay,' Rojer said loudly, 'but like I told you, making demons fight each other is easy.' Of course, what his wives had done was far beyond that, but like Kendall, they were here to test their boundaries.

Amanvah smiled at him, and Rojer knew his confidence was well placed. She touched her choker as she climbed octaves, the song that moments before had the flame demons dancing their victory becoming a lash that drove them north at a frantic run. There was a cold fishing pond barely a mile in that direction. His senses enhanced by the wardsight, Rojer heard the splashes as the flame demons leapt in, and saw the rising clouds of steam that marked their passing.

There was a flash of magic above their heads, and Rojer looked up to see a wind demon plummet to the ground a few feet away, Coliv's spear embedded in its chest. The spear survived the fall. The coreling did not.

The Watcher bowed deeply. 'You are all touched by Everam, it is true. But this will not save you, if you drop your guard. Everam has no time for fools who do not respect Nie's might.'

Rojer expected Amanvah to snap at his haughty tone. Instead, she gave a fraction of a bow. More than he had ever seen her give a mere warrior. 'You speak wisdom, Watcher, and we hear.'

Coliv bowed again. 'I live to serve, Holy Daughter.'

Leesha kept her door shut as she tackled the mounds of paper covering her desk. Outside, Wonda kept visitors away, even Jizell and Darsy. She was in no mood to see anyone.

Wonda's distinctive knock came at the door, and Leesha sighed, wondering who it was she thought urgent enough to disturb over. 'Come in, dear.'

Wonda poked her head in. 'Sorry, mistress . . .'

Leesha did not look up from her papers, pen scratching as

she marked, signed, and annotated. 'Unless someone's dying, Wonda, I haven't the time. Tell them to make an appointment.'

'Ay, that's just it,' Wonda said. 'You asked me to get you at dusk. Supposed to test the Painted Children this evening.'

'It can't possibly be dusk already . . .' Leesha began, but looking through her window at the darkening sky, she realized it was true. Already her office was so dim she was straining her eyes without realizing.

Leesha looked at the barely dented pile of papers beside her and fought down the urge to weep. Dusk came earlier each day as they approached Solstice, making the tasks she needed to accomplish seem that much more insurmountable. Night was a vice, crushing her. New moon in summer had nearly destroyed them. Hollowers died every minute, the entire county holding on for dawn's succour and time to refortify. What would happen if the coreling princes returned when dark was half again as long, and daylight a scant few hours?

'And Stela wrestled a rippin' wood demon!' Wonda was saying as Leesha's carriage made its way home. She and Wonda used to walk the mile from her cottage to the hospit, but now there was no peace for Leesha when she did. Too many well-wishers, petitioners, and would-be advisors.

'Creator, you should have seen it,' Wonda went on. 'Corespawn's thrashing and kicking fit to tear itself in two, and there's Stela on its back, calm as a tree, waiting patiently for her next hold. Broke its spine in two when she found it.'

'Eh?' Leesha shook her head. 'She did what?'

'Ent heard a word I said the last ten minutes, have you?' Wonda asked.

Leesha shook her head. 'I'm sorry, dear.'

Wonda squinted at her. 'When's the last time you slept, mistress?'

Leesha shrugged. 'A few hours last night.'

'Three,' Wonda said. 'Counted. Ent enough, mistress. You know it. 'Specially with you . . .'

'With me what?' Leesha demanded. They were quite alone. Leesha had put sound-muffling wards in the carriage for privacy.

Wonda paled. 'With you . . . I mean . . .'

'Out with it, Wonda,' Leesha snapped.

'In a family way,' Wonda said at last.

Leesha sighed. 'Who told you?'

Wonda looked at the carriage floor. 'Mistress Jizell. Said you needed extra looking after, and were too stubborn to admit it.'

Leesha puckered her lips. 'She did, did she?'

'Only trying to look out for you and the little one,' Wonda said. 'Din't know what it was, but I seen how sick you been since we left the south. It's the demon's heir, ent it?'

'Wonda Cutter!' Leesha snapped, making the girl jump. 'I don't ever want to hear you call my child that again.'

'Din't mean . . .'

Leesha crossed her arms. 'You did.'

Wonda looked like she might be sick. 'Mistress, I . . .'

'This once,' Leesha cut in when she hesitated, 'I'll let it pass. This once, for the love I bear you. But never again. When I want you or anyone else to know my business, I'll tell you. In the meantime, I'll thank you to keep your nose out of it.'

Wonda nodded, her giant woman's body shrunk back like the teenage girl she was inside. 'Ay, mistress.'

It was full dark by the time they returned to her cottage, but the yard was abustle with apprentices, Gatherers, and the mustering Painted Children. It was standing room only in the theatre, where Vika was giving a lesson in warding Cloaks of Unsight. Leesha wanted every Gatherer and apprentice in the Hollow to have one before winter was out.

Vika was seated beside the speaker's podium, drawing wards onto vellum in the lens chamber. The mirrors and lenses bounced the image onto a white screen as hundreds of women copied the marks into their warding books.

'Children are still gathering,' Wonda said, 'and it'll take Roni and the girls a while to set the weights and measures. Why not nap for a bit? I'll come knock when we need you.'

Leesha looked at her. 'No scolding's going to keep you from mothering me now, is it?'

Wonda smiled helplessly. 'Sorry, mistress. Ent like I can stop knowin' something.'

Leesha regretted the harsh tone she had used on the girl. Wonda might only be sixteen, but she carried an adult's responsibilities with a grace few of any age could match. Leesha feared nothing when Wonda was watching over her.

'I'm sorry I snapped at you, Wonda,' she said. 'You're only looking out for me, and I love you for it. You keep at it, even when I'm being . . .'

'Stubborn as a rock demon?' Wonda supplied.

Leesha laughed in spite of herself. 'I'm straight to bed, Mum.'

The way to the cottage door was clear when Wonda moved off to meet the children. They looked at her in wonder, crossing fists over hearts as they gave a *sharusahk* student's bow. Many of them were older than she was, but nevertheless looked to her as their leader.

Leesha quickened her pace, every step drawing her closer to a few stolen moments of peace. She would brew a tea to put her out, and have another ready to counter it when Wonda woke her. Dare she hope for four uninterrupted hours?

'Leesha,' a voice came from behind her, 'glad I caught you.'

Leesha turned, putting a smile on her face that was indistinguishable from the real thing. It was Jizell, the last person in Thesa she wanted to see right now. A visit from Elona would have been preferable.

'Why aren't you in Vika's class?' Leesha said.

'Time was, Vika was my student, not the other way around.' Jizell waved her hand. 'Let the girls learn warding. I'm too old to put my apprentice apron back on.'

'That's enough of that,' Leesha snapped.

Jizell started. 'Eh?'

'Did you not hear my speech?' Leesha pressed. 'Or did you

think you could ignore it because I was once your apprentice, too?'

Jizell's face hardened. 'You've got stones to say that, girl, after all I've done for you. Been working my fingers to the bone since we came to the Hollow when I could've headed back to Angiers a moon ago.'

'You have,' Leesha agreed. 'So much that the other women look to you when I'm not around. And that is why you need to set a better example, for everyone's sake. If you ignore me and skip warding class, what's to stop every Gatherer above fifty from doing it?'

'Not everyone needs to learn warding, Leesha,' Jizell snapped. 'You're asking too much of these women too quick. Piling books and rules on them without even checking to see if they have letters.'

'No,' Leesha said. 'You're asking too little. I nearly died on the road from Angiers because I couldn't ward so much as a circle of protection. I won't see that happen to any Gatherer again, if I can help it. Every woman's life is worth a few hours' study.'

'Won't we all soon have Painted Children to protect us?' Jizell asked. 'The gossips say that's your master plan. A warded bodyguard for every Gatherer.'

Leesha wanted to tear her hair. 'Night, it's just a ripping class! Stop undermining me and go!'

Jizell put her hands on her hips. 'Undermining? How in the Core have I been undermining?'

'You argue requests that will save lives!' Leesha said. 'You ignore rules I set. You act like I'm still your apprentice. Night, you even call me "girl" in front of the other Gatherers!'

Jizell looked surprised. 'You know I don't mean anything by that . . .'

'I do,' Leesha said. 'But the others don't. It needs to stop.'

Jizell gave a mocking curtsy, hurt clear in her voice. 'Anything else you need to get off your paps, mistress?'

Leesha wondered if things would ever be the same between

them after this, but she had learned no good came from running away from problems. 'You told Wonda I was pregnant.'

Jizell only took a moment to answer, but the desperate search for a lie flashed across her aura so brightly Leesha would have seen it with her eyes closed. 'Figured she must already know—'

'Demonshit,' Leesha hissed. 'You're not some fool gossip, letting out scandals by accident. You told her because you wanted her mothering me.'

'Ay, what if I did?' Jizell put fists on her hips. Leesha might be an adult now, but the woman still loomed over her. 'You trust the girl with your life, but not your babe's? You're pushing all of us hard, Leesha, but yourself most of all. You're a woman grown, ay, and can make that choice for yourself, but you're making choices for two, and neither Wonda nor I is going to let you forget that. Keep arguing and I'll tell Darsy, as well.'

Leesha's face heated. She loved Darsy like a sister, but the woman kept a Canon in the apron pocket over her heart. She wouldn't even brew pomm tea for women. This . . . Leesha had no reason to think Darsy or many of the other Gatherers would stand by her if it was known she was carrying any child out of wedlock, much less Ahmann Jardir's.

And with that thought, Jizell started drifting away, blackness closing on Leesha's vision. She felt herself falling, and the jolt as Jizell caught her, but they were distant things.

'Mistress Leesha!' Wonda called, but she was miles away.

Leesha woke in her own bed. She sat up, looking around the darkened room in confusion. It felt like there were weights on her eyelids.

'Wonda?' she called.

'Mistress Jizell!' Wonda rushed to her bedside. 'Gave us all a scare, mistress.'

Jizell appeared with a candle, squeezing Wonda aside. She

lifted Leesha's drooping eyelids with a firm but gentle grasp, holding the candle flame close to check dilation.

'Everything's sunny, Leesha,' Jizell said, caressing her cheek. 'You go on back to sleep. Nothing happening that can't wait until morning.'

Leesha scraped her dry tongue around the inside of her mouth. 'You gave me tampweed and skyflower.'

Jizell nodded. 'Sleep. Gatherer's orders.'

Leesha smiled, snuggling her head back into the pillow and letting blessed sleep claim her.

When she awoke the next morning, Leesha felt stronger than she had in months. Her thoughts were still fogged from the sleeping draught, but it was nothing a good strong tea wouldn't fix.

Jizell was waiting as she shuffled out of her bedroom, clutching her shawl tight. Her mentor moved about Leesha's kitchen as comfortably as she did her own. She pushed a steaming teacup into Leesha's hand, deep black with a dollop of honey, like they had shared on countless mornings. 'Bathwater's hot. See to your privy and take a seat at the table. I'll have breakfast ready before you know it.'

Leesha nodded, but lingered. 'I'm so sorry for what I said.'

Jizell waved a hand. 'You oughtn't be. You were right about most of it. Could have been politer, but a pregnant woman who ent slept right in a month is apt to be prickly. Now go wash up.'

By the time Leesha had finished her bath and tea, her thoughts were clear. She chose her favourite dress and sat to breakfast. As promised, Jizell had a steaming plate of eggs and vegetables waiting.

'Examined you while you were out cold,' Jizell said. 'Child's heart thumps like a Cutter's axe. Strong.' She pointed her fork at Leesha. 'But you're already starting to show. Thamos might not notice with his face buried in your paps, but the rest of the town will be happy to point it out to him, if they haven't already. If you mean to tell him before someone else does, now's the time.'

Leesha kept her eyes on her food. Jizell, like most of the Hollowers, assumed the child belonged to Thamos. 'I'll speak to him. I have to tend the Royal Garden today anyway.'

Jizell laughed. 'That what you've been calling it? Good a name as any. You make sure that garden is good and tended before you tell him about the crop.'

The carriage took Leesha and Wonda right up to the entrance to the Royal Garden. Some of the count's men approached, but Wonda moved to intercept them as Leesha disappeared into the boughs. None save her would pass into the garden with Wonda at the gate.

Her heart fluttered as she passed out of sight. Sneaking into Thamos' Keep was ever a thrill. The fear of getting caught and the anticipation of sex was as strong as a bottle of couzi. But today was different. She would have him one last time as Jizell suggested, but as much for her as for him.

Leesha had once dismissed Thamos as a spoiled fop, good for little more than violence and easily manipulated. But Thamos had proven her wrong again and again. He was not creative, handling things in a by-the-book military fashion, but he was known for his fairness, and folk knew where they stood with him. He never hesitated to use his royal advantages, but neither did he hesitate to stand before the least of his people when the corelings came.

This visit might well end with their betrothal, and Leesha was surprised to find how badly she wanted that. The child would not come for half a year. Who could say what fate the Creator had in store between now and then?

In moments Leesha was through the maze of hedges and

slipped through the hidden door into the count's manse. Tarisa was waiting, escorting her discreetly to a waiting room with another hidden door, leading directly to Thamos' bedchamber.

The count was waiting, taking her into his arms and kissing her deeply. 'Are you all right, my love? There was word you fainted . . .'

Leesha kissed him again. 'It was nothing.' She let her hand drift down, tugging at his belt. 'We can steal an hour, at least, before Arther has the nerve to knock. You can take me twice, if you're man enough.'

Leesha knew the count was up to the task. Thamos fought demons most every night, and she had worked *hora* into his armour and spear. The count was taller now than when she'd met him, and his lust, formidable even then when roused, was doubled now. Since their first night together, there had been no hint of the performance anxiety that had robbed him of stiffness. Already, she could feel his breeches tightening.

Surprisingly, Thamos pulled back, holding her arms at the elbow as he moved his manhood out of reach. 'Nothing? You fell unconscious in front of half the Gatherers in the Hollow and it's nothing?'

Thamos waited for her response, the silence heavy between them. He squeezed her shoulders, putting a gentle finger under her chin to lift her eyes to meet his. 'If you have something to tell me, Leesha Paper, now is the time.'

He knows. Leesha wondered if it had been Tarisa who told him, but in truth it did not matter. 'I'm pregnant.'

'I knew it!' Thamos boomed, grabbing her. For a moment she thought it was an attack, but his crushing embrace only lasted an instant before he lifted her from her feet, swinging her around with a whoop of joy.

'Thamos!' Leesha cried, and the count's eyes widened.

He put her down instantly, staring at her belly in concern. 'Of course. The child. I hope I did not . . .'

'It's fine,' Leesha said, relief flooding her. 'I'm just surprised to see you so pleased.'

Thamos laughed. 'Of course I am pleased! Now you will *have* to become my countess. The people will insist on it, and I would have it no other way.'

'Are you certain of that?' Leesha asked.

Thamos nodded eagerly. 'I can't do this without you, Leesha, nor you without me. The Painted Man may be gone, but together, we can drive back the corelings and rebuild the Hollow into one of the great cities of old.'

Leesha could not deny the tingle his words brought to her. Her heart leapt into her throat as Thamos dropped to one knee, taking her hands in his. 'Leesha Paper, I promise myself . . .'

Creator, he's actually doing it. He has no idea it's not his.

She froze. It was everything she wanted. At worst, she would have six months to plan. There were orphan children throughout the Hollow. Perhaps she could find a babe that looked enough like Thamos to make a switch and spirit Ahmann's child to safety.

Or perhaps she was worried over nothing. She remembered Stefny's words after the council.

Funny thing about children. People see in them what they want to see.

Thamos was swarthier than Leesha and often tanned. Her pale skin would burn, but no tan could take root. The child might be close enough to avoid scrutiny, especially if Leesha quickly delivered additional children, Thamos' true heirs.

I will be a good wife, she promised silently. *A good countess. You will not regret taking me as your bride, even if the day comes when you learn the truth.*

Tears rolled down her nose in fat drops. She hadn't even realized she was crying.

Creator, I think I'm in love.

She opened her mouth, wanting nothing more than to promise herself to this man and make his dreams come true.

But the words caught in her throat. He looked at her with such sincerity, such love, that she could not stand the thought of betraying him.

She pulled her hands away, taking a step back from him. 'Thamos, I . . .'

'What is it, my love? Why are you not . . .' And then, suddenly, he put it together. Even without wardsight, she could see the change in his eyes as he stood.

'Night, the rumours are true,' Thamos said. 'I had three of my men whipped for such talk just last week, but they spoke honest word. The demon of the desert. The man who conquered Rizon, killing thousands and filling all Thesa with a vagrant refugee class that will last for generations. You ripping stuck him.'

'And you stuck every maid in Angiers, to hear gossips tell it,' Leesha snapped. 'I wasn't promised to you when I lay with him, Thamos. We hardly knew each other. I didn't even know you were coming to the Hollow.'

'Those maids weren't killing by the thousand,' Thamos said, making no effort to deny it.

'If they were,' Leesha asked, 'and you could slow their advance and learn their plans by bedding them, would you have hesitated?'

'So you were whoring, then,' Thamos said.

Leesha slapped him. Thamos' eyes widened a moment in shock, then shut tight. His face was a snarl as he balled his great fists.

Leesha was edging her hand towards the pouch where she kept her blinding powder when he gave a shout and stormed away from her, pacing the room like a caged nightwolf. He gave another shout, punching the goldwood post of his great bed.

'Aaaahhh!' he cried, clutching the hand.

Leesha rushed to him, taking his hands. 'Let me look.'

'Haven't you done enough?!' Thamos shouted, his face a mask of anguish, reddened and tear-streaked.

Leesha looked at him calmly. 'Please. You might have broken something. Just sit still for a moment and let me see.'

Thamos limply allowed himself to be led to the bed, where

they sat as Leesha pulled his protective hand away and examined the damaged one. It was red, with the skin torn at the knuckles, but it could have been much worse.

'There's nothing broken,' she said. From a pocket of her apron she took an astringent and cloth, cleaning and dressing the wound. 'Just put it in a bowl of ice . . .'

'Is there at least a chance it's mine?' Thamos' eyes were pleading.

Leesha took a deep breath, shaking her head. She could almost feel her heart twisting and tearing in her chest. There was still a chance with Thamos, and she had just crushed it.

'I love you,' she whispered. 'I swear it. If I could go back and change things, I would. I know I led you on. At first it was to protect the child, but only at first.'

'What was it after?' Thamos asked.

'Because I want to be your countess,' Leesha said. 'More than anything, I want it.'

Thamos yanked his hand away, standing and beginning to pace again. 'If that's honest word, then prove it. Brew Weed Gatherer's tea and flush the child. Start anew, as mine.'

Leesha blinked. It had not surprised her when her mother suggested it, and no doubt Inevera and Araine would want the same. Women could be cold about such things, when they had to. But she never thought Thamos would murder an innocent child.

'No,' she said. 'I drank the tea once – without even knowing if there was a life growing in me or not – and it was the biggest regret of my life. More even than bedding Ahmann. Never again.'

'Augh!' Thamos cried, taking a vase and throwing it across the room. Leesha stiffened. Thamos had to work himself up to violence in the night. Why would it be different here? She rose as well, edging towards the secret door to the gardens.

And Wonda.

But again Thamos surprised her, the rage leaving him with a sigh as his shoulders slumped. His face was one of defeat as he turned to her. 'You realize all Hollow County, and my mother, thinks it's mine?'

Leesha nodded, weeping. Her legs turned to water, and she stumbled back to the bed, covering her face in a vain attempt to hide her sobbing. She sat there for long moments, wretched and convulsing, but then there was weight on the bed, and Thamos put an arm around her.

Leesha leaned in to him, wondering if it was for the last time. She clutched at his shirt, holding tight and breathing deep, remembering his scent.

'I'm sorry to involve you in this,' she said. 'I didn't expect you to start courting me, or that I would fall in love with you. I was just trying to protect my baby.'

'Protect it from who?' Thamos said. 'No one in the Hollow would have harmed the child.'

'The Krasians would cut it from me, if they knew,' Leesha said. 'Or worse, wait till it's born and then take it from me, raising it to believe it's the heir to the green lands.'

She looked at Thamos. 'And your mother might take it hostage, too. Don't deny it.'

Thamos dropped his eyes, nodding. 'She would likely think it best.'

'And you, Thamos?' Leesha asked. She was pressing too soon, but she had to know. 'A moment ago you could not go on without me. Would you see me imprisoned at court with your mother?'

Thamos slumped. 'What am I to do? Rhinebeck still has no son. My mother thinks you may be carrying the next heir to the ivy throne in your womb. How am I supposed to tell her it's the demon of the desert's heir instead?'

'I don't know,' Leesha said. 'There's no need to decide now. There's been no formal announcement of my condition. Let's just act normally and try to figure things out.' She squeezed Thamos' hand, and when he did not pull away she leaned in for one last kiss.

Thamos jumped to his feet as if stung by a bee. 'Don't. Not now. Maybe not ever again.'

He took a step back, waving his hand at the hidden door. 'I think you should go.'

Leesha sobbed as she slipped through the exit, running from the manse as quickly as she could without stumbling.

17

Goldentone

333 AR Winter

The Angierian heraldic coach looked out of place in the Hollow, but Rojer would have known it anywhere. He and Arrick had ridden in it countless times back when his master was still in Rhinebeck's favour.

Only now it belonged to Jasin Goldentone.

Rojer's bow skidded off the strings as the coach pulled up in the Corelings' Graveyard, escorted by a dozen Wooden Soldiers on sleek Angierian coursers. The other Jongleurs and apprentices, following his lead in the bandshell, ceased their playing as well, following his gaze.

Kendall caught his eye. 'Everything all right? You look white as a cloud.'

Rojer barely heard her. His head swam with a mix of panic and fear, remembering the screams and laughter of a bloody night not so long ago. He watched, transfixed, as the footman lowered the steps and moved to open the carriage door.

Hary Roller put a hand on his shoulder. 'Go, lad. Now, before you're seen. I'll give your regrets.'

The words, and the gentle shove the old Jongleur gave, served to snap Rojer out of his daze. Hary took up his fiddle and stepped up to lead the orchestra, drawing the attention of the players away as Rojer slipped away.

Exiting stage right, Rojer picked up speed the moment he was out of sight, bounding the steps three at a time and then out the door, darting around the back of the bandshell quick as a hare. He pressed his back to the wall in the shadow of the shell, watching as Goldentone stepped out of the coach.

The last year had done little to dull Rojer's feelings at the sight of the man who had murdered Master Jaycob and left Rojer for dead in the streets of Angiers at night. In the safety of the shadows, Rojer's lip curled and his hand itched to flick and draw down one of the knives he kept strapped to his forearms. One good throw . . .

And what? he asked himself. *You get hung for murdering the duke's herald?*

But Rojer's muscles would not unclench. He was breathing hard just standing still, his body filling itself with oxygen to fight or flee.

Jasin called to Hary, and the old Jongleur moved down the steps at the front of the stage to greet him. The men shared a hug and a slap on the back, and the knives seemed to fall into Rojer's hands of their own accord.

There was no sign of his apprentices, Abrum and Sali. Abrum who had broken Rojer's fiddle and held him down. Sali, who had laughed as she beat Master Jaycob to death.

But the apprentices were just tools. It was Jasin who had ordered it. Jasin who stood to pay the most for the crime.

'Rojer, what in the Core are you doing?' Kendall's harsh whisper at his back made him jump. How had she managed to sneak up on him?

'Mind your own instrument, Kendall,' Rojer said. 'Doesn't concern you.'

'Core it doesn't,' Kendall said, 'if I'm to be your wife.'

Rojer looked at her, and something in his eyes made her draw a sharp breath. 'For now,' he said quietly, 'all you need to know is that if a demon were about to eat Jasin Goldentone, and all I had to do to save him was play a little ditty, I'd smash my fiddle to a thousand pieces first.'

'Who is Jasin Goldentone?' Amanvah demanded the moment Rojer walked into their chambers. She was in her coloured silks, her bare face beautiful even in her anger.

He'd expected it, but this was quick even so. Kendall and his wives had become thick as thieves in the last few weeks.

'Jasin Goldentone is my ripping business and no one else's,' he snapped.

'Demon's shit.' Amanvah spat on the floor, surprising Rojer with her vehemence. 'We are your *jiwah*. Your enemies are ours as well.'

Rojer crossed his arms. 'Why not ask your dice, if you want to know so much?'

Amanvah gave a tight smile. 'Ah, husband. You know I already have. I am offering you this chance to tell me with your own words.'

Rojer gave her a neutral look, considering. No doubt she had indeed cast the dice on the question, but what the *alagai hora* told her was something else entirely. She might have the whole story – more even than he did – or she might have only a few vague hints with which to pry the information from his lips.

'If you cast the dice, you know all Everam wishes you to,' he countered, knowing it was dangerous ground.

To his surprise, Amanvah's smile loosened a bit. 'You are learning, husband.'

Rojer gave a short bow. 'I've had excellent teachers.'

'You must learn to trust your *jiwah*, husband,' Amanvah said, putting a hand on his arm and drawing close. Rojer knew it was a calculated move, just like her anger, but he could not deny its effectiveness.

'I'm just . . .' Rojer swallowed a lump in his throat. 'I'm not ready to talk about it.'

'The *hora* say there is blood between you,' Amanvah said. 'Blood that can only be washed away with blood.'

'You don't understand—' Rojer began.

Amanvah cut him off with a laugh. 'I am the daughter of Ahmann Jardir! You think I do not understand blood feud? It is you who do not understand, husband. You must kill this man. You must do it now, before he has a chance to strike at you and yours again.'

'He wouldn't dare,' Rojer said. 'Not here. Not now.'

'Blood feuds can last generations, husband,' Amanvah said. 'Fail to kill him, and it may be his grandchildren who revenge themselves upon yours.'

'And killing him will stop that?' Rojer said. 'Or will it just make enemies of his children directly?'

'If he has any, it may be best to kill them, as well,' Amanvah said.

'Creator, are you serious?' Rojer was aghast.

'I will send Coliv,' Amanvah said. 'He is a Krevakh Watcher and one of the Spears of the Deliverer. He will never be seen, and to all the witnesses, your enemy will simply have fallen from his horse or choked on a pea.'

'No!' Rojer shouted. 'No Watchers. No *dama'ting* poison. No getting involved – any of you. Jasin Goldentone is mine to revenge upon, or not, and if you cannot respect that, then this marriage is ended.'

There was silence then. Silence so deep Rojer could hear his own heart thumping in his chest. Part of him wanted to take back the words, just to break the silence, but he couldn't.

They were true.

Amanvah stared at him for a long time, and he met her mask with his own, daring her to blink.

At last she did, lowering her eyes and bowing deeply. Her words dripped venom. 'As you wish, husband. His blood is yours alone.'

She looked up at him. 'But know this. Every day you allow this man to live, his actions will weigh against you when you walk the lonely path to be judged.'

Rojer snorted. 'I'll take my chances.'

Amanvah blew a short, angry breath through her nostrils, turning on a heel and gliding to her personal chambers and shutting the door.

Rojer wanted to chase her. To tell her he loved her and never wanted their marriage to end, but the strength left him and reality closed from all sides.

Jasin Goldentone was in the Hollow, and Rojer could only avoid him for so long.

The invitation came the next morning, a special afternoon meeting of the count's inner council to formally greet the duke's herald.

Rojer crumpled the paper in his fist, but was careful not to leave it where it might be found. Amanvah was still in her private chambers, the air chill around the door.

'I've got to see the baron,' Rojer told Sikvah. Immediately she moved to lay out the appropriate clothes.

Even Rojer's wardrobe had seen Amanvah's touch. She'd been shocked to find the clothes Rojer brought to Everam's Bounty were the only ones he owned. Not an hour later, Shamavah's tailors had been stripping and measuring him.

It was good they were building a manse. At the rate Rojer's closets were filling, they would need to devote an entire wing to his wardrobe.

Not that he was complaining. Rojer now had motley for every occasion, material fine and colours ranging in brightness depending on the nature of the event. Night, he could go a month without wearing the same thing twice. It reminded him of the early days with Arrick, when he had been the duke's herald and they lived in the palace. Even now, the lie of those times exposed, they remained the happiest days he could remember.

Rojer had attempted to pick his own clothes at first, but his wives quickly put an end to that. In truth, they had a better sense of such things than he.

The jacket and breeches Sikvah chose for an informal meeting with the baron were printed with an intricate pattern of muted colour, like a fine Krasian rug. The loose shirt was flawless white silk. It felt like wearing a cloud.

Beneath the flowing cloth, Rojer's medallion hung heavy on his chest. A Royal Angierian Medal of Valour on a thick braided chain, the heavy gold moulding in relief crossed spears behind a shield emblazoned with Duke Rhinebeck's crest: a leafed crown floating above an ivy-covered throne. Beneath the shield, a banner read:

Arrick Sweetsong

But Rojer wore it in reverse, the medallion's smooth back etched with four more names:

Kally
Jessum
Geral
Jaycob

The names of those who had died protecting Rojer. Five names. Five lives, cut short for his. How many was his miserable existence worth?

He pretended to fiddle with his laces for the excuse to touch the medal. For an instant, his fingers brushed the cool metal and a wave of comfort flowed through him, driving away the gripping anxiety. Whatever his brain told him, his heart knew no harm could come to him while he was touching it.

It was a fool's belief, but Rojer was a fool by trade, so that worked out.

Sikvah pulled his hands away like a mother dressing a toddler, fixing the laces herself. Anxiety clenched him again, and he moved his hand back instinctively. Sikvah delivered a sharp slap to the back of his hand. It stung for a moment, then fell away, numb as she jerked the shirt straight.

Rojer jumped back in surprise. 'Sikvah!'

Sikvah's eyes widened, and she dropped smoothly to her knees, hands on the ground. 'I apologize for striking you, honoured husband. If you wish to whip me, it is your right . . .'

Rojer was stunned. 'No, I . . .'

Sikvah bobbed. 'Of course. I will inform the *dama'ting* to issue my penance . . .'

'No one's whipping anyone!' Rojer snapped. 'What is it with you people? Just forget it and find me another shirt. Something with buttons.'

The moment she turned her back, Rojer's hand darted to the medallion, clutching as if his life depended on it.

His talisman was one of the few secrets he still held from his wives. They knew the names, his mother and father, their family friend the Messenger, and the two Jongleurs he had apprenticed under. Honoured dead.

But the stories behind them, the tales of murder, betrayal, and stupidity, these he kept secret.

Sikvah brought the new shirt, a voluminous affair with heavy lace cravat. It was more ostentatious than the occasion merited, but perfect to put a fog over his chest, that he might easily stroke his medallion without drawing attention.

Had she done it on purpose? When Sikvah left the third button from the top undone, Rojer knew she understood, and his heart ached.

Everyone he had ever loved in his life had died and left him alone, but what if the debt was still not paid in full? Would it be Sikvah to die for him next? Amanvah? Kendall? He couldn't bear the thought.

He realized he was clutching the medallion in a grip so hard it hurt. How long since he had done that? Months. After the attack at new moon, very little frightened him any more.

But he was frightened now. Thamos had been cold since Rojer refused to take commission as royal herald of Hollow County. He would not be moved to turn on his brother's herald over a tale of some murdered street performer.

Worse, Jasin might well have arrived with an arrest warrant, for him or his wives. The daughter and niece of the Krasian leader would be valuable hostages, especially now that the Krasians had invaded Lakton.

An accusation against Jasin now might get Rojer nothing but the herald's ire, and Rojer knew well how Jasin Goldentone dealt with ire. He embraced it, stroked it, nourished it.

And then, when you thought he must surely have forgotten, it was knives on a darkened street.

Rojer choked, his next breaths came out in a fit of coughing.

'Husband, are you well?' Sikvah asked. 'I will inform the *dama'ting* . . .'

'I'm fine!' Rojer pulled away, straightening his cravat. The medallion pulled at him, but he ignored the need, reaching for his fiddle and cloak. 'Just need a sip of wine.'

'Water would be best.' Sikvah moved to fill a cup. His *jiwah* no longer tried to stop him drinking alcohol, but neither did they approve.

'Wine,' Rojer said again. Sikvah bowed and fetched the proper skin. He ignored the cup she offered, taking the skin whole and heading for the door.

'Husband, when will you return?' Sikvah called.

'Not until late in the day,' and Rojer was through the door, closing it behind him.

Coliv stood in a shadowed nook just outside the door to the apartments. The Watcher gave Rojer a nod of acknowledgement, but said nothing.

'Post extra *Sharum* around the restaurant,' Rojer said. 'We have enemies in the day.'

'All men have enemies in the day,' Coliv said. 'It is only in the night we become brothers.'

'Just post the ripping men,' Rojer snapped.

Coliv gave a slight bow. 'It is already done, son of Jessum. The Holy Daughter issued these commands yesterday.'

Rojer sighed. 'Course she did.'

Coliv tilted his head. 'This man, Goldentone. He owes you a blood debt, yes?'

Rojer kept his face blank. 'Yes. But I don't want you and my *jiwah* involved.'

Coliv bowed again, deeper this time, and for two heartbeats

longer. 'I apologize for underestimating you, son of Jessum. You greenlanders do know something of the *Sharum* way. There is no honour in a man sending assassins to collect his blood debts.'

Rojer blinked. This from the master assassin? 'Then don't get involved. Even if Amanvah commands it.'

Coliv bowed one last time, shallow and brief. 'There is no honour in assassination, master, but it is sometimes necessary. If the Holy Daughter commands I get involved, I will be involved.'

Rojer swallowed. Part of him thrilled at the thought of Coliv putting his spear through the hearts of Jasin and his apprentices, but it wouldn't end there. Jasin had family. Powerful family with deep ties to the ivy throne. Blood would be paid in blood.

He took the steps three at a time, practically bouncing at the landing and out the back door to Shamavah's stables. Krasian children in tan tended the animals, and they all hopped when they saw him, rushing to be the first to help.

The quickest proved to be young Shalivah, Drillmaster Kaval's granddaughter. The drillmaster, too, had died for Rojer. As had Amanvah's bodyguard Enkido. Two more names to etch into the medallion. Seven lives now, paid for his one.

'Will master need his mottley coach?' the girl asked, her words quick and heavily accented.

Rojer pulled a bright Jongleur's mask over his face in an instant. She didn't see him slip the tiny flower from his bright new bag of marvels. To her it appeared from thin air, and she gasped as he gave it to her.

'*Motley*, Shalivah, not *mottley*. *Motley* means "colourful". *Mottley* means "spotted". Do you understand?'

The girl nodded, and Rojer produced a sugar candy. 'Say it. Motley.'

The girl smiled, leaping for the candy. Rojer was not a tall man, but even he could keep it from the child's reach. 'Motley!' she cried. 'Motley! Motley! Motley!'

Rojer flipped her the candy. Her squeal of glee brought the attention of the other children, looking at him expectantly.

He did not disappoint. More candies were already hidden

in his hand. He gave a stage laugh to cover a heavy heart as he spun, nimbly flicking a candy unerringly into the hands of each.

Their families bled for him, and he repaid them in candy.

The new baron shifted uncomfortably at his great goldwood desk. His giant fist made the quill look like a hummingbird feather as he scrawled something approximating a signature to the seemingly endless stack of papers slid before him by Squire Emet, a minor Angierian lordling Thamos had appointed the baron's secretary.

'Rojer!' Gared cried, rising immediately to his feet as he entered the office.

'My lord,' the secretary began.

'Rojer's got important business, Emet. Yu'll have to come back later.' Gared loomed over the secretary, and Emet was wise enough to gather his papers and whisk out of the room.

Gared closed the heavy doors, putting his back to them and blowing out a breath as if he had just escaped a reap of field demons. 'Thank the Creator. Ready to throw that whole desk out the window, I had to sign one more paper.'

Rojer's eyes flicked to the great heavy desk and the window several feet away. If anyone alive could do it, it was Gared Cutter.

Rojer grinned. He always felt safer around Gared. 'Always happy to provide an escape from paperwork.'

Gared grinned. 'You come by around eleven each morning with a new emergency, I'll thank you for it. Drink?'

'Night, yes.' Rojer had drained the skin, but wine was slow. Gared had developed a taste for Angierian brandy, and kept a bottle in his office. Rojer moved to the service, pouring two glasses. He was quick, and Gared didn't notice as he drained one and refilled it before bringing them over.

They clicked glasses and drank. Gared took only a pull, but

Rojer shot his, moving to fill a third. 'Today it's not a lie. Got an emergency, sure enough.'

'Ay?' Gared asked. 'Sun's up and nothing's aflame, so it can't be too bad. Let's have a pipe and talk about it, before we're off to meet the duke's herald. You think his voice really sounds as good as gold?'

Rojer shot the next glass, filling a fourth before coming to sit on one of the chairs before the great desk. Gared took the other, packing his pipe. Gared Cutter wasn't one to put a desk between him and anyone else.

Rojer took the offered leaf and packed his own pipe. 'You recall how I met Leesha in the hospit?'

'Everyone knows that story,' Gared said. 'Start of the tale of how you met the Deliverer.'

Rojer didn't have the strength to argue. 'Remember you asked who put me there?' Gared nodded.

Rojer emptied his glass. 'It was the duke's herald with the golden voice.'

Gared's face darkened instantly, like a father finding his daughter with a black eye. He balled a meaty fist. 'He'll be lucky if all the Gatherers in the Hollow can stitch him back together when I'm done with him.'

'Don't be stupid,' Rojer said. 'You're the Baron of Cutter's Hollow, not the bouncer at Smitt's.'

'Can't just let something like that lie,' Gared said.

Rojer looked at him. 'Jasin Goldentone is the duke's herald, the representative of the ivy throne in the Hollow. Anything you say to him, you are saying to Duke Rhinebeck himself. Anything you *do* to him, you do to Rhinebeck himself.'

He gave Gared a look that set even the menacing Cutter aback. 'Do you have any idea what the duke would do to you – to the Hollow – if you beat his ripping herald to death?'

Gared's brow furrowed. 'So we should get someone else to do it?'

Rojer closed his eyes and counted to ten. 'Just let me handle it.'

Gared looked at him doubtfully. Rojer was no fighter. 'Want to handle it yurself, why you tellin' me?'

'I don't want you to do anything to Jasin,' Rojer said. 'But I don't expect him to be so magnanimous.'

Gared blinked. 'Mag-what?'

'Generous,' Rojer supplied. 'He might be worried I'm going to do something, and come after me and mine. I'd sleep better if you could spare a few Cutters to keep an eye on his people.'

Gared nodded. 'Course. But Rojer . . .'

'I know, I know,' Rojer said. 'Can't let it fester forever.'

'Stinks already,' Gared said. 'Wish the Deliverer were here. He could rip that skunk's head clean off, and no one would spit.'

Rojer nodded. That had been his plan since he'd first met Arlen Bales.

But the Painted Man was never coming back.

Rojer shifted in his seat. Tension was thick in the air of the count's council chamber as they waited on Thamos and Jasin. Lord Arther and Captain Gamon were even stiffer than usual, though it was unclear if it was news from Angiers or simply the presence of the royal emissary. Inquisitor Hayes looked as if he'd just bitten a sour apple.

Even Leesha had come out of hiding for the meeting. She hadn't left her cottage in the fortnight since she'd fainted in her yard. The Gatherers patrolling her bedside had denied even Rojer's visits. Even now, Darsy guarded her like Evin Cutter's wolfhound.

It wasn't hard to see why. Leesha was pale, face puffy and eyes bloodshot. Not one for makeup, the thick powder on her face spoke volumes, as did the tendons stretched like tightropes on her neck.

Was she ill? Leesha might be the most powerful healer in Thesa, but she had more on her shoulders than even Rojer, and she'd been pushing herself hard. She gave Rojer a weak smile, and he threw a bright – if completely false – one back at her.

Beside him, Gared seemed ready to crawl out of his skin. He'd never let any harm come to Rojer, but the big Cutter had a tendency to break things he meant to fix.

Next to the Baron, Erny Paper and Smitt had their heads together in low conversation. It was doubtful they knew half the drama in the room, but the two men could read the tension well enough to know the duke's herald was not making a social call.

Hary Roller put a light hand on Rojer's arm. The old Jongleur knew more of Rojer's history with Jasin than any present, but he had his mask on, and not even Rojer could see his true feelings.

'He won't start trouble if you don't start it first.' Hary's trained voice offered the words for the two of them alone.

'You think he's had his blood and everything's sunny now?' Rojer asked.

'Course not,' Hary said. 'Secondsong never forgets a slight.'

Secondsong. It was what the other Jongleurs called Jasin Goldentone, back when Arrick Sweetsong had been the duke's herald. It was said he got more patrons from his uncle Janson's connections than any gold in his voice.

Privately, at least. No one called Jasin 'Secondsong' to his face unless they were ready for a fight. Jasin's uncle was good for more than bookings. Master Jaycob hadn't been the first – or the last – time Jasin had gotten away with murder.

Hary seemed to read his mind. 'You're not some two-klat street performer any more, Rojer. Something happens to you, every spear in the Hollow will be out for justice.'

'All bright and sunny for justice,' Rojer said, 'but I'll be just as dead.'

Just then, Arther and Gamon scrambled to their feet, followed quickly by the rest of the councillors as Count Thamos and Jasin Goldentone swept into the room.

Goldentone still had the same oily arrogance Rojer remembered, but service to the throne had obviously agreed with him. He had been thinner the last time Rojer saw him.

Rojer kept his Jongleur's mask in place, open eyes and a painted-on smile, but inside, he thought he might vomit. He could feel the weight of the knives in his forearm sheaths. There were Wooden Soldiers posted at the door, but neither they nor the officers at the table could move faster than Rojer could throw.

But what then?

Idiot, take your own advice, Rojer scolded himself. *Maybe you deserve nothing better than a taste of vengeance and a quick death at the hands of the Wooden Soldiers, but what will happen to Amanvah and Sikvah if you kill the duke's herald?*

Rhinebeck would probably consider Goldentone a fair trade for the excuse to arrest the Krasian princesses and hold them hostage.

So he sat and did nothing, even as the coreling in his breast clawed and shrieked, threatening to tear him to pieces.

Jasin's eyes moved to meet the gaze of each council member in turn as Arther announced him. His gaze lingered a moment on Rojer, and he gave a polite smile.

Rojer longed to cut it from his face. Instead, he smiled in return.

When the introduction was done, Jasin made a show of opening an ornate scroll tube and breaking the wax of the royal seal that kept the paper bound. He unrolled it, his voice rising to fill the room.

'Greetings from the ivy throne to Hollow County in this year of our Creator, 333 AR,' he began.

'His Grace, Duke Rhinebeck the Third, Guardian of the Forest Fortress, Wearer of the Wooden Crown, and Lord of All Angiers, extends his congratulations to his brother and all the leaders and people of Hollow Country for seeing to the safe return of General Gared and Royal Gatherer Leesha from Krasian lands, and the successful defence of the Hollow in the face of the greatest demon attack in centuries.

'But with so many changes and the news from Lakton, there is still much to be done. His Highness requests and commands an immediate audience with Count Thamos and Baron Gared, as well as Mistress Leesha, Rojer Halfgrip, and the Krasian princess Amanvah.'

The coreling inside Rojer stopped its struggle, drowning in those last words. Jasin Goldentone was a tiny subplot of the drama unfolding. Rojer, as well. All of them would go to Angiers – how could they refuse? – but Amanvah would not be coming back. She, and Rojer, would likely be held until they died, or the Krasian army broke down the city walls.

Jasin met his eyes with another pursed smile, but this time Rojer could not muster the strength to return it.

Rojer's stomach churned as Jasin rolled the scroll, breaking the seal on yet another.

'Her Grace, Duchess Mum Araine, mother to His Grace, Duke Rhinebeck the Third, Guardian of the Forest Fortress, Wearer of the Wooden Crown, and Lord of All Angiers, congratulates Baron Gared Cutter on his change of status. To properly introduce him to the peerage and offer opportunity to present the visiting Princess Amanvah, she will be throwing a Bachelor's Ball in the baron's honour upon his arrival in Angiers.'

'Ay, what?' Gared started, and there was laughter around the room until he balled his great fists on the table.

'Apologies, Baron,' Thamos said, but the laughter had not left his voice. 'It means my mother is using your visit as an excuse to throw a party.'

Gared relaxed a little. 'Dun't sound so bad.'

'A party where she will invite every unmarried girl in Angiers with an ounce of royal blood and do her best to broker your marriage to one of them.'

Gared's jaw dropped.

'There will be food, of course,' Thamos said when the baron had no reply. His eyes sparkled with the first light they'd shown in a fortnight. He was enjoying this.

'And music,' Jasin added. 'I shall perform myself,' he winked, 'and let you know which maids are the best to court.'

Gared swallowed. 'What if I don't want any of 'em?'

'Then she'll keep summoning you to Angiers and throwing balls until you do,' Thamos said. 'I assure you, she can be relentless on this subject.'

'And why should she not?' Inquisitor Hayes asked, looking at Gared. 'Your barony needs an heir, and you a wife to tend your home and see that he is educated and raised to lead when you go to join the Creator,' he drew a ward in the air, 'Creator willing, after a long life and many grandchildren.'

'He's right, Gared.' They were Leesha's first words of the day, and all turned her way.

The look Leesha gave Gared was withering, and he shrank before it. 'You've been alone too long. Lonely folk do foolish things. Time you settled down.'

Gared paled slightly, nodding. Rojer was amazed. He knew the two of them had a history, but this . . .

Thamos cleared his throat. 'Settled, then. Lord Arther will be acting count in my absence. His decisions will need to be ratified by this council. The baron and Mistress Paper will appoint representatives to speak in their place.'

'Darsy Cutter,' Leesha said.

Darsy looked at her, eyes pleading. 'Wouldn't Mistress Jizell be a better . . .'

'Darsy Cutter,' Leesha said again, with an air of finality.

'Yes, mistress.' Darsy nodded, but her broad shoulders slumped a bit.

'Dug and Merrem Butcher,' Gared said.

'That's two—' Captain Gamon began.

'They're a matched set,' Gared cut him off. 'I'm still general, as well as baron. I should get two.'

Thamos' eyes flicked around the room, reading the others

without need for debate. Arther and Gamon were not well loved in the Hollow. 'The baron is correct.'

Arther scowled. 'Which shall be general and which baron?'

Gared shrugged. 'Take your pick.'

The moment the count dismissed them, Rojer was out of his chair, not wanting to spend a second longer in Jasin's presence than necessary. He was moving for the door when Leesha's voice checked him.

'Will you join me for lunch, Rojer?'

Rojer stopped and took a breath, turning back with a bright smile painted on his face as he gave his best court bow. 'Of course, mistress.' He put out his arm and she took it, but she refused to pick up her stately pace however he tugged.

They climbed into Leesha's coach, Wonda taking a seat next to the driver and leaving them alone in the carriage. The air was chill outside, winter threatening more with each day, but the inside of Leesha's coach was warm. Still, he shivered.

She knows, Rojer thought as she looked at him. Leesha had always known more than she should about most everything, her guesses almost as good as Amanvah's dice at ferreting out information one would prefer to keep hidden. She'd always wondered what put him in her hospit, and set him running from Angiers the moment his bones had healed. Most likely she'd seen the hate in his eyes and put the pieces together at last. In a moment she would ask, and perhaps it was time to give her the whole story. If anyone deserved it, it was Leesha Paper, who had stitched his broken body back together.

Though many times since, he'd wished she'd let him die.

Leesha took a deep breath. *Here it comes*, Rojer thought.

'I'm pregnant.'

Rojer blinked. It was so easy to forget his wasn't the only drama playing out. 'I was wondering when you'd get around to telling me. Before the babe came, I'd hoped.'

Now it was Leesha's turn to blink. 'Amanvah told you?'

'Ent stupid, Leesha,' Rojer said. 'Jongleurs hear every rumour in the Hollow. Think I'd miss that one? Once it was in my head, the signs were everywhere. You're pale and never so much as look at food in the morning. Always touching your stomach. Scolding every servant that brings you meat that hasn't been cooked to ripping char. And mood swings. Night, I thought you were dramatic *before*.'

Leesha's mouth was a tight line. 'Why didn't you say anything?'

'Waiting for you to trust me,' Rojer said, 'but I guess you don't.'

'I'm trusting you now,' Leesha said.

Rojer gave her a tolerant look. 'You're trusting me now because half the town already knows, and you don't think you can keep a lid on the pot much longer. Night, even Amanvah knew! Had to act all surprised when she told me.'

'You lied to your wife for me?' Leesha asked.

Rojer crossed his arms. 'Course I did. Whose side do you think I'm on? I love Amanvah and Sikvah, but I'm not a ripping traitor. You've waited to the last corespawned minute to trust me, when I could have been helping you all along. Could've made you a ripping folk hero by now for carrying the heir to the Krasian throne. Instead, you've got everyone thinking it's the ivy throne's heir you're carrying. Do you know what the Rhinebeck family will do to you when they find out they've been played? To the child?'

'We'll soon find out,' Leesha said. 'I told Thamos the truth.'

'Night,' Rojer said. 'That would explain how he's been acting. Was hoping it was just that Royals hate a crank bow wedding.'

'I hurt him, Rojer,' Leesha said. 'He's a good man, and I've broken his heart.'

Rojer almost choked. 'That's what you're worried over? All the Core about to break loose around you, and you're worried about Thamos' feelings?'

Leesha pulled Bruna's shawl off the seat next to her, pulling it tightly around her like a Cloak of Unsight. 'I'm worried about everything, Rojer. Myself, my baby, the Hollow. It's too much, and I don't know what to do any more. I just know I can't keep lying. I'm sorry I didn't trust you. I should have come to you sooner, but I was ashamed.'

Rojer sighed. 'Don't add my guilt to your pile of worries. I've kept some important things from you, too.'

Leesha looked up at him, and her tone sharpened like a mother who'd just heard a crash in the next room. 'What things?'

'The night we met,' Rojer said. 'When Jaycob and I were brought to the hospit.'

Leesha's face softened immediately. She and Jizell had spent hours cutting, stitching, and casting him back together that night. And he was the lucky one.

'It was Jasin Goldentone,' Rojer said. 'Wasn't royal herald then, just a pompous ass whose nose I broke in a fight. He and his apprentices started following me and Jaycob, watching our performances, and then, one night, they caught us alone. Beat Jaycob to death and made me watch before trying to do the same to me. Just a lucky break the watch came by in time.'

Leesha scowled. 'We can't let that lie, Rojer.'

Rojer laughed. 'That's what Gared said.'

'You told *Gared* before me?' Leesha almost shrieked.

Rojer stared at her until she had the decency to drop her eyes. 'I'll go to Thamos,' she said at last. 'I am a witness to the event. He'll have to listen.'

Rojer shook his head. 'You'll do no such thing. I doubt Thamos is in a mood to do either of us the slightest favour right now, and you're asking for the mother of all boons.'

'Why?' Leesha demanded. 'Why is putting a murderer in prison such a great boon?'

'Because Jasin Goldentone is First Minister Janson's nephew,' Rojer said. 'His signature is on the payroll of every magistrate in the city, and the royal family couldn't find their stockings without him. You might as well accuse Rhinebeck himself. And with what proof? The only witness was me. With a snap of his ripping fingers, Jasin can have a thousand swear he was elsewhere on whatever night it was.'

'So you're just going to let it go?' Leesha asked. 'That's not like you, Rojer.'

'Ent letting anything go,' Rojer said. 'Just saying Thamos ent our ally here.'

He chuckled. 'Used to imagine I might get Arlen to throw him off a cliff. You can get away with things like that when folk think you're the Deliverer.'

'Killing someone is never the answer,' Leesha said.

Rojer rolled his eyes. 'In any event, secret's best kept, for now. So long as we do nothing, Goldentone's got to worry about what we might. Once there's a move, he can counter.'

'If he's so untouchable, what's he worried about?' Leesha asked.

'He's not worried about punishment,' Rojer said. 'But even he doesn't want to cross the Jongleurs' Guild and Guildmaster Cholls. Cholls saw me hit Jasin, and heard his threats. He's the only one whose word might stand.'

Leesha sighed. 'This is going to be an interesting trip.'

'That's undersaid.' Rojer took out his trusted flask, shaking it. Not a drop left. 'Got anything back at your cottage stronger than tea?'

18

A Whisper of Night
333 AR Winter

The envelope was fine paper, sealed with wax and stamped with Araine's crest, but the note within was surprisingly informal, written in the Duchess Mum's own hand. Leesha could almost hear the old woman's voice as she read it:

> L—
>
> The problem we discussed upon your last visit persists. This business in Lakton makes it all the more urgent. The Royal Gatherer has all but given up. Your expertise is required.
>
> It isn't just Ward Witch the peasants are calling you now, did you know? Leesha Paper, neo-countess of the Hollow. Your name is *expanding*. Something else to discuss while you're with us.
>
> —A

Expanding. The word was like a stone, weighing the paper down. Araine knew about the child. But how much did she know? What had Thamos told her?

Regardless, the tone of the letter was clear. Thamos and the others might have a brief stay in Angiers, but Leesha would not be coming home any time soon. Not if she needed to ensure a royal heir before the Krasians found a way to strike at Lakton proper.

Once the city on the lake was conquered, there would be nothing to stop the Krasians turning their attention to the north. But Euchor of Miln, secure in his mountains, would not join his forces with Angiers so long as he thought he could use the threat to leverage his own issue onto the throne.

Leesha passed the paper wordlessly to Jizell, who read it with a frown.

She shook her head. 'You can't go. They'll keep you locked in the palace until the child is born.'

'I don't see what choice I have,' Leesha said.

'You're too ill to travel,' Jizell said.

'I fainted from stress and exhaustion a fortnight ago,' Leesha said. 'I'm not an invalid.'

Jizell shrugged. 'I'm your Gatherer, and I say otherwise. Send me in your stead. I am Bruna-trained, too. There's nothing you can do for the duke that I can't.'

Leesha shook her head. 'It's not just a matter of skill. It's one of access. Rhinebeck won't even admit he has a problem. Araine needs someone she can hide in plain sight at court. If I need to operate, a Royal Gatherer and potential member of the family is the only one with a chance of being trusted to put the duke under the knife.' She left unsaid that Jizell had consulted her on complicated fertility matters far more often than the reverse.

Jizell raised an eyebrow. 'You'll be lucky if the count keeps you on as his Royal Gatherer, much less promises you now.'

Leesha nodded, biting the inside of her mouth to keep the wave of emotion the words brought from overcoming her. 'Ay, but Araine may not know yet that the child isn't his. In any event, she's canny enough to keep that secret until she has what she needs from me.'

I hope.

'I'm sorry, Stela,' Leesha said. 'I've been ordered to Angiers by the duke himself.'

'But mistress, the blackstem will fade in just a few days.' The panic in the girl's eyes was worrisome.

'We'll take up the experiments again when I get back, honest word,' Leesha said.

'But the others get to keep their weapons when you go,' Stela protested. 'They can still fight. It's the rest of us that have to go back to being nothing.'

'You're hardly nothing, Stela,' Leesha said, but the girl wasn't listening. Stela shifted from foot to foot, scratching at the blackstem wards on her skin. She stood in the shadows away from the window, trying to hold the power just a little bit longer, but even the ambient light in the room was enough to slowly leach the magic from her.

The others whose skin Leesha had warded were much the same. They had taken to dressing in plain robes, much as Arlen had when she first met him, with long wide sleeves and deep hoods, shading the wards from the light. Many would hide in darkened cellars and barns during the day, stealing a few hours of fitful sleep rather than go back to mortal strength. Wonda flushed them out into the light when she could, but she couldn't be everywhere.

There were other problems with the blackstem-painted children as well. Domestic violence on the rise. Stefny had related an argument with the normally passive Stela where she had punched her fist down on a heavy table, cracking it in half. Ella Cutter had struck her boyfriend when she caught him talking to another girl, cracking his jaw. Jas Fisher might have been justified in protecting his mother from his abusive father, but he had nearly killed the man. Leesha had been forced to use precious *hora* just to save his life, and even now it was unclear if he would ever walk again.

Perhaps it was best to let them have a few weeks to cool down before something truly terrible happened.

'Can I come with you?' Stela asked hopefully. 'A guard on your trip north?'

Leesha shook her head. 'Thank you, child, but I will have an escort of Cutters and Wooden Soldiers as well as Wonda to see to my protection.'

'You could tattoo . . .' Stela began.

'No,' Leesha said firmly. 'We don't know what that would do to you.'

'Course we do!' Stela snapped. 'I'd be like Renna Bales, who held back the demons when the Deliverer fell.'

'Absolutely not,' Leesha said. Stela clenched a fist, and Leesha moved her hand away from her teacup to the pocket of blinding powder in her apron.

Wonda was faster, between them before Leesha realized she'd moved. She raised her own balled fist, twice the size of Stela's. 'Ya want to open that hand, girl, and apologize to Mistress Leesha.'

They locked stares, and Leesha worried for a moment that Wonda was only making things worse. Magic heightened the impulse to fight, even against unlikely odds, and Stela was still holding enough to be a problem.

But the girl remembered herself, stepping back and opening her hands, bowing deeply. 'Sorry, mistress. I just . . .'

'I understand,' Leesha said. 'The magic makes a spark of anger into a flame, and a flame into demonfire. All the more reason you and the others take some time off.'

'But what if the mind demons come back at new moon with you away?' Stela pressed. 'Hollow'll need every hand.'

'I should be back by then,' Leesha lied. 'And the mind demons were scattered in their last assault. They'll be back, but not soon, I think.'

'Could you at least paint me fresh?' Stela begged, holding up her arm, the once dark stains of the blackstem faded to a light brown. 'These ent gonna last but another few days.'

Leesha shook her head. 'I'm sorry, Stela. I haven't the time. You'll just have to make do without for a fortnight.'

The girl looked like she had been asked to make do without her arms, but she nodded sadly and allowed Wonda to lead her out.

'Stela's a good kid,' Wonda said when she returned, though they were the same age. 'Understand how she feels. Couldn't you . . .?'

'No, Wonda,' Leesha said. 'I'm starting to wonder if this whole experiment was a mistake, and I'm not about to leave it running while I'm away.'

There was a knock at the door, and Wonda moved to answer. Leesha rubbed at her left temple, trying to massage the pain from her head. There were teas that could numb the sensation, but they left her dizzy and unable to think clearly. Worse, she worried over the effect they would have on her child.

The one cure that always helped was beyond her. Thamos hadn't touched her in weeks, and her own ministrations failed to have the same effect. She would just have to get used to the pain.

But then her mother entered, and it got worse.

'What's this about the duchess throwing Gared a ball?' Elona demanded. 'Parading every half-bloomed flower in Angiers for him to sniff and pluck?'

'Good to see you, too, Mother.' Leesha looked to Wonda. 'Be a dear and make sure Stela and the other Painted Children stand in a sunbeam.'

'Yes mistress.' Like most everyone, Wonda was all too happy to disappear when Elona Paper came to call.

Leesha poured a cup of tea for her mother. 'You make it sound like Duchess Araine is taking him to a brothel.'

'Ent much difference from where I sit,' Elona said, taking the tea.

'For as long as I can remember you've tried to push Gared Cutter into my arms,' Leesha said. 'Now he's got good prospects for the first time in more than a decade, and you want him a bachelor forever?'

'He was with you, I could keep an eye on him.' Elona winked.

'And if you weren't taking care of him, make sure I was first in line to keep his seedpods empty.'

The pain in her eye flared, and Leesha thought she might slosh up. 'You really are a horrid person, Mother.'

Elona snorted. 'Don't play the innocent with me, girl. You're no better.'

'The Core I'm not,' Leesha said.

'Demonshit,' Elona said. 'You look me in the eye and speak honest word that you didn't get a thrill, sticking the demon of the desert behind Inevera's back.'

Leesha blinked. 'That's different.'

Elona cackled. 'Keep telling yourself that, girl. Ent gonna make it any more true.'

The demon was trying to claw its way out of her eye again. 'What do you want, Mother?'

'To come to Angiers,' Elona said.

Leesha shook her head. 'Absolutely not.'

'You need me,' Elona said.

Now it was Leesha's turn to cackle. It sounded disturbingly like her mother's. 'Why? Are you a diplomat now?'

'Duchess Mum's going to try to marry you off to the count,' Elona said. 'You need someone to make the arrangements.'

'These aren't Krasians,' Leesha said. 'I can speak for myself. You just want a last chance to try and stick Gared on the road, and to hiss like a cat at the ladies on his dance card.'

Elona looked ready to spit. 'Those pampered court girls won't be able to handle him, anyway. Cutter baby would split some royal skink like a log, if that tree in Gared's pants don't do it putting the little brat in her.'

Leesha put her cup down, getting to her feet. 'I don't have time to listen to your filth, Mother. You're not coming. You can see yourself out.'

'I have to remind you I might be carrying Gared's child?' Elona asked. 'Ent showing as much as you, but I'm straining my stitches already.'

'All the more reason you let him go,' Leesha said. 'What's

the alternative? Divorce Da and marry Gared? You think the Inquisitor would bless such a union? The count? The Duchess Mum?'

Elona had no ready reply, and Leesha pressed the attack. 'You think Gared will still love you if you cost him his title? Night, do you think he loves you now? The only reason he ever touched you was because you looked like me.'

'That ent—' Elona began.

'It is,' Leesha cut her off. 'Told me himself. You were just an old rag to jerk his cock into while he thought of me.'

Elona stared at her, eyes wide, and Leesha knew she'd taken it too far. Her mother never failed to bring out the worst in her.

The silence hung in the air a moment, then Elona stood, brushing off her skirts. 'You say I'm horrid, girl, but you can be mean as a demon when you want to.'

Leesha watched sadly from the window of her coach as the Hollow passed by. It was foolishness, surely, that she felt she might be seeing it for the last time.

When Leesha was a child, Cutter's Hollow had been a small town of a few hundred people, barely big enough to be on the map. Its paths and structures were so familiar as to be a part of her, and everyone knew everyone else's name. And business.

Little remained of that childhood home, just the Holy House and a few cottages and trees. Even those bore scars from fire and demons.

But from the charred remains had risen Hollow County, a place that would soon match – and likely exceed – the Free Cities in population. In less than two years, tens of thousands had fled here from the Krasian advance, or come from the north to answer Arlen's call to arms against the corelings.

The streets of Hollow County were freshly creted, but Leesha knew them every bit as intimately as the old paths. She had been there at his side as Arlen shaped a pattern of greatwards that could be expanded in ever-increasing circles until Cutter's Hollow was the centre of the warded world.

Perhaps Gared was right. Perhaps Arlen really was the Deliverer.

And you let him slip away. Even with her miles behind, Leesha was not free of her mother's voice.

'It will be a week at least till we reach Angiers,' Jizell said. 'Are you two going to spend all of it staring out the window?'

Leesha started, returning her attention to her coach companions, Jizell and Vika. Jizell needed to get back to her hospit in Fort Angiers, and Vika to visit her husband – Leesha's childhood friend Tender Jona – held for inquisition by the Tenders of the Creator. Leesha had the duchess' word he would not be harmed, but it was nevertheless time he returned home.

Another thing to discuss with the Duchess Mum.

Like Leesha, Vika had spent the last few hours staring out the window, tearing at her cuticles until they were raw.

'I'm sorry,' Leesha said. 'My thoughts were miles away.'

'Ay,' Vika agreed.

'Well bring them back,' Jizell said. 'When's the last time the three of us had a quiet minute together, much less a whole week? We should make the most of it.'

'Shall we discuss work?' Leesha brightened at the thought. Work would take her out of the whirlwind of her thoughts, give her something to focus on beside a vague sense of impending doom.

'We'll get to it,' Jizell said, 'but I don't mean to spend a week straight working, either. I was thinking we might play a game.'

'What kind of game?' Vika asked.

Jizell smiled. 'We'll call it Hag Bruna's Stick.'

Leesha instinctively rubbed the back of her hand. It still hurt when she thought of that stick. It was thick enough for her to hang her full weight on when needed, but light, and her mistress could wield it as deftly as Ahmann did the Spear of Kaji. It was a club, knocking aside fools who stood between her and her patients, but also a whip that could crack across a girl's hand like a shock of electricity. It never left a mark, but could sting for long minutes.

Bruna didn't strike Leesha often, or without cause. Each time had been a lesson. One that would have made the difference between life and death. Like a memory trick, the slaps had trained her from repeating foolish behaviour, reminding her of the power and responsibility of the Gatherer's apron. She had written of every one in her journal, but knew all the stories by heart.

'How do we play?' Leesha asked.

'You start,' Jizell said. 'What was the first time Bruna hit you, and what did you learn?'

'I mixed greyroot with ovara seed, thinking it would cure Merrem Butcher's headache,' Leesha said. She smiled, clapping her hands together and raising the pitch of her voice in imitation of Bruna's shriek. 'Idiot girl! You think being blind for a week is better than a ripping headache?'

They all laughed, an almost foreign feeling to Leesha. And for a moment, the sense of doom faded.

'Me next!' Vika cried.

Rojer had little desire to practise with Kendall and his wives as the slow caravan trundled over the miles. Even more pleasurable pursuits had little interest for him. There had been a hangman's noose slack around his neck for years, but now he could feel it tightening. He sat tuning his fiddle, seeking that impossible perfect tune.

You'll never find it, Arrick said, *but that doesn't mean you should stop looking.*

The women sensed his mood, leaving him to his thoughts as they played Krasian board games and read Kendall passages from the Evejah. There was laughter and Rojer was glad to hear it, even if he could not share in it. There was no telling what Angiers would hold for any of them. Even Kendall, with her skill at charming corelings, would catch the duke's attention. If he tried to make a claim on her, it would be another reason to keep them from ever leaving.

The Hollow had grown so large that a full day's ride from Cutter's Hollow barely had them to the border. But there was an inn at least. The next few nights would be spent sleeping in tents, something Rojer had never cared for. Amanvah's tent was more a pavilion, with half a dozen servants to tend their every need, but for bedding down, Rojer would trade it for a broom closet if the walls were solid and kept the sounds of corelings at bay.

The inn had been cleared in expectation of the royal caravan, but the count took dinner in his rooms. Leesha was not invited to join him, something that spoke volumes in Angierian tea politics.

Jasin, too, was absent from the common, though that was no surprise. He seemed to want to avoid Rojer as much as Rojer did him.

Amanvah, too, would have been pleased to retire, but Rojer did not allow it, loudly inviting Leesha, Gared, and Wonda to join them in the common. He was learning when Krasian customs worked in his favour, for his *jiwah* could not refuse an invitation once made. Sikvah took over half the kitchen, cowing the staff and putting Amanvah's *dal'ting* servants in charge of serving their table. Creator forbid some barmaid offend Her Highness by bowing the wrong way.

Jizell and Vika took another table with a few apprentices, all of them more than happy to have Hollowers serve them. Coliv stood by the wall, watching everything, rigid as a hitching post. Rojer had never seen the man eat.

'Tell us of this Duke Rhinebeck, husband,' Amanvah said between courses. 'You knew him, did you not?'

'Ay, a bit,' Rojer said. 'Back when Master Arrick was royal herald. I learned to read in the palace library.'

'That must have been wonderful,' Leesha sighed wistfully.

Rojer shrugged. 'Suppose you'd think so. For my own part, I couldn't wait to get back to fiddling and tumbling. But Mistress Jessa insisted I learn my letters, and even Arrick agreed.'

'Mistress Jessa was Royal Gatherer?' Leesha asked.

'Not exactly,' Rojer said.

Leesha's eyes narrowed. 'Weed Gatherer.' Rojer nodded.

'What is a Weed Gatherer?' Amanvah asked.

'You'd get along well.' Leesha did an impressive job of adding venom to her voice. She was really quite a natural. 'A Weed Gatherer is the royal poisoner.'

Amanvah nodded her understanding. 'A high honour for a trusted servant.'

'There's no honour in poison,' Leesha said.

'It's more complicated than that,' Rojer snapped. He caught Leesha's eye. 'And I'll not sit and listen to you talk about Mistress Jessa like that. She was the closest thing I had to a mum after mine died. Creator knows I bite my tongue about Elona.'

Leesha snorted. 'Fair and true.'

'So I saw the duke here and there in the palace,' Rojer said, 'usually stumbling to or from the royal brothel. He and his brothers have their own private tunnel there, so they can visit unseen.'

'Of course they do.' Leesha sawed at the meat on her plate like she was amputating a limb.

'This is common in Krasia as well,' Amanvah said. 'Men of power must have many children.'

'Creator, not a chance,' Rojer said. 'All Jessa's girls take pomm tea. Can't have royal bastards running all over the city.' Leesha glared at him, and Rojer coughed.

'They . . .' Amanvah paused, in that way she did when she was searching for the right word in Thesan. 'These *Jiwah Sen* take herbs to *prevent* children?'

'Disgusting,' Sikvah said. 'What kind of woman would make herself *kha'ting*?'

'They are not *Jiwah Sen*,' Leesha told Amanvah. 'They are *heasah*.'

Amanvah and Sikvah put their heads together at that, whispering rapidly to each other in Krasian. Rojer didn't know the Krasian word, but he could well guess its meaning. This conversation was growing more uncomfortable by the second.

Amanvah straightened, carved from pure dignity. 'We will not discuss such matters where we break bread in Everam's name.'

Rojer was quick to bow. 'Of course you are correct, *Jiwah Ka*.'

'Tell me more of Rhinebeck's clan,' Amanvah said. 'How do they trace their blood to Kaji?'

'They don't,' Rojer said.

'Then to the one-time king of your Thesa.' Amanvah waved her hand impatiently. 'Our scholars have speculated that the king's line must go back to the first Deliverer's Northern heirs for the throne to be legitimate.'

'Might be,' Rojer said, 'though I wouldn't go spouting such things at court. The Rhinebecks haven't more than a touch of royal blood to them.'

'Oh?' Leesha asked.

'Demonshit,' Wonda said. 'If Duchess Araine ent royal, no one is.'

'Oh, Araine is royal enough,' Rojer said. 'She was married to Rhinebeck the First's son in an effort to give his coup legitimacy. But Rhinebeck the First was first minister, without an ounce of royal blood. He invented the machine to stamp klats, and it's said he kept one in five the machines made. By the time the old duke died without a son, he was the richest man in Angiers, and every royal house vying for the throne was in his debt.'

Amanvah smiled. 'Your people are different from mine, husband, but not so different.'

'This is Rhinebeck the Third's problem,' Rojer said. 'If he dies without an heir, there are any number of houses with as good a claim to the throne as his brothers'. They might manage to keep power, but it will cost them, and make the succession ripe for interference from the north. Klats are well and good, but Euchor can fill their enemies' coffers with gold.'

'That's not all he can fill them with,' Leesha said, but she did not elaborate.

They moved out of the Hollow proper the second day, but the road leading in was well warded, with caravan camps at regular intervals. They kept moving well after dusk, pressing on to the garrison of Wooden Soldiers at the edge of Thamos' territory.

Rojer was out of the coach the moment the caravan called a halt, stretching his restless limbs with his tumbler's warm-up.

'Gone stir-crazy?' Gared asked, swinging down from Rockslide, his massive Angierian mustang, as easily as any of Thamos' cavalry commanders.

'Needed the stretch,' Rojer said.

'Ay,' Gared said. 'Reckon it's exhausting, sleeping in furs all day with three women.'

Rojer smiled. 'If that's what you think, the duchess needs to find you a bride more desperately than we thought.'

Gared laughed, and Rojer deftly rolled with the blow as the big Cutter accented the sound with his customary slap on the back.

Rockslide turned their way, but Gared had a fat apple in hand. The animal snatched it with a bite that could easily take a grown man's head and turned back, chewing quietly as Gared ran a brush against the stallion's neck.

Rojer shook his head. 'Gared Cutter I met a year ago barely knew which end of a horse was which.'

'A season ago, even,' Gared agreed. 'I could get here to there, but I never liked the corespawned things.' He looked back at the horse, standing proud as if it were doing him a favour by allowing itself to be brushed. 'But old Rocky here's got no patience for raw wood.'

'As fine a specimen as I've ever seen,' Count Thamos said. 'Forgive me, Baron, but I wish every day I'd seen him first.' Rojer turned to see Jasin heeling the count like a dog. Careful to stand well out of reach.

'Offer stands, Highness,' Gared said, holding out the reins with a smile. 'You last a full minute in the saddle, and you can take him.'

Rockslide snorted, and Thamos bowed with a laugh. 'I know weighted dice when I see them, Baron. I'll simply take heart that you ride at my command.'

'Ay,' Gared said, only hesitating a little. With Arlen gone, he had grown increasingly dependent on the count. If the Painted Man never returned, he would soon be Thamos' man through and through.

'The road ahead is unwarded,' Thamos said. 'My garrison commander says the increased traffic has drawn demons by the score. It will cost us additional time, but I do not think we should proceed after dusk from here out.'

'Nonsense,' Leesha said, coming up to them. Thamos glimpsed her, and quickly averted his eyes. 'We have warded weapons and skilled warriors. If your brother cannot ward his roads and keep them clear, the Hollow should offer assistance.'

Thamos' jaw tightened. He raised his eyes to her at last. 'We have warriors, yes. We also have Herb Gatherers. Foreign dignitaries. Jongleurs. These are not people prepared to go out in the night.'

Leesha snorted. 'Rojer alone could protect the entire caravan.'

Ay, don't bring me into this, Rojer thought.

'How dare you speak to His Highness like that, Gatherer,' Goldentone said. 'Prince Thamos is commander of the Wooden Soldiers. He needs no military advice from you. The caravan clearings ahead are filled with beggars these days in any event. Coming in we had to send a squad ahead each day to chase them out before we made camp, and no doubt the filthy rats moved right back in after we passed.'

There was a moment of stunned silence, and then everyone turned their gaze to Jasin, who wilted under the combined glare. Gared balled his huge fists, and Wonda put a hand on the bow hanging from her saddle.

Thamos' voice was low, dangerous. 'Are you telling me, Herald, that you ran peasants from their wards just before dusk each night on your way to the Hollow?'

Jasin paled. 'I was bid to come to you with all haste . . .'

Thamos moved faster than Rojer would have believed of a man in armour, closing the distance and striking Jasin a sharp backhand that dropped him onto his backside.

'Those people are under my brother's protection!' Thamos shouted. 'They are refugees driven from their homes, not beggars and bandits!'

Jasin had been wise enough to stay down, and Thamos kicked him into a roll. 'This is how you represent the crown? By sending those who come to us for aid to their deaths?'

Jasin deftly turned the roll into a tumble that brought him to his knees before the enraged count, his hands clutched together as if in prayer. 'Please, Highness. It was by the duke's own command.'

Everyone had gathered to watch the scene, or stuck heads from carriages. Not just the travellers, the Wooden Soldiers from the garrison were gathering as well, ready to leap to Thamos' command. All equipped with warded weapons and armour.

The count turned to them. 'Are the Wooden Soldiers so unprepared they can't build their own camps? They need to drive the weak out into the night?'

The captain of the garrison came forward, dropping to one knee before Thamos. 'No, Highness, we are not. But the herald speaks true. Duke Rhinebeck himself signed a decree that all who use royal caravan clearings without licence are to be driven out.'

Lines appeared on Thamos' face as his jaw tightened again. 'My brother doesn't have to look peasants in the eye when he condemns them. But your men did.'

The captain put his head down farther. 'Yes, sir. And the Creator will judge.'

'No more!' Thamos barked. His voice rose smoothly as he addressed the soldiers directly.

'Perhaps I have not been clear enough in my expectations of your men. For that, I apologize. But listen you well now, that none claim ignorance later. Every human life in Angiers is your charge. They are yours to protect. Not to drive from the safety of their wards. Not to bully, swindle, or solicit bribes from. Not to touch their women. Am I heard?'

'Ay, Commander!' the soldiers shouted as one.

'AM I HEARD?' Thamos cried a second time.

'AY, COMMANDER!' the men thundered.

Thamos nodded. 'Good. Because those who forget will be hung in Traitor's Square as an example to others.'

Rojer saw Leesha staring at him with tears in her eyes. When the count turned from the crowd she moved towards him, but he smoothly dodged out of her path, coming up to Gared. 'General, ready the men. We'll move on down the road after dusk, culling the demons as we go.'

Gared punched his chest. 'We'll mow them like grass, Yur Highness.'

Thamos turned to Rojer. 'Despite Mistress Leesha's assurance, I do not wish to see any of the duke's guests exposed to any undue risk. Will you cast your spells to keep the demons from the carriages?'

Rojer bowed. 'Of course, Highness.'

'You must be joking,' Jasin said. 'We're to entrust our lives to that . . .?'

Thamos levelled him a look at the edge of patience. 'That what?'

It was such a delight, seeing Goldentone squirm. Rojer began to think he might have a chance to come forward after all. Have the Jongleurs' Guild whisper his villainy in the right ears . . .

Rojer couldn't help but twist the knife. 'Fear not, Secondsong, the demons will never come near you.' He threw his most mocking smile. 'Unless I want them to.'

Rojer knew it was a mistake the moment he said it, but the way Goldentone paled made it worth the risk.

Leesha kept shifting, trying to catch Thamos' eye, but the count turned the other way, striding off. Wooden Soldiers closed at his back, cutting him off from her. She stood frozen a moment, then turned and hurried back inside her carriage.

Leesha stared into the darkness outside the carriage window, and this time Jizell was wise enough to leave her to her thoughts. Behind them, Rojer and Kendall stood on the roof of the motley coach, fiddles at play, while Amanvah and Sikvah sat on the driver's bench, singing in harmony.

With her warded spectacles, Leesha watched the corelings drifting at the edge of the barrier they created. They could see the caravan – it was too big for even Rojer's music to hide – and followed its slow passage, but every time they drew too close, pain drove them back.

Leesha could well understand. The sounds coming from the quartet were harsh, discordant things that sent jabs of pain into Leesha's constant headache until she softened wax to plug her ears.

But even with the world muffled, she could hear the shrieks and shouts as the Cutters and Wooden Soldiers cut a swath through any corelings foolish enough to set foot on the road.

All were aided by Rojer's quartet. Those needing respite could easily drift back into the safe zone of music, and those in the fight benefited from foes distracted by the painful sounds.

Leesha looked sadly at the demon corpses piled by the road-side to wait for the sun. Moments ago, they were the enemy and it was kill or be killed. Now . . . now they were batteries, fuel for her spells. She wished she could spare Cutters to harvest the largesse and ship it back to the Hollow, but they needed every Hollower at hand once they reached Angiers. So much *hora* wasted.

Hours after dark, they came upon the first of the caravan clearings the duke's herald had mentioned. It was a huddled mass of refugees – Rizonan, by the look of them – cowering at the approach of the caravan. Their wardposts were haphazard, and those painted on the ragged carts were giant, clumsy things, hoping to make up in size what they lacked in skill. They wore ragged furs, fires extinguished lest they attract more demons than the shaky protective net could repel. Many were gathering belongings as if ready to flee into the naked night.

But then Thamos' great voice boomed. 'Fear not, good folk! I am Count Thamos, Prince of Angiers and Lord of Hollow County. You are under my protection. Please remain behind your wards. No harm will come to you! We have food and blankets to spare, and will strengthen your wards before we pass. If you have wounded, bring them for our Gatherers to tend. All of you are welcome to shelter in the Hollow, should you wish it.'

The folk started chattering at that. Some gave a ragged cheer, but others looked on with mistrust, no doubt recalling Jasin's passage. Leesha could not blame them.

As the caravan called a halt, Leesha and the other Gatherers were out before the drovers could ready the steps. The sight of their pocketed aprons put folk at ease. Several of them, some with bandages, others with a limp or cough, came forward with a hopeful look in their eyes.

'I'll need to see to the warding,' Leesha said to Jizell.

'Of course,' the woman replied. 'My girls and I can handle a few scratches and sniffles.'

But as they drew closer, more and more heads poked out from the cart beds, and under them. Men, women, and children of all ages. What appeared to be a small camp held close to a hundred people, more than the entire caravan.

Leesha turned as Wonda appeared at her side. 'I want you

patrolling the perimeter with your bow until I'm satisfied with the wards.'

'Beggin' yur pardon, mistress, but I should stay with ya. Don't know these folk, and said yurself the wards ent safe.'

Leesha gave her a patient look. 'I can take care of myself for a few minutes, dear. I still know a trick or two.'

'Ay,' Wonda shifted, 'but . . .'

Leesha put a hand on the girl's shoulder. 'You'll be protecting me by protecting them.' She gestured to the refugees – ragged, hungry, afraid. 'These people haven't felt safe in months, Wonda. Give them that for me, please.'

'Ay, mistress.' Wonda gave one of her awkward bows and moved off, loosening the cuffs of her blouse, rolling the sleeves to uncover her blackstem wards. Leesha knew from experience that nothing made folk feel safer than watching their protector pummel a demon to death with bare hands.

Jasin was with Count Thamos as Leesha approached the head of the caravan. 'What do you mean stay in the carriage? I am—'

'On the very edge of my patience,' Thamos finished for him. 'Your carriage is well warded, more than I can say for these folk. You've run them out once, and now I'll thank you to keep back before you do even more damage to the reputation of the ivy throne.'

The herald slunk back to his carriage, and for a brief moment, Thamos was alone. Leesha ached to go to him, but now was not the time. She didn't even know what she would say if she did. She just wanted him to look at her again.

But there was work to be done. Jizell and Vika had their apprentices triaging those in need, and Rojer was already tumbling and sending dyed wingseeds spinning in the flickering firelight as some of the folk cheered and clapped. He threw snap bangs at the feet of children who had likely not had cause to smile in months. They leapt back, shrieking with delight.

The refugees looked at Amanvah and Sikvah in fear, but

Kendall led the trio, smoothing the way for the Krasian princesses. Soon they had a group of women practising a song of protection.

Leesha walked the perimeter, examining the wardnet. It was as she feared. The Warders in this group were not entirely incompetent, but they were using wards for a circle on an ovoid camping ground. Wards for an oval needed to be shaped differently, a trick beyond most save master Warders. There were no outright holes in the net, but the magic would not distribute evenly, leaving weak points that a powerful demon – or a group of lesser corelings working in concert – might breach.

She focused on the warding, and for a time the other worries left her mind. Some of the wardposts she simply adjusted, rotating a few degrees. She took her brush and paint to others, fixing wards or replacing them entirely. Like clearing debris from a stream, Leesha could see the change in the magic's flow as she worked. Soon the entire net was glowing brightly to her warded eyes.

Another bright glow caught her attention, this one far outside the camp. Leesha looked more closely, expecting a rock demon, but instead she saw Arlen Bales.

Leesha blinked. She was tired, and blessedly alone for the first time she could remember. Had her thoughts wandered?

But no, it was Arlen, waving from a stand of trees beyond the wardlight. 'Leesha!' She could see the touch of magic he imparted on the words, carrying them to her alone.

She glanced around. No one was paying attention to her. She stepped behind a cart by the perimeter, out of sight as she continued to stare into the night.

'Leesha!' Arlen called again, beckoning.

'About time you showed yourself.' Leesha pulled her Cloak of Unsight close and hurried into the night before any noticed her absence. 'You'd best have some ripping good answers for me,' she snapped once she'd made it to the trees without being spotted by the camp or patrols.

But Arlen wasn't there.

'Leesha!' She saw him farther back, where the trees were thicker. He turned and vanished into the shadows, waving for her to follow.

Leesha frowned, stomping after him. 'Are you that terrified of being seen?'

Arlen gave no reply, and she hurried to catch up. He was right at the edge of her vision, his wardlight flickering as he passed through the trees.

But then Leesha lost sight of him. She continued on for several moments, but there was no sign.

'Leesha.' Off to the side now. Had she gotten confused in the trees? She hurried in that direction.

'I'm fast losing patience, Arlen Bales,' she hissed when he did not appear.

'Leesha.' Behind her now. She spun, but there was no one there.

'This isn't ripping funny, Arlen,' Leesha snapped. 'If you don't appear in five seconds, I'm going back to camp.'

If I remember which way it is, she thought. The trees around her all looked the same, and the boughs, still with yellow leaves of autumn, hid any clear look at the sky.

'Leesha.' To the left. She turned, but there was only the dim glow of the trees in the darkness, the fog of magic drifting on the forest floor.

'Leesha.' Behind her again. She began to understand, but it was too late. The calls were all around her.

'Leeeeesha.' It didn't sound like Arlen any more. It didn't even sound human.

'Leesha Paper.' The addition of her surname sent a chill down her spine.

Leeshaaaa.
Leesha Paper Leesha Paper Leesha Paper Leesha Paper
Leesha Paper Leesha Paper
Leesha Paper Leesha Paper Leesha Paper Leesha Paper
Leesha Paper

She turned a slow circle, seeing the movement in the trees. Corelings. It was impossible to know how many. Half a dozen at least, with a mimic leading them. She was invisible to them in her Cloak of Unsight, but they could tighten the noose until she was caught, or broke and ran. The cloak would be scant protection if she were forced to move at speed.

Idiot, Leesha silently scolded herself as Renna's words came back to her. *Minds know who you are. Strike at you, they get the chance.*

It was a compliment of sorts that the minds wanted her dead. A compliment, and a nightmare. She had thought herself safe between Wanings, but apparently the mimics did not share their masters' intolerance of moonlight.

And they're smarter than we gave them credit for, she admitted to herself. This one had played her for a fool, and she'd delivered herself right into its talons.

There was a squirming in her belly, and Leesha remembered it wasn't just her at risk. She'd delivered two, and it was up to her to return them safely to succour.

She saw a small clearing and moved for it, unbuttoning a deep pocket in her dress. She reached within, clutching the long, thin bone she had taken from the mind demon's arm, sharpening the tip and carving its length with wards before coating it in gold. Her *hora* wand.

With her free hand, she reached into a pouch on her belt, scattering warded klats at her back.

Come on then, corespawn, she thought, throwing open her cloak. *You haven't taken me yet.*

They came. Two wood demons swung out of the trees, moving with terrifying speed.

But not faster than Leesha could draw a wood demon repulsion ward with her *hora* wand. The symbol hovered in midair, glowing in her wardsight, and when the demons struck it, their own magic was torn from them and used to fling them back into the trees. They shrieked and vanished with the sound of breaking branches.

If that was not enough to summon aid, Leesha pointed the wand straight up, drawing a light ward. Like a flutist changing notes, she moved her fingers over the wards, imparting more power to the symbol. It flared brightly, turning night into day.

A flame demon spat fire at her, but she drew a siphon in the air, and the power was absorbed. The wand warmed in her hand, and all that passed over her was the demon's foul breath. She threw the power back as an impact ward, and the demon was crushed into the ground like a mouse under Gared's boot.

There was a shriek behind her as a wood demon stepped on one of her klats. The sound was cut short as the coreling stopped moving, a thin coating of rime forming on its barklike armour. There was a high-pitched whine as the demon tried to force its limbs to move, and then a crack across its chest, the sound of an icicle falling from a porch awning. Leesha took aim at the crack, drawing another impact ward.

The demon shattered into countless pieces, but still others came on.

A field demon pounced from the trees, but Leesha's ward threw it back so hard it broke through a trunk a foot thick. A blaze of flame demons scrambled into the clearing, but a moment later their talons were steaming and skidding on a sheet of ice. A moment after that they were frozen solid, the orange light in their eyes and mouths winking into a cold blue.

Leesha heard shouting as Cutters raced towards the flashes and sounds of combat, but it was distant, and still the mimic circled. Were they coming to her aid, or their own deaths? The mimic that tried to take Rojer had effortlessly clawed its way through Cutter and *Sharum* alike until Rojer, Amanvah, and Renna joined forces against it.

Leesha could see it in the trees, a sleek amorphous thing, moving fast. She pointed her wand and sent a blast of magic, heedless of the destruction if it would put the creature down. Trees shattered and the ground heaved, but like a snake, the mimic slithered away unharmed.

The distraction nearly proved her undoing. A copse of wood

demons had surrounded her. One stepped on a ward klat and was immolated in flame as the heat ward activated. The others, four of them, found a clear path.

One took a vial of dissolvent in the face, eyes smoking as the demon clawed blindly at them, only adding to the damage.

She threw more klats, these with lectric wards that caught two of the demons, seizing up their muscles with jolts and shocks.

But the last one was on her, too close for her to draw a ward. She fell back, fumbling at the knife on her belt.

'Leesha!' Thamos roared, smashing into the demon's side with his warded shield. The wards flared, and the coreling was thrown away. Thamos stood tall in his shining armour, and for an instant she felt safe again.

But then a great tentacle wrapped around him, flinging the count across the clearing to crash heavily into a tree. He crumpled, and did not rise.

Leesha sent another blast of magic at the mimic, but again it was too fast. She clipped it, knocking the creature sprawling, but the bulk of the power tore into the woods, reducing hundred-year-old trees to kindling.

Her ears were ringing, but Leesha could hear fighting all around now, as the Hollowers sought to break through the ring of demons and get to her.

She drew a mimic ward in the air over Thamos, then moved to begin a circle of them for her own protection.

She should have started with herself. The mimic lashed out with a thin tentacle, wrapping it around her wrist and pulling her from her feet, unable to draw. She fumbled at the pockets of her apron as it reeled her in close, but she was running out of tricks.

A warded arrow neatly severed the tentacle, and Leesha fell back on her bottom as the tension dropped. The tentacle began to twitch, glistening as it sweated a foul ichor. Leesha shook it off in horror.

Three more arrows struck the mimic's centre mass, crackling

and jolting the creature more each second they remained embedded. The demon screamed, flesh melting away from the missiles. They dropped to the ground, but in that moment of distraction Wonda closed the distance, leaping almost twenty feet to land a heavy blow of her warded fist atop its head.

The demon was flattened, hitting the ground like a soft clay figure struck with a club. But the clay reformed as if under a skilled hand, rising more menacing than before, all spikes and sharp edges.

Wonda was ready for it. Her warded hands and forearms batted its blows aside, and the impact wards on her knuckles struck it like a case of thundersticks. A dozen tentacles, ridged like blades, swiped at her. But Wonda was faster than Leesha would ever have believed, almost as fast as Renna Bales.

And she fought like Arlen – twisting, tumbling, and leaping over tentacles like a fly avoiding the swatter. The demon's head turned into that of a flame demon and it spat fire at her, but Wonda spread her fingers and the heat and magic were absorbed, giving added power to her blows.

She got in close, arms blurring like hummingbird wings as she pulled arrows from her quiver and buried them in the demon with no need for her bow. The creature's scream was a cacophony of pain, a thousand horrors crying out at once.

A new tentacle thrust from its centre mass, striking Wonda full-on and flowing around her to join with itself seamlessly. She was held tight, warded limbs pinned helplessly at her sides, but there was no grip to break.

Leesha raised her wand, but the mimic was wise to the movement, putting Wonda in between the two of them.

'Don't you hold back, Mistress Leesha!' Wonda cried. 'Kill it while you can!'

'Don't be ridiculous,' Leesha said. She kept her wand raised and ready, mind racing. The sounds of combat were all around them, but the mimic must have brought many corelings to the trap, because no other assistance reached the clearing.

'What do you want?' Leesha demanded of the creature, if only to buy a few seconds to think.

The demon tilted its head curiously the way a scolded dog might, knowing it was being spoken to, but unable to understand the words.

Too dumb *to speak*, Leesha thought, *but still smart enough to learn my name and lure me to my doom.*

A screeching noise filled the air, and the demon threw its head back, shrieking. Even Leesha had to cover her ears. She turned to see Sikvah crouched, touching her choker and directing a scream that had the demon's flesh rippling as if from a hurricane wind. How had Sikvah gotten through to the clearing when the others could not?

Just then a speartip burst from the mimic's chest, the blade glowing bright with magic. Thamos planted the butt on the ground and heaved, throwing the demon from its feet.

But the mimic simply grew more limbs, catching itself before it struck the ground. The demon's head reformed into something resembling a snake, with no ears to hear Sikvah's scream.

The last time it had taken the mimic several minutes to adapt to a sonic attack. This one did it in seconds.

It was warned, Leesha realized. *They're learning our tricks.*

The mimic lashed out at Thamos again, but this time he caught the blow, deflecting it off his shield. Leesha drew a freezing ward in the air, and the tentacle holding Wonda snapped off and she landed on her back, struggling to get free of the binding ring of demonflesh.

Finally with a clear target, Leesha raised her wand to blast the demon from existence, but the *hora* was drained, and mustered only a weak push.

Leesha threw her remaining klats, heedless of their effect. The demon was alternately burned, shocked, frozen, and shoved, but it seemed more angered than harmed, its body reforming in seconds to heal the damage.

It became a rock demon, but with eight long obsidian arms instead of two. Every ridge of the carapace looked sharp, but none more so than the wicked talons that topped each limb, edged like shards of glass.

A sweep of its arms knocked Thamos aside, splintering his spear and hooking the edge of his shield, snapping the straps from his arm. It hung limp, more hindrance than help.

The demon bunched, leaping at Leesha, but Thamos screamed, throwing himself bodily in its path. The wards on his armour saved them both, but he was thrown into her in the process. Leesha felt his powerful hands lock on to her arms, twisting himself to take the brunt of the impact as they slammed into the broken trunk of a once great goldwood.

They clutched each other as the mimic charged, but then a bolt of lightning lifted it clear off the ground, slamming it down a dozen feet away.

Amanvah stood at the edge of the clearing, holding what looked to be a lump of gold, bright with magic. The demon began to reform, and she sent another blast of power to knock it back down.

Rojer and Kendall were at her side, fiddles keeping the corelings at bay as the *dama'ting* worked her *hora*. Coliv kept his distance, hurling sharpened steel triangles into the demon, their wards sizzling on impact.

The mimic turned to regard the new threat, but Wonda had worked her knife from its sheath and managed to free herself. Her fine uniform from the duchess was soaked in ichor, but she glowed bright with magic as she renewed her attack.

The demon began to shrink back from the blows, and Leesha knew immediately it meant to flee. She thought to cry a warning, but to what end? The mimic had failed to kill her, and she had nothing left to fight with. The longer the battle went on, the greater the chance one of them might be killed.

A blunt attack knocked Wonda back a few steps, all the time the demon needed to dematerialize and find a vent to flee back to the Core.

Leesha closed her eyes, leaning into Thamos' arm as he guided her back to her carriage. The others gave them a wide berth, and she was glad for it. If almost being killed by demon assassins was the price to be in Thamos' embrace again, it was a bargain.

Thamos held her just a moment longer than necessary when they reached the carriage, and she turned into him, wrapping her arms around him. She felt his chest expand as he inhaled the scent of her hair, and for a moment, she began to hope.

But Thamos shook himself, as if waking from an unpleasant daydream. He let her go abruptly, taking a step back.

'The child?' he asked.

Leesha felt her stomach. 'Fine, I should think.'

Thamos nodded, his aura an unreadable mix of churning emotion. He turned to go, but she caught his arm.

'Please,' she said. 'Can't we at least talk?'

Thamos frowned. 'What is there to discuss?'

'Everything,' Leesha said. 'I love you, Thamos. Doubt everything else in creation, but never doubt that.'

But doubt did colour his aura. She clutched at his cloak. 'And you love me, too. Sure as the sun rises. You protected me with your own body.'

'I would have done as much for any woman,' Thamos said.

'Ay,' she agreed. 'It's the man you are. The man I love. But there was more to it than that, and you know it.'

'What does it matter?' Thamos asked. 'It doesn't change that you lied to me. You bedded me under false pretence, a shield to guard your reputation. You used me.'

Leesha felt tears welling in her eyes. 'Ay. And if I could take it back, I would.'

'Some things can't be taken back,' Thamos said. 'Am I to marry you, knowing in half a year you'll humiliate me before all Thesa?'

The words were a slap, but not so much as those that followed.

'You love me, ay, but you love the babe in your belly more. No matter the cost in lives and honour it may bring.'

Leesha began to weep. 'You would truly have me kill my own child?'

'It's too late for that, Leesha. The time for that choice was in the weeks before you told me.' Thamos sighed. 'It was wrong of me to ask you to drink Weed Gatherer's tea, and for that I am sorry. I don't think I could love a woman who would do something like that simply because I asked.'

Leesha clutched at his arm. 'So you do love me!'

Thamos tore his arm from her grasp. 'Spare me the Jongleur's show, Leesha. How I feel doesn't change your circumstances.'

Leesha stepped back, stung. 'What is your mother planning to do to me?'

Thamos shrugged. 'If she knows you're with child, or suspects the father, it hasn't come from me.'

Leesha breathed a slight sigh. It was a small blessing, but she was in no position to refuse a blessing of any size.

'I won't lie to her face,' Thamos warned. 'Nor will I marry you with another man's babe in your belly. My mother is no fool, so you'd best choose carefully what you say to her.'

19

Tea Politics

333 AR Winter

*L*eesha watched through a crack in the curtain as they passed through the streets of Fort Angiers. People gathered to point and stare at the procession; even Jongleurs on the street paused in their acts as their audiences turned their attention away.

Many of them whispered to one another as the carriages rolled past. Others cried out as if they had no idea she might hear.

'It's the ward witch and her fiddle wizard!'

'Neo-countess of the Hollow!'

'They make you sound downright ominous,' Jizell said.

'Oh, yes,' Leesha said, waggling her fingers and giving her best cackle. 'Beware the ward witch, lest she turn you into a toad!'

Jizell laughed, but Vika shook her head. 'It's funny now with the sun above us, but those demons that attacked you on the road weren't laughing. It was more than a pinch of Bruna's blinding powder and flamework that kept them at bay.'

'Woman's got a point,' Jizell said.

The procession came to a halt before Jizell's hospit, and Leesha watched with envy as Jizell and Vika left the carriage.

What she wouldn't give to go back to the time when her greatest worry was the next case in Jizell's hospit.

She rapped on the side of the coach, and Wonda appeared. 'Pick two Cutters to guard the hospit, and ward off any unwanted visitors.'

'That's not necessary . . .' Jizell began.

'Humour me, please,' Leesha said. 'The men will answer to you, but I'll sleep more soundly knowing they're here.'

Jizell sighed. 'If it's to be Cutters, I'll take women. This is a hospit after all.'

Leesha nodded, and in a moment Wonda had two brawny Cutter women selected. Both could thread a needle with their crank bows, but were better known for their willingness to fight demons in close. Magic had made them larger and stronger still, and they would be as imposing as any man if they stood at the door with their arms crossed.

Leesha was left alone in the carriage for the rest of the journey. Wonda sat up in front, watching all around for signs of threat. She'd blamed herself for the ambush on Leesha, and hadn't let Leesha out of her sight for more than a privy visit since. Even then, she waited only steps away. Close enough to hear things best kept private.

A weight seemed to descend on the carriage as Leesha was left alone with her thoughts for the first time in days. She used to need time alone like others needed water, but lately it led her to dark places.

Arlen, it seemed, had truly abandoned her. Jardir was gone, and Thamos would never be hers. The demons and Inevera wanted her dead, and soon enough, the Duchess Mum would likely want the same.

It was a relief to finally see the duke's palace up ahead. Had it only been six months since her last visit? The whole world had changed. As she took Wonda's hand and descended the steps of her coach, back arched with dignity in her best travelling gown, she felt the weight on her shoulders ease in the midday sun. Araine was not one to waste time with idle words. Whatever was coming, they would have it out before the sun was set, and that was for the best.

First Minister Janson was waiting for them in the courtyard with his son Pawl. It would be unseemly for the Royals to wait outside. He bowed at Thamos' approach.

'Highness, it is good to see you again.'

Thamos clapped him on the shoulder. 'And you, my friend.'

'I trust your journey was uneventful?' Janson asked.

'Hardly,' Thamos said. 'Demon attacks on the road, and your nephew has left a black mark on the throne's reputation.'

'Night, what has that idiot boy done now?' Janson grumbled.

'Later,' Thamos said. 'I know you wanted a chance for him as herald, but he may be better suited to the opera house than diplomacy.'

Janson's nostrils flared, but he nodded, turning to Leesha with another bow.

'It is good to see you looking well, mistress,' he said, glancing meaningfully at her belly. 'Her Grace invites you and your bodyguard to afternoon tea, once you've settled and had a chance to refresh yourselves.'

Rojer eyed Janson warily as he and his wives approached, wondering, not for the first time, just how well the man knew his nephew. Ill fortune was common amongst the minister's enemies as well. What Jasin had done might not surprise the man, or turn him from his kin, but it was likely he knew only that Jasin and Arrick had been old rivals.

The first minister's eyes were unreadable as he gave a shallow bow. 'Master Halfgrip. Fortune has smiled upon you since our last visit.' He turned to Amanvah, bowing much deeper. 'Highness. It is an honour to make your acquaintance. I am First Minister Janson. Please allow me to welcome you to Angiers. Her Grace the Duchess Mum invites you to sup with her tonight at the royal table.'

Amanvah gave a shallow bow in return. 'I am honoured, Minister. I had thought good manners lacking in the green lands, but it seems I was mistaken.'

Janson smiled. 'Apologies, Princess, if you have been treated with anything less than the respect you are due. Please call upon me if there is anything you need during your stay.'

The first minister escorted them quickly inside, signalling servants to lead them to their chambers. They were barely through the great hall when Rhinebeck appeared, his younger brothers Prince Mickael and Shepherd Pether flanking him a step behind, all three so alike in size and manner, and so different from Thamos, many years their junior.

'Thamos!' Rhinebeck boomed, his voice echoing off the vaulted ceiling. He caught his brother in a great bear hug. He kept an arm around Thamos' shoulders as he turned to punch Gared on the arm. 'And you. Last time you were here it was captain. Look at you now! Baron general!'

'Mother is nearly giddy with the thought of finding you a bride,' Mickael said. 'The Baron's Ball is all anyone around the palace has talked about for weeks.'

'And so wise men are getting out of the palace while we can,' Pether said.

Rhinebeck tightened his arm around Thamos' neck, forcing his littlest brother to stoop under it. 'We're off to the hunting fort on the morrow. You and your new baron will have to come.'

Thamos frowned, caught between family and duty. 'Brother, there are important matters . . .'

Rhinebeck waved the words away. 'Matters best discussed away from prying ears.' He gave a slight nod of his head to one of the servants moving about the hall, this one in Milnese livery. Euchor already had a presence at court, it seemed.

The duke turned to Gared. 'What say you, Baron?'

Gared rubbed the back of his neck, looking decidedly uncomfortable. 'Never been too good at huntin' . . .'

'It's true.' Rojer stepped in. 'Your new baron is better suited to knocking trees over than tiptoeing around them.'

Rhinebeck's guffaw was a raw gasping sound. The man was overweight, and his lungs strained. He pointed a thumb over his shoulder at Mickael. 'That's no problem. My brother couldn't hit a tree in the middle of the forest.' Mickael glared at his back as he went on. 'There will be ale as well, and food.' He winked. 'And a few pretty things to look at.'

'You're not married yet,' Shepherd Pether noted.

'Bring your Jongleur as well!' Mickael cried. 'We'll see if he can truly charm the pants from a demon!'

'I can't,' Rojer admitted. 'At least, I've never had opportunity to try. Getting the pants on them is difficult, you see.'

All the men laughed at that. In true Angierian fashion, the Royals spoke as if the women were not present, though they eyed them openly enough. Amanvah and Sikvah waited with patient silence two steps back. Krasian women must be used to this sort of thing, but Kendall, a step behind them, looked less tolerant.

'We'll be glad to go,' Thamos said, though he did not sound glad at all.

'Leesha, welcome,' Duchess Araine said, rising from her tea table as Leesha and Wonda arrived in the women's wing of the palace.

The woman even embraced her, and Leesha found herself savouring it. She had great regard for the Duchess Mum, and more than a little fear of becoming her enemy.

'And Wonda,' Araine said, turning to the big woman and offering her jewelled hand for her to kiss.

Wonda had been practising her etiquette since their last meeting, and while she still chose the wrong fork as often as the right, she was smooth and graceful as she dropped to one knee and pressed her lips to Araine's fingers. 'Y'Grace.'

'Wearing some of the clothes I sent,' Araine noted. 'Stand up and let me have a look at you.' Wonda complied, and the duchess circled her appraisingly. Her pants were loose from waist to knee, giving the appearance of a skirt, but fading to close cuffs that tucked into a pair of thick but flexible leather boots. Her blouse, too, was loose over her broad chest and thick arms, giving a soft look to limbs that could snap most men in half. Bracers kept the sleeves out of her way, protecting the silk – and her arm – from the snap of her bowstring. 'My seamstress outdid herself. Elegant, yet practical. You can fight in these, yes?'

Wonda nodded. 'Ent never felt so fine, but I move like I'm naked.'

Araine looked at her, and Wonda blushed furiously. 'Sorry, Y'Grace. Din't mean . . .'

Araine whisked a hand. 'For what, girl? An apt metaphor? You'll have to do far worse to offend me.'

'What's a metta for?' Wonda asked, but the duchess only smiled, running her fingertips over the delicate wardwork stitched in thread-of-gold on Wonda's fine wool jacket.

It was an Angierian officer's jacket with a distinctly feminine cut, but instead of the emblem of the Wooden Soldiers, this one had held Araine's personal crest, a wooden crown set over an embroidery hoop.

Wonda had removed the crest, replacing it with Leesha's mortar and pestle. Araine tapped the crest lightly. 'If I were the sort to be offended, I might take it amiss that you've removed my crest, after all I've done to finance the Hollow's fighting women.'

Wonda bowed. 'Yuv done so much for us, Y'Grace. The fighting women of the Hollow wear your crest proudly, and shout your name as they charge into battle.' She looked up, meeting the duchess' eyes. 'But I'm sworn first to Mistress Leesha. If the cost of my new armour and clothes is that I can't wear her crest, you can have it all back.'

Leesha expected the duchess to be angry, but Araine looked at the girl as if she had passed some sort of test.

'Nonsense, girl.' With Wonda bowing, she and the diminutive

woman were nearly the same height, and Araine laid a hand on her shoulder. 'If I could buy your loyalty so easily, it would be worthless. Your armour and uniform are yours, and you honour your mistress.'

Wonda bowed her head, breathing deeply at an obvious swell of emotion. 'Thank you, Y'Grace.'

'And let's dispense with all this "Grace" business,' Araine said. 'Fancy titles are fine for the crowd, but grow tiresome in private. You will address me as "Mum".'

Wonda smiled. 'Ay, Mum.'

'Leesha and I have matters to discuss in private, dear,' Araine said. 'Do wait outside and see we are not disturbed.'

'Ay, Mum,' Wonda said, moving swift as a deer from the hunter. She might have professed to serve Leesha, but she was quick to obey the duchess' commands.

Leesha felt a twinge of something akin to jealousy. Leesha had done everything she could to discourage the girl when she'd first appointed herself Leesha's bodyguard, but seeing Wonda comfortably following Araine's commands made Leesha realize just how much she'd come to depend on her.

Leesha and Araine sat. There were no servants present, but a silver tea service had been set on the table along with a selection of edibles. Bruna may not have taught Leesha enough about politics, but she had been quite strict about tea etiquette. Younger and lower of rank, Leesha served, filling the duchess' cup first. Only then did she fill her own and take a small plate.

'How far along is the child?' Leesha was taking a bite of a tiny sandwich when the duchess spoke, and nearly choked.

'I beg your pardon?' Leesha coughed.

Araine gave her a look on the very edge of patience. 'This will go more smoothly if you don't treat me as a fool, girl.'

Leesha snatched a napkin to cough into and wipe her mouth. 'Perhaps four months.' It wasn't a lie, but it wasn't precise, either. Time enough for the child to be Thamos', or not. She'd expected the topic to come up, but once again was caught by surprise by the Duchess Mum's blunt manner.

Araine tapped a painted nail on her delicate porcelain teacup. 'Am I right in assuming it's no relation of mine?'

Leesha only stared, but Araine nodded as if she had spoken. 'Don't look so surprised, girl. I've eyes in all my sons' courts, and you can't expect to keep something like that secret. You and Thamos went from being inseparable to estranged the moment your condition was known. Doesn't take one of your mind demons to see what happened.'

Araine shook her head. 'Another hope for the throne, gone. My dimmest son Mickael is the only one to have produced anything resembling an heir, but none of his idiot brood would hold the throne long enough to warm the seat.'

Her foot began to kick, reminding Leesha of a cat's tail as it readied to pounce. Leesha glanced around, but they were still alone. The sharp, jerking motion of one old woman's slippered foot should not threaten her so, but it seemed to promise violence.

Araine sipped her tea. 'I ordered Thamos to court you the moment you returned to the Hollow. My youngest son has a talent when it comes to women, but even I didn't expect you to tumble the first night.' She looked down her nose at Leesha. 'Still wasn't quick enough, it seems.'

Mesmerized by the twitching foot, it took a moment for the words to register. Leesha looked up. 'Ordered?'

'Of course,' Araine said. 'Thamos has his uses, but he spent more time in the practice yard than the library. He needs a countess with something between her ears, and your courting legitimized him in the eyes of the Hollowers.'

She pointedly placed her empty teacup on the table, and Leesha moved quickly to refill it. Araine took a sip, grimacing. 'You needn't be stingy with the honey, dear. I've lived a long time, and earned it.' She took a delicate silver spoon, putting a generous dollop of honey into the cup.

'It's less bitter than learning everything Thamos and I shared was on his mother's orders.' Leesha felt her vision cloud, and blinked furiously to drive off threatening tears.

'Don't be an idiot,' Araine said. 'I pointed him at you, ay, but I've pointed that boy at many a good match. He wouldn't have stuck if he wasn't interested.'

She pointed her tiny spoon at Leesha. 'And you, child, hardly required me to come hold your legs open. You needed a husband, that much was clear the moment I met you. You've a weakness where powerful men are concerned, and it's going to get you into trouble . . . if it hasn't already.'

'And just what is that supposed to mean?' Leesha demanded.

'Whose is it, then?' Araine demanded. 'One of the would-be Deliverers? It's no secret you shined on Arlen Bales. He was seen coming and going from your cottage at all hours.'

'We were just friends,' Leesha said, but it sounded defensive, even to her.

Araine arched a brow. 'And then there's this business with the demon of the desert. The Jongleurs put you in the pillows with him, as well.'

'There was only one Jongleur in Ahmann Jardir's palace,' Leesha said, 'and he tells no such tales.'

Araine smiled. 'I have other sources in Fort Rizon.'

Leesha waited, but the duchess did not elaborate. 'Who I take to my bed and carry in my belly is my own business, and none of yours. It's no heir, so you can keep it out of your plans and find a better match for your son.'

'Giving up so easily?' Araine asked. 'I'm disappointed.'

'Is there a point to fighting on?' Leesha asked wearily.

'You think this is the first bastard to complicate a royal match?' Araine tsked. 'A Herb Gatherer should know better how these things can be handled.'

'Handled?' Leesha was at a loss.

The duchess' foot stopped twitching. 'You and Thamos announce the child and marry immediately. When the child comes, you deliver in private, and your Gatherer announces, alas, the child is born still.'

Leesha's hands began to tremble, cup and saucer rattling. She set them on the table, levelling the duchess with a hard glare.

'Are you threatening my child, Your Grace?'

Araine rolled her eyes. 'I told you before to keep up with the dance, girl, but you keep missing steps. I've four of my own, and know enough not to come between a mother and her child. I might as well declare war on the Hollow.'

'Not a war you'd be likely to win,' Leesha noted.

Now it was Araine who glared. 'Don't be so sure about that, dear. I've seen all the pawns you can play, but you've not seen all of mine.'

She waved her hand, as if to dispel an unpleasant stench in the air. 'But none of that is necessary. Easy enough to bundle a loaf of bread and bury it, and find a place to hide the child. Announce a few days later that to ease your grief you've decided to wet-nurse an orphan to fill the void in your heart. Creator knows the Krasians have left mudskin bastards from here to the desert flats. Make a show of inspecting a few before you choose, and none will be the wiser. Then you and my son can make a legitimate heir.' She lifted her teacup. 'Preferably more than one.'

Leesha stroked her belly thoughtfully. 'So I can never truly claim the child as my own?'

'You've missed your chance at that, I'm afraid,' Araine said. 'You'd have enemies to the north and south, and your own people would doubt your wisdom.'

'Perhaps they should have a wiser leader,' Leesha said. 'Perhaps your son deserves a wiser wife.'

'Point me to this better woman, and the job is hers,' Araine said. 'Until then, it falls on you.'

She reached up, flicking a finger against the lacquered wooden crown she wore, set with bright jewels. 'The commoners think it easy, to wear a crown. But leaders must make sacrifices. Women, most of all.'

She sighed. 'At least Thamos loves you. It's more than I ever had. After his grandfather bought his way onto the throne, the Royals were on the brink of a coup. Euchor moved soldiers to Riverbridge, ready to crush the battered victor and name himself king. My marriage to Rhinebeck's son was the only thing that held the city together.'

'I never knew,' Leesha said. The Duchess Mum had never been so open with her before, and she was afraid to say anything more, lest she break the spell.

'It seemed like the end of the world at the time,' Araine said. 'Rhinebeck the First did not sit the throne long, and his son had no aptitude or interest in ruling. He visited the palace just long enough to put children in me, and spent the rest of his time in that cursed hunting fort, chasing boar and harlots.

'I was left pregnant and alone with the reins of the city. Did I cry and bemoan my fate? Ay. But I had work to do.' Araine pointed at Leesha. 'And I'll give myself to the night before I let Euchor take the city I've dedicated my life to rebuilding.'

'So this is a Northern palace,' Amanvah said. 'It is not impressive.'

The strangest thing was that Rojer could see what she meant. Rhinebeck's palace fortress had once seemed the grandest building in the world, but after seeing how Krasian royalty lived in Everam's Bounty, suddenly he noticed that the carpet could be softer, the drapes thicker, the ceiling higher.

It was amazing, how quickly he had become accustomed to luxury after spending more than a decade checking for fleas before bedding down in haylofts and two-klat inns.

'Am I the only one thinks the duke needs a slap on the face?' Kendall asked. 'Eyeing our bums without so much as a *How d'you do?*'

'Rhinebeck and his brothers are like that,' Rojer said. 'And to be honest, the rest of the Angierian noblemen aren't much better. Only interested in women as servants and lovers. They'll do all the formal introductions tonight at dinner under their mother's glare.'

'I look forward to meeting this mysterious Duchess Mother,' Amanvah said.

Rojer shrugged. 'You'll find her as vapid and shallow as her sons. None of them has any real responsibilities. Janson's the one who really runs things.'

Amanvah looked at him. 'Nonsense. The man is a puppet.'

'It's true,' Rojer said. 'He paints a dim look on his face when the duke and princes are about, but it's as good as any Jongleur's mask. The man underneath is cunning and ruthless.'

Amanvah nodded. 'But still not in command.'

'Your dice told you this?' Rojer asked.

'No,' Amanvah said. 'I could see it in his eyes.'

'I want you to stick close to Leesha while I'm gone,' Rojer said.

Amanvah tilted her head. 'Is that for our protection, or hers?'

'Both,' Rojer said. 'These people need not be enemies, but neither are they friends.'

'Now,' Araine said, 'if we've spoken enough of your wandering affections, it's time for more pressing matters.'

It wasn't the lemon that made Leesha wrinkle her mouth as she sipped her tea. 'You want to know if the duke is seedless.'

'We both know he is,' Araine said. 'I didn't ask you to come all this way for that. What I want to know is if you can *fix* it.'

'Will he consent to be examined?' Leesha asked.

The Duchess Mum's mouth soured as well. 'He is being . . . difficult in that regard.'

'I can only guess so much without that,' Leesha said. 'I can brew virility herbs . . .'

'Don't you think I've tried that?' Araine snapped. 'Jessa's had him on every stiffener and fertilizer under the sun for years now.'

'Perhaps I can come up with something your . . . *Weed Gatherer* has yet to try.' Leesha kept the bitterness from her voice, but the duchess picked up on it anyway.

'No doubt Bruna ranted at length on the evils of weed gathering,' Araine said, 'but she never had more than a few hundred children to care for, and, as I recall, was never shy about dosing folk without their knowledge.'

'Always to help,' Leesha said. 'Never to hurt.'

'Oho!' Araine said. 'So she was helping when she threw blinding powder in someone's face? Or hit them with her stick?'

'Always for their own good,' Leesha said. 'She didn't poison.'

'Perhaps.' Araine smiled over the rim of her delicate cup. 'But you have, haven't you? All the *Sharum* in your caravan this summer, as I hear it.'

Leesha felt her face grow cold. How had the duchess heard of that? 'That was a mistake. One I won't repeat.'

'A promise like that makes you a fool or a liar,' Araine said. 'Time will tell. You have power, and a day will come when you have to use it, or be destroyed.'

She set down her tea, picking up an embroidery hoop. Her nimble fingers belied her advanced years as she worked. 'Regardless, Mistress Jessa was trained by Bruna herself, and has the royal libraries at her disposal. I'll wager she's forgotten more about herbs than you know. If she says she's tried everything, then she has.'

'Then what do you need me for?' Leesha asked.

'Because you have tools she doesn't,' Araine said. 'Jessa knows her herbs, but she's less skilled with the knife.'

'And if Rhinebeck needs a cut between the legs to let his seed flow?' Leesha asked. 'How are we to arrange that, if he won't even let me examine him?'

'If it comes to that,' Araine said, 'we'll put tampweed and skyflower in his ale and keep him out till it's done. Tell him he drank himself stupid boar hunting and took a tusk between the legs.

'But now there's a third option.' Araine kept her eyes on her hoop. 'Magic.'

'It doesn't work quite like that,' Leesha said. 'The body heals itself, magic just speeds the process. If Rhinebeck was born with a . . . defect, there isn't much I can do.'

'What about the white witch you brought with you?' Araine demanded.

'You want to involve her in this?' Leesha asked.

'Don't be stupid,' Araine said. 'We tell her it's some other nobleman, and have her teach you what you need.'

'If such a thing exists,' Leesha said.

'You'd best hope it does,' Araine said. 'Time's running out. If Melny isn't pregnant by midwinter, we go to the backup plan.'

'And that is?' Leesha asked.

Araine smiled. 'Get Thamos to seed the young duchess.'

'What?' Leesha felt like she had swallowed a heavy stone. For a moment it was hard to breathe, and then it sat aching in her stomach.

'Melny may not be the sharpest spear, but she's got paps to turn the head of any man,' Araine said. 'Not that it will take much to convince Thamos he can save the entire duchy by cuckolding you and Rhiney.'

'And Melny?' Leesha asked. 'Is she just a womb with no say in the matter?'

Araine snorted. 'She'll put her legs in the air and thank the prince when it's done. Girl isn't the sharpest axe in the shed, but she's not entirely dull. What do you think will happen to her if she can't get pregnant before the Krasians turn north and Euchor forces our hand? Princess Lorain of Miln is already in the city with five hundred Mountain Spears, bribing Royals and eyeing poor Melny like an owl eyes a mouse. Her very presence is a slap in the face of the ivy throne.'

She tied off a thread, snipping it with a tiny pair of silver scissors. 'Thamos looks just like his grandfather. None will doubt the child is Rhiney's.'

'Why Thamos?' Leesha demanded.

'I could argue that Mickael is already wed,' Araine said as she started a new stitch, 'and Pether a Shepherd vowed to chastity. But truer is, neither would be able to keep from crowing about it. Rhiney would find out, and do something stupid.'

She looked at Leesha. 'As justices go, it's not without poetry. If you want to keep Thamos' spear dry, then you fix his brother's. If not, you can both have a bastard to hide as you start your life together.'

'Princess Amanvah of Krasia,' Jasin called loudly, his voice bouncing off the vaulted ceiling for all to hear. 'Firstborn daughter to Ahmann Jardir, Duke of Fort Krasia.'

Amanvah bristled at that. 'Duke? Fort? My father is as far above one of your pathetic dukes as they are a peasant's dog, and his empire stretches . . .'

Rojer tightened his hold on her arm. 'He's just doing it to get a rise from us. Everyone knows precisely who your father is.'

Amanvah gave a slight nod, her *dama'ting* serenity returning.

Jasin cast a dim eye at Rojer as they stood in the doorway. 'And her husband, Jongleur Rojer Inn, of Riverbridge.'

It was Rojer's turn to bristle. Normally as husband, he would have been announced first, but the chasm between his and Amanvah's ranks made it impossible. That, he could accept.

But Rojer was a Jongleur master now, and his stage name, Halfgrip, known throughout the land. He had written *The Battle of Cutter's Hollow* and the *Song of Waning*. Jasin made him sound like a juggler brought to entertain the guests between courses.

Amanvah squeezed his arm in return. 'Breathe, husband, and add it to the tally to be avenged.'

Rojer nodded as they paced into the room, allowing time

441

for them to see and be seen. Their lacklustre introduction did little to quell interest, as they were approached by a seemingly endless stream of nobles eager for introduction to the Krasian princess and fiddle wizard who could charm demons.

'Princess Sikvah of Krasia,' Jasin called, 'niece of Ahmann Jardir, Duke of Fort Krasia. Jongleur Kendall Inn, of the famed fiddle wizards of Hollow County.'

Rojer gritted his teeth.

Sikvah steered Kendall in another direction after their introduction. Her rank demanded she be invited, but Amanvah had forbidden her and Kendall from sitting with them. Apparently it did not do for a man to attend a formal dinner with his *Jiwah Sen*.

A small group approached them, led by a man with bright red hair, dressed in subdued heraldic motley in the colours of Duke Euchor. He made a smooth leg before Amanvah, sweeping his cloak over one shoulder in a flash of colour. 'Your Highness,' he looked to Rojer, 'Master Halfgrip. I am Keerin, royal herald to Duke Euchor, Light of the Mountains and Guardian of the Northland, Lord of Miln.'

He waited for Amanvah to offer a hand to kiss, but men and women did not touch in Krasia, especially married women, and *dama'ting* most of all. Amanvah gave only the slightest nod of her head, as if to a servant who had brought her refreshment.

Keerin cleared his throat. 'Please allow me to introduce Her Highness, Princess Lorain of Miln, youngest daughter to Duke Euchor.'

The woman stepped forward, and Rojer saw immediately the rumours were true. Euchor's daughters were all said to take after him in appearance, and Lorain's square face had much in common with the one stamped on Milnese coin.

Her frame, tall and wide-shouldered, had much in common with a man's as well. She looked fit enough to wrestle Wonda. Her hair was still gold with no signs of grey, but her face had none of the softness of youth. She was the shady side of thirty-five, at the least. Old for a political bride.

Amanvah bowed, but it was shallow – an act of respect, but not equality. 'It is an honour to meet you, Lorain vah Euchor. I am pleased to see I am not the only princess in a strange city.'

It was unclear if Lorain registered the slight. The politics of Krasian bowing were a language all their own. But her return bow mirrored Amanvah's in depth and duration – a statement of equality, and a challenge to Amanvah.

But then she did something that put them all off guard.

'The honour is mine, Amanvah daughter of Ahmann,' Lorain said in Krasian.

Amanvah blinked, switching immediately to her native tongue. 'You speak my language?'

Lorain smiled. 'Of course. A properly educated lady can make dinner conversation in all the dead languages, though none of us has ever had the chance to speak with a native. I'm sure you will be flooded with invitations to tea from those of blood eager to practise.'

'Dead languages?' Amanvah asked.

'Ruskan, Limnese, Albeen, and Krasian,' Lorain said.

'My language is hardly dead,' Amanvah said.

Lorain gave a slight bow. 'Of course. But it's been centuries since we've entertained one of your people at court. From the Northern perspective, the language is no longer spoken.'

'Your education will serve you well,' Amanvah said. 'The dice foretell a great resurgence of Krasian speakers in the North.'

Lorain's smile was dangerous. 'I wouldn't be so sure of that.'

A man cleared his throat, breaking the tension between the women.

'Allow me to present my escort, Lord Sament,' Lorain said, switching to Thesan as she indicated the last member of her party. The man wore his rich clothing comfortably, but he looked more bodyguard than escort, his eyes hard. He bowed.

'We'll leave you to mingle,' Lorain told Amanvah. 'I just wanted to make your acquaintance. No doubt we will have time to get to know each other after dinner in the women's wing.'

With that, the Milnese swept off as quickly as they had come.

'Escort?' Amanvah asked.

'Chaperone, more like,' Rojer said. 'Rhinebeck has been through several wives, but none has been able to give him a child. Lorain is the next hopeful.'

'She will likely fare no better, if several have gone before her,' Amanvah said. 'It sounds as if the problem is with him.'

'I wouldn't suggest it in polite company,' Rojer said. 'Lorain has two sons to prove her fertility at least.'

Amanvah looked at him. 'The Duke of Miln sends his rival an aging bride who is not even a virgin? What happened to her sons' father?'

'Euchor divorced them, and sent her south,' Rojer said.

Amanvah snorted. 'A desperate attempt to form an alliance against my father.'

'Can you blame them?' Rojer asked.

'No,' Amanvah said, 'but it will make no difference in the end.'

It was pointless to debate the topic. Amanvah was wise about many things, but where her father was concerned, she saw only what she wanted to see. He was Shar'Dama Ka, and his rule was inevitable.

'Little Rojer, now a married man,' a voice said, and Rojer turned to see the Duchess Mum approaching with Duchess Melny. 'How old were you when I caught you climbing the shelves in the royal library?'

Rojer swept into a low bow. 'Five, Your Grace.' His backside ached as he recalled the incident. The Duchess Mum had only huffed, but it might as well have been a command, for Jessa had a strap in hand the moment she left.

Amanvah ignored the young duchess, meeting the old woman's eyes. Something passed between them, and Amanvah's bow was deeper and longer than before. 'It is an honour to meet the famed Duchess Mother.'

Melny, technically outranking her mother-in-law, might have been offended at that, but she seemed to take it in stride. Araine had little real power in Angiers, but while Rhinebeck's wives came and went, his mother was constant, and the vapid noble-women at court all took their cues from her.

'I trust you've refreshed yourself from your long journey?' Melny asked when the introductions were complete. 'Your rooms were are satisfactory?'

Amanvah nodded, surprising Rojer. Amanvah never felt rooms were satisfactory, but apparently that was something best communicated through servants. 'Of course.'

'I trust the princess from the North was able to mind her manners?' Araine asked.

'It was most refreshing to learn my language is spoken at court,' Amanvah said in Krasian.

Melny's cheeks coloured, and Rojer realized she had no idea what Amanvah had said. Amanvah picked up on it as well, and bowed.

'Apologies, Duchess. I was given to understand by the Princess of Miln that all of royal blood learned to speak Krasian as part of their studies.'

Melny's blush spread, splashing her pale and prodigious bosom with pink. Her eyes found Lorain and her entourage working the room, watching with ill-disguised unease. 'Yes, well . . .'

Araine cleared her throat. 'Baron!' she called, spotting Gared a few yards away. 'Come, let's have a look at you.' She soon had Gared turning like he was modelling the latest fashion, the giant's blush as deep as the young duchess'.

Araine gave a low whistle. 'This won't be difficult at all. The girls will be taking numbers, waiting for a turn to dance with you while their fathers whisper dowers in my ear.'

'I, ah, 'preciate it, Y'Grace,' Gared said. 'Hope I don't step on any toes. Don't know any dances for big rooms like this.' He waved a hand at the high-vaulted ceiling.

'Wait until you see the ballroom,' Araine said with a chuckle. 'As for the dancing, we'll find something you can muddle through. Can't have you looking ill at your own Bachelor's Ball.'

Rojer bowed. 'If it please Your Grace, my quartet would be honoured to handle the music. No doubt we can manage something to make the baron more comfortable.' He slapped Gared on the back, and some of the big man's tension eased.

'A delightful idea!' Araine said. 'You'll be the envy of every bachelor in the city, Baron. We'll find you a bride in no time.'

Gared looked ready to faint.

'I thought . . .' Melny began. All eyes turned to her, and she wilted under the collective stare.

'Yes, dear?' Araine asked.

'Well, that is,' Melny squeaked, glancing to Amanvah, 'it was my understanding that music and dancing were against . . .'

'Evejan law?' Amanvah asked. 'In my land, yes. But I am Hollow tribe now,' she chuckled, 'and *jiwah* to a Jongleur. It has necessitated some . . . change of view.'

She smiled. 'The Baron of Cutter's Hollow is a great *kai'Sharum*, and his seed is being wasted on the ground. The sooner he has a *Jiwah Ka* to give him sons, the better. It is an honour to be part of your Northern courting ritual. At my husband's side, I may study it without impropriety.'

Araine spotted Jasin Goldentone – doing his best to keep his distance – and beckoned him over with a crooked finger.

'You're off the hook for the Bachelor's Ball, Jasin,' the Duchess Mum said when the herald scurried over. 'Rojer and his wives will handle the music.'

'But Your Grace,' Jasin sputtered, 'surely I am more qualified . . .'

Araine laughed. 'More qualified than Halfgrip, fiddle wizard

446

of the Hollow? Be glad that's the only job he's taking from you.'

Jasin's eyes widened, but he knew better than to argue. Araine might be a dim old bat, but when it came to royal parties, her power was absolute.

'I think it's time we took our seats,' Araine said. 'Come, Melny, help an old woman.' The duchess took her mother-in-law by the arm, and Araine leaned on her as they made their way to the table.

Others took the cue and made for their seats, but Rojer could not resist twisting the knife. 'Look on the sunny side,' he told Jasin, 'at least they'll stop calling you Secondsong in the guildhouse now.' He smiled. 'Secondfiddle tumbles so smoothly from the tongue.'

Jasin bared his teeth, but Rojer affected not to notice, tightening his arm around Amanvah's and leading her to their seats.

'Provoking your blood enemies is unwise, husband,' Amanvah said. 'Better to let them think your hatred cooled before you strike.'

'Nothing about vengeance is wise,' Rojer said. 'But I don't trust the afterlife to make Jasin pay for what he's done to me. I want to see him suffer in this life, and that means destroying the thing he holds most dear.'

'His pride,' Amanvah guessed.

'His reputation,' Rojer said. 'Nothing will cut Goldentone deeper than being known as second best.'

Dinner was long and tedious, with endless speeches and false claims of friendship as the Milnese and Angierians glowered at each other, and all cast mistrustful eyes at Amanvah and Sikvah.

But as always in Rhinebeck's palace, the wine was free flowing, and Rojer had been seated next to the Duchess Melny, who laughed easily, her bosom jiggling so hypnotically Rojer almost forgot the punchlines.

Amanvah dug nails into his leg, bringing his attention back to her as she leaned close to his ear. 'If you are done amusing the harlot, husband, I have questions.'

'That "harlot" is Duchess of Angiers,' Rojer said.

Amanvah gave Melny a dismissive glance. The duchess smiled back, oblivious. 'I've seen this before. A man who cannot sire having his *Jiwah Ka* bring him younger and stupider brides year after year, more interested in the act than the result. The only difference here is that his mother,' she nodded to Araine, 'acts as *Jiwah Ka*, and he shames his brides by divorcing them before taking new ones.'

'That's . . .' Rojer paused. 'Actually quite apt. But not something you want to be heard saying aloud. We Northern "savages" are not so blunt about these things.'

Amanvah caressed his arm, but it felt condescending, like one would stroke a pet. 'Then it will be our job to civilize you.'

Rojer changed the subject. 'What questions?'

Amanvah nodded to the far end of the table. The dessert plates had been cleared, and servants were pouring after-dinner wine. A few courtiers not ranking enough to secure a seat at the table had been granted entrance to the dining hall. Coliv appeared, putting his back to the wall behind Amanvah. He had not been allowed to carry weapons openly at court, but Rojer knew that made him no less able to protect his mistress.

At the end of the table, Jasin Goldentone had been joined by a group of sycophants, but he was now flanked by a large, familiar pair that put a heavy lump in Rojer's throat.

'Those two wear the motley, but they are bodyguards, yes?' Amanvah asked.

Rojer nodded. 'Abrum and Sali. Passably competent musicians at their best, Jasin has them sing his harmonies and break bones.'

Amanvah showed no surprise. 'And were any of my honoured husband's bones among those broken by this pair?'

'You've seen my scars, *Jiwah Ka*,' Rojer said. 'Not all come from *alagai* wounds.'

A few minutes later, Araine stood, followed in short order by the rest of the table. Leesha and Melny supported her on either side, sweeping up all the women in their wake as they made their way towards the door.

'What is this?' Amanvah asked.

'The Duchess Mum will entertain the ladies for the rest of the evening,' Rojer said. 'The men will take their wine into the duke's drawing room and smoke.'

Amanvah nodded, allowing Rojer to pull back her seat. 'Take Coliv with you.'

'Absolutely not,' Rojer said. 'Creator love him, but the man will severely inhibit my ability to play the crowd, and these are powerful people, *Jiwah Ka*. They need to be played just right.'

Amanvah looked doubtful, but Gared appeared a moment later, and Rojer was happy for the save. 'Count says we're gonna go smoke.'

Gared waited expectantly for Rojer to join him. He'd been seated between hopeful young noblewomen all night, but Rojer had seen little apart from uncomfortable silence.

'I'll be with Gared Cutter,' he told Amanvah. 'Only a fool will threaten me.'

Satisfied, Amanvah moved to join the women, scooping up Sikvah and Kendall as she went.

Gared let out a deep sigh.

'That bad?' Rojer asked.

'Kareen's perfume gave me a headache,' Gared said. 'Like she dumped a bucket of it over herself. And talks like a mouse. Had to keep leaning in to hear, catchin' a noseful o' stink.'

'Probably whispering to let you lean in and ogle her neckline,' Rojer said.

'And Dinny was worse,' Gared went on. 'All she wanted to talk about was poetry. Poetry! Night, can't even rippin' read! What do I got to say to fancy ladies like them?'

Rojer laughed. 'It doesn't matter. Those women were probably desperate to impress the Bachelor Baron of Hollow County. Say whatever you like. Brag about all the demons you've killed, or talk about your horse. It doesn't matter. They'll laugh and sigh all the same.'

'If it doesn't matter what I say, what's the point of talkin' at all?' Gared asked.

'Passes the time,' Rojer said. 'These people ent done a hard day's work in their entire lives, Gar. Nothin' but time on their hands for poetry and perfume.'

Gared spat. One of the servants gave him a look, but wisely kept silent. Gared had the decency to look embarrassed, at least.

'Don't want a wife like that,' Gared said. 'May not be smart or know my letters, but Creator my witness, I break my back all day and night. Don't want to come home and have to listen to a bunch of ripping poems.'

'You want a woman who's waiting with an ale,' Rojer guessed, 'ready to lift her dress on a moment's notice.'

Gared looked at him. 'Don't know me as well as you think, Rojer. Break my back for Cutter's Hollow, and I need to know my woman's done the same. I can get my own ripping ale.'

He dropped his eyes. 'Like the sound of that last part, though.'

In Rhinebeck's drawing rooms, men were smoking and drinking, debating politics and religion, and generally trying to impress one another. There were several Succour tables with men clustered about them, sipping brandy and acting not the least affected as more money than most Angierians saw in a lifetime changed hands with every throw of the dice.

Jasin was present, but the herald had claimed a corner and

was surrounded by a knot of sycophants that made an unexpected encounter unlikely.

'Gared! Rojer!' Thamos called, waving them over to where he stood with his brothers and Lord Janson. 'Join us!' Keerin, Duke Euchor's herald, was there as well, but with the air of a man trying to join a conversation where he is not entirely welcome.

'Are you refreshed from the road, my sons?' Shepherd Pether asked. 'Thamos was telling us how your caravan travelled at night as well as day, slaying corespawn as you went. A most impressive feat.'

Gared's shoulders lifted and fell. 'Same as any other night, I guess. Killin' demons is sweaty work, but it's not like choppin' a tree. Arlen Bales warded my axe himself. Don't get tired when I swing it at a demon. Feel stronger with every hit.'

The men all grunted and nodded knowingly, but Rojer could see through the façade. Odds were none of them had never even seen a demon up close, much less fought one.

'And you, Rojer?' Janson asked. 'As I understand it, you gain no such advantage when you charm the corelings with your fiddle. Playing through the night must be taxing.'

'Calluses, my lord,' Rojer smiled, holding up his eight fingers. The men were too on guard to flinch, but he could see the shock in their eyes. His crippled hand was a harsh reminder of what lay beyond their wardwalls at night.

'As Gared says, we're used to such things in the Hollow,' Rojer went on. 'I think my fingers could limber a bit more with a spot of Succour . . .'

'Don't bother,' Keerin said. 'I've already tried. They all know better than to dice with a Jongleur.'

'The Duchess Mum raised no fools,' Janson said. Rhinebeck and his brothers looked his way and laughed, acting as if Keerin had not spoken at all.

The herald laughed along uncomfortably, desperate to find

some bit of acceptance. In the moment of silence that followed, he pressed his suit. 'I, too, have some experience with demons. Perhaps you've heard the tale of how I cut the arm from a rock demon?'

Something about that tickled Rojer's memory, but that was all. The other men groaned.

'Not this ale story again,' Rhinebeck said.

'Must've been a little one,' Gared said. 'Don't look like you could reach the arm of a decent-sized rock. What'd you use? Axe? Pick mattock?'

Keerin smiled, seeming to come alive at the words. 'Therein lies a great tale.' He swept a bow to Rhinebeck. 'With Your Grace's permission . . .'

The duke put his face in his hand. 'Had to ask, ay Baron?' He swept the hand at Keerin. 'Very well, Herald. Sing your song.' Keerin swept into the centre of the room calling for attention while the duke signalled for more wine. He had a fine lute, and while he was unlikely to be counted among the great singers, neither was Rojer. Keerin's voice was rich and clear, washing over the room as he cast his spell.

> The night was dark
> The ground was hard
> Succour was leagues away
>
> The cold wind stark
> Cutting at our hearts
> Only wards kept corelings at bay
>
> 'Help me!' we heard
> A voice in need
> The cry of a frightened child
>
> 'Run to us!' I called
> 'Our circle's wide,
> The only succour for miles!'

The boy cried out
'I can't; I fell!'
His call echoed in the black

Catching his shout
I sought to help
But the Messenger held me back

'What good to die?'
He asked me, grim
'For death is all you'll find

'No help you'll provide
'Gainst coreling claws
Just more meat to grind'

I struck him hard
And grabbed his spear
Leaping across the wards

A frantic charge
Strength born of fear
Before the boy be cored

'Stay brave!' I cried
Running hard his way
'Keep your heart strong and true!

'If you can't stride
To where it's safe
I'll bring the wards to you!'

I reached him quick
But not enough
Corelings gathered 'round

The demons thick
My work was rough
Scratching wards into the ground

A thunderous roar
Boomed in the night
A demon twenty feet tall

It towered fore
And 'gainst such might
My spear seemed puny and small

Horns like hard spears!
Claws like my arm!
A carapace hard and black!

An avalanche
Promising harm
The beast moved to the attack!

The boy screamed scared
And clutched my leg
Clawed as I drew the last ward!

The magic flared
Creator's gift
The one force demons abhor!

Some will tell you
Only the sun
Can bring a rock demon harm

That night I learned
It could be done
As did the demon One Arm!

The last words struck Rojer, and suddenly he realized why the tale was so familiar. How many times had Arlen told of the one-armed rock demon that pursued him for years after he cut its arm off as a boy? What were the odds this tale happened twice on the road to Miln?

Keerin ended with a flourish, and there was applause throughout the drawing room, but the sound was noticeably absent from Jasin's corner, and the duke's circle.

Rojer's claps were loud and slow, designed to echo off the room's high-vaulted ceiling. They continued when the rest of the applause had died away, drawing all eyes to him.

'A fine tale,' Rojer congratulated loudly. 'Though I knew a man who told it differently.'

'Oh?' Keerin asked imperiously, knowing a challenge when he heard it. 'And who might that be?'

'Arlen Bales,' Rojer said, and there was chatter throughout the room at the name.

He looked at Keerin with mock incredulity as the colour drained from the man's face. 'You realize, of course, that the boy in your song grew to be none other than the Painted Man, himself?'

'Don't remember a Jongleur in that story,' Gared said, and there was more chatter at that. 'You want to hear a true story?' He slapped Rojer on the back, knocking him forward a step. 'Rojer, play *The Battle of Cutter's Hollow*!'

Thamos put his face in his hand. Rojer turned, bowing to Rhinebeck as Keerin had. 'Your Grace, I need not . . .'

'It's already being played in every alehouse from here to Miln,' Rhinebeck said with a wave. 'Might as well hear it from the source.'

Rojer swallowed, but he took out his fiddle and began to play.

> Cutter's Hollow lost its centre
> When the flux came to stay
> Killed great Herb Gatherer Bruna

Her 'prentice far away
Not a one would run and hide,
They all did stand and follow
Killing demons in the night
The Painted Man came to the Hollow

In Fort Angiers far to the north
Leesha got ill tiding
Her mentor dead, her father sick
Hollow a week's riding
Not a one would run and hide,
They all did stand and follow
Killing demons in the night
The Painted Man came to the Hollow

No guide she found through naked night
Just Jongleur travel wards
That could not hold the bandits back
As it did coreling hordes
Not a one would run and hide,
They all did stand and follow
Killing demons in the night
The Painted Man came to the Hollow

Left for dead no horse or succour
Corelings roving in bands
They met a man with tattooed flesh
Killed demons with bare hands
Not a one would run and hide,
They all did stand and follow
Killing demons in the night
The Painted Man came to the Hollow

The Hollow razed when they arrived
Not a ward left intact
And half the folk who called it home

Lay dead or on their backs
Not a one would run and hide,
They all did stand and follow
Killing demons in the night
The Painted Man came to the Hollow

Painted Man spat on despair
Said follow me and fight
We'll see the dawn if we all stand
Side by side in the night
Not a one would run and hide,
They all did stand and follow
Killing demons in the night
The Painted Man came to the Hollow

All night they fought with axe and spear
Butcher's knife and shield
While Leesha brought those too weak to
The Holy House to heal
Not a one would run and hide,
They all did stand and follow
Killing demons in the night
The Painted Man came to the Hollow

Hollowers kept their loved ones safe
Though night was long and hard
There's reason why the battlefield's
Called the Corelings' Graveyard
Not a one would run and hide,
They all did stand and follow
Killing demons in the night
The Painted Man came to the Hollow

If someone asks why at sunset
Demons all get shivers
Hollowers say with honest word

It's 'cuz we're all Deliverers
Not a one would run and hide,
They all did stand and follow
Killing demons in the night
The Painted Man came to the Hollow

Keerin seemed to shrink as the song went on. Gared roared the refrain along with Rojer, and others in the room took up the song. By the end, the Milnese herald's haughty look was gone.

The applause was louder at the end of Rojer's song, with Gared leading the crowd with piercing whistles and his booming claps and cheers. Thamos joined him, and even his brothers clapped politely, save for Shepherd Pether, who merely sipped his wine.

But from Jasin's corner, there was silence until the rest died down, and then he, too, began a slow clap, walking towards the centre of the room.

'Your Grace—' he began.

'Not now, Jasin,' Rhinebeck cut him off with a wave. 'I think we've had enough of singing for one night.'

Jasin's jaw dropped, and Rojer flashed him a smile. 'Not even Thirdsong tonight, ay? Perhaps we'll call you Jasin Nosong from now on.' Before the herald could react, Rojer turned his back and rejoined the duke's entourage.

'And where is this *Painted Man?*' Pether's mouth was a tight line. Not surprising, since Arlen Bales represented a direct challenge to his authority. Should Arlen be acknowledged openly as Deliverer, Pether's position as the head of the church in Angiers would be effectively meaningless.

'Over a cliff with the demon of the desert, as I told you all in my letters,' Thamos said immediately. 'I was there, and have not heard credible tale of any seeing him since.'

'He'll be back,' Gared said, oblivious to the look Thamos shot him, or the way Pether's lips soured. 'Sure as the sun rises.'

'You believe he is the Deliverer, then?' Pether demanded.

All around them, other conversations died as everyone in the room waited on Gared's response. Even Gared picked up on it, realizing that the entire relationship between Hollow County and Angiers might hinge on his response.

'Was for me and mine,' Gared said at last. 'Can't deny the world's changing, and it started with him.' He looked up, meeting Pether's eyes with an intensity that broke even the Shepherd's glare. 'But I know Arlen Bales. He dun't want a throne. Dun't want to tell folk how to live their lives. All Arlen Bales cares about is killing demons, and that's something every one of us ought to be able to get behind.'

'Hear hear!' Thamos said loudly, raising his glass. His brothers all looked at him in surprise, but the count kept his eyes on Gared, avoiding their stare. The rest of the room responded instinctively at the motion, raising their glasses with a cheer.

Rhinebeck, Mickael, and Pether, sensing the mood, drank the toast with practised smiles, but Rojer could sense the unease that lay beneath.

Leesha continued to be amazed at Araine's masterful performance as a doddering old woman. She had one arm through Leesha's and another through Melny's, no act to the weight she put on them.

There was no denying the effectiveness of the tactic. All the men at court, from the lowest scullery boy to Rhinebeck himself, were trained to leap to her bidding, lest the crone strain herself to exhaustion with the act of crossing the room.

Leesha looked at Thamos as they passed, but the count affected not to notice.

Nothing is settled, she reminded herself. *Not until I make right with Thamos.* She of all people should know that a mother's marriage agreements were meaningless without the child's consent.

Wonda had the door. 'Let an old woman lean on one of those magnificent arms,' Araine told her.

'Ay, Mum,' Wonda said. Melny broke off with practised ease, smiling as she took the lead of the crowd of women in the hall, escorting them to the evening salon.

They approached the end of the hall where two large women stood at attention to either side of a great set of double doors. They were dressed almost identically to Wonda, and wore tabards bearing Araine's crest. They were unarmed, but did not look to need arms to keep out most unwanted visitors. When they moved to pull open the doors, Leesha could see the barest impression of a short club hanging from the back of their belts, hidden by the loose tabards.

They saluted as Araine approached, but their eyes were on Wonda.

'You've become something of a legend in Angiers, dear,' Araine told Wonda. 'Since your last visit, I've made some changes in the palace guard.'

Another pair of women on the opposite side closed the doors, but these were clad in lacquered wooden armour and carried spears.

Araine ignored the discomfort on Wonda's face, turning to Amanvah and Sikvah. She surprised Leesha again, slipping effortlessly into Krasian. 'Be at peace, sisters, and lower your veils. We are in the women's wing of the palace. No men are allowed beyond these doors.'

Amanvah bowed slightly, lowering her pristine white veil and undoing her headscarf. Sikvah followed suit. Unmarried, Kendall's face was uncovered, but she wore her hair in a motley headscarf and removed it with a bow.

The salon was filled with ladies of the court by the time Araine shuffled up the steps and down the hall. Women drank and lounged, discussing art, music, theatre, and poetry. Princess Lorain commanded a knot of women, as did the Duchess Melny, the tension between the groups palpable.

A trio of female Jongleurs in the court heraldic motley

performed near the centre. Two of them, young and beautiful, plucked harps, filling the rooms with soothing sound.

The third was older, tall and thickly set. The motley patchwork of her gown was made of smooth elegant lines of coloured velvet, embroidered in gold. Her voice permeated the room, bounced expertly off walls and ceiling designed to amplify those in the centre of the room. The high soprano aria was from *Scaletongue*, the opera about the mythical Messenger Jak Scaletongue, who could speak to demons, and delighted in tricking them.

Amanvah's eyes locked on the singer in that sharp, predatory way Krasian women had, Sikvah and Kendall's heads swivelled as one to follow, like a flock of birds turning in unison.

Amanvah and Sikvah raised their hands slightly, wiggling fingers in their secret language while continuing to watch the Jongleur. Leesha still had no sense of what the movements meant, but she knew from experience the Krasian women could speak as intricate a conversation with fingers and facial expression as they could with words.

Pretending to adjust her hair, Leesha slipped on a warded earring. It was a tiny silver shell, moulded around a curved bit of dried ear cartilage from a flame demon.

She tilted her head slightly, and caught Kendall's whispered words, even amidst the music. 'Who's that?'

Sikvah leaned close to Kendall, her words the barest breath on the young woman's ear, but Leesha's earring caught them all. 'She is the one who killed Master Jaycob.'

Leesha's stomach tightened. She had written the report to the city watch after the crime. Leesha prided herself on a sharp memory, but it cut both ways, as the image of Jaycob's swollen and bloody body flashed in her mind, bones broken like kindling. He had been beaten to death by someone using their bare hands.

From the size of the bruises, Leesha had always assumed the killer had been a man. There had been a purple handprint on Jaycob's shoulder – where the assailant had gripped him to pull him into their blows. Leesha remembered measuring her own hand against it, like a child measuring against an adult.

One look at the singer's big hands, though, and she knew.

'What do we do?' Kendall whispered.

'Nothing, save the *dama'ting* command it,' Sikvah said. 'This woman owes our husband a blood debt, but until he calls it due, we must endure.'

The Core we must, Leesha thought.

'Creator, that singing is giving me a splitting headache,' she said. Not loudly, but not quietly, either.

Araine immediately picked up on it. 'Sali, quit your warbling!'

The Jongleur had taken a great breath for her next verse, but choked on it instead, coughing with great convulsion. She punched herself in the chest, trying to regain composure, and behind her, Leesha heard Kendall give a tiny giggle.

Leesha raised her voice. 'If the ladies of your salon are as sick of another tired rendition of *Scaletongue* as I, Your Grace, perhaps the Princess Amanvah will bless us with something newer.' She glanced at Amanvah, whose eyes shone with gratitude.

At a nod from Araine, Amanvah and her *Jiwah Sen* swept in on the unfortunate royal troupe, forcing them to stumble awkwardly from the centre of the room.

Kendall had her fiddle out, playing a few notes to warm the strings as Amanvah addressed the crowd.

'In days long past, my people used music to drive back the *alagai*, turning them from their unholy purpose.' Her trained voice easily mastered the acoustics of the room, and her accent, rolling and musical, sent shivers through the crowd, commanding the attention of all, even the displaced Jongleurs.

'It is time,' Amanvah said, 'to return that power to all Everam's children. Listen well.'

With that, she began to sing, Sikvah and Kendall rising to join her, the three of them nearly as powerful alone as with Rojer at their lead. The song was in Krasian, but the melody wrapped them all close, and soon she could see women around the room mouthing the refrain as best they could, excitement on their faces as they remembered childhood lessons in the desert tongue.

And in the corner, Sali stood with crossed arms, seething.

20

Sibling Rivalry
333 AR Winter

Rojer's head was pounding when Sikvah shook him awake. He barely recalled stumbling into his chambers and crawling into bed with her. Amanvah and Kendall had their own rooms in the suite. Rojer looked to the window. It was still dark.

'Creator, what's the ripping emergency?' he asked. 'Unless the walls have been breached, I mean to sleep through till noontime.'

'You cannot,' Sikvah said. 'The duke's man is waiting outside. You leave at dawn for the hunt.'

'Night,' Rojer muttered, rubbing his face. He'd forgotten all about it. 'Tell him I'll join them shortly.'

By the time he pulled on his clothes a breakfast tray had been sent up, but Rojer only snatched a roll on his way to the door.

'You must eat, husband,' Sikvah said.

Rojer waved the thought away. 'Going hunting with Duke Rhinebeck. Believe me when I say there will be food aplenty. Odds are I'll return with a few extra pounds, and not from the game.'

Sikvah looked at him curiously. 'When *Sharum* hunt, they take only water with them. It is a test of survival.'

Rojer laughed. 'For many in the North, as well. But Royals hunt for sport. If the duke's attendants chase a stag before his bow – and he manages to shoot it and not them – the cooks will turn it into a royal feast, ay, but the lodge will be stocked to feed an army in any event.'

He kissed her, leaving Amanvah and Kendall to their beds as he headed towards the stables in search of Gared.

He was fortunate to hear Jasin before he saw him, ducking into an alcove and hiding in the shadow of a statue of Rhinebeck I while he waited for them to pass.

'You cannot mean that Milnese fop and ripping Halfgrip are invited, and I am not,' Jasin growled.

'Lower your voice, boy,' Janson snapped. Gone was the obsequious tone he took with Royals and visitors. Rojer hadn't heard that tone in some time, but he knew it well. Janson had used it often in the last days of Arrick's service to the duke. 'Rhinebeck doesn't want you on the hunt, and that's all you need to know. You'll be lucky to keep your post at all after the mess you've made of your trip south.'

'You're the one who told me to have the soldiers drive the vagrants from the caravan grounds,' Jasin said, dropping his voice to a harsh whisper.

'I didn't tell you to brag about it to the Hollowers,' Janson said, 'and if you so much as breathe a word about my order again, the black dress I have tailored for my sister will be a small price to pay to be free of the headaches you cause me.'

Jasin wisely kept his reply to himself, and a moment later the minister was called away to attend some matter of the duke's departure. Rojer strolled out into the hall, whistling a bright tune. Jasin looked up and scowled.

'Sorry you won't be joining us,' Rojer said as he passed.

Jasin grabbed his arms, shoving him hard into the wall. He wasn't a giant like Gared, but he was taller and stronger than Rojer. 'I thought you'd learned not to cross me, cripple, but it seems you need a reminder of—'

Rojer stomped hard on Jasin's instep, circling his forearms in a simple *sharusahk* move to break the herald's hold. He flicked his wrist, catching a knife in his hand and putting the point to Jasin's throat.

'Not afraid of you any more, Nosong,' Rojer spat. He pressed the knife in, drawing a drop of blood.

Jasin's face went from pink to snow white. 'You wouldn't dare . . .'

Rojer pressed harder, cutting off the words. 'You think I've forgotten what you did to me? To Jaycob? Give me an excuse. I beg you.'

'What's going on here?'

Rojer and Jasin turned as one to see the speaker, Rojer twisting to block the blade from sight as he made it disappear up his sleeve. Lord Janson stood in the hall, glaring at them both. Rojer didn't think he had seen the knife, but there was no telling for sure. Not that it mattered, if Jasin were to accuse him and show the puncture at his throat.

But Jasin smiled, spreading his hands. 'Nothing, Uncle. Simply an old disagreement.'

Janson's eyes narrowed. 'Settle it another time. His Grace awaits you, Master Halfgrip.'

Rojer bowed. 'Of course, Minister.'

'Another time,' Jasin agreed, turning on his heel and stomping back into the palace proper.

'Halfgrip!' Rhinebeck called when Rojer made the stables. It was unclear if he were still drunk from the night before, or if this was a fresh inebriation, but it was barely dawn and already his words were slurred and the wineskin his page carried was only half full.

'You can't mean to hunt in that,' Pether said, pointing to Rojer's motley with a short crooked staff that doubled as a riding crop. The Shepherd had changed from his formal robes into brown and green riding gear, fine silk and suede, with the crooked staff embroidered in gold on his fine wool jacket.

Rojer looked down at his clothes, a bright patchwork of colour that was perfect for performance, but less so for sneaking about the woods. He shrugged helplessly. 'Apologies, my lords, but I had not packed for hunting.'

'No matter,' Prince Mickael said. 'Goldentone has hunting motley. Janson! Send a boy up to fetch a set from the herald.'

Janson bowed. 'Of course, Highness.' He glanced at Rojer, who was wise enough to swallow his grin and look at his feet.

The runner returned with a set of green and brown motley from Jasin, but when Rojer opened the package, it stank like Goldentone had emptied his chamber pot onto it.

Rojer smiled. Still a victory. If he could not easily kill the man, he would settle for a thousand tiny blows.

The royal hunting lodge was a full day's ride east of the city. Keerin and Sament had been invited along, but it was the barest courtesy, and not a true welcome. They had their own entourage, and even on the next day's hunt the two groups kept mostly to themselves.

They were hunting rockbirds, a large species of raptor common in the hills of Angiers. The birds were a slate colour almost indistinguishable from the rocks where they made their nests.

The duke had split them into two groups. Rhinebeck, Thamos, Rojer, and Gared positioned themselves east above a cluster of nesting stones. Mickael, Pether, Sament, and Keerin had been sent to a similar position to the west. Servants led dogs quietly up the path to the stones. When they were ready, Rhinebeck would give the signal and they would loose the dogs, flushing the birds from concealment, right into the hunters' sights.

Rojer and Gared carried conventional bows, arrows nocked at the ready. The duke and Thamos held loaded crank bows with ornate aiming lenses. Each had an attendant with two more, ready to hand off and reload while the Royals fired.

'He's an embarrassment to the crown,' Thamos was saying to Rhinebeck. 'Driving peasants into the night to save a few hours.'

'Rizonan peasants,' Rhinebeck said. 'Squatters trespassing on ground cleared for Messengers and caravans. Most of them bandits who would as soon slit my men's throats as not.'

'Nonsense,' Thamos said. 'Those we encountered were too wretched to be a threat to anyone. Rizon is gone, brother. And Lakton soon enough, if we do not act. If we don't want our lands teeming with bandits, we must absorb the refugees and offer them better. It is the only way. And we cannot do that if Goldentone has them cursing your name.'

Rhinebeck sighed, taking another long pull from his wineskin. He offered it to Thamos, who waved it away, and Gared, who accepted. The young baron was proving impressionable, and was nearly as drunk as Rhinebeck.

'Creator knows I'm not defending Goldentone,' Rhinebeck said. 'That little pissant makes me long for the days of Sweetsong, before the drink turned him sour.' He glanced at Rojer, who kept his face expressionless. It was no secret much of the rift between Arrick and the duke had come after Sweetsong returned from the destruction of Riverbridge with Rojer in tow.

'What about you, Halfgrip?' Rhinebeck asked. 'They say ask a Jongleur if you're looking for gossip. What do they say on the streets about my half-witted herald?'

'He's no more loved in the guildhouse than in the palace,' Rojer said. 'Before Your Grace took him as herald, his patrons were more interested in doing his uncle a favour than they were in his singing. He was known for taking jobs my master turned down. It's how he earned the nickname Secondsong.'

Rhinebeck roared a laugh. 'Secondsong! I love it!'

The sound echoed off the rocks and a dozen rockbirds took flight, muscular wings fighting the pull of the ground to reach the strong winds that swept the hills.

'Night!' Rhinebeck cried, snapping his crank bow up so quickly the bolt came loose and the string twanged uselessly. Rojer and Gared loosed as well, their arrows not coming significantly closer. There were curses from the west as the other group had similar results.

Only Thamos remained calm, raising his crank bow and taking his time as he tracked one of the birds. Rhinebeck snatched another bow from his attendant and had it up while Rojer and Gared were still nocking their second shots. Thamos fired and there was a squawk even as Rhinebeck pulled his trigger with barely a moment to aim.

The rockbird cried as it fell from the sky. Thamos smiled, but it was short-lived as his elder brother glared at him. The count gave a nod. 'Well shot, brother. I confess I am out of practice, but Creator willing, I'll catch up over the next few days.'

There was a moment of silence, and then Rhinebeck's attendant spoke. 'Indeed, sire. A fine shot.' Thamos' attendant nodded emphatically. 'Masterfully done, Your Grace.'

Rhinebeck glanced to Gared and Rojer.

'Rarely have I seen such skill with a crank bow,' Rojer said. Gared remained quiet, so he gave the big man a surreptitious kick in the leg.

'Oh, ay,' Gared said, his voice flat. 'Good shootin'.'

Rhinebeck grunted, slapping Thamos on the back. 'You were always better with the spear than the bow.' He looked to Rojer. 'Your fault, Jongleur, for making me laugh like that.' He chuckled again. 'Secondsong. I'll have to remember that one.' The servants began to breathe again, and the tension bled from the air.

The hunting lodge was a small fortress, built on high ground with thick wardwalls and a full staff year-round. It held a garrison of fifty Wooden Soldiers, and at least two dozen servants and groundskeepers in addition to the score of soldiers in the duke's entourage, along with pages, cooks, and hounds. It even had its own brothel, with comfort women for the soldiers and choicer whores to cater to visiting Royals. Two of these were boys, but their hair and face powders made them seem as women at a glance.

'Disgusting,' Sament said, noticing one of these, but Keerin's eyes lingered, and Rojer knew without a doubt the two would be grunting in the pillows tonight. He wondered if Keerin was the sort to take top or bottom.

Mickael and Pether blamed Rhinebeck for scaring the game, their annoyance only amplified as Rhinebeck held up his prize.

'So Thamos jumps and swings the bow so fast the ripping bolt falls free!' Rhinebeck gesticulated with the drumstick of the rockbird to illustrate his point.

With every retelling of the tale – and there had been many – Rhinebeck added little flourishes with the skill of a Jongleur. He seemed to have internalized the lie entirely.

Everyone had a laugh at Thamos, then. His brothers and their whores, the Milnese, even some of the servants. Gared studied the contents of his cup, and Thamos made a pained sound that the others took for embarrassed laughter.

Rojer, by his nature, wanted to join the merriment. *Never spoil a crowd's good mood*, Arrick had taught, *or act too good to be part of it.*

But over the months he had spent with the man, Rojer had grown to truly like Count Thamos, and could not bring himself to add to his humiliation. He drained his wine instead.

The cooks had done a fine job dressing the prize, but the single rockbird was barely a morsel for a crowd of grown men. Rhinebeck had served it as an appetizer, so all could share in his proud 'victory'. It was gamy and tough, much like the tale they were enduring yet again.

The duke's table was piled with pork, venison, and beef, enough to feed twice the assembled group. Wine flowed freely, and those not drunk already were soon on their way, Rojer included.

Of the royal family, only Thamos had not found company for the pillows, and Rojer caught him watering his wine.

Gared followed his example. He'd withdrawn since the duke

had claimed Thamos' kill. 'You'd think the throne would be enough.'

'My brothers have always been this way.' Thamos' voice was low and tired. 'Time was I would have been the same. My seal was on that bolt, and I would have delighted in showing up Rhiney and the others.' He sighed. 'I might not have cared for the vagabonds in the caravan camps, either. The world looks different since I left Angiers and saw how real folk live.'

He slammed his fist on the table. Rojer glanced around, but the other Royals were making too much noise to notice. 'We're wasting time! To the north Euchor has his eye on kingship of Thesa, and to the south, our enemies mount. People starving all over Angiers, and we're hunting! And doing a poor job of it at that. Just an excuse to get out of the city for more drinking and whoring.'

The count stood. 'I need some air.'

'Going to practise your shooting, brother?' Rhinebeck called, drawing roars of laughter from Mickael and Pether. 'Best be careful, or I'll have to appoint the Wooden Soldiers a new lord commander.'

Thamos grimaced, and Rojer knew the duke had taken it too far. The count was slow to true courage, but he could be reckless when pushed past caring.

'Since your aim is so great, brother, I thought we might dispense with simple game like rockbirds and hunt something worthier.' Thamos looked around the table, catching the eyes of the other men. 'That is, if there are any here man enough to test themselves against real prey.'

There were nervous looks at that, but Rhinebeck had not yet caught on. 'The man who can barely work his bow doubts us? By all means, what shall we hunt? Bear? Nightwolf?'

Thamos crossed his arms. 'On your feet, then. We're going to hunt a rock demon.'

'This is madness,' Rhinebeck said, as they stalked the hills near the hunting fort. It was slow going, for while Rojer, Gared, and Thamos could see perfectly well in wardsight, the others had to rely on lanterns carried by three of the half dozen Wooden Soldiers in their escort. The men carried warded weapons, but they were raw wood, as it was said in the Hollow. Untested against the night.

'You're welcome to go back and cower under the skirts of your favourite whore, brother,' Thamos said, drawing a glare from the duke.

Keerin had done just that, staying behind despite his boasts of bravery. Thamos' brothers no doubt wished they could do the same, but pride would not let them show weakness before their youngest sibling.

Lord Sament had come as well, with two of his Mountain Spears. Like the other Royals, he carried a crank bow and warded quarrels, but unlike the Angierians, Sament had an eager grin on his face.

The group was just small enough for Rojer to cover them with his music.

'Do not drive the demons away,' Thamos told him as they left the safety of the fort's wardwalls. 'Let these men see what we face each night in the Hollow.'

Rojer complied, casting only a thin camouflage over the group, not dissimilar to Leesha's Cloaks of Unsight. The demons could still smell them, hear them, even glimpse the lanterns from the corner of their eyes, but they could not find the source. They prowled at the edge of Rojer's magic, sniffing, searching, but unable to pinpoint their prey.

A flame demon spat in frustration, and Prince Mickael jumped, his deep voice raising to a shriek. The demon caught the sound, head swivelling their way. Wooden Soldiers moved in front of the prince, shields locked and spears ready, but they, too, were shaking in fear.

Thamos glanced back. 'Gared.'

'On it,' the burly Cutter said. He left his massive axe and

machete in their harnesses on his back, balling gauntleted fists. Leesha had warded the gauntlets and infused them with demon bone. He wore only a leather vest and his warded helmet for protection, but Gared strode forward unconcerned.

The demon caught sight of him as he left the protection of the music. It spat fire, but Gared batted at the blast with one hand and it dissipated as it struck the wards. He was upon the creature then, grabbing one of its legs as it tried to scramble out of reach.

The demon might have been fifty pounds, but Gared swung it like a cat with one hand, a smooth arc that brought it over his head and then smashed it back down into the ground. With the breath knocked from it, Gared shifted grip to its throat, pinning it as his gauntleted fist rose and fell, flares of magic flashing in harmony with the spattering sounds and flying ichor.

A pair of stubby stone demons trundled his way, but Gared threw them the flame demon's broken body, and they paused to devour it. By the time they looked up, he had stepped back into Rojer's protective field.

Rhinebeck eyed the stone demons in horror. They were less than five feet tall, but broad, with armour like a conglomerate rock face. He shook like a jelly after someone kicked the table.

Mickael, looking angry at having shrieked in front of the others, spat and raised his crank bow. 'There are our rock demons. Let's shoot them and have done.'

'Pfagh!' Thamos waved a dismissive hand at the stone demons. 'Those are just stone demons. Hardly worthy prey. Rojer?'

Rojer knitted his brows, maintaining the music that kept them concealed, but layering in a suggestion to the stone demons that grew increasingly insistent.

In a moment, it came to a boil. One of the stone demons struck the other, literally breaking its face as the armour shattered.

The demon reeled, then caught itself and struck back in kind as the first one pressed its attack. They crashed to the ground, rolling back and forth as they pounded each other with great stone fists. At last one lay still. The other attempted to rise, but its leg was shattered, and it fell back, unmoving.

'Is it dead?' Sament asked.

Thamos shook his head. 'Demons heal quickly. They'll recover from anything that doesn't kill them outright.'

Sament grunted, raising his crank bow and putting a bolt into the demon's eye. There was a flare of magic as it blasted through the other side of the demon's skull, but in the wardlight they saw other demons approaching.

'We're attracting them,' Pether noted. His tone was flat, but Rojer could sense the hint of panic beneath.

'Of course,' Thamos said. 'And we'll need to do even more if we mean to draw a full-sized rock demon to us.'

'Are we hunters, or bait?' Rhinebeck demanded. 'Because it sounds more and more like you're risking all our lives just to salve your injured pride.'

'Rojer, drive them back.' Thamos pointed to one of the Wooden Soldiers. 'Bring the lantern.' In its light, he pointed to a rock demon print in the dirt, as long as a man's arm. 'We've been tracking this demon for the last half hour. It rose two miles back, where a mudslide uncovered a slice of bedrock.'

'Night,' Lord Sament said, putting his own booted foot in the print and marvelling at the difference. 'It must be fifteen feet tall.'

'Twenty, at least,' Gared cut in, grinning. He so loved to make the raw wood squirm. He held a hand flat above his seven-foot frame. 'Horns taller'n me.'

Rhinebeck let out a slight whine, the crank bow shaking so noticeably in his hands that those in his immediate vicinity took a step back, watching it warily.

The others weren't much better. Mickael was squeezing his crank bow so hard Rojer thought the wood might crack, and Pether appeared to be uttering the first sincere prayer of his life. Even the soldiers in their escort looked ready to soil their fine wooden armour, clutching their spears tight.

Lord Sament looked at them in disgust. 'Is this the courage Angiers wants Miln to ally with? If we send men to fight the Krasians, will you fight shoulder-to-shoulder with them, or cower at their backsides?'

It was an unexpected slap from the previously mild lord, but the naked night had a way of bringing out the truth in a man. The words startled the elder brothers and men-at-arms back to the present.

Thamos pointed to where a pair of ridges formed a narrow pass, gently outlined in the clear light of the gibbous moon. A handful of stunted trees grew high on the steep slopes, naked of leaves in the late season.

'Those trees are too sparse to have drawn any wood demons,' Thamos said. 'Sament, take your Mountain Spears to the northern slope. Brothers, you take the southern.'

'And where will you be, brother?' Rhinebeck's tone made clear there would be a reckoning if they made it home. Rojer feared Thamos had pushed too far.

But if Thamos understood the damage he had done, he showed no sign. His blood was up, and every Hollower knew what that meant.

'Behind those rocks,' Thamos pointed, 'until Rojer lures the demon into the pass. He will take position at the far end, while we move in to the rear with a spear wall to prevent it from escaping the pass while you shoot.'

'Don't spare the quarrels,' Gared noted. 'This is a twenty-foot rock, not some stone demon you can put down with a bolt or two. Even if every shot's perfect, your first volley's just going to piss it off. You'll need to empty your quivers and turn its head into a ripping pincushion.'

'I think I'm going to slosh,' one of the Wooden Soldiers said. Everyone looked as he slapped a hand to his mouth, heaving.

'Sergeant . . . Mese, isn't it?' Thamos asked. The man nodded, eyes wide and cheeks distended with bile.

'Spit it out or swallow, Sergeant,' Thamos said. 'No one's dying tonight if they keep their heads and do as they're told.'

The man nodded, and Rojer had to suppress a heave himself as Mese scrunched his face and swallowed his half-digested dinner back down.

Gared, Thamos, and the Wooden Soldiers moved behind the rocks while the others climbed into position along the ridges. Even with his wardsight Rojer could not make out the men hidden in the trees, which meant the demon would not see them, either. They flashed their lanterns and Rojer raised his fiddle, lifting his chin to let the magic of the instrument send his call far into the night.

It was answered immediately. As Thamos had intended, the sounds of battle had attracted its attention, and the rock was already headed their way. It was a simple matter to lure it along the chosen path.

Minutes later, the demon moved into view, brushing trees aside like houseplants. Its legs were like columns of black marble, and Rojer could feel the ground shake with each footfall.

Rojer adjusted his melody, entrancing the creature as he backed towards the narrow pass. When he was confident the coreling was mesmerized, he turned and moved deeper into the pass, trusting it to follow.

Thamos had chosen the ground well. It would be difficult for the Royals to miss at such range, and the kill would give them all much-needed confidence.

When he was safely out of the line of fire, Rojer altered his melody again, pushing back at the demon instead of drawing it on. As the great beast stood dazed, Thamos set off a flare that lit the night, illuminating the demon clearly.

There was a thrumming from the north, and Rojer's warded eyes saw the Milnese quarrels streak magic through the air and sizzle into the demon's head and neck. It shrieked in pain, and Rojer lost all control of it. He lowered his fiddle and wrapped his Cloak of Unsight about himself to wait.

Another round of bolts flew from the Milnese. Rojer could hear their excited shouts as the quarrels struck home.

But nothing yet from the duke and his brothers. What were they waiting for? Were they too spoiled to work the cranks on their own bows?

As Gared had predicted, the first bolts only angered the great demon. Mad with pain, it rushed Rojer's way in a desperate bid to escape the trap. Rojer brought up his fiddle, loud and discordant, driving it back.

Blocked, the demon ran the other way as the Milnese continued to fire. What were the Royals waiting for?

The count gave a great cry, he and Gared anchoring the shield wall as the rock demon charged their position. They drove into the demon, attempting to send it stumbling back into the killing ground.

But having taken only half the fire, the demon was stronger than anticipated, the pain of its wounds giving it a savage strength. The warded shields knocked it back a step, but the demon kept its balance and smashed a giant fist down on the hard ground, shaking two of the Wooden Soldiers from their feet. A lash of its tail into the breach broke one man's leg, and scattered the others.

With the battle joined, the bowmen could not fire without chancing to hit the men. Only Gared and Thamos kept control. The count rushed to put himself between the rock demon and the injured man, driving it back with measured thrusts of his spear.

Mese moved to stand beside Thamos. The rock fought wildly, but not so much that it gave openings the warriors could exploit.

While the attention was on them, Gared circled around, bashing the demon in the back of one knee with his axe. Its leg collapsed and it fell, catching itself with a clawed arm. The great horned head dipped within reach of Thamos' charging spear.

But then another shriek, this one from above as a wind

demon swept in, taking a screaming Mese in its hind talons. The lacquered wooden plates of his warded armour glowed fiercely, keeping the claws from puncturing, but they did not protect him from the squeeze as it gripped tighter and spread its wings with a great flap. In an instant, it would take to the sky and Mese would be gone.

Thamos changed course without missing a beat, sacrificing the killing blow to save the soldier. He seemed to bounce as he twisted to face the new threat, launching his spear just as the wings caught air and the coreling began to rise.

The count had allotted for the ascent, punching his powerfully warded spear through the demon's chest when it was a dozen feet in the air. It went limp, crashing back to the ridge with Mese shouting but very much alive.

The distraction cost Thamos as the recovered rock demon swiped at him, catching the edge of his shield and launching him through the air to land heavily on his back. The demon gave a roar, launching itself at him.

It would have had the count, but Gared roared and brought his axe down, severing the spiked end of its tail. Spewing ichor, the tail cracked like a whip, knocking Gared from his feet.

Their sights momentarily clear, the Milnese risked another volley, stinging the demon and giving time for Thamos to snatch the spear Mese had dropped. Rojer looked to the south ridge, but there was no sign the Angierians were even there.

Thamos bellowed a challenge to draw the demon's attention from Gared. It hesitated, then struck at him, a measured blow Thamos caught on his shield as he continued to advance.

He had the demon's full attention now, and it was unprepared as the other Wooden Soldiers, led by Sergeant Mese himself, found their hearts and charged in.

Bright with magic, Gared was healing even before he rolled to his feet. He moved in with the angry stride Rojer knew meant the fight had become personal.

He almost pitied the demon.

As Thamos and the others harried the demon back, Gared

swung his axe two-handed, the Baron of Cutter's Hollow chopping wedges from the demon's knee like it was a goldwood tree. In moments he severed the joint entirely, and the demon fell with a boom that shook the entire hill.

And then, a streak of light from the south, followed quickly by several more. The demon was prone now, an easy target, and the Angierians quickly emptied their quivers. The demon's head seemed to explode as bolt after bolt struck home.

Back at the hall, they hung the demon's great horns above Rhinebeck's throne in the dining hall, and spent the night drinking and toasting.

Mese fell to one knee before Thamos, holding the count's fine spear across his arms. 'Your spear, Lord Commander.'

Thamos held up a hand. 'I have others. Keep it, *Lieutenant* Mese.'

The man gaped, taking the spear and reverently laying it at the count's feet as he dropped to both knees. 'My spear is always yours, Lord Thamos.'

He lifted his new spear with a shout. 'The lord commander!'

The other soldiers raised their tankards, sloshing ale. 'The lord commander!'

Rhinebeck and his brothers raised their tankards and drank as well, but Rojer could see hatred and jealousy in their eyes as the men chanted Thamos' name.

Thamos looked to Lord Sament. 'This is Angierian courage, brothers. This is what you ally beside. The peace of the Pact and the loss of battle wards made us all soft, but the heart of a warrior lies in every Thesan breast. Unite with us, and we will drive the Krasians back to the sands where they belong.'

Sament crossed his arms. 'Bold words, but what of the Hollow? Will you hold to the Pact as well?'

'The Hollow is mine,' Rhinebeck cut in angrily, 'and will do as I command.'

Thamos gritted his teeth, but he nodded. 'It is as my brother says.'

'Do you have a plan for this glorious attack, Lord Commander, or is this just brash talk?' Sament demanded. 'Euchor will not commit soldiers for the latter.'

Thamos nodded. 'We send an army to make contact with Lakton and link our forces. Come at Docktown from the land even as the ships of Lakton sweep in from deep water. The siege will be crushed between us, and by the time spring thaws the bodies, we will have secured a permanent border.'

'And Rizon?' Sament asked.

'Will not be won in a season, or a year. But when they see the *Sharum* thrown back, the Rizonans will rise up. They outnumber the Krasians, if only they can regain their spirit.'

'Your plan takes a lot on faith, brother,' Rhinebeck said.

'Indeed,' Mickael agreed. 'Do you even know how many of the desert rats there are in Docktown?'

Thamos lost a bit of steam. 'Not precisely . . .'

'You cannot expect Euchor, or *me*, to commit men on such vague planning,' Rhinebeck snapped.

'We have scouts—' Thamos began.

'Not good enough.' Rhinebeck levelled a finger at him. 'You will take fifty Wooden Soldiers south to view the enemy and make contact with the dockmasters personally. We will see what they have to say of your plan.'

Thamos blinked, and Rojer could hear the trap snap shut. The duke was giving him what he wanted, but fifty men to cross unfamiliar enemy territory? It was a suicide mission, and Rojer did not doubt the duke knew it.

Thamos bowed stiffly. 'As you command, brother.'

'I will join you,' Sament said unexpectedly. 'With fifty Mountain Spears.'

Rhinebeck and the other princes looked at him in shock, but the Milnese lord had that eager gleam in his eyes once more, and they knew he meant his words.

'It's settled, then,' Rhinebeck said.

'When do we leave?' Gared asked.

'The morning after the Bachelor's Ball,' Rhinebeck said. 'But only Thamos will be going to Lakton. You, Baron, will choose your prospective new bride at the ball and return home with her. Hollow County is yours until the count returns.'

If he returns, Rojer thought.

21

The Weed Gatherer
333 AR Winter

Amanvah sipped her tea, watching Araine and Leesha coolly. 'Ask,' she said at last.

'Ask what, dear?' Araine asked.

Amanvah set down her cup and saucer. 'Even if the dice had not told me your question, it is obvious, given the gossip in your court.'

Araine did not rise to the bait. 'Do enlighten us.'

'You want to know if I will use the *alagai hora* to determine the cause of the duke's inability to father, and if I can cure him with *hora* magic.'

Araine stared at her for a long time. 'Will you? Can you?'

Amanvah smiled. 'I have already determined the problem, and yes, I *could* cure it.'

'But you won't,' Araine guessed.

'Would you, in my place?' Amanvah asked.

'Why tell us to ask, if you have no intention of helping?' Leesha asked. 'Why cast your dice at all?'

'Even *dama'ting* cannot resist a mystery,' Amanvah said. 'And I have helped you, by telling you it is possible. The rest you will have to learn for yourselves. I am here as Rojer's *Jiwah Ka*, not a spy . . . or a *ginjaz*.'

'*Ginjaz*?' Leesha asked.

'Turncoat.' Araine's face had darkened. 'You're a long way from home, Princess. We may yet convince you.'

Amanvah shook her head. 'Nothing you can offer will change my mind, nor torture pull from my lips what I do not wish you to know. Solve your own problems.'

'If we fail to, you may be handing Angiers to Duke Euchor,' Leesha said. 'He'd declare himself king, and make war upon your people soon after.'

Amanvah shrugged. 'You seek that as well, or you are a coward. It does not matter. My father is the Deliverer. When he returns to claim your people, they will bow to him. I have no interest in your politicking in the meantime.'

'And if your father does not return?' Araine asked in Krasian. 'If the Painted Man killed him in *Domin Sharum*?'

'The dice would have told me if my father was dead,' Amanvah said. 'But if it were so, then the Par'chin is the Deliverer, and your people will be claimed all the same.'

'You don't know Arlen at all, if you think that,' Leesha said. 'He has no interest in thrones.'

'So long as your spears are pledged to him in the night,' Amanvah said. 'As with my father. But deny this, as the Andrah and Duke of Rizon did, and the Deliverer will take them from you.'

'You'll forgive me,' Araine said, 'if I need more convincing than that before I hand over my duchy to an invading army, or a farm boy from a hamlet the size of my sitting room.'

Amanvah bowed. 'It is not my place to convince you, Duchess. It is *inevera*.'

'Is that Everam's will, or your mother's?' Araine asked mildly.

Amanvah gave a gentle shrug of her silk-clad shoulders. 'They are one and the same.'

Araine nodded. 'Thank you for your candour, Princess, and for your help, such as it was. Will you excuse us, now? I wish to speak to Mistress Leesha in private.'

'Of course,' Amanvah said, her tone and bearing making it seem her own idea to leave as she rose and glided from the room.

Wonda peeked her head in as the woman left. 'Need anythin'?'

'All is well, Wonda, thank you,' Araine said before Leesha could speak. 'Please see we are not disturbed.'

'Ay, Mum.' Wonda seemed to nod with her whole body as she backed out and closed the door.

'Insufferable woman,' Araine muttered.

'Wonda?' Leesha asked.

Araine waved in irritation. 'Of course not. The sand witch.'

Leesha dipped a biscuit in her tea. 'You don't know the half.'

'Can we trust her?' Araine asked.

'Who can say?' Leesha lifted the biscuit, but she had soaked it too long and the end broke off in the cup. 'This is the same woman who slipped blackleaf into my tea on her mother's orders.'

Araine raised an eyebrow at that. 'No wonder you've a distaste for weeds. So she's more interested in politicking than she claims.'

'She's more than she claims,' Leesha agreed, 'though she's proven trustworthy enough since marrying Rojer. I don't think she's lying now, but neither do I think we have the whole truth. She may have hinted us toward a cure because the dice tell her it will weaken the North to keep the duchies divided. Or hidden the cause of Rhinebeck's problem because Euchor will overreach and bring civil war to Thesa even as the Krasians press north.'

Araine squeezed lemon into her tea, though it seemed her mouth could wrinkle no farther than it already had. 'I don't suppose you can make a set of these dice yourself?'

Leesha shook her head. 'Even if we stole a proper set, I haven't a clue how to read them. It takes years of study, as I understand it, and is more art than science.'

Araine sighed. 'Then for all our sakes, I hope you can succeed where every other Gatherer in my employ has failed. It's pointless to guess at prophecies, even if I believed in such things.'

Leesha awoke with a start at the knocking. Her face was numb, and as she rubbed it she could feel the imprint of the book she had fallen asleep on. There was drool on the pages.

What time was it? The room was dark save for the glow of the chemical lamp on her table, illuminating the pile of books of old world medicine she had been studying. Wonda had turned down the lamps when she retired.

The knocking came again.

Leesha cinched her dressing gown tightly as she went to the door, but she had put on weight in recent months, and it strained in the front. She clutched the top in one hand to keep it closed.

Who could it be? She thought to call for Wonda, but they were in the centre of the palace, with guards everywhere. If she wasn't safe here, she wasn't safe anywhere.

But her free hand slipped into her pocket, clutching her *hora* wand as she let go her gown to open the door.

Rojer stood there, and looking haggard. 'We need to talk.'

Leesha relaxed instinctively, but Rojer had a look about him that filled her with dread. What was he doing back so soon? Everyone had expected the duke and his entourage to be away in the hunting lodge a week at least, but they had been gone but a single night.

'Is everything all right?' Leesha felt her chest constrict. 'Is Thamos . . .'

'He's fine,' Rojer said. 'He led the party to bring down a rock demon last night. Hunting rockbirds and boar had little allure after that, and I think everyone wanted to be back in the city to ponder what they saw.'

Leesha breathed out her sudden panic. Thamos had sworn not to wed her with another man's child in her belly, but with Araine's support, she had begun to hope once more. If anything happened to him . . .

'Mistress Leesha?' Wonda was in the doorway to her chambers, rubbing sleep from her face. The knife in her hand was the size of Leesha's forearm. 'Heard voices. You okay?'

'Fine, Wonda,' Leesha said. 'It's only Rojer. Go back to bed.'

The woman nodded, her shoulders drooping as she turned to stumble back to her pillow.

Leesha opened the door to admit Rojer, and he walked in a little too swiftly, jerking his head this way and that as his eyes searched the room. 'Is anyone else here?'

'Of course not,' Leesha said. 'Who else . . .'

Rojer looked decidedly uneasy. 'Thamos hasn't been to see you?'

'No,' Leesha said. 'Why? You're scaring me, Rojer. What's happened?'

Rojer shook his head. His voice was so low she could barely hear. 'Ears everywhere.'

Leesha frowned, but she went to the jewellery box where she kept her *hora*, opening small drawers to take the appropriate bones. These she arranged in a circle around two chairs. She slipped her warded spectacles on, making sure the wards linked and the circle activated.

'There.' She picked up the servant's bell and moved to the circle, reaching her arm past the wards and ringing the bell vigorously. She saw the clapper strike, felt the vibration, but neither she nor Rojer heard a sound.

She took a seat, waiting for Rojer to join her. 'Not a sound will pass through the circle. We can scream at the top of our lungs, and Wonda will keep snoring twenty feet away. Now what's so secret you couldn't even whisper it in an empty room?'

Rojer blew out a breath. 'I think Rhinebeck and his brothers tried to kill Thamos last night.'

Leesha blinked. 'You *think*?'

'It was a . . . passive attempt.' Rojer quickly related how the duke's group had held their fire when the battle seemed to be going against Thamos, only shooting when victory seemed assured. 'They didn't try to hurt him themselves, but from where I stood, they seemed content to let the demons do the job for them.'

'There must be some other explanation,' Leesha said. 'Perhaps there was a problem with their weapons.'

'All of them?' Rojer asked. 'At the same time?'

Leesha huffed. It did seem unlikely. 'But he's their brother, and far removed from the throne. Why would they want him dead?'

'Not so far as all that,' Rojer said. 'The royal families of Angiers are still stung from Rhinebeck the First's coup two generations ago. If the duke dies without an heir, neither Mickael nor Pether will hold the throne without bloodshed, especially with the Milnese buying up allies throughout the city.'

'And you think it will be different for Thamos?' Leesha asked.

'Thamos has his own army,' Rojer noted. 'One already bigger and better trained than his elder brother's. At the rate the Hollow's growing, it may soon be a match for Angiers and Miln combined. And Thamos is a hero, with more than one song to his name. Rhinebeck was too petty to even let his brother claim his own rockbird kill. How do you think he felt when Thamos shamed him in front of the other men?'

Leesha felt a stab of pain and looked down. She kept her nails short so they would not interfere in her work, but they were still enough to dig into her skin when she clenched her fists tightly enough. She forced herself to relax. 'Have you spoken of this to anyone else?'

Rojer shook his head. 'Who would I tell? I don't think Thamos would believe me even if I told him, and Gared . . .'

'Would do something stupid,' Leesha agreed.

'There's already been stupid to spare,' Rojer said. 'I haven't told you all.'

'Those idiots!' Araine clenched her fists, pacing with the strength and speed of a much younger woman.

'What are you going to do?' Leesha asked, when the old woman finally slowed.

'What *can* I do?' Araine demanded. 'I have no evidence but

your Jongleur's word, and Rhinebeck is duke. Once he sets his mind on something he can be stubborn as a rock demon, and I don't have the power to overrule him.'

'But you're his mother,' Leesha said. 'Can't you . . .'

Araine raised an eyebrow. 'Use my magic mother powers? How often do you listen to yours?'

'Not often,' Leesha admitted. 'And I usually come to regret it when I do. But Thamos is your son, too. Can you not beseech—'

'Believe me, girl,' Araine cut her off, 'I'm not above playing every guilt and wile in my considerable repertoire to get my sons to alter course, but this . . . this is pride, and no man lets that go without a spear at his throat.'

She began to pace again, but it was slow, stately. She reached up, stroking her wrinkled chin. 'He probably thinks himself quite clever. If Thamos is killed, he has one less rival. If Thamos succeeds and makes contact with the Laktonians, he can take credit for the whole thing.' She snorted. 'It's the closest Rhinebeck's ever come to an attempt at espionage.'

She turned to look at Leesha, and smiled. 'But just because we can't stop it doesn't mean we can't turn it against him.'

'Oh?' Leesha asked.

'Rhiney and the others have never attempted espionage because they've never needed to. Janson gives them information, and they've never once asked where it comes from.'

Leesha felt a smile tug at the corner of her mouth. 'You have contacts in Lakton?'

'I have contacts everywhere,' Araine said. 'The dockmistress of Docktown was a friend of mine, did you know? Your Ahmann Jardir's eldest son tried to force her to marry him when they took the city.'

'Tried?' Leesha asked.

Araine chuckled. 'She put his eye out with the quill from the marriage contract, they say.' Her face went cold. 'When he was finished with her, they say the lump of meat that was left barely looked human.'

Leesha remembered Jayan. Remembered the savage gleam in his eyes. She wanted to disbelieve, but it was all too plausible.

'We need the Krasians out of Docktown,' Araine said, 'if we're to take back the duchy and press them back to Rizon.'

'Everam's Bounty,' Leesha said. 'I've seen those lands, Duchess. The Krasians are entrenched. It will never be Rizon again.'

'Don't be so sure of that,' Araine said. 'I've been funding Rizonan rebels for months, and they've begun quite a bit of mischief. The Krasians in Lakton will be looking over their shoulders as their "safe" lands burn. They won't see us coming.'

'So Thamos has a chance?' Leesha asked.

'I won't lie and say it's a safe path, girl,' Araine said. 'I know you love him, but he's my son, and the only one worth a damn. He'll be in danger the entire time, but I'll see he has every advantage I can.'

'So now what?' Leesha asked.

'Now,' Araine said, 'you get back to work curing my eldest.'

'You can't possibly expect me to—' Leesha began.

'I can and you will!' Araine snapped. 'Our circumstances with Miln have not changed. Even if Thamos comes back alive and well, he will always be in danger so long as the ivy throne has no heir.'

She waved a hand. 'Let my sons bicker and plot. If we can unite with Lakton and force Euchor into the pact, the ivy and metal thrones won't be worth a klat. The Hollow will be the new capital of Thesa, and Thamos . . .

'Why, Thamos could be king.'

Leesha was distracted throughout dinner. It was her first in Jizell's hospit for quite some time, but the place still felt like home. Jizell and her apprentices had been fixtures about the Hollow the last weeks, and the others, even Sikvah, seemed similarly at ease.

'Delicious, as always,' Rojer thanked Mistress Jizell. 'Every man in Angiers laments he could not take you to wife.'

'A wise man never marries a Herb Gatherer,' Jizell replied, winking. 'There's no telling what she'll put in his tea, eh?'

Amanvah laughed at that, and Rojer smiled. 'That's what Mistress Jessa used to say.'

Jizell's face went sour. 'Both got it from Bruna, if not much else.'

'I'm getting tired of this,' Rojer said. 'Mistress Jessa was never anything but good to me, and if you're going to talk ill of her, I want to know why.'

'So do I,' Leesha said.

'She's a Weed Gatherer,' Jizell said. 'What more is there to say?'

'Ay, what of it?' Rojer snapped. 'I don't see the ripping difference. You both threaten to drug my tea, and mean it.'

'Ay, a Herb Gatherer will use her skill to bully someone that needs bullying,' Jizell said. 'But their primary purpose is to heal and help. Weed Gatherers are the other way around.'

'Not to mention they're all whores,' Vika said.

'Vika!' Leesha snapped.

Vika stiffened, but she did not back down. 'Apologies, Mistress Leesha, but it's honest word. Almost every brothel in the city is run by a Weed Gatherer. Usually apothecary shops with rooms upstairs where they sell more than cures.'

'Most of them were apprentices of Mistress Jessa at one time or another,' Jizell said, 'and she takes a cut. Richest woman in the city short of the Duchess Mum, but it's dirty money, earned off the marriages they destroy.'

Kadie brought the tea, and Jizell paused to add honey, stirring thoughtfully. 'Bruna had already taken me on as apprentice and did not want another, but Duchess Araine insisted she take Jessa as well. The girl was gifted, but less interested in healing than aphrodisiacs and poison. Little did we know Araine was grooming her to run a private brothel for her sons. A way for them to remain under her control even when they were out being men.'

'It is why the *dama'ting* created the *jiwah'Sharum*,' Amanvah noted, 'though my people honour such women, and accept the children they bear.'

'Well not here,' Jizell said. 'Men can't be expected to keep to their wives when there's a brothel in every part of town. You can blame the drunk for pissing on your doorstep, but it's the bartender who put the drink in their hand.'

'And that's why Bruna cast her out?' Leesha asked.

Jizell shook her head. 'She wanted the recipe for liquid demonfire. When Bruna refused to teach it to her, she tried to steal it.'

Leesha's eyes widened. Any Gatherer worth the name knew something of the secrets of fire, but Bruna had claimed to be the last to know how to create that infernal brew. The old woman had kept it close for more than a hundred years, never teaching it to her apprentices. It was only when she felt the knowledge might be lost forever that she decided to teach it to Leesha.

'Why did you never tell me any of this before?' Leesha asked.

'Because it didn't concern you,' Jizell said. 'But now, if you have to deal with that lying witch . . .'

'I think it's time I met Mistress Jessa,' Leesha said.

'We can go now, if you like,' Rojer said. 'Set this whole thing to rest.'

'Isn't it a bit late?' Leesha asked. 'The sun is long set.'

Rojer laughed. 'They're only just stirring now, and expecting guests until the dawn.'

Leesha turned to him. 'You mean to take us to the brothel?'

Rojer shrugged. 'Of course.'

'Can't we just meet at her home?' Leesha asked.

'That *is* her home,' Rojer said.

'Now just a minute!' Gared said. 'Can't be taking women to a place like that!'

'Why not?' Rojer asked. 'It's full of women anyway.'

Gared blushed, balling one of his giant fists. 'Ent taking Leesha to some . . . some . . .'

'Gared Cutter!' Leesha snapped. 'You may be a baron now, but I won't have you telling me where I can and can't go!'

Gared looked at her in surprise. 'I was just . . .'

'I know what you were doing,' Leesha cut in. 'Your heart's in the right place, but your mouth isn't. I'll go where I please, and that goes for Wonda, too.'

'This should be fun,' Kendall said. 'I know a dozen songs about Angierian whorehouses, but I never thought I'd get to see one.'

'And you shan't. A *heasah* pillow house is no place for *Jiwah Sen*,' Amanvah glanced at Coliv, 'or *Sharum*.'

'Ay, Wonda gets to go!' Kendall started, but Sikvah hissed at her, and she fell back with a huff, crossing her arms.

Amanvah turned to Rojer. 'But you would think your *Jiwah Ka* a fool, husband, if you think I will let you enter such a place without me.'

To Leesha's surprise, Rojer bowed to his wife. 'Of course. Please know that I was a child in my time there, and a child only. It was never a place of passion for me.'

Amanvah nodded. 'And it never shall be.'

'Dama'ting, I must . . .' Coliv began.

'You must do as you are told, *Sharum*.' Amanvah's voice was cold. 'I have cast the *alagai hora*. I am in no danger this night.' The Watcher did not protest further.

'No carriages,' Rojer said, as they exited Jizell's hospit from the rear entrance.

Leesha looked at him curiously. 'Why not? There's no law that says we can't ride at night.'

'Ay, but none actually do,' Rojer said. 'Our passage will be noticed, and we're going someplace we've no business going.'

'I thought you said the brothel was a secret,' Leesha said. 'If no one knows it's there . . .'

'Then they'll see Hollower carriages at the doors of Mistress

Jessa's Finishing School for Talented Young Ladies,' Rojer said. 'Which will be curiouser still.'

'What's a finishing school?' Wonda asked.

'A place where young women are taught how to hook rich husbands,' Rojer said.

Indeed, the boardwalk was empty as Leesha, Wonda, Amanvah, and Gared followed Rojer along the twisting streets of Angiers, cutting through alleyways and keeping to the shadows.

Not that there were many places they could be spotted. There were no wardlights, and the streetlamps were few and far between, save in the most affluent neighbourhoods.

They moved swiftly in spite of the darkness, seeing more clearly in wardsight than they did in day. All of them wore Cloaks of Unsight save Amanvah, who had stitched the wards in silver into her robes.

'Eerie, how quiet it is,' Wonda noted. 'Shops'd still be open in the Hollow this time of night.'

'The Hollow doesn't have holes in its wardnet big enough to let wind demons in,' Rojer said. 'Only ones out on the street tonight are guards, us, and the homeless.'

'Homeless?' Wonda asked. 'You mean they put poor folk out at night?'

'More like won't let them in, but ay,' Rojer said. 'I thought it just the way of things, growing up here. Wasn't till I started playing the hamlets that I saw how evil it was.'

As if on cue, there was a crack and part of the wardnet above flared to life. A wind demon had flown too low, bouncing off the wards. The lines of protection spiderwebbed like lightning through the sky for just an instant, but Leesha could see holes big enough for the demon to fit.

The demon saw them, too. It hovered, great leathern wings flapping powerfully as it recovered from the shock. Then it dove, cutting cleanly through the net and sweeping down through the streets, searching for prey.

Leesha itched to draw her *hora* wand and destroy it, but if they worried carriages might advertise their presence, a blast of magic would shout it.

Yet neither could the demon be allowed to hunt. 'Wonda.'

'Ay, mistress,' Wonda said. She looked around a moment, then set off at a run for a rain barrel by the eave of a building. She leapt, foot barely seeming to touch the edge of the barrel as she used it to leap and catch the lip of the slanted roof, pulling herself up effortlessly and running up the roof as she slipped the bow from her shoulders.

She gave a call, so much like a wind demon's that the people huddling behind their warded shutters would take no notice. The demon heard and banked hard, coming for her.

Wonda stood steady, arrow pulled back to her ear as the demon approached. It seemed almost upon her when she loosed, warded arrow flaring with magic as it punched through the demon's chest. It crumpled, falling hard to the boardwalk in front of them.

'Gared,' Leesha said as Wonda made her way back down. 'Please make sure it's dead, and find a trough to leave the body in so it doesn't start a fire when the sun strikes it.'

'On it,' Gared said.

He went over to the demon, but it didn't so much as twitch as he yanked out Wonda's arrow. There was no trough or fountain to be had, so he was forced to hack the demon apart and stuff it in the rain barrel. Wonda went to the pool of ichor in the street, placing her hands in it and shivering as her black-stem wards absorbed the power. The demon's blood would continue to reek, but it would not burn in the sun.

Wonda looked up, her eyes bright as the night strength filled her. 'Want me to keep huntin', mistress, in case there's more?'

'I'd feel safer if you stayed with me,' Leesha said. It was true enough, but she also wanted to limit Wonda's intake of magic until she better understood the effects.

They quickly moved to the inner city, not far from Rhinebeck's palace. The streets here were brightly lit with lamps and patrolled by city guard, but these were evaded with relative ease.

'We're practically back at the palace,' Leesha said.

'Of course,' Rojer said. 'The brothel is connected to the palace by a series of tunnels, so the Duke and his favoured courtiers can have private access, day and night.'

They turned a corner, and there it stood, Mistress Jessa's Finishing School for Talented Young Ladies. It was a grand building, with two wings around a central tower, three floors aboveground. The wards on the tower and building were strong, Leesha saw, carved deep and lacquered hard, polished to shine. The lampposts along the street were warded as well. If the walls of the city fell, the school would be as safe from corelings as the palace itself.

Rojer went boldly to the door, pulling the silk bell rope. Leesha could only assume it worked – they heard nothing outside. A moment later, the door swung open, revealing a giant of a man. He was not as tall as Gared, but broader, with a bull's neck that strained the collar of his fine lace shirt and thick arms threatening to tear the seams of his velvet jacket. His face was crooked, with a nose obviously broken more than once. There was a hint of grey in his hair, but it made him only seem more seasoned. A polished baton hung from his belt in easy reach.

'I don't know you.' It was a simple statement, but the man's tone made it a threat.

'Don't you, Jax?' Rojer asked, throwing back his cloak. 'I've grown some, but I'm still the boy you used to throw so high I could catch the rafters.'

The man blinked. 'Rojer?'

Before Rojer could finish nodding, the man gave a whoop and thrust his hands into Rojer's armpits, swinging him through the air. Gared tensed, but then Rojer laughed, and he relaxed.

'Come in, come in!' Jax said, waving them quickly inside and glancing about before closing the door.

'Caught one of your shows, summer before last,' Jax told

Rojer. 'Mistress and I hid in the crowd and watched. Had both of us in tears by the end.' There was a choke to the big man's voice that seemed incompatible with his huge, menacing frame.

'You should have said.' Rojer punched his arm, but if he felt it, the big man did not react.

Jax pointed a finger at him. 'And you shouldn't have waited so long to visit. You really the Painted Man's fiddle wizard now?'

'Ay.' Rojer nodded to his companions. 'I'm here to make introductions for the Hollowers to Mistress Jessa. Is she available?'

'For you?' Jax asked. 'Of course. Gotta move quick, though. Getting late. Royals will start arriving any time now.'

He led them two stories down a grand spiral staircase covered in red velvet. There was a hallway at the landing, but Jax ignored it, turning instead to push aside a great double bookshelf. It slid smoothly on a wheeled track, revealing an archway covered in heavy laced curtains.

The shelf slid back into place as they passed through the curtain, opening up into an opulent chamber filled with beautiful women. They lounged on soft couches or in semiprivate curtained chambers, ready for the night's custom. All were dressed in beautiful gowns, their faces powdered and their hair artfully arranged. The scent of perfume permeated the air.

'Creator,' Gared said. 'Think I've died and gone to Heaven.'

Leesha gave him a dim look, and he dropped his eyes. 'And to think it was *me* you were worried about coming here.'

The centre of the room had a ceiling two stories high, but around the periphery was a mezzanine presumably leading to private chambers. Jax led them quickly up a staircase to the balcony and through a curtained arch.

Leesha heard sounds below as they passed through, peeking from the curtain to see Prince Mickael arrive with an entourage of men. Her heart thumped in her chest as she quickly closed the curtain.

'I hope there's more than one way out of here,' she said as she joined the others waiting as Jax went to fetch his mistress.

'More than you can count,' Rojer said with a wink.

'Little Rojer Halfgrip!' came a call a moment later, and a woman appeared from a door at the end of the hall.

Jessa was of an age with Jizell – in her fifties at least. But where Jizell had put on the weight of years, Jessa's gown still cinched tight around a tiny waist, and the bosom spilling from the low cut was still smooth and inviting. Her face was painted, but she was beautiful still, with only a few carefully concealed wrinkles to belie her years.

'She reminds me of my mother,' Leesha said, to no one in particular.

'Yuh,' Gared agreed, though from the look in his eyes, he obviously did not think it a bad thing. Leesha wondered if she should send him to wait upstairs. And if he would go if she tried.

Amanvah seemed to be thinking the same thing. She stepped between Gared and the woman as Rojer moved to embrace her.

Jessa tsked as she held him to her bosom. 'It's been over ten years, Rojer. Practically nursed you at my own paps, and you can't trouble yourself to visit?'

'Don't think the duke would have approved,' Rojer said. He pulled back, and Leesha saw his eyes were wet. Whatever her feelings towards the Weed Gatherer, it was clear Rojer loved the woman.

'Let me look at you,' she said, lifting his arms wide and taking a step back as if they were in a dance.

She looked him up and down. 'You've grown into a fine figure of a man. I'll bet you've broken as many hearts as Arrick.'

Rojer backed away, rubbing at the medallion on his chest as he cleared his throat. 'Mistress Jessa, may I present my *wife*, Dama'ting Amanvah asu Ahmann am'Jardir am'Kaji.'

Jessa's smile was bright as she moved to embrace Amanvah, but the young *dama'ting* took a step back.

'Eh?' Jessa asked.

'Apologies, mistress,' Amanvah said, 'but you are unclean, and may not touch me.'

'Amanvah!' Rojer shouted.

'It's all right,' Jessa said, holding up a hand to him, but never taking her eyes off Amanvah. 'Am I to apologize for my immodesty? Should I cover my bosom and my hair?'

Amanvah waved a hand. '*Jiwah'Sharum* wear with honour clothing far less modest than yours. I am not offended by your immodesty.'

'Then what is it?' Jessa asked.

'You are the one that brews the tea of pomm leaves that turns your *heasah* into *kha'ting*, are you not?' Amanvah asked. 'You shame them and weaken your tribe by denying these women the children that come from their unions.'

'Better they not know the fathers of their children?' Jessa asked. 'Better they be unwed mothers before their twentieth year? My girls graduate and return to their lives richer and equipped to find proper society husbands and bear children of rank.'

'So they go to their husbands known to man?' Amanvah pressed.

Leesha cleared her throat, a not-so-subtle reminder about Sikvah, who had not been a virgin when she and Rojer were introduced. Amanvah did not acknowledge the sound, but Leesha regretted the move as Jessa smiled in victory.

'Had a bit of a taste yourself, before you found Rojer?' the Weed Gatherer asked.

Amanvah stiffened. Leesha could see the flare of anger in her aura, hot and dangerous, but she held her outer composure. 'I am a Bride of Everam, but I went to my husband pure and unknown to mortal man as a *Jiwah Ka* should. Rojer knew and accepted that his *Jiwah Sen* had not.'

Rojer stepped forward at the words, reaching out to take Amanvah's hand. She turned to him sharply, but the tenderness in his eyes surprised her, confusion flowing across the anger in her aura.

Rojer reached his free hand up, gently smoothing a lock of hair back into her headscarf. 'I would have accepted you, too, Amanvah vah Ahmann am'Jardir am'Kaji. Don't care about any of that. Don't care about anything. I loved you the moment you first began to sing to me, and I don't think I'll ever stop.'

The confusion left Amanvah's aura, replaced with feelings so intimate Leesha felt ashamed for looking. She removed her warded spectacles, but even in her normal vision there were tears in the young priestess' eyes as she and Rojer embraced.

Jessa watched them, and there was a moist gleam in her eyes as well. She turned away to give them privacy, stepping over to Wonda. 'And you are?'

'Wonda Cutter, mistress,' Wonda said with a bow. The hair she wore over one side of her face to hide her scars waved with the motion.

The mistress lifted a hand. 'May I?'

Wonda hesitated, but nodded. Jessa reached to brush the hair aside as tenderly as Rojer had Amanvah's. She traced the scars with her fingers, and tsked.

'You could hide them better, child, with a bit of makeup,' Jessa said. 'I can have one of my girls teach you how, free of charge.'

'Ay?' Wonda asked.

'Of course,' Jessa said. 'But my advice? Stop hiding them. Be who you are.'

Wonda shook her head. 'Ent no one wants to kiss a mess o' scars.'

Jessa laughed. 'Let me tell you a secret. For every ten men put off by your scars, one will dream of kissing you, just because you're different. Stand tall, and the men will come to you. Women, too, if you've a taste for that.'

'I . . . Ah . . .' Wonda squirmed. Jessa gave another great laugh and let her off the hook.

She lifted Wonda's hand, looking at the wards painted there. 'Blackstem?'

'Ay,' Wonda said.

'A shame you did not bring this Painted Man everyone's talking about. The girls all have bets on whether he's tattooed his cock.'

She left Wonda to sputter at that, turning to Gared. 'Ah, but this is nearly as good. The bachelor himself!' She reached out boldly to squeeze Gared's biceps. 'Sunny thing Jax brought you up here quickly. All the girls would be offering freebies, and no brothel can afford that.'

As if on cue, the curtain parted and a young woman entered, carrying a delicate tea service. Like the others downstairs, she was dressed in a full gown, but her shoulders were bare and her neckline low. The gown was slit high on one side, hidden by the ruffles of her skirt. Each time she stepped that leg forward, there was a momentary flash of thigh. She was tall, and had a bit of meat to her limbs – dancer's muscle.

She smiled at Gared, giving him a little wink, and the Baron of Cutter's Hollow, who faced rock demons without flinching, turned bright red.

Jessa snapped her fingers right next to Gared's face, startling him back to attention. 'But no, the Duchess Mum has plans for you, boy, and she wants you pent. All the girls know you're off limits, even if they're not happy about it.'

She looked at the girl. 'Pour the tea and vanish, Rosal, before the duchess hears of it.' Rosal nodded, moving quickly to a side table and laying out the service.

Jessa winked at Gared. 'Don't be surprised if you see a few of my girls at the Bachelor's Ball. Pick one as Ball Queen, and I can promise you a night to make your head spin. Marry her, and she'll never say no.'

'Sure, Gared,' Leesha said. 'That's all a man needs in a wife.'

Jessa turned a sour look Leesha's way, and everyone tensed. Rojer stepped up to Jessa. 'May I introduce . . .'

'I know who she is,' Jessa said, never taking her eyes off Leesha. Rojer's mouth snapped shut at her tone and he took a step back.

'Little Halfgrip's lovely bride was raised to different customs,'

Jessa said, 'but I'd have expected a student of Bruna to know the way of things better.'

'And just what is that supposed to mean?' Leesha demanded.

'Rosal!' Jessa said. The girl set down the teapot immediately and moved to her side, eyes down.

'Quiz her,' Jessa said. 'What does the wise Mistress Leesha believe are the requirements of the Baroness of Cutter's Hollow?'

Leesha sensed the trap, but she had gone too far and now there was no way forward but to spring it quickly and hope to escape the jaws. She put her spectacles on, examining the girl's aura. 'How old are you, child?'

'I have twenty summers, mistress,' Rosal said.

'How long have you attended Mistress Jessa's school?' Leesha asked.

'Since thirteen summers, mistress,' Rosal said.

'Have you worked in the brothel all that time?' Leesha asked.

There was a flare in the girl's aura. Rosal was scandalized at the notion. 'Of course not, mistress. No girl is allowed downstairs until her eighteenth summer. This is my second and final year. My graduation and debut will be in the spring.' Her eyes flicked to Gared. 'Unless I find a husband at the ball.'

'Can you read?' Leesha asked. 'Write?'

Rosal nodded. 'Yes, mistress. In Krasian, Ruskan, and Albeen.'

'And Thesan, naturally,' Jessa said. 'Rosal is quite the reader.'

'Poems?' Gared asked, the dread in his voice creeping into his aura.

Rosal squeezed her nose as if the notion stank. 'War stories.'

'Military history,' Jessa corrected.

'If one wishes to be dull about it,' Rosal agreed. Her eyes never left the mistresses', but her aura showed her attention was focused solely on impressing Gared. Every word, every pose, was for his benefit. It would have troubled Leesha, but so far as she could tell, the young woman gave honest word.

'Have you had training in mathematics?' Leesha asked.

'Yes, mistress,' Rosal said. 'Arithmetic, algebra, and calculus. We have classes in bookkeeping and inventory, as well.'

'Herb lore?' Leesha asked.

'I can brew the seven cures from memory,' Rosal said. 'For fertility, grind three . . .' Leesha waved her into silence, but not before her words had the intended effect on Gared's aura.

'With books I can prepare others,' Rosal said. 'We all study apothecary, in case men overindulge in powders or spirits while here.'

'Ay, but can she sing?' Rojer laughed, but all the warmth left Amanvah's aura as she glared at him.

'Sorry,' Rojer said. Lower, he added, 'Just trying to lighten the mood.'

The girl shook her head. 'I have never sung well enough for Mistress Jessa, but I can play the harp and the organ.'

'What's an organ?' Gared asked.

Rosal looked at him and winked. 'I can show you mine, if—'

'That's enough of that!' Jizell barked. 'Off with you girl, before I fetch a stick!'

Leesha blinked. How many times had she heard Bruna bark those words? It was like hearing her mentor's voice once more.

But as Jessa watched the girl go, there was no anger in her aura. She was proud of the girl's performance. It was likely no accident that Jax sent Rosal and not some other girl up with the tea.

Gared's eyes followed Rosal, and as she passed through the curtain she gave a tiny wave that sent a shiver through his aura.

Leesha turned back to Jessa, taking her skirt in hand and dipping a curtsy. 'Apologies, mistress. I was unkind.'

'Accepted,' Jessa said at once. 'Now, mistress, would you like to discuss the real reason you're here?'

Mistress Jessa's office was richly appointed with thick carpet and heavy goldwood furniture. There were hundreds of books on her shelves – rare volumes, many of which Leesha had never seen. She had to resist the urge to begin paging through them.

'You may borrow any one,' Jessa said, 'so long as you return it in person before asking for another.'

Leesha looked at her in surprise, and Jessa smiled. 'We started ill, but I want very much for us to be friends, Leesha. Bruna never taught a fool, and Araine thinks the world of you. I've never claimed I could read a person better than those two.'

She smiled. 'And any woman that could hold Thamos' attention for more than a night has got to be special.'

Leesha had been about to smile in turn, but the words chilled her. Jessa was elegant and beautiful, and the mistress of the royal brothel. Had she slept with Thamos? Had any of the girls downstairs? Night, he might have had them all.

Jessa set out a cup and saucer, filling them from a silver tea service that was worth a fortune in metal-poor Angiers.

'The royal brothers visit often,' Jessa noted. 'Rhinebeck and Mickael – even Shepherd Pether has never hesitated to doff his robes here. You'd never know that some of my girls were boys.' Leesha took the cup, willing her hand not to shake.

'But Thamos . . .' Jessa went on. 'Thamos came only once, and never again since. That one always preferred to hunt on his own.'

'And what does that make me?' Leesha asked. 'Prey?'

'In love, both partners can be prey,' Jessa said. 'That's what makes it so delicious.'

'Did you try to steal the recipe for liquid demonfire from Bruna?' Leesha asked.

If Jessa was surprised at her bluntness, there was no sign of it on her aura.

'Ay, I did,' Jessa said. 'The woman was almost ninety, and after the prince was born, she spoke only of returning to the Hollow. I knew I would never see her again, and feared the secret would die with her.'

'Bruna never spoke of you,' Leesha said. 'Not once, in all my years with her.'

Jessa gave a pained smile. 'Ay. None could hold a grudge like Hag Bruna. But I loved her, for my part, and regret we parted ill. When she died, was it . . . quick?'

Leesha stared into her cup. 'I wasn't there. It was a flux that took her. Vika begged her not to go among the sick, told her that she was too weak . . .'

'But nothing could keep Bruna from her children when they were in need,' Jessa said.

'Ay,' Leesha agreed.

'Tried once or twice over the years to patch things up with Jizell,' Jessa said. 'Not as often as I should have, but I was proud, and there was only silence in reply.'

'Jizell can be stubborn as Bruna,' Leesha said.

'And her apprentice?' Jessa asked.

'I have greater concerns than a failed theft, thirty-five years ago,' Leesha said. 'There need be no ill between us.'

'Liquid demonfire isn't even the great power it once was,' Jessa said. 'This desert whore magic makes demonfire seem like flamesticks, I'm told.'

'*Hora* magic,' Leesha corrected.

Jessa laughed. 'That makes more sense! Though whore magic can change the course of duchies, as well.'

Leesha resisted the urge to stroke her belly, though Jessa no doubt knew her condition. 'Indeed.'

'To business, then?' Jessa asked.

Leesha nodded. 'What is your assessment of Rhinebeck's condition?'

'He's seedless,' Jessa said bluntly. 'I've been saying it for twenty years, but Araine won't hear it. She's desperate for a cure that doesn't exist.'

'What is your evidence for diagnosis?' Leesha asked.

'Apart from six wives over twenty years, none of them so much as stuttering her flow?' Jessa asked. 'Not to mention my girls. Whatever the sand witch might say, I don't give pomm tea to Rhinebeck's favourites. Araine would have her son divorced and remarried in an instant if she thought it would secure his line. More than one graduated and proved so fertile her belly swelled just from sitting in a man's lap and tickling his chin.'

It was nothing Leesha did not already know. 'Is that all?'

'Of course not,' Jessa said. She produced a leather-bound ledger, handing it to Leesha, who immediately opened it and began paging through. The book listed all the tests Jessa had run, the herbs and cures she'd tried and the results, all inscribed with a neat hand using the meticulous methodology Bruna had taught.

'I've even had my girls stroke him into a glass so I could look at his seed in a lens chamber,' Jessa said. 'He's precious few tadpoles at all, and those swim in circles, bumping into each other like drunks at a reel.'

'I'd like a look myself,' Leesha said.

'To what end?' Jessa asked.

'There may be a blockage I can clear with surgery,' Leesha said.

Jessa shook her head. 'Even if you had all the resources of the Age of Science, that's delicate work, and assuming the duke will let you anywhere near his manhood with a knife.'

'Then I'll resort to *hora* magic,' Leesha said. 'I know a woman decades past her fertile years cured by it.'

'You think Rhinebeck will let you put a spell on him?' Jessa asked. 'That's asking for the hangman's noose.'

'We'll see,' Leesha said. 'But for now, I'd just like to see his seed. Could you . . .?'

'Acquire some for you?' Jessa laughed. 'Of course. But you could get it yourself if you wished. Pregnant or not, Rhinebeck wouldn't hesitate if given the chance to cuckold his brother.'

'That's not going to happen,' Leesha said.

'You wouldn't even need to lie with him,' Jessa said. 'My girls have given him a taste for a woman's hand. Won't take you but a minute.'

Leesha breathed deeply, burying her revulsion at the thought. 'Will you get it for me, or shall I ask the duchess?'

Jessa saw she had pressed too far. 'I'll have it sent to your chambers on ice as soon as I can procure it. Tonight, perhaps.'

22

Bachelor's Ball
333 AR Winter

There was a rap at the door, and Leesha jumped. She glanced at the clock. Nearly midnight.

It could be Rojer again, but Leesha thought it unlikely unless there was some emergency. Dare she hope it might be Thamos? Late-night visits had been the norm when they were together, and he had stared at her all through dinner. Leesha had pretended not to notice at first, but then she met his eyes, expecting him to look away in embarrassment.

But he hadn't. His eyes held hers, and she could feel the heat in his stare. They had not spoken privately since that night on the road, but he was to head south in just two days, and there was too much still unsaid. He knew it, and so did she.

Wonda had been dozing on one of the chairs, but since Rojer's surprise visit, she had refused to retire before Leesha. She shook herself, casting off sleep and straightening as she approached the door.

Leesha reached quickly into the top drawer of her desk, taking her hand mirror and checking her hair and face. It was vain, but she didn't care. She stuck a finger in the front of her dress, pulling it down and giving her bust a lift.

But it wasn't Thamos. Instead, Rosal sauntered into the room, carrying a lacquered goldwood box.

'Did anyone see you?' Leesha asked, trying to keep the disappointment from her tone. 'The duke . . .'

Rosal shook her head with a giggle. 'I brought His Grace to a boil before I emptied him. He was passed out before I stopped stroking.'

She laid the box on the desk, lifting the lid. The inside was cured and filled with crushed ice. Resting atop the ice were three tiny crystal vials with a thick, cloudy liquid inside.

She closed the lid. 'How fresh?'

'Not half an hour,' Rosal said. 'I took the tunnel.'

Leesha wondered if the duke's brothel tunnel was warded as well as the rest of his walls. 'Pure? No other . . . fluids mixed in?'

Rosal smiled. 'Are you asking if I spit it into the vials? Mistress Jessa would have my head if I delivered a sample like that. I don't even use oil. I pull him dry.'

Leesha shuddered at the mental image of corpulent Rhinebeck grunting and twitching under Rosal's ministration. 'You seem to enjoy your work.'

Rosal shrugged. 'Better than working in my da's lacquer shop, head ready to explode from the fumes. Ent so bad, practising a wife's tricks on the Royals. Mistress Jessa taught us to lead the dance, emptying purses as well as seedpods.'

'So you're there willingly?' Leesha asked.

Rosal nodded. 'Ay. But I won't miss it when I graduate. Looking forward to starting my real life.'

The girl swept back out of the room, leaving just a hint of rose in the air. Leesha immediately began polishing and assembling her lens chamber. She set a drop of the duke's seed on the glass and adjusted the lens until the cells came into focus. Much as Jessa described, Leesha saw few active seeds. She slipped on her warded spectacles, and it was worse. A healthy sample should glow bright with teeming life. Rhinebeck's was grey, like a cloudy sky.

So much for the Duchess Mum's hopes of surgery. If the seeds were not reaching his issue, she might correct that. If they were dead . . .

Gared paced back and forth, clenching and unclenching his huge hands. A young squire watched in horror as his bunched shoulders threatened to tear the seams of his fine jacket.

'Night, Gar, sit down and have a ripping pipe.' Rojer was already sucking on his own, feet comfortably on the tea table.

Gared shook his head. 'Don't want to smell like smoke.' His hair was oiled and tied at the nape of his neck with a velvet bow. His beard was cropped close, and his wool coat was emblazoned with his new crest, a two-headed axe crossed with a machete before a goldwood tree. Gared had stared at the crest for hours when the tailor had presented him the patch for his approval. The man had needed to wrestle it from his hands just to sew it on the jacket.

'A drink, then,' Rojer said, pouring two cups as the big man continued to pace.

'Ay, so I can slur whatever stupid words I manage to stutter out,' Gared said.

'Stop that talk,' Rojer said. 'You're not stupid just because you weren't raised in a manse.'

'Then how come I feel like every other word anyone says is just there to poke fun at me?' Gared asked.

'It probably is,' Rojer said, emptying his brandy. 'Royals are always cutting each other, even as they smile and talk about the weather.'

'Don't want a wife like that,' Gared said.

'Then don't pick one like that,' Rojer said. 'You're in charge tonight, even if it doesn't feel that way. You don't have to marry anyone you don't want to.'

'What if I don't want any of 'em?' Gared asked. 'Duke said I had to go back to the Hollow with a girl to court. What if the Duchess Mum gets fed up and just picks one?'

Rojer gave a short, sharp laugh. 'You stand toe-to-toe with twenty-foot rock demons, and you're more scared of a woman half your size and thrice your age?'

Gared chuckled. 'Hadn't thought of it that way, but . . . ay. Guess I am. Reminds me o' Hag Bruna, only scarier.'

'You've just got stage fright,' Rojer said, taking the brandy he had poured Gared and emptying that as well. 'You'll be fine once it starts.'

Gared started pacing again, but then he paused.

'Ya think Rosal will be here?' He inhaled deeply, as if to catch her perfume. 'Pretty name, that. Smelled like roses, too.'

'Careful, Gar,' Rojer warned. 'I know she was a sight, but you don't want to marry one of Jessa's girls.'

'Why not?' Gared asked.

'Because the duke and his brothers will be laughing the whole time.' Rojer made a face. 'Besides, you want to kiss a mouth that's been on Rhinebeck's pecker?'

Gared balled a meaty fist, putting it right up to Rojer's face. 'True or not, don't want to hear that kind of talk about her, Rojer. Not if ya want to keep your teeth.'

Rojer let out a low whistle. 'You really fell for it, didn't you?'

'Fell for what?' Gared asked.

'Jessa paraded that girl in front of you on purpose,' Rojer said. 'I'll bet she's the mistress' star pupil. Everything that girl did was meant to catch your attention.'

Gared shrugged. 'How's that make her different from the others? Only with her, it worked.'

'I'm just saying, be careful,' Rojer said. 'Jessa's girls can be . . . jaded. They get what they want from a man and make him think it's his idea.'

'My da said that's what all marriage is like,' Gared said. 'Sayin' it's different for you?'

Rojer stuck his pipe in his mouth, neglecting to answer.

Rojer and his quartet stood in a sound shell behind Gared, who stood centre stage with Duchess Araine. The young baron looked very much the bridegroom waiting at the altar.

The ballroom was already filled with the cream of society, Royals, wealthy tradesmen and their wives, all in their finest dress. But outside the great double doors on the far end of the room stood a long line of hopeful young debutantes, waiting to be announced.

The duchess gave a few tugs to Gared's collar. 'You ready, boy?'

'Think I might be sick,' Gared said.

'I wouldn't advise it,' Araine said, brushing a fleck of dust from his jacket. 'But I doubt it would thin your dance card. Not every bachelor has a barony in his pocket. That's worth ignoring a shirtfront of sick for.'

Gared paled, and Araine laughed. 'A young bride to make children with is hardly a death sentence, boy. Glory in it while it lasts.'

She gave him a swat to the bottom with her walking stick, and Gared jumped. 'All you have to do now is stand here while Jasin introduces the debutantes. Once that's done, you can go backstage and empty your stomach before the dancing.'

She shuffled off, signalling Jasin to open the doors. Immediately Rojer put his fiddle to his chin, mirrored by Kendall as they played the first entrance. Each woman had chosen her own entrance music, the song they requested on the dance card. Rojer's quartet had been practising for days to learn them all.

'Miss Kareen Easterly,' Jasin called, 'daughter of Count Alen of Riverbridge.' Rojer changed tune. Kareen had chosen a slow song, both for the intimacy and the chance to saunter down the walkway at a crawl, maximizing her time as the centre of attention.

A poor choice, as it would have Gared's nose buried in the young woman's perfume cloud for the entire dance, at which point he wouldn't be able to get away from her fast enough.

Kareen ascended the steps stage left, then moved to the centre, enjoying the spotlight as Gared bowed to her. She might have stayed there all night, basking in the cheers and applause, had Jasin not opened the door to admit the next woman. Kareen winked at him as she moved slowly to descend stage left.

'Miss Dinese Wardgood, daughter of Lord Wardgood of South Klat.'

Dinny had chosen a waltz that was sure to have Gared tripping over everyone in the room. Odds were she'd compound the punishment by reciting poetry the whole time.

Araine had arranged for many young hopefuls to occupy the seats beside Gared at dinner each night, but none more often than these two. Their powerful fathers were able to buy access the others could not afford. They were the clear political favourites, but unless the rest of the debutantes were farm animals, they had little chance of making Ball Queen.

Dinny gave Gared a hidden wave as she left centre stage, but as with Kareen's wink, the young baron gave no sign he noticed. He kept his eyes on the doors, waiting for something to give him hope.

Rojer played in woman after woman, but Gared remained unmoved.

'Miss Emelia Lacquer, daughter of Alber Lacquer of Merchant Hill.' For a moment Gared remained still, but then he stiffened and leaned forward.

Rojer looked to the door. He should have known. All Jessa's girls chose 'downstairs names' while they were working, cast aside on graduation as they reentered society by their given names.

It was Rosal.

Gared watched intently as she glided down the walkway, though if it was the look of hunter or prey, Rojer could not guess.

From that moment on, Gared only had eyes for her, to the point of ignoring the last few women to enter, save when they passed into his line of sight crossing the stage. Thankfully there were only a few, but much of the crowd had already picked up on Gared's distraction, pointing at Emelia and whispering to one another.

Rojer sighed. Everyone who was anyone was in attendance, including more than a few who had likely been to the royal brothel in the last eighteen months. Emelia had changed her hair and chosen a modest gown, looking quite different than she had at Jessa's, but sooner or later someone was bound to recognize her.

Leesha stood alone at the ball. She had done everything she could to get Wonda into a gown for the event, but finally the girl shrieked, tearing the last dress from her body. Leesha thought the seamstress was going to have a heart attack.

'This ent me,' Wonda said. 'Love you, mistress. Take a hundred crank bow bolts for you. But you and all the demons in the Core can't get me to wear another rippin' dress so long as I live.'

What could Leesha do, but apologize? Wonda now stood by the wall with the other guards. She had cut her hair and oiled it back, proudly showing the jagged lines the demon's claws had left across her face.

Leesha smiled. It was a start. She would have to thank Jessa. Her words had reached the girl where Leesha's could not.

There was a gasp, and she looked up to see Gared ignore the steps, hopping off the stage as easily as other men might from a foot stool. Guests, taken by surprise at the informality, hesitated, then moved to greet him.

But the hesitation was all the time Gared needed to sweep past, his long legs carrying him swiftly across the ballroom to where Emelia stood with her parents. Royals and highborn stood openmouthed at the snub, and Alber Lacquer noticed, even if Gared was oblivious. He twitched nervously as Gared pumped his hand, but Emelia's mother, no small beauty herself, beamed with pride.

Gared had always been a simple man. Direct. It was good sometimes, to remind the Royals that not everything was a secret game of hidden cards.

Leesha had been promised to Gared once, but he was a better man by far now, even if he had been sleeping with her mother. Part of her wanted to advise against the match. Emelia was devious and controlling. But Elona was that as well. And Leesha, if she was honest with herself. Perhaps that was what Gared needed in a woman.

Emelia carried the risk of scandal, but no more than Gared himself, even if he did not know it. If Elona gave birth to a giant, it wouldn't be long before someone figured things out. Even Gared couldn't be thick enough to miss that.

'I'd give anything to know what was going through that mind of yours,' a voice behind her said.

Leesha started, so lost in thought she hadn't noticed as Thamos came up behind her and bowed. But she had been praying for this moment, and she was ready. She gripped her emotions in a cruel fist, shoving them down a dark hole as she turned and dipped into an elegant curtsy.

However hard Wonda had been on the seamstress, Leesha had been worse. She fretted over every stitch and ruffle of her silk gown, designed to hide her growing belly in the shadow of cleavage even the women could not ignore.

She bit back a smirk as she watched Thamos' eyes flick to her chest as she bent. The count was dashing in his polished boots and formal uniform – crushed velvet and silk, with golden epaulets and tassels. A dozen medals of lacquered gold covered his left breast, his dress spear slung over his shoulder in a polished harness encrusted with precious stones.

But if her neckline had caught his gaze, Thamos' handsome face caught hers and held it. His beard was carefully trimmed, not a hair on his head out of place. She wanted to grip it tight, tousling the pristine locks, slick with sweat as he thrust into her.

Leesha felt a moistening between her legs. This was the last night before he was to be sent south, and she meant to have him again before he left. She would die if she did not.

'Nothing of import, my lord,' she said.

'A lie.' Thamos sounded tired. 'But I should be used to that. There is never nothing of import going on behind your eyes, Leesha Paper.'

Leesha swallowed. She supposed she deserved that. 'Gared seems to have chosen his Ball Queen already.' She nodded to the two, staring into each other's eyes. 'I was pondering the match.' She gave her head a twitch towards Wonda. 'And I was thinking of how Wonda had railed against coming in a gown.'

Thamos grunted. 'The girl is wise. My mother's been throwing me these balls for years. I'd rather be fighting corelings.'

'The Baron of the Hollow is not the only eligible bachelor tonight, Highness,' Leesha said. 'The count still needs a countess.'

Just then there were bells, and everyone looked to see the Duchess Mum standing with Kareen Easterly. Crowded behind her stood the Royals Gared had snubbed, trying – and failing – to hide their vexation.

'It looks like the Count of Riverbridge wants the cocktail hour cut short.' Thamos chuckled. 'The Easterlys have better claim to the throne than even my mother. They're not used to being snubbed.'

Indeed, Araine signalled Rojer to begin the first dance, and the Jongleur was not fool enough to refuse. He began the slow song Kareen had inched down the carpet to.

Thamos took a step back, offering his hand with a bow. 'I may yet need a countess, but I have no desire to look for one on my last night in Angiers. Will you dance with me?'

'If I put my arms around you, Highness,' Leesha said, nonetheless taking his hand and moving in close, 'I may not let go.'

Thamos put a hand on her waist. 'You will have to. My mother has summoned us to her garden after the first dance.'

'Now?!' Leesha couldn't believe it. 'In the middle of the ball, with you being sent Creator knows where in the morning?'

'Points I made to my mother,' Thamos said, 'but she said if I value my skin, I was to collect you and come.'

They passed Gared on the dance floor. He was grimacing, and when Leesha caught a whiff of Kareen's perfume, it was not difficult to see why. She felt her sinuses constrict, and a muscle in her temple twitched, threatening the headache to come.

The pain was still mild as Thamos led her from the dance floor and to a side exit. Wonda made as if to follow, but Leesha made a cutting motion and the girl took the hint, easing back to the wall.

They slipped through silent halls, glimpsed only by a handful of servants that knew enough to keep their eyes on the floor.

Even that traffic died as they moved closer to the exit to Araine's private garden. The hall was long and dark, full of shadowed alcoves bearing statues of the dukes of old. Leesha stopped, pulling Thamos up short.

'What is it?' he asked.

Leesha slipped behind the statue of Rhinebeck. It was a flattering portrayal to say the least, but even a flattering like-ness of Rhinebeck was thick enough to cast the back of the alcove into shadow.

'I have a headache.' She yanked, and Thamos offered only token resistance as he was pulled in with her.

For any other couple, the words might mean an end to romantic notions for the night, but it was the opposite for Leesha, and Thamos knew it. Before the count could say anything to break the mood, she thrust her mouth upon his.

He stiffened a moment, but then embraced her tightly, snaking his tongue into her mouth. Leesha put a hand behind his head, gripping his hair, pulling his tongue deeper.

He growled, pawing at her. Somehow her breasts had come free of her gown, and Thamos squeezed them as she pressed closer to him, letting go his hair to reach down and grip him through his breeches. He was hard, and she wasted no time undoing the laces and pulling him free.

'We don't have much time,' he murmured.

'Then don't be gentle,' she said, turning and pulling up her dress as she bent over the pedestal.

Gared did his duty, dancing with every young debutante at the ball. It was awkward to watch. He dwarfed the tallest of the Angierian women, and stepped on a few delicate toes as he tried to keep up with the dances.

But worse was the look of concentration on his face, one more suited to fighting corelings than dancing with beautiful young women. He looked as if he were just trying to survive.

Until it was Emelia's turn. Then the big Cutter's face lit up, and he might have been dancing on air. It seemed he had found his bride, and not all the gold in Riverbridge was going to deter him.

Kendall saw it, too, and lengthened her fiddle solo, giving the two more time to stare into each other's eyes. Amanvah and Sikvah lent their voices to the task, casting a spell over the young couple as easily as they might a coreling.

Jasin kept his Jongleur's mask in place, smiling as he danced with rich royal women while their husbands clustered together, oblivious. But every so often, he looked up to the stage, staring icicles into Rojer's heart.

Rojer allowed himself to smile in return. His revenge was far from complete, and though he did not know what his next step should be, for the moment, Jasin was suffering daily humiliation, and Rojer was enjoying it immensely.

But then Jasin looked pointedly at Gared and Emelia, then back to Rojer, a broad smile on his face.

He knows.

Of course he knew. Unless things had changed since Arrick's day, regular access to the royal brothel was one of the royal herald's perks. Jasin not only knew Emelia was Rosal the whore, suns to klats he'd had her himself.

And Rojer wasn't willing to bet the herald would keep the secret.

Araine and Minister Janson were waiting in the garden when Leesha and Thamos arrived. A few lanterns were hung, but the shadows were deep and foreboding. Despite her trust in the woman, Leesha slipped on her warded spectacles, peering through the shadows for hidden dangers.

'Well this is all very clandestine,' Leesha said. 'Is there a reason we had to leave the ball on Thamos' last night in Angiers?'

'A very good reason,' Araine said. 'I need you to meet my secret weapon, and we can't very well do it inside. Boy smells worse than a chamber pot.'

'Boy?' Leesha asked.

'Briar, dear,' Araine called gently, 'do come out.'

Leesha started as a boy appeared out of a hogroot patch not ten feet away. How had she missed him? With her warded spectacles in place, his aura should have shone like a lantern.

But it didn't. His aura was so dim she thought he might be dying, but he moved with quick and easy grace to the duchess' side. He could not have been more than sixteen summers – tall, thin, and wiry. Over one shoulder was slung a *Sharum*'s round warded shield, but he wore Thesan pants and shirt.

His features were not quite Krasian, but not quite Thesan, either. It was hard to see them clearly, because the boy was utterly filthy.

As the duchess had warned, the stench of him was overpowering. Leesha's nostrils flared, tasting it. There was the stink of stale boy sweat, but stronger was the scent of hogroot. He had bruised leaves and rubbed the plants onto his skin like lotion. His clothes were covered in hogroot stains. The sticky sap had collected a layer of dirt on its surface, but was no less pungent for it.

'Forgive our little ruse,' Araine said. 'Briar claims no demon can see him if he does not wish it, and I wondered if the same were true for your fascinating spectacles.'

Leesha did not reply, but the duchess had her answer already. Had she ever even mentioned the spectacles to the duchess? The woman knew more than she let on.

'Leesha, Thamos, this is Briar Damaj,' Araine said, and the boy grunted at them. It was a guttural sound, harsh and animal.

Damaj. A Krasian surname. It meant he was from the same line as Inevera – and Amanvah – though the relation might be hundreds of generations gone. The Damaj clan could trace their lineage all the way to the time of Kaji.

But Briar was a Laktonian name. The boy was a half-breed, but Leesha hadn't known any Krasians were in the North before the invasion. His features might be common in a few years, but this was the first time she had seen the like. Was he a Messenger's son?

'Pleased to meet you, Briar,' Leesha said, offering a hand. Briar tensed and drew back. She lowered her hand, smiling. 'Demons don't like the smell of hogroot, do they?'

That seemed to relax the boy. 'Makes 'em sick up, they smell too much. Cories hate hogroot.'

Leesha nodded, inspecting the boy's aura. She hadn't known the scent of hogroot was repellent to demons, but it made sense. Hogroot was the primary ingredient in demon infection cures, and corelings were known to avoid patches of the stuff.

But that was not all. She watched the ambient magic drifting along the ground of the gardens like fog. Normally the magic was drawn to living things, unless there were wards in the area. Magic avoided Briar like oil avoided water.

Could hogroot repel magic? That would explain many of its properties, and make the precious herb infinitely more useful.

'Briar has proven invaluable to the resistance,' Araine said. 'He speaks Krasian, and can even pass at a glance. Most of all, he moves day and night. Like your Painted Man, though without the delusions of grandeur.'

Leesha let the barb go. Araine was not exaggerating to call the boy invaluable. He was a resource the duchess would not share lightly, even with her.

'Briar has contacts in Lakton,' Araine said. 'He can guide your force overland from the Hollow, avoiding the Krasian patrols, and arrange a meeting with the dockmasters. They are using a monastery by the lake as a base.'

Thamos raised an eyebrow. 'Does Rhinebeck know of this?'

Araine laughed. 'Of course not. For all Rhiney knows, you'll have found the resistance on your own. But he sent you, and will be held to whatever promises you need to make.'

'And what promises are those?' Thamos asked.

Araine signalled Janson, who handed the count a rolled parchment. Thamos opened it, reading quickly. Leesha leaned in to read over his shoulder.

'This has the Laktonians swearing fealty to me,' Thamos said.

'Why shouldn't we make demands, if we're to commit lives to their aid?' Janson asked. 'They're the ones under siege, not us.'

'Not yet,' Leesha noted.

'Nevertheless, the minister is correct,' Araine said. 'They need us more than we need them right now, a fact we would be foolish to ignore as we open negotiations. Their soldiers will follow your commands if battle is to be met. That part is not negotiable.'

'I understand.' Thamos' voice was tight. 'But you have them swearing to *me*, not Rhinebeck.'

'You are lord commander of the Wooden Soldiers and Count of Hollow County,' Araine said. 'It makes sense for them to ally with you directly.'

Thamos shook his head. 'Rhinebeck will not see it that way.'

'Rhinebeck won't have any choice.' Araine's voice became a lash. 'By the time he hears of it, the treaty will be signed and you'll be out of his reach, with three armies at your disposal. He won't have the strength to oppose you.'

'Oppose?' Thamos asked. 'Am I to take the place of the demon of the desert, conquering Thesa?'

'I'm not asking you to be a conqueror,' Araine said. 'That isn't what we need.'

'Then just what is it we do need, Mother?' Thamos demanded.

'A king,' Araine said. 'Not a demon. Not a Deliverer. Thesa needs a king.'

Thamos stared at her blankly, and Araine stepped up, holding his face in her hands. 'Oh, my sweet boy. Don't think on it now. Think only of keeping safe, doing what must be done, and returning to the ones you love.' She embraced him tightly, dabbing tears from her eyes as she pulled back.

'You have until dawn to settle your business and say your goodbyes,' Araine said. 'Though from the colour in your cheeks when you first arrived, I'd guess you've already settled some of it.'

She turned, sweeping Briar and Janson up in her wake as she left Leesha and Thamos alone in the garden. He held his arms open to her, and she fell into them, embracing him tightly. He squeezed in return, and she began to sob into the neatly bunched wad of cloth where his cloak clasped at his shoulder.

'Don't go,' she begged, knowing it was a foolish request.

'What choice do I have, with my brother and mother unified?' Thamos asked. 'They would strip the Hollow from me. Give it to Mickael, perhaps. He regrets not taking it, now. Pether, too. Neither wanted the place when it was offered a few months ago, but they eye it hungrily, now.'

'They eye it because you built it into something more,' Leesha said. 'The Hollowers know that. Once you're back in your seat, no missive from Angiers could take it from you, if they even dared try.'

'Ay, perhaps,' Thamos said. 'If I wished to war on my brother more than I do the Krasians. But someone needs to turn the tide. If the Krasians take Lakton, it is only a matter of time before they swallow everything south of the Dividing. Who will do it, if not me? Your precious Arlen Bales is gone.'

The words were bitter, but Leesha ignored the barb. 'Take me with you, then.'

'Don't be ridiculous,' Thamos said. 'It's weeks of travel through enemy territory, and you're five moons pregnant.'

'I was strong enough to stand against a pack of coreling assassins,' Leesha said. 'You think I can't hold my own against the Krasians?'

'Krasians fight in the day,' Thamos reminded her. 'Will *hora* protect your child from spears and arrows while the sun shines?'

Leesha knew he was right, but it grated all the same. 'They're just using you. Araine and Rhinebeck, both. A pawn in their political games.'

'And what are you doing, Leesha?' Thamos demanded. 'You knew how it would appear when you made such a show of bedding me. You used me to help hide your indiscretion.'

'I know,' Leesha said. 'I'm so sorry . . .'

Thamos cut her off. 'And now I have a choice. Marry you, and await my inevitable humiliation, or turn my back on the only woman I've ever loved.'

He pulled away. 'Perhaps I'm better off dead.'

He turned on his heel and left her alone in the garden, feeling as if her heart had been torn out.

Leesha stood there a moment, shock and pain freezing her in place. But only for a moment. Then she was lifting her skirts and kicking off her shoes.

'Thamos!' she called, sacrificing dignity to run after him. It could not end like this. She would not let it. She had come so close. He had been in her arms. He had been in *her*. If they must part, let it be with a kiss, and with Thamos knowing she loved him.

Thamos must have been moving fast, or taken a different path from the gardens. She reached the entrance to the palace and there was no sign of him in the hall. She hurried by the statues of dukes past, heading for his rooms. He had to return there to finish preparations for his departure.

There was a sound ahead, coming from the very alcove she and Thamos had used for their tryst. Had Thamos hidden there from her? Or gone there to vent his emotion in the safe embrace of the shadows?

Some things were not meant for shadows. Some things needed the light. Leesha pulled a wardstone from the velvet *hora* pouch at her waist and moved her fingers to activate the wards, filling the alcove with a bright wardlight that banished the shadows like the sun itself.

But it wasn't Thamos hiding there. In nearly the same position she and the count had taken their pleasure bent the Princess Lorain and Lord Sament. Momentum saw the lord pump into her twice more before he reacted to the light, falling back and stumbling, trying to pull up the breeches around his knees.

Leesha felt her face heat, lowering the light and averting her eyes. 'I'm sorry, I thought you were someone else.'

'Sorry or not, you've seen us now.' Lorain had an easier time composing herself, gown falling back as soon as she stood. She advanced on Leesha, menacingly. 'The question is what should we do about that?'

'You are not promised to Rhinebeck. You should not be expected to save yourself for a married man.' Leesha looked at Sament, now decent again. 'I'd heard that Euchor dissolved your marriage, but it was not to a Lord Sament.'

'Sament is a friend of mine,' the lord said, 'and agreed to lend me his name for the trip south. None in Angiers knows what either of us look like.' He reached out, taking Lorain's hand. 'Dissolved or no, I could not just send my wife alone to a hostile court.'

'My father can tear a paper, but he can't take back our vows,' Lorain said. 'I will marry Rhinebeck if politics demand, but he will never be my husband.' She looked at Sament. 'Not even if my husband gets his night wish and dies on this fool's errand to Lakton.'

'I have to go,' Sament said. 'If we succeed at freeing Lakton, then perhaps you won't have to marry Rhinebeck. If not, I'd rather be dead than have to see it.'

Lorain looked at Leesha, her eyes untrusting. 'I expect you cannot understand, mistress. Will you tell the duchess?'

Leesha reached for the woman, ignoring the princess' shocked look as she pulled her into an embrace. 'I understand better than you know. Unless you marry Rhinebeck, you have Gatherer's word I won't speak of it.' She looked to Sament. 'Should that come to pass, you will return to Miln until there is an heir, to ensure the issue is true.'

Sament gritted his teeth, but he nodded once.

'After that,' Leesha said, 'what you do is none of my concern.'

She turned and left them, visiting the ball just long enough to ensure Thamos had not returned there. Everyone seemed taller without her shoes, but she had no desire to dance any longer. She signalled Wonda to follow and returned to her rooms.

She sat at her desk, taking a sheet of the precious flower-pressed paper she made in her father's shop. Her supply was almost gone, and she would likely never have time to make more.

But what was special paper for, if not to tell the man you loved all the words that failed in person?

She agonized long into the night over it, and then sent Wonda to see to it the count did not leave without it in his possession.

Gared was expected to spend time with each of the debutantes when their dances were done, but he signalled Rojer to join them between songs so he was never alone. Each time he drifted inexorably back to Rosal, pulling the chattering young hopefuls with him. Soon the lacquerer's daughter was surrounded by women all unified in their purpose of cutting her down.

'What can a tradesman's daughter know of running a barony?' Kareen wondered.

Rosal smiled. 'Please, my lady. Do enlighten us. Your father, for instance, has run Riverbridge so far into debt he's been forced to double the bridge tolls. The merchants willing to cross are passing on the cost to their clients, forcing men like my father to pay more for materials, which filters down to the peasantry. How would you address the problem?'

'Those are questions best left to men,' Dinny said, when Kareen had no immediate reply. 'As the poet Nichol Graystone said:

'In man and wife the Creator did see
Two souls that beat in harmony
With daily labour, a man doth provide
Food and comfort for his fair bride.
Children and home be her domain;
Thus marital balance is sustained.'

'That was Markuz Eldred, not Graystone,' Rosal noted as Gared's eyes began to glaze over. 'And from a poor church translation. In the original Ruskan it said:

'In man and wife the Creator did see
Two souls to work in symmetry
And in daily labour to provide
Domain and comfort for man and bride
To rear strong progeny in the home
And not bear troubled thoughts alone.'

She looked at Gared, giving him a wink. 'Not my favourite Eldred poem. He did better work in his youth:

'A man from Lakton was so hung,
The women he loved were all stung,
Not a one who could take it,
When he crawled on her naked,
So he stuck it up a rock demon's bung.'

Gared roared with laughter, and it went on thus for the remainder of the evening, Rosal holding her own – and Gared's attention – against a growing tide of detractors.

The giant Cutter's hands were shaking backstage when he told Araine that Emelia Lacquer was his choice for Queen of the Bachelor's Ball.

Araine put her hands on her hips. 'Do you expect me to be surprised? You couldn't take your eyes off the girl all night.'

Gared looked at his feet. 'Know she ent your first choice . . .'

'You don't know as much as you think,' Araine said, 'and we both know that's not a lot to begin with. The lords will be in a frenzy, and Creator knows they'll keep shoving Kareen and Dinny in your face, along with promises of wealth and pretty handmaids, but neither of those girls has what it takes to handle you, or the Hollow. My sons will snicker behind your back but they won't oppose the match, and Emelia's worth ten of any of them, whatever they may think they know of Rosal.'

Gared looked at the duchess in surprise. 'You think I didn't know?' Araine demanded. 'Jessa works for me. She never would have paraded the girl before you if I hadn't approved it.'

The slack look on Gared's face pulled slowly into a wide smile. Araine cut it off before it swallowed his face, raising a finger. 'You do right by that girl, Gared Cutter, and by Cutter's Hollow. I'll have your oath.'

'Swear by the sun,' Gared said eagerly.

Araine nodded. 'And don't get fat. Worst thing a man can do. No one respects a fat man on a throne, and once you lose respect, you're just holding a seat.'

Few in the crowd looked pleased when Gared crowned Rosal Ball Queen, but none was any more surprised than Araine had been. Rojer played something triumphant for their last dance, and the Royals backed off to lick their wounds and lay their plans to change Gared's mind.

As if there were a chance of that. The party shifted to drawing rooms as the ball ended, and still the young couple were inseparable.

Amanvah shook her head at them. 'Don't approve him marrying a *heasah*?' Rojer asked.

'Given the unworthy selection of potential brides, he had little choice,' Amanvah said.

'That almost sounds like approval,' Rojer said.

'Better if my father had given him a proper bride,' Amanvah said.

Rojer smiled. 'I certainly can't complain at his choices in that regard.'

He was a little drunk as they excused themselves from the party and made their way back to Rojer's chambers. The main hall was filled with partygoers heading off to warded carriages, so Rojer led them to a back staircase where they could cross under to the guest wing and then up to their rooms on the fourth floor.

Rojer felt hopeful for once. The wedding would come as soon as Gared could arrange it, and they would soon be back in the Hollow where they belonged. Kendall had a skip to her step, never having performed at such a fancy event. She twirled in her silken ball gown, slashed in bright colours, laughing.

Coliv led the way down the stairs, as alert for trouble as he was in the night, even nestled in the duke's stronghold.

But as he reached the landing there was a *tung!* and he took a crank bow bolt in the shoulder.

Everything seemed to happen at once. Two men in the green and gold tabards of palace guards charged down the stairs above them, shoving hard and knocking Kendall and Sikvah into Rojer and Amanvah. They tumbled forward and Rojer cracked his chin against the last step just before having his breath knocked out as the others landed atop him.

Coliv threw his spear in the direction the shot had come from. There was a grunt of pain in the darkness, followed by another *tung!* Coliv had his shield up in time, but the thin warded metal was designed to stop corelings, not crank bows. The bolt punched clear through, sprouting from the back of the Watcher's neck.

Coliv turned to the guard closest to Amanvah, reaching into his robes and producing one of his sharp throwing triangles. He raised an arm as if he might ignore even this grievous wound to protect his mistress, but then he sank to his knees, choking on his own blood.

They scrambled to rise, but palace guards were coming from all sides now, carrying short, lacquered batons. As one came for him, Rojer flipped out the knives hidden in his sleeves. He threw one, but he was still drunk, and the blade went wide. He clutched the other tightly, unwilling to risk losing his only remaining weapon.

He dodged the first swing of the baton. And the second. Before the guard could recover enough for a third, Rojer was in close, burying his knife into the man's side.

For all the good it did. The blade was small for ease of throwing and concealment. The guard seemed more angered than hurt when he backhanded Rojer across the face with the baton, sending him sprawling. Kendall ran to put herself between them, but the guard kicked her hard in the stomach and she fell back, stepping on Rojer's face in the process.

Rojer tried to raise his knife, but the guard stomped hard on his wrist, and the blade fell from his fingers in a blast of pain. The baton was thrust into his stomach, and when he curled reflexively, the next blow took him in the balls. He screamed, but it was shattered as a third blow put out two of his teeth.

Rojer fell back stunned, seeing Amanvah and Sikvah choked from behind with batons. Whenever they struggled, the guards tightened their grips, choking them into submission. The men had the advantage in muscle and weight, either of them heavier than the women combined.

One of the crank bowmen lay farther down the hall, Coliv's spear in his chest. Kendall was pinned by the other. His spent weapon was slung over his shoulder, and he held her wrists to the floor, kneeling on her thighs so she could not kick at him.

There was a clapping, and Jasin Goldentone came out of the shadows, followed by Abrum and Sali.

'Goldentone?' Rojer croaked.

'Oh, not Nosong now?' Jasin asked. 'You remember respect late, Halfgrip.'

'Golden toad, I said.' Rojer tried to spit at him, but his lips were swelling fast. The slimy mix of blood and spit dribbled down his chin. Still, the move earned him another blow across the face.

'You piece of hamlet shit, you think you can just come to *my city* and humiliate me?' Jasin asked. 'That you can spread lies and threaten my very commission, and not expect retaliation? You should know better than that.

'Not that it was hard to enlist allies.' Jasin nodded at Amanvah and Sikvah. 'Tonight will make me a very rich man. You'd be surprised how many lords will pay good coin for a pair of Krasian princesses to hostage. More when I add proof that the Baron's Ball Queen is a nothing but a royal whore.'

Sikvah pulled at the spear, but her captor tightened it further. 'Best quit your squirming before you give me ideas, girl.'

'No ideas,' Jasin said. 'Not here. We need to finish our business and be gone.'

'They killed Anders,' the guard pinning Kendall said. 'Can't let that go without blood in return.'

'He knew the risks,' Jasin said, 'but you can beat Rojer and the girl to death in recompense.'

'Ay, all right.' The guard grinned, reaching for the baton on his belt.

'No!' Rojer tried to roll away, but the guard standing over

him ground his boot heel into Rojer's wrist, keeping it pinned as his baton repeated its pattern of stomach, balls, and head. Lights spun like drunken dancers before his eyes.

When his vision cleared, he looked at Amanvah. 'I'm so sorry.' His words were a slur.

Amanvah met his eyes with a hard look. 'Enough of this. Sikvah.'

Sikvah kicked straight up, connecting solidly over her shoulder with her captor's face. She grabbed his wrists crosswise and ducked forward, twisting into a throw that sent him tumbling into the far wall and left the baton in her hands. She did not hesitate to throw, striking the man standing over Rojer in the head and knocking him back.

Amanvah struck a precise blow of her stiffened fingers into her own captor's shoulder. The arm fell away limp, and she grasped the other, locking it straight and twisting to bring the man down onto the steps, her foot in his throat.

Sikvah was already moving, springing for the man pinning Kendall. He rose to meet her, but she wove around his attempt to grapple, leaping to hook her leg around his neck. She twisted in midair, using her own falling weight to break his neck.

Jasin did not hesitate, pulling a knife and lunging at Rojer. The man Sikvah had knocked away was recovering, and Abrum and Sali produced clubs of their own as they charged in.

A flick of her fingers, and one of the sharpened triangles Coliv favoured buried itself in Jasin's knife hand. He dropped the weapon and screamed as Sikvah came in.

Rojer supposed what followed was a fight, but it seemed an unfair term for a conflict so one-sided. Sikvah did not fight. She simply killed.

Sali swung her baton, but Sikvah grabbed her wrist and rolled in close, redirecting the momentum into an elbow strike that crushed Sali's throat. She threw the big woman's body into Jasin, stepping like a dancer to meet the masked guard. The guard swung and she spun out of the blow's path, completing the circuit to drive an elbow into the man's spine with an audible crack. He was dead before he hit the floor.

Abrum decided to live, turning to flee the scene, but Sikvah threw a baton, catching him on the thigh. It seemed only a glancing blow, but the leg collapsed and he fell to one knee. She grabbed at his head as she sprang over him, turning a somersault and breaking his neck.

And as quickly as that, it was done.

Jasin was struggling to get out from under Sali's bulk. She'd always had a face like a wood demon, but now it was a blackening horror.

Rojer picked up the knife Jasin had dropped, stumbling to his feet. Amanvah was kneeling over Coliv, staring into unseeing eyes. 'Take the lonely path with honour, *Sharum*. Everam awaits you with rewards in Heaven.'

Rojer felt his throat tighten. He and Coliv had stood alone together in the night. He didn't have the same romantic notions about such things as the Krasians, but there was no denying it was something to bond men.

And now he was dead because Rojer had been too afraid to kill Jasin. Another name to add to his medallion. How many could it hold?

'No more,' Rojer said. He had never killed anything other than a demon, and always wondered if he had it in him. But there was no hesitation now, no desire for a final word. The blade slid into Jasin's eye like a boiled egg, and Goldentone's body gave a last violent jolt as he twisted it.

And that was how the real palace guards found them.

23

Inquisition
333 AR Winter

Rojer tensed at the click of the lock. The door was thick goldwood, banded with steel. There was no window or peephole, only a trap at the bottom just large enough to slide a tray. No way to tell who was on the other side.

But in truth, it did not matter. Rojer had little fight left in him. The palace guards, enraged at the deaths of their comrades, had shown little restraint as they tried to beat a confession out of him. They took their cues from Janson, after all, and the first minister was livid at the death of his nephew.

He was barely conscious when they finally relented, passing out gratefully, only to awaken here.

A single glance from the tiny window told him where he was. The South Tower.

The great Cathedral of Angiers had been built before the Return, with four stone towers, one at each point of the compass. The northernmost held the great bell, which could be heard for miles. The other towers were cells that had held heretics and political prisoners for centuries. Men and women too powerful – or royal – to be executed; too dangerous – or endangered – to be kept in the common gaol.

Rojer knew the famous tales of the towers, had spun quite

a few himself, but never imagined he'd one day be part of them.

Rojer sat up as the door swung open. Through the puffy slits of his eyes he saw Leesha and sighed with relief, collapsing back on the simple bed.

'Rojer!' Leesha cried, rushing over to him as the door slammed behind her. She took his face in her hands, but it was all business as she examined his bruises. Rojer yelped as she stripped the covers back, probing for broken bones and bleeding.

'Ripping savages,' Leesha muttered, getting to her feet. She went to the window, pulling the heavy curtain shut and returning to his side.

'Wha'roo doing?' Rojer asked through swollen lips as she ignored the herbs in her apron pockets, reaching instead for her warding kit.

'Hold still,' Leesha said, taking a thin brush and a jar of ink. 'We don't have a lot of time, and I promised Amanvah to restore you before we talk.'

'Restore?' Rojer asked. Or tried to. His face was refusing to play its proper part in forming words.

Leesha didn't answer, stripping his clothes away with no allowance for modesty and painting wards on his skin. Rojer shuddered when she reached into her *hora* pouch and produced the demon bone, but the pain was too great for him to argue.

The wards warmed as Leesha passed the bone over them, glowing softly and sending a tingle through his skin that penetrated deep into muscle and bone, numbing the pain and reducing the swelling. His vision cleared, lips shrinking back to something of their old agility. There was room in his mouth once more, his tongue slipping instinctively into the gap where the baton had knocked out his teeth. Weariness washed from him, and he felt strong, alert.

He clenched a fist, power surging through him. The door that had seemed to be impenetrable before did not appear so formidable now. He could smash right through and fight his way from the cathedral. Lose himself in the streets. Find a way out of the city . . .

But then the bone crumbled in Leesha's hand, and the mad feeling of power left him.

'Night,' he said as he pulled his clothes back on. 'Easy to see how folk might get addicted to that.'

'Not much I can do for your missing teeth,' Leesha said. 'We can have new ones made of porcelain. They can be tinted to match your remaining teeth, or something more colourful, if you prefer.'

Rojer shook his head. 'The thing I love best about motley is that it comes off.'

Leesha nodded, reaching into her bag and producing a most welcome sight. His fiddle case. 'Amanvah wanted you to have this . . . to pass the hours.'

Rojer quickly opened the case, relief flooding him as he saw the warded chinrest sitting in its velvet compartment. Pointedly, he set it on the bed between them. Amanvah would be able to hear everything, even if she could not respond.

'Rojer, what happened?' Leesha asked.

'I was a fool,' Rojer said. 'Thought we were safe in the palace. Thought I could tweak Jasin's nose and poison his reputation without paying the price.' He hung his head. 'This is all my fault.'

'Don't be an idiot,' Leesha snapped. 'You didn't start this.'

'I did,' Rojer said. 'I started it when I punched Jasin in the nose.'

'My mum punched me in the nose once,' Leesha said. 'I didn't feel the need to murder her and anyone standing between.'

'Not excusing Jasin,' Rojer said. 'That son of the Core got what was coming to him. But I knew what he was, and woke the demon anyway. Now Jaycob and Coliv are dead.'

Leesha took a pocket watch from her apron, looking at the time. 'They only allowed me an hour, Rojer, and we've but a few minutes left. You'll have plenty of time alone to philosophize, but for now I need to know everything you can remember about last night.'

Rojer nodded. 'Jasin came to kill me. He must have bribed

some of the palace guards to help. He said there was a lord who would pay for Amanvah and Sikvah.'

'Did he say who?' Leesha asked.

Rojer shook his head. 'I wasn't in a position to ask details.'

'Go on,' Leesha said.

'They must have known we'd avoid the great hall on the way back to our chambers,' Rojer said. 'They were waiting in the lower hall. They shot Coliv, but he fought to the last, killing almost all of them. He left Jasin to me.'

He deliberately kept things vague, leaving out Sikvah's involvement entirely. He still did not know what to think of that. His sweet, submissive Sikvah had become something terrifying right before his eyes. But whatever she was, she was his wife, and he would not betray her.

'So it was self-defence,' Leesha said.

'Of course it was ripping self-defence,' Rojer snapped.

'That's not what Minister Janson is saying,' Leesha said. 'He says he saw you pull a knife on Jasin a few days ago.'

Rojer looked down. 'Well, ay . . . but only after he attacked me.'

'He attacked you and you didn't say anything?' Leesha demanded.

'Do you go running for help every time someone shoves you?' Rojer asked. 'Or do you just shove back harder?'

'I try not to shove anyone at all,' Leesha said.

'Tell that to Inevera,' Rojer said, and watched in satisfaction as Leesha choked on her next words.

'Well it doesn't matter now,' Leesha said when she recovered herself. 'Janson is claiming it was you that went after Jasin.'

'With my wives and Kendall in tow?' Rojer asked incredulously.

Leesha shrugged. 'It could have simply been an argument that went too far. And when the guards tried to stop it . . .'

'We murdered them all?' Rojer asked. 'Does that sound even remotely plausible?'

'Plausible or no, Jasin is dead and you were found over him with a bloody knife,' Leesha said.

'Find Cholls,' Rojer said. 'Master of the Jongleurs' Guild. I told him months ago that Jasin killed Jaycob and put me in the hospit.'

Leesha nodded. 'I will, but can he be trusted? The first minister seems to have everyone cowed.'

'Put Gared in the room when he's questioned,' Rojer said. 'He was there when it happened.'

'Gared knew?!' Leesha blurted. 'Months before you said anything to me?'

Rojer gave her a level look. 'Gared happened to be in the room when the guildmaster questioned me on my disappearance last year. He didn't know what he was hearing at the time, but it's a safe bet Cholls doesn't know that. My guess is that if he knows Gared's there to contradict him, he won't have the stones to lie.'

'Even if he tells all, it will only strengthen your motive,' Leesha said.

'I already have motive,' Rojer said. 'This will give Jasin one as well.' He put his arms around his knees, pulling them up to the chest. 'How are the women?'

'Amanvah and Kendall are under house arrest until the trial,' Leesha said. 'I've assigned Cutters to stand with the palace guards. They're not happy, but they're safe.'

Rojer swallowed, noting the omission. 'And Sikvah?'

'Sikvah,' Leesha said quietly, 'is missing.'

Leesha's legs ached by the time she reached the bottom of the seemingly endless stairwell. Her sleep was growing increasingly restless as the pregnancy progressed, leg cramps in the night leaving her with lingering pain.

But she was no stranger to the cathedral towers, and as she left the South Tower, she circled the halls until she reached the East, where she began to climb once more.

Rojer was in greater trouble than he realized. Araine herself had been forced to intervene with Shepherd Pether before the furious Janson relented and let the Tenders carry the unconscious Rojer to the protection of the cathedral.

But while he was safe until his trial, there were too many dead for him to walk away from this. And Sikvah? Where was Sikvah? The guards claimed never to have found her after the attack. Had she been spirited away by whatever lord Jasin had been working with? Even the Deliverer's niece was hostage enough to start a war they weren't ready to fight.

The thoughts took her mind from the endless climb to the top of the tower, where she found a cell similar to Rojer's. The guard nodded to her and moved to open the door. They were used to her by now.

'Jona,' Leesha said, as the man looked up from his books. The Tenders had him copying Canons as penance while they debated his fate.

'Leesha!' Jona said, rising quickly and going to her side. 'Creator shine on you. Are you well? You look tired.' He went to the chamber's single chair, removing some books and holding it for her to sit. 'Can I get you some water?'

Leesha shook her head, smiling. 'One would almost forget you're the prisoner here.'

Jona gave a dismissive wave. 'My acolyte cell in Cutter's Hollow was smaller. I have books, and the Canon. I have visits from Vika, and you. What more could I ask for?'

'Freedom,' Leesha said.

Jona shrugged. 'When the Creator wills it, I will be.'

'It's not the Creator's will you need to worry about,' Leesha said. 'It's Rhinebeck's.'

Again the Tender shrugged. 'I was worried at first. They spent weeks interrogating me, and I wasn't allowed proper sleep or books or anything to while away the hours between.

'But now,' he stroked the leather-bound cover of one of his books lovingly, 'I am at peace. The Tenders are convinced I don't know any secrets to give them advantage over the

Deliverer, and my heresy is on the lips of half the duchy. Sooner or later, they'll tire of holding me.'

'Especially with Arlen gone,' Leesha said.

'He isn't gone,' Jona said.

'You can't know that,' Leesha said. 'You weren't there.'

'I have faith,' Jona said. 'What surprises me is that after all you've been through, you do not.'

'If the Creator has a plan, it hasn't been kind to me,' Leesha noted.

'We all have our trials,' Jona said. 'But looking back, what would you change? Would you have married Gared and lived a normal life? Stayed in Angiers while flux took the Hollow? Spat in the face of the demon of the desert when he greeted you with friendship?'

Leesha shook her head. 'Of course not.'

'Would you undo the life within you?'

Leesha put a hand to her belly, meeting his eyes with a hard glare. 'Never.'

'That.' Jona pointed. 'That is faith. You cannot measure it with weights and doses like your herbs. You cannot classify it in your books, or test it with chemics. But it is there, more powerful than any bit of old world science. Only the Creator can see the path ahead. He makes of us what he wants – what the world needs – us to be. But we can have a glimpse, looking back.'

'Thamos has been sent to Lakton,' Leesha said, her voice shaking.

'Why?' Jona asked.

'To avoid a war,' Leesha sniffed, 'or perhaps to start one. Creator only knows.'

Jona laid a gentle hand on her shoulder. 'I only met him for a moment, when he and the Inquisitor sent me here. But I know you, Leesh. You don't give your heart easily. He must be a good man.'

Leesha wanted to vomit. Jona was perhaps her oldest and closest friend, but she had kept secrets from him.

'I've given my heart a bit freely, of late,' she said. 'Arlen spun me around and Ahmann swept me away, but Thamos . . .' She hugged herself. 'Thamos is the only man I've ever loved. And I betrayed him. He's gone off, perhaps to his death, with my scalpel in his heart. How can that too be the Creator's plan?'

Jona folded his arms around her and she leaned in to him, weeping.

'I don't know,' he said, stroking her hair. 'But when this is all behind, you'll see it. Sure as the sun rises.'

The carriage path and great steps of the palace were crowded at the height of the day, abuzz with conversation and business. But as Leesha stepped down from the carriage, courtier and servant alike fell silent, turning their eyes her way.

'Tell me I'm imagining this,' Leesha said.

'Ent,' Wonda said, her eyes roving the crowd for signs of a threat. 'Spent time asking questions in the yard while you were touring Tender's towers. Gossip spread like fire last night. Didn't help that half the ripping city was in the palace.'

Wonda whisked her hand, and four Cutter women moved to flank them, eyes all around. They climbed the steps unmolested, passing through the doors and into the great hall.

It was little better. The palace servants were more professional, but even they watched Leesha and her entourage out of the corner of their eyes.

'What are people saying?' Leesha asked.

Wonda shrugged. 'Tampweed tales, mostly, but they all got the important part right – fiddle wizard from the Hollow killed the duke's herald. Difference is mostly in the spin.'

'Spin?' Leesha asked.

'City's split, just like the Hollow and everywhere else,' Wonda said. 'Common folk think Mr Bales is the Deliverer, powerful ones think he's trouble.'

'What's that have to do with Rojer?' Leesha asked, though she could easily guess. They passed into the residence wing, leaving many of the prying eyes behind, but Wonda did not dismiss the guards. Leesha did not think she would ever be alone again, if her young bodyguard had anything to say about it.

'You and Rojer helped him save the Hollow,' Wonda said. 'The ward witch and the fiddle wizard. Folk think you speak for the Deliverer when he's not around. Even in the cathedral, some are sayin' that if Rojer killed Jasin, Creator decided Jasin needed killin'.'

'That's ridiculous,' Leesha said.

'Ay, maybe,' Wonda said, though she sounded less sure. 'But true or not, anythin' happens to Rojer, folk ent gonna take it well. Liable to get some bodies hurt.'

'If something happens to Rojer,' Leesha said, 'I'm apt to be in a bit of a temper myself.'

'Honest word,' Wonda agreed as they turned a corner, seeing the knot of men in front of the door to the chambers Rojer and his women had shared. Four palace guards craned their necks up, trying to stare down the four giant Cutters Gared had stationed on the opposite wall.

The crowd parted at Leesha's approach, and Wonda stepped forward to knock.

A moment later, Kendall answered the door. 'Thank the Creator!' She stepped aside to let Wonda and Leesha in, their guards joining the throng in the hall.

Kendall was quick to shut the door and drop the bar. 'Did you see Rojer?'

'I did,' Leesha said.

'And is our husband well?' Amanvah asked, appearing at the doorway to her private chamber. The young *dama'ting* seemed relaxed and serene as ever, though Leesha thought she must be anything but.

Leesha nodded. 'No doubt he has already told you so himself.'

'Of course,' Amanvah agreed, 'though men often omit their pain, when they do not wish their wives to worry.'

Leesha smiled. 'I've never known Rojer to be that type.'

Amanvah didn't blink.

'He had been badly beaten,' Leesha said, 'but your *hora* saw to that. He's as strong as ever now, minus a pair of teeth.'

Amanvah gave a fraction of a nod. 'And Sikvah?'

Leesha sighed. 'There's been no word. If someone means to ransom her, they're making sure she's well hidden first.'

'This is intolerable,' Amanvah said. 'They will not even let us leave the chambers to look for her.'

'You're witnesses to murder in the duke's palace,' Leesha said. 'You can't expect them to let you just walk away. There's nowhere you can look that Araine's spies cannot.'

'I do not trust her *chin* spies,' Amanvah said. 'Likely they had a hand in her taking.'

Leesha's eyes flicked to the *hora* pouch at Amanvah's waist. 'May we speak in private?'

'Ay . . .!' Kendall started to protest, but Amanvah silenced her with a hiss, gesturing to her chamber.

Leesha followed, seeing all the windows covered. Even the door was draped with heavy cloth, and when Amanvah closed the door, they were enveloped in darkness. Reflexively she dropped a hand to her own *hora* pouch as she took out her spectacles with the other.

But Amanvah offered no threat. The warded coins on her headdress glowed in wardsight, blending with her aura. Neither of them could read with the facility that Arlen did, but it would be difficult to lie to each other with their auras bare.

'Would you like some tea?' Amanvah asked.

Leesha realized she was holding her breath. She blew it out with a nod. 'Creator, yes.'

There was a slight glow to the teapot, warded to keep the inside hot and the outside cool. The use of powerful magics for something so frivolous said a great deal about the *dama'ting*, who had been using *hora* magic for centuries. Leesha, for all the power she had at her fingertips, understood little of the subtleties of their warding.

'What have your dice told you?' Leesha sipped her tea, and

felt her whole body relax. Perhaps it was not so frivolous, after all.

'The *alagai hora* do not lie, mistress,' Amanvah said, sipping her own tea, 'but neither do they tell us all we would wish. I cast three times today. They have told me nothing of Sikvah's fate, and my husband's future remains . . . clouded.' There was no lie in her aura.

'Clouded?' Leesha asked. 'What does that mean?'

'It means too many divergences for the future to be assured,' Amanvah said. 'Too many plots and wills with an interest in the outcome. He is not safe. This much I can see.'

'He's locked in a tower three hundred feet off the ground, in one of the most well guarded and warded places in the world,' Leesha said.

'Pfagh!' Amanvah said. 'Your greenland defences are pathetic. Any Watcher in Krasia could get to him. Surely his enemies here can manage.'

She shook her head. 'I should have had Coliv kill this Goldentone weeks ago, whatever my husband's wishes.'

'Don't second-guess yourself,' Leesha said. 'Likely it would have been no better. You're playing at politics you don't understand.'

Amanvah shrugged. 'Blood politics never change, mistress. When someone tries to kill you and fails, you see they never have another chance.'

'It will be the courts that kill Rojer, now,' Leesha said.

Amanvah nodded. 'And I expect they would have been more likely to rule in our favour if we were back amongst your tribe.'

Leesha couldn't argue that, but there was something else in Amanvah's aura. Not deception, but . . . 'There's more you're not telling me.'

Amanvah laughed. 'Of course! Why should I trust you any more than these other greenlanders?'

Ungrateful witch. 'What have I ever done to earn your mistrust, Amanvah vah Ahmann?' Leesha asked in Krasian.

'What makes you continue to dishonour me, when I have been nothing but honest?'

'Have you?' Amanvah asked. 'Whom do you carry in your womb, mistress? My sibling, or the next Duke of Angiers?'

Leesha looked at her curiously. 'Your dice told you Rhinebeck cannot be cured,' she guessed.

'You would know for yourself, if you had examined his seed,' Amanvah said.

'I did,' Leesha said.

Amanvah's veil hid her smile, but it was clear upon her aura. 'Did you watch the *heasah* take the sample, or did you trust in her word?'

Leesha started, nearly spilling her tea. She quickly set it down, getting to her feet. 'Please excuse me.'

Amanvah nodded her dismissal. 'Of course.'

Wonda and the guardswomen nearly had to trot to keep up with Leesha as she strode through the halls of the palace, first to her own rooms for a proper vial, and then on to the duchess' chambers.

One of Melny's handmaidens answered the door, ushering Leesha in to the duchess' private chambers.

'Is there something I can do for you, mistress?' Melny asked when they were alone. Ostensibly, she was the most powerful woman in Angiers, but in practice she was nearly as submissive to Leesha as she was to Araine.

Leesha produced the warded glass vial. 'I may be on to a cure, but I need you to procure something for me, quietly.'

Rojer sat atop the desk in his cell, which he had dragged to the window so he could look out over the city as he played a mournful tune on his fiddle.

He wondered if folk below could hear him. He hoped so, for what was a Jongleur without an audience? Even if he could not see them, let them hear his pain.

It wasn't as if there was much else to do by moonlight. The Tenders had given him no lamps, and the warded mask that let him see in darkness was back in his chambers where Amanvah no doubt paced.

It wasn't as if he could demand so much as a candle. Who would he ask? He'd had no more visitors, save whatever name-less acolyte shoved the trays under his door, or took away the empty ones he shoved back. The food was simple fare, but it was nourishing enough.

The window was small – enough for him to put his head out, but not so much as a shoulder in addition. Not that it mattered. Even if he could fit through the tiny aperture, there was nothing below but air. The four towers looked down a sheer three hundred feet.

But anything was better than staring at the walls of his cell, and the view really was spectacular, all Angiers spreading out below him. He watched the flashes of energy light the town as wind demons skittered off the wardnet, and played for Amanvah.

Perhaps the Angierians could hear him and perhaps not, but he knew Amanvah was listening. He played his longing for her, his sorrow, and his fears for Sikvah. His pride and his love. His hope and passion. All the things he had tried to whisper into the *hora*, but words had failed him.

Music never did.

'Husband.'

The bow skittered off the fiddle strings. Rojer was silent, looking around, wondering if he had imagined it. Had Amanvah found a way to speak through the chinrest as well as hear?

'H-hello?' he whispered to it tentatively.

But then a hand appeared, gripping the windowsill, and Rojer fell back with a shriek, tumbling right off the table. The breath was knocked from him as he hit the floor, but years of training took over, and he was rolling the moment he hit, coming into a crouch several feet from the window.

Sikvah peered at him through the tiny aperture. She wore her black headwrap and white veil, but her eyes were unmistakable. 'Do not be alarmed, husband. It is only me.'

Memories flashed before Rojer's eyes. Sikvah crushing Sali's throat. Sikvah shattering the guard's spine. Sikvah breaking Abrum's neck.

'You have never been "only" anything, wife,' Rojer said. 'Though it seems I didn't know it by half.'

'You are right to be upset, husband,' Sikvah said. 'I have kept secrets from you, though not of my own volition. The Damajah herself commanded that I and my spear sisters keep secret our nature.'

'Amanvah knew,' Rojer said.

'She and no other in the North,' Sikvah said. 'We are blood of the Deliverer. She is *dama* blood. I am *Sharum*.'

'What are you?' Rojer asked.

'I am your *jiwah*,' she said. 'I beg of you, husband, if you believe nothing else I say, believe that. You are my light and my love, and if the Evejah did not forbid it, I would kill myself for how I have shamed you.'

'That isn't enough,' Rojer said, crossing his arms. 'If you want me to trust you again, I need to know everything.'

'Of course, husband,' Sikvah said. She sounded relieved, as if he were letting her off easy. And perhaps he was. Her entire meek persona had been an act. Who was to say her relief wasn't as well?

Part of him didn't care. Sikvah had shown him nothing but devotion since they took their vows. Even her killing was for him, and for all that had happened, Rojer could not bring himself to take it back. Somewhere, Jaycob's spirit was resting, his killers given justice at last.

'May I enter?' Sikvah asked. 'I promise to answer your every question in honesty and in sincerity.'

In sincerity? Rojer wondered. *Or insincerity?* It could have been either.

He looked at the tiny window doubtfully. 'How are you planning to do that?'

The corners of Sikvah's eyes crinkled in a smile as she stuck her head through. She twisted and her hand appeared, snaking into the room to push against the wall.

There was a pop that made Rojer flinch, and her shoulder was through. Rojer had seen a great many contortionist acts in the Jongleurs' Guild, but never anything like this. She was like a mouse squeezing through a one-inch crack under the door.

In seconds she was through, dropping into a tumble on the floor and flowing smoothly into a prostrate pose. Kneeling, she spread her hands on the floor, pressing her head to the worn carpet. She wore a silken *Sharum* garb – pantaloons, cinched robe, and headwrap of the deepest black, contrasted by the stark white of her wedding veil. Her hands and feet were bare.

'Stop that,' Rojer said. The Krasians might have enjoyed such shows of submission, but they made him deeply uncomfortable, especially from someone who could kill him with her littlest finger.

Sikvah rolled back to sit on her heels, facing him. She undid her veil, pulling the wrap back to show her hair.

Rojer went to the window, sticking his head out and looking down the sheer wall of the tower. There were no ropes, no climbing tools. Had she scaled it with hands and feet alone? 'Did Amanvah send you to free me?'

Sikvah shook her head. 'I can, if you command it, but the *Jiwah Ka* does not believe that is your wish. I am here to watch over you and keep you from harm.'

Rojer looked around the tiny room with its few furnishings. 'Not a lot of places to hide, if someone comes to check on me.'

Sikvah smiled. 'Close your eyes for two breaths.'

Rojer did, and when he opened them, Sikvah was gone. He searched the room, even looking under the low bed, but there was no sign of her. 'Where are you?'

'Here.' Her voice came from above, but even looking up at the sound, Rojer could not see her among the rafters. But then, as he looked on, one of the shadows unfurled and he caught a flash from her white veil.

Sikvah dropped silently to the floor, seeming to bounce as she struck. Even watching closely, he lost sight of her, wandering the room until her hand snaked out from under the bed to grasp his ankle. He jumped and let out a yelp.

Sikvah let go immediately, appearing a moment later at the door. She stood quietly a moment, then shook her head. 'There is a guard three flights below. He is lax and unlikely to hear, but we should be cautious.'

This time he watched in amazement as Sikvah scaled the stone wall, worn sheer over the centuries, as easily he might climb a ladder.

'When I get out of here, we're reworking our entire Jongleur's act,' Rojer said. 'You're wasted just singing.'

They spoke deep into the night, Rojer lying on his bed, hands folded beneath his head as he stared up into the darkness that cloaked Sikvah.

She told of how she had been given to the Damajah, and sent into the bowels of the Dama'ting Palace. Of the brutal training that followed.

'You must have hated Enkido,' he said.

'For a time,' she said, 'but the life of a *Sharum* is not forgiving, husband. There are no second chances in battle, as there are in performance. Enkido gave us the tools to survive. I came to see that everything he did, he did out of love.'

Rojer nodded. 'It was much the same with me and Master Arrick.' He had always taken care to present the shiny, respectful version of his master to his wives, but Sikvah was baring her life to him, and he did the same in return.

He told of how Arrick tried to leave him and his mother to

die. Of his struggles with wine, and the violence it spurred in him. How he had let the drink – and his own ego – dash their fortunes again and again.

And yet, Rojer couldn't bring himself to hate Arrick, for his dying act had been to leap over the wards and fling himself on a wood demon, that Rojer might live.

Arrick had been weak, selfish, and petty, but he had loved Rojer in his way.

Sikvah spoke without hesitation, sharing more of herself than ever before, but she had yet to have her sincerity truly tested.

'The day we met,' Rojer said. 'And you failed the test of purity . . .'

'You spoke in my defence,' Sikvah said. 'That was when I knew.'

'Knew what?' Rojer asked.

'That you were not like Krasian men,' Sikvah said. 'That when you looked at me, you did not see only property.

'I did not know you that day, husband. I had not seen your face, or heard of your deeds. I knew your tongue, but nothing of your ways, or those of your people. I was not asked to become your wife. I did not volunteer. I was given to you.'

'You're a princess, not some slave . . .' Rojer began, though he knew that even in the North, such things were not uncommon, especially at court.

'Your forgiveness, husband,' Sikvah said, 'but I am what the Damajah made of me. An instrument of her will. If she commanded I marry you, then it was *inevera* I should do so.'

'Why did she?' Rojer asked. 'Why you?' It was a simple question, but he knew it was the beginning of several that would test her loyalty to Inevera, probing deeper into her machinations in his life.

But Sikvah did not hesitate. 'To protect Amanvah, of course. The Damajah wanted a powerful and loyal agent amidst the greenlanders, but she would not place her eldest daughter at risk. There could be no better bodyguard than Enkido, but there are places a man, even a eunuch, cannot go. I, however, could be at Amanvah's side always.'

'And Amanvah?' Rojer asked. 'She is *dama'ting*. Was she at least given a choice?'

There was a whisper of silk above that might have been a shrug. 'The Damajah's words offered a choice, but her will was clear and *dama'ting* or no, Amanvah could no more refuse her than I.'

She laughed. 'I know we have always seemed as sisters to you, but before that day we despised each other.'

'She turned on you, when you failed the purity test,' Rojer said. He paused, waiting for a response, but Sikvah was silent.

'I never asked for the test,' Rojer noted. 'Quite the contrary, I said it was not needed, but Inevera insisted.'

Still Sikvah said nothing.

'And then Leesha lied, saying you passed just to spare you dishonour, yet Amanvah turned on you.'

Silence.

'Did she do it because she despised you,' Rojer asked, 'or was it an act?'

'The Damajah cast the dice before our meeting,' Sikvah admitted. 'She knew you would try to protect me.'

'Bravo,' Rojer said. 'That act had even me fooled.' He supposed he should be angry – enraged even – but he had no energy for it. The past didn't matter. That Amanvah and Sikvah had begun as Inevera's creatures was no surprise. It was what they were now he needed to know.

'Who was he?' he asked.

'Eh?' Sikvah said.

'The man who . . . knew you,' Rojer said. Part of him didn't want to know, but he had been with many women he was not proud of, and was in no position to judge.

'No one,' Sikvah said. 'I broke my hymen in *sharusahk* training. My dishonour to you was a fiction only.'

Rojer shrugged. 'You certainly seemed to know what you were doing.'

Again she laughed, a sweet, tinkling sound. 'The *dama'ting* taught us pillow dancing, that my spear sisters and I could appear the perfect brides.'

Pillow dancing. The very word made him squirm. He changed the subject. 'Why did Amanvah poison Leesha?'

For the first time, there was a pause. 'Amanvah brewed the poison, husband, but it was I who dosed her tea.'

'That doesn't answer my question,' Rojer said. 'You were both in on the plot. What does it matter who did what?'

'The Damajah was vexed when your mistress' influence caused my uncle to create the *Sharum'ting*,' Sikvah said. 'The women of Krasia were ever her purview, and she had another fate planned for them.'

'You tried to kill my friend because she persuaded Jardir to give rights to women?' Rojer asked.

'I put blackleaf in her tea because the Damajah commanded it,' Sikvah said. 'For my own part, I was pleased with Shar'Dama Ka's proclamation. My spear sisters have been allowed to come out of hiding, and earn glory in the night. I regret I was never allowed to do the same.'

'That can change,' Rojer said. 'The secret's out. When we get back to the Hollow, you can . . .'

'Apologies, husband, but the secret remains,' Sikvah said. 'None alive can tell the tale save you and my sister-wives. My ability to protect you and my *Jiwah Ka* would be greatly lessened if others knew of my skills.'

'And if I, as your husband, command that you cease hiding what you are?' Rojer asked.

'Then I will obey,' Sikvah said. 'But I will think you a fool.'

Rojer laughed at that. 'You said you could break me out of here. How?'

'The door is thick, but it is only wood,' Sikvah said. 'I could break it, but it would take time, and rouse the clerics. Easier to slip out the window and climb down to a lower level. Your *chin* Holy Men are not warriors like the *dama*. It would be simple to kill the guards and retrieve the keys.'

'I don't want you killing anyone,' Rojer said. 'Not unless our lives depend on it.'

'Of course,' Sikvah said. 'The *Jiwah Ka* knew you would wish it so.'

Rojer thought of his chinrest, safe in its warded case. 'Is she listening to us now?'

'Yes,' Sikvah said. 'My choker allows her to hear me when she wishes.'

'And can she speak to you as well?' Rojer asked.

'Yes,' Sikvah said again. 'But the *hora* is attuned to me alone. It will not work for you. The *dama'ting* labours even now to craft an earring for you. She apologizes for not having done so sooner. In the meantime, I shall be her voice.'

'And what does she have to say?' Rojer asked.

'That it is late,' Sikvah said, 'and we do not know what the coming day will bring. She bids you sleep while there is still some darkness.'

Rojer stared up into the darkness. 'Are you going to sleep in the rafters?'

'I do not need sleep as you,' Sikvah said. 'I will meditate to restore myself, remaining alert to any threat. Close your eyes, my love, and know that I am watching over you.'

Rojer did as she asked, indeed feeling safe, but there was too much swirling in his thoughts, and he was restless. 'I don't think I can sleep.'

There was barely a sound as Sikvah dropped to the floor. Rojer flinched as she slipped naked into the bed with him.

'The *Jiwah Ka* commands I soothe you to sleep, husband,' she purred.

'Has everything between us been a command?' Rojer asked.

Sikvah kissed him, her lips no less soft now that he knew how hard she could be. 'Just because I am commanded to do a thing, husband, does not mean I do not wish it.' Efficiently, she removed his motley pants. 'Or that I do not take my own pleasure in it.'

Leesha turned the dial, adjusting her lens chamber.

The difference in samples was immediate. There had been few living seeds in the one Rosal provided. This one was positively brimming with them, though they were sluggish and weak.

Drugged.

She looked out the window. The sun was barely cresting the horizon. Would Araine be up at this hour?

It was too important to wait. She sent a runner, and the girl returned almost immediately with a summons from the Duchess Mum.

'You're sure?' Araine demanded when she arrived. 'This isn't some trick of the white witch to bargain for her husband?' The old woman was still in her dressing gown, a surprisingly worn and simple cloth, but she lost none of her regal bearing, and was in no mood for pleasantries.

Leesha nodded. 'Amanvah may be looking to bargain, Your Grace, but she was right. This isn't the same man's issue. Unless you mistrust Melny . . .'

Araine waved the thought away. 'That girl hasn't an ounce of guile, and nothing to gain by lying in any event.'

'Then Rosal lied to us,' Leesha said. 'And I doubt the conspiracy ends there.'

Araine nodded. 'This has been going on since that girl was soiling her nappies.' She tsked. 'Pity. Your Gared will be heart-broken when she's hung for treason.'

'She may only be a pawn in this,' Leesha said carefully. 'Perhaps we can show mercy, if she leads us to the real traitor in your court.' Already she had her suspicions.

'You think Jessa did it,' Araine said.

Leesha shrugged. 'Perhaps. In part.'

Araine huffed, getting to her feet. 'Send a runner to summon the white witch in one hour, then wait in my sitting room while I put my armour on.'

An hour later, Araine was once again clad in fine raiment with her crown in place, staring down Amanvah, who at least had the humility to bow more deeply than the Duchess Mum.

'Do you know who has been drugging my son?' Araine asked.

Amanvah's head dipped slightly, eyes revealing nothing behind her veil. 'I do.'

'Not just who gave it to him, but who ordered it done?' Araine asked.

Again the slight nod. Araine waited, but Amanvah said nothing more. The minutes crawled by as they stared at each other, each a study in royal dignity.

'Will you share it?' Araine asked at last.

Amanvah gave a slight shrug. 'My husband sits locked in a tower alone, just for defending himself under your roof. My sister-wife is missing, and you have done nothing to search for her. Kendall and I remain prisoners in our chambers. Tell me, Duchess Mother, why should I help you?'

Araine's finger began tapping the side of her delicate porcelain cup, causing little ripples in the surface of the tea. 'Apart from the obvious? I could free your husband. Search the city top to bottom for Sikvah. Release you from confinement.'

Amanvah shook her head gently as she stirred her tea. 'Apologies, Duchess, but you cannot. I have cast on this. You do not have the power in your son's court to assure me of any of those things. Your power is great, but you rule Angiers in the details between decrees, and my husband's fate is too public to avoid the duke's notice. The future is full of divergences, but all fates agree that you cannot sway his judgement.'

Araine kept her poise, but her lips disappeared as she pressed them together. There were few things the woman disliked more than reminders of the limits of her power.

'Perhaps not,' Araine said at last. 'There will be a trial – nothing can stop that – but do not be so quick to dismiss my offer. I may not be able to sway my son's judgement, but clemency is one of the few legal powers I still command. Even if Rhinebeck sentences your husband to execution, I can pardon him with a wave of my hand, and not all my sons together could stop it.'

Amanvah stared at her a long time. Then she turned her eyes to Leesha. 'Is this true?'

Leesha glanced at Araine, then back to Amanvah. She shrugged. 'I am no expert in Angierian law, but it is certainly possible.'

'I can produce the necessary documents to prove it,' Araine said.

Amanvah shook her head, getting to her feet. 'That will not be necessary. I will cast on this.'

'Do it here, if you wish,' Araine said, though it sounded more a command than a request. 'I would see this dice magic at work.'

Amanvah considered a moment, then nodded. She looked to Leesha, who set down her tea and went to pull the heavy curtains as Amanvah knelt on the hardwood floor between lush carpets, spreading out her pristine white casting cloth.

Leesha was forced to drag carpets to plug the light seeping in under the doors, but soon the only light came from the glow of the *alagai hora* in Amanvah's hands. Leesha and the Duchess Mum paid rapt attention, but Amanvah muttered her prayers in Krasian, and neither of them could make out much with her lips hidden behind her veil.

She produced a small stoppered vial – presumably Rojer's blood – and dribbled it sparingly over the dice before she shook and cast. It was eerie, watching the wards flare as the dice were yanked from their natural trajectories to form the pattern. Leesha couldn't begin to read what they said, but after staring for some time, Amanvah nodded and sat back on her heels. Leesha took a chemic light vial from her apron, shaking it to cast them all in its luminescent glow.

'I will require three things,' Amanvah said.

'Three things, in exchange for one,' Araine said.

Amanvah shrugged. 'You may attempt to haggle if you wish.' Her tone made it clear the effort would be pointless.

'What three things?' Araine asked.

'You will pardon my husband, myself, and my sister-wives, the moment the trial is done,' Amanvah said. 'Without equivocation or addendum. We will be free to go, and granted your protection until we are back in the Hollow.'

Araine nodded. 'Done.'

'You will grant me daily visitation rights with my husband,' Amanvah went on.

'I can give you an hour a day with him, until the trial,' Araine said.

Amanvah nodded. 'That is acceptable.'

'And last?' Araine asked.

Amanvah turned to Leesha. 'A drop of Mistress Leesha's blood.'

Leesha crossed her arms. 'Absolutely not!' There was no telling what mischief the woman could cause with that single drop. It was an insult simply to ask.

'Leesha,' Araine said, a warning in her tone.

'You don't understand what she's asking,' Leesha said. 'Giving a *dama'ting* your blood is tantamount to handing them a knife and baring your throat. Why should I ever agree to that?'

'Because the fate of my duchy may rest upon it!' Araine hissed. 'Give it to her, or I will have it taken from you.'

Leesha bared her teeth. 'Don't threaten me, Araine. I will defend myself, and the child I carry. If your guards so much as lay a hand on me, I will bring this palace down around your ears.'

Araine's eyes flashed, but Leesha meant every word, and the old woman knew it. She held the Duchess Mum's eyes for a moment, then looked to Amanvah. 'Two conditions.'

Amanvah's eyes crinkled. Krasians did so love to bargain. 'And those are?'

'You use the drop here and now, speaking your question aloud in Thesan,' Leesha began.

Amanvah nodded. 'And the second?'

'You will agree to throw the dice for me once in the future,' Leesha said. 'The time and question at my discretion.'

Amanvah's eyes narrowed. 'Agreed. So long as your question does not directly affect my people or household.'

In answer, Leesha took a lancet from her apron pocket and lifted her finger, poised to puncture. 'Are we all in agreement, then?'

'Ay,' Araine said.

'We are,' Amanvah confirmed.

'Hold out your dice.' Leesha pressed the lancet to the pad of her index finger, squeezing a single drop onto Amanvah's dice.

The *dama'ting* rolled them in her palm until confident the blood had touched them all. Then she turned back to her cloth, hands beginning to shake. 'Almighty Everam, giver of light and life, grant your servant knowledge of what is to come. Show your humble servant the fate of the child carried by Leesha vah Erny am'Paper am'Hollow.'

Leesha felt the child kick as the dice flared and twisted in midthrow. Amanvah bent forward hungrily, reading the hidden meanings.

'Well?' Leesha demanded at last. 'What do they say?'

Amanvah scooped up the dice, returning them to her *hora* pouch. 'I agreed to ask the question aloud for you to hear, mistress, but I never agreed to share the answer.'

Leesha's jaw tightened, but Araine cut off her response. 'Enough! Settle this on your own time.' She looked hard at Amanvah. 'I tire of your games and delays, Princess. We have paid your price. Now cast your dice and tell me who is having my son drugged. Easterly? Wardgood? Euchor? One of my sons?'

Amanvah shook her head. 'Your Weed Gatherer works alone.'

There was a stunned silence, and for once, Araine lost a bit of her regal bearing, eyes bulging like a toad. 'Why?'

Amanvah shrugged. 'Ask her, and she will tell you herself. It is a secret carried too long, and must be lanced like a boil.'

'And the drug?' Leesha asked, when it seemed Araine would take all day to process the information.

'A tincture in his wine,' Amanvah said. 'I cannot say what exactly, but it does not matter. If the doses stop, his seed will recover on its own.'

'That will take months,' Leesha said.

'You can speed the process with *hora*,' Amanvah said. 'I will prepare a bone for the healing.'

She rolled back on her heels, getting to her feet. 'I have fulfilled my part of the bargain. I will see my husband now.'

Araine recovered somewhat at the *dama'ting*'s imperious tone. She shook her head. 'You will sit quietly while I test this information. You will see your husband when I am satisfied, and not before.'

Amanvah's veil billowed as she blew out an angry breath. She and the Duchess Mum locked stares, but after a moment she gave a curt nod. 'I will wait, but if I have not seen my husband and assured myself that he is well by sunset today, I will hold your oath broken.'

Araine's foot began to twitch, but she said nothing.

Leesha struggled to remember Rojer's lessons as she smiled at Rosal and Jessa, come at the Duchess Mum's summons, presumably to discuss Gared's very obvious interest in the girl.

Rojer had taught her much about royal bearing, how to project her voice even when speaking quietly, and how to hold a mask in place, showing only serenity to others no matter what she was feeling inside. It was a lesson she struggled with to this day.

'If you please, mistress,' Leesha said, 'Her Grace would speak to Miss Lacquer alone, before you are called into the discussion.'

Rosal glanced at Jessa in concern, but the woman waved dismissively. 'Go on, girl.'

'I'll make you proud,' Rosal promised.

Jessa touched her shoulder affectionately. 'You could never do otherwise.'

The words struck Leesha, mirroring almost exactly her last words with Mistress Bruna. She wondered what it meant for the women. It might be goodbye for them, as well.

She led Rosal through the doors to Araine's cavernous sitting room. They kept on all the way through, going through another set of doors to a private receiving room with thick walls to deter eavesdroppers.

Inside the chamber, Wonda closed the door, standing to one side of the portal. On the other was another Cutter woman, Bekka, equally huge and menacing. Amanvah sat in a corner by the back wall, staring impassively. The tiny Angierian girl glanced at them nervously before dipping into a graceful curtsy to the Duchess Mum. Gone was the arrogance she had shown Leesha in her chambers.

'Your Grace,' Rosal said, remaining bent so her face was nearly on the floor. 'It is an honour to be summoned. I am your obedient servant.'

'Stand up, girl,' Araine snapped. 'Give a turn and let me have a look at you.'

Rosal did, obediently giving a slow turn, her posture perfect and face like a carven statue.

'The baron wants your hand,' Araine said bluntly. 'Any fool can see it. And a man who wants something that much will usually get it.'

Rosal's cheeks coloured artfully, but there had been no question, and so she remained silent.

'But not this time,' Araine said. Rosal did well to hide her dismay, but even this artful creature had a twitch to her face at the words. 'You'll be more likely to spend the rest of your days in a dungeon cell than the count's bed.'

At this, Rosal's composure fell away, her jaw slackening. 'Your Grace?'

'Whose seed did you bring Mistress Leesha?' Araine demanded. 'I know it was not my son's.'

Rosal froze, eyes wide as a frightened doe. She glanced at the door, but the two Cutter women stepped in front of the portal, crossing their arms.

'I'm not hearing an answer,' Araine said testily. 'Unless you want to end the day hanging from a gibbet in Traitor's Square, you'd best become cooperative.'

'J-Jax,' Rosal said. 'The seed was his.'

'Why?' Araine demanded.

'Mistress Jessa,' Rosal began, and the Duchess Mum gave a hiss. 'She said Mistress Leesha sought to supplant her as Royal Mistress, stealing her position and taking control of the school.'

'I want no such . . .!' Leesha began, but Araine silenced her with a sharp gesture.

'You put the whole duchy at risk for your mistress' reputation?' Araine asked.

Rosal shrank to her knees, tears streaking the pencil around her eyes and the powders on her face. 'I-I didn't . . . Mistress Jessa would have found a cure, if one was to be had. W-what could I do?'

What indeed? Leesha wondered. Mistress Jessa held Rosal's life in her hands. She could not be expected to betray her and hope the duchess took her word over her mistress'.

She felt for the girl, but there was nothing of mercy in Araine's glare. 'Have you been poisoning the duke, as well?'

Rosal seemed genuinely shocked. 'W-what? No! Never!' She paused. 'Sometimes Mistress Jessa give us fertility potions for him . . .'

Araine waved her off. 'I believe you, girl, though it makes your deed no less treasonous.'

'Please, Your Grace . . .' Rosal began.

'Quiet,' Araine said. 'You've told me what I needed to know. If you've an interest in keeping your tongue, keep it still while I speak to your mistress.'

She turned to the door. 'Be a dear, Wonda, and escort Jessa in.'

'Ay, Mum,' Wonda said, opening the door and returning soon after on the heels of Mistress Jessa.

Jessa strolled into the room casually enough, but stopped short at the sight of Rosal kneeling on the floor, tears streaking black down her face. She glanced back, but Wonda had already closed the portal, and she and Bekka blocked the way with arms crossed.

Jessa took a breath and turned back, scanning the room with a predatory eye. She wore a pocketed apron, and Leesha knew well how much mischief she might still cause with its contents.

'I take it Your Grace does not find Rosal suitable for the young baron?' Jessa asked.

'How long have you been drugging Rhinebeck into seedlessness?' Araine demanded.

Jessa took a step forward, spreading her hands. 'This is nonsense . . .'

'Take off your apron,' Leesha said.

'What?' Jessa took another step forward, and Leesha dropped a hand to her *hora* pouch.

'Wonda,' Araine said, 'if Jessa takes another step without laying her apron on the floor, put an arrow in her leg.'

Wonda drew back an arrow. 'Which leg?'

The corner of Araine's mouth twitched a smirk. 'Surprise me, dear.'

Jessa's brow tightened, but she did as she was bid, removing the apron and laying it on the floor as she glared at Leesha. 'Your Grace, I don't know what she's told you . . .'

'Nothing Bruna didn't tell me decades ago,' Araine said, 'though I was too stubborn to listen.'

'What proof . . .' Jessa began.

'This isn't a court,' Araine said. 'I need no magistrate to dismiss you from service and throw you in irons for the rest of your life. You're not here to argue evidence.'

'Then what am I here for?' Jessa demanded.

'You're here to tell me why,' Araine said. 'I've always been good to you.'

'Why?!' Jessa demanded. 'When Rhinebeck treats my girls and I like spittoons? When the Duke of Angiers is fool enough to be led around by the nose by his mother, and throws poor Halfgrip out in the street just for sleeping in the wrong bed?'

'So you thought to replace him with one of his fool brothers?' Araine asked. 'They might have had an extra scrape or two at the whetstone, but none of them is terribly sharp.'

'I don't care how sharp they are,' Jessa said. 'None of the others tried to stick me.'

'Eh?' Araine asked.

'I don't work. You promised,' Jessa said. 'I was to recruit willing girls and train them, but my skirts were to remain down.'

Araine's mouth tightened. 'But Rhiney didn't see it that way.'

'He wasn't even interested in me,' Jessa said. 'All he wanted was to mark every woman in the brothel. He was the duke, his right to spread his seed granted by the Creator Himself.'

'So you took it from him,' Araine said. 'You should have told me.'

'Why?' Jessa demanded. 'What would you have done?'

Araine spread her hands. 'I suppose we'll never know. What I wouldn't have done is put the safety and stability of the duchy in jeopardy for decades on end.'

'Don't be so dramatic,' Jessa said. 'You've no shortage of idiot sons to replace Rhinebeck, and grandsons by Mickael. If it came down to marrying the Milnese bitch or naming one of Mickael's sons his heir, Rhinebeck would have gotten over his sibling rivalry.'

'Once, perhaps,' Araine said. 'But with war brewing, you left us weak for the plucking.'

'That was your stubbornness as much as mine,' Jessa said. 'I expected you to see the night was dark a decade ago and have Thamos slip in and seed one of the endless procession of young duchesses. Instead you sent him on a fool's errand.'

Araine blew a breath out her nostrils, foot kicking as she considered. At last she nodded. 'I'll decide what to do with you later. For now, you can wave to young Master Halfgrip from your room atop the West Tower.' She thrust a chin at Bekka, and the woman came forward and took Jessa's arm in a vice-like grip.

As she was pulled from the room, Jessa's eyes flicked to Rosal, still kneeling on the floor. 'The girl has nothing—'

'—to gain, having you speak on her behalf,' Araine cut her off. She gave a wave, and the guard dragged the woman off. Leesha tensed, wondering if she would resist, but the Weed Gatherer seemed resigned to her fate.

'Night,' Araine said, when Wonda closed the door behind them. She seemed to deflate, and Leesha was reminded just how tiny the woman really was.

But the vulnerability vanished in an instant as the Duchess Mum turned her attention back upon Rosal. 'Now, girl, what am I to do with you?'

Rosal began to sob again, and it wasn't hard to see why. Jessa might warrant a cathedral tower, but Rosal was . . . disposable. Araine could have her hung before the day was out if she wished.

'Amanvah,' Leesha said, surprising herself. 'I'll have my throw of the dice now.'

The *dama'ting* looked at her in surprise. 'You would waste a question before Everam on a *heasah*?'

'On a woman's life,' Leesha corrected.

'I'm afraid I agree with the princess,' Araine said. 'It hardly seems . . .'

'I was engaged to Gared Cutter, once,' Leesha said. 'I may have forsworn him, but I still have an interest in the matter. The Hollow needs him, and he needs a woman who can help shoulder the burden better than those vapid debutantes you keep sitting him with at dinner.'

Araine grunted. 'I can't deny that.'

'Thank the Creator,' Rosal gasped.

'Don't go thanking anyone just yet, girl,' Araine snipped.

Rosal's eyes went wide with fear as Amanvah slipped the curved dagger from the sheath at her belt. 'Hold out your arm, girl.'

Rosal shivered, but she did as she was told. Amanvah's cut was quick, catching the blood in an empty teacup. Araine gestured for Wonda to remove the girl. When she was gone, the duchess turned back to watch as Amanvah knelt on the floor, bathed in the *hora*'s glow as she cast.

'She will be a loyal wife,' Amanvah said, reading the pattern, 'to him, and to the Hollow tribe. She will bear him strong sons, but it will be his daughter who succeeds him.' She rolled back on her heels, looking to Leesha and Araine.

'If I agree,' Araine noted.

Amanvah shook her head. 'Apologies, Your Grace, but you have no choice. The son of Steave will accept no other.'

Araine frowned. 'Then let him take her and be done. I want her gone from my sight before I've chance to change my mind.'

'Mistress!' Wonda burst through the door, holding Bekka in her arms. 'She ent breathin'!'

Leesha came forward in a rush. Amanvah was already drawing *hora* from her pouch.

'Shut the door,' the *dama'ting* said.

Wonda moved to comply, but Araine grabbed her arm. 'Where's Jessa?'

'Gone,' Wonda said. 'Found Bekka lying out in the hall.'

'Find her,' Araine ordered. 'I want every guard in the palace searching for that witch.'

Wonda nodded, and was gone.

'Sometimes I wonder what my life would have been like if Master Piter had just done his ripping job and checked the wards,' Rojer said.

Sikvah, hidden somewhere in the rafters, did not answer. She seldom did, save when he asked her a question directly, or she needed to speak for Amanvah. Even then, she would drop to the floor and come in close, speaking quietly for only them to hear.

Rojer didn't mind. It was enough to know she was there, listening. More than the feeling of safety at her presence, or her warm embrace in the night, it was the sense of companionship she lent him that allowed him to endure his confinement without cracking.

Someone to listen. Someone to care. What Jongleur could long survive without those things? Rojer had seen once great performers become shadows of themselves when their audiences began to thin.

'I'd have had brothers and sisters,' Rojer went on, picturing them so clearly in his mind he could almost name them. 'Mum and Da were young. They seemed old as the trees then, but looking back I see I was supposed to be the first of many.' He sighed wistfully, thinking of childhood games and laughter lost.

'Wasn't an instrument in all Riverbridge, back then,' Rojer said, 'much less someone who could play one. Odds are I'd have gone on to run the inn, married some homely local girl, and had a brood of my own. Never gone anywhere, never seen or done anything special. Might've just been . . . normal.'

There was a snap as the latch of the cell door turned. The portal opened to reveal . . .

'Amanvah!' Rojer leapt to his feet and fair flew across the room.

'You speak nonsense, husband,' Amanvah said quietly as they embraced. 'You are touched by Everam. You could never be normal. If Master Arrick had not brought you to the fiddle, another would have. Sharak Ka is coming, and it was *inevera* that you bring the *Song of Waning* back to Ala.'

'You could have done that without me,' Rojer said.

Amanvah shook her head. 'You may have passed some of your gift to your wives, but it was yours to pass.'

She lifted her veil, kissing him. He tried to tighten the embrace, but she put out her hands, pushing him back while her veil drifted back down in front of her mouth like a curtain after the last act.

'I have but an hour with you each day, husband,' she said, 'until this matter is resolved. There are things we must attend first.'

She clapped loudly, and the door opened again, two burly acolytes hauling in heavy casks of water. Another carried a small wooden tub, just big enough for Rojer to scrunch himself into. Behind them, little more than a shadow, Sikvah flitted to the floor and out the open portal.

'You carried that all the way up here?' Rojer asked, looking at the heavy casks.

The men glared at him looking none too pleased, but they said nothing.

'Do not take their silence for rudeness, husband,' Amanvah said. 'They are forbidden to speak to prisoners. Her Grace has ordered better food for you, and thrice-weekly baths. These men are proud to follow her royal commands.'

The men did not look proud to Rojer as they gave him one last look and huffed out of the room.

'Sikvah . . .' Rojer said quietly, as the door shut behind them.

'Will ensure our privacy for the next hour,' Amanvah said, dropping warded silver stones into the casks. They hissed as magic heated the water.

'Please, husband,' she said, gesturing to the tub. Rojer knew better than to argue, undressing and climbing in. The lacquered wood was cool, and he shivered, breaking into goose pimples as Amanvah lifted the first cask to pour hot water over him.

Immediately Rojer began to calm. This was not the great tub at Shamavah's, but the daily bathing ritual was something he had become accustomed to, and had not even realized he missed.

'I have begun making you an earring,' Amanvah said as she worked at him with a brush and cake of soap. 'But it will be weeks of work, and I hope to see you free long before it is complete.'

'No doubt it will have other uses as well,' Rojer said. 'What greater purpose could magic have for me, than to hear your sweet voice from afar?'

Amanvah embraced him, choking back a sob. Rojer hugged her to him, mindless of how he was soaking her robes.

Amanvah broke off with a sniff, stepping back to remove the wet silk. 'If you put me on my back and spend in me, husband, you will get me with child.'

Rojer had begun to relax at last, leaning back in the tub, but he stiffened at the words, sitting up sharply. 'Amanvah, this isn't the time . . .'

'It is,' Amanvah cut in. 'If I wish to carry your child, it must be now.'

Rojer swallowed. 'I don't like what that says about my chances.'

Amanvah knelt by the tub again, running her hands over his bare chest, no longer washing. 'Nor I,' she admitted. 'Your future is clouded, but not only yours. We are approaching a great divergence, and many in this city may walk the lonely path ere it passes.'

She slid a hand up his neck, cupping his cheek and pulling him into a kiss. 'But there is a pillar in the stream. If you have me now, I will bear your child.'

'So you will survive this . . . divergence?' Rojer asked.

'Until the birth, at least. After that . . .' Amanvah shrugged, kissing his neck.

Rojer flinched. 'Maybe we should wait, then.'

Amanvah looked at him in confusion.

'I don't want to leave you to raise our child alone,' Rojer said. 'You aren't even twenty. If I die, you should take a new husband. One who can . . .'

Amanvah took his face in her hands. 'Oh, husband. I will not be alone. I have my sister-wives, and you do not understand us well if you think we will forsake you if you must travel the lonely path.'

She stood, accentuating the sway of her hips as she walked to the small bed. 'I am *dama'ting*. All Everam requires is that

I bear a daughter and heir.' She lay on her back, opening her legs. 'Give her to me, and I will never need the touch of another man.'

Rojer was out of the tub in a rush, mindless of the wet as he climbed atop her. 'A daughter?'

Amanvah smiled. 'Sikvah already carries your son.'

Janson watched Leesha without watching her. The first minister's full attention appeared to be on the Duchess Mum, but his aura said otherwise. He was intensely aware of Leesha's presence, and frustrated at not knowing the reason. He was accustomed to being Araine's right hand, and did not like that Leesha appeared to be coming between them.

'Fear not, Janson,' she said. 'I'll be gone back to the Hollow soon enough.'

The minister looked at her in surprise. The man had not spoken, but his feelings had been so strong she had responded instinctively.

This is what it was like for Arlen, she realized, once again coming to understand the man too late. There was an ache in her heart at the thought she might never see him again, something the demons had used against her. Likely they had seen the need written on her aura much as easily as she read Janson's.

'Not too soon,' Araine noted. 'You have duties yet.' She turned to Janson. 'Have you found Jessa?'

The first minister shook his head. 'She was seen entering the tunnel, but none claim to have seen her on the far end. I have the school under guard, and we are searching it top-to-bottom.'

'That place is full of secret passages,' Araine said. 'Have the students and staff removed, and have your men rap on every wall. If it's hollow, search the passage or break it down. And by the Creator, tell them to be careful. The witch would have killed Bekka with her poison needle if Leesha and Amanvah had not been on the scene to minister to her.'

Janson bowed. 'It will be done. We are also conducting searches of Mistress Jessa's other properties, and her known associates. The guards at the gate know to search every cart and look under every hood. We'll find her.'

Araine nodded, though her aura was unsure. Betrayal coloured her, but she continued to hold Jessa in high regard. She was dangerous, and Araine was worried she might well slip through their nets.

'Was there something else?' Janson asked. His aura made it clear he knew there was more. She would not have summoned him simply to repeat the same orders she had given hours ago.

'We needed the Krasian princess' help to uncover the plot,' Araine said. 'There was a price.'

Janson's aura shifted, hardening as he realized what she was getting at. 'Halfgrip.'

Araine nodded. 'He will go to his trial, but regardless of what happens, I will pardon him.'

'Your Grace,' Janson began, his voice tightening. 'My nephew was a pompous ass, and often a burden upon the ivy throne, but he was my nephew all the same. I cannot simply let—'

'You can and you will,' Araine cut him off. 'I don't expect you to like it, but it was necessary, and there will be rioting in the streets if he's harmed. He'll stay in the tower until the trial, but when Mistress Leesha returns to the Hollow, he and Tender Jona will be joining her.'

Janson's aura flared hot with rage. So hot Leesha tensed, slipping a hand into her *hora* pouch to clutch at her wand. If he made the slightest move towards the duchess, she would blast him into a thousand pieces.

But then all the burning emotion collapsed, forced down by a will so strong it frightened Leesha as much as the anger. The first minister only bowed stiffly. 'As Your Grace commands.' He turned on a heel and strode from the room, not waiting to be dismissed.

Araine sighed. 'I've often said I'd pay any price to solve my son's seedlessness, but I didn't think it would cost my two closest allies in a single day.'

Leesha laid a hand over hers. 'You have others. Lord Janson will come around, once we are gone from the city.'

But remembering the rage in his aura, she was not so sure.

24

Briar
333—334 AR Winter

Briar woke in the hogroot patch in the duchess' gardens. Mum had offered a proper bed, but Briar hadn't slept in a bed or with a roof over his head for almost a decade. Not since he was six years old, and his carelessness had burned his family out into the naked night.

Fear had kept him alive all those years. That nervous edge alerting him to every sound, every flicker of movement. He did not sleep so much as close his eyes for a few hours now and again, ready to move on a moment's notice. Warded walls and soft beds led a person to forget that the night waited right outside, ready to take everything.

And to forget that was to die.

Briar grabbed hogroot leaves as he got to his feet, stuffing them into his pockets. The weed was common enough, but a person in the night could never have too much.

The commotion at the palace went on until late in the night, cries of murder dying down into a fitful silence as the killer was dragged from the palace to the Holy House. It was none of Briar's concern. There were people in Lakton counting on him to bring help from the duke. Nothing was more important than getting Count Thamos to the monastery.

He went to the stables, but there was none of the bustle he expected. No horses being readied, no soldiers mustering. He caught a stable hand by the arm. 'Where's count?'

The woman looked at Briar, wrinkling her nose. She stank of dung, but the smell of hogroot was distasteful? This is where sleeping in a bed took you. 'Say again?'

Used to watching others from hiding, Briar had barely spoken for years. He understood Thesan and Krasian, but speaking was still foreign to him, and it was difficult sometimes to be understood.

'Sposedta guide the count south. Where is he?'

'Doubt *His Highness* Prince Thamos is going anywhere today,' the woman said. 'This business with the fiddle wizard has the whole city in an uproar.'

Briar squeezed her arm tighter. 'Can't wait. People counting on us.'

'Ay, what am I supposed to do about it?!' the hand cried, yanking her arm away. 'I ent the Duchess Mum!'

Briar started, taking a step back and putting up his hands. He could see his handprint reddening on the woman's arm. 'Sorry. Din't mean to squeeze.'

'S'all right,' the woman said, but she rubbed her arm, and Briar knew it would bruise. People weren't like cories. They were soft. You could hurt them, if you weren't careful.

He went back to the gardens and slipped through the little-used palace entrance there. Guards everywhere, servants bustling to and fro, but none of them noticed his passage as more than a whiff of hogroot in the air. The halls had endless places to hide, if you were quick.

But Mum and Janson were behind closed doors, and Briar only knew a handful of other people in Angiers. None of them could be found. He returned to the garden, crawling into the hogroot patch and closing his eyes.

Some time later there were voices. Briar tensed, ready to flee, but the voices were not directed at him, and he crept closer to listen. Even before he reached them, he knew it was Leesha Paper. The smell of her pocketed apron, filled with dozens of herbs, reminded him of his mother. Briar liked the mistress, even if folks called her a witch. They said the same thing of Dawn.

'Not going anywhere while they've got Rojer held up!' Gared, the Baron of Cutter's Hollow, shouted.

'Keep your voice down,' Leesha whispered.

'Ya seen him,' Gared said. 'He beat up bad?'

Leesha nodded. 'But nothing I couldn't heal with bone magic. He'll need some new teeth, but he's all right now.'

Gared clenched a fist. 'Swear by the son, if that runt Jasin wan't already dead . . .'

'Don't finish that sentence, Gar,' Leesha said. 'It's all the more reason you should go.'

'How's that?' Gared asked.

'You won't help things here,' Leesha said. 'And if you want Rosal to go with you, you'd best take her now, before one of the Royals gets it in mind to stop you.'

When he looked unconvinced, she put a hand on his arm. 'And while you're there, would you be so kind as to ready a few thousand Cutters to return here and escort us home? The roads are so full of bandits these days . . .'

Gared's brows drew tight in confusion, then lifted suddenly. 'Oh, ay. I get it. You want me to . . .'

'I want you ready to see the Hollow delegation safely home,' Leesha said. 'All of us. Whatever the court decides.'

'Duke ent gonna like that,' Gared said.

'I don't imagine he will,' Leesha said. 'I know I have no right to ask it . . .'

'Core ya don't,' Gared said. 'Hollow owes you and Rojer everythin', and ya belong safe at home with us. Duke and his Wooden Soldiers don't wanna throw in with that . . .' He spat. 'Ent no one chops wood like a Cutter.'

'It won't go that far,' Leesha said. 'Show them teeth, but don't bite.'

'Won't,' Gared said. 'So long as Rojer keeps breathin'. I come back and find he ent . . .'

He left the thought hanging in the air and strode off.

Briar looked at the reins the stable hand thrust at him and shook his head. He liked horses well enough, but he didn't trust them. 'I'll run.'

'That won't be good enough, Briar,' Thamos said. 'I mean to press hard for the Hollow.'

Briar shrugged.

'I need you to keep up,' Thamos said.

Briar nodded. 'Ay.'

The count looked irritated, though Briar couldn't understand why.

'You won't be able to keep pace with my cavalry on foot,' Thamos said.

Briar tilted his head. 'Why not?'

The count looked at him a long time, then shrugged. 'Have it your way, boy. But if you lag behind, I'll sling you from my saddle like a deer.'

Briar laughed, surprised the others did not join him. It was a good joke.

Thamos climbed into his own saddle, raising his spear as the city gates opened. 'Forward!'

Briar took off at a run as the cavalrymen kicked their horses into a trot. They kept pace with him for a while, but there was traffic on the road this close to the city, and even those who immediately gave way choked the streets and slowed the count's men. On foot, Briar was able to slip from the road and avoid the traffic and the inevitable stares and questions.

He quickly left them behind, gathering food where he could as he explored the terrain, making note of villages and paths. Mum said he would be coming to Angiers often, so it was best to know the ways. He took careful notice of the hogroot patches, and scattered seeds where there were none. The weed was aggressive, and thrived most anywhere.

Even taking the extra time, he had to backtrack north along the side of the road that evening to find the supper camp. Briar watched in envy from the scrub at the side of the road as the soldiers stood in patient lines to be given a bowl of thick soup and a loaf of bread.

The roots and nuts he'd found filled his belly well enough, but his mouth watered at the smell of the bread and soup. He knew they would give him some. All he needed to do was stand in the line.

But the soldiers all looked alike, in matching wooden armour and cloaks, tabards bearing the count's arms. They belonged. Briar did not. They would stare at him. Call him Stinky or Mudboy, when they thought he could not hear. They would keep their distance, or worse, speak to him.

He wanted bread, but not that badly.

The men were quickly back in the saddle, readying arms as the sun set. They resumed march, killing cories as they went with practised precision.

Already, the demons were learning to avoid the open road, pacing the procession in the trees, watching. Wood demons were patient when prey could outrun them or fight back. Briar saw one demon up ahead swing into a large tree whose limbs stretched out over the road. The demon climbed quickly, perching hidden in the branches as it waited.

The cory let the fighting cavalry pass, but the count and baron rode behind the first ranks at a more stately pace. The others gave the two men a wide berth. Both were lost in their own thoughts. To the woodie in the tree, they might as well have targets painted on their backs.

Briar ran for the tree. Another woodie hissed and tried to block his way, but Briar flapped his open coat at it, and the fresh hogroot stains drove it away, coughing. Dropping his spear and shield, Briar put his foot on a knob in the tree trunk, climbing as quickly as the demon had. He chose his handholds carefully, making not a rustle or sound until he stepped out onto the branch where the demon waited.

The cory looked up as Briar gave a cry and ran out onto the branch, pulling the warded knife from his belt. The demon shifted to spring at him, but Briar was ready, coiling under the sweeping talons. He sprang, grabbing the woodie with one arm as his other thrust the knife into its barklike armour. Magic bucked up his arm, powering a frenzy of stabbing as Briar held his breath.

The cory was under him to break the impact as they struck the road, but it still knocked the wind from him. The fall might have injured him but for the magic coursing through his body. Briar rolled away from the demon and bounced to his feet, knife at the ready, but the woodie was not moving.

'Briar, where in the Core have you been?' Thamos demanded. Briar looked at him, confused. 'Ent been far.'

'I want you checking in regularly,' Thamos said. 'Creator only knows how I'm to find the resistance if I lose you.'

It was a ridiculous statement. How could Briar lose track of so many men and horses? But he nodded before moving back into the trees.

'Li'l stinker killed a woodie that mighta cored us,' he heard Gared say. 'Coulda said thanks before choppin' his head off.'

Briar let himself be seen when the procession stopped for meals, taking his bowl and bread and disappearing once he was sure the count had taken note of him. It was a week by Messenger to the Hollow, but Thamos' Wooden Soldiers did not sleep, absorbing magic enough by night to keep them moving through the day. The men grew increasingly irritable, but they shaved days from their trek, and were close to the Hollow by the third evening.

'Briar!' Thamos called as the boy slipped into the camp for his meal. 'Join us!' He was sitting with Baron Gared and Lord Sament on a fallen log not far from the other men.

'Not too stinky?' Briar asked as he moved over to them.

'Ay, sorry about that,' Gared said. 'Shoulda known yuv got ears like a bat.' He opened his coat, giving himself a sniff. 'Ent none of us are smelling like roses after four days ridin' an' killin' demons.' He glanced at the single carriage in the procession, carrying Miss Lacquer and her mother, and gave a slight smile. 'Well, maybe one or two.'

'We'll be in the Hollow by morning,' Thamos said. 'We'll take the day to prepare and leave the following morning. We'll arrange rooms for you . . .'

Briar shook his head. 'Guide folk to the Hollow sometimes. Know where the hogroot patches are.'

'You can't spend the rest of your life sleeping in hogroot patches,' Thamos said.

Briar tilted his head. 'Why not?'

Thamos opened his mouth, then closed it again. He looked to Gared for help.

'Gonna get cold, come winter,' Gared said.

Briar shrugged. 'Can build a fire.'

'As you wish,' Thamos said. 'How long will it take to get to Shepherd Alin's monastery?'

'Ten days,' Briar said.

'So long?' Sament said.

'Can't take roads,' Briar said. 'Watchers everywhere. Goin' through the bogs.'

'Don't like the sound of that,' Gared said. 'Horses break ankles in wetland, not to mention their riders' necks.'

'Ways twist,' Briar said, 'but I can find dry ground most of the way.'

'Can you draw a map?' Thamos asked.

Briar shook his head. 'Can't read, but I know the way.'

'We'll bring a cartographer,' Thamos said.

'Got food?' Briar asked.

Thamos smiled. 'Still hungry? Ask cook for another loaf.'

Briar shook his head. 'For the monastery. Crowded. Lots of hungry.'

Thamos nodded. 'I imagine so. We don't have time for a proper baggage train, but five hundred mounted Wooden Soldiers can carry considerable supply if there is grazing for the horses.'

Briar nodded. 'Take longer, that many.'

'Thought the duke said to take fifty,' Gared said.

'Do you think?' Thamos said. He reached into his jacket, producing a folded parchment with the royal seal. He pointed to a dark stain on the paper. 'Hard to read with this stain on the paper. It *could* say fifty, I suppose, but that would be madness, of course.'

'Course,' Gared agreed.

'Only a fool would command you send so few,' Sament agreed. 'Indeed, it must say five hundred.'

'Why not five thousand?' Gared asked.

Thamos shook his head. 'We cannot do that without stripping the Cutters from the defence of the Hollow. I will not leave it unguarded. My cavalry will have to do until we know more. I want to be fast and mobile.'

Briar nodded eagerly. The Laktonians had no cavalry. With five hundred Wooden Soldiers, they could defend the monastery from almost anything, and the supply would feed a great many hungry mouths.

'Lookin' forward to seein' the lake,' Gared said. 'Heard it's so big ya can't see the far side.'

Thamos nodded. 'I saw it once before, and it was a sight to behold. But you won't be coming, Baron. Someone needs to see to the Hollow when I'm gone.'

'Make it sound like ya ent comin' back,' Gared said.

'I mean to,' Thamos said, 'but there's no guarantee with the enemy so close. You must be prepared to lead.'

'Folk listen to me, ay,' Gared said, 'but I ent made for papers and policies.'

'We do what we're needed to do, not what we want,' Thamos said.

'Deliverer told me the same thing, once,' Gared said.

'I don't know if Arlen Bales is the Deliverer or not,' Thamos said. 'But if you should see him . . .'

Gared smiled. 'Ay. I'll send him your way.'

They were three days in the Hollow while Thamos gathered his men. Briar spent the time exploring, finding others living in the Gatherers' Wood. Some were his father's people, Krasian, but others were Thesans who had taken to painting wards on their bare skin. They wore only loose robes in the day, and loincloths at night when they killed cories with their bare hands.

Briar kept hidden as he watched them, but he was fascinated. He didn't understand their ways, but thought in time perhaps he could.

They made good time the first few days out of the Hollow, but it was slower going when they entered the vast wetlands surrounding the lake. The cold kept the worst of the mosquitoes at bay, but the men still slapped at them, complaining.

Briar pointed to some tracks. 'Bog demons.'

'I've never seen one,' Sament said.

'Nor I,' Thamos said.

'Short,' Briar said, putting his arms out in front of him. 'Long arms. Bogspit sticks to anything. Burns and eats through, you don't wash it off.'

'How do you kill them?' Thamos asked.

'Step to the side. Boggies can't put their arms sideways. Have to turn.' He lifted his own arm, pointing to the hollow beneath his rib cage. 'Put your spear right here. No armour.'

'You seem to know a lot about them,' Thamos said.

Briar smiled. He didn't know much about maps, but he knew cories. 'Make camp. Can't walk horses through the bog at night. Show you how to make boggie traps.'

Briar twisted to conform with the gnarled trunk of the stooped swamp tree, watching unseen as the Krasian scout made his way through the wetland. The *kha'Sharum* carried a heavy rucksack of supply, noting landmarks on oiled paper.

He was alone. Briar had made sure of it. He wasn't attached to a hunting party, or otherwise likely to be missed. Just a lone scout sent to map the wetlands.

But he was heading right into the path of Thamos and his men. In an hour, he would hear them, or see sign of their passing. Soon after, he would be running to tell his superiors.

Briar clutched his spear. He hated this. Hated killing people. The Krasians looked so much like him that it felt like killing himself each time.

But there was nothing for it. When the scout passed under the tree, Briar fell upon him, spear punching down through his shoulder into heart and lungs. He was dead before they hit the ground.

Briar took his rucksack and papers, leaving the body to sink beneath the murky swamp water.

It was fifteen days before they reached the monastery, as Briar guided Thamos and his men past enemy scouts and dry land with grazing for the horses. Nine Wooden Soldiers were lost to boggies, and seven horses suffered broken ankles and had to be put down. One of the Mountain Spears took a slimy wad of bogspit in the face. Briar packed it with mud and poultices, but it looked like a melted candle when he finally took the bandage off.

The Monastery of New Dawn stood on a high bluff stretching out over the lake. Water on three sides, it was accessible only by a narrow road with a moat that cut clear across to link the waters of the lake. The wooden walls were thick and high, with a drawbridge to allow entry and egress. The docks to the north and south were low on the rocky bluffs – goods and livestock coming by ship had to be taken up a narrow stair cut zigzag into the rock face.

The drawbridge was lowered for them, and they rode inside.

'Creator,' Thamos said, seeing the refugee tent camps inside the walls. The folk were filthy and thin, used now to missing meals.

'I had no idea it was this bad,' Sament said. 'The refugees in the Hollow . . .'

'Have the benefit of being safe in allied territory,' Thamos said. 'These poor souls . . .'

He turned to one of his captains. 'Find the quartermaster and deliver our supply. Learn if there is anything else we can do to provide comfort for these people.'

The man saluted and was off as Briar led Thamos and Sament to the monastery doors.

Tender Heath was waiting for them. The fat old Tender hugged Briar tightly. 'Creator bless you, boy.'

He looked to the count, bowing deeply. 'It is an honour, Your Highness. Welcome to the Monastery of New Dawn. I am Tender Heath. I will take you to the Shepherd.'

It wasn't often Briar was allowed into Shepherd Alin's private offices. The Shepherd wore plain brown robes like Tender Heath, but his inner chambers were richer than anything Briar had ever imagined. The carpeting was thick, soft, and colourful, woven with powerful church warding. Acolytes followed him with ready brooms, lest any mud slip from his sandals.

The seats and couches were great pillowed things – so soft. Heath said he was not allowed to sit lest he stain them with hogroot sap, but Briar walked close to a velvet sofa as they passed by, shivering with pleasure as he ran his fingertips along its length.

Great shelves of lacquered goldwood ran floor-to-ceiling

along the walls, holding countless books. Heath had been trying to teach him to read, but Briar was more interested in the pictures.

The Shepherd was waiting for them in the back office with two other men.

Briar's father, Relan, had taught him all about bowing. The Shepherd's was deep and long enough to be respectful, without relinquishing dominance. The bow of an equal.

'An honour to meet you, Your Highness,' the Shepherd said. 'We hoped Briar would bring back help, but hadn't expected royalty.'

'Or so many Wooden Soldiers,' one of the other men said. He was midsized, with a fine coat. He stood with his feet spread like one more used to the rolling of a ship's deck than dry land. 'And cavalry, no less! It seems the Creator answers prayers, after all.'

'Dockmaster Isan,' Shepherd Alin advised, gesturing to the man, 'and his brother, Captain Marlan.'

Thamos put his hands out in the way Laktonian captains favoured, and they gripped arms just beneath the elbow. 'Please accept my condolences, and those of the ivy throne, over the loss of your mother.'

Marlan spat, ignoring the irritated look Alin threw his way. 'She wasn't lost. She was murdered.'

'Of course.' Thamos turned to Sament. 'May I introduce Lord Sament of Miln, who has brought fifty Mountain Spears.'

'It is good that you've come,' Alin said. 'What happens here concerns all the Free Cities.'

'You don't need to convince me of that,' Sament said. 'Euchor may be another matter.'

'What he needs is a victory,' a new voice added. Briar looked up and smiled widely as Captain Dehlia entered the room with another richly dressed man in tow.

'Captain Dehlia of *Sharum's Lament*,' Heath said. 'She's been a thorn in the Krasians' side since they first came to Docktown.'

'Thanks to Briar,' Dehlia said, running her fingers through

Briar's tangled hair. 'Boy's been sneaking into town for us, spying on the enemy and telling us where to hit.'

She put an arm around him, hugging him close, heedless of the sticky hogroot stains on his clothes. Briar didn't like to be touched, but when it was Captain Dehlia, he found he didn't mind so much.

Shepherd Alin gestured to the new arrival. 'Egar—'

'—third son of Duke Edon of Rizon,' Thamos finished, as the men embraced each other. 'We feared you dead, my friend.'

Egar shook his head. 'After the Krasians struck the capital, I gathered as many fighting men as I could and fled onto the plains. We strike where we can and melt away before the desert rats can catch us.'

'How many men do you have?' Thamos asked.

'I can call five thousand spears, given enough time,' Egar said.

Thamos squinted at him. 'Why are you here, and not in Rizon with your men?'

'Because,' Isan cut in, 'it's time we retook Docktown.'

'It was Briar who made it all possible,' Shepherd Alin said. They were descending what seemed an endless spiral of stairs, past the foundations of the monastery and into the natural caverns of the bluff.

'He discovered the enemy force scouting the lakeshore,' Isan said, 'giving us time to prepare an ambush. We captured or killed over two hundred men that day. Our greatest victory to date.'

They came to a great cavern, cold and damp, the air rank. Briar looked in horror at dozens of Krasian warriors chained to the walls, faces and limbs emaciated.

'Creator,' Thamos said. 'Don't you feed these men?'

Marlan spat. 'When we feed them, they try to escape. And why should they eat when so many above go hungry?'

Briar felt sick. The men, looking so much like his own father and brothers, lay listless and skeletal, soiled with their own filth. He had led the Laktonians to them knowing many of the invaders would be killed, but this . . .

'The ones who talk are fed,' Alin said. 'My Tenders and Children all speak Krasian, but the lesser fighters knew little of use.'

He signalled the guards at the far end of the cavern, and they unlocked a heavy door.

Inside, a Krasian man was strapped tightly to a chair. His black turban and white veil were gone, but still Briar recognized the leader of the Krasian scouts. A narrow table in front of him, his hands were splayed out, each finger held tight in a tiny screw vice bolted to the wood. He was breathing evenly, but he was flushed and bathed in sweat. An old bespectacled man, still in the robes of an acolyte, tended the screws.

'This is Prince Icha,' Alin said. 'He claims to be the third son of the demon of the desert himself, Krasian Duke Ahmann Jardir.'

'And when my father hears of this,' Icha growled in guttural but understandable Thesan, 'he will visit these tortures one thousandfold on every man, woman, and child in the resistance.'

At a nod from Alin, the acolyte adjusted the screws until Icha began to howl. Another nod and he dialled them back until Icha fell silent again, panting.

'Your father is dead,' Thamos said bluntly. 'I watched Arlen Bales pitch him off a cliff.'

'My father is the Deliverer,' Icha said. 'No fall can kill him. The Damajah has foreseen his return. Until then, my brother will be the instrument of his divine wrath.'

'How many men does your brother have in Lakton?' Thamos asked.

'More than there are fish in your lake,' Icha said. 'More than there are stars in the sky. More—'

Alin flicked a finger, and the acolyte dialled him back into screams. The old man hunched over the screws with no more expression than Briar's father mending a broken piece of furniture. Briar wanted to hit the man, or to run away and try to forget the scene. But he could not. He drew closer, and when the pain was at last dialled back, Icha looked up and met his eyes.

'The *chin* will be judged, Briar Damaj, but none so much as you,' Icha gasped. 'Everam sends *ginjaz* to the depths of Nie's abyss in the afterlife.'

'Not a traitor,' Briar said. 'This is my home. You're the *chin*.'

But even as he said the words, he wasn't sure he believed them. He had thought the Shepherd a good man, but what he was doing to the Krasian prisoners was abhorrent.

Perhaps it was time to go back to the bog. Life was easier alone with the cories.

Captain Dehlia put an arm around him. 'Come along, Briar. Don't listen to this animal. You know what they've done.'

Briar nodded, allowing himself to be led away, back through the freezing cavern full of starving *Sharum*.

'This hill,' Thamos said, pointing to the map. 'Do you know it, Briar?'

Briar started. Lost in thoughts of the caverns below, he hadn't been paying attention. He looked at the squiggled lines and blotches of colour on the paper, but he could not make out what was meant to be a hill.

'Colan's Rise,' Dehlia supplied.

Briar nodded. 'Know it.'

'If we can position longbows there,' Thamos said, 'they can cover the bulk of the port.'

'Lots of *Sharum* there,' Briar said. 'Scorpions. Difficult to take.'

'Not for my cavalry,' Thamos said. 'We can trample through and take the scorpions for our own, then continue down the road under covering fire to attack the town proper.'

Shepherd Alin nodded, sliding a finger down the map. 'Drawn to the sounds of battle, they will not see your forces, Egar, coming from the south.'

Egar shook his head. 'We don't know how many warriors they have, but it is doubtless more than our two forces combined.'

'Unless the entire fleet moves to retake the docks and beach,' Isan said. 'We can land thousands of fighting men and women.'

'That will be bloody,' Egar said.

Isan nodded. 'But in six weeks, the lake will freeze, and we will be trapped without supply. The dockmasters are all agreed. We stand to lose far more if we do nothing.'

'When are you planning the attack?' Thamos asked.

Shepherd Alin put down a map with various markings. 'These are the typical Krasian troop positions.' He put down a second map, significantly different. 'And these are their positions during new moon.'

'Waning,' Thamos murmured.

'The sand rats spend the day in prayer, and then move to defend against demon attack,' Captain Marlan said. 'They will not be ready to face our combined forces instead.'

People at prayer, people standing against the cories, and these men were planning to slaughter them. It was no different from what the Krasians had done, unprovoked, but still the thought sickened Briar.

Egar nodded. 'That should be enough time to march, but not if there are enemy troops in the land between. We have to know the way is clear, or I cannot commit my men.'

Alin nodded. 'We will need to interrogate Prince Icha more . . . vigorously.'

Briar flexed his hands, thinking of the screws crushing Icha's fingers, and suddenly he couldn't breathe. He coughed, trying to force air into his lungs.

'Are you all right, boy?' Shepherd Alin asked.

'What if he don't know?' Briar asked. 'What if things changed?'

'He's right,' Egar said. 'I won't commit my men to months-old information. We need to know how many warriors they have in the hamlets *now*.'

'I can go,' Briar said. Anything to keep that horrible old man from adjusting the screws, playing screams like an instrument. 'Know where leaders meet.' He pointed to the maps on the table. 'Steal maps.'

Captain Dehlia put a hand on his shoulder. 'Briar, that's too dangerous. We can't ask you to . . .'

'Didn't ask,' Briar said. 'I'll go.'

25

The Spy
334 AR Winter

'They just sit there, watching us.' Jayan paced before the great dockfront window of his command centre, previously the lavish office of Dockmaster Isadore. 'I wish the cowards would just attack and have done.'

A dozen Laktonian warships stood at anchor halfway between Docktown – now called Everam's Reservoir – and Lakton, still visible in the light of the setting sun. They might once have been fishing and trade vessels, but all had rock slingers on deck now, with archers stationed on the aft and forecastles.

Worst were the newly built scorpions, based on the Krasian design. With the greenland secrets of fire still largely a mystery, it grated on Abban that the Laktonians had so easily stolen the design.

The ships had held the line for months, guarding an invisible border the Krasians had never approached. But for all their armament, the ships were swift, gliding on the lake winds the way a bird might soar overhead. If they decided to attack, it would be swift. Ships switched out of the formation often, and there was no telling if they were crewed lightly to intimidate, or packed with warriors ready to take the docks and beach by storm.

Other ships came and went from the city on the lake, evacuating the dozens of local fishing villages along the lakeshore and desperately foraging for supplies to replace the lost tithe. Jayan sent his half brothers north and south, slogging through the wetlands with their strange demons to crush the hamlets, but most were deserted by the time Icha and Sharu arrived with their forces.

To the south, Sharu had come to a river too wide and deep to cross, and had sent word that he was returning to Everam's Reservoir. To the north, no one had heard from Icha and his men in weeks, and even the *dama'ting* could not divine their fate with assurance.

'They were not cowards when there were ships to reclaim,' Abban reminded. 'The *chin* fear you, Sharum Ka, and well they should. The least of your *Sharum* could slay a dozen fish men . . .'

'A score,' Jayan said, 'without breathing hard.'

Abban nodded. 'It is as you say, Sharum Ka. But do not underestimate the foe. It is not cowardice that stays them.'

'Then what is it?' Jayan demanded.

'There is no profit in attack,' Abban said.

'Pfagh!' Jayan spat. 'This is Sharak Sun, not *khaffit* merchanting.'

'You have said many times the greenlanders are more *khaffit* than *Sharum*,' Abban said. 'There is no gain in taking back the town when we have so many warriors to defend it, and more within a few days' march.' He shivered, signalling Earless to put another log on the fire. 'Better to let the snow and cold weaken us.'

Jayan grunted. All the Krasians were cold and irritable, remembering the last Northern winter. In Krasia winter temperatures would often dip to freezing at night, but the sun in the desert kept the days hot. In the North it was cold and wet for months with no relief. Winter had only just begun farther inland, but this close to the lake the snows came early, slowing their patrols and playing havoc with the scorpions. If the locals were to be believed, much of the lake would freeze in the coldest months, locking the ports until spring.

'So we are left to sit on our spears in this worthless *chin* hamlet?' Jayan demanded.

'The Evejah tells of many winters Holy Kaji was forced to wait out in captured lands, ere the winning of Sharak Sun. Conquest is ever thus, Sharum Ka. Months of moving men and supplies, waiting for the perfect moment to strike,' Abban clapped his hands for emphasis, 'crushing your enemies.'

Jayan seemed mollified at that. 'I *will* crush them. I will take their eyes and eat them. The fish men will whisper my name in terror for generations.'

'Of that, there is no doubt,' Abban agreed, keeping his eyes down, lest he stare at the milky orb of Jayan's right eye. He had commissioned a patch of beautifully warded gold, but Jayan refused to wear it. The young Sharum Ka knew his eye unnerved men, and gloried in their discomfort.

'In the meantime, you can spend the winter in luxury,' Abban waved a hand at the lavish chambers, 'with warmth and an abundance of fine food, even as the lake dwellers shiver on their frozen vessels, gnawing fish heads to fill empty bellies.' He doubted things were so dire, but it was always wise to exaggerate when flattering the Sharum Ka. 'Work has begun again on your palace in Everam's Bounty, and you have greenland *jiwah* to warm your bed.'

'I want glory, not luxury,' Jayan said, ignoring the soothing words. 'There *must* be a way to attack. Now, before the winter comes in force.'

Indeed there was, but Abban was not about to let the boy know that. It was a risky plan under the best of circumstances, and Abban would not trust the timing to a boy whose foolish pride had cost them almost the entire captured fleet.

Of the ten large vessels that survived the *Sharum*'s burning, four had been stolen back by the Laktonians, and two more burned beyond repair. One was lost to a tide of water demons that had claimed several smaller vessels, as well. Abban had sent the remainder to a hidden bay guarded by his own men, where they studied sailing and shipmaking lore pulled from books, bribes, and the tongs of his torturers.

A Sharak horn sat both men up straight. Abban looked out the window and saw the cause immediately. '*Sharum's Lament*.'

Jayan hissed, grabbing his spear and running to the window as if he meant to try and throw it a quarter mile to the sleek fighting vessel that swept in from the north, using the fading light to hide its approach.

Captain Dehlia had renamed *Gentleman's Lament* after taking it back from the Krasians. The flag still had a silhouette of a woman staring off into the distance, but the rejected suitor had been replaced with the silhouette of a *Sharum* on fire. The ship attacked regularly, testing their defences and giving credence to its name. It had been Dehlia and the *Sharum's Lament* that stole the scorpion, allowing the Laktonians to copy the design.

Every time *Sharum's Lament* came in sight, it meant grief and loss for the occupiers, and impotent rage for Jayan. Most often the ship would pull up on the edge of range, loosing flamework from its slinger or a deadly hail of arrows – sailing off before the Mehnding could calibrate their weapons to return fire.

Jayan had tried moving *chin* to the docks and buildings closest to shore, but somehow the captain caught wind of the plan, attacking elsewhere to draw Jayan's forces while other ships effected a daring rescue of their conveniently placed brethren.

Every time they attempted to prepare for or counter *Sharum's Lament*, Captain Dehlia seemed to know their plans and change tactics. There was no telling now if she was simply sailing in to harry, or moving with cunning purpose.

Abban watched carefully as the ship sailed along the shoreline, just out of range. She would veer sharply inward only when approaching her target. All along the docks and shores, Mehnding scrambled and held their breath, knowing they would have only a few moments to target and fire. Jayan had promised a palace to the team that could sink the cursed ship.

But then the ship turned, and Abban felt his sphincter tighten. 'Nie's black heart.'

'Eh?' Jayan asked, turning to look at Abban even as the slinger arm came forward, launching a heavy missile their way.

'Sharum Ka!' Abban cried, throwing himself on the man.

Jayan was heavily muscled, but even he could do little to resist Abban's bulk as he bore the man to the floor. He punched Abban as they struck the carpet, sending him rolling away. 'How dare you lay your unclean hands upon me, you pig-eating camel scrotum! I will kill—'

At that moment there was a crash as something struck the great window. The warded glass Abban had installed held against the blow, but the entire building shook from the impact.

Jayan looked from the window and back to Abban, who managed to get his good knee under him. Again he looked at the window, clouded with bits of wood clinging to the surface, and back to Abban. 'Why?'

The young Sharum Ka was not known for articulation, but Abban understood him well enough. Why would a cowardly *khaffit* risk his own life for someone who had abused and derided him for years?

'You are Sharum Ka,' Abban said. 'Blood of the Deliverer, and the hope of our people while your father remains locked in battle with Nie. Your life is worth far more than mine.'

Jayan nodded, a rare thoughtful look about him.

The words were nonsense, of course. Abban would happily let the boy take a spear for him. More than once he had pondered having the fool killed himself. He might have, if not for the risk of the Damajah's wrath.

But if the Sharum Ka were killed in his presence and Abban survived, Hasik would come for him. It might be that Qeran or Earless could stop him in time, but it wasn't something Abban was willing to bet his life upon. Hasik would be all too willing to die if it meant he could take Abban with him, and that sort of man was not the kind to gamble against.

'You saved me, *khaffit*,' Jayan said. 'Continue to serve, and I will not forget, when I take my father's throne.'

'I haven't saved anyone yet,' Abban said, looking at the fluid and debris still clinging to the warded glass. 'We must get out.'

'Bah!' Jayan said. 'You did not lie when you said your warded glass was proof against any blow. What have we to fear?'

He turned, just as the *Sharum's Lament* launched another projectile, a flaming stinger, from one of her starboard scorpions.

'We must get out!' Abban cried as the missile arced their way. He made a quick series of gestures to Earless, who leapt across the room, scooping Abban up in his arms.

There was a deafening boom and a flare of light to singe the eyes of even a desert dweller as the missile struck the liquid demonfire clinging to the window. Still the warded glass held, blunting the shock and heat of the blast.

Abban drew a ward in the air. 'Everam be praised.' The logical part of his mind knew the glass was performing exactly as it should, but in his coward's heart, it was a miracle. 'Go!' he cried, swinging an arm towards the door. For all the strength in the glass, the building that held it in place was only wood. Already smoke was beginning to seep through the floorboards.

Earless put his head down, charging the heavy door and kicking it from its hinges. The door hit Hasik, who was racing for the scene, but Abban wasted no time on it, gesticulating for Earless to move with all speed. The deaf giant held Abban like a child as he raced down the steps and through the great room below to the back door.

'Fire!' Abban screamed as they raced through the great room. 'Flee!'

It wasn't until they were outside that Abban realized Jayan had been fast on their heels. Abban quickly gestured for Earless to let him down, realizing it must have seemed to all that they had cleared an escape path for the Sharum Ka.

Others joined them, including Khevat, Asavi, Jayan's body-guard, and Qeran. 'You had Earless carry you?' the drillmaster asked in disgust, his voice too low for the others to hear. 'Where is your shame?'

Abban shrugged. 'Where my life is concerned, Drillmaster, I have none.'

'I will put my spear in that witch's heart and fuck the hole!' Jayan cried.

'I will hold her down as you mount her,' Hasik agreed. There was blood in his hair, but he looked ready as ever for a fight.

'Why would I need you to hold her, idiot,' Jayan snapped, 'if I had already put my spear in her heart?'

'I . . .' Hasik began.

'The Sharum Ka does not want your excuses, Whistler!' Abban cried, relishing the moment. 'It should have been you, not a pair of *khaffit*, clearing the path for him.'

Hasik looked as if he wanted the ground to swallow him, and Abban wished the moment could last forever. But then it was gone, and Hasik was baring teeth at him.

'We are blind back here,' Jayan said. 'Go to the docks and find out what's happening.' He pointed, and Hasik ran off like a loyal dog.

'You and the clerics should not remain here, Sharum Ka,' Qeran said. 'Please allow the Spears of the Deliverer to escort you to a safer location where you may direct . . .'

'There!' Asavi shrieked suddenly. All eyes turned to her as she pointed to a *Sharum* exiting the building amidst the smoke and confusion, his night veil raised against the fumes. There was a satchel over his shoulder, black like his robes. The warrior froze, along with everyone else, the moment seeming to last forever.

'Don't just stand there!' the *dama'ting* shrieked. 'Stop him or the streets will run with blood!'

That got people moving, but the warrior was quickest of all, shoving a *dama* aside and moving for the clearest path of escape.

Right Abban's way.

It made sense. Abban was a fat cripple, and far less likely to impede the spy than the *Sharum* and *dama*, and only a fool would venture too close to a Bride of Everam. A good shove would put Abban on the ground, right in the pursuers' path.

But while it was true that Abban was fat and one of his legs wasn't worth a coreling's piss, his cultivated mannerisms were designed to make the infirmity appear far worse than it truly was.

He gave a terrified shriek, shifting his weight to his good leg as the warrior came in. But as the *Sharum* shoved, Abban caught his wrist, tripping him with his crutch and bringing them both to the ground.

That should have been the end of it, but the warrior somehow kept a measure of control, landing on top and forcing the brunt of the impact onto Abban. In that moment, his veil fell away, and Abban got a look at him.

He was young, almost too young for the black. His face was smudged with dirt, but still his skin was light for a Krasian, if darker than most greenlanders'. His features, too, bore traits from both. A half-breed? There was a generation of those coming, but all save a few were still in their mother's bellies, and the others busy screaming and soiling their bidos.

As Abban gaped, the half-breed drew back, then slammed his forehead between Abban's eyes. There was a flash of light, and a muted thud as the back of his head struck the boardwalk. Abban watched dizzily as Earless moved in to grab the warrior, but again the half-breed was quicker, delivering a kick to the *kha'Sharum*'s knee. He took the wind from Abban as he sprang away, just as Earless fell hard atop him. The two of them rolled in a tangle, and there were angry shouts from the warriors hindered in their pursuit.

When Abban's vision finally cleared, the spy was running full speed for the docks, half a dozen *Sharum* on his tail and more looking up as they rushed past.

Surprisingly, Qeran was first among the pursuers, gaining quickly on the spy. His leg of spring steel was not always ideal, but in a dead sprint there were few two-legged men who could hope to match him.

The spy seemed to know it, too. He veered off to catch a rain barrel and throw his full weight against it, spinning it into their path. The barrel moved slowly at first, wobbling even as the spy ran on, but as the weight of the collected water shifted, it moved with sudden swiftness, splashing water as it rolled into the pursuing *Sharum*.

The men scattered, some throwing themselves out of the way, others slipping in the wet as they sought to dodge. One man was tripped by the barrel itself.

Only Qeran kept the pursuit, leaping over the barrel in a spring any cat would envy. He landed in a roll, using his momentum to come back to his feet still running.

Two warriors farther down attempted to slow the spy, but he threw some kind of dust at them, and the men fell away, clutching their faces and screaming.

The dock was littered with barrels, ropes, nets, and other materials, and the spy used it all, zigzagging to use every bit of cover and terrain to slow pursuit.

Still the drillmaster gained. Qeran had dropped spear and shield for speed, but it did not matter. Not even a *sharusahk* master could long keep his feet against Qeran in close quarters.

Abban smiled, limping quickly towards them for the best possible view, and to be first to question the spy before the others did something rash. Jayan and the clerics followed, but he had a lead, and all moved slowly, riveted by the scene.

As Qeran's reaching fingers brushed the cloth of the spy's robe, he turned suddenly, whipping the shield off his back and slamming it into the drillmaster, arresting his momentum and knocking him back. The shield was an old design, dating back at least five years, before the combat wards were returned. Another curiosity.

Qeran caught himself quickly and came back in, but the spy twisted fast to the ground, trying to hook the drillmaster's leg and take him down.

Qeran was wise to the trick, leaping above the sweeping leg, but the spy was not taken unaware. He kept his momentum and whipped the shield around, striking its heavy edge into the drillmaster's metal leg as he came down.

The spring steel recoiled, and Qeran landed uncharacteristically off balance. The spy took full advantage, and they traded a quick flurry of parries and blows. The man was small and impossibly fast, never giving the drillmaster a moment to find his balance. He hit Qeran in the face with the shield, then leapt to kick the drillmaster full in the chest.

Qeran fell back hard, not seriously harmed, but the spy wasted no more time on him, turning and running down the dock.

Ahead, Mehnding warriors from the scorpion and slinger teams had clustered to block his path. The spy looked back, but behind him more than a score of warriors charged past Qeran, Hasik at their lead. It was the first time Abban could recall when he wanted the cursed eunuch to succeed.

The spy turned down a less-used dock, leading out to a section of cove too rocky and shallow for all but the smallest vessels. There were a handful of these tied at the dock, simple rowboats even a *Sharum* could use, but it seemed unlikely the spy could even untie one in time, much less row out of spear range before he was killed. He sprinted for the end of the dock instead. Did he mean to swim?

Hasik mere steps behind, the spy turned sharply, leaping into one of the boats. Hasik lost seconds adapting to the change, but he leapt from the dock, spear ready to skewer the man before he could cut the ties.

'Demonshit,' Abban muttered. Hasik was not known for leaving men alive for questioning.

But the spy never attempted to cut the moorings, hopping two steps across the boat's benches and jumping right out into the water.

Abban held his breath, but the spy did not sink, seeming to bounce off the surface of the water into another leap, where he landed with only a splash about his ankles. He ran three more steps, then turned sharply to the left, still running on the surface of the water.

Hasik struggled to keep his balance on the rocking boat, throwing his spear with surprising accuracy. The spy saw it coming, ducking by mere inches.

'Everam guide me!' Hasik cried, leaping from the boat much as the spy had. Miraculously, he, too, landed on his feet, seeming as surprised as any. With a howl, he took off in pursuit even as other *Sharum* jumped into the boat to follow.

Hasik took two steps, then dropped like a stone with the next. The other *Sharum* fared little better, two of them thrown into the water by the wildly rocking boat. A third made the leap, skidding on whatever Hasik and the spy had landed upon, but he lost his balance, pitching into the water. *Sharum* threw spears at the spy, still running on water, but he was fast getting out of range. At last he slung his shield and leapt, arms outstretched as he cut the water and began swimming.

The *Sharum's Lament* had launched a boat in the confusion, three men rowing with remarkable speed. In moments, they had intercepted the spy and pulled him aboard as spears fell short in the water, lost.

There was a horn, and the *Sharum's Lament* let loose a barrage at the warriors clustered on the dock, killing dozens with burning pitch and stingers, even destroying a slinger and two scorpions. The Mehnding, having left their engines to keep the spy from escaping, were unprepared to return fire.

As they watched helplessly, the launch returned and the warship made one last pass, swinging close for a final starboard barrage, crew jeering. As it turned, they saw Captain Dehlia standing atop the aft rail, baring her breasts as she jeered at them. All around her, the men and women of her crew turned and dropped their pantaloons, slapping their buttocks as the ship sailed away.

Hasik and two of the *Sharum* were still clinging to the rowboat when Abban reached the place where the spy had leapt from the dock. The *Sharum* who attempted to follow Hasik and the spy out into the lake had not resurfaced.

It was no surprise. Krasians were not swimmers, and the heavy armour plates sewn into their black robes pulled those who fell into the lake's cold waters down faster than they could shed the weight.

Abban tried to imagine what it must be like. He had been choked enough in *sharaj* to know how it felt to black out from lack of breath, but to do it surrounded by dark water, not even knowing which way was up . . .

He shuddered.

Qeran was standing on the dock, anger simmering on his features. *Sharum* were ruled by their pride, and the spy had made him look a fool in front of dozens of onlookers. No doubt Qeran would kill the first inferior to look at him wrong.

But *khaffit* or no, Abban was no inferior, and he needed his drillmaster, not some moping child.

'You did well,' he said quietly, coming to stand next to the man.

Qeran grimaced. 'I failed. I should be—'

'Proud,' Abban cut the drillmaster off before he could make some masochistic proclamation. 'You outshone the other *Sharum* in the chase. Such speed! Such skill! Your new leg puts the old to shame.'

'It was still not enough,' Qeran growled.

Abban shrugged. '*Inevera*. Nothing happens, but that Everam wills it. Whatever the spy stole from the Sharum Ka's manse, the Creator wanted our enemies to have it.'

It was nonsense, of course, but *inevera* had always been a balm and a crutch to disgruntled Evejans.

'Like He willed that my leg be lost?' Qeran asked through gritted teeth. 'That I drown in couzi and my own filth until a fat, crippled *khaffit* proves my better and puts a boot to my neck? And now, it is *inevera* that I can't even hold a *chin* spy when I have him in my grasp?'

The drillmaster spat into the water. 'It seems Everam wills nothing but humiliation upon me.'

'There is glory to come, Drillmaster,' Abban said. 'Glory enough for all in Sharak Sun and Sharak Ka. Bad enough I found you wallowing on the floor bemoaning fate. I did not pull you out of it so you could wallow on your feet.'

Qeran looked at him sharply, but Abban met his stare. 'Embrace the pain, *Sharum*.'

The drillmaster's nostrils flared, but he nodded. Abban turned to bow as Jayan approached.

The Sharum Ka looked out over the dark lake. 'How did the spy run across the water like that?' He turned to Asavi. 'I thought you said the *chin* do not use *hora* magic.'

'It was no magic, Sharum Ka,' Abban said, drawing the attention of all. 'I have heard of this phenomenon from men returned from the *chin* villages in the wetland. They build little islands called crannogs, reachable only by stone paths hidden just under the surface of the water. The steps are irregular, easy enough for one who knows the path, but difficult for a demon . . . or man, to follow.'

Jayan grunted, digesting the information as he watched the first of the *Sharum* be hauled back onto the dock. The man shivered, coughing water and soaking the deck, but he seemed well enough.

Until a tentacle whipped from the water, wrapping about his leg. The man had barely a moment to scream before it was cut off with a splash and he was yanked back into the water.

Hasik froze, eyes searching the dark surface for sign of the water demon, but the other *Sharum* began to shout and wave his free arm as he clutched at the boat with the other. 'Everam's balls, throw me the line! Quickly!'

Of course, the commotion drew the demon right to him. A tentacle wrapped around his throat, and his cries were choked off as he was pulled under.

Hasik used that exact moment to attempt to pull himself into the boat. The small craft tipped from his weight, threatening to capsize, but somehow Hasik managed to roll in and shift his weight to right it.

All the boats at anchor were water-warded, and Hasik no doubt thought himself safe until a tentacle wrapped around his ankle. The warrior had already lost spear and shield to the lake, but he clutched at his waist, pulling a curved warded dagger as the boat capsized and he was pulled under.

There was a hush as everyone assembled stared at the surface of the water, watching as the ripples where the warrior disappeared began to fade. *Sharum* were fearless against the demons of land and air. It was fair to say the demons feared them more than the other way around. But water demons, mysterious nightmares that pulled their victims down to drown, terrified them.

Abban was no different, but he could not bring himself to weep at Hasik's fate. He wanted the man to suffer, but after all Hasik had done to make his life an abyss, it was good, too, to have an end.

But then there was a flash, like lightning under the water. It came again, and again, then all went dark. A moment later Hasik broke the surface, gasping for air. He was naked, having discarded his armour lest it pull him down, but he still held the knife. He stuck it in his teeth as he clumsily paddled towards the dock.

'Everam's beard,' Jayan muttered, a sentiment echoed all around as Hasik was thrown a line and hauled himself onto the dock, very much alive. There were puckered wounds all over his skin where the demon's tentacles had latched on, but they were already beginning to close from the magic he'd absorbed in the killing.

As he stood, one of the *Sharum* who helped pull him up gaped at the sight of Hasik's crotch, smooth like a woman's with only a scar and a metal tube where his manhood should be.

Hasik growled, taking the warrior's neck in his mighty arm and flexing, breaking it with a loud crack. He turned from the others as he stripped the man's robes, and the remaining warriors gave him a wide berth as he quickly pulled on the pantaloons and robe. Jayan made no mention of the killing, so his advisors, too, remained silent on the matter.

'I will see to your bodyguard's wounds,' Asavi said.

Jayan caught her arm as she passed, his eyes angry. 'Hasik can wait until you tell us what he almost died for.'

Everyone froze. It was death to touch a *dama'ting* so. She could demand his hand be cut off, or he be killed, and Evejan law would demand it be carried out.

But Jayan was Sharum Ka, firstborn son of the Deliverer, and likely the next leader of Krasia. Abban wondered if any would dare so much as take the *dama'ting*'s side, much less try to carry out a sentence should she deliver it.

Asavi seemed to know it, too, her eyes scanning the reaction of the witnesses. If she demanded punishment and was refused, it would weaken her greatly in the eyes of Jayan's council. Khevat and the other *dama* grated on the new, more vocal role of the *dama'ting* since Inevera's display in the throne room.

She reached out with her free hand instead, seeming only to tap Jayan on the shoulder, but Abban could spot a pickpocket three stalls down the market, and saw the sharp jab of her knuckle.

Jayan's hand dropped away limp, as if he had decided of his own volition to let her go, but his eyes said otherwise.

'The Sharum Ka is right to be concerned,' Asavi said, her voice serene, 'but they are words for your private council chambers, not the open docks.'

'I have no council chambers!' Jayan snapped. 'The water witch set them afire.'

Abban bowed. 'There are other manses claimed by your loyal *kai*, some with a view of the docks, while safely out of slinger range. I will bring you a list to choose from, and see your lieutenant recompensed while we move your possessions. In the meantime, I have a warehouse nearby with a richly appointed office where you may relax until arrangements are made.'

Jayan shifted uncomfortably, eyes flicking to his shoulder, but he simply grunted. 'That will be acceptable, *khaffit*. Lead the way.'

By the time they made it to the warehouse, Jayan was sweating and pale with pain. He collapsed to the pillows, accepting tea with one hand, his other still limp at his side. Khevat and the other men pretended not to notice, but all were aware that something was wrong.

There was a glow from the corner of the room as Asavi sent magic through Hasik, finishing the healing the kill had started. There was a whispered plea to her, but Asavi, eyes flicking between his legs, only shook her head sadly. Hasik looked at Abban, eyes full of hatred, and Abban let him see just the hint of a grin.

'Would the Sharum Ka like me to see to his arm now?' Asavi asked. The other men glanced at her uncomfortably, then back to pale and sweating Jayan. All knew what was coming. Asavi had not been able to take her due in public, so she would have it thrice over behind the curtain.

'If the *d-dama'ting* wishes,' Jayan managed through gritted teeth.

'I could leave it, if you prefer,' the Bride said. 'There is time to save it if I act quickly. If not, it will wither and die.'

Jayan's one good eye bulged, and he began to shake.

'The Brides of Everam do not need clerics and warriors to punish those who would lay hands upon us, son of Ahmann,' Asavi said. 'Our blessed Husband has given us power enough to see to our own protection. It is a lesson you would do well to remember.'

She looked around the room, boldly meeting the eyes of the other men, even Khevat. 'All of you.'

They were bold words for a woman, and many of the men – Khevat especially – bristled, but none was fool enough to contradict her. She gave them a moment, then nodded, gliding over and helping Jayan slip his robe from one shoulder. The spot where the *dama'ting* had struck was black now, and the shoulder swollen. She took the limb tenderly, stretching and turning it as she massaged it back to life. Soon Jayan was wriggling his fingers again, and not long after making a fist.

'The limb will recover fully in a few days,' she said.

'Days?!' Jayan demanded.

Asavi shrugged. 'Kill *alagai*, and the magic will speed the healing.'

'You healed Hasik in an instant,' Jayan pressed.

'Hasik did not lay hands upon me,' Asavi noted.

'Fine, fine!' Jayan said sullenly, cradling the limb with his good hand. 'Now will you tell us what all that business on the docks was about?'

'Your enemies gather and make plans,' Asavi said. 'The dice have long foreseen this.'

'Any fool can guess that,' Jayan snapped.

'The dice also told me to stop the thief who stank of demon root, or thousands would die,' Asavi said.

'Demon root?' Jayan said.

'A *dama'ting* healing herb,' Asavi said. 'They call it hogroot here in the North. The spy reeked of it.'

'Why did you not speak of this sooner?' Khevat demanded. 'We could have had guards sniffing everyone to enter the palace of the Sharum Ka.'

'The dice said nothing of the palace,' Asavi said, 'or the Sharum Ka. The thief could have been anyone, anywhere. The dice foretold we would meet when I caught his scent, and what I must do. Had I spoken of it to anyone, fate may have changed, and the thief evade me as well.'

'He *did* evade you,' Khevat noted. 'All your vaunted *hora* magic, and you could not so much as stop a simple thief?'

'That was no simple thief, my *dama*,' Abban said, bowing. 'He evaded the *dal'Sharum* as if they waded in deep sand, and lasted ten seconds against the greatest living drillmaster. And fearless, running knowingly out amongst the water demons. And let us not forget he had the *Sharum's Lament* to set fire to the palace as distraction.'

'But what was he after?' Qeran mused.

'There's no way to know for sure,' Abban said. 'Only a few lives were lost in the burning of the palace, but the building is lost. We cannot say just what papers are missing amongst the ashes, but it is easy to guess.'

'Troop numbers,' Qeran said. 'Supply trains. Our maps. Our plans.'

Abban bowed to Jayan. 'We have copies of everything, Sharum Ka. Nothing has been lost. But we must assume our enemies now know all.'

Asavi knelt on the floor, drawing everyone's attention. While they spoke, the *dama'ting* had quietly laid out her casting cloth. Now she took out the *hora*, casting all in their eerie glow.

'Guesswork,' Asavi said. 'Everam may show us a clearer path, now that the divergence is past.'

All were silent as she threw, many of them seeing it for the first time since their *Hannu Pash*. When it was over, the Bride looked up, the *hora* light casting her white veils in red as if soaked with blood.

'It does not matter what the spy took,' Asavi said. 'Three duchies unite against us, and your enemies have what they need to attack.'

Jayan's eyes took on an eager light. 'Where? When?' A sane commander might be concerned at an impending attack, but the young Sharum Ka saw only a chance for glory, a chance to prove himself worthy of the Skull Throne.

The *dama'ting* looked back at the dice, eyes flicking over unreadable patterns. Abban had always mistrusted the dice. He could not deny there was magic about them, giving information that could be uncannily accurate, but it seemed their reading was as much art as science, and they did not tell all.

'They will attack from land and water,' Asavi said.

'Oh?' Jayan asked. 'Will they use weapons, perhaps? And warriors? If that is the best your dice can . . .'

Asavi held up the dice and they flared with power, casting the entire room in red light. It seemed they would sear the fingers from the *dama'ting*, but she held them easily, even as the men shrank away from the glow.

All were silent a moment. Abban looked at Qeran, nodding him forward.

The drillmaster looked as if he were being asked to climb into an *alagai* pit, but he went without hesitation or complaint, kneeling before Asavi and putting his hands on the floor. He bent forward, pressing his forehead between them.

Asavi looked at him a moment, and nodded. 'Speak, Drillmaster.'

'Honoured and wise *dama'ting*,' Qeran began carefully. 'It is not for we humble men to question the word of Everam. But if there is anything the dice may tell of where to position our forces, it could mean the difference between victory and defeat.'

'The dice do not speak of such things,' Asavi said, 'because our enemies watch us for hint we see their intent. If their spies note our movements, they will change their plans, negating the prophecy.'

She held up a finger. 'But while they will not say where, they do tell us when. They will attack on Waning.'

Khevat blinked. 'Impossible. They would not dare . . .'

'They will,' Asavi said, 'for the very reason you doubt. They think the Waning will distract us. Make us weak.'

Jayan scowled. 'My father said the *chin* had honour, if of a lesser sort, and were humble before Everam. But it cannot be so, if they would dare attack on the day we prepare for the rise of Alagai Ka.'

'That is only the beginning of their offence to Everam,' Asavi said, drawing all eyes back to her.

'They will attack in the night.'

26

First Strike
334 AR Winter

Heart pounding, Briar ran fast and low, using cover wherever he could find it. Still clad in his stolen blacks, the darkness was a comforting blanket.

There were few cories in the area. Whatever else could be said of his father's people, the Krasians had swept the lands around Docktown clean of demons, so much that even in the night there was little to fear.

But there were other predators out in the darkness.

Thamos had used the distraction of the Waning celebrations to move his forces in close, positioning them behind a small copse of trees near the base of Colan's Rise. The count's horse gave a start as Briar burst from the thicket right in front of them, rearing with a great whinny.

Briar froze, fearing the count would be thrown, but Thamos kept his seat, expertly bringing the animal back down.

'Night, boy,' the count growled, voice low and angry. 'Are you trying to give our position away and get us all killed?'

'They know,' Briar said.

'Eh?' Thamos asked.

'Seen 'em,' Briar said. '*Sharum* moving through the woods to get behind us. Know we're here.'

'Corespawn it,' Thamos growled. 'How many? Are they mounted?'

'Lots more than us,' Briar said. He was not good with numbers. 'But most on foot.'

Thamos nodded. 'Harder to move in secret on horseback. Are they in position?'

Briar shook his head. 'Not yet. Soon.'

Thamos turned to Lord Sament. 'Ready the men. We proceed as planned.'

'You mean to ride right into the trap?' Sament asked.

'What would you have me do?' Thamos asked. 'We won't get another chance at this. Egar and his men are committed, and Lakton without winter supply. We must take that hill and position the archers to cover the Laktonian deployment. The enemy is on foot, and their avenue of attack is narrow. Once we have the high ground, they will have a bloody time getting us out.'

'But they will,' Sament said. 'Once we're on that hill, we'll be trapped there.'

'If we can hold until the docks are taken, it may be we can break through with a charge of horse and escape.'

'And if not?' Sament asked.

'If not,' Thamos said, 'we protect the docks until we die.'

Abban leaned on his crutch by the waterfront window of his warehouse, staring into the darkness. His office spanned the entire top floor with windows on all sides, affording a view in every direction.

Earless loomed nearby, but Abban remained ill at ease. The giant was stronger than anyone Abban had ever met, and well on his way to becoming a *sharusahk* master, but his presence did not lend the comfort of Qeran. The drillmaster was matchless in combat and respected by all, willing – eager, even – to advise and point out when Abban was about to do something foolish.

It was surprising how much he had come to depend on the drillmaster, a man he had once hated with every fibre of his being. The man who had kicked Abban off the Maze wall into a layer seething with demons, simply for failing to fold a net properly.

With his merchant's eye, Abban understood. He had been a liability to his unit, endangering other *Sharum* with his incompetence at war. He accrued debt with no way of paying it back, like a chicken that could not lay. Better the slaughter, from Qeran's perspective.

But Abban had other skills, ones that made him invaluable to the Shar'Dama Ka – and to his sons. It was his plan they executed tonight. If they were victorious, Jayan would claim credit and Abban's part would be struck from history. If they failed, Abban's life wouldn't be worth the dust on his sandals.

Qeran was needed out there in the darkness.

A few feet away, Dama Khevat paced restlessly by the window, the old man taking no more ease than Abban. Only Asavi, kneeling on the floor on her perfect white casting cloth, projected serenity. She watched the men coolly as she sipped her tea.

The Krasians had been careful to appear as if nothing were out of the ordinary throughout the day. Khevat presided over Waning prayers as warriors spent the day eating, resting, and lying with women. Many of the *Sharum* had sent for their families to settle and help hold the town, and others had taken greenland brides when the town was sacked.

But when they mustered for *alagai'sharak*, as all *Sharum* must on Waning, they did not follow the usual path they took to sweep the *alagai* from the town environs, flitting invisibly in their black robes to places where they might ambush the coming *chin*.

'When fire shrieks thrice across the sky, you must strike,' Asavi had told Jayan that morning after reading the dice. The power of the *alagai hora* was shown once more as a line of fire whined into the sky with a shriek that could be heard for miles.

The *chin* flamework was mirrored by another streaking missile from the surface of the lake. A third lit the sky to the south where Sharu had taken his *dal'Sharum*.

In the distance, he heard the Horn of Sharak, and he felt a thrill pass through him. For better or worse, the battle had come.

On cue, roaring fires sprang up in the sling baskets of dozens of Laktonian warships moving swiftly for the shallows. Mehnding crews went to work immediately, but they were still getting the range when flames began to arc through the air. Khevat stopped his pacing to watch the streaking missiles, trepidation on his normally impassive face.

Abban was unconcerned. His engineers and Warders had secured the building, bricking *alagai* corpses into the walls to power the wards. A crude imitation of *dama'ting hora* magic, but effective enough. Boulders would bounce off the walls like pebbles, and no flame could touch them. Even smoke would turn to a fresh breeze before it drifted inside. The whole town could be laid to ruin, but his warehouse would remain unscathed.

He had barely entertained the thought before the Laktonians tried to make it reality. In the past they had restricted bombardment to the beaches and docks, but tonight's missiles ranged farther, blasting through buildings and setting fires throughout town.

'The first night of Waning,' Khevat growled, 'and they would burn women and children from their wards!'

'I suppose it is fitting,' Abban said. 'We gave little thought to their holy day of first snow when we took the town, and I've seen what *Sharum* do to women and children.'

'*Chin* women and children,' Khevat said. 'Unbelievers outside Everam's light.'

Abban shrugged. 'Perhaps. Fools, in any event, if they believe there is profit attacking on Waning.'

Khevat grunted. 'Even if they somehow manage to win the battle, the *Damaji* will not stand for it. They will empty Everam's

Bounty of warriors and kill a thousand *chin* for every *Sharum* lost.'

Briar watched as Thamos bent, putting match to the paper tube he stuck in the ground.

The archers had been ready for them, but there were not enough to stop the charge of Thamos' armoured cavalry. If the Krasians had positioned too many men atop the hill, they would have shown their hand too soon. They left the men on the hill to die.

The fuse sparked to life and the rocket took off with a great shriek, leaving a tail of red fire in the sky behind it. Briar's eyes widened as he tracked its flight. His mother made toss bangs for festival days, but this was flamework like he had only heard tale of. To the south and east, other rockets rose in response, signalling the readiness of the forces to attack.

'They're beautiful,' he said.

'Leesha Paper made them for a different new moon.' Thamos' voice was distant, sad. 'I've seen flamework fail many times, but not hers. Never hers.' He put two fingers into the seam of his breastplate as if to reassure himself something was there.

'I wonder what the Gatherer would think,' Sament said, 'knowing her flamework heralds such bloodshed.'

Thamos turned to him, eyes ready to fight, but a horn sounded below them, stealing both men's attention. The count took a deep breath, seeming to deflate as he let it out.

He put a foot in his stirrup, swinging himself into the saddle. 'It is too late to worry what women think.'

He lifted his spear. 'Archers! Kill anything that moves on the docks until the ships are in! Fire at will!'

Briar ran for one of the great stones by the road, climbing quickly and putting his belly to the rock as he looked out over the approaching forces.

'What do you see?' Thamos asked, riding close.

Colan's Rise was sheer rock on three sides, with only one rock-strewn road leading to its top. 'Too much cover to shoot,' Briar said. 'They're charging on foot. Archers held behind.'

'To be fresh and ready when they retake the hill,' Thamos said. 'If they manage it, they can rain arrows on the docks as the Laktonians deploy.'

Briar moved to climb down, but Thamos checked him with a pointed finger. 'Stay right there, Briar. This is soldiers' business.'

'My home,' Briar growled. 'My fight, too.'

Thamos nodded. 'But you fight in ways others cannot, Briar. You alone can escape this hill, and make sure others know what happened here.' He reached into his armour, removing a folded bit of paper.

'You alone can get this to Leesha, if I do not live through the night.'

Briar felt his throat tighten as he took the paper. He liked the count, but there were many *Sharum* coming.

Too many.

Thamos gave a wild cry, kicking his mare and leading the charge down the road.

Briar felt a surge of hope, watching the heavy horses. He had expected the charge to slow when they reached the *Sharum* spears, but the Wooden Soldiers and their horses wore lightweight wooden armour strengthened by warded lacquer. They turned the enemy spears even as the giant mustang mowed the men like grass, leaving nothing but bloody clippings behind.

But as they reached the base of the hill, great lights flared as the Krasians put fire to bowls of oil. Mirrors caught and angled the light as the horses came into the sights of the enemy archers. They launched indiscriminately into the press of warriors, heedless of their own men in the line of fire.

Arrows began to find seams and weaknesses in the Wooden Soldiers' armour. Men screamed and horses reared in pain, even as enemy troops moved to surround them on the open ground.

Thamos gave a signal and his cavalry turned like a flock of birds to race back to the high ground.

It was a temporary respite, but already the *Sharum* gained ground, and more warriors were flowing up the hill. In the oil lights Briar could see their robes were not black or tan, but green.

That explained why their commander was so willing to waste their lives taking the hill. They were not Krasian at all, but Rizonan men pressed into service. They would do the bleeding, and then their masters would take the hill.

Briar remembered Icha, remembered the sympathy he had felt for the man under the torturer's screws. That treatment had been cruel, and wrong, and pointless. But it was nothing compared to what the enemy was willing to do.

Briar knew then that nothing would stop the Krasians from taking Colan's Rise. He rubbed his fingers against the paper the count had given him. If he was to escape, it had to be soon.

The main road was too dangerous, so Briar moved to the far side of the bluff to scale down the sheer walls. With his climbing skills and the blacks he still wore, he could go where others could not.

Or so he thought.

At first Briar rubbed his eyes, thinking they were playing tricks on him. His night vision was strong, honed by a lifetime living in the darkness, but even it had limits.

He froze, straining against the dim starlight and the fires now raging on the waters below as Captain Dehlia and the others attacked the port.

There it was again. Movement on the cliffs. All over the cliffs.

There were *dal'Sharum* scaling Colan's Rise, hundreds of them.

He scrambled the other way, racing through the archers. '*Sharum* on the cliffs! *Sharum* on the cliffs!'

'I see one!' an archer called, firing down into the rocks. He must have missed, because he cursed, pulling another arrow.

All around the bluff, archers were confirming the approaching warriors, taking their eyes from the docks as they attacked the closer targets. But the *Sharum*, black-clad and flat against the steep slope, were difficult targets, and more arrows were wasted than Krasians killed.

Thamos rode up to the sergeant in charge of the Laktonian archers. 'Tell your men to stop wasting arrows and keep firing on those docks! I'm leaving a hundred horse to guard them.'

'And the rest of us?' Sament asked, riding up next to him.

Thamos pointed down the hill. 'The rest of us are going to destroy the archers they have waiting to position here. They may take the rise, but they will not benefit from it.'

He looked to Briar. 'The chaos in our wake . . .'

Briar nodded. It would be easy to slip away unnoticed with four hundred heavy horses as a distraction.

The count gave a shout, kicking his horse before he had time to rethink his course. The Wooden Soldiers thundered down the hill, sweeping the *chi'Sharum* aside. Unlike previous sallies, they kept on as they reached open ground, heading straight for the ranks of elite *dal'Sharum* archers.

The Krasians had not anticipated the move, but their surprise was short-lived, and they began to pepper the horsemen with a withering fire that thinned their ranks. The horses could not run in full armour, and as arrows began to find the gaps, they screamed and fell, often taking out neighbours in their fall.

Still they picked up speed, and suddenly they were on top of the archers, laying about with cavalry spears as their great horses trampled and crushed. The bowmen had no defence, and were quickly overrun.

Thamos led the attack, his spear a blur as his horse leapt to and fro. Sament rode close beside him.

But as the archers were destroyed, the Krasian army moved in. These were not *chi'Sharum*, given spears and pressed into service. These were true *Sharum*, bred to battle and trained since childhood, many of them mounted themselves. They closed in from all sides, breaking Thamos' ranks and shattering his ordered men into chaos.

Still the battle raged. Sament kept close to Thamos, the two lords standing out in their bright armour. Sament batted a spear from Thamos' path with his shield. Thamos skewered the man, then swung the *Sharum*'s body into the path of an enemy horse. Sament was ready, putting his spear into the rearing animal's throat.

They seemed to be dominating the field around them, but from a distance Briar could see they were being separated from their fellows. Herded.

Briar knew he should flee. Should take his lead into the night and deliver news of the loss of the hill, and the letter to Leesha Paper.

But he could not bring himself to go. He pulled up his *Sharum* veil and flitted from stone to stone, getting closer to the battle.

Thamos and Sament fought their way into a ring, and suddenly found themselves in the clear. The *dal'Sharum* had circled an area of open ground.

There in the centre of the circle was the Krasian leader, Jayan, marked by his white turban and veil.

'You fight well, greenlander,' Jayan called, raising his spear. 'Shall we test your mettle against a true foe?'

Abban took up his distance lens – another gift from the Damajah. His Warders had painstakingly taken the device apart, studying the design, the warding, and the shard of demon bone that powered it. It had not taken long to produce more of them, and all his ship captains, Qeran included, had them now.

The device allowed him to see in Everam's light – wardsight, the greenlanders called it. With it he could see the enemy ships as if they were right before him in bright day, with every hand illuminated and the wards on their hulls glowing as if written in fire.

The water was dark, all its drifting magic drawn to the ships' wards, but underneath the surface Abban could see the glow of demons, drawn to the commotion. They circled like a whirlpool, waiting only for a gap in the wards to pull whole ships down to Nie's embrace.

On the docks and beach, the enemy slingers were taking a heavy toll. The demonfire was concentrated farther inland – the *chin* did not wish to destroy the docks. Their slinger baskets were filled with stones the size of a man's fist, scattering to smash through fortifications, warriors, and engines alike. Scorpions added precise kills to the chaos, taking out shooters and *kai* when they stepped from cover.

And still, the withering fire from Colan's Rise.

'They cannot hold,' Khevat said, pointing to galleys moving in behind the barrage, large enough to be seen in only the light of wards and fire. 'The *chin* will overwhelm them when they land their forces.'

'*If* they land, honoured *dama*,' Abban said.

Asavi appeared beside them, looking out onto the lake. Abban pretended to adjust his lens, stealing a glance at her through it. As he suspected, her many jewels glowed fiercely with magic, particularly the warded coins at her brow. No doubt she could see as well as he in the darkness.

'Leave war to true men, *khaffit*,' Khevat said. 'I was studying the conquests of Kaji before your father wore his bido. There is nothing the *dal'Sharum* can do to stop the landing. They will have to prevail on open ground.'

Abban wasted no time arguing, skimming his lens to the south, finding what he sought at last. There, coming in fast from their hidden cove, his small fleet was nearly invisible on the dark water, unnoticed by the enemy.

The lead vessel was *Everam's Spear*, commanded by Drillmaster Qeran and crewed entirely by men from Abban's Hundred, a sleek galley with twenty oars to a side and square sails that could catch most any wind. But the black sails were furled, the galley shooting like an arrow for the enemy fleet under oar power alone. The fore and aft castles had no slingers, only specially designed scorpions and many, many men.

Two more galleys followed, and a score of smaller vessels – these carrying neither slinger nor scorpion, their holds packed with *Sharum*.

Abban produced a second warded distance lens, a cheap copy of his own, but effective enough. He wanted his old teacher to see this.

'You are right, Dama, not to put faith in the *dal'Sharum* to stop the enemy. Watch now as my *kha'Sharum* do what they could not.'

Khevat looked doubtful, but he raised the lens to where Abban pointed. 'Our captured ships. What of it? A handful of ships cannot sink so many.'

'Sink?' Abban tsked. 'Where is the profit in that? If we are to win this war, Dama, the enemy fleet must become ours.'

A moment later, Qeran's ship was in range of a large Laktonian galley, an elegant vessel with great pointed sails and wide deck lined with armament on both sides.

The Krasians fired great barbed stingers that stuck and held fast in the enemy ship's hull. The trailing ropes were attached to heavy cranks, and muscular *chin* slaves bent their backs, drawing the ships in close.

Before the Laktonians knew what was happening, agile *kha'Sharum* Watchers were already running up the taut ropes like *nie'Sharum* on the top of the Maze walls. They carried no shields, but all had half a dozen throwing spears on their backs, and by the time planks were dropped for the other warriors to follow, the biggest threats on deck were eliminated.

In moments, Abban's warriors swept the deck. He saw Qeran among them, the drillmaster easy to spot with his missing leg. He killed with an efficiency that would have frightened Abban, if not for the man's aura. Abban could not read hearts like Ahmann or the Damajah, but the glory of victory was bright around him.

You see, Drillmaster? Abban thought. *I have given back all you have lost.*

When the deck was clear and the ship firmly in the hands of the Hundred, Mehnding were brought aboard, the teams running to man the *chin* armament. A skeleton crew was left in place, and Qeran leapt back to *Everam's Spear* even as the lines were cut.

All across the lake, Laktonian ships were being similarly boarded by teams of *Sharum* that had rowed silently into position. The greenlanders might have the advantage in ranged fire, but in close-quarters killing, there were none in all the world to match the *Sharum* of Krasia. Jayan had given Qeran men, and the drillmaster had run them mercilessly back and forth across tilting ship decks until they found their water legs.

Qeran himself had taken four ships, and the rest of his fleet another sixteen, before the cries of alarm reached the rest of the Laktonian fleet.

Only then did the Mehnding on the decks open fire, aiming for the enemy ships that had pulled up to the docks and struck ground on the beach. As the Laktonian troops disembarked, the Mehnding rained the greenlanders' own demonfire down on them. *Chin* warriors screamed and burned as Abban's pirates turned their attention to the next ships in line to unload. Great chains were slung, tearing sails and splintering oars to leave the ships dead in the water.

The Laktonian captains, still outnumbering the pirates, shifted fire to the new foe, but the Mehnding archers let fly flaming arrows, catching their sails and strafing their decks while the *chin* fire teams struggled to recalibrate.

Sharum's Lament appeared, the agile vessel tacking around the others to bring its armament to bear. The advantage of surprise was soon lost, and the numbers began to tell. But unlike the greenlanders, *Sharum* warriors were ready to die. When their ships were damaged, they were more than willing to ram the enemy and leap the gap, fighting in close.

But still it seemed the battle on the water would be lost, and the Laktonians escape back to their stronghold. There was one last trick Qeran could try, but the drillmaster had argued long and hard against it, and even Abban agreed it was a desperate move that might do more harm than good.

Jayan lowered his veil. 'I am Jayan asu Ahmann am'Jardir am'Kaji, firstborn son of Shar'Dama Ka and Damajah, Sharum Ka of all Krasia.' He gave a slight nod from his saddle. 'May I see your face and have your name, *chin*, before I send you to Everam to be judged?'

'Don't . . .' Sament began, but Thamos ignored him, sticking his spear in the ground within easy reach, unfastening his helm.

As he lifted it away, Jayan's eyes widened. 'You. The princeling who came with the Par'chin to . . .'

Thamos nodded. 'I am Prince Thamos, fourth son of Duke Rhinebeck the Second, Lord Commander of the Wooden Soldiers, third in line to the ivy throne and Count of Hollow County.'

Jayan bared his teeth. 'The one who dared touch the Deliverer's intended.'

There was an angry murmur through the *Sharum* at this.

'Leesha Paper chose me even before Ahmann Jardir fell to his death.' Thamos pointed at Jayan with his spear. 'And you will share his fate. I challenge you to *Domin Sharum*.'

Jayan laughed, and after a moment, the warriors joined him.

'*Domin Sharum* is honourable combat before Everam, *chin*.' Jayan pointed his spear back at Thamos. 'You have attacked men in the night on Waning. You have no honour.'

'We have your brother and his lieutenants,' Thamos said. 'Harm us, and you will never see them again.'

'Icha?' Jayan asked.

Thamos nodded. 'And three *kai*, half a dozen drillmasters, and more than fifty *Sharum*. Grant me honourable combat, and they will be released.'

Jayan turned to his *dal'Sharum*. 'See how even *chin* warriors attempt to bargain for their lives like *khaffit* merchants!'

The Krasian warriors jeered, many around the ring spitting at Thamos.

Jayan turned back to Thamos. 'Keep my brother and his men! If they were weak and stupid enough to be captured by *chin*, they deserve no better. We will come for them soon enough.'

He raised his veil. 'But if you wish me to kill you personally for thinking you could cuckold the Shar'Dama Ka, that I will grant.'

Thamos was quick to replace his helm and snatch up his long spear, kicking his horse to circle counter to Jayan as he readied himself.

Neither man hesitated long, kicking their great mustang into nearly identical charges, spears lowered.

At the last moment before they struck, Jayan lifted his spear to take aim at Thamos' chest. Thamos, unexpectedly, tossed his long spear expertly in the air, catching it in a reversed grip much closer to the head.

Jayan's spear struck the count full in the chest, but there was a flare of light from the wards on Thamos' armour, and the weapon shattered.

And then Thamos was in close, able to put force and speed to a series of rapid spear thrusts, poking holes at Jayan's defences, searching for an opening.

Jayan tried to ride off and regroup, but the count was the better horseman, his mare herding Jayan's stallion like a sheepdog, keeping them locked close as the count continued the battering.

Jayan moved his shield with frantic speed, and under its wide shade and his own glass armour, he found shelter enough. But he was on the defensive, and without a spear to strike back. It seemed the count would soon manage to find a seam in his armour and deliver a killing blow.

Jayan shoved against his shield, knocking Thamos back just enough to strike at his mount. The back of the mare's neck was armoured, but its throat was not, and Jayan buried the broken haft of his spear into it.

The giant mustang reared and gurgled, stumbling on hind legs as its forelegs kicked wildly. Thamos kept his seat until the animal began to topple, managing to throw himself clear of its bulk as they struck the ground.

Briar thought it would end there, but Jayan rode back to his lieutenants, dismounting and taking up a six-foot infantry spear.

Thamos was back on his feet as Jayan began striding towards him. He left his ten-foot cavalry spear in the mud, pulling a three-foot Angierian fencing spear from its harness on his back as he waited for his enemy to come.

Jayan growled, his feet set in the stance Briar's father had taught him long ago. His skittering steps forward were fast and economical, spear resting on his shield arm. His arm was a blur as he pumped the weapon much as the count had on horseback, searching the wooden armour for weaknesses to exploit.

Thamos took most of the barrage on his shield and breast-plate, thrusting his own spear low at the gap between the armour plates on Jayan's thigh.

But Jayan twisted the limb out of the weapon's path. With his shield hand he grasped the harness straps on Thamos' back and hauled, driving a knee into his stomach as Thamos was flipped onto his back, momentarily stunned.

But again Jayan let the advantage go, circling while the count shook himself and rose to his feet, growling. He hunched low, tamping feet like a cat.

'I may not see the dawn, but neither will you,' Thamos promised.

Jayan barked a laugh. 'You have great balls, *chin*. When I have killed you, I will cut them off and shove them down your throat.'

Thamos came in fast – faster than Briar would have thought possible. The wards on his armour were glowing now as his fencing spear whipped through the air in thrusts and parries.

Jayan picked them off confidently now, his skittering steps

never losing balance. He circled away from one thrust, spinning around to strike Thamos hard in the face with the rim of his shield. The count stumbled back, and Jayan pressed in, delivering hard jabs into his armour that battered and stung, even if they could not penetrate. Thamos was herded like an animal into the centre of the ring.

The count struck back with a shield attack of his own, but Jayan was ready for it. He dropped his own shield and reached in to take the biceps of Thamos' shield arm. He pivoted clockwise, straightening the arm, then thrust hard into the gap beneath Thamos' helmet.

The count stood shaking a moment, then dropped limply to the ground.

At last Qeran gave the signal, and the slinger teams let loose another volley, casks of heated tar that shattered against the hulls of the enemy ships making their final press for the port.

Marring the wards.

The effect was immediate. Abban saw the glow of water demons as they came streaming towards the vulnerable ships, and caught a rare glimpse of the creatures as they broke the surface here and there to break hulls with tentacle and snapping claw. A few braved the open air long enough to slither onto the ships, sweeping the decks as easily as a wedge of *Sharum*.

The surface of the lake turned to a churning froth, men and women screaming as they were pulled under.

Then, as they looked on in horror, a huge demon came close to the surface. The water heaved in great spumes as tentacles the size of Sharik Hora's minarets rose around one of the largest vessels, wrapping about the hull and squeezing. The deck splintered in the crush, hapless sailors flailing as they were sucked down. In moments, the entire ship vanished beneath countless tons of water.

Khevat turned his dark glare on Abban. 'Is this your doing, *khaffit?*'

Abban swallowed, but after what he had just witnessed, there was little the cleric could do to frighten him.

He straightened, steeling himself. 'It was, *dama*. Do not blame Drillmaster Qeran. He argued most vehemently against the plan, and Jayan was never told.'

Khevat only stared. It was a negotiation tactic Abban knew well, giving one's adversary the rope for his own hanging, but Khevat was a *sharusahk* master, and the ranking cleric in Everam's Reservoir. If he decided to kill Abban here and now, there was nothing Abban could do to stop him.

Best to convince him otherwise.

'Look,' Abban said, pointing to the chaos on the water. As instructed, Qeran and his captured ships retreated with all speed when the demons began their feeding frenzy. 'Most of our captured ships are safely away, and the enemy fleet is destroyed. Already the few that remain are fleeing back to their floating home. Even the *Sharum's Lament* runs from us, and I daresay Captain Dehlia is not showing her breasts this time.'

'You gave our enemies to the *alagai*,' Asavi said, her voice low, dangerous. 'Gave them to *Nie*.'

'I did,' Abban said. 'There was no other choice, if we were to defeat the attack and escape with enough ships to end the stalemate. Should I have left our men to die?'

'They are *Sharum*,' Khevat said. 'Their souls are prepared, and they know the price of war.'

'As do I,' Abban said. 'I know the price, and I paid what I must for victory. These men attacked in the night, on Waning. They are no brothers of ours, no enemies of Nie. Indeed, they do Her bidding, and so I gave them to Her.'

He pointed a finger at Khevat, a simple action that was nevertheless reason enough for a *dama* to kill a *khaffit* by Evejan law. 'I paid the price for our men, and I paid it for you.'

'For me?' Khevat asked.

'And the Sharum Ka, and even Qeran, who would have

refused the order had he not sworn an oath to obey me. All of you may go to the Creator with no weight on your souls. The soulless *khaffit* has spared you responsibility. Let Everam judge me, when I finally limp to the end of the lonely path.'

Khevat stared at him a long time, and Abban wondered just how soon he would be standing before the Creator. But then the *dama* turned to Asavi, a question in his eyes.

The *dama'ting* searched him with her eyes, and it was all Abban could do not to squirm under her gaze.

At last she nodded. 'The *khaffit* speaks the truth. He is already doomed to sit outside the gates of Heaven until Everam takes pity and grants him another life. It is *inevera*.'

Khevat grunted, moving to the window and laying a hand on the glass as he watched the ships burn.

'These men were no brothers of ours,' he agreed at last. 'We did not make them attack in the night. *Inevera*.'

Abban blew out a breath he hadn't realized he was holding.

27

Dama in the Dark
334 AR Winter

'They said I was cursed by Everam, to bear three daughters after Ahmann,' Kajivah told the crowd, waving a hand at Imisandre, Hoshvah, and Hanya. The Holy Mother was clad in plain black wool. She wore the white veil of *kai'ting*, but unlike the other women of Ahmann's blood, Kajivah had taken to wearing a white headwrap, as well.

Inevera, watching from the royal tier as the Holy Mother gave the blessing over the Waning feast, wished she could be anywhere else. She had heard the idiot woman give this speech a thousand times.

'But I always said Everam blessed me with a son so great, he needed no brothers!' The crowd erupted in a roar of approval at the words, warriors stomping feet and clattering spears on shields as their wives clapped and children cheered.

'We thank Everam for the food we are about to partake of, richer fare than many of us knew before Ahmann led us from the Desert Spear into the green lands,' Kajivah went on. 'But I wish to thank the women who worked so hard preparing the feast as well.'

More applause. 'We honour the *Sharum'ting* who stand tall in the night, but there are other ways to give honour to the Creator. The wives and daughters who keep the bellies of our men full, their houses clean, their cribs full of children. We honour today the men who protect us from the *alagai*, but also the women who brought them forth and suckled them, who taught them honour and duty and love of family. Women who are modest and humble before Everam, providing the foundation our fighting men depend upon.'

The cheering increased, with women wailing in love and devotion. Inevera saw more than one woman openly weeping, and couldn't believe it.

'Too many of us are forgetting who we are and where we come from, lowering our veils and coveting the immodest dress of the Northern women. Women daring to wear colours, as if they were the Damajah herself!' Kajivah swept a hand at Inevera, and there were boos and hisses. Inevera knew they were directed at immodest women, but she could not help but prickle at the sound of hisses to her name.

'The Damajah was wise in giving the Holy Mother this task,' Ashan said. 'The people love her.'

Inevera was not so sure. It seemed harmless enough, asking Kajivah to plan feasts. It kept her busy and out of Inevera's way. But somehow the fool woman was winning the hearts of the people with her uneducated ways and conservative values. It was a time of change for their people. They could not continue the insular ways they had developed over centuries in the Desert Spear if they were to win Sharak Sun.

Kajivah showed no sign of slowing, warming to a sermon like a *dama* who'd caught the *Sharum* with dice and couzi. For a woman with an empty head, Kajivah could talk for hours if unchecked.

Inevera stood, and instantly the crowd fell silent, women falling to their knees and putting hands on the floor as the men, from Damaji to *Sharum*, bowed deeply.

The sight used to comfort her. A reminder of her power and divine status. But there was power, too, in leading the cheers of the crowd. Too much, perhaps, for a simple woman like Kajivah.

'The Holy Mother is indeed humble,' Inevera said. 'For none has worked harder to prepare this grand feast than Kajivah herself.' The crowd roared again, and Inevera gritted her teeth. 'We can do her no greater honour than sitting to it. In Everam's name, let us begin the feast.'

'I fear we may have opened a djinn bottle with that one,' Inevera said.

Her mother, Manvah, sipped her tea. It was her first visit to the royal chambers, but if she was impressed by the opulence around her, she gave no sign.

'Having dealt with the woman directly, I would have to agree,' Manvah said. Manvah's pavilion in the new bazaar provided many of the implements used in the Waning feast, earning her an invitation. Her *khaffit* husband, Kasaad, had been asked not to attend.

It had been a risk, slipping her in for a private audience, but Inevera needed her mother now more than ever. The eunuch who ushered her through the secret passages had been drugged. He would wake with no memory of the woman, and with her veil in place Manvah would look like any other woman as she slipped out from the passage into the public section of the palace.

'I thought her a poor haggler at first, but after enduring a few of her tantrums, I see I undercharged.' Manvah shook her head. 'I'm afraid I advised you poorly in this case, daughter. I will deduct it from your debt.'

Inevera smiled. It was a joke between them, for Manvah made Inevera, the Damajah, weave palm for her whenever her daughter came to her for advice.

'They aren't an act,' Inevera said. Manvah had taught her early how a proper tantrum could aid in haggling, but it was always calculated. A good haggler never lost their temper.

Kajivah had no control over hers.

'Yet the people love her,' Manvah said. 'Even *dama'ting* hop when she speaks.'

'Nie take me if I can understand why,' Inevera said.

'It's simple enough,' Manvah said. 'It is a time of great upheaval for our people, leaving many without sure footing. Kajivah gives them that, speaking in a way the masses can understand. She walks among them, knows them. You spend your time here in the palace, far removed.'

'If she were not the Deliverer's mother, I would poison her and be done,' Inevera said.

'Ahmann would not appreciate that upon his return,' Manvah said. 'Not even you could hide such a thing from the divine sight of Shar'Dama Ka.'

'No.' Inevera dropped her eyes. 'But Ahmann is not coming back.'

Manvah looked at her in surprise. 'What? Have your dice told you this?'

'Not directly,' Inevera said. 'But they made reference to the corpse of Shar'Dama Ka, and I can see him in no futures. Barring a miracle of Everam, our people must go on without him until I can make another.'

'Make?' Manvah asked.

'Of all the mysteries the dice have revealed to me,' Inevera said, 'none struck so hard as the knowledge that Deliverers are made, not born. The dice will guide me to his successor, and how to shape him.'

Inevera expected Manvah to gasp as she had, but in typical fashion, Manvah absorbed the information with a grunt and went on. 'Who will it be, then? Not Ashan, surely. Jayan? Asome?'

Inevera sighed. 'The moment I cast the dice for Ahmann, a boy of nine, I saw the potential in him. I would have thought it a fluke, but after years of searching I found it in another, the Par'chin, who was younger than Asome. Never before or since those two have I seen a boy or man with even the hope of following the Deliverer's path. One of my sons may yet need to take the throne, but they will only be holding it for the one to come next.'

'None rise willingly from a throne once it is sat,' Manvah said.

'And so it is my hope to hold them off as long as I can,' Inevera said. 'There is still time, Everam willing. Neither boy has proven himself in any significant way. Without deeds, neither of them can wrest power from the Andrah. My concern this day is how to keep Kajivah in check.'

'I hate to suggest it,' Manvah said, 'but the answer may well be spending more time with her.'

Inevera stared at her blankly.

'And making your raiment a touch more modest.' Only the corners of Manvah's mouth were touched by her smile, but it was unmistakable.

Ashia watched impassively as Asome cut his hand, squeezing blood over Melan's dice.

Her husband had done this often since word of the impending attack on Docktown had come to them. Asome's hands were covered in bandages.

Asome and Asukaji still stared at the process in fascination. Growing into womanhood in the Dama'ting Palace, Ashia had seen the casting ritual countless times, but even she found her eyes drawn to it. There was beauty in the *alagai hora*, and mystery. She tracked the dice as Melan threw, breath held in anticipation of that exquisite moment when the dice were struck from their natural trajectory, moved by the hand of Everam.

She knew in her heart the power came from the bones and the wards, but Ashia did not believe any but the Brides of Everam could summon His hand. To any other, they would just be dice.

But for all their power and closeness to Everam, Ashia did not covet white robes and *dama* blood. She, too, felt Everam's touch. It thrummed through her when she killed *alagai*. Not the magic, though that was a heady sensation of its own. She felt it even that first night, when she killed with an unwarded spear. There was a sense of rightness, an utter calm and surety that she did His good work. It was her purpose in life. The gift of *Sharum* blood.

Melan looked up, veiled face glowing red in the wardlight. 'Tonight. The divergence is now, or it will never be. When Jayan returns, he will come for the Skull Throne. If you do not act tonight, he will take it.'

For an instant, Ashia lost her centre, swept away by a memory.

'Let him defeat you,' the Damajah told Ashia.

'Eh?' Ashia asked. She had only just been raised to *Sharum'ting*, she and her spear sisters to be sent to the young Sharum Ka for the first time.

Inevera had claimed the young women as her bodyguard, but they were still *Sharum*, and subject to Jayan. He was to 'assess' them this night, to deem their worthiness and where he would position them in *alagai'sharak*.

'Jayan is proud,' Inevera said. 'He will seek to dominate you in front of your sisters, to ensure you do not threaten him. He will challenge you to spar under the guise of assessing your *sharusahk*, but the fight will be very real.'

'And you wish me to . . . lose?' Impossible. Unthinkable. How many years had she been forced to feign weakness – Asome the *push'ting*'s timid bride? The Damajah had promised that would change when she was given the spear.

'I *command* you to lose,' Inevera said, her tone sharpening. 'Show him your mettle. Earn his respect. And then lose. If you do not, he will kill you.'

Ashia swallowed, knowing she should be silent and nod. 'And if I kill him?'

'He is the firstborn son of the Deliverer,' Inevera said. 'If you kill him, every *Sharum* and *dama* in Krasia will call for your head, and the Shar'Dama Ka will not deny them.'

She said nothing of her own part in that, but Jayan was her firstborn, as well. Ashia knew Inevera's oldest son vexed her, but she loved him, too.

'I know this command pains your *Sharum* heart,' Inevera said. 'But I give it in love. I am the Damajah. Your pride, your life, are mine.' She laid a gentle hand on Ashia's shoulder. 'I value the first less than the second. Everam has a plan for you, and it is not to die for the sake of a man's frail ego.'

Ashia nodded, shrugging off the hand as she knelt, putting her hands on the floor and pressing her forehead between them. 'As the Damajah commands.'

There had not been many witnesses. Jayan knew the *Sharum'ting* had his father's favour, and did not wish to discredit them publicly. It was just her and Shanvah, Jayan, Jurim, and Hasik. Shanvah's father Shanjat, first among the *kai'Sharum*, should by rights have been there as well. His absence was telling.

The Sharum Ka and two elite Spears of the Deliverer. Even if she and Shanvah could kill them all before they raised the alarm – a prospect of which she was by no means certain – dozens of warriors had seen them enter the audience chamber. There would be no lasting escape.

Jayan grinned as the two women placed their hands on the floor before him. 'My timid cousins! Shying from every sound and never speaking in more than a whisper. Who but Everam could have imagined you spent years learning *sharusahk* in secret?'

'There are many mysteries in the Dama'ting Palace,' Ashia said.

Jayan chuckled. 'Of that, I have no doubt.' He undid the clasp of his cape and opened his armoured robe, standing bare-chested in his pantaloons. 'But while you learned at the hands of women, I studied at the feet of Shar'Dama Ka himself. I must judge your prowess, if I am to find a place for you in *sharak*.' He held a hand out, beckoning.

Ashia's breathing was steady as she rose. She, too, removed her cape and unslung the shield from her shoulder, passing them to Shanvah. She did not remove her robe, but she slid her hands into its many pockets with practised efficiency, removing the ceramic armour plates within and stacking them neatly on the floor.

She was lighter when she rose to her feet, gliding out onto the floor to begin circling opposite Jayan.

His stance was strong. Jayan was not lying when he said the Shar'Dama Ka had taught him, and her uncle was the greatest known *sharusahk* master. Perhaps he could win the battle fairly. It would bring no shame to Enkido to be defeated by the Deliverer's son, and Ashia would prefer to lose in truth than dishonour them both by throwing the match.

But then he came at her, and Ashia was the faster. Instinctively she tripped him, jabbing her toe into a convergence point that numbed his foot momentarily. He lost balance as he passed, and Ashia stole the energy, slipping her hand under his armpit and using it to throw him onto his back.

A hush fell on the room. The men looked dumbstruck, having expected a very different result. Ashia wondered if she had already gone too far; if the men would kill her to save face for their Sharum Ka.

But after a moment, Jayan forced a laugh, getting back to his feet, stomping to restore feeling to the numbed appendage. 'A fine throw! Let us see what else you have.'

He kept better guard this time, delivering a flurry of punches, kicks, and open-hand blows. Ashia dodged most of them, diverting the others with minimal contact. She made a few halfhearted strikes of her own, assessing his defences.

He was good, as *Sharum* went. One of the best. But many of his blocks left convergences open, giving her points she could use to disable, cripple, and kill.

Instead she leapt over one of his circle kicks, somersaulting away to put space between them.

'You are wise to retreat, sister,' Jayan said. 'I would have had you there.'

Ashia's jaw tightened. She could have killed him three times over by now. Her eyes flicked to Shanvah.

Her spear sister knelt serenely, but she worked the fingers of one hand into a question. *Why are you giving up advantages?*

Why indeed? Ashia wondered. The Damajah had commanded it, of course, but what example was she setting for Shanvah and future *Sharum'ting* if she allowed Jayan to defeat her?

'You cannot circle forever,' Jayan called. 'I have given you too much energy already. Come, show me what strength you have when you are not stealing mine.'

Ashia shot in so quickly Jayan was unprepared. She parted his arms with cobra's hood, and then bent forward and held his waist as her right foot came up over her back to kick him in the face.

He stumbled back and she spun to the floor, hooking the back of his knee with hers and pulling him off his feet.

Jayan was no novice at ground fighting, twisting and shifting his weight to offer minimal targets and leverage. But Ashia was in close now, where the *dama'ting sharusahk* Enkido had taught was its deadliest. Precise strikes broke his lines of power as she worked into a submission hold atop him, her forearm cutting off his windpipe and the artery supplying blood to his brain.

Jayan shook, sweat broken out on his face, and she saw fear in his eyes. And, at last, respect. She imagined herself forcing a submission from him, but the Damajah's words came to her again.

Show him your mettle. Earn his respect. And then lose.

Jayan made a weak pull at her choking arm, and Ashia eased back slightly, as if the effort had made a difference.

Jayan caught a breath, and with a surge, he came forward, punching her hard in the face. Unprepared for such ferocity, Ashia fell back as he landed blow after blow, striking her face, her body, blows meant to do lasting damage.

He rolled her onto her stomach, pinning her under his weight as he took hold of the collar of her robe from behind, pulling in opposite directions to close off the air and blood to her head, much as Ashia had done to him.

Did he mean to kill her? She did not know. If she had taken it too far, humiliated Jayan past reason, he would not hesitate. He was the Deliverer's firstborn, and if he killed her, he would get no more than a scolding from his father and the support of all others.

Even now, she could turn it around. Even now, with the world blackening around the edges, she could strike the convergence in his elbow, sucking a breath as his grip loosened then reversing the hold.

Let him defeat you.

Ashia wanted nothing more than to show Jayan and these men that she was their better, but that was not the way she had been taught.

Battle is deception, Enkido taught. *The wise warrior bides their time.*

She reached a shaking hand towards Jayan's arm as her vision shrank down to a dark tunnel, the light at the end ready to wink out at any moment. But instead of striking the convergence, she slapped twice, weakly.

The sign of submission.

Jayan grunted, loosening the hold. Ashia drew a breath, sweeter than any save the first one Enkido had allowed her, those many years ago.

But though he seemed to have accepted her submission, Jayan did not roll away, keeping her pinned, his mouth close to her ear.

'You fight well, cousin, but you are still only a woman.'

Ashia gritted her teeth, saying nothing.

'How long?' Jayan whispered, shifting atop her. 'How long since my *push'ting* brother last treated you as a wife? I expect it was just the once.' He ground his hips into her backside, and Ashia could feel his erection. 'When you are ready for a true man, come to me.'

'Jayan must not take the throne,' Ashia said. 'He would have to kill my father to do it, and he would not be wise in his rule.'

Asome nodded. 'Help me stop him.'

'How?' Ashia asked. 'If he is to find victory this night, we cannot change it even if we wanted. And I will not help you steal the throne in his absence. The Damajah has spoken. Shar'Dama Ka will return.'

'The dice say he *may* return, girl,' Melan said. 'Not that he will.'

'I have faith,' Ashia said.

'As do I,' Asome agreed. 'I do not ask you to help me take the throne, *jiwah*. Only to help me win glory to match my brother, that his claim be diminished and the Andrah hold power until Shar'Dama Ka comes again.'

'How?' Ashia asked again.

'It is Waning,' Asome said. 'Tonight I will go out with my newly raised *dama* brothers and fight the *alagai*.'

'It is forbidden,' Ashia said.

'It must be done,' Asome said. 'You heard the *dama'ting*. The Damajah cannot keep Jayan from the throne, nor can the Andrah. Only I can do it, and only tonight. Tomorrow will be too late.

'I do this because I must,' Asome added. 'For the good of all Krasia. For the good of the world. But I am afraid.'

He held out a hand to her. 'No doubt you felt much the same, the first night the Damajah bade you to defy Evejan law and claim your *Sharum* birthright. I beg you, if ever you were a wife to me, stand with me now.'

Ashia hesitated, then took his hand. 'I will stand with you, husband. With pride.'

Ashia watched the Damajah from the shadows as Inevera entered her chambers. She remained alert to the slightest danger to her mistress, but still her thoughts reeled. It was her duty to serve the Damajah in all things, but Asome was her husband, and the son of the Deliverer.

Where did her greatest loyalty lie? To Everam, of course, but how could she, barely worthy of His notice, judge His plan? Was that not the job of the Damajah? She should inform her of Asome's plan – now – and let Inevera judge Everam's will.

But she hesitated. Perhaps she could not know His plan, but in her heart, the voice of Everam was clear. Sharak Ka was coming, and there was little room for those who would not fight. Asome had a warrior's spirit, a warrior's training, but as she had been, he was forbidden to use it, even as Nie's forces mounted.

The Deliverer had given the right to fight to *khaffit*, to women, even. Why not the clerics? Was the cowardice of old men to dictate the lives of the young, even as the *alagai* tore Everam's Bounty apart?

Once Asome killed an *alagai*, there would be no stopping it. He was the *dama* son of Shar'Dama Ka and the Damajah, and his glory would be boundless. Not even the Damajah could halt it then.

But until that moment, his plans could still be thwarted, costing Everam warriors and putting an unworthy boy on the Skull Throne.

Inevera stopped as she passed, looking right at Ashia as if the shadows that cloaked her were not there. Ashia froze. She knew she could not hide from her mistress, but it was always unnerving when the Damajah looked at her directly when she was concealed. 'Are you well, child?'

'It is nothing, Damajah,' Ashia said, quickly finding her centre and letting her fears and doubts fall away.

But Inevera narrowed her eyes, staring, her divine Sight peeling away Ashia's centre like the layers of an onion. 'The coming night troubles you.'

Ashia swallowed the growing knot in her throat, nodding. 'It is Waning, mistress.'

'Alagai Ka is attempting to lure us into relaxing our defences by not appearing,' the Damajah agreed. 'You and your sisters must be extra vigilant, and rush to inform me if you witness anything out of the ordinary.'

'I will, Damajah,' Ashia said. 'On my love of Everam and my hope of Heaven, I swear it.'

Inevera continued to scrutinize her, and it was all Ashia could do to hold her centre. At last, the Damajah nodded. 'Return to your chambers and spend the remaining hours until muster with your son.'

Ashia bowed. 'I will, mistress. Thank you, mistress.'

Ashia held young Kaji close as she watched Asome and Asukaji prepare for the coming night.

Her own preparations were quick and efficient, the result of years of training. Her weapons and armour were oiled and laid out in precise fashion. Though she lounged in a plain robe of silk in their private chambers, she could be armoured and ready to fight in moments.

Her brother and husband, however, paced and preened like pillow wives. Their hands were wrapped tightly in white silk, only the first knuckles exposed. Much like Ashia and her sisters, Asome had painted fighting wards on Asukaji's finger and toe nails, layering clear polish over the symbols to harden and protect them.

Asukaji clenched his fists, moving through a series of *sharukin* with the precision of a master, flexing his fingers to bring different combinations of wards into play.

'Try it with the silvers,' Asome said, and Asukaji nodded, going to a lacquered wood case on his vanity. Inside were two pieces of polished, warded silver, shaped to be slipped over the fingers. They rested comfortably to protect his top knuckles, giving her brother fists that would strike the *alagai* like thunderbolts.

Asukaji went through his *sharukin* again, layering in moves to make the most of the new weapons.

'Now the staff,' Asome said, taking Asukaji's whip staff from its stand and throwing it to him.

The whip staff was a glorious weapon – six feet of flexible Northern goldwood, carved with wards of power and capped on either end with warded silver. Asukaji caught the staff, spinning it into a blur he incorporated into his *sharukin*. The whip staff moved faster than the eye could see, and in the hands of a master, the supple wood could bend to strike around defences that would deflect a rigid weapon.

Ashia looked to Asome, wearing only his alagai tail, the weapon all *dama* carried. The barbed tips of its prongs were no doubt warded, but it seemed like little compared to the myriad weapons her brother was preparing to bring into the night.

'What of you, husband?' Ashia asked. 'You have not so much as painted your nails. What *dama* weapon will you bring to *alagai'sharak*?'

Asome pulled the whip from his belt, hanging it on its hook on the wall. 'None. Tonight I fight as you did on the night the *Sharum'ting* revealed themselves.'

Ashia hid her surprise. 'You will fight spear and shield, like your honoured father?'

Asome shook his head. '*Dama* are forbidden the spear, and a shield would slow me, when I must be fast.'

Ashia looked at him, understanding slowly dawning on her. 'Husband, you cannot mean to fight with *sharusahk* alone.'

'My father did it, when he was only a *kai*,' Asome said.

Ashia knew the story. One of the first legends of the Shar'Dama Ka's rise. 'Your honoured father had spent years in the Maze by then, husband, and his own retelling had it an act of last resort. To go unarmed into Waning is . . .'

'Madness,' Asukaji agreed, but Asome glared at him, and he dropped his eyes.

'Anyone can kill *alagai* with weapons,' Asome said. 'My

Sharum brothers do it every night. It is not enough if I am to win glory to match my brother.'

He clenched one of his bandaged hands into a fist. 'Either Everam wills me to succeed, or He does not.'

They went into the night wrapped in black cloaks, Asukaji and the *dama* sons of the Deliverer. Only Asome walked boldly in the night in his white robes. *Sharum* looked at him with apprehension, remembering the Shar'Dama Ka's forbiddance that clerics go out at night. But they recognized Asome, blood of the Deliverer himself, and none dared hinder him.

There were no *alagai* close to the city proper, held back by walls, wardposts, and regular patrols. They had to range far before the sounds of battle came to them. At last they came to Hoshkamin, Asome's younger brother, wearing the turban of Sharum Ka as he directed men culling field demons on a wide plain.

Hoshkamin looked at them in surprise. 'You should not be out in the night, brother! It is forbidden!'

Asome stood before him, slender where Hoshkamin was thick with muscle; clad only in silk, where Hoshkamin wore the finest armour; weaponless where Hoshkamin carried spear and shield of warded glass.

And yet it was Asome who dominated, Ashia saw immediately. There were but two years between them, but that was vast for men not yet twenty. Asome leaned in, and Hoshkamin took a step back.

'The Deliverer is not here to stop me,' Asome said quietly. 'Nor is our elder brother.' His smile was dangerous, predatory. 'Will you try?'

He didn't raise his voice, or make a threatening gesture, but Hoshkamin paled visibly. He glanced at his men, no doubt imagining the shame if his elder brother were to beat him in front of them while he wore the white turban.

Hoshkamin took two steps back, giving Asome a respectful bow. 'Of course not, brother. I only meant that it is dangerous in the night. I will assign you a bodyguard . . .'

Asome whisked a hand dismissively. 'I have all the bodyguard I need.'

With that, Damaji Asukaji and Asome's *dama* brothers cast aside their cloaks, their white robes bright in the flames and wardlight. Hoshkamin and the *Sharum* stared, speechless, as they strode into the field of battle.

Asome went first, striding towards a reap of field demons being harried by a unit of *dal'Sharum*, their shields locked in a V-formation.

He walked right up to the apex of the V, brushing aside the *Sharum* at point with a gesture. Surprised at the sight of a *dama*, the Deliverer's son, they fell back instinctively. Ashia and her spear sisters followed with Asukaji and the others.

One of the demons was quicker to take advantage of the break in formation than its fellows, leaping at Asome with a roar. Ashia tensed, ready to charge and interpose herself should the *alagai* prove too much for her honoured husband.

She needn't have worried. Asome flowed easily around the jaws and talons, catching the demon by the horns and turning a full circle that converted all the energy of the demon's leap into a twist that cracked its neck like a whip. Trained *Sharum* jumped at the sound, and hopped back as Asome threw the demon's lifeless body at their feet.

Two more charged at him, but Asome was ready, snatching the wrist of one and turning to pull its arm straight as he laid his free hand against its shoulder joint. Again he turned the demon's momentum against it, twisting it to the ground and breaking its arm effortlessly as he put it into the path of the other.

The second demon lost barely a moment clawing its way over the first, talons digging deep wounds as it tamped and pounced. But a moment was time enough for Asome to shift his stance and catch its wrists, pulling it off balance as he fell back. He hooked a leg around its neck, getting in too close for the demon's jaws. They rolled in the dirt a moment, but Ashia knew her husband had the hold, and even *alagai* needed to breathe.

Soon it lay still, and Asome rose. The other demon hissed at him, limping weakly on three legs. Asome hissed back, moving in.

'Everam's beard,' Hoshkamin whispered as the demon retreated to match Asome's advance. The other *Sharum* echoed him, muttering oaths and drawing wards in the air.

The other demons of the reap hesitated momentarily in confusion, but now they gathered themselves, readying a charge that would surely overwhelm Asome.

Asome saw it, too, chopping his hand in the air at them. '*Acha!*'

With that, Asukaji and the other *dama* gave piercing battle cries, raising their weapons and charging past Asome into the fray, leaving husband and wife standing together.

Ashia turned to Micha and Jarvah. 'Inform the Damajah of what you have seen. Now. Do not deviate or slow until our mistress has heard your account.'

The women looked at each other, then bowed deeply to Ashia, running at speed back towards the city.

Asome looked at her curiously.

'Many oaths conflict this night, husband,' Ashia said. 'But I will keep them all, if I can.'

Asome bowed. 'Of course, wife. I would ask nothing less of you. But you should have waited.' He winked. 'The best is still to come.'

They turned together, looking out on the field as the clerics waged *alagai'sharak*. Asukaji waded into a knot of demons, whip staff seeming to strike them all at once. Flashes of magic sparked and popped around him as he spun.

The younger brothers distinguished themselves as well. Though they were but fifteen, they had been trained in *sharu-sahk* since they could stand, each marked by the distinctive fighting style of his tribe. Maji, trained by grand master Aleverak, used no weapon save warded nails and silvers. He let the demon he faced do most of the work, powering the heavy blows that rocked it back.

Dama were denied blades by Evejan law, including the broad-bladed arrows and throwing knives Mehnding *Sharum* favoured. Mehnding *dama* used bolas instead, and Savas was no exception. A slender warded chain connected two heavy balls of warded silver. Savas took the legs from a field demon, immobilizing it as he beat it senseless with his silvers.

Hallam, the Sharach brother, used the *alagai*-catcher favoured by his tribesmen, its metal cable warded. He caught a demon by the neck, tightening the loop until the magic popped its head off. Tachin and Mazh, the Krevakh and Nanji brothers, had small wooden pegs hammered into their staves, like the rungs of a ladder. Ashia watched Tachin run up the side of his staff to leap ten feet in the air, somersaulting over a charging demon to land behind it. As the creature whirled about in confusion, he landed a flurry of explosive blows with his silvers.

They ranged through the night, Hoshkamin and his warriors following his older brother as Asome led his *dama* brothers to glory.

As it had been for several months, there was no sign of Alagai Ka, but it was Waning, and the *alagai* were stronger and more numerous. And there was something else.

'They are attacking strategic positions,' Ashia said. The demons lacked the precision they had under the control of the minds, but they clustered in places where defences were weakest, attacking wardposts to increase their range.

Asome nodded. 'Perhaps Father stands at the cusp of the abyss as Mother foretold, holding Nie's princelings at bay, but She has *kai*, as well.'

'The changelings,' Ashia said, tightening her grip on her spear.

'Melan foretold we would find one in the night,' Asome agreed. He looked at Ashia. 'For this test, wife, we must fight side by side.'

Ashia nodded eagerly. A mimic had taken Enkido, and she would show this one the sun in her master's honour. 'Your glory is boundless this night, husband. I am proud to stand with you.'

An hour later, the attack came without warning as a large wood demon surrounded by fighting *dama* lashed out, its arm becoming a great horned tentacle. The blow knocked half a dozen men back. The wards embroidered in silver thread on their robes deflected the worst of it, but all were stunned, shaking heads and placing hands on the ground as they tried to push up even to sitting position.

Hoshkamin rushed in to protect his *dama* brothers. The shields of his warriors were better at turning the mimic's blows, but the demon spun, lashing through the thin gap between the shields and the ground. *Sharum* screamed in agony as they collapsed, many with severed feet.

Ashia was relieved to see Hoshkamin had escaped that fate. *Dama'ting* magic could heal much, but even they could not grow back that which was cut away. She gave a cry as she rushed in, hoping to distract the creature from her brothers in the night as they regrouped.

Asome followed, but her husband had absorbed no magic in the night's battle, and could not keep pace. It was good. Asome had surpassed all expectations, but without so much as a warded nail, this foe was beyond him.

Tentacles whipped at her, but Ashia was ready. She dodged the first, leapt over the second, and caught a third on her shield, never slowing her advance. Two more lashed out as she drew in close, and she dropped her shield in order to dive between them.

She hit the *Ala* in a roll, bouncing back to her feet and using the momentum to add power to her two-handed thrust into the demon's heart.

Magic exploded with the blow, shocking up Ashia's arms and filling her with power such as she had never felt. The changeling's black eyes widened in shock, and Ashia stared back hard, wanting to see its unholy life melt away. 'Everam burn you in the name of Enkido!'

The demon shrieked at her and she tried to pull the spear free and thrust again, but found it held fast. Still staring into the creature's dark eyes, she understood her mistake.

A rock demon's arm grew from the mimic's chest, knocking the wind from her as it clutched her tightly and bore her to the ground, talons scraping against the plates of warded glass woven into her robes. The claws did not pierce, but it mattered little as Ashia felt her ribs crack.

Her spear, punched clear through the demon's torso, melted free like a spoon through hot resin, sloughing onto the ground just out of reach. There were other weapons concealed in her robes, but Ashia could not reach them while held in the crushing grip.

Everam, I am ready, she thought. She had served Him in all things, and would die on *alagai* talons, as her *Sharum* blood demanded. There was no dishonour. This was a creature like the one that had killed her master, like the one that fought the Deliverer on even terms. It was a good death.

As the changeling drew back for a killing blow, Asome leapt past her. She wanted to cry out, to tell him to flee, but even if she had the breath, she would not dishonour him so.

We will walk the lonely path together, Ashia thought. What more could any couple ask for? Everam had joined them in life. It seemed only fitting they should also die as one.

But then Asome struck, and there was a flare of magic so bright it burned Ashia's warded eyes. As if she had looked at the sun, the image stayed with her a few moments, even as she blinked and shook her head. The talon that held her eased its grip as the creature was rocked by explosions of magic, then pulled away entirely.

Ashia clenched her eyes tight for a moment, then opened them.

Asome held the demon's arm in a grip that smoked and burned, bright with magic. Her husband had stripped to a simple white bido, discarding even his sandals and the wrappings that had covered his hands.

She saw now why he had hidden his hands these last days. His fists – his entire body – was covered in raised scars. Like his father, Asome had cut wards into his flesh, that his very touch be anathema to the children of Nie.

His glow had been dim before, when he fought without the aid of the symbols, proving himself before Everam and the *Sharum*. But now the wards were written in fire across his skin, and he glowed so brightly that there was a halo around him all could see, warded sight or no.

He ducked and twisted, delivering powerful blows that knocked the demon back, parrying its return strikes, but even he seemed unable to do lasting damage. They fought for several moments, and instead of continuing to lose ground, the demon seemed to be strengthening, gaining firmer footing as it took Asome's measure and adapted.

Asome saw it, too. 'Brothers! Form a ring! Nie's servant must not be allowed to escape!'

He barely got the words out before the demon struck hard, one of its flailing tentacles slipping past Asome's defences. Magic stopped the limb short of connecting, but the impact still sent him flying through the air.

Ashia was already moving, diving into a roll and coming up with her spear in hand. She studied the mimic in her warded sight, but it was unlike any demon she had faced before. Every demon – every living thing – had lines of power. The essence of *dama'ting sharusahk* was breaking these lines by striking the points where they converged.

But the demon's lines were as amorphous as its body, growing and retracting, ever changing. She sensed a pattern in it all, but it was beyond her ability to grasp, her attention focused upon simply staying alive.

The magic she had absorbed on her initial blow surged through her, making her impossibly fast and strong. Horned tentacles came at her from all sides, but she spun her spear, picking them off.

The demon hawked and spat fire like a flame demon, but like a flame demon its eyes squeezed shut and in that instant she quickstepped around it to come from another angle. This time she made no effort to strike a killing blow, instead thrusting the spear rapidly back and forth to strike half a dozen shallow ones.

Each wound flared brightly at first, the demon's ichor giving off raw magic like smoke from a fire. But then the loss stemmed, and the area around the wound dimmed as the demon's flesh knitted back together.

The changeling shrieked, and this time she wasn't fast enough as it spat lightning at her. Pain like she had never imagined wracked her body, jolting limbs rigid as she was thrown through the air. She thought she would lose the spear, but when she struck the ground it remained locked in her frozen grasp. She could not have let go if she wanted.

Then, as quickly as it came, the pain dissipated and her muscles unclenched. Her entire body burned, but there was still magic coursing through her, and already it was easing. She looked up to see Asome back in the fight, hammering at the mimic while his brothers struck at it from all sides.

Savas caught two tentacles in his bola, and the warded chain held them fast, unable to melt away. Another was caught in Hallam's *alagai*-catcher.

But even these seemed minor inconveniences. The demon would writhe from the bolas soon enough, and it swung Hallam to and fro by his *alagai*-catcher pole. Others lent their strength to the task, but they were sorely pressed and out of the fight.

Asome continued to pound at the demon, and as she retrieved her shield, Ashia could see a pattern beginning to emerge in the creature's magic. Even this fiend had a limited supply, and she watched as it ebbed and flowed, healing its wounds, powering its blows, reshaping its body.

With every blow he struck, Asome grew a fraction brighter, the demon, that much dimmer. If they could keep it at bay long enough, his victory was inevitable.

Ashia moved back in, stabbing hard where the creature was held by the men at the catcher pole. She hacked the blade of her spear through a tentacle at its base, severing the limb. The demon repaired the damage, but the tentacle, and the magic it had contained, lay in the dirt, no longer part of the whole.

The changeling grew eyes on its back, whipping horns and talons through the air to fend off the assailants, but Ashia could see its lines of power, and knew its attention was fixed on Asome. It knocked him sprawling, then opened a jaw that grew rapidly to gigantic size.

Ashia didn't know if it meant to bite him in half or swallow him whole, but didn't give it the chance, accepting the lash of a tentacle to get in close and stab hard. The sharp horns tore her robe, ripping away armour plates and finding soft flesh beneath. She hit the ground spitting blood, praying to Everam that Asome had used the distraction to recover.

Indeed the demon had hesitated, but Asome did not use the opportunity to flee. As the creature roared in pain through its impossibly wide jaws, Asome coiled up and sprang right into its mouth.

The force of his leap took him past the rows of jaws and down the *alagai*'s throat. Ashia could see its lines of power shatter as it pulled in all its strength to heal the damage Asome's warded skin was no doubt doing inside. Limbs melted back into the blob, save those the *dama* held trapped in warded silver.

The amorphous pile bucked and thrashed. Choked, the demon could not shriek. Ashia could see it losing cohesion, and knew its end was inevitable, but would it take her husband with it? He was still alive, still fighting, but even he could not go forever without breath.

Forcing herself to her feet, Ashia stumbled back in. The *dama* fighting around her were denied the blade, but her curved knife was a foot long and sharp enough to shave the hairs from a spider's leg. She stuck it to the hilt in the gelatinous mass, cutting a deep line.

The wound bucked from the inside, spattering her with ichor, but she did not relent, slashing deeper. At last, one of Asome's warded fists punched out into the night air, bright with power. His other hand appeared, the two gripping the wound and tearing it apart from the inside.

Mouths broke across the surface of the demon, joining in one last cry before it collapsed, motionless.

Asome stood there, covered in ichor and glowing like the sun. Like her blessed uncle.

Like Kaji himself.

His *dama* brothers and the remaining *Sharum*, including Hoshkamin and Asukaji, fell to their knees before him. Ashia felt it, too. She understood what had happened, but the instinct to kneel was strong. It was only by an act of will that she kept her feet.

'Nie's power grows again at Waning, brothers!' Asome called. 'This is but the first of Her *kais* to come. With my father chasing Alagai Ka to the edge of Nie's abyss, it is not enough for the *Sharum* to hold the line against Her. Every man must fight, if Sharak Ka is to be won! My father made the weak *khaffit* into *kha'Sharum*! The *chin* into *chi'Sharum*! Even women, like my blessed *Jiwah Ka*, were called as *Sharum'ting*!'

He swept a hand over the assembled *dama*. 'Of all in Krasia, it is only we, the clerics, who waited to be called! But the wait is over, brothers! As my father called others to the fight, so do I call upon those in white to join in *alagai'sharak*! It is only fitting that it should be blood of the Deliverer to first step into the night. I name you *shar'dama*, warrior-clerics, and we will guide Krasia through its darkest hour!'

There was a stunned silence, and then all the assembled men broke out in cheers. Even Hoshkamin, the Sharum Ka and Jayan's creature, could not help himself as he punched a fist in the air, joining the cry.

'*Shar'dama! Shar'dama! Shar'dama!*'

Kajivah was asleep in the nursery as Ashia and Asome crept into their palace chambers. Asukaji and the other *dama* went to see the *dama'ting* for their injuries, but Ashia and Asome, flush with stolen magic, had already healed every scrape and bruise.

There was no mistaking what Asome was about as he pushed into Ashia's pillow chamber. She felt it, too, pulling him along with one hand as she pulled down her veil with the other to kiss him.

The thrill of battle, the pride in each other, and the charge of battle whirled in them both, an aphrodisiac neither could resist.

Ashia tripped her husband, flinging Asome onto the bed and crawling atop him.

'I am told these greenland beds have better uses than sleeping.' She kissed him again. Asome's member stood in his robes like the pole of a tent.

'I am still . . . *push'ting*.' He groaned as she squeezed it.

'Tomorrow, perhaps,' Ashia said, pulling off her own robes. 'Tonight, you are my husband.'

28

Shar'Dama

334 AR Winter

'You have broken my decree, and that of the Shar'Dama Ka,' Ashan said from his seat on the Skull Throne. The anger in his voice was apparent to all, and it was not an act. From her perch above the throne, Inevera could see it dancing on his aura. 'Going into the night at Waning and fighting *alagai'sharak*. What have you to say for yourselves?'

There was silence in the great hall as all held their breaths, waiting for an answer. The throne room was filled to capacity, with every *dama* in the city in attendance, as well as ranking *Sharum* and *dama'ting*. Word of the night's battle had reached every ear in the city by now, talk of the *shar'dama* on everyone's lips. Inevera doubted the djinn could be put back in the bottle now that it was out.

Asome stood out in front, unrepentant, with Asukaji at his side. Behind them stood his *dama* half brothers with the *Damaji* of their respective tribes. Most of the old men were livid with rage, auras crackling. They had been forced to take Ahmann's sons as their heirs, but with the Deliverer gone and a crime to pin at their feet, many were praying fervently that this might be their chance to rid themselves of the boys and regain direct control of their tribes.

Inevera had wanted to settle the matter in private, but Ashan, in an uncharacteristic show of will, had refused. He wanted the distance of the throne, fearing he might throttle the boys if they stood close in private.

It was a feeling Inevera understood well. The balance of power in the city already shifted as if built on a foundation of sand. Ahmann's *dama* heirs were only newly raised to the white, still too young and inexperienced to take and hold control of the tribes. The dice had told her of Jayan's victory on the lake, and he would surely use the triumph to further his claim to the throne.

Yet for Inevera the deepest cut was Ashia. Her sons were expected to wrestle for power. The spear sisters' loyalty should have been absolute. Micha and Jarvah had not known – it was clear on their auras when they came to her – but Ashia had stood before her, knowing her husband's plans, and put Asome's honour above her duty to her mistress.

But that was a problem for later. Inevera was pulled from her thoughts as Asome drew breath to speak. Unlike the tension and anger in the others, Asome's aura was cool and even, convinced of the righteousness of his path, safe in the knowledge that Everam was on his side.

'Holy Andrah,' Asome said, bowing deeply before Ashan, 'it is said amongst the *Sharum* who accompanied you and my father to meet with the Hollow tribe that you, yourself, fought *alagai'sharak* with them. Is this not so?'

There was a buzz through the room at that, *dama* gasping and whispering to one another.

Ashan's eyes narrowed. 'The Shar'Dama Ka commanded I follow him into battle and I obeyed, defending myself by tripping and throwing *alagai* into the path of *Sharum* spears. I did not take up warded weapons and kill.'

'And yet your honour was boundless,' Asome said. 'I did not take up weapons, either. The first *alagai* I killed were by *sharusahk* alone, with no magic to aid me. It was only when Nie set Her *kai* against us that I fought as my father did, turning their own power against them.'

Another buzz through the crowd.

'And yet it was that very thing your father forbade,' Ashan reminded him. 'Here, in open court, he forbade you to fight at Waning.'

'My father made that decree to punish my arrogance,' Asome said, drawing looks of surprise. Indeed, all Ahmann's sons were arrogant, though none to Inevera's knowledge had ever admitted it. 'My wife had gone into the night, killing *alagai* at the Damajah's command.' He looked up, meeting Inevera's eyes. 'With no warning to me beforehand. What husband would not rage at such a sight? What man not feel the sting? I spoke out in anger, attempting to deny her the spear.'

Asome turned, taking in the assembled court. 'But I was wrong! Wrong to deny the honour to any who wished to take arms against Nie and stand unified in Sharak Ka. For make no mistake, brothers and sisters, Sharak Ka is near! My mother has foretold that the Deliverer has gone to the edge of Nie's abyss, and when he returns it will be with all Her forces at his heels! The armies of the Deliverer must stand ready when that day comes, strong at his back as he turns to face that fell horde and cleanse their taint from Ala once and for all!'

He turned back to Ashan. 'Why do *dama* spend lifetimes studying *sharusahk*? To bully *Sharum* and *khaffit* to our will? That is not Everam's way. Not the way of Shar'Dama Ka. At every turn, my father added to his forces from unlikely places. *Khaffit. Chin.* Women. The creation of the *shar'dama* was inevitable, Holy Andrah. My father denied me honour to teach me this, but I have learned. I have grown. And now, with my father facing trials far from here, it is the duty of all *dama* to lead his people in his absence.'

Again his eyes swept the crowd. 'And so on the second night of Waning, I call upon all *dama* to take up the fight, staining their white robes with demon ichor and sending a message to Nie's generals that we of Krasia are not weak in the night. That we will stand not only when the Deliverer is with us, but when he needs us most to stand on our own. Every *Sharum* unit has a *dama* advisor. Go with them into the night and see firsthand the great work they do, the sacrifice they make. Join in *alagai'sharak*, and become what you were meant to be since the first time you stood in the bowels of Sharik Hora and began the *sharukin*!'

There was a roar at that, some *dama* and *Damaji* screaming in protest, but many more crying out in support, eager for the honour Asome offered.

'You must support him,' Inevera whispered into Ashan's earring. She had said it before, but now there was no other choice. When Ahmann had first brought back the fighting wards and offered true battle against Nie, the Andrah and *Damaji* had resisted, fearing the loss of power. *Sharum* had defected in droves, flocking to the Maze and Ahmann's call. If they resisted, it would only be a matter of time before Asome did the same.

Ashan was angry at his sons, but he was no fool and saw it, too. 'There is wisdom in your words, my son. The blood of my brother Ahmann, Shar'Dama Ka, runs strong in you – all of you. You honour Everam with your words.' He rose from the Skull Throne. 'And so I, too, will fight this night, and stain my robes.'

'As will I.' Ancient, one-armed Aleverak stepped forward. 'Too long have the *dama* cowered like women in the Undercity while *Sharum* shed blood in the night.'

Others stepped forward, some in passion, and others, their auras told, out of fear of being seen as cowards. The wind blew, and none could resist it.

'Shar'dama! And my brother is first among them! They chant it in the streets while I sit here in the cold doing nothing!'

Jayan threw the letter into the fireplace, followed by his couzi bottle. The ensuing fireball consumed the paper instantly, and everyone took a step back. Thankfully, the blaze did not spread.

Bring the Sharum Ka a fresh cup, Abban's fingers told Earless, *but leave the bottle on the tray.*

The mute *kha'Sharum* did as he was bidden, eyes firmly on the floor. Even stooped he was the tallest man in the room, but Earless' silent subservience was as good as a Cloak of Unsight. Jayan took the cup without so much as glancing his way.

'You will not find the path to glory at the bottom of a couzi cup, Sharum Ka,' Khevat said.

Jayan made a show of throwing back the cup, wiping his mouth with his white veil. Khevat rankled, but said nothing as Jayan stormed up to him. 'Then where will I find it, Dama? You were sent here to advise me, were you not? How long will your son keep the Skull Throne if my brother's power continues to grow?'

'My son never should have had the throne in the first place,' Khevat said. 'That was the Damajah's doing.'

'And what would you have done instead?' Jayan asked.

'The law is clear,' Khevat said. 'The throne should have passed to you. You are the eldest son. Your holy father gave you command of *alagai'sharak*, and you are the one in foreign lands, fighting Sharak Sun for the glory of Everam. Your brother has only killed a handful of *alagai*.'

'And started a movement that will tear the clergy asunder, much as your father did,' Abban said.

Khevat glared at him. 'Your opinion was not asked for, *khaffit*.'

Abban bowed as Jayan looked his way. 'As the Sharum Ka says, honoured Dama, we are here to advise.'

'You are the one putting couzi in the Sharum Ka's hands,' Khevat said. 'How can you hope to advise a path to glory?'

'How indeed?' Jayan asked, but there was none of his usual derision. 'I would hear the *khaffit*'s advice.'

Abban smiled. 'The Sharum Ka already knows what he will do.'

Jayan crossed his arms, but he was smirking. 'Do enlighten us.'

Abban bowed again. 'The Sharum Ka could have returned to the capital for the winter. The city on the lake is all but taken, and cold will keep the siege better than warriors. The *chin* rebellion in Everam's Bounty is crushed. Why remain here at the head of his armies, with little to do until the thaw?'

'What course is left to me?' Jayan asked. 'With the lake frozen and the Hollow tribe outnumbering us to the north?'

'East, to see for yourself the destruction your warriors have wrought upon the heathen monastery that launched the attack upon us,' Abban said. 'Your siege engines will gather snow if left so close to the lake, but the Old Hill Road to the north is yet clear.'

'You can't possibly be suggesting the Sharum Ka attack Angiers,' Khevat said, but Jayan was smiling widely now. 'We do not have enough men to hold such a prize.'

'Hold?' Abban asked. 'What hold? Sack. The Northern walls are nothing. Kick in their gate and you can flood the merchant district with ten thousand warriors. Empty the warehouses, take anything else of value, and be back in Everam's Reservoir before winter sets in full.'

Jayan looked disappointed. 'You want me to take thousands of *dal'Sharum* north simply to steal a few wells?'

'Burn the palace down if you wish,' Abban shrugged. 'Take hostages, post the duke's head on the wall. Whatever you like, so long as you do it quickly and be gone before their neighbours can move against you.

'After that, you will have the largest, most seasoned army in the world, mobile and well supplied, and wealth to surpass even your father's. What matter then, who sits the Skull Throne? Kaji himself spent more years in the saddle than he ever did upon a throne.'

Jayan looked at Khevat, who seemed mollified. 'It is a bold plan, Sharum Ka. If the Watchers of the Hollow tribe should spy your movements—'

'They will not,' Jayan cut him off. 'My Watchers have spied

on the Hollow tribe for some time now. Their patrols do not yet range to the far side of the great wood.'

Khevat looked to Asavi. 'Perhaps we should consult . . .'

'I have already cast the dice at the Sharum Ka's request,' the *dama'ting* said. 'The Deliverer's son will shatter the gate and pour thousands of *dal'Sharum* into the city before the first day is out.'

Jayan moved to a tapestry map of Thesa on the wall, pointing with his spear. 'How many warriors remain in Everam's Reservoir?'

He did not look to Abban, but as few of the others could count so high, the *khaffit* was quick to answer. 'Thirty-five thousand *Sharum* remain in the wetlands. One hundred twenty *kai'Sharum*, six thousand, four hundred and six *dal*, nine thousand, two hundred thirty-four *kha*, and nineteen thousand, eight hundred and seventy-six *chi*.'

'I will take twenty thousand *Sharum* east.' Jayan turned to Khevat. 'Dama, you will accompany me to the monastery and remain there with a thousand men to refortify it to receive the spoils from Angiers, away from prying eyes.'

Khevat bowed. 'Yes, Sharum Ka.'

'Captain Qeran will take command of the siege of Lakton under my brother Sharu, who will command our land forces.'

Qeran and Sharu bowed. 'Your will, Sharum Ka.'

'Jurim. My father's pact with the Hollow tribe does not forbid us to steal a few wells. Here and here.' Jayan pointed to villages along the southern border of Hollow County's influence. Technically Laktonian, the hamlets were too far from Docktown to be of strategic value, and the Hollow tribe had annexed the land. 'Take three hundred men. Do not stay in one place longer than it takes to loot and burn or strike in a predictable pattern. Let them think there may be many times your true number.'

Jurim bowed, looking gleeful at the prospect.

'It will not be enough to bring their warriors into our lands, but it will draw their attention and patrols to the south.' Jayan's finger skirted the map east from Docktown through the wetlands until it met a thin line heading north. 'While I take my men north along the Old Hill Road. We will skirt the Hollow entirely and take the Angierians unaware.'

He smiled. 'And they will be ill prepared, once Dama Gorja delivers his message.'

29

Dama Gorja
334 AR Winter

The note was written in Darsy Cutter's blocky print. Like the woman herself, her missives wasted little time getting to the point. Instead of one long letter as some might write, Darsy's correspondence was a stack of small notes, each its own problem.

> Mistress Leesha,
>
> Painted Children have ceased to mind. Don't report for inspection. Started painting themselves with more than just blackstem. Stefny Inn caught Stela with permanent tattoos under her dress. Yon Gray tried to bring them in line, and Callen Cutter broke his arm.
>
> They live in the woods now, like they say the Deliverer did. Those that sleep at all do it during the day, out of the sun. Gared's been letting it go because they take a heavy toll on the corelings, but even he's losing patience.
>
> Said you had a plan in case something like this happened. If you've got a trick up your sleeve, now's the time for it.
>
> —Darsy

'Corespawn it,' Leesha said.

Wonda looked up from polishing her bow. 'Corespawn what?'

'Things are falling apart in the Hollow,' Leesha said. She rubbed her heavy belly. 'And if I stay much longer, I won't be fit to travel until the child comes.'

'How can we leave without Rojer?' Wonda asked.

'We can't,' Leesha said. 'But I'm losing patience with Janson's endless delays. I don't give a coreling's piss if Jasin was his nephew. He tried to kill Rojer twice, and it's his own fault what came of it.'

'Doubt that's gonna sway anyone,' Wonda said.

'They'll be swayed if Gared has to show up with a few thousand Cutters to collect us and escort us home,' Leesha said.

Wonda looked at her a moment, then went back to polishing her bow. 'Think it'll come to that?'

Leesha rubbed her temple. 'Perhaps. I don't know. I hope not.'

'Be bloody, it does,' Wonda said. 'Them two might lock horns sometimes, but Gar thinks of Rojer like a little brother.'

'We all do,' Leesha agreed. 'But the duke and his brothers are stubborn. If Gared shows up with an army, they might let us go, but the Hollow will be on its own.'

Wonda shrugged. 'Like the count well enough, an' the Duchess Mum, but the Hollow'd do just fine without 'em. Need us more'n we need them.'

'Perhaps,' Leesha said again, but she wasn't so certain.

There was a knock at the door. Wonda answered it, finding one of Duchess Melny's handmaidens.

'It's a good sign,' Leesha told Melny, 'but too early to get excited.'

'Demonshit,' Araine said. 'Girl bleeds every fourth Seconday, dependable as sunrise. Now it's Fifthday, and not a drop. Don't need a Gatherer's apron to know what that means.'

'Means I've got a babe in me,' Melny said.

'Ay, I'm not denying it,' Leesha said, and Melny's face lit up. 'But I wouldn't go shouting it from the balcony. This early in a first pregnancy, the odds are even on it coming to term.'

'It will!' Melny insisted. 'I can feel the Creator's hand in it, giving us the child when we need it most.'

'Even so, it can't hurt to wait a bit before telling anyone else,' Leesha said. 'There's still time.'

'Not as much as you think,' Araine said.

Leesha had to hurry to keep pace as Araine led the way through the women's wing of the palace. She was so used to the Duchess Mum's doddering invalid act, this seemed another woman entirely.

Something is very wrong, Leesha realized, for her to have dropped the performance out in the open hall.

She smelled him the moment she entered the chambers. Araine had opened the windows and filled the room with fresh flowers, but the stench was unmistakable, even in the outer room. She felt a twinge behind her left eye, and knew it had just triggered a headache that would have her whimpering in bed by day's end.

Briar waited in the receiving room, looking – and smelling – even filthier than last time. There was blood on his clothes, still wet from slogging through melted snow. What she could see of his flesh was covered in scrapes and bruises.

Leesha went to him, swallowing a gag. Pain blossomed behind her eye, and she swallowed that, too, searching him for injuries.

The boy was haggard, as if he hadn't slept in a week. His feet were bloody and blistered, but there was no infection. The rest of his injuries looked painful, but superficial.

'What happened?' she asked him.

Briar's eyes flicked to Araine, and it was she who answered as Leesha continued to tend the boy.

'Thamos led an attack to retake Docktown,' Araine said. 'A joint effort with Lakton and the Rizonan resistance.'

'Why wasn't I told of this?' Leesha demanded.

'Because I don't trust you where the Krasians are concerned,' Araine said, bluntly. 'You would have opposed the attack.'

Leesha folded her arms. 'And what has Your Grace's brilliant military strategy accomplished?'

'We lost,' Briar said quietly, and began to weep.

Leesha reached for him instinctively, breathing through her mouth and holding the boy as he cried, tears leaving streaks in the mud and hogroot resin staining his cheeks. A thousand questions swirled about her, but at the moment only one mattered.

'Where is Thamos?' she asked.

Still weeping, Briar shook his head. He reached into his robe, pulling out a folded bit of paper, stained and filthy. 'Told me to give you this.'

'Eh?' Araine asked. Briar had obviously left this out of his initial report.

Leesha took the paper in shaking hands. The words, written in haste, were smeared, but in Thamos' unmistakable hand. The message was short:

> My Darling Leesha,
> I forgive you. I love you.
> Doubt anything, but do not doubt that.
>
> Thamos

Leesha read it three times, vision clouding as her eyes filled with tears. The sob burst from her despite her best efforts, and she dropped the paper, covering her face. Briar moved to her, holding her much as she had him.

Araine bent and snatched the paper from the ground, grunting as she read it.

'Will they even give us back his body to bury?' Leesha asked.

Araine pulled her shawl tighter and moved to the window,

staring at the grey winter sky. 'I expect an emissary will be sent from Krasia soon. If they demand money, we'll give it to them, no matter the cost.'

'They don't want money,' Leesha said. 'They want war.'

Araine turned and met Leesha's eyes. 'If that's what they want, we'll give them that, too. No matter the cost.'

The Krasian emissary came two weeks later, a single *dama*, escorted by two *dal'Sharum*. The palace guards confiscated their weapons, eyeing them with open hostility, but the Krasians exuded the infuriating confidence of their people, acting no less haughty unarmed and surrounded by enemies than in their centre of power.

Leesha watched them from the royal box, a row of seats behind the throne's dais. The sun was low in the sky, beneath the high windows of the throne room. The natural light was dim, and her warded spectacles could dimly see their smug auras.

With her were the Duchess Mum, Wonda, and Princess Lorain of Miln. Melny's flow had still not come, and Araine had forbid her to attend.

This was the first time Leesha had seen the Milnese princess since the news of the Krasian victory. Like Araine, Lorain had known of the attack in advance. Lord Sament was to ride beside Thamos as his cavalry led the charge, and there had been no word of him since.

Lorain had vanished into her heavily guarded embassy, Mountain Spears patrolling the walls and grounds until news of the emissary came. She seemed to have aged in those days. There were dark circles around her eyes that even paint and powder could not fully conceal, but at their centre, her stare was hard.

Rhinebeck and his brothers glared down from their dais, but the Krasians were uncowed. The *dama* strode forward boldly, followed by the *Sharum* carrying a large lacquered box between them.

Guards stopped the *dama* before he could halve the distance to the throne, and the man gave a shallow bow. 'I am Dama Gorja. I bear a message from my master, and speak with his voice.'

He unrolled a large parchment, beginning to read:

'Greetings Rhinebeck the Third, Duke of Angiers, in the Year of Everam 3784—

'I testify before Everam that you have broken faith with the Creator and His children on Ala, attacking on sacred Waning in the night, when all men are brothers. In accordance with Evejan law, you must die for this.'

There were angry rumbles through the court at that, but Dama Gorja ignored them, continuing to read:

'But Everam's mercy is infinite, and His divine justice need not extend to your people, with whom we have ever wished only friendship and brotherhood. Set your affairs in order and kill yourself for ordering this abomination. On the first day of spring, your successor will deliver your head to me and be allowed to touch his forehead to the carpet at my feet. Do this, and your people will be spared. Fail, and we will hold all Angiers responsible, and bring Everam's infinite justice down upon you all.

'I await your response – Jayan asu Ahmann am'Jardir am'Kaji, Sharum Ka of Krasia, Lord of Everam's Reservoir, firstborn son and rightful heir of Ahmann asu Hoshkamin am'Jardir am'Kaji, also known as Shar'Dama Ka, the Deliverer.'

Rhinebeck's face was bright red as the *dama* looked up from the parchment. 'You expect me to kill myself?!'

Dama Gorja bowed. 'If you love your people and wish them to remain untouched by your crime. But even in the south, it is known that Duke Rhinebeck is fat, corrupt, and seedless, a *khaffit* who does not deserve his throne. My master expects you to refuse, and invite Everam's divine wrath.'

'Everam has no sway here, Dama,' Shepherd Pether said.

Dama Gorja bowed. 'Apologies, Highness, but Everam holds sway everywhere.'

Rhinebeck looked like he was choking on a chicken bone, his thick-jowled face nearly purple. 'Where is my brother's body?' he demanded.

'Ah, yes,' Dama Gorja said, snapping his fingers. The two *Sharum* approached the throne with their lacquered box.

Leesha felt a mounting dread as that box drew closer. Janson and half a dozen Wooden Soldiers intercepted it before they made it to the steps, and the *Sharum* stood impassively as the first minister looked inside.

'Night!' Janson cried, turning away in horror. He snatched a kerchief from his pocket, heaving into it.

'Bring it here,' Rhinebeck commanded, and two of his guards took the box up to the throne. Pether and Mickael stood from their seats, stepping up to see as Rhinebeck opened the box.

Mickael gasped, and Pether heaved. He was not as fast as Janson, catching the bile on his hand and the front of his pristine robes. Rhinebeck only looked coldly at the contents, then waved the box away.

'I'll see that box, Wonda,' Araine said.

'Ay, Mum,' Wonda said, and she intercepted the guards, steering them to the royal box.

Janson rushed to her. 'Your Grace, I do not advise . . .'

But Araine ignored him, opening the box. Leesha stood quickly. She had already guessed the contents, but she had to see it for herself. The horror inside was what she expected, but worse.

Inside were two great sealed jars of warded glass, filled with what looked like camel's piss. In one floated Thamos' head, the other, Lord Sament's. Thamos' genitals had been severed and shoved in his mouth. Sament's mouth was filled with dung.

The sight cut through her like a demon's talons, but she had hardened her heart, and gave no sign of her pain. Lorain, too, had more anger in her gaze than horror.

The same could not be said for Araine. Leesha had seldom

seen a hint of emotion from the woman, but this was too much for even her regal aura to bear. Leesha watched her powerful spirit collapse as she reached out and took the jar with Thamos' head, clutching it tightly as she wept.

'Guards!' Rhinebeck shouted. 'Drag these desert rats to the dungeons!'

Dama Gorja's aura changed at the words, his smug arrogance changing to a thrill of victory. He had been hoping for this response. Goading it, even.

Gorja bowed deeply to the dais. 'Thank you, Highness. I was prepared to simply leave, as it is written in the Evejah that an emissary is as a man in the night, inviolate. Even in your heathen culture, these rights are granted a Messenger. As your guest, I could not honourably strike at you.' He smiled. 'But since you choose to compound your crime, I am free to kill you myself.'

Rhinebeck's snort of derision caught in his throat as Gorja whipped around, driving the heel of his hand into the nose of the closest guard. Cartilage crumpled and bone shattered, the shrapnel driven into his brain. Leesha saw his aura wink out, and he fell to the floor, dead.

The two *Sharum* exploded into action as well, breaking bones and bending joints in directions they were not meant to go.

Dama Gorja was at the steps of the dais by then, moving with impossible speed. Janson produced a knife from somewhere, but Gorja caught his wrist and pulled, hardly slowing his stride as he flipped the first minister onto his back on the hard stairs and continued.

He could have taken the knife, Leesha knew, but Evejan clerics were forbidden to use bladed weapons. Gorja needed no weapon in any event. His aura flared brightly when he began his attack. There was magic at work.

In an eyeblink, the *dama* was on Rhinebeck, landing heavy blows. The duke's aura had already winked out as the force of the leap tipped the great chair back. Gorja took no chances, continuing to punch as he rode it down atop the duke. By the time they hit the dais floor, Rhinebeck's head looked like a melon cast from the South Tower.

Mickael leapt to his feet. The prince was fitter than Rhinebeck, larger than Gorja and with greater reach. He grabbed the *dama* roughly by his shoulders, attempting to pull him off his brother.

Gorja barely looked back, backhanding Mickael with a closed fist. There was little leverage to the blow, but the lower half of Mickael's face exploded with a crack and burst of blood, teeth, bone, and flesh left hanging in a ruined mass.

The *dama* planted his foot, using the momentum of his rise to add force as he whipped around and sank his fist into Mickael's chest. The sound of his ribs shattering echoed from the ceiling as the prince was thrown from the dais. He landed twenty feet away, aura snuffed like a candle.

Shepherd Pether attempted to flee, but the *dama* caught his robes and casually flung him back into his seat. 'Stay, infidel, that we may further debate Everam's sway.'

It happened so fast the duke and prince were dead even as Leesha was rising to her feet, but as Gorja gripped the front of the Shepherd's robes and raised his fist, she lifted her *hora* wand and let loose a blast of magic that lifted the *dama* off his victim and threw him clear across the room. He struck the wall, cracking stone and leaving a great webbed crater as he fell to the floor.

Leesha felt the burst of magical feedback buck up her arm, filling her with strength. She felt giddy with it, until the baby kicked hard in response. She gasped, clutching her stomach.

The *Sharum* had killed the guards by now, though one had taken the thrust of a spear in the fighting, bleeding but not out of the fight. Other guards rushed forward, but they would not be in time to save Pether as the freshly armed *Sharum* rushed up the steps to finish the *dama*'s work and end Rhinebeck's line.

'Corespawn you!' Leesha was terrified of what the magic might be doing to her child, but she could not stand by. Again she raised the wand, loosing two more blasts that picked off the assassins one by one.

The baby was beating the inside of her belly like a drum, as if it were trying to burst free months early – and might manage it. Leesha was weeping as she lowered the wand again, wrapping her arms around the lump of her stomach.

'Mistress, look out!' Wonda cried. Leesha raised her gaze, seeing Gorja, scorched and bloody but still bright with power, kill two guards and race her way.

An arrow streaked over Leesha's shoulder, aimed right for the *dama*'s heart, but Gorja swatted it aside like an annoying horsefly.

'Corespawn it,' Wonda growled, dropping her bow and charging in front of Leesha, meeting the *dama* head-on.

Gorja thought to shove past her as he had the others trying to hinder him, but Wonda's armour was infused with demon bone she could draw upon for strength and speed, just as the *dama* appeared to be doing. She caught his arm and twisted into a throw.

But Gorja never lost control, shifting to meet the new attack. He leapt ahead of the throw, kicking Wonda in the face and landing in position for a throw of his own.

'No you don't!' Wonda said, throwing her weight against the move and keeping her feet. The *dama* adjusted as well, until Wonda surged back in, smashing his nose with her forehead.

At last the *dama* was off balance, and she put him on the ground hard, cracking the stone floor. The *dama* contorted on the rebound, hooking Wonda's ankle and bringing her down as well.

The *dama* paid for the move, Wonda landing atop him and pumping short, powerful punches into his body. She bashed his head into the stone again.

But Gorja was squirming around even as she pummelled him, and kicked up suddenly, crossing his legs around her throat. Wonda was pulled back with a choked gasp, hitting the ground flailing as Gorja added torque to the hold.

Wonda could not reach the *dama* to attack, clutching helplessly at his legs as he strangled her to death.

The child still wild in her belly, Leesha dared not use the wand again, but neither could she let Wonda die. She looked frantically for a weapon, but Lorain had beaten her to it. The thickset woman had taken her chair by the back, and she struck hard with it.

Again the *dama* shifted, getting a forearm up in time to block the blow. The chair shattered against it, and Gorja grabbed the front of the princess' dress, pulling her down as well. He put his arm across her throat, cutting off her air even as his legs continued to choke the life from Wonda.

Leesha was moving before she knew it, magic filling her limbs with an inhuman surge of strength. She forgot about the baby, about Thamos, about her Gatherer's oath. Her whole world shrank to a single target. Dama Gorja's head.

Her stomp drove it down into his chest. Leesha felt vertebrae pop as the impact whipped down his spine, and at last the *dama* collapsed.

The room fell silent, but for the three women gasping for breath. Wonda and Lorain were taking great lungfuls, but Leesha's breathing was sharp and quick, like the beating of her heart. She stood there, knowing the fight was over, but struggling to control a mix of anger, adrenaline, and magic that threatened to overwhelm her. She wished there were more foes to fight, as if the power might tear her apart if she did not give it release. Night, was this what Wonda and the others felt when magic-drunk in battle? It was terrifying.

Around the room, everyone stared at the scene, dumbstruck. Even Araine had lifted her tear-filled eyes from the jar at her lap, staring openmouthed at Leesha. She could see fear of her in their auras, and could not blame them.

The darkening room was alive with magic, swirling angrily

in the air, drawn to the violence. Leesha shut her eyes to block it out, forcing her breaths to deepen. The baby continued to kick and squirm violently.

Caught up in the magic, Leesha could feel the life within her like never before. It was strong. The magic had obviously not harmed it, but that did not mean the effect was good. Leesha had seen magic force children into their full growth before their time. Might the baby come early, too big to birth without dangerous surgery? Or would the power wreak some other change? Arlen had feared this when he refused to be with her, and now Leesha was left with the same problem without him.

She shook off the problem for later, opening her eyes and helping Lorain to her feet. Wonda was already on one knee, and held a hand out to forestall aid.

'Don' worry about me, mistress.' She gulped another great breath. 'Be fine in a minute.'

Leesha could see the magic coursing through the woman, drawn naturally to her injuries, and knew it for true. She let Wonda have her pride, turning to the corpse of Dama Gorja.

Even now, she felt nothing. She had incinerated two of his men, and crushed the *dama*'s spine. These were not demons, but human men. Still, there was none of the guilt she might have felt in a more introspective moment. These men would happily have murdered everyone in the room as easily as Leesha might pluck herbs from the dirt.

One of the *dama*'s fists remained tightly clenched, and she pried it open to find a crumbled bit of demon bone, its power expended. She blew softly, and it was swept away like dust.

At last, Janson shook himself, stumbling up the steps of the dais. He looked down at the body of Rhinebeck, shuddered, and reached into the gore for the lacquered wooden circlet the duke had worn.

'The duke is dead!' the first minister cried. He descended a step, reaching out to help Shepherd Pether to his feet. 'Long live Duke Pether!'

Shepherd Pether looked at him, confusion and fear in his aura. 'Eh?'

There wasn't enough left of any of the royal brothers for a proper interment, and three royal funerals too much for even the ivy throne to bear. A week after the attack, the city still on lockdown, Thamos, Rhinebeck, and Mickael were given rites as at the great Cathedral of Angiers.

Pether himself presided over the service, seeing no conflict in keeping his position as Shepherd of the Tenders of the Creator even as the wooden crown was placed upon his brow. After the initial shock wore off, he assigned artisans to create new raiment and ceremonial armour to befit his dual status.

Leesha stood straight-backed and stone-faced on the receiving line after the service. She had wept for Thamos privately, but her grief was not something she was ready to share. She accepted the condolences of Angierian Royals whose names she did not know or care to know, smiling wanly and giving a brief, mechanical squeeze of her hand before dismissing them by turning her eyes to the next in line.

Still, the line seemed endless. She did her duty and endured it all, but she was hollow inside.

Back in her rooms, she collapsed on her bed, only to be roused a moment later by Wonda. 'Sorry to disturb, Mistress Leesha, but Mum wants to see you.'

Leesha climbed wearily to her feet, checking her hair and arching her back before leaving her chambers again, not giving a hint of what she was feeling to the servants and guards in the hall. They were in mourning, too, and needed to see her strong.

Lorain was sitting before the Duchess Mum as Leesha entered the receiving room. The Milnese princess looked at Leesha and nodded, but her eyes said more. There was something between them, now. Not friendship, perhaps, but trust. And a mutual debt.

Lorain turned back to Araine, resuming their conversation as if Leesha were not there. 'Will His Grace agree?'

'The crown's ballooned the boy's already swollen head, but it's a head my son wants to keep. Pether may prefer sticking boys dressed as girls, but if it will get your father to send us a few thousand Mountain Spears . . .'

Lorain nodded. 'I'm no more interested in his touch than he is in mine, but if it will pay those desert rats back for what they did to my husband, Pether can bring his bugger boys to bed with us for all I care.'

Araine grunted. 'You will never take the throne. Not even as regent, should you produce a son not fully grown when Pether dies.'

Lorain nodded. 'My father may want a claim to your throne, but I do not. I will never be denied access to the boy, though. And my children will be brought here and live in the palace with their full royal status.'

'Of course,' Araine agreed. 'But their title will be honorary, with no Angierian lands or positions accorded to them beyond what they earn.'

'I will have my Mothers alter the contract accordingly,' Lorain said. 'We'll be ready to sign in the morning.'

'The sooner, the better,' Araine agreed. Lorain stood, squeezing Leesha's shoulder as she left.

'Have you recovered, dear?' Araine asked, gesturing for Leesha to sit.

Leesha lowered herself to her seat. 'Well enough, Your Grace.'

'Call me Araine in private,' the Duchess Mum said. 'You've earned that, and more. I might have lost four sons that day, and not three.

'Pether will sign this in the morning, as well,' Araine continued, handing Leesha a royal decree. The papers made Leesha Countess of Hollow County and a member of the royal family, though she and Thamos had never married.

'It's common sense,' Araine said as Leesha looked up from the parchment. 'You've effectively held the role for months in any event, and I daresay your people will accept no one else. Gared's a good boy, but better a baron than count, especially with that scandal-ridden new bride.'

'I expect he'll be relieved to hear it,' Leesha said.

'You'll return immediately,' Araine said. 'And take Melny with you.'

'Eh?' Leesha asked.

'Everyone's forgotten Melny for the moment, and I want to keep it that way,' Araine said. 'Miln and Angiers must ally, and now. No one knows that girl's carrying Rhinebeck's baby, and if it gets out, the child will cause undue complications. The kind settled with spears.'

'Lorain would never kill an unborn child,' Leesha said.

'Never say never,' Araine said, 'but I was thinking more about her father, or Easterly and Wardgood using it as a rallying point against Miln. Wouldn't surprise me to find one of them kidnapped poor Sikvah as well.'

'That brings us to the matter of Rojer,' Leesha said. 'He's coming with me when I go, and the charges against him will be dropped.'

Araine raised an eyebrow at her tone, but she nodded. 'Done.'

Leesha rose, returning to her rooms to begin preparations. They were ready to leave in two days, but by then, the Krasian army was at the walls, and the city in panic.

30

The Princess' Guard
334 AR Winter

Rojer looked out from the tiny window of his cell, the tower affording him an all-too-clear view of the Krasian forces massing at the South Gate.

After months in this cursed cell, this was supposed to have been his release day. Instead, the whole city was on alert, and he'd been forgotten.

'Knew it was too good to be true,' he muttered. 'Gonna die in this cell.'

'Nonsense,' Sikvah said from the shadows above. 'I will protect you, husband. If the walls are breached, we will be long gone before they reach the cathedral.'

Rojer did not look at her. He seldom even tried now. Sikvah was seen when she wished it, and no other time. His eyes stared in mounting horror as column after column of warriors assembled, wheeling great rock slingers into position.

'Did you know this was going to happen?' Rojer asked.

'No, husband,' Sikvah said. 'By Everam and my hope of Heaven, I did not. I was privy to many of the secrets of the Deliverer's Palace before we were wed, but never did I hear of any plans to expand beyond the borders of Everam's Bounty in the near future. Everam's Bounty was a land of vast riches, and people to bring to Everam's will. Wisdom dictated we stay there half a decade, at least.'

'And then resume conquest.' Rojer spat from the tower window.

'This is not news, husband,' Sikvah said. 'My blessed uncle never hid his path from you. Sharak Sun must unite all peoples, for Sharak Ka to be won.'

'Demonshit,' Rojer said. 'Why? Because some book says so?'

'The Evejah—' Sikvah began.

'Is a ripping book!' Rojer snapped. 'I don't know if there's a Creator or not, but I know He didn't come down from Heaven and write any books. Books are written by men, and men are weak, stupid, and corrupt.'

Sikvah did not respond immediately. He was challenging everything she believed, and he could sense her tension, her desire to argue, warring with her sacred vow to be a submissive wife.

'Regardless,' Sikvah said after a moment. 'This must be Jayan's doing. My cousin has the strongest blood claim to the Skull Throne, but no real glories to his name. No doubt he strives to prove himself to our people so they will accept him in my blessed uncle's absence.'

'Your blessed uncle fell off a cliff months ago and hasn't been heard from since,' Rojer said. 'Do you still think he's coming back?'

'There was no body,' Sikvah said, 'and signs he was alive when they landed. I will not believe the Deliverer is dead. He will return when he is needed most. But what will his sons and *Damaji* wreak in his absence? Will our armies be stronger when Sharak Ka comes, or will my fool cousins spread them so thin they shatter?'

She dropped down silently beside him, looking out the window, careful even at this height not to be seen from without. 'Everam's blood. There are nearly fifteen thousand *Sharum* out there.'

'The fort's home to sixty thousand, give or take,' Rojer said. 'But I doubt there's two thousand Wooden Soldiers left after Thamos went south.'

'Do you think it's true, what they say?' Sikvah asked. 'That he attacked my cousin's forces on Waning? At night?'

Rojer shrugged. 'My people don't see the night, and Waning, like yours do, Sikvah. Twice now, Jasin tried to kill me in the night. And the duke and his brothers, when they turned on Thamos on the hunt.'

'Yes, but these were not men,' Sikvah said. 'Goldentone, Rhinebeck, these were soulless *khaffit*. I saw Count Thamos fight. A fool, perhaps, but he had a *Sharum*'s heart, and the *alagai* quailed before him. I cannot imagine him acting so dishonourably.'

Rojer shrugged again. 'Wasn't there. Neither were you. But what does it matter, now that his head was sent to his mother in a jar?'

'No mother should witness such a thing,' Sikvah agreed. 'My cousin has little high ground on which to stand.'

Columns of smoke rose to the east, where the Krasians had sacked the local hamlets. There were dozens of them within a day of the city walls.

'If they've come so far north,' Rojer asked, a lump forming in his throat, 'does that mean the Hollow has fallen?'

Sikvah shook her head. 'The Hollow is strong, and blessed by Everam. This many warriors might have conquered it, but it would have taken weeks, perhaps months. These men are fresh, with no wounded or damaged equipment.'

She looked to the east where the smoke rose. 'They went east around the great wood, likely skirting the Hollow entirely.'

'There's that, at least,' Rojer said. 'Maybe Gared's already on his way here with ten thousand Cutters.'

Please, Gar, he begged silently. *I'm too young to die.*

Duke Pether shifted nervously, lines of sweat streaking the powder on his face. No doubt the Shepherd was unaccustomed to standing before the altar instead of presiding over it. A third son given to the church, Pether had likely never expected to wear the wooden crown, much less get married with an invading army at the gates.

Princess Lorain, in contrast, stood straight and resolute, eyes on the Tender as he hurried through the vows that would seal their alliance and allow her to commit her soldiers to the fight. Not that her five hundred Mountain Spears were likely to make much difference against twenty thousand *Sharum*. Messengers had been dispatched the moment the enemy forces were spotted, but there was no way of knowing if they had gotten through.

It was morning, though dawn was still an hour away. The ceremony was blessedly quick, just oaths and an awkward kiss. Leesha didn't envy either of them the wedding night, but the needs of their people outweighed their personal comfort. It seemed such a simple thing, creating a child, but Leesha knew as well as any how it could impact the world.

'Man and wife!' the Tender called, and the new duchess nodded to Bruz, the captain of her guard. The man sent a runner to muster the Mountain Spears, then fell in behind her as she and Pether stepped down from the altar. The attendees gave a ragged cheer, but most of the pews were empty, people manning the walls or barricading themselves in homes and shelters.

Araine was the first to bow to the new couple, but the others quickly followed. Leesha bent as far as she could manage in her current state. Even Amanvah bowed, a telling move. She was desperate to see Rojer freed.

'Enough,' Pether snapped, drawing everyone erect once more. 'There will be plenty of time for bowing and scraping tomorrow, if we live to see it.' His shrill tone made clear his expectation on the matter.

Lorain's face was stone as she looked at her new husband, but her aura was a mix of irritation and disgust. 'Perhaps, husband, this is something best discussed in private?'

'Of course, of course,' Pether said, waving the royal entourage into the vestry beside the altar and down the hall to his private offices. Rhinebeck's palace was his, now, but there had been no time to move, and the Shepherd was reluctant to leave the lavish office he had spent a decade arranging.

There in his place of power, surrounded by the symbols of his faith and reminders of his own greatness, the duke seemed to regain something of himself, straightening his back. 'Janson, what is the status of our defences?'

'Little different than it was twenty minutes ago, Your Grace,' Janson said. 'The enemy is massing, but if nothing else, we learned this week they will not attack until dawn. We have archers on the wall, and men to repel attempts to scale, but the real danger is the South Gate. There are companies of men guarding the other gates, but the enemy has positioned their engines to strike there.'

'Will it hold?' Pether asked.

Janson shrugged. 'Unclear, Your Grace. The enemy did not haul boulders all this way, and they are unlikely to quickly find stone of sufficient size to break the gate. It should withstand most bombardment.'

'Most?' Pether asked.

Janson shrugged again. 'It has never been tested, Your Grace. If it falls, the courtyard will be the last hope of stopping the charge before the enemy can spread out into the city.'

'If it fails, we're lost,' Pether said. 'After the losses at Docktown, we don't have enough Wooden Soldiers to man the wall and hold that yard if twenty thousand Krasians come pouring in. Men are streaming in from the levies, but we don't even have weapons for them. They're not going to hold back trained cavalry with carpentry tools.'

'Nothing is lost,' Lorain said, her voice hard. 'Captain Bruz will take the Mountain Spears to the courtyard. There are only three avenues for enemy coming through the gate to take. Each a choke point we can hold with limited men.'

Pether turned to Leesha. 'And the Hollow, mistress? Do you think we can expect help from the south?'

Leesha shook her head. 'I gave Briar *hora* to speed his journey to the Hollow with news of Gorja's attack, but even if Gared got right on his horse, it will be days yet before he can arrive with any sizable force.'

She shrugged. 'I suppose it's possible the Hollowers caught sign of the Krasians on the march and mustered sooner, but I wouldn't place any wagers on it.'

'And your Painted Man?' Pether asked. 'If ever he were the Deliverer, now would be the time to prove it.'

Lorain snorted, and again Leesha shook her head. 'You've better odds with the Hollow, Your Grace. If the Painted Man is still alive, he's off chasing demons and left politics behind.'

'What about you, mistress?' Pether asked. 'You threw lightning at Gorja and his warriors.'

'And nearly miscarried as a result,' Leesha said. 'I won't be doing that again save as a last resort with a spear pointed at my belly. There is little I can do in open daylight in any event. I may be able to strengthen the gate, however.'

Everyone looked up at this. 'How?' Pether asked.

'With wards, and *hora*,' Leesha said, 'if we can shroud the gate in darkness.'

Pether looked to Janson. The minister's eyes flicked to Araine, who appeared to do nothing more than shift her feet slightly.

Janson nodded immediately. 'We can have every tailor in the city stitching bolts of cloth, Your Grace.'

'See to it.' Pether looked around. 'Any other ideas? Anyone with a mad plan brewing, now's the time to speak it.'

Silence hung in the air like a weight, and Leesha took a deep breath. 'There is one thing . . .'

'Let me speak to him,' Amanvah said.

Pether shook his head. 'Madness.'

'You asked for mad plans, Your Grace,' Leesha said. 'For what it's worth, I believe her.' She could not explain her wardsight, and the sincerity she saw in the woman's aura. The Royals were more likely to think her mad than trust her words.

'Jayan is my brother,' Amanvah said. 'Firstborn son and daughter of the Deliverer and Damajah. Send me out now while they wait for the sun, and he will speak to me. Perhaps I can turn him from this course. The Evejah forbids any, even the Sharum Ka, from harming or physically hindering a *dama'ting*. He cannot prevent me from returning, or attack the city with me in it.'

'And what guarantee do we have that you will return?' Lorain demanded. 'More likely you will embrace your brother and bless him with knowledge of our defences and command structure.'

'You have my husband,' Amanvah reminded her. 'And my sister-wife, whom the dice tell me remains imprisoned some-where in the city.'

'What better way to free them,' Pether asked, 'than have your brother knock down the walls of their prisons?'

'If you care at all,' Lorain noted. 'Perhaps you've tired of your *chin* husband, and plan to wipe the slate clean and return to your own kind.'

Amanvah's eyes flared, and her aura shone with rage. 'How dare you?! I offer to hostage myself for your stinking *chin* city, and you insult my honour and husband.'

She advanced on the duchess, and though Amanvah was shorter and half the thickly set woman's weight, Lorain's aura flashed with fear, no doubt remembering the casual way Dama Gorja had killed his way across the throne room.

'Guards!' Lorain shouted, and Bruz was in front of her in an instant, levelling his polearm at Amanvah. It had a wide, curving blade affixed to the end that would serve equally well to chop or stab. Leesha could see glittering wards etched into the steel.

Amanvah looked at the man as if he were a bug to squash, but she stopped, holding up her hands. 'I offer no threat, Duchess. I am simply concerned for my husband's safety. If you believe nothing else, believe that. The dice tell me he is in grave danger if he remains imprisoned.'

'We're all in danger, with your brother at the walls,' Lorain said as six Wooden Soldiers burst into the room, surrounding Amanvah. 'But if you are so concerned for your husband's safety, you're welcome to join him.' She signalled the guards to take Amanvah away.

'Have women search her before she goes to the tower,' Araine said. 'We don't want her smuggling in demon bones.'

One of the guards reached for her, but Amanvah breezed past him with a few well-placed taps that sent him stumbling from her path. She quickstepped over to Leesha, removing her *hora* pouch. She stripped off her jewellery, including her warded circlet and choker, slipping them into the pouch and pulling the drawstrings tight. She handed it to Leesha as the guards massed again, this time guiding her away at spearpoint.

'I'll keep it safe for you,' Leesha promised. 'I swear by the Creator.'

'Everam will hold you to that,' Amanvah said as she was escorted to the tower.

Leesha was still warding the South Gate when the sun came up. Janson had made good his promise. The gatehouse was bathed in darkness, the doorways and portcullis draped in thick cloth. She wouldn't have even known dawn had come, if not for the boom and shudder as the Krasian slingers opened fire.

The impact threw Leesha from her feet, but Wonda was there to catch her. There was a clatter of stone as debris rained down to the ground. The enemy had not found any boulders to hurl. That was a blessing, at least.

'Ent safe here, mistress,' Wonda said. 'Need to go now.'

'We're not going anywhere until I finish my work,' Leesha said.

'The child . . .' Wonda started.

'Will be taken from me if this gate is breached,' Leesha cut her off, 'if its half brother doesn't simply cut it from my womb.'

Wonda bared her teeth at the idea, but she made no further protest as Leesha went back to work painting wards on the great wooden gates and heavy crossbars. Wonda had downed three wind demons flying over the city, and gutted them in the gatehouse, filling buckets with their foul, magic-rich ichor.

Leesha wore delicate gloves of soft leather as she dipped her brush in the thick, reeking fluid and drew more wards, the smooth, curving lines glowing brightly in wardsight. Each linked to its neighbours, forming a net that would distribute strength throughout the wood. Even now the wards brightened with each impact, effectively healing the wood of damage. So long as the gatehouse remained dark, the barrier would only strengthen as the bombardment continued.

Creator, let it be enough, she prayed.

When she finished the net, Leesha drew her *hora* wand. Manipulating the wards on its surface with her fingers, Leesha released magic into the web in a slow, steady stream. The wards about the gate grew brighter and brighter, while her wand dimmed steadily.

The gloves offered some protection from the feedback as the magic did its work, but not much. She felt the tingle in her fingers, spreading like a thrill through her. The baby, motionless a moment before, began to kick and thrash, but there was nothing for it but to endure as she emptied the wand's power into the gate. The item could be recharged, if they lived till sunset.

Again there was a boom as the gate was struck, but this time it barely shook.

'That it?' Wonda asked. 'We can go?'

Leesha nodded, heading for the stairs.

'Ay.' Wonda cast a thumb over her shoulder. 'Way out's this way.'

'I know.' Leesha continued to climb. 'But I want a look from the top before we go back to the palace.'

'Night!' Wonda spat, but she darted up the steps, slipping past Leesha to take the lead.

There were drapes on both sides of the door to the top floor of the gatehouse, a full storey above the rest of the wall. The gatehouse was thick stone, with twenty-four windows – eight north and south, four each east and west. The narrow apertures afforded cover to the fifty archers stationed there.

The north windows looked out over a great fountained courtyard, the cobbles cluttered with abandoned merchant stalls and carts. Some had been hastily stripped of their contents, but most had been abandoned as the vendors were evacuated.

Three avenues branched from there, one east, one west, and another straight north towards the centre of town. Lorain had stationed two hundred of her Mountain Spears there, with another one hundred and fifty positioned east and west. The men stood at attention, ready should the Krasians manage to breach the gate.

At all other sides of the gatehouse, archers knelt by the windows. Those facing south fired in a steady stream, boys running to refill quivers as they emptied. The men looking out over the wall tops shot only periodically, but the fact they were shooting at all was worrisome.

Leesha moved to the east wall, looking out as Wooden Soldiers and volunteers cut grappling lines and pushed back ladders. Here and there a few Krasians made the wall top, cutting a swath through the defenders until the archers picked them off. The Wooden Soldiers fought bravely, but the dal'Sharum were bred for this.

Leesha took a breath, steeling herself as she moved to the south wall. Wonda took the lead again, speaking to Lord Mansen, the captain commanding the archers. The man glanced doubtfully at Leesha, but knew better than to protest.

'Peers, you're relieved,' the sergeant called to one of the archers, the man positioned by the eastern corner window.

Wonda was at the window before Leesha could take a step, looking out to ensure it was safe. She pulled back suddenly, along with all the other men. Another boom shook the gate-house, and debris flew through the windows, a heavy dust and bits of shattered brick.

Wonda waited a moment, then peeked out again, coughing. 'All right, mistress. Quick now, while they reload. And then we go.'

'Honest word,' Leesha agreed. But as she looked out over the Krasian troops, her heart sank. Twenty thousand. It was a number she understood logically, but looking at the reality was something else entirely. There were so *many*. Even if they failed to breach the gate, those scaling might overwhelm the wall guards eventually.

Gared, she begged silently, *if ever there were a time for you to do something right, this is it. We need a miracle.*

The majority of the host held back, a huge cavalry and thousands of footmen, ready to charge should the gate collapse. Mehnding sling teams hauled rubble from the burned hamlets into the baskets of their engines. Most fired blindly into the city, but one had been hauled in close to fire with accuracy on the gate. Mansen's archers were focusing their arrows on those warriors, but others stood with overlapping shields to protect the men as they worked.

The Krasians returned fire. There was a shriek and a scorpion stinger punched through one of the Angierian archers. The broad-bladed head burst from his back as he was flung across the room, dead.

Everyone stared at the ruined thing knocked all the way into the north wall. Leesha's instinct was to rush to the man, but her mind knew it was pointless. No one could survive a blow like that.

'If you're still alive, quit gawking and shoot!' Mansen roared, snapping the men back to their work.

Wonda shifted nervously, but Leesha ignored her, daring another peek from the window, looking at the ammunition the Mehnding were loading. Most of it was large chunks of shoddy masonry like that which had shattered against the gate a moment ago. If that was the worst the sling teams could bring to bear, the gate was safe.

But even as the thought crossed her mind, she saw a cart being hauled in with a piece of solid stone. A statue of Rhinebeck II with a heavy base, the whole thing twenty feet tall. It would be the greatest test yet, but the wards would hold against even this.

I hope, she thought.

Yet even as the statue was loaded, the *kai'Sharum* raised his hand for the teams to hold. Archers continued to fire on both sides, and men fought and fell from the wall, but the heavy artillery halted.

'What are they waiting for?' Leesha asked.

She learned a moment later, when the windows all darkened at once as Krasian Watchers abseiled down from above, twisting through the narrow apertures.

The men were all in black, carrying no spears or shields. They did not have their distinctive ladders, but Leesha had known Watchers before, and recognized them by their silence, skill, and exotic weapons.

Several archers went down, kick-daggers punching into heads and necks as they tumbled into the room. Wonda barely yanked Leesha out of the way in time.

Brief skirmishes followed as the Watchers cut the remaining archers apart like they were chopping herbs. Even when they fought in close, arms were flinging sharpened steel at the reserves in the centre of the room.

One came at Leesha, but Wonda latched onto him, and his flailed punches and kicks did nothing to hinder her pitching him bodily out the window. Famed for their silence, the Watcher screamed as he fell.

Wonda whirled for the next assailant, but no others threatened them. Half the *Sharum* had already disappeared through the door to the stairwell, and the others were moving in that direction, killing any who hindered them.

Leesha thought they came to remove the archers, but

hearing the screams of men from below, she saw now that was incidental.

'They're going to open the gate!' Leesha cried, cursing herself for a fool. All the wards in the world wouldn't mean a thing if the Krasians simply turned the cranks.

Wonda had her bow in hand, and even in the close, chaotic space, put an arrow through a *Sharum* about to reach the door. She had another nocked an instant later, but another Krasian made the stairs in that time. She shot the third, but then a press of the Wooden Soldiers blocked her sight as they tackled two of the Watchers.

Leesha ran to the north windows. 'Krasians in the gatehouse! To arms!'

The Mountain Spears did not budge from their positions, but Wooden Soldiers and volunteers raced for the gatehouse.

They would be too late, Leesha knew. Already she could feel the floor rumbling as the Watchers raised the portcullis. Even if the Angierians retook the gatehouse and closed it again, the damage would be done. Even indirect sunlight could suck the power from her wards, rendering them useless.

'Night,' Leesha said, rushing back to look back at the sling teams. They had the statue loaded, but continued to wait, appearing to stare right at Leesha.

There are more Watchers on the roof, Leesha realized. They gave some signal, because the sling teams leapt to action. Leesha watched Thamos' father flying through the air, and could only consider the irony that Araine's husband should be the instrument that ended her rule.

The entire gatehouse shook with the impact, roaring with the sound of splintered wood and twisted metal. Leesha stumbled, but again Wonda was there to steady her. The last Watchers had disappeared, barricading the door behind them. Archers, not always the heaviest of men, threw themselves against the heavy portal fruitlessly. It had been built to keep invaders out, but it served just as well turned on the defenders.

She could hear the fight in the gatehouse intensify as the

Wooden Soldiers desperately tried to close the heavy iron portcullis before the gates gave way.

On the outside, a group of *chi'Sharum* were tasked with the ram. Leesha could not believe her eyes as the men, born and raised in Thesa, took up the great goldwood trunk while others surrounded them, shields held high to form a tortoise shell over the rammers. Despite the complex formation, they picked up speed as they crossed the open ground. Archers on the wall fired helplessly, arrows splintering off the shields. Men with cauldrons of boiling oil had been positioned on the gatehouse roof to defend against this, but the Watchers had taken the roof, leaving them defenceless.

The boom as the ram struck carried the sound of breaking wood, and Leesha knew the gates would not last much longer.

The rammers drew back, readying for another charge. Leesha looked down at the cluster of men below sadly. 'Creator forgive you.'

They charged again, but Leesha had reached into her basket and produced a thunderstick by then. She put match to it and threw, blasting the tortoise apart and splintering the ram.

Men screamed, and when the smoke cleared, Leesha saw them, bloody bits of humanity scattered across the ground like an abattoir.

They weren't all dead. That was perhaps the worst of it. Some wailed in such agony that Leesha felt sick to her stomach.

These are the secrets of fire Bruna protected for so long, she thought, *the ones she trusted me with on Gatherer's oath to do no harm.*

And I've turned them into death.

It made no difference in the grand scheme, as there were new men with a fresh ram making for the gates even while Leesha tried to keep from sloshing up. The gatehouse shook, and there was a cheer from the Krasian army as Jayan waved his flag, signalling the charge of his heavy cavalry, right through the city gates.

Rojer screamed himself hoarse as Watchers scaled the gatehouse, but none could hear him so high up. Next to him, Sikvah stiffened, and he fell silent, hearing the sound of footsteps climbing the tower.

Were they coming to free him, at last? Perhaps it was Amanvah's demand for negotiating a surrender with her brother.

Sikvah coiled and sprang, scaling the wall with handholds he couldn't even see. In seconds she was back in the shadows of the rafters.

The cell door slammed open, but though Amanvah was on the other side, she was not there to oversee his release. Her hands and feet were shackled, and from the bruises on the faces of her captors, she had not taken the manacles willingly.

Amanvah was shoved roughly into the room, stumbling over her chains and hitting the stone hard. Rojer rushed to her side.

He expected the guards to leave, but they pressed into the room, two, four, six. All told, a dozen men crammed themselves into his tiny cell, until it seemed he could not reach an arm in any direction without touching one.

All were palace guards, like the ones that had struck after the Bachelor's Ball, armed with heavy batons. Rojer knew their faces, but not their names.

'Sorry for the press,' their sergeant said. 'Minister din't send enough men last time, but Janson don't make mistakes twice.'

'Should've known Jasin couldn't pull that off without help,' Rojer said.

'Jasin couldn't pull his boots off without help,' the sergeant said. 'Won't say any of us miss the little pissant, but you've gone and made the minister very cross.'

'You can't possibly think you can get away with murdering me right in the cathedral,' Rojer said.

The sergeant laughed. 'Whole city's eyes are on the gate, sand sticker, and it ent demons on the other side you can charm with your fiddle. No one gives a rip about you or your Krasian bitch right now. Your guards are all cowering downstairs, ready to barricade themselves in the crypts if the Krasians break the gate.'

He tilted his head, leering openly at Amanvah, her silks pulled tight over her curves. 'Not that I can blame you. P'raps the men can have a bit of fun before we cram you two through that little window.'

'No!' Rojer cried.

The sergeant laughed again. 'Don't worry about being left out, boy. Got a few men gonna be more interested in your arse than hers. It's a holy house, after all.'

There was a blur across his throat, as if a shadow had fallen across him, but then he was falling towards them in a spray of blood. Sikvah flitted like a fly across the room, stabbing another man in the throat as she used him as a springboard back into the shadows above.

'Night, what in the Core was that?!' one of the guards cried. All of them were staring upward now, Rojer and Amanvah forgotten.

'You all right?' Rojer asked her.

'No,' Amanvah said. 'I have reached the end of my patience.' Something about the words was more frightening than anything she had ever said.

There was another blur, Sikvah dropping from above like a wood demon to put a blade in a man's chest. She killed two more in the chaos that followed, again vanishing into the rafters.

'That's it, I'm getting out of here,' one of the men said. He and two other men ran for the door, but it slammed shut, the lock clicking loudly.

'Janson wants them dead!' a voice on the other side barked. 'You want the door open, get it done!'

The men turned from the door angrily, but then Sikvah fell like a spider on the one in the centre, shattering his spine. She hit the floor with a bounce, using the momentum to power the knives she stuck into the men on either side.

'It's the other one!' a guard called, and three of the remaining four leapt at her, swinging clubs.

The fourth pulled a knife, lunging for Rojer and Amanvah. Rojer tried to pull her to safety, but the chain linking her feet was short, and she stumbled again. Rojer reversed direction, coming in hard and delivering a powerful snap kick from his *sharusahk* training into the man's crotch.

But his foot struck armour, and he felt something snap as pain blossomed. His bellow was cut off as the guard swatted him aside with his baton, lifting the knife to finish off Amanvah.

'No!' Rojer didn't think as he leapt into the knife's path, shielding Amanvah's body with his own. He felt the thud against his back, and suddenly there was a sharp bit of metal sticking from his chest, his shirt reddening around it. There was no pain, but he could feel the cold of the metal inside him, and understood, distantly, what had happened.

Amanvah understood it, too. He could see it in her eyes, her beautiful brown eyes, always so serene, now wide with horror.

There was a jolt, and the assailant's hand fell away from the knife's hilt. He collapsed dead to the floor next to Rojer.

Sikvah began to wail, but like the pain, it was a distant thing. His second wife lifted him from Amanvah as gently as a babe. 'Heal him!' she begged. 'You must . . .!'

'The *chin* took my *hora* pouch!' Amanvah snapped. 'I have nothing with which to work.'

Sikvah tore the choker from her throat. 'Here! Here is the *hora*!'

Amanvah nodded, moving quickly to block the window. Sikvah laid Rojer gently on the bed, then stripped off every bit of warded jewellery from her person, smashing the priceless items with the hilt of her knife. They gave her incredible powers, but she destroyed them without a thought for him.

It was such an act of love, Rojer's eyes began to tear. He wanted to tell her to stop, that it wouldn't save him and she would need their power in the days and nights to come.

Amanvah was with him, then, cutting away his clothes as if there weren't a knife through him. As if there were something she could do. He was dying. Dying, with so much undone.

There was a thin brush on Rojer's writing desk, and Amanvah used his own blood to draw the wards, working quickly as more continued to well around the cloth wadded over the wound.

In moments, she raised the *hora*, and there was a warm glow at his chest, bringing a euphoria that deadened his pain. Amanvah looked to Sikvah. 'Withdraw the blade slowly, sister. The magic must repair his organs in your wake.'

Sikvah nodded, and began to pull. Rojer could feel the blade moving, inch by slow inch, pulling at his insides and cutting anew. He felt it, body convulsing, but there was no pain. It was as if his body were a player, miming the act of dying.

The bones in Amanvah's fist crumbled, and Sikvah pulled the knife out the last few inches in a rush, immediately pressing a cloth against the wound.

Amanvah moved to inspect his back. 'His spine is intact. If I sew the wound . . .'

But Rojer could feel the burning inside, and the erratic beating of his heart. He rolled to face them.

'K—' The sound came with a bubble of blood that burst and spattered in Amanvah's face, but she did not flinch, his blood mixing with her tears.

He paused, gathering his strength. 'Keep singing.' It came out as a gasp, and he fell back, struggling to simply breathe when there was so much to say. His wives each took one of his hands, and he clutched them with all his strength.

'K-keep learning. T-teaching.'

He looked off to the side. 'Kendall . . .'

'Husband?' Sikvah asked, and he shook himself, realizing he had been slipping away. Darkness was closing on him, shrinking his vision to a pinhole, with a light at the end to follow.

'Give Kendall my fiddle.'

Leesha rushed to the northern windows of the gatehouse, praying the portcullis had been closed in time, but instead she saw the gateway spewing forth an endless stream of Krasians. The flow split around the fountain, hundreds – thousands – of screaming warriors with long spears lowered like lances as they galloped towards the handful of Mountain Spears guarding the avenues.

To their credit, the princess' guard did not break ranks, keeping their polearms extended before them, as if any spear could hold back two tons of galloping horse.

Captain Bruz raised his own weapon as the avalanche came down upon them. At the last moment, he brought his mountain spear down with a shout.

The courtyard erupted in hundreds of explosions, like a box of festival crackers thrown on a bonfire. The air filled with smoke, and the Krasian charge broke against it as surely as a demon against the wards.

Horses screamed, some rearing so far they fell backward, others collapsing in mid-run, throwing their riders to smash against the cobbles.

The Krasian cavalry had no time to pull up. Those behind smashed into the front ranks, shattering bones and helplessly ramming their lowered spears into the backs of their fellows. From above, Leesha could see the impact ripple back through the charging horses until it lost momentum.

There was one moment, as the *Sharum* shook themselves off. Some horses leapt back to their feet, often riderless. Many stayed down. There was a dazed confusion.

KA-CHAK!

The Mountain Spears worked a bar on their weapons and levelled them again, firing another deadly barrage into the chaos.

The secrets of fire, Leesha realized. She had known Euchor had them – had seen the very plans for the weapons the Mountain Spears now fired.

But she had never dreamed he would actually be mad enough to use them, or that they could be mass-produced so quickly.

He had them all along. The thought was chilling, but it made sense. Euchor had always been hungry to become king of Thesa. Miln, after all, had once been the nation's capital.

KA-CHAK!

The enemy was in full rout now, those still able wheeling their horses and heading back through the gates. Half the Mountain Spears fired again, then began to reload as the other half fired.

When all had reloaded, the Mountain Spears began their advance. Behind them, thousands of men from the levies followed, some with weapons and others with heavy tools. The leaders had despaired for these men in open combat, but they were ideally suited for bashing in heads and cutting throats as they moved through the enemy wounded. Leesha watched them work, and sicked out the window, spattering the turban of one of the fleeing *Sharum*.

The Mountain Spears retook the gatehouse in minutes, flowing up to the wall tops and spreading out, reloading with practised precision.

The enemy forces were in disarray, the cavalry riding back through the ranks of infantry that had been on the march in their wake. The Mehnding looked confused, unsure where to direct their fire and perhaps wondering if they, too, should flee.

That moment's confusion was all the Mountain Spears needed. They opened fire on the sling and stinger teams first, and even the wood and hammered steel of their shields was no protection. They were devastated, collapsed torn and bloody atop their engines of war.

Again the Mountain Spears began to reload. Five hundred men, each with three shots to their flamework weapons, and they had reloaded how many times now? Four? Leesha had to grip the windowsill for balance as she sloshed up again.

'Time we got back to the palace, mistress,' Wonda said as a dozen Mountain Spears finally unbarred the door, marching past the flustered archers to take position at the windows.

Leesha nodded, hurrying for the door, but she was not quick enough, wincing with every blast of the flamework weapons.

Leesha was pale and worn by the time she returned to her chambers. She knew she should find Araine and report, but there seemed little point. The Krasians were broken, and the whole city would know it soon enough.

The horror of it all kept flashing in her memory. The Mountain Spears firing at the backs of fleeing Krasians. Levies brutally finishing off the wounded.

Bodies blown apart by her thunderstick.

Was she any better than Euchor? She had preached for years about why the Herb Gatherers kept the secrets of fire, but when truly pressed, she had not hesitated to kill with them. She was a Weed Gatherer. A better killer than healer.

Wonda kept her bow in hand, even as they passed through the halls of the women's wing. None challenged them. The two women were filthy and reeking of blood and smoke, but immediately recognizable to all.

Wonda opened the door, and all Leesha could see was the inner door to her bedchamber. She made for it directly.

But the moment Wonda closed the door she let out a yelp. Leesha turned to see her on the floor, somehow pinned helplessly by tiny Sikvah. The rooms around her had been ransacked.

Amanvah appeared in front of her. 'Where are they?!'

'Where are what?' Leesha demanded.

Kendall came out of Wonda's room. 'They ent hidden in there.'

'Ay!' Wonda yelled from where Sikvah held her prone.

'Sorry, Won.' Kendall shrugged.

'Where have you hidden my *hora* pouch?' Amanvah snapped, drawing Leesha's eyes back to her. She did not wait for an answer, hands digging at the pockets of Leesha's apron.

'Take your hands off me!' Leesha tried to shove the woman away, but Amanvah diverted the attack easily, glancing up only long enough to punch a knuckle into Leesha's shoulder. The limb went numb a moment, then filled with tingling. It would recover shortly, but for now it hung limp, useless.

'Ah!' Amanvah held up her *hora* pouch and turned from Leesha as if she were no further matter. 'Kendall! Sikvah!'

Sikvah let Wonda go, and the women followed obediently as Amanvah headed for Leesha's bedchamber. It was only then

Leesha realized the young *dama'ting*'s pristine white robe was soaked with blood.

Wonda was up in an instant, a long knife in her hand. Leesha raised an arm to forestall her. 'Amanvah, what's happened?'

Amanvah looked back. 'Come and bear witness, daughter of Erny. This concerns you, too.'

Leesha and Wonda exchanged a worried look, but followed cautiously after.

Sikvah had overthrown the bed, clearing the floor and putting the mattresses over the thickly curtained windows. Leesha slipped her warded spectacles back on as the door was closed, leaving them in utter darkness.

Amanvah knelt in the centre of the room, bathed in the red glow of her dice. She was covered in blood, but none of it seemed to be her own. She gripped a bloody wad of her robe and squeezed, hand coming away soaked red. She slipped the *alagai hora* into that hand and began to roll them in her palm, coating them.

'Whose blood is that?' Leesha asked, dread growing in the pit of her stomach. Her baby roiled as if it meant to kick itself free.

'Everam, Creator of Heaven and Ala, Giver of Light and Life, your blessed son, Rojer son of Jessum of the Inns of Riverbridge, son-in-law to Shar'Dama Ka and my honoured husband, has been murdered.'

Leesha's throat constricted at the words, and she thought she might choke. Rojer? Dead? Impossible.

Her thoughts were cut off as Amanvah continued. 'Where must Sikvah lie in wait for the one responsible, that our vengeance be swift in bringing him to your infinite justice?'

She cast, and there was a flash of magic as the dice were twisted to fate's pattern. Leesha did not believe the messages were Heaven-sent, but she could not deny the *alagai hora* had very real power.

Amanvah studied the symbols a moment, then looked to Sikvah. 'The lavatory in the southeast corridor, fourth floor.'

Sikvah nodded and vanished. Even in wardsight her aura changed, becoming a blank veil of energy, blending like a Cloak of Unsight with her surroundings. There was the barest blur as she slipped from the door, somehow not letting light into the room in the process.

'She's going to kill someone?!' Leesha demanded, grabbing Amanvah's wrist as she gathered up her dice for another throw.

Amanvah gripped the dice in her fist and rotated her wrist, reversing the grip and bending Leesha's wrist back so far Leesha feared it would break. The pain was intense, making it difficult to think.

'Do not touch me again,' Amanvah said, releasing her with a shove back. Wonda moved forward, but a glare from Amanvah checked her.

'Yes,' Amanvah went on. 'Sikvah is doing what I should have ordered her to do months ago. Destroy the enemies of the son of Jessum. It is my failure, and now honoured Coliv and blessed Rojer are on the lonely path.'

'Amanvah,' Leesha said, 'if someone killed Rojer, we can tell . . .'

Amanvah hissed, cutting her off. 'I am through waiting for corrupt *chin* justice while our enemies strike. I need neither assistance nor permission to avenge my husband.'

'And suffer the same fate?' Leesha asked. 'I cannot help you if you have this man murdered.'

Amanvah gave her a withering look. 'You can, and you will.' She pointed to Leesha's belly. 'Your child has cousins growing even now in my and Sikvah's wombs. Children of the son of Jessum, tied to yours with blood. Will you trust them to your *chin* justice?'

Leesha stared at her, knowing she was beaten, but hating to admit it. 'Corespawn you, no.'

Leesha hadn't needed to fake her weeping at the sight of Rojer brought down from the tower. She'd thought herself drained of tears forever after the massacre in the courtyard, but seeing her friend, pale and bloody, brought new reserves. She had waited too long, thinking Rojer safe in the South Tower. Amanvah was right. She should have pressed harder.

'Rojer dead in the tower,' Araine said later at tea. 'Janson found sliced open on the commode.'

'Both within hours of each other,' Lorain noted, 'right under our noses.'

'Let us not forget a dozen palace guards,' Leesha noted. 'One of whom murdered my friend in his cell after you agreed to his release. Men who reported to Janson for orders and pay. Why were a dozen armed guards crammed into Rojer's cell, do you think?'

'I'm sure I don't know,' Araine said. 'What I do know is that they are dead. Palace guards, Leesha. *My* guards. Dead, while Amanvah is missing.'

'Perhaps her brother sent men to rescue her while we were distracted at the wall,' Leesha said, 'and they took the opportunity to dispose of a dangerous minister in the process.'

'Or perhaps the witch managed to smuggle in some demon bones,' Lorain said.

Leesha nodded. 'Perhaps. Or perhaps there are other explanations still. Regardless, it seems the matter is resolved, and I would as soon leave it behind us.'

'How can you say that?' Araine demanded. 'You wish no justice for your fiddler? Don't you care?'

'That *fiddler* has saved more lives than the Mountain Spears have taken,' Leesha snapped. 'He was my best friend in all the world, and my heart is broken that he is gone.'

She leaned in, eyes hard. 'But I have watched this cycle long enough. Two years ago Jasin Goldentone killed Rojer's master and put Rojer in my hospit. Then Jasin tries to finish the job, and Rojer is imprisoned for defending himself. Now Rojer is dead, likely at Janson's command, and Janson is dead in return. How many deaths does it require to end this?' She shook her head. 'Nothing can bring Rojer back to me, and so I want nothing more than to take him back to the Hollow and lay him to rest.'

'Perhaps you have the luxury of letting things go,' Lorain said, 'a week's ride to the south. But the murder happened in the palace. The killer must be found, and Rojer's body is evidence.'

Leesha visibly lost patience, slamming her teacup down on the table so hard it rattled and spilled. It was an act only, but she thought Rojer would have been proud of her performance. 'Unacceptable. My people and I have been held prisoner in Angiers too long. Baron Cutter will be in the city soon with thousands of Cutters. When he gets here, he's going to have questions about how his best friend was murdered in your care, and one way or another we *will* be leaving.'

'Is that a threat?' Lorain demanded.

'It is a fact,' Leesha said.

Lorain shook her head. 'Angiers is no longer weak . . .'

'Don't think your little trick impresses me, Princess,' Leesha said. 'I know more of the secrets of fire than you. You've saved Angiers, but what you've unleashed may be worse still. We do the demons' work for them when we should be banding together.'

Lorain snorted. 'You can't possibly believe all this Demon War Deliverer business.'

'I don't believe in the Deliverer,' Leesha said, 'but there can be no denying the demons are mounting against us. I felt one in my mind, and know what they are capable of. Your new weapons will be worthless against them.'

'We shall see,' Lorain said. 'But we stood against the demons for three hundred years. It was not us who attacked.'

Leesha nodded. 'All of us have been . . . compromised in this battle. There is blood enough for all our hands.' She looked at each of them in turn. 'I saved your son's life, Araine. And yours, Lorain. Both at the risk of my own, and the life within me. Pray, let us part in peace, as allies.'

The two duchesses looked at each other, already speaking

volumes by expression alone. Araine nodded to Leesha. 'Take Rojer and your new apprentices and go in peace.'

New apprentices. Jizell would be closing her hospit to take position as Royal Gatherer to the Duchess Mum, and sending the rest of her apprentices south with Leesha to train in the Hollow. Among these 'apprentices' was the pregnant Duchess Melny, and – unbeknownst to Araine – Amanvah and Sikvah.

The duchesses would have questions when those two re-appeared back in the Hollow, but those were questions best answered by Messenger and not face-to-face. Leesha had no intention of leaving the Hollow again with anything short of an army of Cutters to escort her.

31

Whistler

334 AR Winter

Abban had never seen *Sharum* flee before. Everam his witness, he could not remember a time they ever had. It was an ugly, disorganized thing, born of panic.

Thousands of *dal'Sharum*, the elite of Jayan's forces, had ridden into the city. Only a handful made it back out, screaming and bloody. Those who did abandoned the field entirely, racing their chargers back the way the army had come without anything approaching a plan. They left the rest of the forces – siege crews, *kha* and *chi'Sharum*, and Jayan's personal guard – standing confused in the churned mud of their passing. Others took their cue, abandoning their posts and following.

'Everam's beard,' Abban breathed as the enormity of the defeat began to dawn on him.

He turned to Earless. 'Fetch my trunk.' As the mute *kha'Sharum* rushed from the tent, Abban turned to his other bodyguard, his son Fahki. 'The maps and papers, boy, quickly. We must flee before—'

Just then the tent flaps burst open and Jayan stormed in, followed by Hasik and two *kai'Sharum* Spears of the Delivered.

'So much for your bold plan, *khaffit*!' Jayan barked.

'*My* plan?' Abban asked. 'I merely agreed with the wisdom

698

of the Sharum Ka. It was the *dama'ting* who seemed to promise victory.'

'The *chi'Sharum* cowards are surrendering,' Hasik said, peeking through the tent opening. He stepped outside, and shouting and chaos filled the tent until the heavy flap fell back in place.

'Better than turning their spears on us,' Abban said. 'Without spoils or *dal'Sharum* whips to propel them, there is nothing for them to gain in sharing our defeat.'

'I will kill that lying witch when we return to Everam's Reservoir,' Jayan said.

'She did not lie, precisely,' Abban noted, still gathering papers and stuffing them into a satchel Fahki held. 'She promised you would shatter the gates and enter the city, and indeed you did.'

'Leaving out that my men would be slaughtered moments later,' Jayan growled.

'I have never cared for *dama'ting* prophecies,' Abban said. 'They never tell all.'

'Don't they?' Hasik asked, entering the tent once more.

Jayan turned to him. 'What's that?'

'The *dama'ting* prophecies are not meant to tell us what we wish to hear,' Hasik said. 'They are to tell us Everam's will. I did not truly believe it before today.'

'Everam's balls, Whistler!' Jayan shouted. 'What are you babbling about?!'

'I asked Dama'ting Asavi if I would ever have my revenge on Abban the fat *khaffit*,' Hasik said. 'She told me there would come a day of smoke and ruin, when the Sharum Ka would lose Everam's favour.' He slipped a curved blade from his sleeve. 'And on that day, none could stand against my wrath.'

'What are you doing?!' Jayan gave a shrill whistle. 'Whistler! Heel!'

The two *kai'Sharum* were fast, moving instantly to stand side by side in front of Jayan, weapons at the ready.

Hasik charged in fearlessly, his face stone as he swatted away a spear thrust and kicked hard against the *kai'Sharum*'s shield, knocking him across the floor to crash into Abban's table, landing in a flurry of papers.

Hasik stepped into the space before the other *kai* could adjust position. He pivoted, thrusting his curved knife into the armpit of the warrior's shield arm where there was a small seam in the impenetrable glass armour all the Spears of the Deliverer wore.

Jayan launched his own attack before Hasik could withdraw the knife, a spear thrust for his unarmoured throat. Hasik saw the move, ducking away from the thrust. It skittered off the helm under his turban instead, taking part of his ear with it.

Hasik laughed, grabbing the spear shaft just under the head and pulling it aside while he punched out hard, fist wrapped around the heavy knife handle. Jayan's nose crumpled, and he fell back, senseless.

'Flee, Father!' Fahki cried, shoving the satchel into his hands and propelling Abban towards the exit. His intent was good, but the boy was still an idiot, continuing to push even as Abban's crippled leg buckled. He fell to the floor, Fahki landing on top of him.

The surviving Spear of the Deliverer was back on his feet amidst a cloud of swirling reports. He had lost his spear, but drew a knife to match Hasik's and moved in, shield leading.

The shield should have been a telling advantage in a knife fight, but Hasik feinted a thrust, then dropped his own knife, spreading his arms and locking his hands around the shield. He twisted, lifting with savage strength. The *kai* was thrown bodily over Hasik, and Abban heard the snap of his arm at the apex of his flight.

He landed on his back, and Hasik effortlessly broke his other wrist, taking the *kai*'s knife to replace his. With the man prone he gripped his breastplate and yanked, snapping the fastenings and baring his chest for a knife thrust.

Abban's leg screamed at him, but he ignored it, pulling hard on both Fahki and his crutch to get to his feet.

Jayan groaned, pushing himself onto one arm. 'Whistle, what . . .?'

Hasik leapt upon him, thrusting his knife into Jayan's mouth. His face was a demon's snarl as he pushed the curving blade up into the brain of the Deliverer's first son.

'My name!' Hasik pulled the blade free and thrust it in again. This time it slid easily to the hilt. 'Is not!' He yanked the blade out and stabbed a third time. 'Whistler!'

It was then that Earless returned. The mute stood at the entrance to the tent holding Abban's treasure trunk.

Abban said nothing, but raised his hand in the sign for kill, thumb pointed at Hasik.

Silently as a diving wind demon, Earless took three running steps forward. Filled with gold, the trunk weighed over two hundred pounds, but Earless easily raised it over his head and threw. It struck Hasik in the back, knocking him from Jayan's lifeless body.

Protected by his own glass armour, Hasik was not seriously injured, but he stumbled to his feet, off balance as Earless closed the distance between them, grappling Hasik and bearing him down.

'Quickly, boy!' Abban shouted, limping towards the exit. 'Come!'

The combatants rolled across the tent floor. Earless, heavier and in control, came out on top, pinning Hasik's knife hand with a knee. He held Hasik's other arm down at the wrist, pummelling him about the face with his free hand. They were powerful, terrible blows, but Abban had watched Hasik fight in the food lines since they were boys in *sharaj* and knew it would not end there.

One of the punches knocked Hasik's head to the side, and he bit hard into the wrist of the hand Earless used to hold him prone. The giant could not speak, but his toneless roar of pain was all the more terrible for it, an animal cry bereft of humanity.

The moment the grip weakened, Hasik had his hand free, cutting off the mute's cry with a punch to the throat. He surged, reversing the pin, and saw Abban drawing near the tent flap.

'Not this time, *khaffit*!' Hasik cried, throwing the knife.

Abban threw his arms up, but the blade was not aimed for

his head or chest. It sank into the thigh of his good leg, and Abban fell again with a scream.

'Father!' Fahki cried, rushing to him.

'Flee now,' Abban told him. 'Find warriors and tell them Hasik has killed the Sharum Ka.'

'I won't leave you,' Fahki said, squatting to try and haul Abban to his feet. Hot blood ran down his leg but Abban gritted his teeth and planted his foot, leaning heavily on his camel crutch. He cried for help, but in the chaos outside, no one heard him through the heavy canvas walls.

Hasik and Earless were on their feet now, trading blows meant to cripple and kill. Earless was holding his own – barely. Both men's faces were bloodied and beginning to swell. One of Earless' eyes was filling with blood, and Hasik's nose was flat against his cheek, broken.

But he was smiling. Their army was destroyed, Jayan dead, and Hasik fighting for his life, but the brutal eunuch was smiling like Abban had never seen.

Abban tried to take a step, but even with Fahki to support him, the pain was unbearable.

Hasik managed to get inside Earless' guard, catching him by the ears. He pulled hard as he drove the crown of his helmet into Earless' face. His helmet spike tore a jagged hole in the mute's forehead.

The giant shoved Hasik back hard, then gave a cry, clutching at his head.

'Looking for this?' Hasik laughed, holding up the ear he had torn free. 'Now you truly *are* earless!'

The giant came back in, angry for the first time. His punches would have knocked out a camel, but Hasik batted them aside easily, getting in close and heel-kicking him in the stomach. Earless was knocked back into the central pole of the tent, cracking it in half and bringing the canvas roof down.

Abban gritted his teeth and moved for the exit with all his strength. One step. Two. But it was not enough as Hasik appeared from the tangle of canvas.

'Behind me,' Abban said, gripping Fahki's arm and pulling him out of Hasik's path. 'It's me he wants.'

'I won't let him—' Fahki began, moving to stand before his father.

'Don't be an idiot,' Abban cut him off. 'You are no match for him.'

'You should listen to your father.' Hasik was still smiling. 'Run and leave your father to *inevera*.' His eyes flicked to Fahki's spear. 'Or I will fuck you with your own spear.'

'As Shar'Dama Ka did to you?' Abban asked.

The smile fell from Hasik's face, and Abban thrust his camel crutch out, pressing the release that sprang a six-inch electrum from its tip. The blade was poisoned with tunnel asp venom, the deadliest poison known.

But Hasik moved faster than he thought possible, grabbing the camel foot at the base of the crutch and turning the blade aside. He yanked it from Abban's hands, sending the *khaffit* sprawling, and broke the crutch over his knee.

Fahki gave a cry and charged, thrusting with his spear. His spearwork was fine, but he was only a boy, and Hasik one of the deadliest killers alive. He knocked the tip aside with the bladed half of the crutch, stomping hard on the side of Fahki's knee. The boy screamed and dropped to one knee, using his spear for support.

Hasik kicked the spear from under him, guiding Fahki's fall with kicks and whips of the crutch shaft to put the boy on his back.

Then Hasik thrust the electrum blade of the crutch up Fahki's arse. The poison worked fast. Fahki began to convulse wildly, his mouth white with foam.

'You took my cock, but I still fuck in my way,' Hasik said to Abban as he stalked in. He was smiling again.

There was a rustle of canvas and a toneless cry as Earless freed himself from the tangle and tackled Hasik about the legs.

It was a momentary advantage only. Hasik had both arms free, and even as they fell he was driving extended knuckles into the mute's eyes and neck. He landed heavier blows as they hit the floor, and at last the mute lay still.

'There will be no coming back from this,' Abban warned as Hasik rose for the final time. 'The Damajah will find you. Your life is over.'

Hasik laughed. 'Life? What life? I have nothing, *khaffit*. You have seen to that. Nothing but daily humiliation.'

He smiled. 'Humiliation, and my revenge.'

'Then kill me, and have done,' Abban said.

Hasik laughed, drawing back a fist. 'Kill you? Oh, *khaffit*. I'm not going to kill you.'

32

The Night of *Hora*
334 AR Winter

'The attack is done,' Melan told the clerics. 'It was a slaughter.'
Ashia watched as the men wrung their hands and shifted their feet. News had come a day ago that Jayan had taken the bulk of his forces north to attack Angiers, greatly exceeding his authority as Sharum Ka. The clerics had been begging *dama'ting* for foretellings ever since. If Jayan succeeded – as he likely would – he would almost certainly move for the Skull Throne.

The Damajah had grown tired of their dramatics, retreating to her own chambers to divine in private, leaving Melan to divine in her stead.

The black-veiled *dama'ting* added dramatics of her own, casting the glowing dice from the twisted ruin of her right hand. It was whispered in the Dama'ting Palace that she had been forced to hold her first, imperfect set of dice up to the sun, burning her down to the bone. Melan had grown the nails long, and with the rough melted scars the hand looked like nothing so much as an *alagai* talon.

The *dama'ting*'s dice had been drained throughout the morning by the incessant questions of the clerics, with no news to show. They had been forced to wait for sunset to try again.

Ashia was the only other woman in the room, but none

dared protest her presence. Her husband wanted her presence more and more, of late. Asome was under tremendous strain, and had come to rely on her support in recent days. He was *push'ting* still, but since they had lain as man and wife, Ashia dared hope they might find a way to keep their union on Ala without making life Nie's abyss.

'He did it?' Ashan had an edge to his voice. 'Jayan has taken Fort Angiers?' It was a closed court, with only the highest-ranking clerics in attendance. Ashan sat the Skull Throne, with the *Damaji* and the *dama* sons of the Deliverer at the base of the dais, lining Melan on two sides as she knelt upon her casting cloth.

'It is no surprise,' Damaji Ichach sneered. 'The *chin* are weak.'

Melan leaned in closer, tilting her head as she continued to study the pattern. 'No. The *dal'Sharum* were broken. They are in full retreat. The Deliverer's firstborn is dead.'

There was a stunned silence. To a one, the *Damaji* had not wanted impulsive young Jayan to take another great victory so soon. But the alternative was too horrible to bear. The *dal'Sharum* broken? The Deliverer's son slain? By *chin*?

Victory after victory under Shar'Dama Ka had led their people to a national pride that for the first time in centuries began to transcend tribe. A sense they were all Everam's chosen people, Evejans, and it was *inevera* the *chin* should be yoked and bent to Evejan law.

It was Sharak Sun, the Daylight War that would unite all humanity for Sharak Ka.

Defeat was unthinkable.

'Are you certain?' Asome asked. Melan nodded.

'You are dismissed,' Asome said, and the woman nodded, scooping up her dice back into her *hora* pouch and beginning to fold her casting cloth.

'Stay,' Ashan commanded. 'I have further questions.'

Melan finished folding her cloth and rolled back onto her feet. 'Apologies, Andrah, but the Damajah has commanded I attend her immediately with any news.' She turned to go.

Ashan opened his mouth at the disrespect, but Asome cut in before he could speak, stepping right in front of the steps to the throne. 'Let Melan see to my mother, Uncle. There is much we must discuss that does not concern the *dama'ting*.'

Ashan looked at him curiously, and Asome bowed. 'Apologies, honoured Andrah, but your failed leadership has brought us to this point. Jayan would not have dared such a foolish attack if my father sat the throne. This is a clear sign of Everam's displeasure at your rule.'

He turned to sweep the room with his gaze, meeting the eyes of the other men. 'It is time to accept that my father will not return. With my brother dead, it is *inevera* that I sit the Skull Throne in his place.' He looked at Ashan. 'It is your right to attempt to deny me. Know that if you do, there will be no dishonour in your death.'

Ashan scowled. 'That is only if you can kill me, boy. But first, you must look to the *Damaji* to clear your path.'

'Indeed.' Asome nodded, turning his back to Ashan as he strode down the aisle until he had passed the other men. 'Damaji! Stand forth!'

As one, his *dama* brothers all took a stride into the aisle, bowing in unison as they turned to face their respective *Damaji*. 'Apologies, honoured Damaji,' they said as one, 'but I must challenge you for leadership of the tribe. It is your right to attempt to deny me. Know that if you do, there will be no dishonour in your death.'

'Outrageous!' Ichach shouted. 'Guards!'

Asome smiled. 'No guards can hear you, Damaji. Melan has sealed the room in wards of silence, and barred the doors.'

Ashia and Asukaji were an island of peace amidst the sudden tension as men took battle stances. She froze, unsure what to do. Asome had clearly planned this, but she had not been privy to it.

Suddenly *Let Melan see to my mother* took on an ominous tone. She turned a questioning glance at Asukaji just as her brother threw the garrotte around her throat. She was fast, but not fast enough. He crossed his fists, pulling tight as he danced behind her.

Ashia choked, her head whipped to the side, but she went with Asukaji's pull and bent forward, setting one foot firmly and snapping the other up behind her to scorpion-kick him in the back of the head.

Her brother held on, but Ashia managed to get a finger under the chain around her throat, pulling in an obstructed breath.

Choking. In the end, it was always choking.

She continued to kick and elbow Asukaji with her free arm, but he had the hold, accepting the flailing blows and tightening his grip as their feet danced the floor, seeking to gain leverage even as each denied it to the other.

Ashia caught her feet for a moment, but when she lifted one leg for a kick, Asukaji was ready, hooking her other leg and taking her down to the marble floor.

'Did you really begin to think you were his *jiwah*?' Asukaji demanded. 'That you mean a thing to him? You spend one night under him and think you can supplant me? Asome is mine, sister. Now and forever.'

Indeed, Asome glanced at them, his aura flat and cold. Asukaji might as well have been squashing a bug.

Ashia pulled her finger against the chain until it bled, but could not manage to work in another. She felt her face swelling, and knew it was only a matter of time.

She watched as the *shar'dama* executed their *Damaji*. It could not be called anything else. The *Damaji* were all *sharusahk* masters, but not a one of them was under sixty years old, with several much older. Many had gotten fat, as well. Asome's half brothers were all young and strong, close to the prime of their lives.

But it was more than that. All of them had scar-warded their hands by now, and each clenched a fist that glowed powerfully with *hora* magic. The power absorbed into the scars, giving them inhuman strength and speed, and stealing any honour from their victories as one *Damaji* after another fell to their brutal attacks.

In seconds all were dead save ancient Aleverak, who danced back and forth with Maji. The ancient *Damaji*, too, had taken *alagai* in the night. He was still thin and withered, but stronger than he had been in decades. Thus far neither had landed a telling blow, hold, or throw.

But even as her vision began to blur, Ashia could see Aleverak was only taking the boy's measure, his aura calm as he explored Maji's defences and probed for weaknesses.

She saw it in his bearing when he locked on to his target. The *Damaji* could not see in Everam's light, but he, too, had noticed Maji's increased abilities, and the fist he kept clenched tight as he fought.

Aleverak could not see the lines of power that kept Maji's fist clenched, but he shattered them as easily as Enkido, kicking a toe into the young *dama*'s wrist. His hand opened reflexively, and though he recovered quickly, balling his fist again, the damage was done.

Caught up in the ongoing conflict, no one, not even Asome, took note of the shard of demon bone that fell from Maji's grasp, bouncing across the floor.

But all could see the shift in the battle. Aleverak's expression remained neutral, but Maji's grew fearful as the *Damaji* began to press more fiercely. He took a step back.

Savas stepped forward to aid Maji, but Asome held a hand to stay him. 'This test is for him alone, brother.' Savas did not look pleased, but he bowed and stepped back.

A moment later, Maji was prone on the ground with Aleverak's hand around his throat.

Ashia chose that moment to renew her struggle, a last attempt before she lost consciousness. Asukaji, distracted by the battle, returned his attention to her, tightening his grip further, but it did not matter. Her grasping fingers closed around the bit of demon bone. She could feel the magic tingling against the wards painted on her nails, filling her with new strength.

'Your father, Shar'Dama Ka, swore me an oath, boy,' Aleverak said. 'That he would never challenge my rule of the Majah, and that Maji could fight my son for leadership on my natural death.'

Asome bowed. 'I know this, honoured Damaji. But I am not my father. His oaths are not mine.'

'It is said in the Evejah that oaths spoken by fathers are binding to their sons,' Aleverak said. 'And oaths spoken from the Skull Throne bind us all. Had you kept that pact, I would not have stood against you this night.'

He sneered. 'Instead you break oaths and attack in the night like an honourless *chin*. And so your victory will not be complete.' He glanced down to Maji. 'You have no other Majah to supplant me.' With that, he snapped Maji's neck.

The new *Damaji* all stepped back, clearing the floor for Asome and Aleverak. The ancient *Damaji* took position before the steps to the Skull Throne, blocking Asome's path.

Ashan stood ready atop the steps. Tradition demanded he wait until the path between them was clear, but her father had a warrior's heart. He was eager for the fight.

'You honour our people this night, Damaji,' Ashan said. 'Everam will open the gates of Heaven to you Himself.'

'We're not dead, yet,' Aleverak said as Asome came at him.

Ashia could see no glow of *hora* about her husband. He might have allowed his brothers to win dishonourably, but he fought as tradition dictated.

He struck hard and fast. Aleverak slipped to the side, but Asome was ready for the move, twisting to drive an elbow into Aleverak's armpit. He caught the limb as it lost strength, pulling the old man off balance. He grabbed the *Damaji*'s belt, lifting him clear off the ground, then planted his knee and broke Aleverak's spine across it.

Asome let the *Damaji* collapse, limp and forgotten, as he rose to his feet, eyes on Ashan.

Ashia had managed to slowly work another finger into the chain. It was not yet leverage enough to break free, but she wheezed in a breath, and it doubled her power.

Asukaji tightened his grip. 'Everam's beard, do me the honour of dying before my hair greys, sister.'

Ashia had a third finger in place now, but she made choked sounds and fell limp while she gathered her strength.

Ashan strode down the steps from the throne, and Asome gave ground before him, that they might stand as equals on the floor. His brothers cleared the dead from the path between them.

'Does your mother know your betrayal, boy?' Ashan asked. 'You, whom I raised as my own son?'

'My mother knows nothing,' Asome said. '*She shall ever be blind to her sons*, the dice told Melan about my mother, and it has proven true time and again.'

'She will not let you keep the throne,' Ashan said.

'She will give up hers as well,' Asome said. 'My grandmother is a more fitting Damajah. Her beatification will be my first decree as Shar'Dama Ka.'

'First you must reach the steps,' Ashan said.

As the *Shar'Damaji* looked on impassively, Asome and Ashan battled for the Skull Throne.

Aleverak lasted longer. Asome parried his uncle's first three blows, setting Ashan up for an aggressive kick inside his guard. He deflected the blow, but could not prevent Asome leaping to hook his leg around Ashan's neck. His own weight did the rest.

Ashia's father was a *sharusahk* grand master before his fortieth year, but Asome broke him like a *nie'Sharum*. The snap of his neck echoed in the great hall.

Asome looked to his brothers. They hurried to kneel in proper order along the path to the throne, foreheads pressed to the floor as Asome began his ascent.

It was then, with all eyes on her husband, that Ashia struck, throwing her head back as she yanked hard on the garrotte chain. She felt Asukaji's nose crumple, and his grip loosened, allowing her to slip the chain.

All eyes turned to them in surprise, but Ashia did not hesitate, delivering a precise strike to the nape of her brother's neck, shattering bone and severing his spinal cord.

'Asukaji!' Asome roared, his cold aura at last turning hot.

But he did not stop his ascent, taking the remaining steps in two great bounds to reach the dais. Ashia burst into a run for the rear exit that would take her to the royal quarters.

Asome leapt onto the throne, eyes turning to glare hate at her as he roared, 'Kill her!'

Ashia threw herself against the exit to the Damajah's wing of the palace, but as Asome warned, Melan had sealed all the doors with *hora* magic. She might as well have thrown her shoulder against the city walls.

She rebounded in a new direction, darting for one of the great pillars as the sons of the Deliverer turned their fury her way.

The moment their line of sight was blocked, she rolled to a second pillar, springing high and climbing quickly. By the time her cousins rounded the pillars and saw she was gone, she had already slipped into one of the alcoves used to guard the Damajah.

Everam's spear sisters had their own exits from the throne room, and the *dama'ting* had not barred these.

The wards of silence around the court had kept the outside guards in ignorance. They stood calmly at their posts, easily avoided until she got to the open hall. Any moment, Asome would break the seals and put the entire palace on alert, but for now the way was clear. Her duty was to protect the Damajah, who might even now be facing a coup of her own.

'Everam forgive me,' Ashia whispered, running in the opposite direction.

'No, I most certainly will *not* give him to you!' Kajivah held her infant great-grandson protectively as Ashia reached for him.

'It isn't safe for either of you,' Ashia said. 'Asome is killing the *Damaji* in the throne room. I will take you into the Damajah's protection until the unrest has passed.'

Kajivah took another step back, but Ashia caught her grandmother's thumb and gave a half turn, catching Kaji smoothly as he fell from her grasp.

'How dare you lay hands upon me, you . . .!'

Ashia nestled her son into her breast, binding him to her in a sling of silk. Half awake, the boy began sucking at her robe, seeking a nipple. 'He is my son, Tikka, not yours. If you would keep him safe, we must go. Now.'

'*Your* son?!' Kajivah demanded. 'Where is your nipple when he hungers? Where are you when he cries? When he soils his bido? Off fighting *alagai*. And then I find you covered in demon blood, trying to crush the life from him . . .'

Ashia felt her face heat. 'It wasn't like that. That was an accident.'

Kajivah lifted her veil and spat at Ashia's feet. 'The accident was being cursed with a deviant granddaughter who brings shame to our family.'

It was so ludicrous Ashia had to laugh. 'Are you that foolish, Tikka? Can you truly not see my "deviance" is your doing? You pushed me and my sisters into the Dama'ting Palace without a thought of what it meant. I am what you have made of me, and nothing more.'

'And now you expect me to seek the Damajah's protection?' Kajivah asked. 'The very woman who twisted you is to protect me from my own grandson?'

Ashia pulled open her veil, showing the angry red line across her throat. 'My own brother tried to kill me this night, Tikka. No one is safe.'

'Asukaji?' Kajivah asked in shock. 'What did you do to him?' She came at Ashia in a rush, beating with her fists. 'Witch! What did you do to Asukaji?!'

Ashia turned away to protect Kaji, diverting the blows easily. She caught the woman's arm and put her thumb on a pain convergence, guiding her for the door. Every time Kajivah made to go any direction save the one Ashia wished, she sent a jolt of agony through the old woman, quickly overcoming resistance.

They made it to the hall before there was a shout, half a dozen *Sharum* rushing in on either side to block their path.

'Thank Everam we have found you safe, Holy Mother,' the *kai'Sharum* leading them said. 'Your grandson is eager for news of your safety.' He turned, levelling his spear at Ashia. 'Give the child to the Holy Mother and step back. Now.'

Ashia reached a hand behind her, wrapping it around the shaft of one of the short stabbing spears she wore crossed at her back. 'My son belongs with me.'

The *kai'Sharum* smiled. 'And so he will be. The Shar'Dama Ka is most eager for his *Jiwah Ka*'s safe return as well.'

'So he may kill me himself?' Ashia asked.

'You have little choice, Princess,' the *kai* said. 'Will you fight instead, using your own son as a shield?'

It was Ashia's turn to smile. 'Do not fear for my son, *Sharum*. Fear instead for any fool enough to point a spear his way.'

'Enough.' Kajivah moved in, reaching for Kaji. 'It's over, Ashia.'

Ashia let out a breath, slumping as she took her hand from the haft of her spear. She turned to her grandmother, fumbling at the knot of the sling that bound her son to her breast.

But when Kajivah was in close, their bodies momentarily blocked the sight of the surrounding warriors. Ashia struck the old woman with a quick, precise blow, making a show of catching her as she collapsed.

'Tikka!' Ashia threw a panicked look at the warriors. 'Help her! The Holy Mother needs help!'

The men froze, forgetting the weapons in their hands as they leaned in to the scene, unsure of what to do. The thought of laying hands upon the Holy Mother no doubt frightened them more than facing a horde of *alagai*.

Ashia struck in the confusion, her hand flicking sharp warded glass at the warriors closest to her.

The men were armoured, but Ashia could clip a fly's wings with her throwing glass. One warrior's head was tilted just enough for her to slip a glass into his jugular. *Sharum* did not have nose guards on their helmets, so another caught a glass between the eyes. There was a tiny crack as it broke through the thin bone and drove up into his brain.

The confusion only mounted as the dying warriors stumbled back into their fellows. One *Sharum* was quicker than the others to catch on, but stepping forward he exposed the gap in the groin of his armour, allowing her to sever the knot of muscle connecting thigh to hip. As the warrior's leg collapsed, he left her a clear path to the *kai'Sharum*.

Kaji woke and let out an irritated cry as Ashia put one of her stabbing spears into the *kai*'s throat. She pulled the other spear from its harness as she kicked the *kai* into the path of another warrior. A quick stab into the ensuing chaos, and the warrior's spear arm fell lifeless to his side as she leapt past.

She was through the press then, the way clear before her. A quick sprint and she could climb into one of the secret ways . . .

'Bura! Kamen! Take the Holy Mother to Shar'Dama Ka!' a voice boomed. 'The rest of you, after her!'

Ashia looked back. A red-veiled drillmaster had taken command of the men, leading the charge himself as two warriors laid down their spears and stripped their cloaks to make a stretcher.

Already she had killed three men, and crippled two more. Honourable warriors following their leader's commands. *Sharum* now lost to Sharak Ka.

But she could not let the men take Kajivah to Asome, where he might use her to supplant the Damajah. Nor could she allow the warriors to go back to her husband with word that Inevera had custody of their son.

She looked down, and Kaji met her eyes. She knew then Kajivah had been right. She had let duty separate her from her child, and almost lost him as a result.

'Be brave, Kaji,' she whispered. 'Though we walk the edge of the abyss together, I will never leave you again.'

Each of her spears was a two-foot shaft tipped with a foot of razor-sharp warded glass. Ashia popped caps from the ends and joined them with a twist as Kaji gave a yawn and closed his eyes.

Even the drillmaster pulled up as she charged, unsure how to attack without harming the child. She was under his guard before he knew it, and past before he realized he was dead.

She fell into her breath, watching in Everam's light the lines of power running through the four remaining warriors as she picked her targets. A stomp broke the ankle of the first, giving her plenty of time to parry a thrust from the second. Ashia spun her spear in two hands, slipping the second blade down the edge of the next man's shield, severing his spear hand. He fell away in horror, clearing the path to the next warrior. This one was ready, but Ashia stepped back, parrying another blow from the second warrior even as she lined up a killing blow for the first. The man had not found balance on his remaining ankle, and a simple shove opened a gap in his defences.

She expected the warrior with the severed hand to need longer to recover, but the man gave an inchoate cry and rushed her with his shield.

With nowhere to dodge, Ashia twisted, taking the blow on the armour-plated robe at her back. She kept her spear held out crosswise before her, creating a safe zone around Kaji as she was driven into the other warrior.

But while the men took a moment to regain their balance, Ashia's quick feet never missed a step. A shove and a trip put the warriors on their backs. The lines of the *Sharum* with the severed hand were dimming fast as his life bled away. She turned to the other, snuffing out his aura with a quick thrust before turning to face the last man standing in her path.

Bura and Kamen had Kajivah's stretcher in hand by then, already rounding the far corner followed closely by the warrior whose arm she had disabled initially. Ashia snatched a discarded spear and threw, taking the fleeing man in the back.

The last warrior had his shield up, knees bent and ready to spring. His spear was lowered at her chest, pointed at Kaji.

But the tip shook.

'Find your courage and come at me, warrior,' Ashia said. 'Die with honour in your duty, and Everam will welcome you at the end of the lonely path.'

The *dal'Sharum* took a breath, then gave a great cry and leapt at her, spear leading in a fine thrust.

Ashia killed him quickly, with honour.

'Witch!' Ashia saw as he fell away that the warrior with the crippled leg, forgotten on the floor, had raised himself on his good leg.

The spear had already left his hand, bound for her heart. The armour plates in her robes could have easily deflected such a blow, but Kaji, strapped above them, could not.

With no time to dodge, Ashia dropped her weapon and wrapped Kaji in her arms, twisting to take the blow on her side. The plates there were smaller, with gaps to allow freedom of movement. The point deflected from one, then sank into the gap in between.

Ashia was knocked back a step. For a moment she thought the blow nothing, but the weight of the spear pulled at her when she moved, embedded deep in her side.

She did not know the extent of the damage, but it was as irrelevant as the pain. She pulled the blade from her body and turned it on the thrower, then snatched up her own spear and sprinted after Bura and Kamen.

It was easy enough to get ahead of the men. The palace was riddled with paths known only to the *Sharum'ting*, allowing her to pass through walls while the men were forced to take a longer route, slowed by their holy charge.

Ashia was braced above an archway, waiting for them to pass. Kaji fidgeted, and her hastily bound wound ached, soaking her robe, but she was deep in her breath, and these things did not touch her.

Heralded by their frantic gasping, the warriors approached. She let Bura run past the arch, falling silently upon Kamen.

Kaji gave a laugh as they dropped, and the unfortunate warrior looked up just in time to see death coming. When Kamen dropped his end of the stretcher, the sudden drag cost Bura his balance, and she had him.

'Tikka!' Kaji cried, seeing Kajivah. Ashia gritted her teeth as she lifted the woman's dead weight and slung her across her shoulders.

Down the hall she heard the shouts of more warriors, combing the palace for her.

—Your firstborn is dead.—

Inevera stared at the dice, sorting through the mixture of emotions that passed through her.

It was the duty of all *dama'ting* to produce a female heir, but she had put her own needs aside for her people, using the dice to bless Ahmann with two sons first, one for *sharaj* and the other for Sharik Hora. The boys had been born out of duty, but as they grew within her, Everam worked His subtlest magic, for in that miracle she had come to love the infants as they suckled her breasts.

As they grew, the boys vexed her in equal measure. She had thought her sons would take after Ahmann, but they were their own creatures. For what son of the Deliverer could be anything but a disappointment?

Jayan was *Sharum* to the core – brutal and wilfully ignorant. From cradle to the Maze, he had never wasted a moment on caution or personal safety, leaping without a glance below. As a leader, he was apt to solve problems with the spear rather than wisdom. He was clever in his way, and might have made a name for himself, but the only name anyone ever needed to hear was his father's. Too much decision had been thrust upon him before he was fully a man.

The dice had never been much use with her own children, but she had always known in her heart he would die young.

That fear trebled at word he was heading north.

—*Doom befall the armies of the Deliverer*—the dice had said—*if they should march north with enemies unconquered at their back*—

Confirmation of Jayan's death brought a wave of anguish, made worse by the guilty feeling of relief that the moment she'd dreaded for so long had finally come.

There would be time to fill tear bottles later. She envisioned the palm bending before the wind of her pain and focused her breath until she was ready to cast again.

—Three times will your power be challenged tonight.—

This gave her pause, and for a moment, she felt a touch of fear. Her eyes flicked to the single entrance to her casting chamber. Outside Micha and Jarvah waited with Damaji'ting Qeva, ready to defend her with their lives. Other *Sharum'ting* waited outside her chambers, as well as eunuch guards trained by Enkido himself.

If the news of Jayan's defeat reached the *Damaji*, there was no telling what they might do. None of them could be trusted, schemers all. They would not hesitate to act if it was in their interests.

She lifted the dice a third time. 'Almighty Everam, Giver of Life and Light, give your humble servant knowledge of what is to come. Who will challenge me this night?'

The dice flared and fell into a complex pattern as always, but the message was simple.

—Wait.—

There was a cry outside the chamber.

Melan looked up as Inevera entered the room. She had removed her white headwrap, holding her mother's black one in hand.

Qeva lay at her feet, aura extinguished in death. Across the chamber by the doors lay Micha and Jarvah. Their auras were flat and dim, and they lay unmoving.

To Inevera's shock, Melan laughed. It was so unexpected, she hesitated.

'Come, Damajah!' Melan cried. 'Can you not see the irony? Is this not precisely how we found you with my grandmother all those years ago?'

It was true enough. Inevera had not wanted to assume leadership of the Kaji Dama'ting prematurely, but when Kenevah had threatened her plans to put Ahmann on the Skull Throne, she had not hesitated to kill the old woman.

'Perhaps,' she allowed, 'but it was not matricide as well.'

'Of course not,' Melan sneered. 'The weaver's daughter could never harm her sainted mother. How is Manvah? Still in the bazaar? Perhaps the time has come to pay her a visit.'

Inevera had heard enough. She raised her *hora* wand, firing a blast of magic at Melan.

The instant she raised the wand, Melan's hand darted into her robe, holding a warded piece of rock demon armour, plated in gold. The magic bent around the warding, tearing apart the room and leaving Melan untouched.

She's ready for me, Inevera realized. 'How long have you planned this betrayal, Melan?'

Melan held up her burned, misshapen claw of a hand. 'Do you have to ask?' She snorted. 'Longer. Since your first bido weave, I have dreamed of this day.

'But Everam spoke to you. The dice named Ahmann Jardir Shar'Dama Ka and you his Damajah. What could I do, but obey?'

Melan pointed one of her talons at Inevera. 'But you failed to foretell Ahmann Jardir's defeat, and have not kept our people unified in his absence. Everam favours you no longer. The dice have spoken against you ever since the Northern whore supplanted you in the pillows. It is time for a new Shar'Dama Ka and a new Damajah.'

Inevera laughed. 'You don't have what it takes to satisfy my *push'ting* son.'

'No woman does,' Melan agreed, 'and I haven't the recognition our people need in any event.'

'Kajivah.' Inevera spat the name.

Melan clapped her misshapen hand. 'How delicious that you yourself handed me the weapon. Asome will have beatified her by now, and she will occupy your pillows by the throne . . . a few steps down. A figurehead and blunt instrument, but one we've learned to aim quite effectively.'

Inevera raised her *hora* wand. 'You won't be aiming anything, Melan. You walk the lonely path tonight.'

Something struck Inevera then, knocking her across the room. If she had not been strengthened by magic, the force would have left her broken and helpless. As it was, she was thrown like a doll and hit the floor with a jolt that sent pain lancing up her limbs and the wand clattering from her grasp. She looked in the direction the strike had come from, the room momentarily spinning.

But then the whirl resolved into Dama'ting Asavi, who was supposed to be hundreds of miles away.

Advising Jayan.

'You killed my son,' Inevera said.

'It was your own prophecy that spoke his doom.' Asavi put a hand to her breast. 'Since the wise Damajah chose not to reveal it to her son, who was I to speak it to him?'

He would not have listened, in any event, Inevera thought. But it did nothing to lessen the pain as the words cut into her, nor the anger blowing through her like a hurricane.

Melan and Asavi spread out to opposite sides of the room, keeping Inevera between them so it became difficult to see them both at once. Their auras were brightening, each having activated a *hora* stone to strengthen herself for the fight to come. Their jewellery and the items in their hands all shone with power.

Too much power for Inevera's comfort. Her eyes flicked to her *hora* wand, but Melan kicked it farther away.

Made from the limb of a demon prince, the weapon was more powerful than all Melan and Asavi's *hora* combined. So powerful that Inevera had come to rely on it overmuch, and had few other items of offensive magic on her person. She took comfort, at least, that it was useless to her enemies without hours to study how she had positioned the wards of activation.

But even disarmed Inevera was not defenceless, as Asavi learned when she raised a flame demon skull and sent a jet of fire at her. One of Inevera's rings tingled and the fire became a breeze as it passed over her.

Inevera wasted no time, darting right into the fire and kicking the skull from Asavi's hands. She followed through into a full spin, meaning to drive an elbow into the woman's throat, but Asavi was no novice to *sharusahk*. She slipped a hand under Inevera's elbow and pulled it along its natural circuit as she dropped her own weight, attempting a takedown with wilting flower, a *sharukin* that would shatter the line of power in her leg.

Inevera adapted quickly, turning her thigh to protect the convergence point. Asavi's fingers missed only by an inch, but it was enough, and her leg remained planted as she used Asavi's own momentum to drive her hard into the floor.

But before she could press the advantage, Melan threw a handful of wind demon teeth at her. The wards cut into the teeth activated, sending them flying with speed to make the air crack.

She threw a hand up, halfway between her face and chest. One of her bracelets was warded against wind demons, and a flare of magic protected her vitals.

Other parts of her body were not so fortunate. Wind demon teeth were sharp as needles and thick as straw. One punched a hole through her stomach, another her hip.

Inevera Drew hard on her jewellery again, healing the punctures, but two of the teeth were embedded in her thigh, and she did not have time to pull them free.

She stomped down, but Asavi had already rolled out of the way and kicked back onto her feet. Melan was raising a tube made from the leathery wing of a wind demon, and she knew what was coming next.

With nowhere to run, Inevera dropped to the ground just as the blast of wind struck her like the hand of Everam, slapping her down onto the floor so hard she felt floorboards crack beneath her.

Asavi threw a wardstone as Inevera lifted her legs to kick herself upright. It skittered across the floor, leaving a trail of ice in its wake. Power enough to freeze an enemy solid.

Inevera Drew on her ruby ring, the gold moulded around a circlet of flame demon bone, and her body was filled with warmth to fend off the cold as she kicked the stone towards Melan.

The woman had been readying another gust of wind when the cold stone came her way. Desperately she turned the tube of demon wing and loosed. She succeeded in blowing the stone away, but she foolishly aimed the blast at the floor, and the rebound knocked her from her feet.

Inevera closed the distance between her and Asavi, driving pointed fingers into her shoulder. Asavi was not quick enough to block fully, but she tapped Inevera's forearm just enough to protect her convergence point, turning a crippling blow into one merely painful.

With Inevera in close, Asavi caught her shoulder, holding her in place as her knee drove into Inevera's kidney, once, again. Inevera accepted the blows for the chance to hook Asavi's knee with her free arm, again taking the woman down. She snaked her other arm around Asavi's leg as well, preparing to twist it from the socket.

She was not able to complete the move, but it had the desired effect. Unwilling to let her lover be maimed, or to strike with magic while she was in its path, Melan moved in close to join the fight.

Inevera had to drop Asavi's leg to block Melan's whip kick,

striking a return blow to her chest that would have broken the breastplate of a normal woman. But Melan, too, was strengthened by magic, and resisted the blow as she fell back, kicking Inevera hard in the crotch.

Unlike other points, where an inch meant the difference between striking a convergence or not, much of a woman's power centred between her legs, and the target was difficult to miss. Nerve clusters screamed in pain and Inevera's legs went momentarily weak. Asavi was ready, kicking at them and at last taking her down.

Rather than be pulled, Inevera threw her weight into the fall, catching Asavi by the back of her neck and rolling to put the woman on top just in time to catch Melan's driving knee in the back. Inevera kicked the two women into each other, rolling to her feet and sprinting across the room for her *hora* wand.

As fast as she ran, Melan's throw was faster. Like a glowing coal, the *hora* stone streaked through the air to land between her and the weapon, impact wards blowing a gaping hole in the floor and striking her with debris. She had no wards against wood, and it left her bloodied and pincushioned with splinters. Amidst the smoke and dust, she lost sight of her wand.

There were shouts from outside, drawn to the commotion, but Asavi threw another impact stone at the doorway, collapsing the frame to prevent any from coming to Inevera's aid.

Again Inevera Drew for healing, but she felt the reservoir of power in her jewels dwindling. She could not continue depleting *hora* at this rate.

Desperately, she reached into her *hora* pouch, closing her fingers about the familiar contours of her dice. She did not even need to look at them as she held them aloft and summoned light.

Light wards were among the first *nie'dama'ting* carved into their dice, that they might work further by Everam's light. Even a novice could do it. Melan and Asavi laughed at the effort.

But Inevera's dice were carved of mind demon bone, focused

by pure electrum. The light she called shone like the sun itself, and the women shrieked, turning from the glare.

By the time they caught their senses, Inevera had caught Asavi's arm, torquing it back until she felt cartilage pop and the woman screamed.

The move cost her a slash of Melan's talons across the face. Blood began to flow into her eyes as she caught the follow-up blow and struck a convergence that sent Melan stumbling back.

She had to pause to pull her forearm across her eyes, wiping the blood away. Again she Drew for healing, but this time she felt the well run dry as the bleeding slowed. Asavi camel-kicked her away, pausing as she too Drew for healing.

The next minutes were a blur. Inevera was forced to focus almost entirely on defence as the women pressed her from both sides. They had come prepared, their auras continuing to glow brightly even as Inevera's dimmed and she began to slow.

More, Asavi and Melan had been fighting together their entire lives, designing their own *sharukin* to fight in perfect harmony. Blocking one opened Inevera to attacks from the other, and the women took full advantage.

Inevera found herself missing more and more blocks as her power waned, and the few counters she managed amidst the pummelling were easily blocked. It became clear they were toying with her, savouring the moment.

'Accept your fate,' Melan said, landing a kick to the side of the head that sent Inevera reeling.

'Everam has forsaken you,' Asavi said, kicking her back the other way.

'It is your own fault,' Melan said, punching Inevera in the jaw so hard it took her feet from under her.

Asavi was positioned to catch her as she fell, dropping to one knee and driving Inevera hard into it. Inevera coughed a spatter of blood as the air was blasted from her, and Asavi hurled her onto her back. 'You have grown complacent in your power, coming into battle with little more than your dice, flawed since you coated them as the Evejah forbade.'

Was it true? Had the dice turned from her? Had she truly fallen from Everam's favour? If so, what had been her failing? Not confirming the death of the Par'chin? Coating her dice? Allowing Ahmann into *Domin Sharum*? What might she have done differently?

But then she remembered something, and her hand dropped to her *hora* pouch.

'They warned me,' she croaked.

'Eh?' Melan asked.

'The dice.' Inevera gasped as she reached into the pouch. 'They warned me my power would be challenged. Everam has not forsaken me. This is just another test.'

It was forbidden in the Evejah to Draw on one's dice for anything save light and foretelling, lest the *hora* might become so drained as to cause false foretellings. More, the items were the most precious thing a *dama'ting* owned. They were her key to the white, her guide through life, the heart of her power. No *dama'ting* would risk harm to her dice.

But Inevera had already lost her dice once, leaving her blind until she could carve a new set. The price was high, but she was stronger for paying it.

Now, she had dice carved from a mind demon's bones, and coated in electrum. She closed her fingers about the seven dice, Drawing hard on their power for one last burst of strength and speed.

Melan and Asavi had not expected the move, but neither were they caught unaware. As Inevera came back, they moved in perfect sync, Asavi to block, and Melan to counter.

Faster than asps a moment ago, the women now seemed to move like plodding camels. Inevera's kick connected with Asavi's chest before her hands were in place to block, knocking her back with plenty of time to pivot and catch Melan's attack, pulling her into a throw that sent her clear across the room.

At a safe distance, both women reached for their *hora* pouches once more, but Inevera was faster, raising the fist that clutched her dice and pointing a finger, her sharp nail tracing a cold ward in the air.

Asavi literally froze, a thin rime of white coating her skin. Inevera had not intended to kill her – yet – but she had not anticipated the raw power of the dice. The woman's aura snuffed like a candle.

Melan shrieked, letting loose a blast of lightning, but Inevera turned, sketching a quick ward in the air. Her hand tingled as the energy was absorbed back into the dice.

Gaping, Melan fumbled with her *hora* pouch, pulling free another fistful of wind demon teeth. Propulsion wards activated as she threw, but Inevera traced the ward in reverse, and the teeth ripped back through the thrower.

Melan gave a sharp cry and fell back, groaning and labouring for breath, riddled with holes. Inevera kept her dice in hand, ready to ward, but the woman's aura gave no sign that she might continue the battle.

'Killed . . . Asavi . . .' Melan said through clenched teeth.

'The same fate she wanted for me,' Inevera noted. 'But you don't fear cold, do you, Melan?' She drew quick wards in the air, and a bright flame hovered above her hand. 'Fire has ever been your bane.'

Melan flinched, crying in pain as she curled reflexively, clutching her scarred hand close. 'I will tell you nothing!'

Inevera laughed. 'I have my dice, little sister. I need nothing you can tell me. Any value you might still hold vanished the moment you mentioned my mother.'

'Forgive our failure, Damajah,' Micha begged when Inevera revived her. Jarvah was only just stirring from the healing magic when one of Inevera's earrings began to vibrate, signalling that someone had entered one of the secret passages the spear sisters used.

Be silent, Inevera's hands signalled. She flicked her fingers, and Micha helped get Jarvah out of sight as Inevera raised her *hora* wand.

The hidden door opened silently, but it was no attacker. Instead she found Ashia, with Kajivah slung over her shoulder and a bundle strapped to her chest. The spear sister's robes were torn and wet with blood, her white veil splotched red. She left bloody footprints behind her.

'Succour, I beg, Damajah.' Ashia laid Kajivah down and uncovered the bundle, revealing her infant son.

'What has happened?' Inevera demanded, moving to inspect the woman's wounds. There were bruises and superficial cuts, but a spear had pierced her abdomen and come clear through. She was pale, her aura dim. She would need *hora* magic if she was to survive.

'Jayan is dead,' Ashia said, 'his forces shattered.'

Inevera nodded. 'I know.'

'The *shar'dama* killed their *Damaji* and took control of the tribes in response,' Ashia said. 'All save Maji, who was defeated.'

This was news, and dire. It had been Inevera's intention all along that Ahmann's *dama* sons take control of the tribes, but at a time of her own choosing. The idiots risked everything, and she realized just how far her control of them had slipped.

'And Ashan?' she asked, already guessing the answer.

'My father is dead,' Ashia said. 'Asome sits the Skull Throne.'

Worse, still. She had already lost Jayan. It would be devastating if she were forced to kill Asome, as well.

'I turned to Asukaji when the slaughter began,' Ashia said, 'just in time to catch a chain around my throat as he tried to kill me.'

'Then your brother, too, is dead,' Inevera guessed.

Ashia nodded, coughing blood, then, and swayed on her knees. Inevera signalled and Micha and Jarvah were there in an instant. 'Take the child.'

Jarvah reached out, but Ashia tightened her grasp reflexively and Kaji began to cry. Ashia squinted as if she did not recognize her spear sister, confusion and fear in her aura.

That more than anything frightened Inevera. When had she ever seen fear in Ashia's aura? Not even when the *alagai* built greatwards around the city.

'By Everam and my hope of Heaven, I swear I will not harm him, sister,' Jarvah said. 'Please. The Damajah must see to your injuries.'

Ashia shook her head, and some of the confusion left her aura. 'I have walked the abyss to protect my son tonight, sister. I will not be parted from him.'

'You will not be parted,' Inevera said. 'You have my word. But you may clutch too tightly when the magic takes you. Let your spear sister hold Kaji. They will not leave your side.'

Ashia nodded, relaxing her grip. Jarvah took Kaji, holding the thrashing infant beneath the armpits at arm's length. She looked like she would prefer fighting a rock demon. The *Sharum'ting*, denied their own childhoods, had none of a mother's instincts.

Inevera snatched the child from her, bundling his limbs tightly in the blanket. She took the neat bundle and pushed it into the crook of Jarvah's elbow. 'Micha, take the Holy Mother down to the vault. We will meet you there shortly. Go quickly and tell no one.'

'Yes, Damajah.' Micha bowed and vanished.

Inevera swept into the throne room at dawn, her *Damaji'ting* sister-wives at her heel. The room was already filled with *dama* and *Sharum*, causing a great din at the news. Before them, their second sons lined the path to the throne, save for Belina, who glared hatred at Damaji Aleveran. Aleverak's eldest son, Aleveran had taken the place of his father to lead the Majah – at least for now.

None of the *Damaji'ting* approved of their sons' coup, but

ties of blood ran deeply in them all. Inevera felt it herself, looking up the steps to Asome, his face grim, eyes still puffed from tears no doubt shed over Asukaji.

There is always a price to power, my son, she thought. Even now, sympathy for the boy mingled with the pain of Jayan's loss. Some might claim the younger killed the elder, but the truth of the dice was harsher. Asome had goaded his brother, but it was Jayan who defeated himself.

'It is good to see you well, Mother. I feared for you last night.' Asome had wisely uncovered the windows of the throne room, filling it with light that bounced around the room on dozens of new mirrors, but Inevera did not need to read his aura to know the lie.

'I fear for all of us,' Inevera said, continuing on as her sister-wives took their place left of the throne, opposite the new *Damaji*. 'So much that I have taken Kajivah and my grandson into my custody. For their own protection, of course.'

'Of course.' Asome gritted his teeth as she began to ascend the steps. She knew he wanted to stop her – every man in the room did – but while it was one thing to have your mother quietly killed, it was another to attack the Damajah in the light of day before the entire court.

'And Ashia?' Asome asked. 'My traitorous wife must face justice for killing her brother and my palace guards.'

Inevera resisted the urge to laugh at the irony. 'I am afraid your *Jiwah Ka* was mortally wounded in the battle, my son.'

Asome pursed his lips, clearly doubting. 'They must be returned, now that the danger is past. I would see the body of my wife, Kaji must lead his tribe, and my holy grandmother . . .'

Inevera topped the steps and met his eyes, and he did not dare finish the sentence. As Shar'Dama Ka, Asome's power exceeded her own, but it was untested, and they both knew Inevera could have both of the hostages killed long before he found them.

'The danger is not past!' Inevera said loudly, her voice echoing through the room. 'I have consulted the *alagai hora*, and the dice foretell doom, should they leave my protection.'

She did not bow, striding as an equal to her bed of pillows beside the throne.

33

A Voice in the Dark
334 AR Spring

Six cycles passed, cold months come and gone as the demon worked, shaving the metal of his shackles away atom by atom. The first lock was ready to shatter, and the others grew weaker. Soon he would be ready to escape, but still his captors remained vigilant.

The prison began to heat, light seeping in through the curtain weave. Soon the day star would rise in full.

He was about to curl back down when a sound came from below. His gaolers, coming again to bark at him.

There were five of them, the same that had struck in the Enemy's tomb. For reasons unknown, they had foolishly cut themselves off from their drones. Their minds were warded, but they had not learned to mask their auras well, and the glow about them showed the Consort much.

First came the drones. The male was magically and mentally dim, but loyal as a rock drone. He circled the ward mosaic, taking position behind the Consort.

The female drone was brighter than her sire, but this was not surprising. Demon females always dominated their sires – something the Consort knew well. The Hive Queen was his progeny, after all.

With the lesser drones behind him, the Unifiers entered. First came the Heir, who carried the weapons of the Enemy, powered by the bones and horns of the Consort's ancestors, including his own grandsire.

The Consort swallowed a hiss. The Heir had gone to great lengths to protect the body of his own ancestor, yet he flaunted his enemies' bones arrogantly. It was an insult the Consort would repay a thousandfold when he was free.

But the Heir's surface aura was one of barely contained action. His every instinct screamed for him to kill the Consort and have done. He would not act unprovoked, but he would take any excuse to strike.

The Consort was careful to give none. His posture did not threaten, but he met the Heir's eyes, watching.

Next to enter was the Explorer, who found the Enemy's tomb and brought back the fighting wards the Consort and his brethren had worked so hard to suppress. Immediately following was his mate the Hunter, who feared nothing when the kill was scented. Both had covered their flesh in powerful wardings, powered from within by stolen Core magic.

Heir. Explorer. Hunter. Each was bright with power, but even now, all three could not match the power the Consort held in reserve, if he were free to use it.

'Mornin',' the Explorer said. 'Hope the accommodations are to your liking. Sorry we can't be better hosts.'

The Consort watched him with bemusement. The Explorer always opened with some insincere platitude. They played the game over and over, but never learned the rules.

The Heir's aura chafed at the Explorer's lead. Older and more experienced, he was accustomed to dominance, but the Explorer's magic was brighter, and in the end, magic always led.

It was a small rift in their alliance, but like the links of his chain, the Consort could worry it in time.

'How do we know it even understands us?' the Hunter asked. The female lacked patience, quick to anger. Another crevice to widen.

'Maybe its mouth ent suited to our speech,' the Explorer said, 'but it's getting every word.'

He moved along the wall, eyes on the Consort. There was something new in his aura. Impatience. 'Only, I'm thinking it *can* talk. I think maybe it just doesn't *want* to.'

'Can't imagine why,' the Hunter said.

'Because it is a creature of Nie,' the Heir said.

'Thing is, demon, you ent much good to us if you can't talk.' The Explorer took one of the curtains in hand, pulling it aside.

The Consort shrieked, throwing up arms to shield its eyes as the cell was filled with blinding brightness. Like molten stone, it burned his skin.

The Explorer let the curtain drop, and the Consort immediately Drew on his reserve, healing the damage. The pupils of the humans had not even dilated, but it was more light than the Consort could bear for long. He would be drained of power even before the day star rose to burn him into oblivion.

'Got anything to say?' the Explorer asked, still clutching the cloth.

It was a ploy. The Unifiers had kept him too long to kill him now. But the Consort's eyes still burned, and the auras around him were unreadable. He could not risk it.

The Consort Drew hard, rolling to the side and strengthening a claw to shatter the lock he had eroded. A twist of the chain freed one of his legs, and he reached out, snatching the broken pieces of lock in his talons.

A short burst of power sent metal flying through the room. Neither the Consort nor his magic could leave the circle at the centre of the mosaic, but once in motion, the projectiles flew uninhibited.

The Heir batted one piece aside with a wave of his weapon. The Explorer dissipated, letting it pass harmlessly through him. The Hunter was struck, but her aura brightened, healing the damage instantly. The female drone angled her shield and diverted the missile harmlessly.

The male drone was dim, but quick and alert. He stepped

precisely as the Consort anticipated, and the twisted bit of metal missed him to strike the wall behind at precisely the right angle to rebound into the back of his head, knocking the warded wrappings he wore askew.

Dazed, the drone stumbled onto the mosaic and collapsed, one limb falling forward, the barest fingertip crossing the circle.

But even that breach was enough for the Consort to slip into his mind, crushing the drone's will like an insect.

The others rushed to him, but they pulled up short when the drone got to his feet and placed himself in front of the Consort, his spear and shield held at the ready.

'Shanjat, stand aside,' the Heir said.

'Your drone no longer controls this shell,' the Consort replied, using the warrior's mouth to form the clumsy, inefficient vibrations of their speech.

The Heir pointed the hated weapon at him. 'Shanjat is ready for Heaven, demon. We will not release you for him.'

'Of course not,' the Consort agreed. 'He is only a drone. He does not expect you to save him. He begs your forgiveness for his failure.'

'There is no dishonour in being defeated by a superior foe,' the Heir said, emotion colouring his aura and clouding his judgement. How easily they were manipulated!

'Indeed,' the Consort agreed. 'You were correct that I cannot form your words, but this drone will serve hence as my voice.'

The female drone made a low sound, her aura colouring with a delicious blend of pain and anger. The Explorer reached again for the curtain. 'Just for now, Shanvah. You'll get your da back.'

She would not, of course. The Consort had already severed the drone's will and replaced it with his own. He could access the drone's thoughts, feelings, and memories, but without the Consort's will to animate it, the body would wither and die. 'What price for my freedom?'

'The path to the Core,' the Explorer said.

'They are all about, for one such as you, Explorer,' the Consort said.

The Explorer shook his head. 'A real one. Kind you use to march your prisoners down to demon town.'

'A dangerous path, and winding,' the Consort said. 'Countless twists and turns. Too much for this primitive drone to impart, but I can guide you.'

'We cannot simply trust this servant of Nie,' the Heir said.

'No one trusts anyone,' the Explorer said. 'Just talking, is all.'

The Heir chafed at the Explorer's dominant tone, and the Consort turned to him, both heads swivelling at once. 'Your Nie and Everam are fictions. Soothing grunts to ease your fear of the dark.'

'More lies,' the Heir said.

The Consort shook the drone's head. 'You want to know why we have something, instead of nothing. Perhaps the worthiest question one of your primitive intellect can muster. The mind court has pondered this for millennia. There are many plausible answers, but none of them resembles the ridiculous fantasy the Mind Killer used to inspire his warriors.'

'Mind Killer?' the Heir parroted.

'The one you call Kaji,' the Consort said. 'Though in truth it was pronounced *Kavri*.'

'How can you know this?' the Heir demanded.

'I knew him, in my fashion,' the Consort said. 'All my kind did, in those cycles.'

'You were alive in the time of Kaji?' the Heir demanded. 'Three thousand years ago? Impossible!'

The drone smiled. 'Five thousand one hundred twelve. You've lost count many times, over the years.'

The female drone dared speak to her betters. 'He lies.'

'He is the prince of liars,' the Heir said.

'Night, what is the matter with you?' the Hunter snapped. 'Ent here to argue scripture!'

The Heir's aura filled with anger at her tone, and she leaned in, fearless before the kill.

'Enough,' the Explorer said quietly, his submissive tone

belying his dominance as their auras shamed and they stood down.

'Why would you take us there?' the Explorer asked.

'Because the journey is long, and you are mortal. The time will come when your guard grows lax, and then I will be free.' The Consort let out a false aura, granting sincerity to his words.

'Fair enough,' the Explorer said.

'And because the surface will soon be swept clean,' the Consort added.

'Eh?' the Explorer asked.

'You understand nothing of what your actions in the desert have brought upon your people,' the Consort said.

'There will be swarm.'

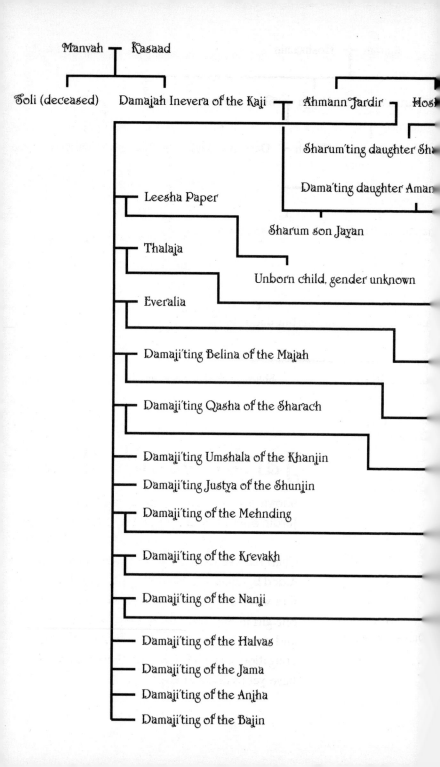

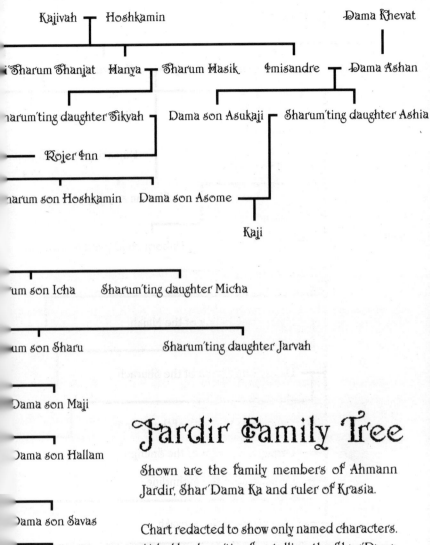

Jardir Family Tree

Shown are the family members of Ahmann Jardir, Shar'Dama Ka and ruler of Krasia.

Chart redacted to show only named characters. Aided by dama'ting foretelling, the Shar'Dama Ka's wives have each delivered two boys and one girl in their first three years of marriage, and continued to conceive normally after the obligation was met. Most of these children have yet to come of age.

Krasian Dictionary

Abban am'Haman am'Kaji: Wealthy *khaffit* merchant, friend to both Jardir and Arlen, crippled during his warrior training.

Ahmann asu Hoshkamin am'Jardir am'Kaji: Ahmann, son of Hoshkamin, of the line of Jardir, of the tribe Kaji. Leader of all Krasia. Believed by many to be the Deliverer. See also: Shar'Dama Ka.

Ajin'pal (blood brother): Name for the bond that forms on a boy's first night fighting in the Maze, when he is tethered to a *dal'Sharum* warrior to keep him from running when the demons first come at them. An *ajin'pal* is considered a blood relative thereafter.

Ala: (1) The perfect world created by Everam, corrupted by Nie. (2) Dirt, soil, clay, etc.

Alagai: The Krasian word for corelings (demons). Direct translation is 'plague of Ala'.

Alagai hora: Demon bones used by *dama'ting* to create magic items, such as the warded dice they use to tell the future. *Alagai hora* burst into flame if exposed to sunlight.

Alagai Ka: Ancient Krasian name for the consort to Alagai'ting Ka, the Mother of Demons. Alagai Ka and his sons were said to be the most powerful of the demon lords, generals, and captains of Nie's forces.

Alagai'sharak: Holy War against demonkind.

Alagai tail: A whip consisting of three strips of braided leather ending in sharp barbs meant to cut deeply into a victim's flesh. Used by *dama* as an instrument of punishment.

Alagai'ting Ka: The Mother of All Demons, the demon queen of Krasian myth.

Aleverak: Ancient, one-armed *Damaji* of the Majah tribe in Krasia. One of the greatest living *sharusahk* grand masters.

Amanvah: Jardir's eldest *dama'ting* daughter by Inevera. Married to Rojer Inn.

Andrah: Krasian secular and religious dictator, second only to the Deliverer and Damajah.

Anoch Sun: Lost city that was once the seat of power for Kaji, the Shar'Dama Ka. Rediscovered by Arlen Bales, it was found to contain the secrets to battle warding.

Asavi: Dama'ting of the Kaji tribe. Former rival of Inevera as *nie'dama'ting.* Lover of Melan.

Ashan: Son of Dama Khevat and closest friend of Jardir's during his training in Sharik Hora, Ashan is *Damaji* of the Kaji tribe and part of Jardir's inner circle. Married to Jardir's eldest sister, Imisandre. Father of Asukaji and Ashia.

Ashia: Jardir's *Sharum'ting* neice. Daughter of Ashan and Imisandre. Married to Asome. Mother of Kaji.

Asome: Jardir's second son by Inevera. *Dama.* Known as the 'heir to nothing'. Married to Ashia. Father of Kaji.

Asu: 'Son' or 'son of'. Used as a prefix in formal names, as in Ahmann asu Hoshkamin am'Jardir am'Kaji.

Asukaji: Ashan's eldest son by Jardir's sister Imisandre, and heir to the Kaji tribe. *Dama.*

Baden: Rich and powerful *dama* of the Kaji tribe. *Push'ting.* Known to possess several items of *hora* magic.

Bazaar, Great: The largest merchant area in Krasia, located right inside the main gates. It is run entirely by women and *khaffit.*

Belina: Jardir's *dama'ting* wife from the Majah tribe.

Bido: Loincloth worn by most Krasians under their robes, the bido is most commonly noted as the sole clothing of young Krasian boys and girls in training.

Chabbavah: *Dal'ting* woman killed in an attempt to be raised to *Sharum*.

Chin: Outsider/infidel. This word is also considered an insult, meaning that a person is a coward.

Chi'Sharum: Greenland adult men too old to go through *Hannu Pash* are levied and trained in the *chin'sharaj*. Those who pass are inducted into *chi'Sharum*. Generally used as fodder in combat.

Cielvah: Daughter of Abban. Raped by Hasik, leading Abban to have Hasik castrated.

Coliv: Krevakh Watcher, bodyguard to Amanvah.

Couzi: A harsh, illegal Krasian liquor flavoured with cinnamon. Because of its potency, it is served in tiny cups meant to be taken in one swallow.

Crownsight: Enhanced wardsight from Crown of Kaji.

Dal: Prefix meaning 'honoured'.

Dal'Sharum: The Krasian warrior caste, which includes the vast majority of the men. *Dal'Sharum* are broken into tribes controlled by the *Damaji*, and smaller units answerable to a *dama* and a *kai'Sharum*. *Dal'Sharum* dress in black robes with a black turban and night veil. All are trained in hand-to-hand combat (*sharusahk*), as well as spear fighting and shield formations.

Dal'ting: Fertile married women, or older women who have given birth.

Dama: A Krasian Holy Man. *Dama* are both religious and secular leaders. They wear white robes and carry no weapons. All *dama* are masters of *sharusahk*, the Krasian hand-to-hand martial art.

Damajah: Singular title for the First Wife of the Shar'Dama Ka.

Damaji: The twelve *Damaji* are the religious and secular leaders of their individual tribes, and serve the Andrah/Shar'Dama Ka as ministers and advisors.

Damaji'ting: The tribal leaders of the *dama'ting*, and the most powerful women in Krasia.

Dama'ting: Krasian Holy Women who also serve as healers and midwives. *Dama'ting* hold the secrets of *hora* magic, including the power to foretell the future, and are held in fear and awe. Harming a *dama'ting* in any way is punishable by death.

Daylight War, the: Also known as Sharak Sun. Ancient war during which Kaji conquered the known world, uniting them for Sharak Ka.

Desert Spear, the: The Krasians' term for their city. Known in the North as Fort Krasia.

Domin Sharum: Literally translating as 'two warriors', *Domin Sharum* refers to a strict ritual of single combat under Evejan law.

Draki: Krasian unit of currency.

Drillmasters: Elite warriors who train *nie'Sharum*. Drillmasters wear standard *dal'Sharum* blacks, but their night veils are red.

Enkaji: Damaji of the powerful Mehnding tribe.

Enkido: Eunuch servant and *sharusahk* instructor of the Kaji *dama'ting*. Made personal bodyguard to Amanvah, killed by a mimic demon.

Evejah, the: The holy book of Everam, written by Kaji, the first Deliverer, some three millennia past. The Evejah is separated into sections called Dunes. Each *dama* pens a copy of the Evejah in his own blood during his clerical training.

Evejan: Name of the Krasian religion, 'those who follow the Evejah'.

Evejan law: The militant religious law the Krasians impose on *chin*, meant to force nonbelievers to follow the Evejah under threat rather than belief.

Everalia: Jardir's third Kaji wife.

Everam: The Creator.

Everam's Bounty: After Fort Rizon with its vast farmland was taken by the armies of the Deliverer in 333 AR, the city-state

743

was renamed Everam's Bounty to honour the Creator. It is the Krasian foothold in the green lands.

Everam's light: Wardlight, and the ability to see otherwise invisible flows of magic using warded sight.

Fahki: Dal'Sharum son of Abban. Raised to hate his *khaffit* father.

Gai: Plague, demon.

Gaisahk: Form of *sharusahk* modified by Arlen Bales to maximize the effect of his warded flesh.

Ginjaz: Turncoat, traitor.

Greenlander: One from the green lands.

Green lands: Krasian name for Thesa (the lands north of the Krasian desert).

Hannu Pash: Literally 'life's path', this represents the period of a boy's life after he has been taken from his mother but before his caste (*dal'Sharum*, *dama*, or *khaffit*) is set. It is a period of intense and brutal physical training, along with religious indoctrination.

Hanya: Jardir's youngest sister, four years younger than he. Married to Hasik, mother to Sikvah.

Hasik: Disgraced bodyguard to Jayan, castrated by Abban. Called Whistler because his missing tooth causes his *s*'s to whistle.

Heasah: Prostitute.

Hora magic: Any magic using demon body parts (bones, ichor, etc.) as a battery to power spells.

Horn of Sharak: Ceremonial horn blown to begin and end *alagai'sharak*.

Hoshkamin: Father of Ahmann Jardir; deceased. Also Jardir's third son by Inevera.

Hoshvah: Jardir's middle sister, three years younger than he. Married to Shanjat. Mother of Shanvah.

Hundred, the: The *kha'Sharum* and *chi'Sharum* warriors in Abban's employ. Taking their name from the one hundred *kha'Sharum* warriors given him by Jardir, Abban has increased their numbers well beyond that.

Ichach: Damaji of the Khanjin tribe.

Imisandre: Jardir's eldest sister, one year younger than he. Married to Ashan. Mother of Asukaji and Ashia.

Inevera: (1) Jardir's powerful *dama'ting* First Wife. Kaji tribe. Also known as the Damajah. (2) Krasian word meaning 'Everam's will' or 'Everam willing'.

Jamere: Abban's *dama* nephew and heir apparent.

Jardir: The seventh son of Kaji, the Deliverer. Once a great house, the line of Jardir lasted more than three thousand years, slowly dwindling in number and glory until its last son, Ahmann Jardir, restored its renown.

Jayan: Jardir's first *Sharum* son by Inevera. Sharum Ka.

Jiwah: Wife.

Jiwah Ka: First wife. The *Jiwah Ka* is the first and most honoured of a Krasian man's wives. She has veto power over subsequent marriages, and can command the lesser wives.

Jiwah Sen: Lesser wives, subservient to a man's *Jiwah Ka*.

Jiwah'Sharum: Literally 'wives of warriors', these are women purchased for the great harem of the *Sharum* during their fertile years. It is considered a great honour to serve. All warriors have access to their tribe's *jiwah'Sharum*, and are expected to keep them continually pregnant, adding warriors to the tribe.

Jurim: Kai'Sharum Spear of the Deliverer who trained with Jardir. Kaji tribe.

Kad': Prefix meaning 'of'.

Kai'Sharum: Krasian military captains, the *kai'Sharum* receive special training in Sharik Hora and lead individual units in *alagai'sharak*. The number of *kai'Sharum* in a tribe depends on its number of warriors. Some tribes have many, some just one. *Kai'Sharum* wear *dal'Sharum* blacks, but their night veils are white.

Kai'ting: Jardir's mother, sisters, nieces, and *Sharum* daughters. *Kai'ting* wear a white veil with their blacks. Striking one means death or the loss of the offending limb.

Kaji: The name of the original Deliverer and patriarch of the

Kaji tribe, also known as Shar'Dama Ka, as the Spear of Everam, and by various other titles. Kaji united the known world in war against demons some thirty-five hundred years past. His seat of power was the lost city of Anoch Sun, but he also founded Fort Krasia.

Kaji had three artefacts for which he was famous: (1) The Spear of Kaji – the metal spear he used to slay *alagai* by the thousand. (2) The Crown of Kaji – bejewelled and moulded in the shape of powerful wards. (3) The Cloak of Kaji – a cloak that made him invisible to demons, so he could walk freely in the night.

Kajivah: Mother of Ahmann Jardir and his three sisters, Imisandre, Hoshvah, and Hanya. Also known as the Holy Mother. While not a trained cleric, she has great (if largely undefined) religious power among the commoners, who adore her.

Kasaad: Inevera's father. Crippled *khaffit*. Former *Sharum*.

Kaval: Gavram asu Chenin am'Kaval am'Kaji. Drillmaster of the Kaji tribe. One of Jardir's *dal'Sharum* instructors during his *Hannu Pash*. Killed by a mimic demon.

Khaffit: A man forced to take up a craft instead of becoming a cleric or warrior. Lowest male station in Krasian society. Expelled from *Hannu Pash*, *khaffit* are forced to dress in the tan clothes of children and shave their cheeks as a sign that they are not men.

Kha'Sharum: Able-bodied *khaffit* whom Jardir has made into low-skill infantry. *Kha'Sharum* wear tan robes, turbans, and night veils to show their *khaffit* status.

Kha'ting: Infertile women. Lowest female caste in Krasian society.

Khevat: Father of Ashan. Most powerful *dama* in Krasia.

Lifan: Bespectacled and weak-looking Sharach *kha'Sharum* who serves as tutor to Fahki and Shusten. One of Abban's Hundred.

Little sisters: Inevera's term for her sister-wives.

Lonely road: Krasian term for death. All warriors must wall the lonely road to Heaven, with temptations on the path to test their spirit and ensure that only the worthy stand before Everam to be judged. Spirits who venture off the path are lost.

Maji: Jardir's second Majah son, a *nie'dama* who will have to fight Aleverak's heir for the Majah *Damaji* throne.

Manvah: Mother of Inevera. Wife of Kasaad. Successful basket weaver.

Mehnding tribe: The largest and most powerful tribe after the Majah, the Mehnding devote themselves wholly to the art of ranged weapons. They build the catapults, slings, and scorpions used in *sharak*, quarry and haul the stones for ammunition, make the scorpion bolts, etc.

Melan: Kaji *dama'ting* daughter of Qeva. Granddaughter of Kenevah. Former rival of Inevera. Lover of Asavi.

New Bazaar, the: Rebuilt Great Bazaar in the outer city of Everam's Bounty.

Nie: (1) The name of the Uncreator, feminine opposite to Everam, and the goddess of night and demonkind. (2) Nothing, none, void, no, not. (3) Prefix for Krasian children in training.

Nie'dama: Nie'Sharum selected for *dama* training.

Nie'dama'ting: Krasian girl who is in *dama'ting* training but is too young to take her veil. *Nie'dama'ting* are given great respect by men and women alike, unlike *nie'Sharum*, who are less than *khaffit* until they complete the *Hannu Pash*.

Nie Ka: Literally 'first of none', a term for the head boy of a *nie'Sharum* class, who commands the other boys as lieutenant to the *dal'Sharum* drillmasters.

Nie's abyss: Also known as the Core. The seven-layered underworld where *alagai* hide from the sun. Each layer is populated with a different breed of demon.

Nie'Sharum: Literally 'not warriors', name for boys who have gone to the training grounds to be judged and set on the path to *dal'Sharum*, *dama*, or *khaffit*.

Nie'ting: Barren women. The lowest rank in Krasian society. Also known as *kha'ting*.

Night veil: Veil worn by *dal'Sharum* during *alagai'sharak* to hide their identities, showing that all men are equal allies in the night.

Oot: Dal'Sharum signal for 'beware' or 'demon approaching'.

Par'chin: 'Brave outsider'; singular title for Arlen Bales.

Pig-eater: Krasian insult referring to *khaffit*. Only *khaffit* eat pig, as it is considered unclean.

Push'ting: Literally 'false woman', Krasian insult for homosexual men who shun women altogether. Homosexuality is tolerated in Krasia only so long as the men also impregnate women and add to their tribe.

Qasha: Jardir's Sharach *Damaji'ting* wife.

Qeran: One of Jardir's Kaji *dal'Sharum* drillmasters during his *Hannu Pash*. Later crippled, he is taken in by Abban to train his *kha'Sharum* Hundred. Bodyguard and advisor to Abban.

Savas: Jardir's Mehnding *dama* son.

Scorpion: A Krasian ballista, the scorpion is a giant crossbow using springs instead of a bowstring. It shoots thick spears with heavy heads (stingers) and can kill sand and wind demons outright at a thousand feet, even without wards.

Shalivah: Krasian girl working at Shamavah's restaurant in Cutter's Hollow. Kaval's granddaughter, whom Rojer dotes on out of guilt that her father was killed saving his life.

Shamavah: Abban's *Jiwah Ka*. She speaks fluent Thesan and is assigned to oversee Abban's operations in Hollow County.

Shanjat: Kaji *kai'Sharum* who trained with Jardir. Leader of the Spears of the Deliverer and wed to Jardir's middle sister, Hoshvah. Father of Shanvah.

Shanvah: Sharum'ting niece of Jardir. Daughter of Shanjat and Hoshvah.

Sharach: The smallest tribe in Krasia, with fewer than two dozen warriors at one point. They were rescued from extinction by Jardir.

Sharaj: Barrack for young boys in *Hannu Pash*, much like a military boarding school. The *sharaji* are located around the training grounds, and there is one for each tribe. The name of the tribe is a prefix, followed by an apostrophe, so the *sharaj* for the Kaji tribe is known as the Kaji'sharaj. Plural is *sharaji*.

Sharak Ka: Literally 'the First War', the great war against demonkind the Deliverer will begin upon completion of Sharak Sun.

Sharak Sun: Literally 'the Daylight War', during which Kaji conquered the known world, uniting it in Sharak Ka. It is believed that Jardir must do the same if he is to win Sharak Ka.

Shar'dama: Dama who fight *alagai'sharak* in defiance of Evejan law.

Shar'Dama Ka: Literally 'First Warrior Cleric', the Krasian term for the Deliverer, who will come to free mankind from the *alagai*.

Sharik Hora: Literally 'heroes' bones', the name for the great temple in Krasia made out of the bones of fallen warriors. Having their bones lacquered and added to the temple is the highest honour that warriors can attain.

Sharukin: Literally 'warrior poses', practised series of movements for *sharusahk*.

Sharum: Warrior. The *Sharum* dress in robes often inlaid with fired clay plates as armour.

Sharum Ka: Literally 'First Warrior', a title in Krasia for the secular leader of *alagai'sharak*. The Sharum Ka is appointed by the Andrah, and the *kai'Sharum* of all tribes answer to him and him only from dusk until dawn. The Sharum Ka has his own palace and sits on the Spear Throne. He wears *dal'Sharum* blacks, but his turban and night veil are white.

Sharum'ting: Female warrior, mostly used to describe Inevera's personal guard. The *chin* Wonda Cutter was the first to be recognized by Jardir.

Sharusahk: The Krasian art of unarmed combat. There are various schools of *sharusahk* depending on caste and tribe, but all consist of brutal, efficient moves designed to stun, cripple, and kill.

Shevali: Dama advisor to Damaji Ashan.

Shusten: Dal'Sharum son of Abban. Raised to hate his *khaffit* father.

Sikvah: Hasik's daughter by Jardir's sister Hanya, and Amanvah's personal servant. Offered to Rojer as a second bride.

Skull Throne: Made from the skulls of deceased Sharum Ka and coated in electrum, the throne is powered by the skull of a mind demon, casting a forbiddance that prevents demons from entering the inner city of Everam's Bounty. The seat of power for Krasia's leader.

Soli: Dal'Sharum brother of Inevera. *Push'ting.* Lover of Cashiv. Killed by Kasaad.

Spears of the Deliverer: The elite personal bodyguard to Ahmann Jardir, made up mostly of the *Sharum* from his old Maze unit.

Spear Throne: The throne of the Sharum Ka, made from the spears of previous Sharum Kas.

Stinger: The ammunition for the scorpion ballistae. Stingers are giant spears with heavy iron heads that can punch through sand demon armour on a parabolic shot.

Sunian: Artefacts from the city of Anoch Sun. Also the name of its people.

Tachin: Dama son of Jardir, Krevakh tribe.

Thalaja: Jardir's second Kaji wife, mother of Icha and Micha.

Tikka: Grandmother (informal term of affection).

'Ting: Suffix meaning 'woman'.

Tribes: Anjha, Bajin, Jama, Kaji, Khanjin, Majah, Sharach, Krevakh, Nanji, Shunjin, Mehnding, Halvas. The prefix *am'* is used to denote both family and tribe, as in Ahmann asu Hoshkamin am'Jardir am'Kaji.

Undercity: Huge honeycomb of warded caverns beneath Fort Krasia where women, children, and *khaffit* are locked at night to keep them safe from corelings while the men fight. Still being constructed in Everam's Bounty.

Vah: Literally 'daughter' or 'daughter of'. Used as a suffix when a girl is named after her mother or father, as in Amanvah, or as a prefix in a full name, as in Amanvah vah Ahmann am'Jardir am'Kaji.

Waning: (1) Three-day monthly religious observance for Evejans occurring on the days before, of, and after the new moon. Attendance at Sharik Hora is mandatory, and families spend the days together, even pulling sons out of *sharaj*. Demons are supposedly stronger these nights, when it is said Alagai Ka walks the surface. (2) The three nights each month when it is dark enough for mind demons to rise to the surface.

Watchers: Watchers are the *dal'Sharum* of the Krevakh and Nanji tribes. Trained in special weapons and tactics, they serve as scouts, spies, and assassins. Each Watcher carries an iron-shod ladder about twelve feet long and a short stabbing spear. The ladders are light, flexible, and strong. They have interconnecting ends (male/top, female/bottom), so ladders can be joined together. Watchers are so proficient they can run straight up a ladder without bracing it and balance at the top.

Zahven: Ancient Krasian word meaning 'rival', 'nemesis', or 'peer'.